# TRIUMPHANT
## *Hearts*

*Love Is the Strongest Remnant
After the Battle
in Four Complete Novels*

SUSAN DOWNS
TAYLOR JAMES
SALLY LAITY
JERI ODELL

BARBOUR BOOKS
*An Imprint of Barbour Publishing, Inc.*

*Remnant of Light* © 2002 by Taylor James.
*Remnant of Forgiveness* © 2002 by Sally Laity.
*Remnant of Grace* © 2002 by Susan K. Downs.
*Remnant of Victory* © 2002 by Jeri Odell.

ISBN 1-58660-522-4

All Scripture quotations, unless otherwise noted, are taken from the King James Version of the Bible.

All Scripture quotations for *Remnant of Victory*, unless otherwise noted, are taken from the HOLY BIBLE, NEW INTERNATIONAL VERSION®. NIV®. Copyright © 1973, 1978, 1984 by International Bible Society. Used by permission of Zondervan Publishing House. All rights reserved.

Scripture quotations marked NLT are taken from the *Holy Bible*, New Living Translation, copyright © 1996. Used by permission of Tyndale House Publishers, Inc. Wheaton, Illinois 60189, U.S.A. All rights reserved.

Published by Barbour Books, an Imprint of Barbour Publishing, Inc., P.O. Box 719, Uhrichsville, Ohio 44683.  http://www.barbourbooks.com

Member of the
Evangelical Christian
Publishers Association

Printed in the United States of America.

# TRIUMPHANT
## *Hearts*

# Remnant
# of
# Light

Taylor James

*In memory of the twentieth-century martyrs around the world, who number more than those who died for their faith in all other centuries combined. . . .*
*And for Peter Terbush, a fine son, brother, man, friend. . .hero.*
*He gave his life that another might live.*

# Prologue

Wednesday, September 13, 1922

*And unto the angel of the church in Smyrna write; These things saith the first and the last, which was dead, and is alive; I know thy works, and tribulation, and poverty, (but thou art rich) and I know the blasphemy of them which say they are Jews, and are not, but are the synagogue of Satan. Fear none of those things which thou shalt suffer: behold, the devil shall cast some of you into prison, that ye may be tried; and ye shall have tribulation ten days: be thou faithful unto death, and I will give thee a crown of life. He that hath an ear, let him hear what the Spirit saith unto the churches; He that overcometh shall not be hurt of the second death.*
Revelation 2:8–11

By late afternoon in the ancient Christian city of Smyrna, enemy troops were lighting twenty fires for each one extinguished by the fire brigade. The smell of the burning city infiltrated the very fabric of the populace as only smoke can. With the billowing smoke came all the fear that uncontrollable fire brings.

Elena Apostologlou and her sister, Sophia, had sewn treasures—money, jewels, and important papers—into each of their garments in the hope that something might survive their trek to the safety of the Theatre de Smyrna, an American enclave in the city. Whispering a prayer, Elena followed her sister and their beloved father, Andreas, from the sanctuary of their villa.

As soon as they stepped through the massive front door of their neoclassical home and into the quayside road, the trio experienced the full measure of their city's ransacking. Over the five-day span since the Turkish army had occupied the city again, the sounds of looting and killing had seeped through the thick walls of their home. Yet nothing compared to being out and among the carnage.

The scene looked like something out of the Middle Ages. Elena's senses filled with fiendish displays of barbaric butchery, and she instinctively drew closer to her family. They exchanged frightened looks of disbelief as they witnessed the almost diabolical delight the soldiers found in causing others agony. Like a sweat-drenching nightmare, the late afternoon sky glowed orange and red, while clouds of smoke, ash, and embers descended upon them all.

But the sounds were even worse than the abominable sights. The frantic cries of humans and animals permeated the heavy air and filled Elena's head with a vile timbre. She could focus on an individual cry of pain, yet still hear the wail of a mass agony of souls. The anguished din rose commensurate to the roar of the fire now breathing down on their city like a vast, evil, flame-throwing dragon.

The thick crowd of people moved as one body toward the choppy, churning water of Smyrna's famous sea harbor, where they would hopefully find a launch that would take them to a ship. The pain of seeing his beloved city in the clutches of this antichrist had already taxed her father's weak heart to its limit. So Elena followed Sophia in a deliberately slow pace.

She could feel as well as hear walls crashing in the fire several streets up, and the ground shook beneath them, a man-made earthquake. They were within sight of their father's office building when the thundering hooves of a Turkish cavalry filled the road. A report of rifle fire resounded through the crowd.

Pandemonium reigned.

The three of them could do nothing more than crouch and duck their heads down low. There was nowhere for them to go. People screamed all around them. Camels, chickens, dogs, and horses raced around, trampling and being trampled in their frightened frenzy. And still the shots rang out, indiscriminate ones meant to terrify and kill. They accomplished both in a horrible way.

With an arm around both his daughters' shoulders, Elena's father held them under his protective grip and struggled to keep his children safe. She could hear him reciting the Lord's Prayer.

Elena kept waiting to feel the cold bite of metal rip through her skin. She watched the man in front of them throw his little girl, then his wife, upon the ground. He had no sooner flung his own body over the both of them than a shot hit him and made his body stiffen, then relax. When Elena reached out to try and help, the shot she had been dreading hit its mark.

But the bullet didn't hit her.

It plowed into the dear flesh of her father's body, which had been protecting her own, and the force slammed him against her.

"*Baba!*" Elena and Sophia screamed together as he crumpled to the ground.

"*Baba*, no!" Elena dropped to the earth beside him. Where the bullet had pierced him, his life flowed in a steady stream of dark red. She pressed her hand, sheathed in a white linen glove, against the wound. But despite her best efforts, his blood—his life—continued to seep out. Turning her glove crimson, it ran into the pavement of the city that had been home to their ancestors for three thousand years.

"*Baba!*" She shook her head in horror at the sight of the red liquid now trickling from the side of his mouth as well. "No," she rasped. "No. This war cannot have you! Please. No!"

"Elena." Sophia spoke sharply from the other side of their father, and Elena looked into her tear-filled eyes. "Listen," she commanded. "He is trying to tell us something."

In their home of safe haven over the past few days, she had witnessed the deaths of so many refugees from this Greco-Turkish War that she now recognized all the signs. Their father, like the others, would soon leave them. With tears of despair washing unchecked down her face, Elena leaned in to hear her father's last words. As she did, she faded into another reality amid the volley of bullets whistling around them and the resulting mayhem.

"My daughters," he choked through the blood that filled his mouth. "Fear none of those things which thou shalt suffer." He admonished them with the same love that they had never doubted. Elena immediately recognized his words as those spoken by the Lord to the church in their very own city.

"God's truth, His wisdom, and His light will guide you." His gaze lit upon Sophia, his eldest child, then turned to his younger one. Elena bit her lower lip as she nodded her understanding of his choice of words. Her deceased American mother's name, Letta, meant "truth," Sophia's, "wisdom," and her own, "light," all attributes of the Lord's and of those who follow in His footsteps.

Blood dripped from her father's mouth, and he coughed weakly. Elena felt certain that his heart was giving out, yet he struggled for enough breath to speak his final words to them before he left.

"Promise me. . .you will escape this tribulation," he managed to say as he fought for air, ". . .and you. . .will both live. . .to be. . .very happy, very kind. . . old ladies. . . ." His lips turned up into a weak smile. ". . .Older than I am now," he rasped.

"*Baba*. . ." Elena bit her lower lip and shook her head back and forth. "Don't—"

"Please. . . ," he begged, and from the gurgling sound coming out with his words Elena knew that his lungs were fast filling with blood and drowning him. She had never felt more helpless. "I know. . .you never. . .break your. . ." He stopped speaking, but Elena knew that it wasn't because of want.

Seeing and understanding the need in his eyes, both girls vigorously nodded their heads. "We promise, *Baba*. . . ," they spoke together, assuring their dear father of their pledge.

"We will grow old. . . ," Sophia declared.

"Very old," Elena agreed.

"And. . .bitter. . .ness. . . ?" He shook his head slightly. "No. . . ."

"No. No bitterness, *Baba*," Elena quickly assured him. His entire life he had preached against hatred, anger, and bitterness. She wouldn't dishonor him now by letting it grow. "No bitterness against those who did this to you."

His lips curved up slightly at their corners, and he gave them one last smile. His eyes then turned to something beyond their shoulders, and his face, in spite of his pain, radiated an otherworldly light as he whispered out a perfect sentence, his last. "He has come to guide me home."

"*Baba*. . ." As Elena called out, his face paled before her gaze, and his lips, beneath the red of the blood still trickling out between them, slowly turned to blue. She pushed her hand harder against the hole the lead had carved into his beloved flesh, a child's futile effort to keep a much-loved parent with her, if only for a few seconds longer.

"No. . . ," she whined. "No. . .come with us, *Baba*." She leaned harder still on the wound. "Don't turn us into orphans," she implored of his gentle blue eyes, eyes that now gazed unseeingly up at her, making the lids of her own squeeze shut in agony. "Don't leave us," she cried, sounding more like the little girl of five she had been when her mother had died than a young woman of eighteen.

Even when she felt her sister's fingers wrap around her own and remove her hand from her father's wound, she couldn't move. "Elena, look at him," Sophia commanded, a measure of the sublime touching her tone. "He is not here any longer. Our dear *Baba*. . .this body is no longer his home. Look. He has left it. He has moved on to a better place."

Through her excruciating, breath-robbing pain, Elena could, by a miracle of God, hear the wisdom in her sister's voice. Like a resounding thunder, and yet, as soft as a caress, her tone was not something she could ignore. There was truth in her sister's words, a truth that demanded attention. Slowly opening her eyes, Elena looked, and as she did, she saw the evidence of Sophia's testimony. The man who had been their father was no longer there. He looked as if he had come out of the body that had been his home for seventy-two years and moved—somewhere else.

" 'For God so loved the world, that he gave his only begotten Son, that whosoever believeth in him should not perish, but have everlasting life.' " Elena heard Sophia speak the most loving, the most truthful words of the Lord's, found in the Gospel of John: John, the very apostle of Christ who had taught Polycarp, the first bishop of Smyrna.

"It's true," Elena whispered with a joy only a Christian could feel, could comprehend, in the face of death. "Our father has only departed. He has not perished." The radiance she felt belied the horror of what she had just experienced.

Sophia nodded her head, and, while not taking her eyes from the beloved face, she reached into her pocket and pulled out a handkerchief of the purest white. Gently, she wiped the blood from her father's gray mustache, his beard. That done, she looked at Elena and, wordlessly, they discarded their blood-soaked gloves, and together they reached out and closed their father's unseeing eyes.

A bullet whizzed past their heads, bringing into focus once again the bedlam that surrounded them. As Elena looked around, she saw the man and the woman who had been running ahead of them. She had seen the man die. But as she looked through the eerie light cast by the roaring, citywide fire, she now saw that his wife had been killed too. With a groan that sounded like something issuing from a wounded animal, she lunged toward the couple.

Sophia grabbed her arm and held her back. "Elena. What are you doing? Have you gone mad?"

"The girl!" Elena shouted. "They threw themselves on top of their little girl to protect her. Even if she survived the barrage of bullets, she won't survive much longer without air."

Understanding and horror dawned simultaneously in Sophia's face. Sophia joined her in pushing aside the large man and his wife. Too numb in the nightmare of the moment, Elena felt nothing for the couple. But they had died protecting their child, and she knew that they must get the girl out from under her parents' combined dead weight.

Blood covered the little girl, and for a moment Elena feared that the child too had fallen victim to a Turkish bullet. But when air reached her small face and she opened her eyes, Elena knew the girl was uninjured. At least physically.

"Come, Darling." She held out her arms to the girl. The young girl was in a trance, but upon seeing Elena, she blinked.

"Elena?"

She looked closely at the features of the little girl, now camouflaged beneath the blood and the dirt covering her face.

"Rose! Is that you?" Elena exclaimed as she recognized her favorite charge from the previous July. Of Armenian ancestry, eight-year-old Rose had been one of Elena's swimming students. She was one of the sweetest little girls in the world. Her kindness toward others was well known within the American school she attended in Smyrna, both among the teachers and students.

"Elena!" The girl wrapped her arms around Elena's neck, but as she did, her gaze fell upon her parents lying to the side. Backing up from Elena, she caught sight of the blood on her arms, on her chest, on her legs, and just about everywhere on her body. Her screams rent the air.

*"Mairig! Hairig! Mairig! Hairig!"* Over and over in her native Armenian she cried out for her parents. A litany of despair. Of pain. Of mourning.

Afraid that Rose would attract the attention of the soldiers, who would, without remorse, run her through with a sword, Elena pulled her close in a tight hug, quieting her mouth against her chest. "You mustn't cry out." She nodded over to the soldiers who were still firing into the crowds but had moved down a bit farther. "They will come back and hurt us. And your mother and father don't want that. They gave their lives so that you might live. And live you will."

"But how? I'm so. . .afraid," Rose whimpered, and her grief-stricken face, smeared with her parents' blood, touched deeply into Elena's soul. "Without my *Mairig* and *Hairig*. . . ," she squeaked out but bravely gulped back her cries. Even though tears still streamed down her little face, she didn't scream out again.

"You have Sophia and me. And now we have you. From this moment on, you are our sister." She glanced over at Sophia for confirmation of the idea. As Sophia nodded her golden head in affirmation, Elena continued, "We were all three made orphans this night, little Rose. But we will be safe."

"How do you know?" The little girl's soft wails rose to a piercing crescendo. But she bit her lips to keep from screaming, and blood, this time her own precious supply, seeped out from between her teeth. Elena knew Rose had plenty of experience at stifling screams. In all likelihood, she and her parents had been hiding from the Turkish soldiers in the suffocating heat of their home's attic since the soldiers had entered the city five days earlier. But, like Elena's family, Rose and her parents had been forced from their home when the fires were set.

"Because my trust is not placed in just a person," Elena answered the little girl. "Nor in those ships out there." She motioned to the ships—American, British, French, Italian, and more, all ostensibly allies of Greece—which the Christians of the city had thought of as safe haven. "Only with God. He will keep us safe. He has to, so that my sister, Sophia, and I can fulfill our *secret* promise to our father." She nodded toward her sister as she spoke, purposefully placing emphasis on the word secret.

Rose's dark eyes widened. "What *secret* promise?"

"To live a long life."

"They are coming back this way!" Sophia shouted out in terror. "We must go!"

Elena glanced up to see only daggers, dripping with blood, marching in their direction. Grabbing Rose in her arms, she turned to look one last time at the precious body that had housed her father. Sending it a final, sad smile and a blown kiss, she turned, and, with Sophia by her side, they ran as fast as their feet could carry them away from the approaching soldiers.

"We have to get to the Theatre de Smyrna," she heard Sophia shout from her side.

"I know." But a frantic glance in its direction showed that the way to the theater they had been instructed to take by the American consul general was now cut off by Turkish soldiers. Their only chance was to run the next street up. "Maybe the consul general hasn't left the consulate yet," Elena said. Panting and sweating in the heat of the city burning on a hot summer day, they took off up a side road in that direction. Elena still clutched Rose in her arms.

Just as they reached the point where they could see the stately neoclassical edifice of the American consulate, they caught sight of the consul general and his wife rushing down a guarded pathway and past the American sailors on their way to their car. Even under the best of circumstances, Elena, a very good athlete, knew that she wouldn't be able to reach him or the American servicemen in time. A sea of frightened people blocked their way.

As still as a statue, except for the tears that ran unchecked down her cheeks, Elena watched the car move through the crowd in the opposite direction from where they stood.

"He's gone. The consul general is gone," Sophia breathed out.

"May God protect him," Elena whispered into Rose's blood-matted hair. "Next to our father, the consul general is one of the best men I have ever met."

Sophia nodded. "Just like the Greek soldier, Christos, who brought the wounded one to our house last Thursday."

Elena knew the soldier had made a great impression on her sister. A huge man, Christos had carried his friend for days across battlefields to what he had thought would be the safety of Smyrna before going to join his routed army at their debarkation point. Now he represented to them all the individuals who were trying to help people survive in this city of anarchy.

Even beyond that, Elena was aware that something wonderful, perhaps something God-inspired, had passed between her sister and the big man. And she sensed the importance of Sophia's thoughts about him—in this world turned upside down and inside out.

Until the previous Saturday, Smyrna had been considered one of the most beautiful cities in the world. Some even said it was second only to Paris. Now both its beauty and its identity were being obliterated forever. Elena knew Sophia was nearly in shock over the many losses they had faced in such a short time. "Yes, Sophia, just like Christos."

She grunted when a large woman bumped against her shoulder. The road was filled to capacity with frantic people running for safety.

"All of our friends will assume that we're safely at the Theatre de Smyrna," Sophia stated in a monotone when the car with the consul general could no longer be seen. Her entire demeanor spoke of a defeated person. "We. . .are. . .alone."

Elena sharpened her gaze on her sister. Through the smoke-filled air around them she could see Sophia's trembling lips. Fear gripped her as she heard the despondency creeping into Sophia's voice.

"No, Sophia," she admonished. "We are *not* alone. God is with us. He will see us safely out of Smyrna. Don't get discouraged. Please," Elena begged. "Don't despair. I need you."

Sophia had been named perfectly. Wisdom filled the very essence of her nature, and Elena could tell as her sister breathed in and out deeply, trying to find enough oxygen in the smoky atmosphere to feed her system, that she was endeavoring to keep the debilitating, negative emotion from gripping hold of her. After a long moment, she reached out for Elena's hand and squeezed it. "As I need you, Dear."

Rose wiggled to be put down and placed her small hand over those of the two older girls. "And I need both of you," she said.

Elena offered the young girl a smile of comfort. "We are family now. Sisters. For always." As she said the words, she looked down. A gasp escaped her lips when she glimpsed their interlocked hands.

All three of them bore the sacrificial blood of their parents.

Elena knew she would remember the sight throughout the remainder of her days. But for now, the sight made her all the more determined to find a way out of their burning city. Their parents died trying to get them to safety. Elena refused to let their deaths be in vain.

# Chapter 1

*Thursday, September 14, 1922*

*And now for a little space grace hath been shewed from the LORD our God,
to leave us a remnant to escape.*
Ezra 9:8

Elena awoke to sunlight on her face. And with the light came a good heat.
A normal heat. A heat that didn't claw at her lungs or burn her skin.

Yet even with the realization, another pain, a deep pain, started somewhere around her stomach and rose with bile to her throat. A heartrending knowledge filled her thoughts. This would be the first day of her life that she would not see her father or wish him a good morning. An unbidden, keening moan came from the depths of her soul as she cried for the father she had loved.

Elena knew that her father was now forever safe. She knew he was alive in Christ. She accepted, with childlike faith, the fact that he was in heaven experiencing a grand reunion with her mother.

But, oh, she missed him. She missed him so badly. And a vision rose within her—a tormenting vision of her father's body lying on that dirty street with the blood flowing out of his mouth from the mortal wound. Her heart filled with a pain that seemed to flow through her veins and pumped through every vessel in her body, even to the tiniest capillary.

She realized the hurt of having been orphaned at the age of eighteen, in such a terrible way, would cripple her if she allowed it to take control. She couldn't let it rule her.

She forced herself to stop the sounds of mourning that flowed from her innermost being, and she opened her eyes. They were caked with salt from her tears and from the sea she had swum in the previous night in escaping Smyrna. She had to rub her fingers over them to help pry the lids apart. Gritty and rough, the salt pulled at them, pulled many of her lashes out too, but she hardly noticed.

She looked up to the sky. It wasn't the Aegean blue she was used to seeing. Rather, it was vividly red. The sun seemed to have a hard time filtering its rays through the smoke of Smyrna's smoldering remains.

Seagulls flew in the strong wind above the Italian flag, which rose above the stern of the ship. Elena's gaze stayed glued to the squawking gulls. They sang their same, ancient song.

Elena's chapped and cracked lips turned up slightly at their corners, and she smiled, even though the taste of blood accompanied the movement. Gulls were something normal in a world turned traitor to her, something to feast her eyes upon, to draw comfort from, to focus upon now, and to live.

She watched them play in the sky for a few minutes, then slowly turned her head to look for Sophia and Rose and the others who had shared the little rowboat with them in escaping Smyrna. She smiled when she saw Rose's heart-shaped face as she lay next to her, safe and secure. Sophia slept on the other side of the child, and the other women and children occupied the deck just beyond her.

She squinted. She didn't see Christos, Sophia's Greek soldier, who had miraculously appeared the previous night in their time of greatest need.

They had returned to their home for the rowboat, which Elena had remembered their father storing in the garden shed. There, Christos had not only saved them from rape and death at the hands of a gang of Turkish soldiers, but he had helped them escape the burning city as well. Elena knew, even with the precious rowboat, they would never have accomplished their flight without Christos's strength.

Not seeing any men at all, she assumed that Christos was sleeping in a section cordoned off specifically for them. She turned the other way, and her eyes widened when she saw she was lying along the edge of the ship with only an inch separating her from a fall into the choppy sea. She was desperately thirsty but even more exhausted. A kind person had covered her during the night, and now she pulled the blanket tighter around her shoulders and scooted closer to Rose. Realizing that her head was resting upon a ringed lifesaver, she only had the energy to wrap her arm through it before oblivion, sweet and deep, overtook her once again and she slept.

But it wasn't the sweet sleep of an untroubled soul.

The ship swayed back and forth in the wind, first rising high out of the water only to slam back down into the sea. The push of humanity, as on the burning streets of Smyrna, seemed to have followed Elena. She felt herself being shoved against something both sharp and long. She struggled to awaken, even as her fingers clawed at the pillow her head rested upon, but she couldn't pull herself into consciousness—not even when she felt herself falling. Falling. Falling.

Only when her body submerged into the sea and the water sucked her into its depth did her eyes open. Only then did she know that her nightmare was once again a reality, and she had been swept off the boat into the deep blue sea.

When she had fallen overboard, her body was still wrapped in the thick blanket, and it was now pulling her down into the water's depths. She struggled to free herself from the blanket's weight. Thankfully, she had discarded her shoes last night when she and Christos opted to swim next to the rowboat in order to allow more room for women and children in the boat's hull. She would have failed in her attempts to survive now with the added weight of shoes. With her lungs nearly bursting, she pushed the heavy blanket from her. She followed the rising bubbles of oxygen and pushed herself toward the surface light using all her strength.

Waves crashed upon her face.

She gulped in seawater, which irritated her already raw throat. Gasping and coughing, she struggled to keep afloat. If her hands hadn't grazed against the lifesaver she had rested her head upon during the night, she doubted that she would have been able to get her breathing under control as well as keep herself afloat.

Clutching the ring, she turned her back to the waves and coughed out the water that threatened to fill her lungs. Moments later, she looked toward the ship. It was steaming away from her, the black smoke coming out of its smokestack like a flag of mourning, mocking her.

No one—not Sophia or Rose, or even Christos—seemed to realize that she had fallen overboard. As the ship moved farther and farther away, Elena knew that she was on her own. By the time those on board realized that she was missing, they would be long gone. And she would appear as nothing more than a dot on the sea.

A sense of surrealism assailed Elena. *Had she really fallen off the ship?* Was it possible for her to have lived through the horror of seeing her father and hundreds of other Christians killed, to have witnessed the utter destruction of Smyrna, only to tumble from their rescue vessel to be drowned at sea?

She felt so utterly miserable; she knew it was all too true. Her throat burned. Her back ached from her fall against the hard sea surface. The salt water stung the numerous raw blisters on her face and hands caused by flying embers as they fled the city.

A tidal wave of panic swelled from the pit of her stomach and swept over her. But Elena knew she couldn't allow it. She knew enough about people washed overboard to understand that panic was more her enemy right now than the neverending sea that surrounded her.

If she didn't panic, she would survive.

She made her body breathe in and out, calmly, smoothly, while she forced her mind to consider her advantages. The rough seas were beginning to calm, and she could swim. She had a life ring, and she was in the Aegean Sea, a body of water that was filled with boats and islands. A new day was dawning, so she had at least twelve hours before darkness engulfed her. And the water this time of year was not dangerously cold. She knew that Sophia, Rose, and Christos were safe. But, most of all, she knew that she wasn't really alone.

God was with her. He was her trust. He would give her all she needed to survive. And even though she couldn't begin to imagine what good He could bring out of her falling into the sea, especially after all that had happened during the last five days, she would trust Him to provide for her. Now was definitely not the time to stop trusting.

As the sun rose higher into the sky, Elena settled into the life ring, pulled her body as close as she could to conserve her body heat, and she waited.

She was so tired. And so very thirsty. "I thirst." The Lord's words as He hung upon the cross held new meaning for her.

After floating in the sea for a couple of hours, her body was freezing, and she had to kick her feet to generate warmth. However, her head was burning in the rays of the sun. She could see her cheeks expanding below her eyes and knew that her face was swelling severely. The burns she had sustained in the fire had been minor, but after baking all day in the sun and soaking in saltwater, she shuddered to think how they would become.

Wiggling around, careful not to lose her grip on the life preserver, Elena reached down to remove her petticoat in order to use it as a covering for her head. As she did, her hands brushed against something hard and round in the pocket of her dress. She frowned, wondering if some sort of fish had taken up residency in her pocket.

But remembrance swooped in on her when her numb hands inspected what was caught in the billowing folds of her dress. A grin, which made her cracked lips bleed again, split across her swollen face.

An apple!

She remembered she had pushed the fruit into her dress pocket just before leaving home the day before. "Oh, dear Lord," she croaked. If she had had enough liquid in her system for tears, they would have fallen down her cheeks in blessed relief. For Elena knew that this apple might just save her life.

Of all her father's wealth, this apple, which their cook had bought the previous, peaceful week at the fruit market, was, at this moment, the most precious thing he had owned. It was worth more than all the gold, all the works of art, all the money he had had in banks, because this apple, God's very bounty, would sustain Andreas Apostologlou's youngest daughter's life.

Elena bit into the fruit, and the sound—that wonderful popping sound—reverberated in her head. For that half-hour in which Elena kept company with her apple, she didn't even feel the crinkles of her shriveling skin. She forgot where she was, how thirsty, how tired, how cold her body felt, and how hot her head burned. The apple became more than just nourishment and liquid to her. It became Elena's hold on life.

When she had eaten three-fourths of the fruit, she forced herself to stop. Nothing could be seen on the horizon, and she knew that she would have to keep the rest for later. If she were indeed called upon to spend the night in the sea, she would need the apple to get through it. Just to hold it, lick it would help. That decided, she placed it back into her pocket for safekeeping.

And she waited.

And as she waited, she prayed.

If God couldn't send a boat to her, she prayed He would at least send her some sort of company. A seagull, or a turtle, even a school of friendly fish. She knew God was with her, but still, she felt so lonely—something she had never been before. There had always been someone with her. Most often her father or Sophia. But now she had lost both, and even her new little sister, Rose. All within a matter of hours.

"Lord, Lord," she implored, calling out to Him as she had so many times during her eighteen years. "Please send a boat. . .someone. . .don't let me stay out here all night alone. I can't. . .can't. . ." She groaned from deep within her soul.

She had no sooner stopped praying than she saw something moving toward her. She blinked her eyes.

But it wasn't a boat. It seemed to be swimming in the water. A dolphin?

She slightly shook her burning head. No. The form wasn't slicing through the sea like those streamlined mammals normally did.

A dog then? But it couldn't be.

She squinted her eyes and tried to focus on the object. It sure looked like a dog. Yet the idea that a dog could survive out in the Aegean Sea was absurd.

She squeezed her eyes shut and shook her head before opening them once more. Perhaps she was hallucinating.

Chills had been racking her body, and she hadn't been able to stop coughing for the last couple of hours. She was quite certain that she was running a high fever.

But as the object came closer, she also knew that she wasn't imagining things. It *was* a dog.

As big, brown eyes gazed up at her from a sopping face, the fluke of a dolphin's tail emerged from behind the dog, and Elena knew how the dog was being kept above water. The dog used his weak paws to paddle up beside her, and Elena made a sound that was as much a laugh as she could manage.

"Oh my, oh my," she said as she reached for his forelegs. Growing up along the shore of the Aegean, she had heard all the legends about dolphins and how they saved shipwrecked people. But never had Elena considered them to be more than just sailor's fancy, and even less something that might happen in modern days. Elena knew all she had heard was true when the grinning face of a large dolphin swam from beneath the dog and greeted her with a high-pitched squeal. It seemed to be giving her an admonishment to care for the canine creature. Then and there, she was firmly convinced that dolphins really *do* understand, and they *do* help those in need.

Pulling the dog close to her, Elena somehow managed to drape his legs across the life preserver without upsetting her own hold. "Here, Boy, here," she cooed to him. Elena knew if she could see his tail, it would be wagging slowly from side to side. As it was, he looked at her with grateful eyes and flicked his dry tongue about her face. The dolphin swam around them like a sentinel guarding treasure.

Even though Elena understood that her prayer for company had been answered, she also recognized that the dog, unquestionably another refugee from the destruction of Smyrna, was in a desperate condition. He needed what remained of her apple more than she did. Without the liquid it would afford him, she was sure he would die. And without him, Elena was almost certain she would too.

Reaching into her pocket, she pulled out the apple, and slowly, with love, she fed him. With each bite the dog's eyes seemed to light up a bit more. After he had finished, she laid her head against his, and his breath—life—fanned her face. With the dolphin swimming around them both, she rested.

However, after awhile, her chills and cough threatened to make Elena totally lose her hold on reality. Just then, the dolphin nudged her softly. Elena watched as it spun around and started slicing though the water away from them.

"No. . .don't go. . . ," she croaked out, fear lacing her voice. "Please don't go. . . ." But it turned back to her only long enough to whistle something in his language before taking off at a high-speed swim toward the sun, which sat just above the surface of the sea like a bobbing ball.

Wrapping her arms tighter around the dog, Elena couldn't help the dry sobs that she poured out onto his neck. Where the dog was companionship of an earthbound nature, the dolphin had been not just company but a source of security as well. She was in his watery world, his domain, and somehow having him close had made her feel protected.

But now he was gone, and she was so cold, so tired, so miserable, that her body didn't even feel like her own.

Still, she had the dog. She had to focus on this blessing. And he needed her as much as she needed him. With the sea lapping all around them, they clung together, eye to eye, his ragged breath mingling with her own. And they were the best of friends.

Even though all seemed hopeless, even though she had cried as if it was, Elena knew that all hope was not lost. She had to live, so she *would* live. Her father's dying request had been for Sophia and her to live to be very old ladies. Elena, for her part, wouldn't disappoint him. Besides, she had to survive in order to meet Sophia and Rose at the Lincoln Memorial in Washington the following May.

She thanked God for their having made that impromptu date the previous May when they—her father, Sophia, and she—had attended the dedication ceremony of the memorial built to honor Abraham Lincoln. A shudder shook her body as she considered how she would have located her sisters otherwise. She had no fear that Sophia would forget their planned picnic on May 30, 1923—a year to the day after that moving ceremony. She was certain that they would be reunited there. Because of this assurance, at least Elena knew that she didn't have to worry about never finding her loved ones again.

Time passed.

Elena wasn't sure how much.

Through fits of coughing, she watched the sun sink into the sea. With its disappearance, she closed her eyes. She didn't want to see the night. To feel it was enough.

An hour passed—maybe a little less, maybe a little more—while she and the dog she had named "Buddy" hugged one another. Suddenly, she felt a change in her canine friend. His ears twitched. And then his head moved against her cheek. When a small yap came out of him, Elena's eyes popped open.

And she gasped.

The silhouette of a ship loomed on the horizon against the backdrop of a majestic sky. And the ship was gliding across the sea toward them.

Elena's befuddled brain knew that she had to get its attention somehow; otherwise it would plow straight past them. Just as she started to slap her numb and impotent hands against the water, at least fifty streamlined bodies jumped up and out of the sea and started dancing and singing around the two castaways. Elena's mouth dropped open in amazement as she surmised that her dolphin friend had returned with his pod and that they were performing a dance—a rescue dance for her and the dog—upon the moonlit surface of the Aegean Sea.

The dog gave a little bark to the dolphin as it swam up next to them and gently nudged both of them with his pointy nose. Elena reached out and rubbed him. "Thank you," she croaked. The dolphin's smile seemed to broaden. With a happy glint in his eyes, he squeaked in his dolphin way, then swam off to frolic with the members of his pod.

Through eyes that were practically swollen shut from saltwater blisters and burns, Elena watched their ballet, and, thankfully, those on board the ship did too. Just as a light shone down upon the company of playful dolphins, and thus upon her and the dog, unconsciousness claimed Elena. As on the previous night when their little rowboat had been rescued by the Italian ship in Smyrna's harbor, she slipped into the sweet, sweet release of knowing others would now care for her.

While she slept, the moonlight dance of dolphins and the sweet breath of a dog stayed within her mind and calmed her soul.

# Chapter 2

*Jesus answered and said unto him, Verily, verily,
I say unto thee, Except a man be born again,
he cannot see the kingdom of God.*
John 3:3

I'm fearful that she may have pneumonia."

A woman's pleasant but concerned voice sounded as though she stood far above her. Yet even as Elena endeavored to identify the speaker, blackness claimed her once again.

"*Baba*, no! *Baba!*" Elena startled to a hazy wakefulness to hear someone screaming. "Sophia, Rose, Christos, come back! Mamma!"

At the final word, the realization hit her. She was the crying girl.

"Shhh, Darling, shhh." Again she heard the sweet voice speak to her. Could it be her mother? Elena's befuddled brain wondered. Had she gone to be with her mother in heaven? But, no. Heaven had no pain, no confusion. And Elena's body was filled with both.

A cooling cloth pressed against her forehead. "Be still, dear girl. Be still. You are safe." Elena grabbed hold of the admonishment like she had so recently grabbed hold of the life preserver. She forced herself to quiet down, and soon oblivion claimed her, something much sweeter than the chilled and aching reality of a body that had betrayed her. Consciousness hurt—hurt more than Elena, who had never been sick a day in her life, wanted to hurt. She slept, but whenever she detected the cooling hands of someone lifting her head and pouring liquid down her parched and burning throat, she accepted the offering with a grateful heart.

Although her body slept, her mind didn't. It shifted and shimmered with images.

Images—red and orange—of fire and screams, which could be doused only by replacing them with the sweetness of a dog's breath against her cheek or the dance of dolphins on a starry night.

And a ship.

The mental picture of a ship before her in the sea would bring relief from the raging of the fire, the screams of people running, running, always running.

23

And she would sleep.

Until the next time.

But somehow even with the terrible nightmares filling her fevered sleep, Elena knew that they were exactly that.

Nightmares.

No longer reality.

And even though they startled her, they were not to be compared to the living ones she had so recently experienced. In the realm of bad dreams, there came the cooling hands of a mother to soothe her. In the actual days of wartime reality, the real-life nightmare world, there had been no comforting touch.

Time passed. But Elena had no idea how to count out the days or hours. Only the woman with the calming hands knew, the wonderful hands Elena would forever trust, forever remember. They were "mother" hands, hands Elena had missed for the last thirteen years of her life. Hands for which Elena expectantly waited to see the face to whom they belonged.

❧

"*Anne*," Auhan addressed his mother, Fatima, in Turkish as he reached down to rub the ache he knew had to be in her slender shoulders. "You must rest."

His mother hadn't caught more than an occasional nap in days. She had single-handedly doctored the young woman whom the crew of their little steamship, the *Ionian Star*, had picked out of the Aegean Sea several days earlier. All onboard had affectionately taken to calling the rescued woman "Dolphin Girl."

His mother squeezed his hand. Then, with a gentle caress, she studied it in the special way that told Auhan she was thinking about her older son, Mehmet. Auhan and his older brother had identical hands, even down to their matching moles just above the knuckle of their right thumbs. He knew his mother wondered where his brother with the same hands might be. Even though many soldiers—both Turkish and Greek—had died in the Greco-Turkish War, Auhan knew that she believed that her eldest child wasn't among the dead. Auhan didn't share his mother's opinion.

With a sigh, she let go of his hand and turned back to the girl. "I cannot let the sea have her, Auhan. It will *not* end like before," she spoke softly but with determination in her tone.

Auhan knew that his mother's mind had now shifted to his older sister. She had drowned when she had been fifteen and he only twelve, his brother sixteen.

In the light of the lone candle that burned on the bedside table, Auhan glanced over at his father, Suleiman, who sat on the far bunk in the cabin. The older man's lips pursed together beneath his bushy mustache, and he gave his head a gentle nod, a nod of understanding. Auhan's father, his brother, and he had all thought

24

that they were going to lose this dear woman to a broken heart at that time too.

Auhan turned back to his mother. "This girl will not die." He said the words with a conviction he could not have explained, yet somehow believed. "You have saved her, *Anne*. You." He put the emphasis on his mother's work. Unlike the murmurs to "God" he had heard coming from his mother, he would not let Allah—God—Whomever—have any of the credit. Neither the Muslim Allah nor the Christian God, if there were any difference, was very high on his list of "likes." Auhan seriously doubted that the Almighty would ever be. It wasn't that Auhan didn't believe in Him. He simply didn't like Him. At least not the Almighty he knew.

"*Anne, your* work has saved her," he repeated, and his eyes went to the dog that slumbered at the girl's feet. The sight still amazed him. *A dog, not only in their cabin, but sleeping—sleeping—on a bed.* Amazing and yet wonderful too.

Auhan had always loved the creatures. But the Muslim religion forbade people to have dogs as pets. They believed angels would not enter a house with a dog, and they even ordered all black dogs put to death. Due to his love of dogs, he had secretly spent extra time with their watchdog at their farm, and he was glad his parents hadn't separated the girl and her dog. In his opinion, after what the two had been through together, such a thing would have been cruel.

"Not only have you saved the girl but the dog too, *Anne*," he pronounced and watched with interest as his mother leaned over and gently ran her hand over the golden fur of the dog's long body.

"Poor thing," she murmured with compassion in her tone. "He suffered so much."

The dog had sustained numerous burns to his neck and back, and they estimated he had been in the salty sea for at least a day. His mother had doctored both girl and beast, just as she had doctored Auhan through his bout with malaria the previous year.

Yet, his mother couldn't cure him of his guilt, his doubt, his deep-seated anger. Auhan was sure no one could ever help him. And since his parents' revelation, all these emotions had only intensified.

Last year, after all he had seen with his own eyes of what had become of many of the Christians who had been forced into cruel winter deportations by his government, his parents had hoped to encourage him. So they confessed that their bloodline was composed more of apostatized Christians—Greeks, from the earliest days of Christianity—than of the Turks from the medieval steppes of Asia. But the knowledge hadn't helped Auhan. He wasn't sure his being descended from an apostatized people was a better alternative.

Besides, if he had both Turkish and Greek blood running through his veins, who was he? He shook his head. He wouldn't let these thoughts play in his mind right now. They were circular ones, which led nowhere except to more disillusionment, more confusion. But the realization occurred to him—there *was* something he could do to help his mother. He could assist her with this girl who had invaded their cabin.

He frowned. "Invade" was a harsh word and the wrong one. It wasn't the girl's fault she had been found adrift upon the sea. But then, whose fault was it? He almost didn't want to know.

"Tell me what to do, *Anne*," he quickly spoke to quiet his mind. "It's past midnight," he said and pointed to the blackness beyond the porthole. "I will care for her as you sleep."

Fatima's tired gaze flitted toward her son. He could tell his offer had startled her, but not any more than the voicing of it had surprised him.

Since the previous year, he had not only deserted from the Turkish army, but he'd deserted from life in general. Deep, dark depression had caused him to have nothing to do with anyone, hardly even with his father or mother. He hadn't wanted it to be that way. It wasn't something he had decided upon. In fact, Auhan hated his behavior. He felt like a prisoner. He was. A prisoner of his mind.

He knew his mother didn't want to leave the girl in anyone else's care, not even the ship's doctoring seaman. But, for him to show an interest in something—someone—would be too enticing an occurrence for her to pass up.

As he anticipated, his mother stood and relinquished the care of the girl to him.

"Every half an hour, spoon a little bit of soup into her mouth," she instructed, motioning to the table behind the girl, which held a covered bowl of broth. A weary, affectionate smile lifted the corners of her mouth as she regarded the girl. "Bless her heart, unlike most who fight liquid being poured into them when so ill, she normally tries to help."

She motioned to a ceramic bowl filled with water on the trunk beside her. "Keep the cloth cool upon her head." Auhan nodded in understanding. He couldn't help but notice that the cloth she had fixed around the girl's golden head was actually one of his mother's own scarves.

"Be careful not to let the burned areas get wet," his mother continued. She pointed to a big burn on the "Dolphin Girl's" left cheek near her ear and to her hand, swathed in the white cloth Fatima had sterilized the moment she had realized the extent of the burns. "Praise God, her burns have not become infected. But they must be kept dry," she admonished.

"I can do that." Auhan nodded and sat on the trunk his mother had been using. "What if she starts to shake?" On occasion, he had noticed the girl's body wracking with chills.

Fatima motioned to the dog at the end of the bed. He had practically recovered after a couple of days of rest and nourishment. However, except when Auhan took him above deck to relieve himself, he didn't leave the girl's side. "He keeps her feet warm, which is good, because her chills seem to originate there. If she does start to shiver, you must cover her with another blanket and rub her arms and legs, but only until the chills subside. Afterwards her temperature will rise and then her legs and arms will have to be bathed with spirits to draw out the fever. Call me if that occurs," she admonished.

Auhan knew his mother wouldn't want him, a young man, to perform such a deed for the girl. They weren't certain of the girl's age, but judging by her stylish clothing and youthful physique, his mother had estimated her to be somewhere between seventeen and twenty years old.

After casting one more loving look in the young girl's direction, Auhan's mother walked over to his father, who, standing, sent a grateful look to him for finding a way to get the woman to take a much-needed rest.

❧

As his mother slept, Auhan followed all her instructions.

Keeping his distance helped him to retain a small hold on normal life. Yet, in spite of his need to remain aloof, he saw something special in this girl. She tugged at his ability to care and feel—a part of him he thought mortally wounded the previous year—the day he had come upon the mass grave.

He would never forget that horrific moment. Seeing the remains of people—old men, woman, children, *babies*—hundreds of them, had broken the fun-loving, youthful part of Auhan's soul. Even with the repercussions of the Great War still touching their lives, up until then he had believed the world was a pretty nice place. Until that moment, he had never seriously considered the talk in the army camp about the rulers of his nation ordering the deportation—a convenient term for execution—of so many Christians, people, perhaps, like the young girl before him. But coming upon that fresh mass grave had been all the proof Auhan had needed. Running into the woods nearby, he lost the contents of his stomach as well as any desire to be part of a nation that deliberately killed babies.

*Babies*. Auhan loved babies. He loved children in general. He had always dreamed of teaching them music. But music had died in him that day too. He glanced over at the leather case that contained his beloved violin. He doubted he would ever play another note.

Shaking his head, he remembered—as much as his brain would allow—the day he happened upon that grave. He had thrown his gun aside and started to walk. He had walked and walked and walked. For days, weeks, he just kept walking. Amazingly, the malaria, which he contracted somewhere along his demented wanderings, had actually saved his life. For when a roving band from the Turkish Army found him, they attributed his desertion to illness. They shipped him home to where his mother nursed him back to health. But despite the restored health of his body, he knew the state of his mind was even worse than the sick body of the girl before him.

Deep lines creased his forehead as he watched her. Her breathing came ragged and rapid, and her skin appeared pallid as her body struggled to heal itself. A wave of compassion flooded over him. Yet another wave quickly followed and overcame him—one of anger—when he considered that such a fragile creature as this slight girl should have experienced such pain.

He felt quite certain he knew what had happened to her. Smyrna.

They had heard all sorts of conflicting press reports about what had been going on in that golden city before their ship had set sail. Many news reports had said his countrymen had gently retaken control of the city. But a smoky haze had risen from the metropolis, like a towering mountain extending thousands of feet into the sky. A fiery glow had been visible from their ship even during the daylight hours. And the girl they had found was a living testimony to an entirely different story. Often he had heard the girl cry out in her uneasy sleep, "*fotia*," the Greek word for fire. Auhan knew without being told that the thick haze and red glow they had seen had caused the devouring of the buildings, the vegetation, the people, the animals of that great city. He looked down at the dog by the girl's feet.

Again the image of the grave pressed itself into his brain. One image in particular he could not shake—the sight of a little baby still wearing a sweater knitted from soft blue wool. The image tormented him every night. And haunted his every waking moment. Without a miracle, he doubted it would ever cease. And since Auhan didn't believe in the Almighty's goodness, he knew he could never expect such a thing.

He shook his head. He didn't realize how vigorously until the dog lifted his own head to regard him with a wary eye.

"It's okay, Boy," Auhan said. But the dog didn't seem reassured. With his mouth closed, he maintained a steady and tight gaze watching Auhan.

They continued their stare-down for a few heartbeats until finally a ghost of a smile touched Auhan's lips. It was the first one in over a year.

"What's your story, Boy? You love her, don't you?" He stated the obvious as he motioned to the girl.

The sound of his voice seemed to, at last, reassure the animal. Giving a great big yawn, the golden beast lowered his head to the girl's feet once again, and his eyes slowly closed.

Looking at the dog, Auhan sighed. He had forgotten how nice it felt to talk to the creatures, even if in secret, as he had with his father's farm dog. He expelled a deep breath. The fact that he had always had to hide his love of dogs was just one more thing in a long list of things that bothered Auhan. All the rules and regulations, the dos and don'ts in life. And for what? To placate an Almighty who didn't care?

Covering his face with his hands, Auhan rubbed his fingers over his eyes. An old, familiar heaviness pressed on his chest and nearly cut off his breathing whenever he thought too much, too deeply.

How Auhan wished he could start life all over again. To go back into his mother's womb and be born an innocent little baby right now—today—and not have to deal with all the emotions that tugged and pulled at him so hard and made it difficult to draw air into his lungs.

He wished to not only start a new life in a new land but to be *totally* reborn.

He heaved a shaky sigh.

But he knew it was only a wish. A senseless wish. A little child's daydream. Reality was his life with its knowledge of the evil doings in the world; reality was the war being fought daily within his mind; reality was never being able to truly start life all over again—even in a new land, in America.

At twenty, Auhan, with the burden of knowledge, of knowing evil, of having met it face-to-face at the mass Christian grave, felt older than time itself.

Bitterness splintered through him. Why had he been forced to learn just how evil man could be? Why had he needed to learn about evil, period? Why?

He lowered his hands from over his eyes and sat back. A choking tightness wound itself deep inside him. With sweat beading upon his forehead, upon his chest, and even upon his back, he forced himself to stop thinking.

To stop.

Stop.

Glancing at his father's timepiece, he saw it was time to get more liquid into the girl. She also had a definite war waging within her. A physical one.

He reached for the spoon. Then, taking care not to touch her numerous burns, he gently lifted her dainty head. He poured the healing liquid past her cracked and bruised lips and down her throat. The back of her neck was hot, so hot it burned against his fingertips in an unnatural way. She moaned slightly in protest to the hurting movement, and yet her tongue moved around her mouth, and she did all she could to work the soup into her system.

Auhan recognized in her a will to live as strong as any he had ever seen. He had no such will last year when he had been so gravely ill. It had been his mother's will that had made him physically well again. But he was convinced. If this girl hadn't possessed her own fierce will to live, she would have succumbed to the sea long before being rescued.

On that fateful evening, he had been standing out on deck regarding the infinite stars when the dolphins started jumping up and down and all around. The sailors trained a light down upon them and discovered the girl and the dog in the middle of the cavorting, dancing dolphins. The sight was one of the most amazing things those hardened sailors and he had ever experienced. Auhan knew he would never forget the sight even if he should live to the turning of the next century, which was something he didn't expect. As she and the dog clung to each other, she had looked so small, so vulnerable, and yet somehow strong too.

The captain, seamen, and the few passengers aboard the cargo ship all decided the girl's spirit must contain a matchless quality. In order for the dolphins to have responded to the girl and come to her rescue in such a magnificent way, the innocent creatures must have recognized something very, very special about her.

Auhan held to such a belief, and, therefore, he wasn't surprised to see that the more time he spent around her, the more she intrigued him. He understood why it might be so. Nevertheless, the feeling caught him off-guard. He couldn't even remember the last time someone had been able to arouse his attention. It felt strange, like a long-unused muscle being utilized again. Yet, it also felt good.

Still. . .dolphins coming to a person's aid? A dog for a companion in the choppy sea? Such things didn't happen every day, and only a dead person could ignore such an occurrence.

A humorless sound, a distant cousin to a laugh, escaped him. Throughout the previous long months, he had considered himself as good as dead. Her coming and proving him otherwise was both an unexpected and a welcome gift.

Bending a little bit closer, he studied her closed eyes. He wondered about their color and finally decided that they could either be blue like a sapphire or brown with bits of golden light to match her hair. And her name—Auhan wondered about that too.

Amazed by his pleasant thoughts, encouraged by them, he exhaled with a deep *whoosh* and glanced back at his mother. He had fed the girl ten times, and still his mother slept, safe in the arms of his father.

Auhan would not awaken her.

Even when, after a few minutes, chills started to course through the girl's body, Auhan decided against rousing his mother. He would follow his mother's way, and, as if he were a doctor or a nurse, he would care for the girl. As he lifted the spare blanket over the girl's shivering body and gently, yet vigorously, rubbed her slender limbs to help warm them, he was amazed to realize he really wanted to help—and not just for his mother's sake.

The dog, seeming to understand the girl's need for warmth, inched his way up against her side. Auhan smiled at him. The dog blinked back, then placing his paws against the girl's arms, he sat and looked at her in loving concentration. To Auhan, the animal seemed to almost will his sea companion to open her eyes. He understood. He too wished the "Dolphin Girl" would awaken.

And open her eyes she did. The very next morning.

# Chapter 3

*Likewise the Spirit also helpeth our infirmities:*
*for we know not what we should pray for as we ought:*
*but the Spirit itself maketh intercession for us with*
*groanings which cannot be uttered.*
Romans 8:26

With clouded vision, Elena regarded the woman before her. This wasn't her very own mother, as her unconscious brain had falsely registered. Yet, the truth didn't diminish the beauty of the slender woman who stood above her, beaming with love.

"Dear girl." The woman ran her soft touch over the uninjured part of Elena's forehead. "Welcome back."

Elena blinked to clear her blurred eyes. She moved her parched and numb lips into a smile. Her mouth hurt. Every square inch of her body ached. And she felt utterly exhausted. But before sleep could capture her once again, she had to thank the woman for her care. Elena suspected that she had long been tending to her needs.

"Thank you," she whispered in Turkish, glad her brain had registered the fact that the people around her spoke in that tongue. But even as unconsciousness moved upon her once again, Elena felt no fear. These people were not her enemies. They were her friends.

"Sleep, Daughter. Sleep," she heard the woman say, and Elena felt assured that these people were not just her friends but her family now.

❧

Watching from behind his mother's shoulders, Auhan startled at the stirring of a now unfamiliar emotion when the girl's eyelids suddenly parted. As he had suspected, her eyes were brown with golden pinpricks of light, which made his own widen as he gazed into them. A light emanated from her soul and filled the cabin with a joy he hadn't felt in years—since before the Great War. He couldn't help but wonder how brightly these eyes would sparkle when she was in better health. Perhaps they would be too brilliant for him to return a steady gaze.

"Her fever is down, praise God," Fatima exclaimed. The deep, even breathing of the girl indicated her improving health.

However, his mother's words sliced into the heart of Auhan's confusion like a knife does a loaf of bread. "Don't you mean Allah?" he retorted at her use of the Almighty's title.

She had been using the Christian name, God, more than the Muslim's Allah since they boarded this American vessel. In truth, he liked neither name. To his way of thinking, his mother's work had healed the girl. Not an uncaring Almighty.

Slowly, Fatima turned her head. In the light coming through the portholes, the wisps of gray amid the dark hair escaping her scarf gleamed like platinum. She regarded him with such patience, a twinge of regret for his words seized Auhan.

"God," his mother answered with neither fear nor doubt creeping into her voice. Even as feelings of annoyance slashed through him, Auhan recognized this lack of fear had to be a heady feeling for his mother. She had grown up in a society that not only allowed but encouraged a fellow Muslim to kill a neighbor suspected of having Christian leanings. His mother had such leanings all of his life. Maybe even all of her own. She looked away from him and down at the girl again. "It is the God of Jesus Christ who has saved her," she declared with boldness.

Auhan sighed. That statement rankled and made his anger boil within him as fiercely as hurricanes do the Atlantic, the ocean they were soon to enter.

"It is *you* who has saved her, *Anne*," he corrected. "Neither God nor Allah— whichever name you choose—had *anything* to do with her being saved. And besides, how do you know for certain that she is a Christian?" Even to his own ears, he sounded like a child throwing a tantrum. "She just thanked you in Turkish."

"Many Greeks speak Turkish. And whenever she cries out, it is in the Greek language." Auhan knew his mother spoke the truth.

She reached into her pocket and drew out a pure white handkerchief, unfolding the cloth with reverent respect. The contents revealed from within the folds of the pure, white fabric made Auhan step back, almost as if he had been struck. His spirit had. Struck by the object in his mother's hand. An object he had never seen her hold before.

"I know because of this." She held up a cross that appeared to be both very old and, undoubtedly, extremely valuable. Precious jewels heavily studded the piece. "I found it sewn into her clothing."

Auhan looked between the girl and the ancient emblem of her belief. Had her God saved her from death in the rough sea? It was a nice thought. But he didn't give it more than half a second to sit in his brain before anger swooped in to replace it.

"The question should be, 'How come her God allowed her to even be in a situation of such danger in the first place?' " No. Auhan would not believe that God, as revealed by Jesus Christ, was any better than Allah, as revealed by the Koran.

In fact, the God of Jesus Christ seemed weaker. At least Allah was strong in war. His people weren't being killed in death marches or being fished from the sea as this girl had been. God, as represented by that cross, seemed to sit back and let others violate His people—men, women, children, *babies*—in the worse possible way. And wasn't the Great War a case of Christian fighting against Christian? What did that say?

The truth was, Auhan believed that neither God nor Allah cared for people. Auhan didn't care which interpretation of Him people used.

Evil was in charge of the world.

Not God.

Not Allah.

Not an Almighty.

He looked at the cross again and then at his mother. His very tired mother. Out of three children, the woman had only one child left—one very bitter, very angry, very confused child. Auhan knew that she held hopes that his brother still lived. But that was a hope Auhan didn't share with her. After all, why would Allah allow his mother's oldest son to live if he hadn't allowed her only daughter the same privilege? And, at the moment, his mother was also homeless. Her home was this room on this rolling little steamship in the middle of this big sea.

Yet even as he thought about their homelessness, Auhan knew it to be something good. He believed his parents had made the correct decision in leaving their home. Who knew what plans the politicians were cooking up for the people in their area of the world this year—both Turkish and Greek? At least now they were still able to emigrate to America.

Auhan had a feeling that soon the gates to that golden land would be closed. His mother could not have taken such news at this point in her life. She had dreamt of going to America for as long as he could remember and had worked toward it just as long. His family would not be arriving in the New World as paupers.

"Auhan." He heard her call his name and realized he had been staring at her. He blinked his eyes and looked at her again, really focusing on her this time. Remorse filled him to see the deep lines of concern etched in her classically pretty face—concern he knew he had placed there.

"I'm sorry, *Anne*. Don't worry." The shadow of a smile touched his lips. "I will be fine." He wasn't sure his assurances were true, but he wouldn't add to either of his parents' anxieties by saying otherwise. He glanced at his father, who, in his normal way, had been silently observing everything.

"I *do* worry, my son," his mother insisted as she wrapped the cross in the fine cloth and placed it back into the pocket of her dress. She just managed to complete the task before the boat dropped sharply on a wave. Auhan reached out for her elbow, but his steadying hand was unnecessary. His mother had already caught herself and adjusted to the rolling of the Mediterranean Sea. Both he and his mother had discovered themselves to be true seamen on this trip.

He let go of her, and he braced his feet farther apart to counter the motion of the ship. He wanted to explain. He owed her that much and so much more.

"What I'm feeling inside, *Anne*," he touched his hand to his forehead, "is dark and gray and ugly—something only *I* can push out of me. I'm not sure that I will ever be able to—" He licked his lips as he watched her eyes fill with tears. This was the very reason he hadn't told her his feelings before. He felt horrible about making his strong mother cry.

"But, *Anne*," he said with a sigh, glancing back at his father to include him, "*Baba*, I promise you both that I *will* try." He paused. "I am trying."

He startled to discover the absolute truth of the declaration. He hadn't realized his intentions until that moment. But since the girl had come to be with them, he had been trying.

Auhan didn't want to be a zombie. But if he didn't allow himself to think, then the little baby in the blue sweater could not haunt his mind—at least, not as easily. Yet since the "Dolphin Girl" had come, he *was* thinking again, and sometimes even thinking nice thoughts. He didn't know why the girl should make such a difference to him. He just knew for some reason she had.

His mother took a deep breath. "I believe you, my son." She reached up and pulled him down to her level in order to kiss the right and left points of his forehead, something she had done for as long as he could remember. Then she stood back, and, blinking tears from her clear, green eyes, she regarded him with such an intensity that he stood a little taller.

"I also believe two other things. First, that this move to America will be partly responsible for saving you." He could tell from the way she paused, with an expectant tilt to her head, that she had been nearly certain that he would refute her observation.

He didn't. How could he? He too suspected their moving away from the old, war-torn land and starting fresh in the new would help him. Already, just being on the ship had helped. He had discovered a real love for sea travel. That and the girl proved to be two good reasons to get up every day. Before leaving home, there had been times when he hadn't left his bed or his shuttered room for days.

When he didn't make a comment, his mother continued. "Second—" She looked away from him and placed her hand across the sleeping girl's cheek. "I believe this girl—and her God—will fill the part of you that the move doesn't. There is light in her." She turned back to Auhan. "A light you need, my son."

*A light he needed?* Auhan wanted to scoff at his mother's proclamation. He knew he would have if he hadn't already challenged her. He felt guilty about doing so again.

But he watched the sleeping girl carefully during the next couple of days. He couldn't deny the joy she brought to their little world every time she awoke. His mother seemed happier, as did his father. And yes, even he.

Here the girl lay, sick and bruised, far from everyone she knew, and yet she had a strength about her, an inner radiance, that both astounded and mesmerized Auhan. Despite his resolve not to, he found himself waiting for the moments when she opened her eyes. He didn't try to analyze why. But he knew somehow, even in her weakened state, she was transforming his feelings of despair.

Each time he gazed into her eyes he felt a stirring within his soul, as if a spark were trying to ignite—to find life. For the first time since he had discovered the mass grave, Auhan found himself truly interested in someone.

With the first fluttering of her lids, his pulse jumped to a quicker beat. He watched as her gaze would first search out his mother, smile at her; then search out his father, smile at him; and then look for him.

She would smile, and he would smile back. Always. With not just a little turning up of his lips but a great big, broad grin. Then his mother's eyes would dance in delight, and his father would chuckle in mirth as he had long ago, when the daughter of his own body had been alive.

Auhan knew his mother had been correct. Even with all the "Dolphin Girl" had been through, she illuminated the world around her. The darkness that had settled upon his soul the previous year was now not as great because of her. And when the girl laid her hand upon the dog's head, as she always did before allowing her eyes to close in sleep, Auhan couldn't help but wonder from where her strength came.

The image of the cross his mother carried in her pocket flashed into his mind. He knew she still carried it because he had seen her take it out several times and look at it in a longing way. Was that cross—what it stood for—the source of the girl's strength, her happiness? Had Jesus actually been more than just a prophet? Contrary to what the Koran wrote about Jesus in Sura al-Nisa' 4:157, "They crucified him not," had Jesus, in truth, died on the cross only to live again? Could He truly be God's Son?

Auhan shook his head. He was so confused. Once again, he wished he could talk over such things with his brother. He missed Mehmet fiercely. Of the two, Mehmet was the thinker, but he had always challenged his younger brother to do the same.

Before coming across the mass grave, Auhan had been a deeper thinker than most of his friends. But he hadn't allowed himself to dwell on such contemplations for such a long time now. Somehow, though, he knew that he was coming to the point where he would have to face his beliefs—or lack thereof—directly. They were, after all, sailing to a new land, a place where a person was allowed to think and believe what they wanted without fear. But did he really want to think that much? Would the little baby in the blue sweater allow him the freedom of such thought?

Every time the girl awoke, she left something behind. Something elusive but something right and true. Lovely and pure. A feeling that reached deep down inside of him and quickened his soul—much akin to the feeling he used to get when he played his violin. Only better. Much better. Her very eyes possessed a wonderful ability to scatter joy all around her.

ᴥ

Elena remained too weak to manage more than the "thank you" she had uttered the first day she opened her eyes, but she wasn't too weak to pray for the wonderful people who had taken her in. She prayed that the Lord would work in their lives in His own glorious way and bring peace and grace to their souls—particularly to the young man.

Something about him seemed familiar to Elena, although she couldn't place what it was. She certainly sensed he was hurting. His eyes reflected a pain much deeper than the physical pain that racked her body. Her body would recover with care and time. Yet, Elena sensed that the young man's hurt was a spiritual pain, a pain only God could heal.

Elena feared the young man would never find peace without the direct intervention of Jesus.

# Chapter 4

*For false Christs and false prophets shall rise,*
*and shall shew signs and wonders, to seduce,*
*if it were possible, even the elect.*
Mark 13:22

When Elena awoke early the next day, she felt a fresh physical energy flowing through her. Although her muscles still hurt fiercely, the general ache of fever no longer compounded her body's pain. Her throbbing headache had disappeared. Her head felt heavy but not in an aching way. She looked over at the dog sleeping by her side. Her fingers slowly uncurled, and she rubbed his golden fur.

The dog lifted his great head, and his soft brown gaze met hers. As they had when in the sea, woman and dog looked lovingly at one another.

"Dear Buddy," Elena croaked out after several minutes had passed, with a voice that seemed very foreign to her. "We made it, Boy. We made it." He nudged her hand in reply, and she patted his snout as tears of happiness slid from the corners of her eyes. "Thank you for keeping me company in the sea, Buddy. I don't think that I could have survived without you." He rewarded her words of gratitude with a gentle thump of his tail and the dearest doggie grin she had ever seen. Her smile deepened, and she realized her lips no longer hurt. As she moistened her lips with her tongue, she could still feel scabs, yet they didn't pull as before.

With expectancy for the new day, she turned her head toward the porthole. But the color filtering through the window was not the blue she had anticipated. Rather the light glowed red, like the red of Smyrna burning. Like her father's blood. Sad tears flowed from her eyes while she whimpered, "*Baba.*"

And again.

"*Baba. . .*"

At her outcry, the young man who had been dozing in a chair near her bed moved quickly to her side. His gaze flicked between her and the red sky beyond the porthole. "It's okay. It's just the sunrise," he said, patting her shoulder.

"It's just. . .so. . .red," she whispered. She covered her eyes with her hand in an attempt to block the terrifying color of glowing fire from her view.

"Soon it will be blue," he assured her. At his words, she lowered her hand to look at him and found comfort in his smiling face. "Here." He slipped a hand under her head to gently lift her up. "Since you're awake, please have a sip of broth." He brought the cup to her lips with his other hand. She did as he instructed and drank heartily in an effort to quench her neverending thirst.

Rather than dwelling on her thoughts of Smyrna, she forced herself to concentrate on his hands as they held the cup. They looked like the hands of an aristocrat —long and slender with clean and trim nails. Elena had seen someone else with such hands recently. But the memory of exactly where was trapped somewhere within her brain.

"How are you feeling?" He moved the cup away from her lips and placed it on the table behind her head.

"Much better." She gave him the most encouraging smile she could muster. Yellow sunlight now bathed the cabin, and Elena studied the kind stranger. He looked every bit as handsome as Elena's muddled brain had registered during the previous days of semiconsciousness. His high forehead matched the nobility of his hands. But along with his good looks and slender build, she noticed his brooding quality, sensed his uneasy mind. Visible not only in his dark eyes, the cloud of grief seemed to wrap around his entire body. She wondered what had happened to place such sorrow there.

"What's your name?" he asked softly. She noted he was unable to meet her gaze as he spoke. He looked at the dog instead.

"Elena," she responded.

"Elena," he echoed. "Your name means 'light.' "

"I like the way you say it," she said, surprising herself with her own straightforwardness. "And your name is?"

"Auhan."

She nodded her head. Now she had a name to use when praying. "Thank you, Auhan, for caring for me."

He motioned to the bunk where an older couple slept. "It was my mother who nursed you. She didn't leave your side for days."

*Days? How many?* She frowned, and the motion made her forehead sting. She reached up with her right hand to explore her face but stopped when she noticed, for the first time, the bandage wrapped around the back of her hand. She raised her left hand. She was perplexed to see bandages encasing it too. Only a portion of her fingers protruded from the dressing. Then, she remembered. The fire falling from the sky. The burning of her skin. Her father dying. The bitter memories engulfed her, and her eyes closed as an involuntary quiver shook her body.

"Elena. . ." Auhan stroked her uninjured fingers.

The sound of his voice and the feel of his fingers around her own were like lifelines to her. She forced her eyes to open and to look into his.

From the language he spoke she knew he was Turkish. All human reasoning told her that she should hate him because of that fact. His race had destroyed her city, killed her father, separated her from her sisters.

But human reasoning didn't rule Elena. God ruled her. Neither this man nor his parents were to blame for what had happened to her and her family—to all the Christians in Smyrna. This Turkish family had been a blessing to her, not a bane.

"Do you want to tell me about it?" Auhan prompted her with a comforting half-whisper, and she slowly nodded her head. She did want to talk about it. All of the happenings in Smyrna had been roaming around her subconscious for days, and somehow she knew that she had to get them out. But she worried she was not yet strong enough. Perhaps she needed a few more days of rest before telling the ugly tale. Before telling about the evil that had invaded the streets of her city.

"Auhan." Sleepiness tinged the voice of the woman on the cot as she spoke. "Is she okay?"

Auhan smiled back at his mother. "*Anne*. I'd like for you to meet Elena. Elena, may I introduce my *Anne*, Fatima."

"Oh!" the older woman exclaimed as she quickly scrambled out of bed and across the space of the small room. The smile she leveled down at her seemed so familiar to Elena. "Dear girl," she breathed out, and Elena watched in amazement as her deep, green eyes filled with tears of happy relief.

When the other woman reached out her hand and brushed it against her cheek, Elena's eyes briefly closed at the wonderful and familiar touch. "Finally, your fever is totally gone! You are better!"

Elena smiled up at her. "Much better, *Anne* Fatima." She used the Turkish word for "mother," which Elena could see pleased the woman very much. "Thanks to you."

Fatima shook her head, and Elena watched in question as she dug deeply into the pocket of her dressing gown for something. "No. It is thanks to God that you are well." She held up the cross.

Elena gasped as she recognized it. "My mother's cross. . .the one. . .I had sewn into my dress. . ." She looked from the woman to her son, whose hand still covered her fingers. The woman gave the credit of her recovery to God. And she was holding up the cross.

Elena wiggled the fingers of her free hand through the dog's fur. They had also allowed Buddy to stay with her, not only in this cabin, but also on her bed, something she knew a Muslim family would never condone. Did that mean that this family was a rarely heard of Turkish Christian family? Elena had to know.

"Are you. . ." She paused and looked between the mother and son and the older man who sat on the far bunk. "I mean, do you believe in Jesus Christ?"

A shadow seemed to cross Fatima's face, and Elena felt the blood rush to her own face at having asked such a personal question of people who were, in truth, still strangers to her. But as the woman spoke, Elena's regret evaporated like fog touched by the rays of the sun.

"I'm not proud to admit this," Fatima began, "but our ancestry is that of apostatized Christians. The people of our bloodline renounced Jesus Christ in order to live in their homes without the terrible discriminations, including the dreaded blood tribute of earlier years, imposed upon Christians by the Ottoman Empire."

Elena knew she referred to the hundreds of years when agents of the sultan had combed the empire for the ablest Christian boys between the ages of ten and twelve. Those boys found to be of top physical and mental quality had been taken from their family, forcibly converted to Islam, and made into the elite fighting corps of the sultan, the Janissary corps. The boys were never to be seen by their families again—except as adversaries sent to kill the very ones who had given them life, their Christian parents. In the face of this terrible crime against humanity, Elena marveled that throughout the middle and late medieval ages so many Greeks, Armenians, and other Christians hadn't apostatized after finding their homeland under the rule of the nomadic conquerors, the Seljuk and Ottoman Turks from the steppes of Asia. Most modern Christians would agree—to have one's child taken because of the "crime" of being a believer would be even harder than giving one's own life for one's faith. Elena wasn't a mother yet, but she was sure this must be so.

"However," Fatima continued after a lengthy pause, her voice barely above a whisper, "I would like. . .to find. . .the God of my ancestors once again." Elena, seeing how Fatima rubbed the cross between her fingers, regarded her with curiosity. Such soft words, so few, and yet words that Elena knew had the ability to change the dear woman's entire life. Wonder filled Elena as, letting go of Auhan's hand, she reached out and placed her fingers over Fatima's, which now held tightly to the cross, the cross of Jesus Christ. "He's so easy to find, *Anne* Fatima. So easy."

Fatima carefully covered Elena's wounded hand with her other one and lowered herself to the side of Elena's bed. "When you are well," she implored, her green eyes intense with longing, "would you help me?"

Making a little half laugh, half cry sound, but which equaled total happiness, Elena sent up a silent prayer to God for His having literally washed her into the path of this wonderful, searching woman. "It would be my greatest delight, *Anne*

Fatima," Elena responded truthfully, and, reaching up, she wrapped her arms around the slender woman's shoulders in her famous, impromptu hug.

❧

Watching as the two women held one another close, Auhan thought that not only their eyes but their entire bodies seemed to radiate a golden joy.

But joy wasn't what Auhan was feeling, golden or otherwise. Anger, confusion, and a multitude of emotions he couldn't even begin to identify battled within him like a skirmish full of ricocheting bullets. His fingers, his now empty fingers, clenched into a fist.

When Elena had let go of his hand to touch the cross in his mother's hand, he had felt as though he had been cast out into the darkest night and exchanged for something, or Someone, who didn't care as much as he was beginning to. But despite the blood that surged and pounded like the ocean within his head, he forced himself to calm down and to think.

What exactly did his mother mean by saying that she wanted to "find" the God of her ancestors? That was something Auhan had never heard before, and annoyance flickered through his thoughts. Did his mother really believe there was much of a difference between the two religions? Was she planning on exchanging one impotent way of regarding the Almighty for another?

Auhan looked between the two women. They seemed to be communicating on a different plane, one on which he didn't belong. His mother looked happy. Yet her happiness went beyond that of human control to a realm that was, for him, very suspect.

Hearing his father arise from his bunk, Auhan glanced his way. But the older man was watching his wife. Auhan saw a smile curve his father's lips beneath his thick mustache. Judging from the glint in his eyes, his father found pleasure at the sight of his happy wife.

Auhan wished he felt the same way. He just didn't. He couldn't believe he could trust his mother's source of joy. Then again, Auhan didn't believe there was anything in this evil world that he *could* trust.

His mother might be happy today, but what about tomorrow? Had they so quickly forgotten Elena had been fished from the sea only a few days before? Where had the God of Jesus Christ been then?

*Probably off in the same place He had been when the baby—the Christian baby—in the blue sweater had been thrown into that mass grave,* Auhan thought as seeds of anger flowered within him. The walls of the cabin seemed to press upon him, and Auhan knew he had to get out.

"Excuse me," he said, a metallic quality lacing his voice. He grabbed his cap and motioned to the dog to follow him out of the room.

From his peripheral vision he caught a glimpse of his mother's eyebrows arching upward. He knew she was surprised by his abrupt departure. Yet, he also knew her to be a very wise woman. Unlike most mothers, she wouldn't challenge him. And now, more than ever, he appreciated her for it.

As his feet clanged through the hollow passageway and the paws of his companion tapped behind him, Auhan continued to ponder his mother's declaration. To believe in God as revealed by Jesus Christ was, in Auhan's opinion, an even weaker alternative than to believe in Allah as revealed by the Koran. To believe in Allah at least didn't require much thought. No one had to "find" Allah. They just had to follow the rules. Belief in Jesus required too much on the part of humans. *And for what?* Auhan wondered as he swung open the deck's door. *To be forgotten when evil reared its ugly face?*

The ocean wind pushed at Auhan when he stepped out onto the middle deck, and sea spray washed over him. He stood still and filled his lungs with fresh air. He liked the feel of the spray upon his face—as if it washed him clean each time he stepped into its path.

Walking over to the railing, his hand idly stroked the dog's head, and he gazed out over the sea and sky. Regarding the unbroken seascape made him feel free. The way music once made him feel.

For music resounded from the sea.

Carried on the wind.

Singing not in billowing voices of nature's grandeur but in whispers. Gentle murmurs upon his soul.

Auhan filled his lungs with a deep, rejuvenating breath. He liked to stand on the deck. He could breathe deeply there. Surrounded by the unbridled, expansive sea, he could almost live with himself.

# Chapter 5

*I will receive you, and will be a Father unto you,*
*and ye shall be my sons and daughters, saith the Lord Almighty.*
2 Corinthians 6:17–18

Where is this ship heading?" Elena asked as she ate the soft-boiled egg that Fatima patiently spooned into her mouth. Elena felt stronger and stronger by the hour and now even sat up in bed.

"To America," Fatima responded, and Elena's eyes widened.

*Home.* Feelings of excitement bubbled up as her gaze skidded over to the porthole.

She was going home. To the land of her birth. The miracle of God's provision caressed her mind like a soft ocean breeze would her skin.

"America," she breathed as she studied Auhan's face. He sat on the opposite bunk. "But how—?" she asked. The Italian rescue ship had been taking the refugees from Smyrna only as far as Athens's port of Piraeus.

"Don't worry, Elena," Auhan answered her quickly, motioning to his father sitting beside him and to his mother before her. "My parents have already agreed. If you are amenable to the idea, they will adopt you. They have all the necessary papers to enter America, and as their daughter you will not be turned away."

Elena's eyes sought out Auhan's parents. With big smiles covering their faces, the older couple nodded their agreement. Their generous offer touched a chord deep within Elena's heart, and as a slow smile moved across her face, she whispered up yet another prayer of thanksgiving to God for bringing her to these wonderful people.

"I thank you." Emotion made her tone husky. "That is one of the nicest things anyone has ever offered to do for me." She reached out and touched both of their hands in turn. "Since my parents are now both gone from this earth, I would count it an honor and a privilege to be known as your daughter. But," she said with a shrug of her shoulders, "you don't have to do so in order to get me into the United States." She paused, then declared in perfect English, "I am American."

"What?" Fatima's mouth dropped open while Auhan's eyes widened momentarily, then narrowed.

"You. . .are. . .American?" he asked in broken English. His parents had taught themselves and both him and his brother to write in English. They could read almost anything and possessed extensive vocabularies. But neither he nor his parents had heard the language spoken by a native speaker before boarding the *Ionian Star*, where they heard the seamen speak it. To hear Elena speak English —and those particular English words—stunned him. The ramifications behind her pronouncement were huge.

With her eyebrows rising slightly, Elena nodded her head, confirming her proclamation.

"Then what were you doing adrift in the Aegean Sea?" Auhan asked with a caustic tone in his voice.

"Although my mother was American, my father. . .was. . . ," Elena stumbled over her first past tense reference to her father. "He was. . .a Greek man. From Smyrna."

Fatima thumped the bowl with the egg onto the table, and Elena jumped at the clatter. If *Anne* Fatima hadn't immediately reached for her fingers and squeezed them in a comforting way, Elena would have worried that the other woman disliked hearing she was part Greek.

"You often screamed out for your *Baba*—your father—in your sleep." Fatima stroked her hair. "And for ones called Sophia, Rose, and Christos. Who are they?"

Elena tipped her head downward slightly. Elena recognized the time had come for her to address some important issues. "Sophia is my older sister. Since my mother died when I was but a child, Sophia and I have always been particularly close. Rose is my informally adopted little sister. Sophia and I took her in when her parents were killed, at the same time our father was shot. . .the last night. . . we were in Smyrna," she explained and squeezed her eyes shut as the image of that horrible moment on the quay swooped in on her. She could feel the blood drain from her face and felt her lips start to tremble, but at the pressure of Fatima's fingers on her own, she opened her eyes and looked into the loving eyes of the woman who had nursed her back to health.

"We are very sorry to hear about your father," Fatima murmured her condolences. "But you must not think of such sad things. You are not strong enough. You must think of only good things, good memories with your father. Tell us only if your sisters and the one called Christos yet live, and then we will ask no more." She flashed Auhan a mother's look of admonishment before returning her gaze to Elena.

Elena knew *Anne* Fatima was right. She could not dwell on her father's death. Her father's physical life, as she knew it, was gone. Yet, the spirit that had made him Andreas Apostologlou still lived. Elena knew with certainty she would meet him again someday. And on that day, he would have a brand new body. One unmarred by bullets.

"Thank you, *Anne* Fatima." She squeezed the other woman's fingers as much as her injured ones allowed. "I will only think of things that help me to get well."

As she had done her entire life, Elena resolved to give all bad thoughts to God.

"Good." Fatima smiled and nodded for her to continue.

"Yes. My sisters and Christos live. We were rescued from the sea by a very overcrowded Italian ship. I was sleeping against the edge when I—" She grimaced at the thought. "I quite literally fell overboard. That's how I ended up in the Aegean Sea."

"Why didn't the ship come back for you?" Auhan asked in a judgmental tone.

She shook her head vehemently to dispel any suspicions that someone from the ship was at fault. "No one saw me fall. Most likely, by the time my sisters or Christos even discovered that I was missing, the ship had steamed miles away."

"And who is this Christos?" Auhan asked. If Elena didn't know better, she would have suspected a jealous motive behind the question.

"Christos is a Greek soldier whom Sophia and I had met only a few days before." She paused and had to think exactly when it was. "The Thursday before the Turkish soldiers. . ." Remembering her audience, she stumbled on her words. But at their looks of encouragement, she continued, "before the Turkish soldiers entered the city. Christos had carried a wounded soldier from the battlefields all the way to our doorstep. He left him with us to care for him." She remembered back to that day, the last day Smyrna had been. . .Smyrna.

"Christos wouldn't even come in to rest. His only concern was for his friend. But something happened between my sister and Christos." Elena thought she could see a noticeable easing of Auhan's shoulders as he drew a deep breath.

"They hardly exchanged words before he shuffled away, but they definitely experienced a strong emotional exchange. And, when we met again the following Wednesday—"

"But how did you meet up with him again on Wednesday?" Auhan interrupted. "I overheard before leaving port that all the Greek soldiers had left for Greece before the Turkish troops entered Smyrna."

Elena felt the need to cough, but she tried to suppress it. "I think Christos. . ." She paused and swallowed and prayed that she wouldn't cough. Once she started, she knew that she wouldn't be able to stop for several minutes. "He was the only. . ." She swallowed again and took a sip of her tea. "Greek soldier left," she finally answered, glad that, with the help of her soothing chamomile, she had avoided a coughing fit.

She explained how Christos had not only saved her and her sisters from a brutal attack outside their home when they had returned for their rowboat but had, in fact, gotten them and the other women and children who had occupied their rowboat aboard the Italian ship in the harbor. "We all owe our lives to Christos. From the soldier he carried to our home—who was Turkish, by the way—"

"Turkish?" Auhan interrupted and made a disagreeable sound. "A Greek helping a Turk?" he challenged, with thinned lips.

Elena's eyes flashed. "Tell me, Auhan," she responded without allowing even a breath to intervene. "Is it any stranger than a family of Turks helping a Greek?" She held out her hand to indicate the three of them.

She patted her chest with her bandaged hand. "I am American, but I am Greek too. Both facts of which I am very proud." Elena always had been. She was a product of the oldest democratic nation in the world and one of the newest and best, a position she knew was very unique. And, both modern countries—the USA and Greece—had always been allies—a very special relationship that very few countries in the world today could claim. If Auhan wanted to take issue with her dual nationalities, she knew it was better for him to do so now rather than later.

Elena watched as Auhan's jaw hardened in defiance, but after a moment he expelled his held breath and sent her a half smile. She returned it with a full one of her own.

In that instant, something happened between them. A spark. A sigh. Something as exciting as a festive summer fair and as calm as a good book read together by the fireplace on a cold winter's night. A nice feeling that seemed to soften Auhan's heart as much as her own.

"I suppose you are right," he finally admitted. "This Christos carrying the Turkish soldier to safety is not really any different than our caring for you."

"Besides," Elena continued after a moment, "I think that Christos would help anybody in the world in need. He didn't consider that man his enemy. In fact, they were friends. Christos is truly a man of God." She noted the slight stiffening of Auhan's spine at her declaration. "And someday," she hurried her words and turned to stare, unseeing, out the porthole, "I think that he's going to be my brother-in-law. He and my sister, they had only just met, but you know, love does come quickly under such extraordinary circumstances."

"I can see how that might happen," Fatima interjected. When Elena turned back toward her, she discovered *Anne* Fatima studying her and Auhan. The mother visibly bit the inside of her cheek while a slow, mischievous smile creased her cheeks. Fatima reached for the egg and spooned a little bit more into Elena's mouth. "So you will meet up with your sisters and Christos again soon."

❧

His mother spoke in the encouraging way of all mothers, but Auhan wondered just *how* they might find each other. Even so, he kept his questions to himself. Elena was still much too weak to consider such a task. Auhan knew, though, for family members to locate one another after a political separation could prove to be a difficult feat to accomplish and sometimes took years—if ever. He was glad that his parents had the foresight to set up a rendezvous point in America in the eventuality that any of them should become separated. If by chance his brother still lived, at least he, as well as they, knew when and where to meet one another again. It was a date they would keep each year until they were reunited.

"But for now," he heard his mother continue, "you must sleep. We will talk more later," she said as she gave the last of the egg to Elena, and, removing the wool shawl from around Elena's shoulders, she proceeded to fix the covers around the girl's slender form.

"*Anne* is right," Auhan said, and getting up, he motioned for Buddy to follow him. "We will take a walk up on deck." But as he reached for his hat, he flashed Elena a smile. "Soon, I hope that you will be able to come with us."

Auhan couldn't help but think as he watched her, everything about her glowed golden. Her eyes. Her hair. Her skin. Her spirit. Golden and bright.

The idea of being out in the elements didn't seem to appeal to Elena at all. She snuggled deeper down into her covers in a protective way. "I trust that is so," she responded with only her head poking out of the blanket. "To sit on the deck of a ship and just watch the sky pass before me *used* to be one of my favorite things in the world to do, something I gladly did for hours."

"Really?" Her words caught Auhan's interest. An image popped into his mind of the two of them sitting up on deck watching the clouds skitter across the sky. He was surprised to realize how much he liked the idea.

Elena nodded her head. "Although, after my mother died, we lived primarily in Smyrna, my father never wanted us to lose contact with America as our home too, so he took Sophia and me to America every summer."

"An ocean crossing every year?" Auhan asked with raised brows. By the standards of their village, his family had been considered well off. Yet, this was the first voyage they had ever been able to afford. He watched with interest the changing expressions crossing Elena's face as she nodded.

"I love every aspect of sailing across the sea," she continued, remembering her journeys. "The sound of the engines." She cocked her head as if listening to the noise of the self-propelled ship beneath them. "The vibration." She motioned to the glass of water and the liquid that jumped lightly within it. "The wind in my hair, the sea spray on my face, the seagulls greeting a ship after crossing the ocean, the dolphins." She smiled, a poignant turning up of her lips in remembrance of the dolphins that had saved her. "But mostly," she looked in the direction of the porthole, "I just love watching the sky." She sighed, and pulling her arm out of the blanket, she reached out her hand to touch the cool glass of the window and the firmament beyond. "Not just the sun rising in the morning or setting in the evening," she qualified, "but any time of the day or night and in any weather. I could just sit and look at it forever." She sighed wistfully, and turning back to Auhan, she caught her breath at how his eyes looked as they regarded her.

Holding a usually absent sparkle, they gleamed down on her like polished stones. She realized that for the first time since they'd met, he looked genuinely happy about something. She felt special in an unfamiliar way. A womanly way. She had never cared about pleasing a man before. Yet, where Auhan was concerned, pleasing him mattered a great deal to her.

"Since this is my first voyage, I've only just discovered that I too like watching the ocean sky," he admitted. It thrilled her to know that they had something in common.

"Maybe," he paused, and the sweetest grin moved his lips before he ventured to ask, "maybe soon, when you are better, you might enjoy sitting on deck with me where we might regard the sea and the sky together?"

Elena's eyes widened and that unfamiliar, womanly feeling intensified. Was he asking her for a date? If so, Elena knew that the idea appealed to her. In spite of the brooding quality so often evident in him, there were other attributes about him, elusive, but things that she knew were good and true, to which her spirit responded. She sensed that many of his best traits were locked deep inside of him. A slow, returning smile curved her lips, and she prayed that she might help bring out those special traits. "That would be delightful," she replied, feeling more like her elegant sister, Sophia, responding to one of her many suitors, than herself.

Auhan's gaze stayed on her for a moment longer, probing, searching. Trying, Elena thought, to understand what this reaction between them was—something she herself couldn't quite understand. Then, with an almost self-conscious nod, he turned, and, with the dog at his heels, he left the room. For a long moment, Elena stared at the doorway in wonder over what was happening between herself and Auhan. *Anne* Fatima's softly spoken "thank you" broke the comfortable silence.

Hearing a catch in the dear woman's voice, Elena pulled her gaze toward *Anne* Fatima and away from the door where the dog and the man had just exited—the man who was quickly becoming very special to her.

"Thank you?" Elena asked, genuinely perplexed. "For what?"

"For coming to us."

Elena stilled the woman's hand in the motion of tucking her into bed. "Dear *Anne* Fatima. It is *I* who must thank *you*."

But Fatima shook her head in adamant denial. "No. You have brought healing to our lives. To the life of our child." She motioned over to her husband, who nodded his ever silent, ever watching, ever observant head in agreement. "Your God has," Fatima qualified fearlessly, and Elena closed her mouth on the argument she had been about to offer.

For Auhan's parents to see a difference in their son meant that God *was* working in his life. Her prayers *were* being answered. *Oh, dear Lord,* Elena whispered within herself to the God whom she knew always heard. *Thank You. Thank You.*

"Please." *Anne* Fatima wore a pleading expression. "Just keep praying to your God for our son."

Elena's eyes widened at how closely the dear woman's words echoed her own thoughts. "Always," she whispered as *Anne* Fatima's loving hands finished settling her down for a nap.

But just before sleep overtook her brain, Elena did what *Anne* Fatima asked and even more. *Please God,* she prayed, *please bring Auhan and his dear parents to You. I want them to know the fullness of life—both now and eternally—known only by those who know Your Son. In the name of Your precious Son, Jesus, I pray.*

Her prayer was a simple one, yet one with mighty implications. And with its "*amen,*" Elena knew that she could sleep soundly.

God was, as always, in control.

# Chapter 6

*Who is a liar but he that denieth that Jesus is the Christ?*
*He is antichrist, that denieth the Father and the Son.*
1 John 2:22

The next day, Elena patted Buddy's clean, golden fur with the fingers of her right hand while she raked the fingers of her left hand through her own clean hair. *Anne* Fatima had surprised her by washing it for her earlier that morning. As she worked, she lamented about how miserable Elena must have felt at having her hair caked with salt from the sea. She had used a home-made shampoo scented with chamomile, which now fragranced the air around Elena like a refreshing spring breeze.

Although Elena still felt weak, she felt like a new person with her hair falling soft and shiny around her shoulders. When *Anne* Fatima, her work done, came up to the side of the bed, Elena smiled up at her as her right hand continued to caress Buddy. They were alone in the cabin.

"You love that dog, don't you?" Although she phrased it as a question, it was actually more of a statement.

"*Anne*, his coming to me in the sea was a miracle." Elena's reply held no hesitation as she reached for her teacup and took a sip of the golden liquid within. Ever since she had become strong enough to sit up in bed, there had been an ever-present cup of chamomile next to her. She loved the herbal tea. With each sip she couldn't help but think how wonderful it would have been if someone had offered that drink when she had been adrift in the sea. The consumption of liquids was something Elena would never take for granted again. "Just when I didn't think that I could go on any longer alone," she continued, "God sent Buddy and the dolphin to me." Elena had already explained to them all how that had happened. "But I think that the dolphin coming to Buddy's aid and keeping him afloat in the choppy water before finding me was the greater miracle."

"Miracle," Fatima murmured in concurrence and pulled the cross, Elena's cross, out of her pocket. Because of its value, they had agreed she would hold it for safe-keeping until Elena was strong enough to look after it herself. Of the numerous

51

pieces of jewelry Elena had sewn into her clothing, only the cross and her mother's wedding ring set had been found when Fatima had washed out her tattered clothes. The rest were either on the charred streets of Smyrna or sitting at the bottom of the deep, blue sea.

Seating herself on the trunk next to Elena, Fatima seemed to study the cross before turning to Elena and, with hesitation, voiced a question. Elena could tell the thought had long been on the dear woman's mind. "How do you live, Elena, without grief overwhelming you?" she finally asked. "You lost so much, and yet," Fatima looked at her with true, open-minded inquiry in her sharp green eyes, "you are like a light to us all."

A quick smile spread across Elena's face as she reached over and took the older woman's hand in her own. Elena's thumb rubbed the soft flesh of the woman whom she had grown to love deeply, then she moved to touch the metal of the beautifully crafted cross now warmed by Fatima's touch. "Dear *Anne* Fatima, it is God who gives me the power to live. Whenever my problems start to overwhelm me, I immediately give them to Him." She had been constantly doing that in regard to her father's death, her separation from her sisters, and the death of her city, of Smyrna, since consciousness had returned to her.

Fatima's fine brows came together in a quizzical frown. "*Give* your problems to God?" She placed a marveling emphasis on the word "give."

Elena started to take a deep breath, but it made her cough, so instead she took a sip of her tea, then another and another before placing her cup back on the chest beside her. She didn't want a coughing fit to interrupt her. "When God created us, *Anne*, He never intended for us to live life without Him. Through sending His Son, Jesus, to earth, God made it possible for us to have the relationship with Him He had meant for us to have from the very beginning."

"Jesus really is God's Son?"

"He is, indeed."

Fatima shook her head. "Islam, the religion my family has been following, teaches that although Jesus was a great prophet. . .He was not, however. . .God's Son and. . . ," Fatima looked down at the cross in her hand, "that He was neither killed. . .nor crucified."

"But He was," Elena refuted in a soft voice. She rubbed the cross—the oh-so-important reminder of the actual cross of Jesus—which was responsible for bringing all who made the choice to believe in God's redemptive work back into fellowship with Him.

"Jesus said He came not to be ministered unto, but to minister and to give His life as a ransom for many," she paraphrased the New Testament verse. "*Anne*, Jesus ransomed His life on that cross for you, for me, for all of us. That was the very reason for which He came into the world. Only by dying on the cross could He achieve ultimate victory for humans over sin, death, and Satan and bring us back into full fellowship with God. In this way, this most glorious and love-filled way, He—God—serves us."

Fatima's mouth quirked into a dry line. "We are taught to minister to Allah. We are his servants, and we should always submit to him."

Elena had never been happier that her father had insisted that she and Sophia memorize Scripture verses than at this moment. Her fingers itched to pick up her dearly loved Bible and to flip through its much worn pages as she talked to Fatima.

But she couldn't. Her Bible, like so many other Bibles in Smyrna, along with thousands of illuminated Greek manuscripts and letters from the earliest days of Christianity, were now gone. Burned to ashes.

Asking the Holy Ghost to guide her words, Elena spoke. "The Apostle John, a man who was very close to Jesus, wrote, 'But as many as received him'—Jesus—" Elena qualified, " 'to them gave he power to become the sons of God, even to them that believe on his name.' "

"Sons?" Fatima questioned, tilting her scarf-covered head to the side.

"Sons," Elena affirmed. "And because of this, if we believe that Jesus is who He Himself said He is—God's Son—then we become, by adoption, God's children. Jesus, God's begotten Son, came to serve us. He came to break the chains of darkness, which would then enable us to live in the light of God's love once again. *Anne* Fatima, children are not their parents' servants, but rather their parents' joy."

Earlier, while she had been washing her hair, Fatima had told Elena how her two sons and her little daughter had been the joys of her life since the days of their births.

"Please tell me more," Fatima prompted a bit breathlessly, and Elena was glad to do so.

"Jesus is God, but Scripture tells us that He 'made himself of no reputation, and. . .was made in the likeness of men: And being found in fashion as a man, he humbled himself, and became obedient unto death, even the death of the cross,' " Elena repeated her favorite Bible verses, those found in the second chapter of Philippians.

She could never think of them or repeat them without chills of sublime wonder coursing from one shoulder blade to the other, especially when she spoke the next words. " 'Wherefore God also hath highly exalted him, and given him a name which is above every name: That at the name of Jesus every knee should bow, of things in heaven, and things in earth, and things under the earth; And that every tongue should confess that Jesus Christ is Lord, to the glory of God the Father.'"

"But, this is something I find very confusing."

Elena startled at the sound of Auhan's voice. She turned to look at him as he stood in the doorway with his father. She had been so intent on her conversation with *Anne* Fatima, she hadn't heard them return to the cabin.

He pulled his cap from his head as he continued. "My brother and I used to discuss such things. While some Muslims view the Trinity as a union between God and Mary giving birth to Jesus, I understand Christians worship three gods —the Father, and the Son, with the Holy Ghost—not Mary—being the third party. Am I right?"

Elena shook her head from side to side. "No, Auhan. We believe in one God. One perfect and indivisible God."

"But, Father, Son, and Holy Ghost." He shrugged his shoulders. "Aren't they three different persons?"

Even though Elena knew that the question was a hard one, one of the hardest, to answer, the fact that he was even asking sent tremors of hope coursing through her. Her father, in spite of war and discrimination, had possessed a heart full of love for his Muslim neighbors. He had often told her that a Muslim who submitted uncritically to the authority of the Islamic religion, a recited, dictated religion, would never be able to see the truth about Jesus. To think with the rational mind God gave to humans was the first step.

While Islam was characterized by submission to Allah and his commands—no questions asked—the Christian God trusted people to use the brain He Himself had put into their heads. Consequently, the Christian God, unlike the Muslim's Allah, didn't fear questions. Quite the contrary. God welcomed them.

Even though she knew Auhan didn't realize it, just his inquiry meant he had crossed the first and most difficult hurdle. As she answered him, hope filled her—hope for his eventual salvation and maybe even hope for a future together with him.

"Yes, three different persons, Auhan, but still, one God. A unity in a Trinity." She wanted to keep everything simple.

She knew a person trained in the Muslim faith found the triune nature of God something very difficult to grasp. But Elena, backed by nearly two thousand years of her ancestors' belief in the redemptive work of Christ on the cross, also understood that without the mediation of the Son of God, God the Father would have remained in isolated splendor, being too holy for sinful man to even approach. And, without the Holy Ghost living in the midst of His people and dwelling in the believer, man would have been left on his own to try to follow God's holy precepts, an impossible task.

Elena studied Auhan's face before plowing ahead, praying all the while for the right words to dispel his suspicions. "After Jesus died on the cross and was resurrected, just before He was taken up to heaven, He told His disciples, 'All power is given unto me in heaven and in earth. Go ye therefore, and teach all nations, baptizing them in the name of the Father, and of the Son, and of the Holy Ghost.' "

Although Auhan didn't offer a verbal response, she sensed a dubious air settling around him like a disagreeable cloud.

"Auhan, Jesus spoke of 'Father, Son, and Holy Ghost' together in one phrase to mean God—one God. But for now, the main thing you need to know and believe can be summed up in this one verse, 'For God so loved the world, that he gave his only begotten Son. . . .' " Her voice faltered, and she stopped speaking at the remembrance of the last time she had heard those beautiful words of promise. Sophia had spoken them on the quay right after their father had gone on to Paradise. As Elena continued to say the verse in her mind, her voice merged with the echoed memory of her sister's recitation. " 'That whosoever believeth in him should not perish, but have. . .everlasting. . .life.' "

Once more, the glorious assurance of knowing her father wasn't gone from her forever—that he hadn't perished—filled Elena with an inexplicable joy.

She turned her head and looked out the window. Elena could never describe this sensation, yet she felt as if the very arms of God reached down from heaven and enfolded her soul within His protective grasp.

"Oh, my! Could it really be so very simple?" *Anne* Fatima exclaimed.

Elena turned to look at her, and the sight nearly left her breathless. Her eyes shone like emeralds washed by the sea. She seemed like a little girl opening the best present she could have ever imagined receiving. She was. The gift of salvation.

"That's basically it," Elena agreed, her voice tight with emotion. "But not only did He die for us, *Anne*, but He was resurrected as well. That's what Pascha, Easter, is all about. Jesus was killed; He was crucified, but after being dead for three days and in His tomb, He rose again to life. He didn't just ascend to heaven without dying on the cross as the Koran claims. Jesus was horribly tortured; He died—a historical fact witnessed by thousands—and three days later He rose again to life. Life! By doing all this not only did He mark the way for us back to God—Himself—but He conquered death for us too."

"And the Holy Ghost?" Fatima asked. "We have been taught that the Comforter whom Jesus referred to is the prophet Mohammed, and the Holy Ghost is the angel Gabriel who brought messages from God to both Mary and Mohammed."

This was not the first time Elena had heard about the Muslim belief that the Comforter was Mohammed and the Holy Ghost was someone other than God. But, as always, such false doctrine made chills run up and down her spine. From their childhood, so many people like Fatima had been falsely taught about the Holy Spirit. The Comforter and the Holy Ghost were One and the same—the very One who lives within a believer. For *Anne* Fatima to so misunderstand this fact truly saddened Elena.

Coughing in agitation over these troubling thoughts, Elena reached for her chamomile and took a sip before offering a gentle answer to her precious friend, again using the inspired words of the Bible. "Jesus said, 'I will pray the Father, and he shall give you another Comforter, that he may abide with you for ever; Even the Spirit of truth; whom the world cannot receive, because it seeth him not, neither knoweth him: but ye know him; for he dwelleth with you, and shall be in you. I will not leave you comfortless: I will come to you.' "

*Anne* Fatima looked as if a light had been turned on within her soul. She seemed to understand everything. However, Elena could tell Auhan was doubtful by the firm set of his jaw.

⁂

In truth, it did indeed sound to Auhan as if the Counselor was the third person of the one God Elena described. Still, he just wasn't sure. No matter what his distant ancestors might have believed, he still wasn't even certain that he wanted to know more about God, Allah—Whomever. The Almighty was still pretty low on his list.

Even so, Elena's enthusiasm about the subject electrified the air. Her eyes seemed to sparkle with an inner fire. Sunbeams poured through the porthole and surrounded her hair with a halo of heavenly light. As Elena continued her treatise, Auhan knew she addressed him now rather than his mother.

Elena looked him straight in the eye as she spoke. "Another time, Jesus said, 'But when the Comforter is come, whom I will send unto you from the Father, even the Spirit of truth, which proceedeth from the Father, he shall testify of me: And ye also shall bear witness, because ye have been with me from the beginning.' "

"Jesus said that?" A frown tugged at the corners of his mouth. "That the Comforter would testify about Him?"

Elena nodded. "So how could the Comforter possibly be Mohammed? Mohammed does not testify about Jesus being God's Son, and neither was Mohammed with Jesus when He spoke these words."

"No, of course not," Auhan agreed. "Mohammed didn't live until more than six hundred years after Jesus."

"That's right." Elena face brightened again at his response.

"It's all so amazing!" his mother exclaimed.

"Amazing and true—and the reason why I am able to turn my problems over to God, *Anne* Fatima," Elena said, returning to the original question. "He is not only my heavenly Father but my friend too."

Radiance seemed to fill his mother's face as she nodded. "I think I understand now. It's as if a veil," she moved her hands as if she were removing a cloth from her face, "has been taken away from my eyes, and for the first time I can see, can understand, that which I only sensed before."

She looked down at the cross in her hands. "God is a personal God who is not only above me as my heavenly Father," she paused, as though savoring a sweet, new wonder, "but He is with me in Jesus Christ and in me through the Comforter, the Holy Ghost." She turned to him.

"The Comforter whom Jesus talks about is another nature of God, Auhan. It's true!" She crossed her arms across her chest. "I feel it here."

He looked for a long moment at his mother. He was glad to see her so joyful, yet he still felt very unsure. He glanced over at his father but found no help there. The older man wore an enigmatic expression that gave nothing away.

Auhan turned to Elena. As expected, she wore the same radiant expression as his mother.

He wondered, could something that made others so happy be wrong? He didn't know. However, he did know he had ruined enough moments for his mother during the last year, and he resolved not to mar this one by voicing any more doubts or by leaving the cabin, as he had the last time the discussion had turned religious.

"What do I have to do?" Fatima asked Elena. She responded by touching a bandaged hand to his mother's arm.

"Scripture tells us, 'But as many as received him, to them gave he power to become the sons of God, even to them that believe on his name: Which were born, not of blood, nor of the will of the flesh, nor of the will of man, but of God.' "

The phrase "born. . .of God" jumped out at Auhan, but Elena didn't notice the look of wondering inquiry he sent her way. She continued her explanation of the recited scripture to his mother.

"*Anne*, to all who believe in the redemptive blood of Jesus Christ, God gives them the right to be counted as sons and daughters. All you have to do is to repent of your sin—tell Him you're sorry. Confess your belief in Jesus Christ as His Son. Then, accept the gift of His salvation, which He bought for us with His atoning death."

"That's all?" There was an incredulous note in his mother's voice.

"That's it," Elena replied. "Believe me, *Anne* Fatima, afterwards you will find yourself really wanting to please God. But your salvation won't depend on what you do. Your salvation has already been bought by Jesus. All you have to do to please God, to be counted as God's daughter, is to believe Jesus, believe He spoke the truth when He said, 'I am the way, the truth, and the life: no man cometh unto the Father, but by me.' "

Auhan realized just how amazing such a concept must be to his mother. The idea seemed too incredible to him as well. Like his mother, he had been raised to believe that one must earn Allah's mercy and the rewards of heaven through good deeds. He could hardly grasp the idea that God, through Jesus, freely gave salvation to them who would simply repent and believe.

In answer to Elena, his mother's chest swelled on a deep, new breath, as though she breathed in a new air of freedom.

"Would you like me to pray with you?" Elena offered.

Fatima shook her head. "No. I wish to go and commune with my God alone." Casting a smile at each of them, she turned and walked out of the cabin.

As she left, Auhan's mind filled with questions concerning what had just happened to her. There was so much about this whole discussion that he didn't understand. He determined to ask Elena more questions.

But later.

Later.

# Chapter 7

*And having spoiled principalities and powers,*
*he made a shew of them openly, triumphing over them in it [the cross].*
Colossians 2:15

The following days proved to be glorious ones. Not only did God's light fill both *Anne* Fatima's heart and their little cabin, but Elena's physical healing seemed to progress at a modest rate as well. Each day she witnessed a major improvement. Her cough was breaking up, and her burns were healing. Although her energy remained low, she rejoiced that she no longer had to stay in bed. She could sit for several hours at a time in an easy chair and sip her ever-present cup of chamomile while enjoying the movement of the ship beneath her, the wonderful ship that had not only rescued her but was carrying her home to America.

One morning her eyes spied a violin case tucked away in a far corner of the cabin.

"Oh my," she exclaimed and looked toward Auhan. He sat on his mother's bunk holding his hands apart and aloft as he helped her turn a skein of yarn into a manageable ball. His long and slender, aristocratic hands with their blunt nails convinced Elena that he owned the instrument.

"Do you play the violin, Auhan?" She motioned toward the case.

The guileless words no sooner left her mouth than Elena knew she had stumbled onto a sensitive subject. *Anne* Fatima paused her yarn rolling. Auhan's expression turned to stone. Elena flicked her gaze toward Auhan's father. Like her, he seemed to be waiting for his son's answer.

"I used to," Auhan answered, tight-lipped and hard.

Elena looked at his hands. She studied them. She didn't see any scars, nor had she noticed him favoring his arms or hands in any way during the time she had been with them. Quite the contrary. Now that she thought about it, she had often noticed his fingers moving as if they fingered musical chords. She drew in a quick breath of amazement as the realization struck her. He had been doing just that. She had thought the strange movement just a nervous trait. She now knew otherwise.

He might not pick up and play the instrument, but the instrument often played him. She quickly surmised that his reason for not plucking and bowing on his violin must be of the mental, not physical, kind.

"I love the sound of the violin." She sensed that she, in blissful ignorance, might broach the subject of his musical abilities, even though he had strictly tabooed the issue for discussion by his parents.

From the moment she voiced her question, she had sensed a definite current of anticipation shooting back and forth between the couple. They appeared to wait with near breathless expectancy to see how their son would respond to her inquiry. Elena's own curiosity prodded her on as well, although Auhan obviously wished she would drop the matter.

She paused just long enough to measure her words. "My father often invited musicians into our home to give performances. String quartets were our favorites. One group in particular played the most wonderful rendition of Beethoven's 'Ode to Joy.'" She closed her eyes in remembrance and sighed. "Their music was sublime. We all loved it."

Opening her eyes again, she looked back at him. His jaw muscles rippled to show his tension, and he purposefully avoided her gaze by scrutinizing some indefinable point near the ceiling of the cabin.

She offered him the most encouraging smile she could muster, despite his refusal to look at her. "I'll bet with those long fingers, you make sweet music."

"He makes the most wonderful sounds emerge from any instrument," Auhan's father spoke from his bunk, with the gravelly voice of a person unaccustomed to speaking. Elena looked at him in surprise. Although he often sent smiles and good feelings in her direction, the older man rarely uttered a word.

Nodding in appreciation of the information, Elena turned back to Auhan and ventured to say, "I'd love to hear you some—"

"I don't play anymore," he growled, slinging the skein of yarn onto the bunk. He grabbed his cap and stalked out of the room, not even motioning, as he normally did, for Buddy to follow him.

Elena stiffened. As she listened to his feet thump along the passageway, she decided Auhan dealt with all the topics that disturbed him by stomping away. She threw a disgusted look at the door through which he had, yet again, disappeared in a masculine huff. When she regained her strength, he wouldn't find it so easy to walk away from her. She regarded the empty doorway for a moment longer. Then, when she could no longer hear his hard footfall, she turned her eyes back to his parents. Her heart went out to them.

They sat apart and yet together in a world of parental misery. The defeated slouch of their shoulders, their vacant stares, their short, quick breaths—each evidenced their sadness and pain.

Not knowing quite what to do or what to say, Elena looked down at her ever-present sidekick, Buddy. As if he picked up on the tension in the air, he let out a soft "harrumph" and rested his chin upon Elena's knee in that canine way meant to impart comfort. Elena placed her hand upon his head. Just rubbing the tips of her fingers in little circles upon his crown acted as a tranquilizer, one she wished she could offer to Fatima and Suleiman.

As much as Elena wanted to ask what the violin had to do with such a display of mood on Auhan's part, she didn't feel that she should pry. More than anything, she was beginning to get annoyed with Auhan's sulking temper. She liked him, sometimes more than she knew she should, but she was also perturbed with his thinking that he could continually hurt his parents in this way. Surely they weren't to blame for whatever had caused him to stop playing that curvaceous instrument.

Just when Elena decided nothing further would be said, Fatima's low, hurting voice drifted across the cabin's screaming silence in the wake of Auhan's departure.

"Our two sons are extremely gifted young men." Tears shimmered but did not fall from *Anne* Fatima's intense eyes.

"Auhan's soul sings through the instrument," she motioned over to the violin case, "as our eldest does through words." She paused, and the muscles of her face tightened, making her look years older than her reported age of forty-one.

"But Auhan was terribly traumatized last year by things that happened when he was with his army—things he hasn't even told us about in full." Her thin shoulders shuddered beneath her dark dress in the distressed movement of a mother who felt helpless. "Our other son. . .we don't even know for certain if he lives," she whispered. Opening her fingers, she dropped the ball of yarn onto the bunk, and tucking her elbows against her chest, she cradled her face in her hands.

Elena's heart broke for *Anne* Fatima. The poor woman didn't even know if her firstborn son was alive, and every mile they traveled took her farther and farther away from their homeland.

Elena leaned toward the head of her bunk and wiggled her fingers under her pillow until she felt the cloth containing her mother's cross. Since she was now well enough to care for both it and the wedding ring set, *Anne* Fatima had returned the jewelry to her the previous day. With the cross in hand, she pushed the rings back under her pillow and slowly rose from her chair. She hadn't stood unassisted since her ordeal, and her knees shook as she took small, hesitant steps over to the older woman. Bracing herself against the wall, she held out the cross to Fatima.

"*Anne* Fatima, I want you to have this." Elena knew a new Christian needed a reminder of her faith—especially when dealing with something as difficult as having one of her children missing somewhere in the world.

Fatima regarded the cross for a long moment as it dangled from its gold chain in front of her eyes. Suddenly, she jumped to her feet.

"You shouldn't be walking on your own, dear girl—" She just managed to place her steadying grip beneath Elena's elbows as the boat rolled on a wave. In the same moment, Elena felt herself losing her balance, and she grabbed hold of Fatima's arms. "Especially in such rough seas." Waves crashed against the hull of the ship to punctuate the older woman's admonishment.

Elena gave a nervous, self-conscious laugh. She couldn't believe how weak she still felt. "I'll sit." When she did, she immediately held the cross out to Fatima once again, not wanting to forget her original purpose in approaching the other woman. "Please," she fought to stay the cough that rose within her from the exertion of her small walk, "accept this, dear friend. Please."

Fatima looked from Elena to the cross and back again. She made a negative gesture with her hand. "No, I can't. It's too valuable." Elena knew Fatima was well acquainted with expensive jewelry. She had told Elena how her jewelry—the selling of much of it, the careful protection of the rest—had enabled her family to make this move.

"It is valuable." Elena didn't try to deny its worth. "But mostly because of the meaning behind it and because it belonged to my mother. But I know she would be very pleased for you to have it." She coughed a little, but she refused to let a coughing fit swallow the words that needed to be said. "You have not only been God's instrument toward saving my life, but you now understand the meaning behind the cross and believe the truth for which it stands." Her throat muscles worked as she tried to suppress yet another cough.

While Fatima handed Elena her cup of tea, a small smile creased the older woman's lips. "Like my ancestors long before me, I now know."

Her newfound knowledge and faith seemed to give *Anne* a great deal of satisfaction—as if a cycle had somehow successfully been completed.

After a few sips of the warm liquid, Elena had her coughing reflexes under control again. She placed the cup on the bedside chest and reached out to take *Anne's* work-worn hands within her own. She nestled the cross in her palms.

"The cross of Jesus is yours, my dear friend in Christ. You understand its meaning—its redemptive meaning—probably better than most. Please take this symbol of that most glorious event in history and, whenever doubts about either of your sons invade your mind, look at it and keep faith. God will look after your sons."

Fatima's eyes clung to the cross now cradled lovingly within the palm of her hand. "More than anything I'm afraid that it might be too late and that they may not find the faith of their long-ago ancestors."

Elena knew that she was voicing her deepest fear. She shook her head. "It is never too late. Let's just keep praying."

Looking over at her ever-silent husband, Fatima appeared on the verge of tears. The two gazed at one another with a love that had weathered many storms in life. Elena could tell Fatima would not have changed him for all the men in the world—despite his quiet nature. He gave his wife a short nod of his gray head, encouraging his wife to accept the cross. Fatima looked back at Elena and relayed the nod. "Dear Daughter, I would be honored to accept your mother's cross and the reminder it stands for. Thank you."

❧

Elena fell asleep praying for the brooding young man, Auhan. The last prayerful thought she remembered before she drifted off to sleep had been a request that he might once again take his violin in his beautiful hands and draw melody from the instrument.

A musician!

Elena had no musical talent of her own, but she loved listening to music. Like most who could neither carry a note in song nor play a tune, she had a great respect and appreciation for those who could.

Her father had always told her that people with such passions—writing, teaching, playing an instrument, painting, drawing, doctoring, creating stained glass windows, figuring scientific calculations—any creative thing, if they didn't do what they had been fashioned to do, they could never be totally content. Talent came with a price—the price of obedience to use what God had given them. And when a person didn't use their talent, the fear that their talent would be taken away haunted them, tormented them.

Auhan returned later in the afternoon just as Elena awakened from her second nap of the day. Although no one mentioned the earlier episode, she had learned a great deal about Auhan as a result of his behavior. She now knew part of his problem stemmed from his no longer playing the violin as well as what had happened to him the previous year. Elena believed these two things, combined with his doubts about the Almighty, held him in the grip of lonely and confused misery. With a degree of certainty, Elena thought he owed his alienation to a deep sense of guilt.

She had often read guilt in his expressive eyes. The encompassing emotion enveloped him like a dark cloud and turned him into a sullen young man. Of course, she had no idea why he felt guilty. She doubted if even his parents knew why. But her father had taught her the real issue had little to do with why a person feels guilty. Ridding them of the debilitating emotion was the important thing. Guilt ate away at a person like a cancer. God never intended people to contend with their guilt by themselves.

Elena's young heart went out to Auhan. She knew all sin and its resulting guilt could be assuaged only by the power of the risen Lord, the Lord Jesus Christ. She wanted the free gift of salvation, deliverance from all his sins, to be Auhan's. In spite of his moods, he was becoming more and more dear to her. Although he was one of the most handsome young men she had ever met, her reasons went deeper than such a superficial attraction. She had often caught a look in his eyes, a flicker—as if his soul held a wick just waiting to be quickened. She hoped to be on hand when the spark burst into flame. She could just imagine how bright his deep-set brown eyes would shine.

# Chapter 8

*Humble yourselves therefore under the mighty hand of God, that he may exalt you in due time: Casting all your care upon him; for he careth for you.*
1 Peter 5:6–7

Days sailed by, one upon another.

Although the ocean had been blowing a tempest for nearly half a week and the little ship rocked and rolled in the heavy sea, Auhan was amazed by how it didn't bother the ladies in his cabin in the least. He had overheard fellow passengers speaking, and he knew the few other female passengers aboard the *Ionian Star* were suffering greatly.

He marveled even more at Elena. With her regained health, the recollection of what she had gone through and lost came into sharper focus. Yet, although she mourned the loss of her father and often talked about her sister and little Rose, the light shining from Elena's soul seemed to shine brighter and brighter as her body became stronger and stronger.

The change in his mother equally astounded him. With all the love of a child for his parent, Auhan had always wished such an all-encompassing happiness for her. Yet even when he had played the violin expressly for her, she hadn't looked as joyful as she did now.

Almost, but not quite.

Auhan recognized his mother was not only happy, she was at peace. He had made her glad when he played his violin. Proud too in that manner in which parents specialize and upon which children thrive. But, ever since his mother had made the decision to return to the religion of her ancestors, the inner tranquillity, which had always eluded her before, now radiated from her. He hadn't even realized this serenity—this peace, which seemed different from anything a mere mortal could give to another—had been the missing quality. She seemed lighter somehow. Freer. No longer carrying heavy emotional burdens on her slender shoulders. Her every step reflected this new freedom. She bounced everywhere she went.

He had noticed the cross hanging around her neck, but he withheld any comment. Although he was still very suspect of spiritual matters, he knew he liked the way his mother's new belief had helped her. The realization softened his heart a little toward the Christian God. Finally, the God of Jesus Christ seemed to be helping someone.

The light shining from his mother's eyes, which used to be so dull in comparison, gave him a moment's pause each time she held his gaze. Her eyes were almost as bright and radiant as Elena's.

Almost.

Not quite.

Yet, Auhan felt certain that with time, they might blaze just as brightly. Somehow.

☙

They had been in the Atlantic for several days when their little ship sailed into a perfect calm. After days of rough seas, it was a pleasant change, even to those unaffected by the motion of a ship. For Suleiman, who didn't possess a stomach in tune with sea travel, the reprieve brought back into the older man's cheeks a color that had been missing.

The sun shone brightly into the cabin, and to Elena, it felt more like a midsummer's day than one of the first days of autumn. As more of a summer person than a winter one, she savored the feeling.

An unexpected knock on the wall to the side of the opened cabin door brought her attention to a distinguished-looking man wearing a blue uniform replete with a double row of shiny brass buttons traveling down its front.

"So, how's our 'Dolphin Girl' today?" The man's words possessed the clipped sounds of a decidedly New England accent. Regarding him, Elena felt certain she had to be looking at the captain of the *Ionian Star*.

Of medium height, but with a sturdiness of body brought on by life aboard a ship, the mariner looked as if a traveling drama company had cast him to play the captain's role in a production. From his white-trimmed whiskers and his ruddy complexion to his twinkling but ever observant eyes, he epitomized Elena's idea of how an American sea captain should look. At first sight, Elena liked him.

"Captain," Auhan exclaimed in English. His tone held more excitement than Elena thought he was capable of showing. He immediately stood and offered the distinguished man his seat. Auhan obviously held a great respect for the man.

"A nice...surprise...this...is," Fatima spoke in halting but gracious English. She rose from her bunk and went to stand before the captain. "A tea...you would... like? Yes?"

"That would be lovely, Madam," he responded with equal grace. Then he trained his sharp yet kind eyes on Elena. "Dear 'Dolphin Girl,' I am so glad to see you looking so well. I must say, you gave all onboard this vessel, myself included, quite a scare."

Elena rolled her eyes and nodded. "I gave myself quite a scare too." She smiled as the older man chuckled. The sound reminded Elena of her father. She rejoiced in hearing the laugh.

"But what do you mean by 'Dolphin Girl'?"

"Don't you know? That's what you are called by all onboard this ship." He looked around the cabin at the others. "You didn't tell her about how she was saved?"

Elena didn't even give Fatima, whose mouth was poised to answer, the time to respond.

"Oh, I remember, Captain," Elena assured him. "The moonlight dance of the dolphins jumping and leaping all around me in the sea is not something I shall ever forget. I just didn't realize all the other passengers were aware of my unusual rescue."

He answered with a respectful bow of his head. "I have heard my fair share of dolphin stories in my more than fifty years at sea, but never have I actually witnessed such a rescue in action." He shook his head and reached over to pat Buddy. "Auhan told me about how the dolphin had first saved this dog, brought him to you, then saved you both." He shook his head again. "What an amazing God we have," he proclaimed.

Elena's eyes opened wide, even as her spirit made an excited leap within her. Regarding him with a new, specific interest, she felt compelled to ask, "Are you. . .a . . .believer, Captain?"

"Most definitely," he answered without hesitation. Smiling his thanks to Fatima, he took the cup of tea that she held out to him. "That is one of the reasons I try to travel in the Levant as much as I possibly can," he continued to Elena. "I not only like sailing those historic waters, but often I try to take excursions in which I might visit the sights of early Christianity. The Near East—Asia Minor—has always been one of my favorite places."

A pleased smile curved Elena's lips. Now she understood there was a lot more to this captain than just his seafaring abilities. "That's wonderful, Captain. Since you have the opportunity, how marvelous it is for your Christian walk that you take it."

The captain nodded in agreement while he placed his teacup and saucer on the table. "It has helped immensely. I firmly believe if not for the rational minds of those early Greeks when the apostles walked Asia Minor's beautiful land, Christianity would never have reached the northern shores of my ancestors in far-off Britain—and most other nations of people, for that matter, even the distant, then-future shores of America. For that, all of Christendom should forever be grateful."

Elena's brows came together in a quick frown. "The Christians of the world certainly didn't act too grateful while they sat safely on their ships in Smyrna's harbor and watched the destruction of one of Christendom's oldest cities," she shot back before realizing how bitter she sounded. Color flooded her face. "Forgive me," she whispered and looked down.

"So," the captain said. The word spoke volumes. "That is what happened in Smyrna. Many conflicting press reports have come over the wireless. One hardly knows what to believe." He raised his hands in a show of helplessness before letting them fall back onto his knees. "But I had suspected as much."

His words reminded Elena of something her father had told her during their trip to Washington the previous May. "My father believed that if the Greco-Turkish War should end with the defeat of the Greeks, before this century passes, few people will realize Asia Minor was predominantly a Greek land—and a Christian one—much, much longer than it has politically been a land of the Turks."

"I believe your father to be correct," the captain replied.

Elena continued, feeling free to talk to her countryman about these issues she had longed to voice for days. "Near the beginning of recorded history—nearly three thousand years ago—Smyrna was peacefully settled by Greeks who offered a better way of life, a civilized life. A life that appealed to all who experienced it. Their culture and civilization—the polis, city—made Asia Minor one of the most advanced places on earth for much more than twenty-five hundred years."

The city of her father's ancestors was now gone, and Elena ached with the knowledge. "Even after Asia Minor's occupation by the Ottoman Turks—who used Greek know-how to build their empire—it was the Christians of the land who were the backbone of the economy. Up until last week." She shrugged her shoulders slightly. "That's how it always was."

"As a transporter of cargo I am very aware of all of this," the captain concurred. "One has only to walk through Asia Minor and see the graceful ruins of a civilization, both ancient and medieval, to realize their beauty surpasses much of what is to be found in our modern world, my dear." The captain obviously wanted to impart comfort. "If a person doesn't have such an opportunity, one need only pick up a Bible and read the letters penned to the Greek cities or study church history for a powerful reminder."

Elena dipped her head. "But I don't think many will do as you suggest," she reflected. "My father also told me people are too lazy to learn the truth. And even if they want to learn, press reports today cannot be trusted. Soon, even history books will be changed to reflect the angle the governments find most beneficial. They cater only to the god of commerce—the god they are coming to worship more and more in this twentieth century."

The captain's eyebrows rose in obvious surprise at her knowledge of political matters.

"You are a very bright young lady," the captain responded after a moment.

Elena offered him a self-conscious smile. "My father wanted my sister and me to be aware of what was going on around us." A look of sadness crossed her face. "Actually, in spite of his teachings, we were, until last week, very naïve."

She remembered how her father had wanted them to remain in Washington the previous May until the Greco-Turkish War was resolved. They had insisted on returning with him to Smyrna rather than face separation from their much-loved and respected father. Neither Elena nor Sophia ever imagined Smyrna, in these modern days, could be pillaged and utterly destroyed.

"Any wisdom you see in me now, Captain," she continued after a moment, "has come from the bitter pill of experience. I've witnessed things people should never have to see."

The captain's lips pursed together beneath his mustache. "Oftentimes experience is the best teacher, my dear, albeit the hardest."

"Captain, do you know about all the Christians who were killed under cover of the Great War by the Turkish government?" Again her words left her mouth before she took time to consider them.

ॐ

She was asking the captain, but Auhan's heart nearly skipped a beat at her mention of this occurrence, a small portion of which he had stumbled upon the previous year. He hadn't realized she knew about the executions, his country's so-called "deportations" of Christians. Knowing about them, how could she be so open to him, a former Turkish soldier?

As if he were watching one of those new moving pictures he had heard about, he watched as the captain again nodded his head, this time with a seriousness of movement Auhan was sure he normally reserved for matters pertaining to the safe running of his ship.

"In 1917 our president, Woodrow Wilson, wanted to declare war on the Turks because they were strong allies of the Germans. But the lobbying of American missionaries prevented his doing so for the ostensible reason that a declaration of war would have meant abandoning the millions of Christians—Greeks, Armenian, American missionaries, and others—living there."

Auhan was amazed as he watched Elena dip her head in knowledgeable concurrence to this tidbit of recent history. He had no idea the then-president of the United States had desired to declare war upon the Turks.

"Ironically, if the missionaries hadn't lobbied against the declaration, things would have probably been much better for the Christians of the Near East," the captain commented. "For most regrettably and sadly," he continued with a gravity of expression, "what followed was the worst mass extermination of people our modern time has ever seen. The Armenians and the Greeks have suffered terrible things under Turkish rule." He glanced Auhan's way, as if he dared him to refute it. But Auhan wouldn't. He knew better than most the truth found in the captain's words.

*

"So tell me, Captain," Elena persisted. She could feel Auhan watching her, but she averted her gaze and studied the epaulets on the captain's coat. "Why did the Christians allow it to happen again, just last week? Why did all those allied ships filled with men representing Christians from England, France, America, Italy—friendly nations, allies of Greece—just sit in the harbor and watch thousands more brethren die?"

The captain pursed his lips, and Elena waited for his response as he weighed his words.

"I don't really think most of the men onboard the ships really knew what was going on."

Elena nodded her head in agreement. "You are correct, of course, Captain," she replied. "I remember many of the sailors had stricken looks upon their faces."

"And those few who did, well. . ." The captain opened his hands before him. "My dear, just because a person labels himself a Christian doesn't necessarily mean that he is. . .actually. . .a. . .Christian. And further, how many people in positions of authority are true believers—people who have a deep and personal relationship with God, as revealed by Jesus, the Christ? I personally doubt many politicians—presidents, prime ministers, generals, kings, queens—are truly Christians. Otherwise, we wouldn't have all these terrible wars. I believe most in positions of authority—most, but not all," he qualified, "are more concerned about commerce and the accumulation of wealth for themselves and their nation. The Christians of Smyrna got in the way of those who worship that god you mentioned a few moments ago, the god of commerce."

She dipped her head. "But, please forgive me. You have come for a friendly visit—I don't know what made me speak of such things." Remorse filled her words. She feared she showed a total lack of the social graces. If Sophia had been here, she would have received a thorough scolding upon the captain's departure.

But the captain showed no sign of being offended. With a kind, sad smile, he offered, "Seeing your city destroyed is motive enough for such talk, my dear."

Elena looked up at the captain and, taking a deep breath, whispered, "It used to be so pretty."

"I know. I've gone into Smyrna many times when picking up cargo. It was one of the prettiest cities in the Levant."

Elena nodded in agreement. In her mind's eye, she saw again her final glimpse of Smyrna that last horrible night she swam next to the rowboat toward the rescue ship. The city had groaned, lamented, as flames licked upward, trapping thousands of people in an area a mile and a half long by one hundred feet wide. And the desperate, frantic wails of the people filled her head.

"Elena," she heard Fatima call out to her and realized that her breathing had become fast and hard. She blinked and forced herself to slowly draw in large, controlling breaths of air.

"I'm sorry," she murmured and gave Fatima a reassuring smile. "Sometimes, when I remember back to Smyrna burning. . . ." She gave a slight shudder. She couldn't go on.

With the gentle comfort of a grandfather, the captain gave her arm a soft pat and rose from his chair. "When you are stronger, we shall talk more. To talk is something good. But it is infinitely better to give to God those thoughts that are too hard or too heavy for you to carry." Elena's gaze flicked over to Fatima's.

The older woman smiled at Elena and then turned to the captain to explain their reaction. "That. . .she do, yes. Give problems. . .to God. I do too, that."

The captain regarded Fatima with a look of wonder. "You are a believer, Madam?"

Fatima glanced down at Elena, and they exchanged another of the special mother-daughter smiles they had become accustomed to sharing over the last few days. This little interchange communicated more than a thousand words ever could.

Fatima turned back to the captain and answered him. "When I come to ship." She paused. Crinkling her eyelids together in concentration, she corrected herself. "When I came on ship. No, I was not. But now. Yes."

"I wish I had known," the captain returned. "You could have come to Sunday service yesterday."

"You have church?" Fatima asked, puzzlement drawing lines on her face.

"I hold a service each Sunday. To pastor those of my crew and passengers who are Christians is my very favorite duty as captain. I would be very pleased for you all to come to service on the next Lord's Day, Kyriakie," he qualified, using the Greek word and meaning for the day of worship.

"Only my mother and Elena are Christians," Auhan interjected.

The captain regarded him with a steady, measuring gaze. "You would still be welcomed, Son. Since next Sunday is the last Sunday before arriving in New York, we are planning an extra special service too. One of my sailors, who is pretty handy with the fiddle in a folksy kind of way, has agreed to play."

A charge like a lightning bolt passed between Elena and Auhan, but she tore her gaze away from Auhan as the captain continued to speak. From the way the captain's blue eyes narrowed, Elena knew he had noticed the tension electrifying the air.

"The sailor doesn't like performing in formal settings. He enjoys the foot-stomping fiddle playing below deck much more. Nonetheless, we have a standing agreement that he will play for my church service the last Sunday before arriving in port."

"When do we arrive, Captain?" Elena asked and glanced back at Auhan. She was saddened to see a deep, brooding look settling in his eyes once again.

"God willing, early next week. We'll talk more, young lady." He walked toward the doorway and then turned back to them. "Goodness, I almost forgot the reason I came by—other than to meet the 'Dolphin Girl.'" His eyes held a twinkle as he looked down at her. "I wanted to suggest that you come and sit up on deck. We should be having several days of smooth sailing. Why don't you let the healing rays of the sun touch you?"

"Oh." Elena's eyes widened, and she was both amazed and very happy to realize the idea appealed to her. She must truly be getting better. Until that day she had felt no desire to be out in the elements. But with joy filling her, she realized the thought of the sun's rays touching her skin didn't bother her at all anymore. "I'd like that, Captain, very much. Thank you."

He nodded his head, then frowned. "You don't have a fever any longer, do you?"

Elena laughed. "The only fever I have now is cabin fever."

"Good." He sent her his ready smile. "That is a fever I can help cure. I'll have a sailor set up a canopy on the upper deck and place a chair there for you." He glanced down at her bandaged hands. "You don't want to let your burns feel the sun yet."

She slightly dipped her head in agreement. "Thank you, Captain."

"Don't mention it, my 'Dolphin Girl.'" His eyes filled with merriment as he smiled down on her. He turned to Auhan. "Shall I have one of my sailors carry her up on deck or will you be able to manage it?"

"It will be my honor, Sir. Besides," Auhan glanced down at Elena and shocked her—thrilled her—by winking, "this 'Dolphin Girl' and I have a long-standing date to sit deckside."

As the captain looked from one to the other, Elena felt heat rising in her cheeks, and she knew they were turning red. He gave a hearty chuckle, which reminded Elena so much of her dear father.

"Now why doesn't that surprise me?" Placing his hat upon his head, he touched its brim. "Until later." He turned and walked briskly up the passageway away from them.

Elena looked up at Auhan.

He looked down at her.

He smiled.

She, of course, smiled back.

# Chapter 9

*In him was life;*
*and the life was the light of men.*
*And the light shineth in darkness;*
*and the darkness comprehended it not.*
John 1:4–5

Two hours later, Auhan ambled over to where Elena sat, waiting, on her chair. Fatima and Suleiman had just left the cabin to retrieve cleaning supplies. They planned on cleaning the room from top to bottom while Elena was out.

"Don't you look nice," he commented. Looking up at him, Elena noticed a special sparkle in the depth of his dark, chestnut eyes—a sparkle she had never noticed before.

Blushing slightly, Elena tore her gaze away from the unfamiliar but very welcome glint. She glanced down at the soft china blue dress she wore for her reintroduction to the outside world. Of plain cotton, it was probably the least expensive dress to have ever touched her skin. Yet, because the garment had belonged to Fatima, who had stayed up late several nights altering it to fit Elena's smaller frame, it was also her most beloved one.

Elena completed her outfit by draping a white, lightweight shawl around her back, and then she turned back to Auhan. "Promise you won't drop me?" she bantered, wanting to hide the nervous thrill she felt at the idea of Auhan carrying her.

She hadn't considered this part of their "date" the first time he mentioned their sitting together on deck. But she had been able to think of little else since Auhan had declared to the captain his intentions to transport her outside. Elena was finally beginning to understand how her sister felt about Christos. The idea of being so close to Auhan, as near as his carrying her would bring them, did unexpected but very pleasant things to her heart.

What had started out as prayers for Auhan were now day-long thoughts of him. Elena couldn't seem to stop thinking of him. She wasn't quite sure when her unceasing prayers for him had turned into her constantly dreaming of a life together with him.

"I wouldn't drop you any more than I would the most precious crystal in the world." Warm amusement flavored his voice. His words made Elena's nerves quiver all the way to her toes.

Reaching down, he placed one arm beneath her legs, which the long length of the dress concealed in a decorous way. His other went across her shoulders.

The ease with which he lifted her from the chair surprised her. Christos had carried Sophia when she fainted by the side of their home after having been attacked, but Christos was a huge man. Auhan wasn't much taller than Elena and of slight build. Feeling the rippling motion of his muscles beneath his jacket, she learned how his strength had been deceptively hidden by his size. For a moment, he just held her against him, as if gauging her weight.

"As I thought, you're lightweight," he commented, and she could hear the smile in his voice.

Not quite knowing where to rest her gaze, she looked down at her fingers as they lay upon her chest. Excitement and wonder at being so near to him sent funny little tremors through her body. He smelled of rope hemp and ocean breeze, a heady, masculine scent that left her weak and slightly woozy. Being this close to him made her aware of him in an adult way, a way in which she had never felt before.

His breath brushed warm against her neck when he spoke again. "But, if you could just place your left arm around my shoulders, it would be even easier for me." Mirth deepened his voice still further.

"Oh." She felt heat rush to her face as she quickly did as he requested. Her color intensified when he chuckled. A gloriously male sound rumbled out from his chest.

"Elena," he said as he left the cabin, the dog at his heels, "you are adorable. We have been sleeping in the same room ever since you came aboard, and for the first time since we've met, you are properly dressed." He glanced down at her dainty feet. His mother had even found a pair of ankle-strap pumps for her. "And yet, you are embarrassed."

"It is because I am dressed," she countered, but seeing his brows rise in a manly way of question, she huffed out a breath and quickly continued to explain that which she felt was obvious. "What I mean is, for the first time, I am not a sick patient."

"Ah. . ." He nodded his head, and she was conscious of a subtle glint in his eyes as he suggested dryly, "You mean, you are a woman?"

She looked at him squarely in the face. She had seen how he had looked at her when he thought she hadn't been noticing. She had very good peripheral vision, and she knew that he "liked" her every bit as much as she "liked" him.

"Aren't I? A woman, I mean?" she asked in direct challenge.

With her face just a scant two inches from his own, he wondered if she had any idea about the inner turmoil she stirred to life within him. He suspected she was too young and too inexperienced to really understand what a woman could do to a man. These two qualities about her didn't bother him in the least.

But to address her question. Was she a woman? Most definitely. His own body pressed, as it was, against her own made him all too painfully aware of this fact. Actually, she was a woman who felt wonderful in his arms. Even more, one to whom he didn't want to say good-bye when their ship arrived in New York City in a few days.

"You are," he finally answered, not able to control the deep huskiness in his voice any more than he could still his wildly beating heart. "A very beautiful one, at that."

Her lips parted and curved in a spontaneous, timid response, and Auhan felt as if all the flowers of spring were contained within her smile.

"Thank you, Auhan." She reached up with her right hand and gently touched around the burned area on her left cheek as well as the one at the hairline on her forehead. "It's nice to hear," she shrugged her shoulders slightly, "—after all this."

"Ah. . .Elena." He shook his head, quickly denying that she had any reason to worry. "Those scars might fade away." He looked directly at the burn on her cheek—the worst one—and paused to study it. Almost the size of an American silver dollar, it was red and sore looking. The pain it had caused her—still gave her—ate away at him. But swallowing his anger, refusing to let it divert his thoughts or mar their outing, he continued, "But if the scars never disappear, you are beautiful. You don't need to depend on physical appearance to be beautiful," he qualified. "That light which shines out from your soul is so bright, it's all a person sees when they meet you."

Her eyes widened as though she was surprised to hear him being so complimentary. Perhaps she simply enjoyed hearing his words of true compliment. "What a nice thing to say, Auhan. Thank you." She paused, and Auhan watched as she kneaded her lower lip with her teeth.

"I pray. . . ." She hesitated and, with a look of uncertainty, searched his face before she ventured to speak her mind. "I pray that it is. . .a light. . .which you will someday come to have."

He dropped his smile, but he continued to search her face for answers. In truth, Auhan longed to possess such a light within his own soul. He sensed the light illuminating Elena's soul came from an unlimited source. He almost wished Elena, as the friend she had become, could just give him a share of her inner light. But he also knew such a dream was senseless, as nonsensical as his wish to be reborn. To be handed such a gift, free and clear, would be too easy, and in this evil world in which they lived, it was not to be expected.

Not wanting to say or do anything that might ruin this day, he murmured, "I hope you are right." Even as he spoke the words, he was surprised to realize how much he really meant them. He would like to have the light she possessed—the light his mother now seemed to enjoy as well. But in order to be a bearer of such light, he sensed he would first need a soul free of guilt and anger. But he didn't expect such a thing could ever happen.

Not to him.

Not after the horrors he had seen. Not without a fresh start. A whole new life. And people just weren't given a second chance, even if they moved, as he was doing, to a land far, far away. The emotions forged by the former life would still be with a person. Hanging onto him. Pulling him down.

He came upon the doorway to the deck and twisted around so as not to bump either Elena's legs or her head against its hard edges. He stepped out into the sharp clearness of the sparkling day. Elena's laughter, a bubbly and light, infectious sound, filled the air and brought a quick and genuine smile to Auhan's lips as his attention returned to Elena and, thankfully, away from the contemplations of his mind.

"Oh, Auhan." She motioned out to the glorious day. "Look how beautiful the world is. So lovely," she sighed. "The clouds, the sky, the sea." She craned her neck and looked down into the placid water. "If only it had been this calm when I had been adrift in it." Auhan heard a wistful note to her voice. "I know things could have been many times worse," she hastened to qualify. "But this—it's like looking at a mirror of the sky."

Laughter, like water gurgling from a mountain spring, bubbled out of her again. Being near the edge of the ship didn't seem to bother her, so Auhan walked closer to the side. "Even the ship is almost perfectly reflected in it." She pointed down to the image of the *Ionian Star* portrayed in the peaceful, green sea through which it glided.

Auhan understood what she meant. A most remarkable day, it was as if the ship moved across a placid summer lake and not one of the vastest bodies of water on earth. But more than the ocean, it was the woman in his arms whom Auhan wanted to watch.

Like a baby being introduced to the world, she looked all around her until she settled her gaze on the horizon and the fluffy white clouds drifting above it. He could tell she was using all her senses, not just sight, to experience this moment. Tilting her head slightly to the side, she appeared to be listening to the ship-generated breeze as well as feeling it upon her skin. From the way her chest rose and fell with a few deep breaths, he was certain she was sniffing the ocean-scented air. By the way her mouth slightly parted, he had no doubt she tasted the saltiness of the sea upon her red lips.

Her red lips. . .

He watched them as she moved the tip of her tongue across their smooth contour. With a start, he noticed the cuts and blisters, which had been a part of them ever since he had met her, had all but disappeared somewhere between yesterday and today. Yesterday, her mouth had still possessed a bit of puffy redness around its rims. Today, her lips looked smooth and so perfect, so appealing. He wanted nothing more than to lower his own lips to them, to taste them, to feel them, to—

The direction of his thoughts drew him up sharp. He pulled his eyes away from her face and to the horizon upon which she still gazed. He hadn't noticed a woman in so long that the feelings growing within him for Elena had gone unrecognized. Until now.

Now, all was different—and much more complicated. With Elena he felt much more than just a desire to kiss. He wished for a life together with her, a chance to see her smile every single day of his existence.

Turning abruptly away from both the railing and his thoughts, Auhan nearly swiped a sailor across his weathered face with Elena's pointy shoes. He instinctively drew back, even as the sailor ducked. Although the sailor had been trained to guard against dangerous parts of the ship or cargo that had worked its way loose, he was obviously surprised by having to maneuver in order to avoid the sharp tips of a woman's shoes.

"Hey, Mate," he called out. A wide, toothless grin split his face.

"I apologize." Auhan rushed to take the blame while Elena placed her hand over her mouth. She bent her knees back trying to lower the offending shoes. "I'm sorry too."

"No reason for either of ya to feel sorry, Ma'am," the sailor was quick to assure her. "Me and me mates," he motioned to the three sailors who hovered behind him, twirling their hats, "just wanted to see how ya was doing. We was the ones who spied ya among all them jumpin' dolphins and pulled ya from the sea th' other night," he declared, his chest puffing out with pride.

&#10086;

"Oh," Elena gasped and landed a smile upon each of the other men who stood looking on like embarrassed schoolboys. Elena's heart went out to them, as did her free hand. In turn, she took each of their hands in her own, not caring when they motioned to their hands, soiled from work. She hadn't minded their dirty hands the night they had pulled her from the sea. She certainly didn't mind them now.

Then she spoke to each individually—to the spokesman first. "Thank you." They were two very common, often uttered words. Yet, she hoped the emotion she put into them left no doubt about the depth of her gratitude.

"Me pleasure, Ma'am," he responded, beaming as proudly as a new father might.

She turned to the next man. He had the softest blue eyes she had ever seen, even lighter in color than Sophia's.

"Thank you," she repeated to him her heartfelt appreciation.

"Me pleasure too, Ma'am. I am just glad to see ya so well." He blushed beet red when his mate jabbed at him, but he deflected the jab with expert agility. Elena smiled at their antics and turned to the one with curly brown hair and matching whiskers who had poked the second man.

"Thank you too, Sailor." She matched her tone to his outgoing personality.

Sweeping his cap before him, he gave a little bow. "Just try and stay closer to shore when you go for a swim in the future, Missy." A bright smile accompanied his admonishment, and Elena knew for certain that she was addressing the jokester of the group. Her father had told her there was always one on every ship. Normally of above-average intelligence, the crew's jokester made life aboard a seagoing vessel "interesting" for everyone else.

"I will, indeed," she assured him and turned to the youngest man in the group. With hardly any whiskers on his face, he could not have been any older than she. Rather, she guessed him to be a couple of years younger.

"Thank you," she repeated the words but tried not to lose even a bit of their meaning as she reached for his hand and gave it a gentle squeeze. She'd thought the second sailor had been embarrassed, but this one couldn't even look her in the face. Lighting his gaze anywhere but at her, he plopped his hat back onto his head in order to be able to touch its brim in response.

"Hey, Boy." The jokester pulled the young sailor's cap off when he left it there. "Don't you know it's impolite to wear a hat in the presence of a lady?"

The boy looked as if he wished the sea would swallow him up, and Elena, always a bit of a joker herself, had a hard time containing the laughter threatening to bubble out from her. She was grateful when the toothless spokesman spoke up.

"We just wanted to make sure for ourselves that the 'Dolphin Girl' was as fine as the captain said." Elena caught Auhan's mirth-filled glance at the sailor's use of her new title.

She looked back at the sailor as he motioned to his buddies with his cap. "We all are happy to see you're fine."

"Thanks to you men and the dolphins," she murmured. "I'll never forget your finding me." Her face turned very serious. "I'm going to leave my name and the address with the captain so you may reach me. If any of you should ever need anything in the future—next month, next year, in ten years, or more," her gaze again lit upon each of the men, "please let me know. I would like to be able to help you or your families in the same measure you have helped me."

"Naw," the spokesman offered in quick response. "We don't want nothin'. Besides, the dolphins are the ones what saved ya. We never would've seen ya if they hadn't started jumpin' and movin' around like a bunch of bunnies in a forest."

Elena smiled at his analogy and thought, perhaps, he missed seeing trees and land creatures after having been at sea for so long. "Regardless, if ever I can be of assistance in any way, please let me know. I would not be here today if it hadn't been for your quick action. My father—" She paused and remembered back to the many times her father had assisted people. Of all his wealth, all his works of art, his assets, her father had never lost track of the fact that people were his greatest treasures—both close friends and strangers on the street. Her father had believed very strongly that God had so blessed him with wealth in order that he might prove himself a worthy steward and use his monetary means to help others. Elena would not forget his lesson or example. She lightly licked her lips and continued, "My father would want me to do so."

The sailors stuffed their hats back onto their heads and touched their brims to her in a show of respect. Then, Auhan returned their salutation with a nod of his own head and proceeded to carry her to the upper deck with Buddy close at his heels.

# Chapter 10

*Help those women which laboured with me
in the gospel. . .whose names are in the book of life.*
Philippians 4:3

The canopy tented an easy chair in the shadiest part of the deck. The captain had thought of everything for her. Within easy reach, a small table held a teapot and several cups, all decorated with an interesting botanical design. A crate had been set in front of her chair so she could rest her legs.

Auhan lowered her to her feet with tender care.

Elena stood for a moment and enjoyed the vibration of the moving ship beneath the soles of her leather shoes. Then she turned a happy face toward Auhan.

"It's so wonderful to be outside again," she sighed. Not wanting to tax her strength, she sank into the chair and placed her legs upon the crate, taking care to arrange her skirt neatly and modestly around her legs.

Auhan lowered himself to the café-style chair provided for him, and they sat in companionable silence for several minutes while the surrounding sea played out its ancient tune.

The fresh, ocean-scented air wafted on the gentle breeze while the sounds of the sailors and the hum of the engines from deep within the bowels of the vessel provided welcome background sounds. Elena savored the moment. Being out on deck with Auhan proved to be even more wonderful than she had anticipated.

She treasured the ability to sit comfortably with someone in silence. To communicate by talking might be necessary, but to communicate by just *being*—what a rare gift! Silent music filled the moment with a profound harmony—one that she suspected Auhan had been unable to capture and enjoy in a very long time.

"Thank you for bringing me out," Elena murmured after a few minutes. She turned her face to his and let out a peal of bubbly laughter. "And for holding me while I talked to the sailors." She nodded toward his back. "It must be hurting you."

"Not at all." He flashed her a smile. "Didn't I tell you that you were a lightweight?" He studied her with such intensity that his perusal sent a heat of embarrassment rushing to her cheeks.

She smiled but chose to bring the subject back to the sailors. "What a nice group of men. I thank God for them."

Auhan nodded. "I must say, they were sharp. When they realized you were in the middle of the jumping dolphins, they didn't waste even a second in getting you aboard. I overheard one of them say if they didn't move fast, they would lose you." He pointed to a lantern hanging on a peg just a short distance from them. "When they shone the lantern upon the sea and saw you, the stern of the ship had practically passed you by."

"I didn't know." She looked out at the huge expanse. From the safety of the ship's deck, the sea seemed so friendly. Yet, she knew how fast the raw elements could wear down a human or a land animal should one be tossed into the ocean's depths. She glanced down at her much-loved Buddy.

"Do you think, after what has happened, you will ever want to swim again?" Auhan ventured to ask. "You were literally trapped in the sea."

A wry smile curved her lips. "Well, not today—even with it being so beautiful—" She sighed. "But, I'm sure I will swim again. By next summer, a trip to Virginia Beach will find me in the water." She cast him a sideways glance. "After all, it is my love of swimming that helped to save me. If Sophia had been the one to fall overboard or little Rose—" A slight shudder passed through her. She didn't even want to consider the ending of that sentence. "The fact that I have spent so many hours in the water saved me that day," she said, going back to her original thought. "Although I knew my situation wasn't good, I wasn't afraid of the water. Both Sophia and Rose would have been."

She took a deep breath and sighed. "But I do wish I could thank Buddy's and my dolphin." The dog looked up at the mention of his name, and sitting on his hind legs, his tail swished back and forth on the deck's surface like a mop. Elena brought her face close to her canine friend—just as they had been when in the sea together—and she spoke sweet nothings to him while scratching behind his ears.

The affection she shared with the animal passed back and forth between them, a viable thread of devotion, until a deep chuckle emanating from Auhan drew her attentions away. He appeared to be watching something in the distance.

"Well, look, there's a dolphin you can thank."

At the thought of a dolphin swimming near the ship, Elena's pulse immediately quickened. But when she saw Auhan's hand pointing upward and not down into the water as she had expected, she blinked and frowned slightly even as she trained her line of vision to follow the direction of his finger.

"Oh!" she exclaimed. "Cloud art." She gazed at the huge cloud in the perfect shape of a dolphin, spreading across the wide expanse of the eastern sky. "One of my favorite things to do when on an ocean voyage is to try and find objects in the shapes of clouds. But this—" she chortled. "This doesn't require any trying." She moved her hand in an arc.

"It looks as if this dolphin has just jumped out of the water, and he is only pausing in the sky before returning to the sea." She shook her head. "Amazing."

"Yes," Auhan agreed. "Amazing." Something in his voice alerted Elena to the fact that he wasn't referring to the cloud.

She turned back to him. His eyes, his deep and beautiful eyes as unfathomable as the sea, now regarded her, and she had the crazy but wonderfully disconcerting sensation that he was talking about her. He thought she was amazing.

Feeling flustered and very young and inexperienced, she turned back to the cumulus-cloud dolphin fashioned by the supreme artist. She wanted to keep the mood light. She pointed to the mammal's famous grin, which appeared to extend hundreds of miles across the sky.

"It looks just like our dolphin's smile." She patted Buddy's head, then stayed her hand on the dog to help control the strange, adult feelings now bombarding her.

"How about the giraffe over there?"

Elena turned to see where he pointed. "It is a giraffe," she agreed, even as she cocked her head to the side to accommodate the slightly bent shape of the form. "It's not as easily recognizable as the dolphin, but I definitely see the very long neck of a giraffe. It looks as if it's eating leaves from a tree, a tree made of clouds, of course," she qualified with a smile.

"Your turn," Auhan prompted her to find another shape.

She promptly complied. "Straight ahead. A tiger. You can even see his stripes."

"And how about the motor car over there?" He pointed to a formation that did look remarkably like a Ford Model-T, but Elena only laughed.

"That's the first time I've heard of someone finding an automobile in the clouds."

"Well, why not?" He sighed, almost pensively. "I hope someday to be able to buy one."

She watched him as he looked with true longing at the shape of the vehicle. She had grown up with her father owning automobiles, both in Smyrna and in Washington. Thus, she had never really thought about how some people—young men in particular—might yearn for one. Reaching over, she took his hand in her own.

His fingers wound around hers, and, as on the first morning when she had awakened without a fever, the feel of their hands clasped together felt right; a completion somehow.

He turned to her. A smile crinkled the corners of his eyes—his beautiful eyes, which held secrets she could only guess, but which also held responsive warmth.

Slowly, as if from a great distance, she watched as the curve of his mouth moved closer and closer to her. When she felt the warm softness of his lips brush against her cheek, her eyelids fluttered shut, and her entire body tingled as though warm sand trickled across it on a hot summer day.

"Auhan," she whispered his name and swayed toward him, not wanting this closeness to end. He made her feel so womanly. Unlike a moment ago, she didn't feel at all uncomfortable now. His touch made everything right.

"I'm sorry," he murmured, his face just a scant inch from her own. "I shouldn't have—"

She placed her right forefinger against his lips, stilling his words. "Don't." The looks they exchanged roamed one over the other—deep, dark, velvet brown. Merging. Touching. Meeting. "Don't apologize for something so perfect," she whispered.

"Elena. . ." He transformed her name into a melodious song accompanied by the gentle breeze. A moment before, his lips had touched hers and made the music of her soul leap to glorious life. The movement of his lips touched, tender and soft, against her own. So loving, so warm, so pure was Auhan's kiss, Elena wished it could go on forever. Elena had never been kissed by a man before. Yet she knew, as Auhan's lips left hers, she would never want to kiss another. She had been falling in love with Auhan for the last several days. Now, with his kiss, she was certain. She had stopped "falling" and was wholly, totally "in" love.

"Dear Elena." He caressed the side of her mouth with his fingertip.

"Dear Auhan," she returned. With a sigh as soft as the breeze, she rubbed her cheek against his hand.

After a moment, the most enchanting moment of both their lives, he whispered into her ear, "Dear Elena, where do we go from here?"

She knew what he was asking.

But she also knew she did not want to answer him.

Her answer would be the same as his.

And it was one neither wanted to voice.

Until he made a decision about Christ and resolved his problems, they couldn't take their relationship any further. A wide chasm of theological thoughts and beliefs separated them.

But he was waiting for an answer. She opened her eyes and twisted her head toward the bow of the ship. "How about—New York?"

He laughed.

She laughed back.

He laughed louder, a young, carefree sound she had before never heard issuing from him.

Laughter continued to bubble up and out of her until tears sprang to her eyes.

As they were involved in mutual merriment, a combination of release and relief, the captain found them.

"Now, what have we here?" His husky voice interrupted them, but Elena could tell from the look he gave them he was very pleased to find them laughing.

Dabbing her eyes with a handkerchief proffered by Auhan, Elena continued to smile. She couldn't have done otherwise. "Captain." Elena offered her hand to the grandfatherly man as Auhan stood and gave him his chair. "I am just enjoying my first day out in the world again."

" 'Dolphin Girl.' " He reached for her fingers after he sat in the chair offered by Auhan. "So I see. And for that I, like Auhan, am very happy." He glanced up at Auhan and nodded his pleasure.

"We were enjoying the cloud art, when. . ." Her cheeks flushed with heat. She suspected that the captain knew they had shared much more than just a fun moment of observation, but she would not enlighten him as to what had further occupied them—their first kiss.

"When," the captain finished for her, "the wonderful, carefree feeling of the day combined with some funny comment to make you both laugh—long and hard." With a grateful heart for his insight and tact, Elena lifted her shoulders in acquiescence. "I'm glad." The older man released her fingers with a gentle squeeze. "You two young people deserve a little fun in life."

Auhan caught Elena in his gaze and they shared a look—that secret look of a close couple who are getting closer by the moment.

The private glance did not escape the notice of the wise, old captain. Between his beard and his mustache, his lips curved upward in acknowledgment before he spoke. "There is a reason I dropped by, other than to receive pleasure out of seeing you out on this beautiful day, my dear," he said to Elena. "I know your first name, but for my records I need to know your last."

"Yes, of course," she murmured. "My name is Elena Maria Apostologlou."

The captain's brows came together in a thoughtful frown. "Apostologlou?"

"That's right."

"You aren't by any chance related to Andreas Apostologlou, are you?"

A surprised gasp emanated from Elena upon hearing the name. "He was. . .my father."

The captain's sharp intake of breath was his immediate answer. "Your father? Andreas was your father?"

Elena minutely nodded her head.

"Oh, dear girl." The captain reached out for her hands again. He scanned the clean bandages still protecting their burned areas. "Auhan told me you lost your father the last night you were in Smyrna. I just didn't realize your father was Andreas." Visibly shaken by the news, the captain inhaled in deep, controlling breaths. "I am so sorry. I knew your father well. He was one of the most honest, fair men I ever had the privilege of carrying cargo for, not once, but many times." He gave a poignant smile.

"I always wondered if his name might have had something to do with the forming of his character. Doesn't the first part of your last name mean 'apostle' while the ending denotes someone coming from the Constantinople area of the world?"

"That's right," she concurred in breathless wonder. She was amazed by the captain's knowledge. Most people, even those familiar with things Hellenic, didn't realize that Greek names normally had interesting meanings and, quite often, Christian ones; hence their many letters. Her father had taught her to be very proud of her long, very old and significant last name.

The captain took another deep breath and said, "If ever a man lived up to his name, it was your father. He was truly like an apostle of Christ."

"Thank you, Captain," Elena responded. "I always thought so too."

"Many did, my dear. Many did. If there were more men—more Christians— in the world like your father, wars would never take place."

⁂

Auhan watched as a solemn Elena nodded her head. The captain's reference pointed out something that had always bothered him about Christianity and was a major stumbling block to his believing in God as revealed by Jesus Christ. Christians fighting Christians seemed like a contradiction to him, and he was beginning to think the captain felt the same way. It was the second time the man had mentioned something similar. Auhan wanted to pursue the subject further. But when he saw the poignant expression shadowing Elena's features at the captain's mention of her father, he held his tongue. This was her day. Her time to enjoy. He almost wished the captain hadn't asked for her last name. Serious topics had no place in today's magic.

But he didn't fault the captain. Who would have thought the giving of her name would have caused the atmosphere to turn so heavy? Auhan wanted to change it back to the light and carefree one of before. Looking up in the sky, he knew how.

"Elena," he interrupted the weighty silence, "why don't you show the captain your dolphin?"

The quick smile that readily spread across her face told of her relief in changing the subject. She launched into a lighthearted explanation about her wishing to thank the dolphin who had saved her and Buddy and how they had found the one she now pointed out in the clouds.

Watching her animated, intelligent face, Auhan knew they would discuss serious topics again.

But not today.

He looked out over the calm sea and smiled as she and the captain continued to chat.

No. Today was not the day to speak to Elena about anything but happy things. Now was a time of celebration, to rejoice in her being alive.

Reaching for the teapot, he poured all three of them a cup of the brew while listening to Elena as her bubbly laughter filled the air.

It was music of the most excellent kind, and Auhan breathed in deeply of the moment.

# Chapter 11

*The people answered him, We have heard out of the law*
*that Christ abideth for ever: and how sayest thou,*
*The Son of man must be lifted up? who is this Son of man?*
*Then Jesus said unto them, Yet a little while is the light*
*with you. Walk while ye have the light, lest darkness come upon you:*
*for he that walketh in darkness knoweth not whither he goeth.*
*While ye have light, believe in the light, that ye may be the children of light.*
John 12:34–36

As Auhan stood at the railing of the ship late that night, he heard the deep sounds of the captain's voice coming from behind him. "When I consider thy heavens, the work of thy fingers, the moon and the stars, which thou hast ordained; what is man that thou art mindful of him?"

The poetic words surprised Auhan. They were beautiful; but even more, they expressed exactly what he had been thinking as he gazed out over the star-filled sky of the soft, North Atlantic night. What was man compared to such awesome worlds as those that sparkled above him? And even more, why should Auhan even expect a God of such vastness to care about insignificant, little, warring humans?

Auhan turned to the captain as he came to stand beside him. "How did you know my exact thoughts?"

"It's what all young men who are thinkers consider when they look out over a night such as this," the captain replied and motioned to the heavens above.

Auhan turned back to the night scene. The sky was so full of stars, it looked like a blanket of soft, white cotton had been placed over a blue-black bed of deepest velvet.

"Thinker?" he questioned. His brother was the thinker, not he.

"Aren't you?" the captain challenged.

Auhan blew air out from between his teeth. "I have been considering things a great deal lately," he admitted in his heavily accented but 100 percent grammatically correct English.

"If that makes me a thinker, then I guess I am," he replied and paused. "It's just—" he began, but stopped and sighed, then sighed again.

"Go on," the captain prompted.

Auhan lifted his hand and nodded heavenward. "Is God mindful of man?" he asked, using the exact words the captain had just spoken.

"Let's finish seeing what the rest of the eighth psalm says." The captain spoke with love in his voice and seemed to worship the Creator as he gazed out over the infinite sky and recited the Scripture. The fact that the captain so obviously believed every word he spoke touched a chord deep within Auhan's soul.

" 'What is man, that thou art mindful of him?' " the captain repeated, " 'and the son of man, that thou visitest him? For thou hast made him a little lower than the angels, and hast crowned him with glory and honour. Thou madest him to have dominion over the works of thy hands; thou hast put all things under his feet: All sheep and oxen, yea, and the beasts of the field; The fowl of the air, and the fish of the sea, and whatsoever passeth through the paths of the seas.' "

The captain paused as emotion filled his throat. Then, with a resounding tone, he finished his recitation. " 'O LORD our Lord, how excellent is thy name in all the earth!' "

Silence settled between the two men, yet it was a friendly one. Comforting. Auhan really didn't understand everything the captain said—he wondered about this "son of man"—but the fact that the words meant so much to this man of authority whom Auhan had grown to greatly admire during the past two weeks gave him cause to ponder.

"I must admit, Captain," he spoke after a thoughtful moment, "between watching how you conduct your life and Elena hers and now seeing the change in my own mother, the Christian faith is beginning to seem very—" he paused and scanned his brain for the correct word, "—interesting to me."

"But?" the captain asked, and Auhan turned to him in surprise. "There is something which you wish to ask. I sensed it earlier today when on deck with our 'Dolphin Girl.' " Again, the captain's ability to note Auhan's mental musings impressed him. He didn't even try to deny his questions.

"I didn't want to say anything then." He shrugged his shoulders. "Elena needed happiness today. Nothing else."

"I agree. She needed today. But tomorrow or the next you might ask her anything you so desire. If she is anything like her father," he paused and chuckled, "and after having dolphins come to her rescue, I have no doubt she is—you'll find her to be a young lady of much understanding and knowledge. What we have seen in her so far is just the beginning, I'm sure. You will do well to bring your questions to her. The communication will draw you closer together. That's the key to a good relationship with another person—especially a young woman with whom you are growing very fond."

Auhan smiled into the darkness. He couldn't see the other man's eyes, but from the timbre of his voice he knew they had to be twinkling like the giant star Antares. He needn't even attempt to deny his feelings. "I do like her. Very much."

"Then don't be afraid to talk to her."

"I'm not. We've already shared some interesting conversations. But, I wanted today to be special for her, free from anything save good thoughts," he repeated his earlier words.

"Both smart and considerate of you," the captain acknowledged. "But," he asked after a quiet moment, "might I help you with your questions, or at least one of them now?"

Auhan nodded and breathed deeply of the clean, ocean-scented night before plunging into the profound waters of a theological discussion. "Like I said, your faith is beginning to seem very interesting to me." He turned to the captain. "But what about Christians fighting Christians?"

He doubted anyone could help him with his other questions, such as how the Christian God could allow little babies to be killed and thrown into mass graves. . . or how he could permit Elena and others like her to go through the tortures they had just experienced during the destruction of their city. No. No one could answer such tormenting questions.

*Elena probably could.* He frowned as the thought zipped through his brain, and he spoke quickly to cover both the surprise and unease it brought to him.

"I can somewhat understand why groups of diverse religious backgrounds might war with one another. It isn't right," he qualified, "but, I can see how so much divides and it might happen, such as with the Greeks and the Turks." He took a deep breath. "But Christians against Christians? Such a thing doesn't make any sense to me at all, and wasn't that what the Great War was all about?" The conflict had always presented a major stumbling block to Auhan's belief in the authenticity of Christianity.

"No, the Great War was never about Christians fighting Christians," the captain was quick to refute. "Rather, it was about imperialism and economics and greed; about groups of people wanting more than another, an age-old problem between humans and one not inclusive only to those who call themselves Christians."

But if Auhan was ever to believe in the God of his ancestors, he needed more convincing evidence than this. The captain's answer seemed too pat. He pressed on. "But the Germans, Austrians, and Hungarians are all Christians—and on the other side, the English, the French, and the Russians. These groups fought one another and brought other nations into the fray as well," Auhan pressed on.

"For the most part, yes, those nations mentioned are predominantly Christian." The captain didn't try to refute the commonly-held fact. "But what people forget, and some such as yourself don't even realize, is that Christianity is not a huge group of people who simply *call* themselves Christians. Rather, Christianity is about Christ. If a person wonders about Christianity, he is not to look at me or at that lovely girl sleeping below or at any other person or nation of people in this world. Only at the man—the God—from where we get the 'Christ' of the word 'Christianity.' Christ is the perfect one. Not me. Not Elena. Not the English or the French. Not the Germans or the Austrians. Not the Hungarians or the Italians or the Greeks or any other race of people. Christ is perfect and just and everything good in the world, the only true good to have ever existed.

"And, too," the captain continued, "many people who say they are Christians have no idea what being a Christian really means. A Christian isn't a group or a denomination to which one belongs or a set of traditions one follows in order to go to heaven. Rather, a Christian is one who has made a decision to turn from a life of sin and has asked Christ to help as he or she seeks to live a holy, loving lifestyle."

"My mother made a choice to be a Christian. Is she, then, a true Christian?" Auhan asked.

"It would seem so. But even still, Christ is the One you should look to. Not your mother. Because no matter how closely a person follows the life of Christ, we all fall short. We aren't perfect. Oh, we often get better and better as we study and learn and pray—we should, actually—but still sometimes a Christian might do something that makes another wonder about Christianity and say, such as yourself, 'Well, if the Germans and the English are fighting each other, then what good is Christianity?' But Christianity is not the English or the Germans or the Greeks or the Austrians or the Americans or the Hungarians. Christianity is Christ."

"So, you are saying I shouldn't look at another person when judging whether to believe the message of Christ or not?"

"Not entirely. You can look at Elena or at your mother or at me and wonder if the way we live our lives—with the Lord Jesus Christ at the very center of our being—is something you would like to experience for yourself. But if we do something you don't like, you shouldn't let that be the measure by which you judge Christianity."

"Then, Jesus Christ is the—measure?" Auhan asked. He wasn't too sure about the meaning of the word "measure" as used in this context, but he guessed it to be something similar to a musical measure and that the captain meant it was a criterion to follow.

"That's right." The other man paused. "You see, Son, even if there were no Christians in the world—no people who believed the message Jesus Christ came to earth to give—that would not negate the truth of His message or of His redemptive act. He is. Jesus Christ is God's Son whether you believe it or I believe it or anybody in this world does. His truth is not dependent on people's belief." He paused. "But conversely, our salvation *is* dependent on His truth. He came to earth for us. Like a parent wanting to rescue His child, He came to earth to save us."

"But why then should Christians fight one another?" Auhan went back to his original question.

"Personally," the captain breathed out a heavy sigh, "I don't believe people who have made a conscious effort to follow Christ make war on one another. I'm not saying believing Christians won't serve their country and fight in wars, for that comes under the scriptural directive to follow the laws of our individual countries."

"So, what you're saying is that only non-Christians are behind wars?" Auhan persisted, somewhat appalled. He didn't know if he agreed with that idea. In fact, he was almost certain he didn't.

The captain grimaced. "I guess it sounds that way. Maybe that is what I personally believe. Any sort of official statement to the effect might cause lots of problems. So, let me qualify myself a bit." He paused and seemed to think a moment. "If by non-Christian you include in that group people who are only traditional Christians —people who call themselves Christians because their parents were, and theirs before them, and so on back into time, yet who have never made a personal, conscious choice to believe Christ's message—then yes." He shook his head.

"That's not to say those born in the tradition of Christianity, such as myself, don't have a great advantage over those who are not. They do. But that advantage also brings responsibility—the responsibility not to take one's faith for granted and the responsibility to teach others. Christ demands a response from each person, whether he or she comes from a family of believers or not."

When the captain finished, Auhan took a deep breath, then blew it out from between his teeth in a half-whistle. "That's a lot to consider, Sir."

The captain patted him on the back. "Well now, that's why God gave humans good brains. We have the ability to think through things. Personally, I think He gave us our brains in order for us to use them to find Him. Unfortunately, most don't take the time to do so. But I'll tell you something else, Son. When we say 'yes' to Christ and the Spirit of God moves into our hearts to live within us, He gives us a whole new life. When the learned Nicodemus—" The captain paused when a sailor approached.

"What is it, Sailor?"

"Excuse me, Sir, but you are needed above."

The captain nodded, dismissing the sailor, then turned back to Auhan. "I'm sorry, Son, but duty calls." As he spoke, he straightened his cap and prepared to leave. "Just remember this: When you answer 'yes' to Jesus, 'yes' that you believe Him, then you are reborn a new man. A new man in Christ. And He is able to give you that rebirth because He is God, not just a prophet of God. Think about it." The captain turned on his heels and walked away with the clipped, authoritative steps of a man whose mind was already on the job before him.

Auhan turned to look out at the starlit sea again. Somehow, it seemed to be even brighter than a few moments before.

*Rebirth.* . .the word replayed in his mind as Auhan breathed deeply of the ocean air. *Was it possible?*

He smiled. He was beginning to think that many things were more possible than he had ever considered before.

❧

Two days passed—glorious days in which Auhan and Elena laughed and talked, looked for art in the clouds, and just enjoyed being a young and happy, seemingly carefree couple.

The third day, Elena told Auhan she felt strong enough to walk out to the deck on her own. Even though he missed the closeness of carrying her, he thrilled to see her renewed strength and energy. He discovered a new joy in having her by his side, of using his strong arms to support her, of just being a couple perambulating together. He hadn't anticipated such a pleasant bonus. Auhan had often seen happy couples strolling along as they were doing now, and he had always thought those other couples were a bit foolish. Perhaps he had been the foolish one.

As he guided Elena toward the canopy, she motioned to the glorious day which once again surrounded their ship and exclaimed, "Oh, Auhan, when the sun set that day when I was in the sea, I didn't know if I would ever see the world like this again." She placed her hand on her dog's head and sank into her seat. "Except for Buddy and the dolphin, I don't know if I would have made it." Auhan's jaw clenched upon hearing the slight catch in Elena's voice, and he reached out to instinctively ruffle Buddy's soft fur.

Even though the captain's explanation of a few nights ago about Christians fighting Christians made sense, Auhan still had a hard time with the suffering that the millions of Christians of Asia Minor—and particularly this woman who had become very dear to him—had gone through. How could God allow it? It was totally beyond Auhan's thinking that Elena could still consider God as her friend. He didn't see how she could think God actually loved her after He had allowed her to be so grievously hurt, both physically and mentally.

"I'm so sorry you had to go through all that, Elena." He seated himself across from her. "If I could have prevented it, I would have." Her eyebrows lifted in question when he put emphasis on the pronouns.

"What are you saying?" Her lips formed a firm line across her face. "That God didn't prevent it?"

She knew him too well. He didn't even try to deny it. How could he? It was exactly what he meant. "That's right," he agreed. In spite of everything, all Auhan could conclude was that God hadn't helped her just as he hadn't helped all those people—those Christians—in that mass grave or others like it.

"If God is your friend, then why did He allow you to suffer in the sea on top of all that you had already endured?" Doubt flavored his words.

"God didn't bring the suffering, Auhan," she sighed, and he detected a weary note to her voice. "Men did. Men who made wrong choices." She raised her bandage-covered hands in the air even as the pitch of her voice rose. "It amazes me how God is always blamed for the mistakes and meanness of people."

The thought caught Auhan's attention, and he would have given it more consideration if she hadn't totally staggered him with her next statement. "But even with what I went through, God did bring good to me." Her voice softened, and as he wondered what good she could possibly mean, she reached out and brushed the tips of her fingers across his right cheek with her right hand. "He brought you to me, dear Auhan," she whispered, and her eyes became as soft as liquid gold. "And I am beginning to think a day spent in the sea was worth meeting you."

His gaze narrowed. That was the last thing he had expected her to say, and he didn't know how to respond. Or how he felt. Wonderful? Frightened? Flabbergasted? To think that such a girl would think such a nice thing about him. The realization was almost too much.

She shrugged her shoulders as though embarrassed by his sudden quietness, but she continued with a determined tilt to her jaw. "Maybe for us to meet was the reason I was 'allowed' to fall off that rescue ship, Auhan."

Auhan looked away from her honest eyes and out at the mighty ocean. Quietly, with his voice as smooth as the water's surface, he asked, "Do you really think God let you fall overboard so that we could meet?" To part of him, it seemed totally absurd. To another part, both amazing and wonderful.

"It's possible," Elena admitted after a moment, and he let out a deep breath, one that carried a large weight with it.

"I do have feelings for you, Elena." He wouldn't even try to deny them. He wasn't sure when they had started—probably while he stood on deck that night and watched the sailors pull her out of the sea with all those dolphins jumping around her. "But, because I haven't felt anything but anger and bitterness for so long, I don't know if I can do anything with these feelings—if I can offer you anything," he qualified. "I'm crippled, Elena. In my mind, my soul, I'm crippled."

It was more than he had admitted out loud to his parents or even to himself before.

"Dear Auhan." She looked at him with such compassion, he felt as though she had reached out and caressed him. She had. She had caressed his hurting, weeping soul.

"Don't you know, until God lives in our hearts, we are all crippled?"

He stood up so suddenly, Buddy growled a sound of fear and confusion, and Elena rested a hand on the dog's golden head to reassure him. "God! Why would I want such an impotent God living within me? You don't know what I've seen. The wicked things I've seen done to God's so-called people, even while they called out to Him for help." He nearly spat the words, and he saw the horror of what he had seen reflected in her eyes.

❧

She recognized his stare of terror-filled panic. She had seen painfully similar abominations in Smyrna. The horrors would take control of her too. If she let them.

But a fresh, sudden thought, a terrible thought, went through Elena's head, and she licked her cotton-dry lips. "Auhan, while fleeing Smyrna, I overheard a group of Turkish soldiers taunting a family they were about to murder—'Why doesn't your God save you now?' they snarled." Her face became pale as she remembered. She had blocked the wretched scene from her mind until this moment—until Auhan's statement about other Christians in other parts of the empire calling out to God triggered the memory. And her blood ran cold once again.

Auhan fell to his knees beside her. Remorse covered his features. "I'm so sorry, Elena. I shouldn't have marred this moment with such talk."

She ignored his placating words. "Are you taunting me with the same question?"

Auhan's face turned ashen. "No, Elena, no." He shook his head back and forth, absolutely denying it. "I didn't. I mean, I never—" He buried his face in his hands. "Elena, no. I'm not taunting you. Please, you must believe me," he pleaded. "I'm just wondering why? Why would God allow so many thousands of His people to die? Why didn't He rescue them? Why did He allow deportations that killed thousands of mothers and their children? Thousands of babies." Babies in blue sweaters.

Elena looked out into the still sea. But she wasn't seeing the mighty Atlantic Ocean or looking for the still unseen freedom-loving shores of her other home, of America. Rather, she was seeing the fleets of Western ships filled with Christians as they floated in the harbor of Smyrna a couple of weeks ago. They had done nothing—absolutely nothing—to help bring the people, the remnant of believers from one of the oldest Christian lands in the world, to safety.

In mute dismay, Elena shook her head.

God had sent help to the Christians of the Smyrna Protectorate. He had sent help in the form of the strongest nations on earth—and even that of her other country, America. Those nations, filled with Christians, simply sat and watched as their allies, their Christian brothers and sisters, were slaughtered. Not until the Greeks and Armenians were trapped between the burning city and the deep, wind-churned harbor did some—some, but not all—start to help. But that was after thousands had been murdered in cold blood. Her father included.

How evil had laughed in the inferno of those hours.

She could still hear its awful sound. Among all the cries of agony, torture, blood being spilled, evil's cackles, snarls, and snickers still resounded in her head.

Her body shook.

But she could feel Auhan's warm arms as they enfolded her, could smell his wonderful scent, and could feel his heart—his life—beating against her palm.

Then, she heard his voice. He was calling out to her.

"Elena, Elena," he repeated her name over and over. "Dear." He was rubbing her face. "Please, Darling."

That endearment got through to her. Still plagued with horror-filled visions of her city's indigenous population being slaughtered, she turned to him and picked up the fabric of their conversation as if there had been no interval.

"Tell me, Auhan," she said, her voice flat but demanding. "What exactly do you believe about God?"

His eyes reddened and filled with unshed tears as he shook his head negatively. "That is not something. . .you. . .want. . .to know," he rasped, his voice sounding scraped and stripped.

"Maybe not," she admitted. "But it's something I have to know before I can help you."

He gave a bitter laugh. "No one can help me."

"God can."

"God is impotent," he spat in reply.

"Is that what you believe?" If that were it, she would deal with it. But somehow, she felt certain there was more to it than that. To say God was impotent was just a battle cry.

Muscles twitched along his jaw, and she could see a war raging within his soul. Like Smyrna's war, like all wars, it was ugly. Hideous.

"I was a Turkish soldier," he ground out after a moment. "Doesn't that bother you at all?"

"Did you kill any civilians?" she asked, her voice barely above a whisper.

"No." He shook his head from side to side in fierce denial. "Never."

"Then," she paused and moistened her lips, "perhaps you were as much a victim as I?"

He shook his head. "No. Not a victim like you." He paused. "I held a gun."

She flinched. "But you didn't use it on civilians?" she questioned again.

He shook his head again in adamant refute. And she believed him. Totally. She hadn't forgotten he had been a Turkish soldier. Not once. Not even as she had been falling in love with him had she forgotten. But she had been certain too that he had never hurt a defenseless person. Having him volunteer the information was all the proof she needed. Putting the unpleasant facts behind her, as she had so many other things, she nodded and returned to her original question. "Auhan, please tell me what you believe, what you truly believe. You have rightly admitted you are crippled. I want to help. But I have to know what you believe in order to do so."

He shook his head as a tear fell from the corner of each of his red eyes.

"Auhan." She leaned toward him and wiped his teardrops away. "I know you weren't taunting me with your question." Her countenance and her voice offered him sweet assurance. "I understand. If you'll let me, I'll do my best to help you discover the answers to all your haunting questions."

Auhan looked at her, really looked into her eyes. He knew that she wouldn't stop pressing him for an answer until he told her. He also knew his trying to convince himself that she wasn't strong enough to know the truth was a lie. She was the strongest person he knew.

"Please, Auhan. Not knowing is the hardest thing for me," she said, reading his mind as easily as if it had been an open book.

In slow acquiescence, he nodded his head. He could understand her need to probe. He would feel the same way if the roles were reversed. With lips that barely moved, he opened his heart, his dark and cold dungeon of a heart, for the first time in over a year.

"I believe. . ." He shook his head as the somber words left his mouth. He didn't want to speak. He knew with their voicing, he would destroy any chance of a life together with her. He sighed and began again. "I believe that evil rules this world, Elena. Not God. Evil."

Slowly, a smile, a sad one, but still a smile, touched her colorless lips. Auhan never felt more shocked in his life when she replied, "Dear Auhan, you are absolutely correct."

# Chapter 12

*And out of the ground made the L*ORD *God to grow every tree that is pleasant to*
*the sight, and good for food; the tree of life also in the midst of the garden,*
*and the tree of knowledge of good and evil.*
Genesis 2:9


*Blessed are they that do his commandments,*
*that they may have right to the tree of life,*
*and may enter in through the gates into the city.*
Revelation 22:14


E vil does rule this world, Auhan. And yet God is still sovereign." She looked
out over the mighty body of water and smiled a sweet smile of hope.

Auhan shook his head as if to clear his confusion. "That's a contradiction, Elena." The calmness of his voice amazed him. He felt anything but calm.

Her eyes held not the slightest glimmer of doubt when she looked at him. "No, it's no contradiction. Although God is sovereign, that is to say, He possesses supreme power, evil does indeed have a sphere of influence, a rule, here on earth." She frowned in thought.

"You see, Auhan, that's exactly why God sent His Son to earth. To break the hold the evil one has over people."

He looked at her in amazement. "How can you say such a thing? How can you even believe it? Especially after what you have just lived through?" He made an ill-tempered grunt. "*Barely* lived through, I should say."

"Because it's true," she insisted. Even though he shook his head in disagreement, she continued. "Auhan, we don't know when Satan became God's enemy. We don't even know when he, the most glorious of all God's angels, fell into sin. But we do know evil came into this world through his lying, tricking words."

She leaned forward as though to punctuate the importance of her words. "We read in the Bible, in the third chapter of Genesis, 'And he said unto the woman, Yea, hath God said, Ye shall not eat of every tree of the garden?' " Elena's eyes widened with the question.

"The conniving serpent had expertly planted the seed of doubt within her innocent mind, and the poor woman replied, 'We may eat of the fruit of the trees of the garden: But of the fruit of the tree which is in the midst of the garden, God hath said, Ye shall not eat of it, neither shall ye touch it, lest ye die.' "

Auhan made an impatient motion with his hands. "This is just a children's story."

Elena vigorously nodded her head up and down, and she surprised him again by agreeing with him. "That's right, it is! It's God's story to His children—to us."

Auhan was too bewildered by her response to reply. In truth, the thought was an amazing one. God's story to His children? His children? Was that what the Bible was?

"How do you suppose the evil one responded to God's words as repeated by the woman?" Elena didn't wait for a response, but answered her own question.

"With a nice big contradiction, that's how. He told her, 'Ye shall not surely die: For God doth know that in the day ye eat thereof, then your eyes shall be opened, and ye shall be as gods, knowing good and evil.' " Elena paused and looked deeply at Auhan. "What a lie. Evil was not something we ever had to know, needed to know about." She gazed toward the eastern horizon, while Auhan looked into his soul.

How often had he wondered why? Why had he had to learn about evil at that grave? It was an amazing thought to hear Elena say God hadn't wanted him to know about such depravity. God had never intended for him to come to that moment in his life. Neither had He wanted Elena to face evil in her home city. But what made their reaction to evil so different? The darkness of it all had nearly killed him, whereas Elena, in spite of everything, still shone with hope and light.

He found himself listening with rapt attention as she continued. "Believe me, evil is not something we want, and God never wanted us to have to know it or to have to fight it in our lives," she repeated with fervor.

"Even though He would not keep its knowledge from us if we so chose to have it, He didn't want us to know it. No more than your parents or mine ever wanted us, as their children, to eat or do something that was bad for us, which would cause us harm or even death." Her words sparked with passion as she spoke.

Auhan couldn't help but think of his sister. She had been warned by their parents, as had all three of them, not to go too close to the water. She had disobeyed, died, and brought immeasurable pain upon them all.

In spite of his disbelief, Auhan found himself interested in what she was saying. That she believed it made it important to him. "You know, there is something most people don't notice when reading about the fall of man in Genesis. The Bible tells us there were two trees in the middle of the garden."

"Two?" He frowned. He didn't recall ever hearing this fact. He'd only heard about the one tree.

She nodded her head. "Right next to the tree of the knowledge of good and evil stood the tree of life."

"The tree of life?" He was certain he had never heard about that tree.

She nodded her head. "God didn't warn the man and the woman not to eat from the tree of life. Before they disobeyed God, they could have eaten from it at any time they so desired."

Auhan felt Elena might be hitting upon a topic few people ever considered. She definitely had his interest. It was as if, for the first time, everything—all his thoughts and questions—were coming into accord. One of the things he loved most about playing the violin was tuning it, something he had never been able to do with his life, not even before the war. He continued to listen, as she seemed to speak one more remarkable word upon another, words he wanted to hear with a desire stronger than any yearning he had ever felt—even stronger than his love of playing the violin. He longed to believe. And her words seemed to be answering the fervent hope of his soul.

"The woman and the man disobeyed the only commandment God had, up to that time, given to them. The only one. Don't you think, Auhan, God gave them this one command because it was important to their welfare? He loved them so much, He didn't want them to have to deal with evil. God had created a world apart from evil. A world of freedom. Humans needed only to trust God's commandment, have faith in His judgment. God gave the command in order for the tree of human history to remain unmarred by the evil one. So simple. As simple as a child listening to—or ignoring—his parents." She sighed with a sound that held the sadness of the ages.

Auhan pursed his lips in contemplation. "But if God is sovereign and all-knowing, surely He knew what would happen—how they would choose. Couldn't He have prevented it?" Elena's face brightened at his inquiry.

"I believe even though He knew how His creation would choose when confronted with the evil one, the pain that choice would bring to Him was still worth all the joy." She smiled and swept away from her face the strands of hair that the gentle breeze had pushed into her eyes. "Kind of like earthly parents. All people are wise enough to know that, although children are a blessing, in many cases they bring much pain to their parents' hearts. But even with knowing this, people still want children. Yearn for them. We have children in the hope they will become wonderful human beings. Yet God knew, even before He created us, exactly how many would actually turn out to bring joy to Him. And, even though He knew not all of us would make the right choice when confronted with the question of obedience, God considered His resulting suffering and pain worthwhile."

Auhan still had a hard time believing that God considered humans as His children, and he wasn't quite sure about the "choice" Elena referred to, but he didn't interrupt her with his doubts. He wanted to hear her out. The information her brain contained fascinated him, and, well, something was stirring within him. He wasn't sure what it was exactly, only that it was something nice, something bright, as if, for the first time ever, the music of his soul was beginning to play to the correct melody.

"To answer the second part of your question, God couldn't have prevented our choice, not without taking away human volition, that is, our humanness. We have to be held accountable for our actions. The decision made by the man and woman gave evil the right to invade the perfect world God had made for them, and they immediately stopped living in the light of God, and darkness revealed them."

"Darkness revealed them?" Auhan questioned the seeming contradiction, and Elena nodded in response.

"Upon looking at one another, they saw they were naked—because for the first time in their existence, they were. Man and woman, God's created children, no longer had the 'clothing' of God's light to cover them."

Auhan looked at her in amazement. Maybe that first man and woman no longer had the light of God's "clothing," but Elena certainly did. Even when sick in bed, she had looked as though God's light had been wrapped around her like an exquisite mantle. He knew now it was this very thing that had made him take note of her from the beginning, that had gotten his attention when nothing else could.

Elena was clothed in the light of God's love.

His eyes widened.

Where had that thought come from? He had never thought such a thing before. But, to his amazement, he didn't want to stop. He felt something not only stir, but now jump, within his soul. It was as if he were coming alive after having been dead. All he wanted was to hear more.

"Go on." He heard his voice speak the words, but he didn't feel like the words came from him any longer. Yet, even that made him glad. He didn't like the person he had become, a person without hope, without love, without light, a person who believed evil was in control of the world.

When Auhan looked at Elena, her eyes sparkled as though she too sensed something was different about him. He wondered if she realized that an entirely new feeling now radiated from him. For the first time, he felt his spirit was in one accord with hers.

"Even though His children disobeyed, He was already working on a plan to make things right again. Before we even leave the third chapter of the book of Genesis, God spoke Himself into the world. He spoke Himself into the very fabric of the world's future population so that He could act and solve the problem of the separation between Himself—a holy God—and sinful man. God came into the world through the right door—the door of human bloodline—and He offered Himself to correct the rift standing between Him and the people He longed to call His children. Jesus Christ—the Son of man—"

"Jesus Christ was the Son of man?" Auhan interrupted her, remembering the verses the captain had recited the starry night on deck. If Christ was the same Son of man he had referred to, it certainly explained a lot.

"Jesus Christ is the Son of man." Elena corrected his tense and continued. "He was born a human baby. He lived among us, revealed God—who is Himself—to us, taught us, and then hung on that cross, died on that cross, and took our punishment for all the wrongs we have ever done, will ever do," she qualified, "in order to make everything right. He did this to prevent mankind from being under the dominion of the evil one any longer. It's done. The work is complete. All we have to do—all anyone of any race anywhere in the world has to do—is to tell Him we are sorry for our sins and believe Jesus is who He Himself said He is—God."

Auhan dropped his gaze and studied the floor while he concentrated on her words.

"If Jesus' sinless life doesn't prove to you who He is, if all the prophecies about Him don't prove it, if all of His miracles don't prove it, if His teachings don't prove it, if His dying on the cross and then being resurrected doesn't prove it to you. . ." She paused and touched her hand to where his heart beat beneath his jacket and vest. "Then, please, let the Comforter, the One Jesus sent when He ascended to heaven, the One who can live within your heart, prove it to you. It's all real. It's all true. It's God's story of redemption to His children—the most fantastic 'children's' story ever penned. Jesus is the One who conquered evil. He is the One who provides a way for us to reach the other tree in the middle of the garden again—the tree of life. Because of man's bad choice, evil does influence this world, Auhan. But. . . ," she paused, and Auhan looked up to see her smile, "God still rules supreme."

Hot tears slid from the corners of Auhan's eyes and down his face. He didn't even try to wipe the tears away. Instead, he reached for her hands and intertwined her fingers in his. Speaking softly but with sincere desire, he said, "Elena, I want to be a part of such a belief. What do I have to do?"

She cried out, squeezing his hands in hers. "Oh, dear Auhan, just believe. Just believe that Jesus Christ—God's Son—came to earth to save you from the grips of the evil one. Just believe He came to pay the price of your guilt in order that you might be born a whole new person."

At those words, his shoulders heaved, and for the first time since he was a little boy, sobs, great, big, heaving sobs, erupted from his body. He cried for himself. He cried for what he had seen. He cried for Elena and her family and the thousands of families in Smyrna and in Asia Minor. He cried for the baby in the blue sweater. And as his sobs subsided, he prayed and asked the Lord Jesus to live within his heart.

Auhan believed. He was a new person in Christ. His desire to be reborn had just come true. And he knew he would never relinquish his new life. Not ever.

# Chapter 13

*Rejoice in the LORD,*
*O ye righteous. . . . Praise the LORD with harp:*
*sing unto him with the psaltery*
*and an instrument of ten strings.*
*Sing unto him a new song;*
*play skilfully with a loud noise.*
Psalm 33:1–3

After Auhan's birth into the kingdom of God, Elena and Auhan sat on the deck for hours in the pure lighting of the ocean sun. They talked and laughed and grew closer and closer to one another and, as a couple, closer to God. They were now both members of the same spiritual family, God's family; and on that seafaring deck, their love blossomed into the most beautiful of blooms.

By the time the sun sat very low in the sky, Elena knew she would spend her life together with this man. She didn't want to leave the magic of the deck, but her body was still on the mend, and Auhan insisted she needed her rest. Before she went to bed, however, they agreed on one more thing Auhan needed to do on this most remarkable day.

The pitter-patter of the dog preceded them into the cabin. *Anne* Fatima stopped in the motion of slinging her shawl around her shoulders when Auhan guided Elena over the threshold. "I was just about to come looking for you two," she exclaimed. Dropping her shawl onto a bunk, she quickly crossed over to Elena. With concern etching lines in her face, Fatima placed her hand against her forehead while Elena waited patiently. The dear woman sighed, and the lines left her face when she seemed assured that Elena's temperature was normal. *Anne* Fatima turned back to her son, obviously intent on admonishing him for keeping her out so long. But *Anne* Fatima stayed her words of reproach when she saw Auhan reach for his violin case. A gasp escaped the devoted mother, and her gaze searched the cabin for her husband.

Elena watched as Suleiman rose from the side of his bunk and reached for his wife's outstretched hand. Elena watched as, together, they considered their son.

Lines of wonder painted their classical features when Auhan gently, almost reverently, laid the leather case on his bunk, unlatched it with great care, and lifted the lid.

Reaching down, he ran his fingertips over the smooth varnish of the meticulously crafted instrument. Elena thought he looked as though he were greeting an old friend. Her eyes widened when she looked closely at the red-toned violin. Auhan had told her earlier that his violin was a very special instrument—a gift from a very old, childless, Greek merchant who had recognized Auhan's great talent.

But the instrument before her eyes far surpassed anything she had envisioned. She didn't claim to know much about violins. However, she had seen a good number of them up close when musicians performed in her father's salon in Smyrna. With certainty, she knew this one before her now was of exceptional quality. Very likely it was a sixteenth-century creation from an Italian school. *Perhaps, from the workshop of Stradivari himself,* she thought with a tingle of excitement.

Taking meticulous care, Auhan lifted the intricately crafted violin from its velvet bed. For a moment he just cradled the instrument in his arms as he would a baby. He cast a conspiratorial smile in Elena's direction, and her heart beat glad within her chest. Then he nestled the violin beneath his chin. He started plucking at the strings to tune it, and he finished the task with such quick and expert ease, he looked like he had done the task as recently as the day before. Elena moved to stand beside Fatima as Auhan turned to his parents. Picking up the bow, he touched it to the strings. He paused and presented them all with a smile so full of light, they all answered with matching grins.

Then.

Then.

Auhan made music.

The most wonderful, the most meaningful rendition of Beethoven's "Ode to Joy" Elena had ever heard came forth from the movement of Auhan's hands, from his body, from the music within his soul.

Auhan played and played. He bobbed and bowed. He was one with the instrument, one with the melody. The sound seemed to transcend the physical as sweet music rose above the din of the ship's engines and floated out over the ocean to God above.

Tears ran down Elena's face, down his parents' too. And when Auhan played the last glorious note and the final sound drifted out of the cabin into the never-never land of silent-but-remembered melodies, Auhan looked over at Elena.

For a long moment, they gazed into each other's eyes. Words weren't necessary to convey the hope, the love filling their hearts.

At Elena's gentle nod, Auhan, still holding the violin in his hands, walked over to his mother and father. "*Anne, Baba.* No more tears." He reached into his pocket and pulled out a clean handkerchief, then handed it to his mother. "No more tears for me. I am healed."

He looked down at the cross that hung from his mother's neck.

"The cross of Jesus Christ has healed me; it has made me whole. Made me well. Made me—" He paused as emotion clogged his throat. "Made me into a whole new man."

Fatima cried out, a mother's sweet cry filled with pure joy. Elena watched as the woman hugged her child close. "Oh, Auhan, my dear, dear boy." She pulled back and looked up at her husband.

"Suleiman?" she asked. "I believe in the God of our ancestors. Our son believes now too. But what about you?"

He looked between his son and his wife and then shifted his gaze to Elena. He ran his large hand over the short, silky locks of her golden hair and cleared the emotion from his throat before testing his little-used voice. "E–le–na," he stammered. He paused and swallowed hard again.

"Dear Daughter." He pronounced the words with deliberate slowness. "I am a man of few words, but this I must say."

Elena encouraged him to continue with a nod and a smile.

"The night the sailors fished you from the sea. . ." His Adam's apple bobbed up and down as he struggled to speak his mind. "I knew you were special." The quiet man spoke a little faster with each word.

"You brought light into our cabin. Into our hearts. You shared this light with us all. First my wife. . ." He encircled his wife's shoulder and drew his wife close.

"And then with my son." He smiled at Auhan and reached out to run his long fingers over the rich wood of the violin. Elena couldn't help but notice his trembling hand.

"I had lost all hope my son would ever play again." Again he had to pause as he struggled to regain control of his fragile emotions. Then, standing tall, he took a deep, rejuvenating breath and spoke with renewed strength and confidence. "As our Auhan played those beautiful notes, I realized I had never really cherished hope in my heart." He exchanged a tender glance with his wife, and his voice softened to a whisper. "My wife, she had hope. Yet, I felt such things only through her."

He looked at Auhan, then back again to Elena. "But listening to Auhan's music. . ." His lips pursed in determination, and he nodded his head in a quick jerk. "While Auhan played, I came to understand. I can never have my own hope without this Light. I need the Light."

A glint of excitement sparked in his eyes as he spoke directly to his son. "I need the Light of my ancestors to shine within me too. The Light you have embraced, my son. As you bowed and expressed your soul with that song. . ." His face broke into a wide smile as he looked at Elena, then his son, and then stayed his gaze on his wife. "In that moment, I gave my soul over to the Christ, to the One whom Auhan's melody must glorify."

"Suleiman!" Fatima exclaimed and placed her hand upon her husband's dear face.

He looked deeply into his wife's eyes, and his joyful smile erupted into a rumble of laughter. He shook his head in amazement. He whispered, "This old, cold heart of mine could no longer ignore such a Light as Elena brought onboard."

Along with *Anne* Fatima and Auhan, Elena allowed herself to be drawn into Suleiman's strong-armed embrace, and they all celebrated this happy moment of eternal significance. As the ever quiet patriarch pounded her on the back in a most uncharacteristic display of emotion, her heart pounded in her chest with boundless bliss. She could almost hear the angels in heaven as they too rejoiced.

The next morning—another beautiful day—as their little ship drew them closer and closer to the shores of America, Auhan and Elena invited both of Auhan's parents to accompany them up onto the deck.

Although not even twenty-four hours had passed since they had declared their love for one another, it seemed like so much longer. A lifetime. To Elena, it seemed as if they had known each other forever. If Elena hadn't seen such a love blossom between Christos and her sister on the catastrophic streets of Smyrna, if she hadn't heard again and again throughout her life how quickly her parents had fallen in love, she might have been suspect. But she wasn't. Elena counted the love she and Auhan felt for one another as just another blessing from God.

"Do you have the ring?" she whispered into Auhan's ear. She referred to her mother's engagement ring, which she had taken from the handkerchief under her pillow earlier that morning. In acknowledgment, Auhan patted the pocket in his vest that protected the heirloom. Elena returned his smile. She could hardly wait to see his parents' reactions.

"*Anne, Baba,*" Auhan addressed his parents when they were all seated under the canopy, sipping tea. "Elena and I have something we'd like to tell you."

"Actually," Elena gently corrected him as she pushed a windblown strand of hair from her face, "we have something we'd like to *ask* you." Auhan gave her a quick and loving smile before turning back to his parents.

His mother looked as if her curiosity would make her jump out of her skin, whereas his father's eyes held a knowing glint. Elena suspected he knew exactly what was going on, especially when she caught him sending his son an encouraging wink.

She rejoiced in the realization that Suleiman's newfound faith in the God of his ancestors had rejuvenated him. According to Auhan, the father he remembered from his childhood had now returned.

Auhan sat a little taller in his chair. "A couple of weeks ago, you offered to adopt Elena as your daughter."

Fatima nodded her head and smiled broadly. "Elena is our daughter now." She paused and qualified, "Our daughter in Christ."

Auhan's smile matched that of his mother's. "That's true but, well, as her adoptive parents, I would like to ask you both a question."

Fatima was perplexed. "You?"

"Dear." Suleiman reached out and gently squeezed his wife's hand. "Let the boy—" His thick mustache quirked as he corrected himself, "I mean, let the *man* speak."

Fatima nodded and sat back in her chair to listen and wait, albeit impatiently.

Auhan rose and walked to the right of Elena's chair. Buddy was on her left. Placing his hand upon her shoulder, Auhan addressed his father as seriously as any young man standing before a girl's parent might.

"As Elena's adoptive father, Sir, may I request your daughter's hand in marriage?"

The words had no sooner left his mouth than *Anne* Fatima made a sound of pure glee, jumped out of her chair, and wrapped her arms around Elena.

"You will be my daughter two times—no, three times over, darling girl," she exclaimed, and both women, with smiles and nods, looked happily into each other's eyes. The miracle of a new mother for Elena wrapped around her, and Fatima's face mirrored her joy in finding a new daughter. The mother and daughter in heaven were not now, nor ever would be, forgotten. But, the gift of a new person to love helped ease the pain of missing the one who was no longer on earth.

"Well now," Suleiman drawled. "I'm not so sure, young man," he said, causing all three to turn to him in surprise. "Just how do you propose to support my dear daughter?" Elena couldn't keep her mouth from dropping open in shock when she realized he was totally serious.

She forced her mouth closed and looked between the three of them as they silently regarded one another. Finally, she could contain herself no longer. "I haven't said much before, but my father was a very wealthy man. There will not be a need for Auhan—"

"Forgive me, Dear," Suleiman kindly cut her off. "However, I didn't ask how your father supported you. I asked how this young man was planning on doing so."

Elena looked to Auhan in dismay. In truth, they hadn't even talked about that, nor even about his profession. Money had never been an issue for Elena, and, thanks to those of her father's assets safely tucked away in banks in America, it still wouldn't be. "Really, *Baba* Suleiman," she began. But at the slight pressure of Auhan's fingers against her shoulder, she stopped.

"Your adoptive father brings forth a very good point, Elena, and one I have given thought to," he said, and her mouth again dropped open in surprise. He turned back to the older man and answered. "I will be seeking employment with an orchestra. If I am not good enough for that, then I will make, sell, and repair violins, Sir. If that is not enough, I will give music lessons to all who want to learn to love the violin as much as I do."

Suleiman stood and regarded his son for a moment. When a great big smile showed beneath his mustache—the biggest Elena had ever seen come from him—she breathed a sigh of relief. "That is acceptable work for a man who wishes to marry my daughter." He paused, and, reaching out, he took hold of Auhan's upper arms with both of his large hands and squeezed them. "And more than acceptable for my son. I'm proud of you, Auhan. Proud."

"Oh!" Fatima clapped her hands together. "A wedding to plan," she exclaimed, and they all laughed at the dreamy element in her voice. "I just love to plan celebrations! When do you plan to marry?"

Auhan looked down at Elena with a sheepish grin. "We really haven't discussed dates yet."

"Well," Elena gave her shoulders a little shrug, "I was thinking toward the end of next June."

"June?" Auhan questioned and knelt down beside her. "Beloved? That's so far away. Is it. . .because of your mourning for your father?"

She shook her head. "No, my father never agreed with that custom. He always said a Christian should not mourn for long the passing of another Christian. 'For to me to live is Christ, and to die is gain,' " she quoted from the first chapter of Philippians. "My father is in heaven with Jesus. How can I mourn that?"

"Then what is it, Beloved?" He shrugged his shoulders. "Why can we not marry sooner?"

She offered him a wistful smile. "Because," she softly answered, "I would like my sisters to be at my wedding."

"And you hope to be reunited with them by next June?"

As Elena softly nodded her head, Fatima interrupted. "Auhan, June is good," she encouraged. "You should be reunited with your brother by then too."

Auhan looked up at his mother, and Elena saw a passing shadow of pain cross over his features. "Do you really believe he will be able to make it to the Lincoln Memorial, *Anne*?"

"I do," his mother insisted.

Elena swiveled her head between the two as if she were hearing things. "What did you say?" she breathed out. Auhan's English was heavily accented, but she was certain that she had heard him say in English, "Lincoln Memorial."

Auhan turned to her and explained. "In the event my brother, my parents, or myself were separated by this war and unable to be reunited before my parents sailed for America, we set up a rendezvous in America. My mother is a great admirer of Abraham Lincoln, so we decided to meet each May thirtieth at the memorial built in his honor in Washington—"

Elena could feel the blood drain from her face, and Auhan laid a comforting hand on her arm.

"Beloved? What is it?"

"Auhan. What is your brother's name?"

His eyes narrowed and crinkled in confusion, but he answered her. "Mehmet."

Her heart began to pound wildly.

"Mehmet!" She covered her lips with her hands in a vain attempt to contain her surprise.

Auhan fell to his knees beside her and held her hands tightly in his own. "Beloved?" he questioned with a worried frown. "Please, what is it?"

She smiled at him even as tears fell from the corners of her eyes. "Mehmet is your brother? Lincoln is your brother?" She lowered her gaze to his hands. She turned and twisted them within her own, and as she did, she finally remembered where she had seen identical ones.

"Of course he is," she answered herself. "Your hands are exactly the same." She gave a slight laugh as her thumb traced the mole on his right thumb. "You even have a mole in the same place."

"Elena." Auhan's voice was very deep. "What you are saying is true. Mehmet and I do have identical hands. But, how do you know this?"

A look of comprehension came over *Anne* Fatima, and she clapped her hands in prayer as she lifted her face heavenward. "Oh, dear Lord, thank You. Thank You."

Elena reached out with her other hand and squeezed the older woman's. "He lives, dear *Anne*. He lives!"

"The Turkish soldier?" Fatima questioned, and Elena vigorously nodded her head. "Yes."

"Turkish soldier. . . ?" Even with question in his tone, Auhan voiced his dawning understanding. "The one Christos carried?"

"Auhan." She turned back to him and swallowed to get control of her racing heart so that she could tell her story, her wonderful, amazing story. "On the night my sisters and I met Christos the second time—the night we were all fleeing Smyrna—I found out from him that the wounded man he had carried to our house was Turkish and," she paused, "that his name was Mehmet."

Auhan gasped.

"But," Elena continued, "when Christos first left him at our house, we thought the wounded man was an American because he was wearing an American issue serviceman's shirt." She paused as she thought back to that time. "And the only thing he said in his feverish state was 'Lincoln.'" She gave a slight laugh. "Assuming that Lincoln was his name, my sister, father, and I called him Mr. Lincoln."

She watched as Auhan's eyes grew wide with wonder. "Mehmet. . .is truly Christos's Turkish friend? The Turk he carried to your house?"

With her face beaming, Elena confirmed his question. "Yes. Yes, he is."

Even as joy filled his face, gravity quickly swept over it.

"But you said the man was very sick. Do you think he survived?"

"He was very sick when Christos brought him to our house. His leg was terribly injured," she confirmed, not wanting to give false hope. "But he had a will to live, and because a friend of ours at the American consulate was able to get him aboard an American naval ship in the harbor, I think he must have made it."

She turned to Fatima and Suleiman, who were looking at her with all the ageless hope of a parent for their child. "Mehmet was alive when I last saw him on Monday, the eleventh of September. That's when he was taken aboard the American naval ship. I don't know if the doctors were able to save his leg, but I'm certain—I'm *certain* the doctors on that warship were able to make him well."

Tears streamed down Fatima's face, and Elena knew the mother's tears were happy tears, amazed tears, relieved tears, all at once.

"He must have been saying 'Lincoln,'" she whispered, "to remind himself of his rendezvous with us." She touched her hand to her chest and turned to her husband. "Suleiman, he lives! Our son lives!" she exclaimed. "The girl we fished from the sea, her family is responsible for giving our son life."

"No. It was mostly Christos," Elena corrected her. "If Christos hadn't carried him to Smyrna, Mehmet would have, without a doubt, succumbed out on the battlefield. Christos carried him on his back, literally, for days."

Suleiman shook his great head and, drawing his wife against his chest, gazed out over the vast sea surrounding their ship and said, "What an amazing God we have."

Auhan helped Elena to her feet and wrapped his arms around her. "Only God could have orchestrated this."

The two couples stood for several long moments with perfect peace and hope enfolding them. Elena broke the silence by pushing slightly back from Auhan.

"That's not all," she said. The others all turned to her with question in their eyes.

"You see, last May—" She paused and looked off into the horizon.

*Was it only four months ago?* The question pierced her thoughts. *It seemed like a lifetime ago.*

She swallowed hard as a somber realization struck her. *It was a lifetime ago. My father's life*. She shook her head to dispel the sad musing and turned back to them.

"My father, Sophia, and I attended the dedication to the Lincoln Memorial—"

"You attended it?" Fatima interrupted her. "That's why our rendezvous is set for May the thirtieth—the anniversary of its dedication. I so wanted to be there for the actual ceremony, but—we waited—" She shrugged her thin shoulders. "In case Mehmet made it back to us."

Elena wagged her head in joyous amazement. "While we were there, we too agreed to a rendezvous at the memorial exactly a year later. I am certain I will meet my sisters and Christos on that day." She faced Auhan and turned the conversation back to his original question.

"That's the reason why, my dear love, I want to wait until June to marry."

Auhan shook his head slowly from side to side. "God had the merging of our families planned before we ever met."

Elena smiled over at him and reached into his pocket, already acting as a wife might. She pulled the ring from its hiding place and held the precious stone so the rays of the morning sun caught its lines and flashed out its light.

"Dear Auhan, He had the merging of our families planned—even before the beginning of time."

"Amen," Suleiman interjected. Then her beloved Auhan took the ring from her hand, and, bending down on one knee, he asked her, before God and his parents, to be his wife for all their earthly life.

Elena, of course, agreed.

# Chapter 14

*For the Lord himself shall descend from heaven with a shout, with the voice of the archangel, and with the trump of God: and the dead in Christ shall rise first: Then we which are alive and remain shall be caught up together with them in the clouds, to meet the Lord in the air: and so shall we ever be with the Lord.*
I Thessalonians 4:16–17

*May 30, 1923, Memorial Day*
*Lincoln Memorial*
*Washington, D.C.*

Everything was so different last year. Yet, so much was the same. The secular shrine gleamed timelessly on its knoll with the serene statue honoring Abraham Lincoln sitting within. Elena held onto the arm of the handsome young man whom she had grown to love during the last few months. Her feelings of affection for Auhan, which were born aboard the *Ionian Star*, could not compare to the love she felt today, after eight months of courtship. She never would have thought possible the depth of affection she now felt for Auhan.

But her thoughts turned to bittersweet memories of her family as they approached the spot where she had stood between Sophia and her father last year to watch the dedication ceremony of the Lincoln Memorial.

She sighed and looked up at Auhan in anxious anticipation. "Do you think they will all come?" In truth, Elena had expected to find Sophia and, thus, Rose and Christos through their mutual bank accounts long before this prearranged meeting. The fact that Sophia had not yet contacted the banks seemed to indicate she still hadn't arrived in America. And Elena had started to worry.

Auhan reached over and patted her right hand in its snowy white glove, which rested upon his left arm. "I believe. . ." He paused for a brief moment as though to confirm his forming words in his own heart. "I believe our God is in the miracle-making business, Elena."

His eyes looked upon her with a contagious brightness. "And this day we are going to be taking part in the miracle of a grand reunion, a reunion between loved ones and friends, something not unlike the reunion all believers will share when Jesus returns to earth."

With his words, worry erased itself from Elena's face, and a smile curved the corners of her lips. His faith amazed her. He had gone from having had none when she met him the previous September to being so full of faith, he was now a constant source of edification to her.

"You're right, of course, Auhan. They will all come today. My sisters, Christos, your brother." She spoke with faith ringing loudly in her voice. "Yes, they will all come," she reiterated with conviction. She looked back up toward the statue of the seated President Lincoln and the pavilion built to house it, which had been fashioned after the Parthenon of Athens. In the gleaming light of the Lincoln Memorial's white marble there existed the complete antithesis to that which had run rampant across the city of Smyrna during those black days the previous September.

In the light of the early morning sun, the monument gleamed pristine and new. But the sight of it brought her thoughts back to similar Greek edifices to be found throughout the Hellenic world of the Mediterranean. She glanced back at the Washington Monument, which shot up into the sky. Further on, the United States Capitol building gleamed in the light of the rising sun. It was all so beautiful. Beautiful and new. She sighed.

Auhan leaned toward her and asked with softness lacing his words, "What are you thinking?"

Elena slightly shook her head. "So many things, but mostly I hope America—this land founded and built by people who believed Christ is God's Son—is never taken over by a people who don't believe in Him, as we saw happen in Asia Minor. This is my greatest hope for this country, this beloved land."

"Mine too, my dear," Auhan nodded his head. From the moment he had set foot upon America's green and golden shores, he had fallen in love with this land. It was his home now. And one he never planned to leave. He leaned over and planted a kiss upon Elena's forehead. He had started doing so when she had fretted that her scars had left her looking ugly. Auhan had taken to kissing them as a way of assuring her that, although they did exist, they were not displeasing, at least not to him. It was a habit now, but one he never took for granted. Those scars, only partially hidden by her hair, were a poignant reminder of what evil had cost her, cost them all.

So many lives had been lost, and many more were still being uprooted by it. Earlier in the year, the Treaty of Lausanne had implemented a "population exchange." This exchange enforced the relocation of almost one and a half million Greeks, whose families had built some of Asia Minor's most glorious cities during the previous 3,000 years, in addition to the displacement of well over 300,000 Turks who had settled in Greece. Auhan shook his head. So much pain. How could governments justify forcing people—any people—from their home?

But Auhan wasn't naïve. Although he never talked about it to anyone, he remembered the mass grave.

He knew that the population exchange was actually the only way the governments of the allied powers, after their poor decision making during and after the Great War, could save the remaining Christians of Asia Minor. If the Christians weren't forced out by international politics, they would, at the hands of the Turkish government, suffer the same fate met by millions of martyred Christians—Armenians, Greeks, and others—over the previous thirty years. And more little babies would have to suffer like the baby in the blue sweater who still came to haunt Auhan.

Auhan slightly shook his head and sent a prayer heavenward, asking God to take away the tormenting image of the child.

As always, God did.

Where it used to stay within his head for days at a time, it now came to torment him only at odd moments. Auhan suspected it always would. But with the Lord Jesus Christ in his life, the vision no longer debilitated him.

He looked over at his parents. They stood directly in front of the Lincoln Memorial, just below the first step leading up toward the statue. In excited expectation, they were casting their eyes about for Mehmet. Auhan was so grateful to God they had left their home while they could. They would have been caught right in the middle of the population exchange and would never have made it to America otherwise.

Auhan looked back at the Capitol in the distance. Elena was right. He hoped Christianity was never forced from this land as it had been from Asia Minor and so many other areas of the world. He hoped people never forgot the liberty brought to people through their belief in the truth of Jesus Christ.

Reaching into his pocket, he took out an American silver dollar and turned to the side with the eagle. He looked at the inscription engraved between its wings. "In God We Trust." Auhan silently read America's motto and sighed. He just hoped the people of America never forgot that the God referred to on their money was God as revealed by Jesus Christ.

Elena tensed by his side, bringing his attention back to her. "What is it?"

"There," she breathed out and pointed in the direction of the Washington Monument. The silhouettes of three people—a very tall man, a woman, and a young girl—could be seen walking toward them. "It has to be them. No one is as tall as Christos." She qualified what made the three, just visible near the far end of the recently completed Reflecting Pool, different from the other elegantly clad people strolling in the morning sunshine.

Auhan chuckled. "This is America, Elena. Many tall men grow here." He wanted to keep things light, just in case the three were not her Sophia, Rose, and Christos. He didn't want her to get excited, only to be bitterly disappointed.

"We will wait until they get a little closer." She paused and squinted against the sun. "Oh, I wish the sun had decided to rise in the West today. I can't see anything with the glare."

Auhan chuckled, glad to hear her joke. As long as she could make light of the situation, she would be fine—even if the people coming toward them were not three of the four for whom they anxiously awaited this day.

When the threesome were closer to the Lincoln Memorial than they were to the Washington Monument, Elena started walking toward them, pulling Auhan along with her. Buddy, as always, was right at her heels. "Come on," she said. "We'll just stroll casually in that direction until—"

"El–e–na!" a woman's voice called out, and Elena held out her hand for Auhan to stop.

"Sophia?" Elena squeaked out the name, her volume barely louder than a whisper.

"El–e–na," the woman called out again.

Elena responded with a half-laugh, half-sob. "So–ph–ia!"

"Elena?!" came the return, this time in a chorus of three voices—that of a man, a woman, and a child.

"It's them, Auhan! It's them." She waved her arms in a wide, swooping arc and began to shout as she took off in a run toward the trio. "It's me! It's me!"

Laughing and sobbing, Elena covered the distance between herself and her sister as if wings were on her feet. Within seconds their arms were around one another, and they were kissing each other—laughing and crying all at the same time.

"Sophia! Rose!" Elena swept both her tall, elegant sister and the beautiful little girl into her arms. "Oh, we've found one another! We've found one another!" As she reached for Christos, she wished she had another pair of arms with which to hold her dear ones.

She felt herself being lifted off the ground in a mighty embrace. "Christos," she squealed in happy surprise.

"Give your brother-in-law a hug, little Elena," he boomed out with a voice that matched his body. Not the least surprised by his news, Elena hugged him closer.

"I knew you were going to be my brother one day. I just knew it," she bubbled. When Christos put her down, she reached for her sisters again. "Dear Sophia. I'm so happy for you. Knowing you had Christos and Rose kept me from worrying about you."

Sophia wiped the corners of her eyes with her crochet-bordered handkerchief. "And, dear sister, it was their faith that edified me enough to function without knowing for sure if you would be here today."

"God never took His eyes off of me," Elena assured her sister as she allowed her to scrutinize the telling burns on her face. She hastily relayed the fantastic story of her rescue at sea, taking care to credit the special family that had nursed her back to health.

Feeling a tug on her skirt, Elena reached down and scooped a giggling Rose into her arms. "Little sister, I'm so glad to see you."

"Me too, but—" Rose paused and rolled her shining eyes. "I don't think you should call me your little sister."

"Why not? Don't you want to be my little sister any longer?" Elena searched the girl's grinning face for a clue as to why she would say such a thing.

"Yes, but," Christos interrupted, and with a wide smile cutting across his face, he took Rose from Elena with one arm while his other went comfortably around Sophia's shoulders, "what Rose probably means is that you are now her aunt, not her sister."

Elena's mouth dropped open as she stared at first Christos, then Sophia.

"After we married, we legally adopted Rose as our daughter," Sophia explained.

Elena thought her happy heart could not contain any more good news. Bringing her face right up next to Rose's, she said, "So now you have a father, a mother, and an aunt."

Rose nodded her head vigorously. "But that's not all," she exclaimed and looked over at her new mother as if she might burst.

Understanding the look, Elena exclaimed, "You have a secret!"

A grin spread across Rose's pixie face, and she bobbed her head up and down so hard, her curls bounced around her shoulders like puppets on a string. Sophia laughed in her delightful, refined way. It was a sound from their past that thrilled Elena all the way down to her toes, even as she regarded her sister in happy question.

"Come now, tell me," Elena insisted with her eyes wide and bright.

"Well," Sophia looked shyly but lovingly up at Christos. "Rose will have a sister or a brother soon too."

Elena's eyes widened even more as she noticed, for the first time, her sister's expanding figure. "A baby!" she whispered and hugged Sophia close to her again. "I'm so happy for you—" Her look included the three of them. "For all of you."

Elena reached for Auhan's hand. "We have news too. This very wonderful man, Auhan, is soon to be my husband."

"What? When?" Sophia's surprise registered in her monosyllabic questions.

"As soon as we can get your dresses made," Elena said. "We waited so that you could be at our wedding."

"Oh, Elena, Auhan. Your news gladdens my heart." Sophia threw her arms around both Elena and her husband-to-be in a congratulatory hug. And, even though Elena knew her sister was more than a little curious to know all about this handsome young man with the Turkish name, she also knew Sophia trusted her to choose the right mate.

"We so wanted to wait for you to be at our wedding," Sophia explained to Elena, "but Christos and Rose didn't have the necessary immigration documents for entry into America, and such things take many, many months, years, to receive—if ever. We were advised that our marriage and Rose's subsequent adoption would be the most expedient way for them to obtain the proper permissions."

Elena watched as Sophia looked into her husband's eyes. She gave him a dimpled smile and breathed a deep sigh of contentment. "Since Christos and I knew from the time we met in Smyrna that God intended us for one another. . .well, we saw this as the answer—"

"You obviously made the right decision," Elena interrupted. She remembered back to how Sophia's thoughts of Christos had kept her sister going after their father had died.

Sophia gave Elena a smile and a gentle nod before she continued. "We decided on a quiet but lovely ceremony at a sixth-century chapel in Athens. Then, as husband and wife, we were able to legally adopt Rose as our daughter." Elena gave in to her urge to tousle little Rose's hair as her sister spoke.

"Only two things survived from all the treasures I had sewn into my clothing before we fled Smyrna. My papers verifying my American citizenship and one of Mother's necklaces. We were able to sell the necklace, and we lived off the proceeds of the sale." She continued after a brief pause. "But God knew what He was doing. If I hadn't had those things, we wouldn't have made it here today."

Christos shook his lowered head from side to side. "Greece has opened her doors to all the refugees fleeing Asia Minor, and the population of the country is increasing at an astronomical rate. But, there is much misery. After these many years of war, Greece is so poor."

"It still took months for us to accomplish all the necessary requirements for our passage here," Sophia said. "Our ship arrived in New York only yesterday, and we traveled directly from there to here." She motioned down to their clothes, and Elena noticed they were still wearing traveling outfits.

"So, that's why you haven't gone to the banks," Elena commented. "I left messages for you, telling you where I was living. I must admit, I was getting concerned when I heard nothing from you." She looked over at Auhan. "I don't know what I would have done if I hadn't had my man of faith to strengthen and support me."

Sophia extended her hand to Auhan in a show of gratitude. Then she turned again to Elena.

"You do understand, don't you, why I couldn't wait for you to be at our wedding? I know we had planned for—"

Elena signaled for her sister to stop. "Dear Sophia. I don't mind. Not at all." She laughed gaily. "The only things to have survived my journey were our mother's cross, her engagement ring, and. . ." Elena paused long enough for suspense to fill the air. "Her wedding ring."

"Her wedding ring!"

The wedding ring had always been intended for Sophia, the engagement ring for her. She knew how much it meant to Sophia to have something of their mother's.

"It's sitting safely in my jewelry case, waiting for you in the home I bought for us all near the Capitol." Elena sent Christos a quick smile.

"Actually, the ring is waiting not for you, but for Christos." A look of bewilderment colored her sister's face, so Elena hastened to finish her sentence. "For Christos will be the one to place it on your finger." Sophia's expression portrayed her utter happiness as Elena shifted to a more serious note.

"But dear Sophia, more than anything, I'm so thankful that you weren't left orphaned and alone." Her look included Rose and Christos. "I'm thankful you joined together to make a family. I might not yet be married to Auhan, but in his parents, I have had the love of a mother and a father." She pointed to the older couple, who stood by the marble stairs of the memorial. "They are the very special people who took me into their cabin and into their hearts after my ordeal in the sea. They are the ones who nursed me back to health. Come, let me introduce you."

Amid much talking and laughing, the happy band walked over to Fatima and Suleiman. Rose and Buddy frolicked around the adults with the youthful abandon that every dog and child should have. The two were becoming fast friends.

Fatima held out her hands to Elena as they approached. "Your sisters?" she asked. At Elena's nod, Fatima opened her arms to Sophia and Rose. "Oh, I'm so glad. So thankful you are reunited."

"Thank you, dear people, for caring for my sister." Sophia's gaze included them both.

Suleiman smiled beneath his mustache. "Ah, my dear. I think your sister cared for us every bit as much as we cared for her."

Sophia laughed and looked at her sister with a knowing glint. "She has a way of doing that."

From out of the corner of her eye, Elena noticed Auhan shaking hands with Christos, and she seized upon the lull in her circle of conversation to eavesdrop on the pair's dialogue.

"Excuse me, Sir, but have we met before?" Christos squinted, and his brow furrowed in deep curiosity as he studied Auhan. "You seem so familiar, and I'm never one to forget a face."

"No, Christos, we haven't met," Auhan rasped. "But you have met my brother."

Elena knew her beloved well enough to know that he was fighting to maintain control of his emotions. Over the past months, Auhan had often spoken of the day when he would meet Christos and get to thank him face-to-face for carrying his brother across the battlefields to safety. If Mehmet managed to keep the rendezvous with his family today, it would be due to the aid and compassionate spirit of this gentle giant, Christos.

"Look carefully, Christos," Elena instructed, and Christos's brows knit together as he obviously searched his brain to try to place the familiar stranger. "Think. Who does he remind you of?"

Elena tilted her head to her sister. "Sophia? How about you? Do you notice anything familiar about Auhan?"

Sophia looked at Auhan carefully. "He does remind me of someone," she shook her head. "But I can't—"

"Look at his hands, Sophia," Elena prompted.

Auhan lifted his hands for all to see while Suleiman and Fatima smiled at each other. Sophia reached out to Auhan and held his hands with her gloved fingers. "They seem so familiar—"

"Mehmet," Christos whispered, for once without a loud voice. He looked from Auhan's hands to his face. "You're Mehmet's brother?"

Auhan nodded.

Christos turned to the older couple. "And you. . .are Mehmet's parents?"

"Lincoln?" Sophia breathed out the name by which she still thought of Mehmet—the young man she had diligently nursed over a period of several days the previous September in Smyrna. At everyone's affirmative nods, Christos and Sophia exchanged looks of total amazement before they turned back to the others.

"But, how did you. . ." Christos motioned between Auhan and Elena. "I mean— Mehmet? He lives?"

"Yes, my friend," a man's soft voice answered from behind the happy group. "He lives."

And, as a single body, Elena and the precious members of her family all turned in the direction of the one speaking. She could hardly believe her ears. Or her eyes.

There stood Mehmet! He leaned on a cane, but he was standing—and on two legs, not one.

Joy and laughter and everything good filled the air surrounding the happy, complete reunion of family and friends. Their voices tumbled together in melodious cacophony as they became acquainted or reacquainted with one another. Elena rejoiced along with *Anne* Fatima, *Baba* Suleiman, and Auhan to hear that Mehmet too had learned to trust the God of his distant ancestors.

And they all marveled at how God had woven the fabric of their lives together so miraculously.

For Elena and her beloved family, Memorial Day of 1923 was the first of many such days of reunion and remembrance—one which they were to keep each and every anniversary of the Lincoln Memorial dedication. For the rest of their lives. Their very long lives.

## TAYLOR JAMES

Taylor James is married to a physician and is the mother of two nearly grown children. A native of Virginia, she loves traveling the world over, seeing new places, and meeting new people. She combines her traveling experiences with her love of writing, history, and God to write stories which are both uplifting and informative.

Her favorite Bible verses are to be found in Paul's letter to the Philippians: "Therefore God exalted him to the highest place and gave him the name that is above every name, that at the name of Jesus every knee should bow, in heaven and on earth and under the earth, and every tongue confess that Jesus Christ is Lord, to the glory of God the Father" (2:9–11 NIV). This truth is what she hopes to convey in all her novels.

# Remnant
## of
# Forgiveness

Sally Laity

*To Marjorie Burgess, a shining star, a loving heart, an inspiration to us all, this book is lovingly dedicated. Her unwavering faith and courageous hope have been a true reflection of our Lord Jesus Christ. Thank you, Margie.*
*Special thanks to Dianna Crawford and Andrea Boeshaar.*
*May God bless you always.*

# *Prologue*

*Poland, 1945*

A chilly spring wind wailed across the ashes of Warsaw, as if mourning the loss of the once proud capital's soul. Only the multistoried Polonia Hotel and a few other buildings remained unscathed—the ones the German armies had required for headquarters or troop barracks. The rest had been bombed or gutted by fire. Gone were the tree-lined streets and magnificent landmarks renowned throughout Europe. The main marketplace, the *Rynek,* lay in rubble. Twisted and blackened ruins marked the demise of the formerly luxurious railroad station. Even the Blue Palace, frequented in bygone days by pianist and former premier of Poland Jan Ignacy Paderewski, had been reduced to waste. Block by block, building by building, the bombs, cannons, and fires of the methodical and relentless Nazi destruction had spared nothing, not even cathedrals or hospitals. The latter they had torched while beds and corridors still teemed with helpless, trapped patients. The smoky pall of long-dead fires still lingered in the air, along with the sickeningly sweet odor of burned human flesh.

*It is all as Josep told us,* Marie Therese conceded bitterly. *Warszawa is dead.* Having learned to hold her emotions inside, she could not even speak for the heaviness that pressed upon her spirit as the young man affiliated with the Polish Relief Organization drove her and her Jewish friend, Rahel Dubinsky, along a crater-pocked street.

In this city, which used to bustle with streetcars and happy children, they passed not even one automobile, only horse-drawn carts or bicycle-propelled pushcarts. What little trading still took place occurred on street corners, by ragged people in crudely constructed wooden shacks. Girls in Polish uniforms directed traffic, assisted by Red Army soldiers, and additional Soviet troops patrolled the city.

But most heartbreaking of all was the sight of the one-legged children, in nauseating numbers, hobbling about on such sticks as they could find, silently holding out grubby hands to passersby. Hatred for the German forces and their maniacal leader who had committed suicide to save himself from the world's retribution rose like bile in Marie's throat.

The depth of the rubble at *Stare Miastro*, the oldest section of town, forced Josep Klimek to park his rickety vehicle, and Marie and Rahel got out.

The faint drone of motors drifted toward them on the breeze, and Marie raised her gaze off into the distance, where a handful of battered trucks carted away loads of debris. Except for the absence of that distinctive, abrasive squeaking, the sound seemed reminiscent of the Nazi tanks which had rumbled through the city six years ago, rendering an end to her peaceful and idyllic life as the daughter of a professor and a French-born mother. . .a life that would never again be the same, once her father had spoken out against Adolf Hitler.

And it was even worse for her friend, Rahel.

Even before the German occupation, anti-Semitism had been strong in Warsaw. But nothing could have prepared the girls for the sight of the Ghetto, where Rahel, her family, and the rest of the Jewish population had been imprisoned behind barbed wire, enduring starvation and disease before their ultimate liquidation at Nazi death camps. The two could only stare in open-mouthed horror at the four square miles which had been utterly pulverized by the German army.

It broke what was left of Marie's heart to see tears roll from Rahel's sunken brown eyes and down her sallow cheeks, making dark splotches on the faded coat. "Nothing is left," the devastated girl cried, her expressive face contorted with grief. "Nothing. I cannot even tell where Papa's shop used to be."

Marie put an empathetic arm around her friend's gaunt shoulders. Small comfort, but she had nothing else to offer.

"I had hoped to spare you," Josep reminded. The bearlike young man who had befriended the girls since they'd come back to Warsaw returned to the truck and waited for them to join him inside. Then he restarted the engine and inched forward again, steering around huge craters and the debris in their path to head out of the city, his truck bed packed with supplies for a village to the north.

"You are still positive I am to let you out in the middle of nowhere?" he asked a few minutes later. "Such a foolish scheme I cannot condone." He wagged his head, a shapeless charcoal felt hat shadowing the glower on a ruddy face lined beyond his thirty years.

Rahel stared straight ahead. "I am positive. I will tell you where."

"But two young women alone—even dressed like boys! It is folly." He cut them an incredulous scowl. "The Russian soldiers are worse than the Nazis. They are not so disciplined, and for women or young girls they have no respect at all. Right across the river, on the *Praga* side, they are shipping trainloads of Polish refugees to slave camps in Siberia. My head Ania will have if harm comes to either of you."

"Do not worry," came Rahel's calm assurance. "We will be careful. There are places to hide. We will watch for your return."

Marie Therese held her silence. Since their release from the concentration camp, Rahel had hinted of a secret she had harbored throughout their captivity. But she had yet to disclose the particulars.

The two of them had been through so much—even after Ravensbruck had been liberated. The majority of the freed Polish captives begged to return to their homeland to see what, if anything, remained of farms, businesses, or relatives of whom they'd received no word in months. Thanks to the efforts of the brave souls sympathetic to their cause, small groups of refugees were shepherded by night through Russian-occupied Eastern Germany, a harrowing journey none of them would likely forget.

When the pathetic lot finally gained the Polish border, the Polish Red Cross and other relief organizations took over. Among them were Josep Klimek and his wife, Ania, two more individuals doing the work of angels. The couple took Marie and Rahel into their care. For today's venture, they had even supplied the girls with men's clothing so they would more easily blend in with other workers around Warsaw. Hunching deeper into the scratchy jacket she wore, Marie drew a troubled breath and let her mind drift to the past as the truck wheezed and coughed its way up a lengthy rise.

Barely nineteen, it seemed a lifetime ago that she'd been a giggly schoolgirl in uniform, walking home from classes with her brothers and younger sister, blushing whenever a handsome boy glanced in her direction. As the daughter of a prominent college professor, she had traveled in far different circles from Rahel's and would never have been allowed to associate with someone of the Jewish faith. Now this young, painfully thin woman was her only friend in the world. Like a sister. Both of them, along with a number of other naturally attractive and appealing young women, had been dispersed to various locations in Poland and Germany for the private entertainment of the Nazi officers.

Her and Rahel's destination had been Ravensbruck, the infamous German extermination camp.

Strange how such a horrendous place could create an incredibly strong bond between individuals forced to suffer the unspeakable shame and agonies they had endured.

But what would become of them now? They could never return to the innocence of their lost youth.

Pondering her hollow future, Marie Therese almost envied the emaciated souls who'd met their end in the gas chambers. No amount of years would ever completely banish the memory of that squat, square concrete building smack in the middle of the grounds, the thin, acrid vapor rising in a constant stream from its huge smokestack. Nor would she forget the horrendous, hellish sounds which emanated day and night from the punishment barracks, the lice and fleas, the constant gnawing hunger. Or parading naked before the snickering SS guards to the icy showers and humiliating medical examinations. . .and worse.

So much worse. . .

As the truck bumped and lurched over the unpaved country road, Marie deliberately forced her thoughts away from the horror to concentrate on the single good element of that despicable camp: an older Dutch spinster with the unlikely name of Corrie ten Boom. With a small Bible she and her sweet, frail, even older sister Betsie had somehow managed to smuggle past the guards, the dear woman had instilled a measure of hope to the wretched captives amassed in flea-infested Barracks 28.

Every night until lights-out, the pair would take turns reading Scripture passages. Some were familiar to Marie Therese. But what struck her most was the way Corrie spoke *of* God and *to* Him—as if He were her very closest friend. Her words, spoken in Dutch, had to be translated by other women to be understood by the different nationalities. Marie surmised that somewhere along the line from Dutch to German, and then on to French, Russian, Polish, and Czech, the original thoughts acquired a far-too-lofty idealism that couldn't possibly be taken literally.

Nevertheless, in the cold dark of night, as the searchlight swept in regular intervals over the barracks walls, sending flashes of thin light through the rag-stuffed broken windows, those very promises brought an inner warmth to Marie beyond any the threadbare blankets provided to her body. And a hope that at least some of what Corrie had related was true.

Someday, somehow, she would obtain a Bible and search things out for herself. But for now she could only struggle to follow the older woman's admonition to dwell on thoughts of a loving God rather than on cruelty and hatred, however impossible that seemed at times. A ragged sigh came from deep inside.

"Here!" Rahel declared with force. "Stop."

Josep stomped on the worn brakes, and the old truck lumbered to a halt.

Marie Therese peered at the open, rolling countryside dotted here and there by woods. Traces of new green had begun to soften the stark winter-bare bushes and trees framing the fertile farmland. But the absence of freshly plowed furrows made the fields appear lonely and desolate, like a canvas waiting to be painted.

Rahel's bony elbow jabbed Marie's ribs, urging her to quit gawking and get out. "Do not forget the shovel," the dark-eyed girl reminded her.

Marie Therese nodded and opened the door, stepping down from the running board. From the truck bed she retrieved one of two digging tools Josep always carried with him. Rahel claimed the other.

"I'm going on now," he called to them, "to deliver these goods. In two hours I should be back. Maybe a little longer. Be careful. Keep your eyes peeled. Russian convoys come through all the time to plunder whatever is left from the towns and villages," he added grimly.

"We will be careful."

At her friend's confident statement, Marie gave a dubious smile and a nod to their benefactor and watched after the lorry as it chug-chugged over the next rise and vanished from sight, leaving a silence broken only by the sighing wind.

Marie turned to see her friend already well on her way toward an irregular grove of trees some distance away, the oversized tan coat flapping with each step. She only hoped the two of them did appear to be men, just in case. Tugging her hat more snugly over her hair, she hastened to catch up. "Where are we going?"

"Not far."

A stand of trees rose up from a spot where the contour of the land hid the road from view. Approaching the grove, the Jewish girl slowed, her dark eyes focusing on one tree in particular, studying the gnarled roots, its position among others. Then a corner of her lips curved in a tiny smile. "We will dig here." She jabbed the pointed end of her shovel into ground moist from recent rains, stepping on the dull side to add her weight.

Marie Therese followed suit, amazed to find herself quickly winded by the uncustomary exertion.

When they'd dug about a foot down, Rahel's shovel struck metal. "Ah!" She fell to her knees and sat back on the heels of her too-big shoes, a satisfied smile adding a sparkle to her wide-set eyes. "Just where we left it, Papa, Aron, and I." She brushed aside the remaining layer of soil, revealing an object flat and round.

"What is it?" Marie panted, leaning on the handle of her own mud-caked shovel to catch her breath.

"Our future, yours and mine." Grasping what turned out to be the edge of a milk can lid, Rahel gave a mighty yank, but to no avail. "You must help. Take hold of the other side."

Marie sank down and added all the strength she possessed, grunting and tugging along with Rahel. On the third try, it popped open with a loud squeak of protest and clunked to the ground.

Rahel reached inside the hollow interior of the buried container and withdrew a cotton sack, dumping out its contents.

Marie stared incredulously at more jewelry, loose gems, and *zluty*, Polish money, than she had ever seen at one time in her life.

"Papa was a wise man," Rahel explained, gathering the items and stuffing them back inside the bag. "He saw this war coming well in advance, knew that deep trouble would come upon our country. One day he brought our family here—for a picnic, we thought. But once we had eaten the food in the basket, he and Aron buried our savings at the base of this tree, in case we survived whatever was ahead." She paused, her chin trembling. "I. . .never imagined I would be the only one left to come back to reclaim it. Mama, Papa, my four brothers. . ." She met Marie's gaze through a sheen of tears.

It was the most the young Jewess had ever said at one time since their months of enforced silence. Reminded of her own wrenching loss, Marie Therese leaned close and hugged her hard, struggling to contain the anguish she dared not give in to. There weren't enough tears in the world to relieve that depth of sorrow.

A scant moment ago, they'd been utterly destitute and alone in the world. But things had changed. They were still ragged, to be sure, pale and gaunt from near starvation, and dirty from digging. And still alone. But no longer destitute.

As she watched Rahel cinch the mouth of the sack and tuck it securely inside her coat, a verse Corrie ten Boom had often quoted flooded Marie's mind. *My God shall supply all your need according to his riches in glory by Christ Jesus.* "But— are you sure you want to share your family's treasure with me?" she asked.

"Of course. Why should I need all of it, just one person? You are my very dearest—indeed, my only—friend in this world. I will give some to Josep and Ania for helping us. And you will take half of what remains. I insist. You will need it."

*"Nie!"* Marie exclaimed. "I cannot take so much."

Rahel regarded her evenly. "I have been thinking about this for a long time. When I realized we were going to survive Ravensbruck, the thought came to me. I shall go to Palestine, my people's homeland. I have never been there. I shall live in Jerusalem, our Holy City. Make jewelry, perhaps. Like Papa. He would like that."

Marie brushed straight blond bangs from her eyes and stared, awed by the dreamy expression subtracting lines of suffering, one by one, from Rahel's exquisite features. In their place, her classic beauty rose to the fore, despite the pallid complexion and dirt smudges, despite ill-fitting clothes and the dull, chopped hair peeking out from beneath her boyish hat.

"And what about me?" Marie asked, a sudden sense of awe surging through her as she tucked a few strands of lifeless hair back inside her cap.

"You, dearest friend, will go to America. The land of hope."

"Go to America!"

"Josep and Ania have contacts to help us reach the American sector. They say Jews are the only ones who have no trouble leaving Poland. Josep can obtain forged papers stating you are Jewish, get us both to Switzerland. From there we can go where we want." Smiling sweetly, she took out the sack and reached into it, withdrawing a Star of David on a fine gold chain. She slipped it over Marie's head, letting the medallion fall inside the shirt Marie had tucked into her baggy trousers. "There. This will help."

Still somewhat in awe, Marie fingered the necklace through her shirt. "But I don't know a soul in America."

"And who do you know here? Our families have been taken from us." Rahel stood and spun in a slow circle, her thin arms flung wide. "Look around. Where are the crowds that used to leave the city to bask in the quiet countryside? There is no one in sight. The only people we have seen are strangers. You must go where there is life. Make a new start."

The notion took on credibility as Marie Therese mulled it over. And gradually she understood the wisdom in her friend's words. She would go to America.

But a single thought sank into her heart, cruel and cold as the Ravensbruck barracks. A new life would be a thousand times lonelier.

In America she would not have Rahel. . .the only one who understood her special shame. Her curse.

# Chapter 1

*New York City, Spring 1946*

"What means this—*babe*, this *chick?*" Mary Theresa asked, moving to the dressing table for a closer look at herself. "Like infant I am? My legs, they are too skinny?" Turning sideways, she eyed her reflection in the pinkish light streaming through the bedroom's dotted swiss curtains.

Mr. and Mrs. Chudzik had fed her well in the six months she had been living in their home. Even she could see that her once emaciated frame had lost the bony contours. And her honey blond hair had grown considerably, recapturing much of its former length and shine. With her now Americanized name—from Marie Therese to Mary Theresa, her new, fashionable hairstyle, and a wardrobe with an abundance of long sleeves to conceal the evidence of her imprisonment, only her halting English set her apart from other young women her age.

She repositioned a bobby pin in the poufed roll of hair behind her ear as the mirrored images of Christine and Veronica Chudzik, the young daughters of the household, conquered the giggles brought on by her questions.

"No, Silly," dark-haired Veronica said, her heart-shaped face sobering. Two years older than her thirteen-year-old sibling, she always assumed the lead. "It is nothing. Babe and chick are *dobrze.* Good. It means the young men think you're pretty."

Mary frowned. Young men were the last thing on her mind and would likely remain so. "Much better to use proper English. *Nie rozumiem.* I not understand foolish American words."

"But you're learning," Christine reminded her, childish features alight with leftover remnants of mirth. "I think Mama is right. You learn faster if we only use Polish to explain things. It makes you have to start thinking in English."

Mary could only agree, though she'd considered the stringent household rule somewhat harsh at first.

"And," Veronica piped in, "you start your job next week. Soon you'll be out on your own and settled into your new apartment." She drew her knees to her chest and hugged them.

Christine brushed a flaxen braid over her shoulder, her smile wilting. "I'll miss you when you leave. It's been fun having you share our room."

This lovely room. Mary Theresa glanced around. So much fancier than hers had been in the Old Country. Rose-patterned wallpaper, cheerful rugs on the varnished floor. And so big for just two girls, she'd thought upon arriving. The spacious apartment in a multistoried brownstone building in Manhattan's Upper East Side had all but swallowed her up with its roominess. Her own tiny walk-up, more than a dozen blocks away and off Second Avenue, would be nowhere near so elegant. How had Rahel Dubinsky fared in Jerusalem?

Swallowing down loneliness for her dear Jewish friend, she crossed to the pair and put an arm about each of them. The sweet innocence that shone from their azure eyes was a sad reminder of a part of her own life that could never be undone. "And already I am missing you. Little sisters you are to me." Mustering all her effort, she feigned a cheery air, a wry smile tugging at her mouth. "Perhaps you teach me more foolish words, so I am knowing what these Americans say."

"Girls," their mother's voice called from the floor below, "I could use some help with supper."

"Yes, Mother," Veronica answered, getting up. She grinned at Mary. "We'll work on your English later."

The threesome hurried downstairs, the girls heading to the kitchen, and Mary Theresa to the linen closet for a fresh tablecloth. Mrs. Chudzik liked supper to be special, since it was the one meal when the whole family gathered together, first at the dining table, then afterward around the big radio in the parlor.

Mary had taken to the couple at once. Their plump, short frames were the exact opposite of her own late parents', but both Mr. and Mrs. Chudzik were intelligent and loving and showed real concern for her. The family-like atmosphere reminded her of her own roots. And the fact that their children were both girls had been a bonus. Mary found it hard not to feel uncomfortable in the presence of men, young or old.

Tonight would be one of the last she'd be with these kind people who had helped many newcomers over the years to adjust to life in the new land. It was important that her transition to American life took place as smoothly as possible. So as they had done with others, they'd taken her into their home and their lives, made sure she attended Mass regularly, and treated her as a member of the family. She tried not to think about how much she would miss them all. Or how truly alone she would be living in a place by herself.

She felt as if she'd spent the last few years of her life saying good-bye to everyone she ever knew.

❧

Leaden clouds dragged across the city, enshrouding the tops of skyscrapers and coating their sides with drizzle, leaving a sheen on the streets below. The fine mist added streaks in the line of small, sooty glass panes high up on the Olympic Sewing Factory on 34th Street. Only the sickliest light penetrated the window grime even on the best of days, and on dull ones the windows were utterly worthless.

Inside the ancient building, a raft of black electrical cords dangled from the high ceiling like so many snakes, the exposed light bulbs casting a harsh, brassy glare across endless rows of women bent over their work. The incessant clacking of Singer sewing machines drowned out any hope of conversation—something which was not advisable during working hours, close confines or not. Everyone knew that too much visiting resulted in raised quotas.

Occupying one of the Singers, Mary Theresa grabbed a cutout shirtsleeve and partially finished cuff from the stacks at her side and positioned them for assembly before starting her treadle. As a newly-hired, inexperienced employee, she'd been delegated to one of the older foot-powered models which interspersed the lot at random. The more proficient laborers used the much faster electric machines. Mary had worked steadily all morning, determined to reach her quota by day's end.

Most of all, she did not want to attract undue attention from the taskmistress, Mrs. Hardwick. With her large-boned, stocky frame, sharp nose, and short, frizzy hair, the woman seemed a replica of one of the guards at Ravensbruck. She was only slightly more pleasant in the somber suit, plain white blouse, and black-laced shoes which made up her typical attire.

"Pssst."

Mary cut a glance at Estelle Thomas, at the electric machine to the right.

Her coworker did not slow her own work but tipped her head pointedly toward the floor.

A stack of finished sleeves had toppled off Mary Theresa's machine. She smiled her thanks to the friendly brunette and snatched them up, brushing the bottom one free of dust before eagle-eyed Mrs. Hardwick skulked by to find fault. The last thing she needed was for the woman to dock her pay or raise the quota to some unattainable number as punishment.

Mary found the job at the sewing factory tedious, but her limited English did not instill enough confidence in herself to seek something better. The long hours occupied a good part of her existence, and the wages, however meager, did provide her living expenses. Only a small sum of the money from Rahel remained in the savings account Mrs. Chudzik had opened for her—a balance she hoped to add to for night classes in English, typing, and shorthand someday. The greater part of the funds had paid for the necessary bribes and her fare to America, plus room and board to the Chudziks during the months she stayed in their home. It had also purchased new clothes and some necessities for her furnished apartment.

At last, the noon whistle shrilled. The rows of machines ceased operation, their cacophony immediately replaced by the drone of chatter and of chairs scooting back to form circles here and there among the tired-looking mass of women.

"Finally!" Estelle exclaimed, her thick-lashed sable eyes sparkling as she brushed a wisp of damp, curly hair from her temple. "I'm starving." She cleared her work space for room enough to eat, then reached into her bottom drawer and withdrew a lunch sack.

Mary did the same. "I too feel hungry."

The willowy young woman peered up at the windows, and a grimace replaced the ever-present smile on her rosy lips. "I hate it when the weather's too cool and miserable for us to go outside for a breath of fresh air." Removing the waxed paper from a sandwich, she set it out, releasing the unmistakable smell of tuna salad into the room's stuffy atmosphere while she poured hot tea from a thermos bottle.

"We stop the work for short time. That I am glad for."

Estelle nodded, her piquant face serene as she bowed her dark head for a quick prayer of thanks before taking a bite.

Somewhat uncomfortable at public displays of that nature, Mary waited respectfully until her new friend's prayer ended, then devoured her own cold cheese sandwich. It was a far cry from the sumptuous fare she'd enjoyed with the Chudziks, but it was the best she could throw together before dashing out the door to catch the trolley this morning.

"Think you'll make your quota this time?" Estelle asked, her feminine features accenting her sincerity.

Mary Theresa cocked her head. "I try. I keep trying till I do. Maybe today. Maybe soon."

"You're a good worker. I think you'll make it." A confident nod accompanied the statement.

"And if I do, it is because you help," Mary had to admit. "I know nothing when I first start here."

"Hey, we all had to start sometime, Mary. And I've enjoyed having such a conscientious worker next to me. The last girl was forever grousing about one thing or another. Never failed to put me in a bad mood—to say nothing of constantly aggravating Mrs. Hardwick." Rolling her eyes, she finished the last bite of her sandwich, then washed it down with some tea.

Gobbling her own food so quickly had done little to satisfy Mary's appetite. She tried not to notice the delicious-looking cookies her new friend was unwrapping, liberally speckled with chunks of chocolate and walnuts.

"Would you care for one?" Estelle asked, holding them out. "I don't think I can eat them both."

"If you are sure." More than grateful for the treat, Mary nodded her thanks.

"I am. In fact, I'll be baking more tonight—my brother's orders. Now that sugar rationing has ended, we've been enjoying some treats we've been missing." Her eyes widened. "Hey! Why not come home with me after work? I could use the help with baking, and you could have supper with us. I live only a couple of stops past yours. I'll see that you get on the right trolley afterward."

Mary stopped chewing. "I. . .think not. But thank you."

"Please, Mary?" Estelle urged. "I really like our working here together, and I've mentioned you so often to my family, they're dying to meet you. You do live alone, right?"

"Yes, but—"

"Then wouldn't you enjoy a good hot meal—with some other people as nice as me?"

The light tone and big grin assured Mary that the girl was teasing. But she wasn't altogether certain she should accept the offer, tempting or not. She opened her mouth to voice a polite refusal, but the bell to resume work cut her off.

"At least think about it," Estelle pressed as she swung around to her machine and turned it on. "Promise?"

"I will think about it."

In truth, it was all Mary Theresa thought about for the endless hours which made up the remainder of the workday. She'd been out on her own for three weeks now, and though the Chudziks occasionally popped in to see how she was faring, it wasn't the same as living with them. No lively chatter enlivened her tiny kitchen table at mealtimes. In fact, their parting gift, a small table radio, only made Mary homesick for the laughter that would erupt among the family over a humorous comment by Jack Benny or George Burns and Gracie Allen. When the programs ended, even the most lively big-band music seemed a letdown.

She had started skipping Mass also. The ornate beauty of the cathedral seemed impersonal, and once-beloved rituals no longer offered the kind of substance for which her heart yearned. She finally tucked her rosary and prayer book into one of her drawers, rarely taking them out. Mary still wore the Star of David Rahel had given her and had added a tiny crucifix to the chain. It seemed somehow symbolic of the friendship which had drawn them together.

But after years of being crammed into a too-crowded barracks, plus several months of sharing a room with two sweet, bubbly girls, the solitude she had once yearned for now seemed oppressive. She almost looked forward to coming to work, simply to hear other voices—and even more important, because of the growing friendship between her and Estelle. What could it hurt to accept that invitation, to liven up at least one lonely evening?

"Well, have you decided?" her coworker asked hopefully after the quitting time bell sounded and the muslin covers were being placed over the machines. "Please say yes."

Mary just smiled. Even if she had intended to refuse, Estelle's expression would have thwarted that plan. "I will come," she told her, and the two of them grabbed their umbrellas and handbags and filed out with the rest of the throng.

"Do I look all right?" Mary asked when they emerged into the dwindling light of day, where a playful gust of wind snatched long gold hairs from her neatly pinned roll and tossed them into her eyes. She tied on a triangular *babushka*. "I am dirty from factory."

"No worse than me," came Estelle's cheery response as she opened her umbrella. "You can freshen up at my house. Oh, I am so glad you're coming!" And with that, she linked an arm through Mary Theresa's, unmindful of such mundane matters as puddles or umbrella spokes that bumped together all the way to the trolley stop.

*I hope I will be as glad*, Mary thought. *Or will this just be more people I will grow to love. . .only to have to give them up?*

# Chapter 2

That's it. I'm outta here." Jonathan Gray shoved his chair back from the card table by the parlor windows and unfolded his long legs to stand.

Nelson Thomas peered up from the checkerboard and smirked at his lanky best friend. "Isn't that a touch extreme? You've only lost six games. . .in a row."

The off-duty policeman didn't crack a smile. "Just isn't my day, Buddy. I gotta get to the precinct anyway. I drew the night shift this week." He plunked his uniform cap atop his sandy head and crossed the width of the room in three strides.

"Catch a lot of bank robbers," Nelson quipped, lacing his fingers behind his neck to stretch his shoulders.

"Will do. Gotta keep the streets safe for Mr. Average Citizen. See ya." With a mock salute, the cop shut the front door almost noiselessly behind himself.

While his pal clomped down the steps and away, Nelson returned his attention to the scattered red and black pieces. He scooped up the checkers and replaced them in their cardboard container, then folded the game board and stood it on end beside the bookcase. He debated about working some more on the picture puzzle he'd started before but decided against it.

At that moment, his mother bustled into the room, her slight form creating a breeze which stirred the graying permed hair framing her rosy cheeks. A frown etched twin lines above her button nose. "Jon left?" she asked, drying her hands on a dish towel. "I was going to invite him for supper."

"He was in a hurry, Mom. Had to go to work."

"Oh, and just when I made too much. Well, I suppose we can eat leftovers tomorrow." Draping the damp towel over the shoulder of the bib apron covering her housedress, she gathered the empty iced tea glasses the two men had drained, then headed back up the hall toward the kitchen.

Watching after her until she left his range of vision, Nelson marveled over her inherent need to mother all the young people who darkened their doors. Especially the ones like his pal, who had no moms of their own. Stray young people, stray puppies and kittens, they were all the same to her. Dad had picked a real gem for himself.

*Thought I had too. Once.* Immediately shrugging off that painful reminder, Nelson used his crutch as leverage to ease himself to a standing position and hobbled to the overstuffed easy chair he preferred, ignoring the vinyl-covered hassock as he sank onto the seat cushion. He switched on the radio, turning the dial in search of some lively Benny Goodman or other upbeat tunes. Anything to keep his mind too occupied to dwell on that loss. . .or the other one.

The front door opened, admitting his sister, Estelle, on a round of giggles that made her sound twelve years old instead of just two years younger than his own twenty-three. She and a honey blond Nelson had never seen before stuck closed umbrellas into a stand just inside, then looped their shoulder bags and kerchiefs over the hall tree.

Assuming the pair would head upstairs to Stella's room, Nelson relaxed against the comfortable chair back and focused again on Glenn Miller's rendition of "Little Brown Jug."

But they didn't leave. He cringed as his sister's footsteps headed his way, hers and the other girl's. And Stella knew he wasn't at ease around strangers—hadn't been since he'd come home from the war. Later, he'd drive that point home to her one more time, make her understand. After all, a guy deserved some privacy.

"Nel-se," she sing-songed, making two syllables out of one as she came up beside him, "I've brought my friend from work home with me. She's going to help me bake cookies after supper."

"That's swell, Sis," he said, not bothering to camouflage his facetious tone.

"I'd like you to meet Mary Theresa Malinowski," she went on. "You've heard me mention her before. Mary, this is my brother, Nelson. He likes to boss his baby sister around, but I don't let him get to me."

Reluctantly, he slid his gaze up to meet the visitor's.

Nelson stared into a face as gorgeous and perfectly rendered as any porcelain doll's. And the largest, most beautiful eyes he had ever seen mesmerized him. A luminous, celestial blue-green, and fringed by long, silky lashes, they were filled with what appeared to be outright. . .*fear.* She looked twice as uncomfortable as he, if such a thing were possible. He offered a reserved smile. "Glad to meet you, Mary."

"I too am pleased," she whispered with an almost imperceptible nod, her creamy skin every bit as white as the blouse she wore with her plaid skirt. But the way she shrank a fraction backward added the anticipated dash of doubt to the polite words issued by those rose-petal lips.

It didn't appear as if Estelle noticed anything unusual, however. "Well, come on, Mare. I'll introduce you to Mom. It's still a little early for my dad to come home from our butcher shop, but he's always in time for supper."

As they walked away, Nelson beheld Mary's cameo-like profile in awe.

Mary Theresa struggled to gather her composure. A father she could deal with. But had Estelle mentioned a grown brother at home? If she had, that little detail had gotten lost in the noise of sewing machines being started up again after the noon break. If she'd caught it, she never would have agreed to come here.

But turning away from Nelson Thomas in the upholstered chair, her gaze had landed on something she had not noticed before—the turned-up trouser leg. He was missing his left limb from just below the knee. Her heart contracted. Except for some grim lines alongside his mouth and a slight downward turn of his light brown eyes, Estelle's lean, mahogany-haired brother had an amiable enough face. Even handsome, in a timeless sort of way—if she were the least bit interested— which of course she was not. Reinforced by a determination to ignore that square jaw and those finely honed features, she steeled herself against what nevertheless might turn out to be a very long evening and tagged after her friend.

The Chudziks' apartment had been quite lovely, furnished in fine woods and rich textiles. But this tenement house, Mary decided on the way through the hall, emit- ted a nearly tangible quality of homeyness that the more elegant residence had lacked. Even though the floral runner showed definite worn paths, and the drapes and slipcovers looked faded and threadbare in spots, the whole place seemed to welcome her and make her feel at ease.

The delicious aroma of beef stew grew stronger as they neared the kitchen and entered. This room also exuded a decidedly cheery atmosphere, whether from the red and white decor and crisp gingham curtains or the roomy expanse of work space, she couldn't be sure. At least, not until Estelle approached the stove and tapped the shoulder of the petite-framed woman standing in front of it.

"Mom?"

She paused from stirring the pot of stew and turned around, the smile on her face looking as if it had been born there and never left.

"Yes, Dear."

"I brought company for supper. This is Mary. Mary Theresa Malinowski. We work together at Olympic. I've told you about her."

The smile broadened, adding an engaging light to small hazel eyes as she reached out to lay a hand on Mary's forearm. "Yes. How lovely to meet you, Mary. I'm so glad you've come."

"Mrs. Thomas," she answered, noting the sincerity in the woman's expression and manner. It differed very little from Estelle's, she realized, appreciating the strong resemblance. No wonder her daughter had seemed so pleasant and help- ful to a brand-new employee, growing up with such a mother.

"Can we do anything to help?" her friend asked. "Set the table? Make lemonade?"

"Not a thing. It's all done. You two just run along and have a nice visit. We'll

141

eat as soon as your father comes in from work."

"Well, come upstairs then, Mary," Estelle suggested. "We can freshen up before supper."

Mary snagged her handbag from the hall tree on their way to the staircase and accompanied the young woman to her room.

They'd barely finished sponging their faces and running a comb through their hair when the summons came, and the two of them hurried down to the dining room, where the rest of the family had already gathered around the oblong maple table. Mary admired the embroidered red roses on the tablecloth as she and Estelle each claimed one of the two remaining places.

Not without a twinge of uneasiness did Mary notice her chair was directly across from her friend's brother. And gracing the wall behind him she spied a beautifully framed portrait of Christ, without the sacred heart she was accustomed to seeing. *The old nuns at school would be shocked,* she thought with chagrin. Not only had their prize student consorted with Jews but now was being entertained by Protestants!

"Ah. Stella has brought a guest, I see." Light from the fixture overhead glinted on the receding hairline and bifocals belonging to the congenial-looking man who occupied the head of the table as he glanced from Mary to his daughter. His wiry, muscular build and strong hands gave evidence of hard work.

"Oh, I almost forgot," she said lightly. "Dad, this is Mary Theresa Malinowski, my friend from work. I imposed on her good nature to help me make cookies after supper."

"I see. Well, how do you do, Mary? We're glad you could join us."

"Mr. Thomas," she said politely, noting that the man seemed every bit as gracious as his wife, and he possessed an open, honest face that put her at ease.

"Now that everyone's present and accounted for, we'll return thanks," he said with a jovial smile. He bowed his head, and everyone followed suit.

"Dear Lord, thank You for Your wonderful provision day by day and for the opportunity to share our bounty with friends. Please bless this food and our conversation around the table. And thank You for bringing Mary to our home. May this be the first of many happy visits. We ask You to grant her a special blessing this evening and in the days to come. In Jesus' name, amen."

"Amen," the others echoed, and Mary crossed herself.

Having used recited prayers for so many occasions in her life, the intimate tone of Mr. Thomas's prayer brought Mary's prison mate, Corrie ten Boom, to her mind. As the older man began ladling rich stew from the china tureen into bowls and passing them around, she marveled at the way some people seemed able to approach Almighty God in such a casual, friendlike fashion.

"Would you care for bread?"

Estelle's voice coaxed Mary back from her musings. . .as did the realization that Nelson was staring at her. "Oh. Yes, thank you," she mumbled, lowering her lashes. She accepted the heaping plate and removed a slice before passing it to Mrs. Thomas on her left.

"So, Mary," the man of the house began, "tell us about yourself. Have you and your family been in New York long?"

She didn't relish becoming the center of attention, much less receiving personal questions that might lead to her shameful past. But after filling her spoon with succulent beef broth to cool, she met his gaze. "My family is no more. From Poland I come to stay with American family. With the English language they help me till a job I could get."

"Oh, you poor dear," Estelle's mother murmured, administering a loving pat to Mary's arm, her expression revealing a tender heart.

Her husband blanched. "I didn't mean to pry. Forgive me."

Mary feigned a tight smile to no one in particular. "It is. . .how you say. . .okay."

"Mary works on the machine next to mine," Estelle piped up. "She's only been with Olympic for a couple weeks and should be making her quota any day now. She lets me talk my head off whenever I want—when we're allowed to visit, of course. Usually the noon break."

"But do you keep her supplied with aspirin?" Nelson muttered with a subtle curl of his lip. "For the headaches."

"No headaches," Mary responded. "I am liking her talk."

He smirked. "Just wait till the novelty wears off."

"Novelty?" Mary had to ask. "This I not understand."

"Don't pay any attention to that brother of mine," Estelle said, rolling her eyes. "It's best to ignore him."

But Mary Theresa caught the mischievous twitch of Nelson's mouth, and the sight resurrected the long ago days when her own brothers would tease her mercilessly. And somehow, she didn't mind the bittersweet memory, even if the present banter did happen to be at her expense. She returned her attention to the hearty stew before her as the father of the house began regaling everyone with amusing stories about some of his butcher shop's regular customers and how glad everyone was to see the end of meat rationing.

After they'd finished the stew and generous slices of fresh apple pie, Mr. Thomas reached behind him for a small leather-bound book on the lace-doilied buffet and read aloud a collection of Scripture verses pertaining to hope.

Once more, Mary was transported back in time to Ravensbruck. She could hear in her mind the surprisingly strong voice of the older woman from Holland, hear again some of the very same wondrous promises that had remained in her memory to this day. It seemed a fitting end to supper, one she would ponder later in her solitude. But now, however, as Estelle stood and began clearing the table, she knew it was on to dishes and baking.

Hours later than normal, Mary Theresa finally got back to her apartment. She still smelled of cookie dough, could still taste the satin sweetness of the chipped chocolate, melted and warm from the oven. After hooking the handle of her umbrella over the doorknob, she switched the floor lamp on, then draped her raincoat over the camelback sofa which dominated her combination dining/sitting room. As she kicked off her loafers, her gaze surveyed her surroundings.

Compared to some of the other residences she had seen in America, her diminutive abode seemed stark and uninviting. The Chudziks had seen to it that she had curtains and linens and other basic necessities. But the walls lacked adornment. The whole place needed some bright, homey touches. Perhaps some weekend she'd prevail upon Estelle to come shopping with her. The girl had made no mention of a regular boyfriend, and she might know where to find some good bargains, assuming she wasn't always busy with her family.

Her family. Mary's heart swelled at the remembrance of the kind people who made up Estelle's world, the way they had taken her in. She couldn't help smiling. Mrs. Thomas had fluttered about the kitchen like a mother hen, yet never really intruded, while her daughter and Mary baked a double batch of cookies. Her husband, who had not repeated his blunder of probing for personal information at the table, had retired to the parlor after supper to read the evening paper.

But Nelson. Mary's smile took a pensive turn when thoughts surfaced of her friend's brooding older brother with the perceptive brown eyes. Despite definite laugh lines alongside his mouth, smiles had been few. He hadn't exactly been friendly, but neither had he been unfriendly.

In truth, Mary didn't quite know what to make of him. And perhaps that was just as well.

# Chapter 3

Mary brushed lingering bread crumbs from her polka-dot dress, then took another drink of the hot tea she'd brought for lunch.

"Looks like you're doing great today," Estelle commented between bites of her sandwich as she eyed Mary's stack of finished sleeves.

"Yes. My quota I should make, I think, this time."

"I wouldn't be surprised." Her friend paused. "My parents sure enjoyed meeting you last night. I hardly ever take someone home with me. They really like you." She offered her two cookies from the batch they'd baked.

"Thank you." Mary lifted one of them to her nose and inhaled deeply. "So much better it smells than this place."

"I agree. Completely."

"I am liking your family too. So friendly they are." Munching the treat, she mentally replayed the visit.

"Even Nelson thought you seemed. . .let's see, how did he put it? Oh, yeah. Decent. He thought you were pretty decent."

Mary swallowed a little too quickly, but recovered. "What means 'decent'?" She suspected she already knew the definition, but some American words had a variety of meanings. In this particular instance, she needed specifics.

"Oh, you know. Swell. Nice. It's about as much of a compliment as he gives these days, grump that he is."

Estelle's response unraveled the tightness around Mary's spirit.

"He's been in a black mood ever since he came home from the rehabilitation center," she went on. "Thinks his life is over. He hardly does anything except sit around and mope. He never used to be like that."

"Wounded at war your brother is?"

Estelle nodded. "In France. He almost didn't make it, really. He was in the hospital for quite a long time, before—" The end-of-lunch bell overpowered the last part of the sentence.

Pursing her lips, Mary Theresa wrapped the remaining cookie and tucked it inside her handbag, then moved her chair into place to resume working.

She didn't want to think about Nelson Thomas. At all. He was too attractive.

And, too—his own word fit perfectly—decent. Too decent for someone like her. No man would ever want her now. She'd accepted that cruel reality long ago. But still, the teasing remarks he'd made to his sister and the quirk of his mouth when he had chided Estelle made Mary miss her own siblings, particularly Aleksandr and Patryk, the two who had been closest to her own age. How unfair it was that such handsome, strong youths had been put to death merely to satisfy the whim of a Nazi lunatic who hadn't known either one of them—or any others among the countless millions who had been exterminated. She only hoped her brothers had not been first made to suffer.

"Pssst."

A quick look at her coworker, and Mary caught the warning in her eyes. Mrs. Hardwick was marching purposely toward them. Plucking a set of sleeve parts from her work piles, Mary immediately positioned them under the presser foot on the machine and started pumping the treadle. She felt the keen stare boring into her back when the woman paused momentarily behind her before slowly moving on.

Halfway through the afternoon, while Estelle left her machine to replenish her supply of shirt sections, Mary went to use the facilities. It drew a stern glower from the supervisor but couldn't be helped. In the briefest of moments, she was back at her station and working steadily until the end of the shift.

This had been her best day yet. She'd kept a running tally of each dozen she added to her basket and knew she'd done it—finally reached the magical number which at first had seemed an impossible goal. With a triumphant grin at Estelle, she stood to collect the completed sleeves to be turned in and logged next to her name in the ledger.

She felt the blood drain from her face as she stared at the pathetic pile.

In the middle of covering her electric machine, Estelle stopped. "What's wrong?"

"Gone!" Mary croaked through her clenched throat. "Almost half of my sleeves. Gone."

Her coworker leaned to peer into Mary's basket, her expression registering shock. "It can't be. I watched your work accumulating all through the day. I know you had to have made your quota."

The heavy footsteps of the supervisor grew louder on her approach. "Got a problem here, Malinowski?"

Mary's insides turned over at Mrs. Hardwick's insinuating look.

"I–I—"

"Someone helped herself to Mary Theresa's finished pile," Estelle answered for her.

"Is that right? And who might that be?" the woman challenged, cold gray eyes darting from her to Mary and back. "The girl hasn't made her quota once in all the time she's been here."

"She would have today," Estelle insisted.

Mrs. Hardwick tapped the toe of one black shoe impatiently and tucked her chin. "Well, we don't really know that, now, do we?"

"I. . .am sorry," Mary somehow managed. "Harder I will work tomorrow."

"You're right about that, little lady," she answered, each word precise and flat. "Your quota will rise by two dozen, beginning tomorrow morning. I suggest you get here early and spend more time at your machine and less at the lavatory."

*Two dozen more!* Mary swallowed her rising panic and stood tall. "Yes, Madam."

"And if you aren't turning in your daily requirements by the end of this week, there are plenty of other applicants waiting for work. Remember that." Without further comment, the supervisor turned and hiked away.

Once Mrs. Hardwick was out of earshot, Estelle hugged Mary. "I am so sorry. I can't figure out how such a thing could have happened."

"It is. . .all right," she whispered. "This quota I make. I make the new one."

Subdued, they gathered their belongings and left to catch the trolley, neither of them making their usual small talk along the way. But once they were seated and on the homeward journey, Estelle shook her head. "I don't know how you could be so gracious to that old witch."

Mary shrugged, recalling more of fellow prisoner Corrie ten Boom's admonitions at the death camp. "A job she has, like us. To turn in much work done each day. What is expected I will do."

Estelle regarded her evenly. "You sound like our pastor. 'Turn the other cheek.' I used to think I could do that without any effort at all. But not today. My temper's always been my worst fault. And this afternoon it would have given me great pleasure to punch her in the face."

"A good teacher I had," Mary admitted. "And wise. So wise." She averted her attention to the passing buildings, especially enjoying the little groups of children at play on the side streets. So healthy and carefree they looked, as children should.

A few silent moments lapsed.

"Doing anything for supper tonight?" Estelle asked, a ray of hope gleaming in her face.

Mary had to smile. "Yes. A hot bath I am taking. Then a bowl of soup. Chicken noodle."

"My favorite."

"Sometime soon I make two cans. For you to eat with me."

"I would like that. Truly. But everybody should have some real home cooking now and then. Ever had pasties?"

Confusion clouded Mary's mind. "The word I not know."

"They're delicious," Estelle answered. "Kind of a meat and potato pie, served with broth or gravy over top. My mom makes the absolute best ones in the world. I'll invite you over next time we're having some."

"Already it is making me hungry," Mary teased. Standing to pull the cord, she gave her friend's shoulder an affable squeeze. "My stop this is. See you tomorrow."

"Bright and early," Estelle teased. "Don't forget."

❧

"We're off to prayer meeting, Son," Nelson heard his father say on his way into the parlor. He wore his customary suit and tie, his Bible under one arm. "Sure you won't come with us?"

Nelson returned his gaze to the open book he'd been trying to concentrate on, without success. He shook his head.

"Maybe next time, then," his mother suggested, tugging on white cotton gloves that complemented her church hat as she joined them. "The pastor's been presenting a wonderful study on 'The Cross through the Scriptures.' We're enjoying it immensely."

"That's good, Mom. I'll see you both when you get home." He buried his nose a fraction deeper, to miss seeing that pained look on her face. His parents meant well, he knew. But what they didn't seem to acknowledge was that he could no longer dredge up much enthusiasm for churchgoing—even though Pastor Herman had once been one of his biggest heroes. Sure, church had been pretty important before he went off to join the army, but that was then. A lot of water had gone under the bridge since those days. A lot.

He made another attempt to read the same page, then gave up and closed the book.

Barely ten minutes elapsed before Stella breezed in. "Oh, no. I missed Mom and Dad, huh?"

"You got it."

"Rats." Without removing her cardigan or hanging her shoulder bag, she plopped on the couch adjacent to his chair, letting her head fall back in defeat, her hands crossed atop her abdomen. "I got held up past quitting time at work. And I really need more practice on that new choir number for Sunday too."

Nelson cocked a brow. "So what do you want from me, a piggyback ride?"

Straightening, Estelle leveled a glare on him, one that gained heat by the second. "If you must know, I don't want anything from you," she snapped. "You've been nothing but a pain since you came home, and I've about had it up to here with that poor-me attitude of yours." With a huff, she rose to her feet.

He opened his mouth to respond, but she didn't give him a chance.

"I had a bad day at work—or at least Mary did—and now I'm missing church because of it. So I'd appreciate it if you'd just—just—"

"Wait a minute, Sis," he cut in calmly, raising a palm like a traffic cop. "What happened at work? Why don't you calm down and tell big brother your troubles? It'll make you feel better."

Her expression gradually softened, turning to a blush with her sheepish smile. "Sorry for blowing up, Nelse. I didn't mean what I said. I promise."

He gave an offhanded shrug. "I know. But I probably deserve it. Everybody else is walkin' on eggshells around me. At least you level with me, get honest once in awhile."

"Honest, maybe, but hardly tactful."

"Hey, that's what sisters are for, right? But for now, the subject is you, not me. So what happened at work?"

Estelle moistened her lips. "It concerns Mary, really. She's been trying hard to make her production quota—"

"And?" he probed, impatient, yet not knowing why.

"Well, the thing is, she finally did it this afternoon. She was so proud."

"So? What'd they do, throw the girl a party? Is that why you're late? I thought you said this was a bad day."

"This would be a little easier if you'd quit cutting in," she reminded him.

With a repentant grin, he gestured for her to take the floor once more.

"Anyway," she continued, "I watched her working all day long, saw the pile growing higher and higher in her basket. I know she made her quota, if not better than that. . .only, when she went to turn it in, someone had snitched a good half of it, if not more."

Nelson raised both eyebrows this time, but did not say anything.

"Mary was absolutely white with shock. Old Lady Hardwick was her usual magnanimous self, full of tea and sympathy. Ha! Insults and insinuations were all that came out of that mean mouth. She upped Mary's requirements two extra dozen. And she has to do it by Friday or she's out of a job. That's only two days from now."

"The woman's all heart. Sounds like my old drill sergeant back at boot camp."

Estelle almost laughed but turned serious again. "But you know what surprised me the most? Mary. She just squared those shoulders of hers and said she'd work harder. She'd made this quota, and she'd do that one too. It's the strangest thing. I was mad enough to spit nails at whoever took advantage of such a sweet-spirited girl. And there she is, telling me Mrs. Hardwick has a boss too and depends on the rest of us to keep her level of production high."

"You don't say." Nelson rubbed his jaw with a thumb and forefinger, trying to envision that wisp of a gal holding her own before the hard-nosed supervisor of Olympic Sewing Factory. No wonder Stella had been so upset with him for being such a smart alec.

Again he felt there was something indefinable about that Polish beauty. Mary seemed on a higher plane than most of the other girls he'd known. And her eyes. . .they had a haunting quality that caught at a person's heart. Coming from Poland, she had to have known a fair amount of suffering—especially if the rest of her family no longer existed. In all likelihood, her loved ones had met their ends at the hand of some beast of a Nazi.

And he'd lost only a leg.

Maybe a guy could afford to take a few lessons from Mary Theresa Malinowski.

# Chapter 4

Curled up on her couch in a flannel robe, her hair wrapped in a towel, Mary smiled at the banter between Jack Benny and his man, Rochester, issuing through the radio speaker. Even when she couldn't quite understand the jokes, she tried to enter into the spirit of the audience's laughter. After all, the more exposure to English, the better. She figured eventually she'd catch on to American humor. She kept the radio on most of the time she was home to help banish the awful stillness of the apartment, a quiet so deep she doubted she'd ever get used to it.

During the musical interlude between the end of the program and the beginning of the next, her thoughts drifted backward to the day's events at the factory. Someone else, among the throng of women who toiled long hours at Olympic, must have had a desperate need to reach a quota. But in dredging up the sea of faces which were still only vaguely familiar, Mary couldn't imagine who might have stolen her work.

In the death camp, poor performance resulted in a short walk to the ovens. . .an incentive for putting forth one's best efforts. But here at the factory the task of attaching cuffs to sleeves had finally become automatic for Mary. She had not the slightest doubt she'd be able to produce enough to keep Mrs. Hardwick satisfied.

It had been thoughtful of Estelle to stand up for her, though, and then, later, to suggest she come to another family meal. Listening to her friend's father reading Scripture after supper made her realize how much she missed the nightly readings she'd grown to rely on in the Ravensbruck barracks. She'd spied a Bible on the night table in Estelle's room and another on a bookshelf in the parlor. Perhaps on her next visit she might actually touch one, even open it. Let her eyes feast on the written words that had given her strength to survive.

Footsteps outside, followed by a knock on the door, startled her out of her reverie.

Mary got up and turned off the radio. Clutching the throat of her robe, she padded to answer the summons. "Who is outside?" she asked before turning the latch.

"It's me, Veronica."

"And Christine," a second voice supplied.

With no little relief, Mary let them both in, then glanced around for the girls' parents.

"It's just us," Veronica told her. "Mother and Father wanted to visit a sick friend from our parish, and we convinced them to drop us off on the way."

"We hope you don't mind," her sister added. "They said they wouldn't be too long."

"Mind!" Mary grabbed their petite forms in a huge hug. "Being alone I mind much more. Please, sit down. I change quick." She dashed to the bathroom, where tomorrow's skirt and blouse hung in readiness for the morning. Seconds later, she emerged dressed, with her damp hair fastened in a barrette at the nape of her neck.

"We stopped at the corner for some ice cream," Veronica said, holding out a small brown bag. "Chocolate, just for you."

"How well you know me, my little sisters. Oh, so glad to see you I am." Accepting the treat from the older girl, Mary stepped to the tiny kitchenette off the main room. She set the pint onto the sink's drain board and made short work of dipping the contents into three dishes.

"How is your new job?" Christine asked, delving into hers the minute she was served.

"Fine. It is fine. Sleeves I make. For men's shirts."

Veronica turned up her pert nose. "Sounds boring."

"A living it is," Mary responded quietly. "To learn to sew is good." She took a leisurely spoonful of ice cream and studied the dear little faces she so sorely missed. Veronica's rich brown hair was as shiny as ever, parted in the middle with bangs. And Christine's braids sported bows that matched her navy jumper. In many ways, the tiny blond resembled Mary's dead sister, Janecska, which she found strangely comforting. "Everyone is well at your house?" she asked the younger girl.

She nodded. "Only it seems like someone is missing, without you."

"Have you made any friends, Mary?" Veronica placed the spoon in her empty dish, then set it on one of the lamp tables bracketing the sofa.

"Yes. One."

"A handsome man?" she teased, grinning.

For a split second, the face of Nelson Thomas taunted Mary's consciousness. She opened her mouth to offer a negative reply, but Christine spoke first.

"Mother told us not to be nosy," she rebuked Veronica, then turned to Mary. "Sissy only thinks about boys 'cause she's got a new boyfriend."

Her sibling rolled her eyes to the ceiling. "Jason's *not* my boyfriend. Besides, he has too many freckles."

"My friend is from work," Mary blurted in an effort to restore the peace. "Estelle is her name. To her house I went last night for visit. We make cookies."

"I hope she's nice," Christine mused.

Mary nodded. "Very nice family she has. Friendly."

"Any brothers?" Veronica asked, that impish sparkle back again.

"Not of your age," she said with a wry grimace.

Christine made a face at her sister, then turned. "What's it like to work in a factory, anyway?"

For the next few minutes, she entertained the young pair with the lighter aspects of being new on a job, relishing the carefree sound of their girlish giggles.

But all too soon another knock signified the end of the visit, and Mrs. Chudzik came to collect her daughters.

"Some tea you would like?" Mary asked after returning the plump little woman's warm embrace.

"No, thank you, Dear. The girls need to get to bed for school. Perhaps another time. Everything okay with you?"

"Fine, yes."

A round of kisses and hugs and good-byes, and the lively bunch took their leave.

Mary held onto the knob as she watched the threesome head for the car parked out front. She mustered her brightest smile and waved down at Mr. Chudzik, then closed the door once again, not wanting to see them drive off.

Not wanting to hear it either, she hurried to the radio and turned it on, sighing when "Little Brown Jug" brought yet another reminder of Estelle's brother.

≈

*Ho ho ho, you and me. Little brown jug, how I love thee.* Nelson whistled under his breath to the accompaniment of the Glenn Miller tune as he shucked his shirt and trousers and slipped between the cool sheets, his crutches on the floor beside his bed. Not in the mood for a recanting of how wonderful the church service had been or how he should have been there, he had purposely retired to his room before his parents came home. Even with his bedside radio playing, they were considerate enough not to disturb him, which suited him just fine. He doused the light.

Cupping the back of his head, he gazed up at the darkened ceiling. He'd barely been out of this house in the three months since he'd been home. His friend Jon had been trying to persuade him to go out with him to a movie or a baseball game, and his mom and dad were forever after him to start going to Sunday and Wednesday services again. But Nelson couldn't abide other people's stares, the looks of pity—or worse, eyes averted altogether. He had plenty to occupy himself right here. Books, board games, daily crossword puzzles, radio programs. One of these days he might even tune in to *Stella Dallas* or *Pepper Young's Family*. . .see what Mom thought was so wonderful about soap operas.

A grim smile tweaked one side of his mouth. Some exciting life. And a far cry from the career in engineering which once had been his dream. He rarely allowed himself to indulge in poignant recollections of the bustling office where he'd apprenticed before going into the army. He could still picture that place, cluttered with rolls and stacks of blueprints, drawers filled with stubby drawing pencils and slide rules, hard hats perched atop file cabinets. That life was for the able-bodied, not someone who was half a man.

Even as he lay there, he felt a nagging tingle in his missing foot, as if nobody had informed his brain the shattered limb had been left behind in some field hospital across the ocean. The doctors at rehab alleged that those phantom itches would eventually subside. Nelson hoped it was true. He rolled onto his side and punched his pillow to a more comfortable shape.

Was Stella right? Had he sat around with a chip on his shoulder since coming back from the war? If so, it was a wonder his family could put up with him. He'd make a better effort at being cheerful from now on. Be more like. . .Mary.

Nelson made no attempt to banish visions of the fair, golden-haired beauty that drifted across his mind's eye. His family loved him and naturally sympathized with him over the wounds he'd suffered on the battlefields of France. But Mary Theresa was probably the only one who could really understand the depth of his loss. That conviction caused a peculiar expectancy in his stomach, an eagerness which pressed up against the underside of his heart.

Maybe she also needed someone to talk to. . . .

◖◗

"Hey, Mare, you can stop now," Estelle quipped a whole minute after the noon bell.

Mary nodded. Her shoulders sagged, and she ceased pumping the treadle. "This sleeve I wanted to finish. That is all."

Estelle eyed the growing stack in Mary's basket, then scrunched up her face. "You work any faster and you'll even beat me!" She lowered her voice to a conspiratorial whisper. "Then the old bat will raise everybody's quota! Honestly," she added with a mischievous smirk, "the woman's stocking seams are so straight, her garters must hang from her shoulder blades."

Unable to stop a self-conscious grin as she unwrapped her sandwich, Mary met her friend's gaze. "To make only my quota I want today—plus one more. I do it; you will see." She bit off a corner of the bread.

"I believe you will. I've been watching you hunched over that old machine all morning without even stopping for a breath. Where in the world did you get such determination?"

*If you only knew,* Mary thought. "Hard teachers I had."

"I had no idea Polish schools were so strict."

"Not Polish," Mary corrected. "In Germany, the hard teachers." At the confusion clouding her friend's face, she sought a change of subject while she filled her thermos cup with steaming tea. "Some company I have last night. My American little sisters."

"Oh," Estelle breathed. "Your host family. How nice."

"Yes. To see them is good, Veronica and Christine. They bring ice cream. Chocolate, my favorite."

Her coworker smiled. "It's very considerate of those people to keep track of you, make sure you're doing okay. Speaking of favorites, Mom says she'll make some pasties next week. Tuesday, perhaps. Will you come for supper?"

"I will come." The words popped out of their own accord, before Mary could muster a refusal.

The rest of the afternoon passed so swiftly, she remembered only a blur of white fabric passing from her left to the workbasket on her right. The quitting bell caught her by surprise. But she knew she'd made her goal—that, along with not just one, but two extras. With no little satisfaction, she clipped the threads on the final sleeve and added it to the others. Then she stood, easing the kink in her back.

"Good going, Mare!" Estelle murmured at her side. "Wait'll Hardwick checks your total today."

Mary picked up her work and straightened her shoulders, smiling all the way to the production counter.

Later that night, in her bed, she tried not to dwell too much on next week's meal with Estelle's family. She dared not let herself become attached to people. It only hurt later, when they were no longer around. She would simply enjoy each day as it came. Be thankful for the present, as Corrie ten Boom would have said.

And, her conscience admonished, no doubt Corrie would do whatever she could to encourage a soul who still suffered from the cruelties of war. . .like Nelson Thomas.

Even if he did happen to be a man.

The realization lingered on the edges of her heart.

# Chapter 5

Despite her misgivings about becoming too attached to Estelle's family, Mary couldn't help counting the days until Tuesday arrived. Home-cooked meals were a real treat in light of her limited cooking ability, and she was curious to see whether Mrs. Thomas's meat-and-potato pies were as tasty as her friend alleged.

She selected an emerald jumper from her wardrobe, plus a complementing print blouse with dark green piping around the collar and sleeves. The ensemble would look fairly presentable by the end of the day—at least, so she hoped. There was no reason she needed to dress up, she told herself, but a guest in someone's home should at least look neat.

Her skill and performance at the factory had continued to improve since she made her quota, which increased her confidence. But it was the friendship with Estelle that made her look forward to each weekday, especially this one. She relished even the smallest chance to spend time with her wavy-haired coworker. Lunchtimes seemed far too short in comparison to the hours when the noisy atmosphere precluded any real communication.

Humming as she uncovered her Singer, she smiled at Estelle and stowed her lunch bag and purse in the machine's bottom drawer.

"Ready for a bright new day?" Estelle asked cheerily, sweeping a glance around the dreary facility already filling with employees.

Mary's gaze followed the same course. "A place to work, it is."

"I can think of lots of places where I'd rather spend my time."

"Perhaps." A spark of mischief brought a saucy grin. "But me you would not have." The quip surprised even Mary. When had she last felt the lightness of spirit which made her want to joke with someone?

Estelle bubbled into a giggle. "Now I know why I like you. When you're around, a person doesn't *need* sunshine."

The trill of the starting bell prevented Mary from having to concoct a response. With a playful nod, she took her seat and focused on her production goal, hoping that this day too would pass quickly.

Unaccountably restless, Nelson leaned on his crutches and idly plunked a few notes on the upright piano which dominated a length of parlor wall, then gave up and made his way to the front window.

The usual after-school baseball game occupied the neighborhood boys out on the street, while a bit farther down the block, young girls chanted rhymes in the measured cadence of double Dutch, happy sounds which carried through the screens. Both sights made him feel old. It didn't seem so long ago that he and Jon would have been among those boisterous boys, and Stella would have been out there taking turns jumping rope or manning the ends for others. Where had those simple years gone?

"Such a nice day," his mother commented, coming to join him. "I always look forward to the warm days of summer."

"You like humidity, huh?" he wisecracked, still watching the kids at play.

"No, not humidity. The flowers, the fresh garden vegetables. I like knowing I'll soon be canning again, putting up a supply for winter when the cold days come and we're snowed in."

Nelson had to smile. Hectic canning days were among his most vivid memories of childhood. . .Mom and Stella, dwarfed by assorted piles of garden produce, their hair damp and frazzled and forming tiny ringlets around their faces as they worked. He could still conjure up the familiar smells of scalded, peeled tomatoes and peaches, the cinnamony scent of apples being cooked down to make endless quarts of sauce. And what a bounty for the pantry and cellar shelves! On the cold, rainy battlefields of Europe, he'd have given almost anything to find such delectable fare in his mess kit, instead of cold, monotonous K-rations.

"Yeah, I know what you mean," he finally answered.

She slid an arm about his waist. "Can I get you anything? Fresh coffee? Tea? Lemonade?"

"Now that you mention it, I guess I am kind of thirsty. Thanks, Mom."

"Stella should be off work by now. She's bringing Mary Malinowski home with her for supper. My heart goes out to that little gal." She sighed. "All alone in the world, trying to adapt to life in a whole new country. So much pain in those young eyes, yet never a complaint. Even to Stella."

Had it been anyone else, Nelson would have taken the comment about not complaining as a personal affront. But he knew his mom, and knew her words came from deep inside. And he, too, sensed the war had taken an immeasurable toll on the young Polish woman. He'd caught the haunted longing in those eyes several times himself, when Mary wasn't aware of it.

"Makes a body want to say some extra prayers," his mom added on a wistful note, returning to the kitchen.

Until then, Nelson had been trying hard not to think about Mary Theresa. He'd convinced himself no woman could possibly be as naturally beautiful as she'd seemed on her first visit. And it might not be wise to get involved in problems he probably couldn't help her with either. He took a seat in the easy chair, and in moments his mother brought him a tall glass of lemonade. "Thanks again."

She gave his arm a loving pat. "I do hope the girls come soon. I need your sister to try on the dress I've almost finished. Meanwhile, I'd better get back to what I was doing."

It wasn't more than a few minutes later when the two chatterboxes arrived, their cardigans draped over their shoulders in the mild early evening. Their talking ceased abruptly with the bang of the screen door behind them.

Nelson made an effort to appear deeply engrossed in Ernie Pyle's *Brave Men* but found the touching accounts of real-life wartime heroes far too moving for now. So he merely stared at the pages, occasionally turning one in pretense.

"Hi, Nelse," Stella said airily.

"Sis," he returned, looking up. "Hello, Mary."

The visitor offered a shy smile.

His heart thudded to a stop. Not only was she *as* beautiful as he'd first thought, but even *more*, if that were possible. Yet there seemed something far beyond her mere outward appearance that called out to his spirit whenever she was near. Something that made him think maybe he should try to help her, after all. All the more reason to focus his eyes on Ernie's book. Before he'd made sense out of the top paragraph, however, his mother reappeared, greeting the girls with her usual enthusiasm.

"Oh, Stella," she continued in a breathless rush, "supper won't be ready for a little while. Could you try on that new dress I've been working on? I'm sure your brother can keep Mary entertained for five minutes. I shouldn't need longer than that to mark the hem. Would you mind, Dear?"

Not entirely sure to whom she'd addressed the last question, Nelson shot her a glance.

"Sure, Mom," his sister answered. Then she turned to her friend. . .who stood frozen, her eyes wide with fright. "I hope you don't mind, Mare. I'll be back in a jiffy." Showing her to the couch, she leveled a glower on Nelson. "And *you*, big brother, be your old charming self. Mary has yet to see that side of you."

*My charming self,* he thought with chagrin as his sister and their mother retreated to the sewing room off the kitchen.

Almost directly across from him now, Mary Theresa perched poker straight, her ankles crossed, her hands together in her lap, studiously refraining from glancing in his direction. Then her gaze drifted to the coffee table, where his mom's frayed Bible remained from this morning's reading.

An audible span of seconds ticked by on the mantel clock, a poignant silence which hung in the air between them.

He cleared his throat. "I've. . .uh. . .worked up a little song and dance routine," he began, "in case an awkward moment ever came along. . . ."

Her lips parted in obvious confusion, and her eyes hesitantly met his, as if she couldn't decide whether she should laugh.

Nelson flashed his best smile and his most offhanded shrug. "Best joke I could come up with. Sorry." A wave of relief washed over him as surprise skimmed across her face.

She held his gaze for a flicker of a moment, then lowered her eyes. "It—it was not what I expect. To make the joke."

"Little wonder," he admitted, "considering what a boor I was last time you were here. I hope I didn't offend you."

"No. You did not. I. . .understand."

"Know what? I think you probably do." He paused. "But if it's all the same to you, I'd like to apologize, anyway. And this evening I will try to be charming, like my baby sister advised."

Mary brightened, relaxing even more. "A good friend Estelle is. Big help when first I start job."

Watching Mary as she spoke, Nelson noted the way her attention inevitably returned to the Bible in front of her—and lingered with an almost tangible yearning. "It's Mom's," he said quietly.

Those lovely turquoise eyes turned to his in question.

"The Bible. I noticed you admiring it."

She pinkened slightly. "It looks. . .loved," she murmured.

Nelson perused the leather-covered volume lying on the coffee table between them, realizing that the term he would probably have used to describe his mother's Bible was *worn out*. But now, seeing it through Mary's eyes, it took on a whole different quality. "It is that," he agreed. "Mom reads it morning and night, and whenever else she finds time. She's done that as far back as I can remember. Lately, she's started memorizing the Psalms."

"Many Psalms are there?"

The question caught him off guard. From her apparent interest, he'd expected her to be more familiar with God's Word. "A hundred and fifty," he explained. "So she's got a big task ahead."

"Someone else I once met knew much Bible," she said, her breathless voice so soft Nelson had to strain to hear it. "She would read to us, tell us. . .things."

"Us?"

But before she could explain, Stella and Mom breezed back into the parlor, which appeared to relieve Mary greatly.

His sister went immediately to their guest and plopped down on the arm of the sofa beside her. "I am so sorry, Mare, to leave you here with our resident grump. I hope he hasn't dragged you into his bad mood."

Nelson hiked his brows. "I'll have you know Mary and I got along just fine without you. Between us, we've managed to solve all the world's problems since the dawn of time."

"I can imagine." His sister's chin flattened in disdain. "Well, I've come to rescue her, anyway, so you can go back to whatever you were doing before we came home." Rising, she offered Mary a hand.

"As you wish," he answered facetiously, but the impish grin faded as he looked up at their visitor. "Maybe we can talk again sometime, Mary Theresa, about things."

❧

Following Estelle to the second floor to freshen up, Mary drew what felt like her first real breath since arriving at the Thomas house. In her wildest imaginings, she wouldn't have pictured herself being left alone with her friend's brother for any length of time. Nor would she have expected to maintain a calm appearance. But, amazingly, Nelson had managed to put her at ease. . .at least on the surface. Underneath, she had been as jittery as her sewing machine's vibrations.

He seemed so different from the way he'd been last time she'd come. So much more pleasant and *likable*. But being a part of this family, how could he be otherwise?

*But you must not grow fond of him,* her wiser side lectured. *You must not even think of becoming close to any man.*

"So," Estelle said, as the two of them sank down on the patchwork quilt covering her single bed, "what did you and Nelse talk about all that time?"

"Mostly he talks. I listen."

Her friend giggled. "That's my brother, all right. Hey, we have a few minutes before Dad comes home and calls everyone to supper. You can be first to wash up, if you like."

As Mary walked down the hall to the bathroom, the few moments of solitude felt strangely like a reprieve. Any minute now and she'd find herself across the table from Estelle's handsome brother. . .the young man who was becoming *friendly*. . .the young man who was starting to make her believe there could one day be restoration for her shattered trust.

His lips made music of her name. She knew better than to assign too much importance to something so simple as that, yet he made it sound so. . .intimate. Meeting her flushed reflection in the mirror above the sink, she splashed cool water on her face.

And he wanted the two of them to talk again. About things. Well, should the unlikely occasion ever arise, she would allow him to talk all he wanted. But she wasn't about to let the conversation revolve to her. Once this kind family discovered the kind of girl their daughter had befriended, Mary would no longer be welcome in their home.

Besides, even if she did allow herself to become interested in Nelson, what purpose would it serve? He couldn't possibly want her. No man would ever want her.

No, she had no plans of revealing her secrets. Not to Estelle, and especially not to Nelson.

# Chapter 6

Would you care for another slice, Mary, dear?" Mrs. Thomas asked, the pastry server poised in readiness. "We wouldn't want you to leave the table hungry."

Mary's glance made a quick circuit around the loving Thomas household. Having polished off three entire meat pies, none of them could possibly still be hungry, least of all her. "No, thank you. Is full I am. Very good are the pasties."

"Why, thank you," the kind mother beamed, pleasure pinkening her button nose.

"I knew you'd like them," Estelle said. "Mom's are better than anyone's. She makes the flakiest crust around."

"Far be it from me to disagree," her father added pleasantly, patting his stomach. His thick brows arched higher, toward the receding hairline of his wavy, graying hair. "It's a favorite meal in this house."

"I second that," Nelson said with a nod. "They were great, Mom."

Feeling increasingly at ease around Estelle's parents, Mary astonished herself by voicing a favorite. "As child I loved *holubki*, stuffed cabbage. To have that I sometimes wish." Then, regretting having drawn attention to herself, she quickly sipped water from her glass, hoping she hadn't initiated a barrage of personal questions.

Mrs. Thomas sat forward in her chair at the foot of the table, hazel eyes alight. "Stuffed cabbage? Is it made with ground beef and rice? Tomato sauce?"

Mary nodded. "Yes."

A satisfied smile plumped her rosy apple cheeks, and she sat up straighter, evening out the bib of the apron protecting her cross-stitched gingham housedress. "Well, isn't that interesting? I happen to make that dish myself. I just wasn't aware it had a foreign name. I'll prepare some next time you come to supper."

"Hey," Nelson cut in, "this is swell. More of the foods I missed out on when I was in the army." A grin as teasing as a summer breeze added a glimmer to his light brown eyes. "Any other delectable delights you have a hankering for, Mary?"

"What is served now I am liking," she said, stifling a maddening blush before it could make an appearance. It was ridiculous that he should affect her so.

"Well," Mr. Thomas said, unwittingly coming to her rescue, "let's put the icing on this tasty meal." He reached around to the maple buffet behind him for the

162

book of Scripture readings. . .another delight she hungered for.

❧

Nelson watched Mary Theresa's face while his father read the evening devotional selection, a collage of verses pertaining to humility. *A person would have to be blind to miss that deep yearning,* he realized. When had he last savored—or even paid much attention to—Bible passages that were so familiar to him that he'd taken them for granted most of his life? He'd owned a variety of Bibles since he was a young boy, the latest version being a classy, gold-edged Scofield edition his parents gave him the Christmas before he'd gone off to the army. But it had gathered so much dust since he'd come home from rehab, he'd finally put it inside the drawer of his nightstand to assuage his guilt. He couldn't remember the last time he'd opened it.

Or the last time he'd prayed, for that matter.

He'd prayed his head off in battle, with mortar rounds and shrapnel exploding around him. . .right up until a shell came along that had his name on it. His and army buddy Mike Parsons's. Mike had died instantly. That's when Nelson decided nobody was listening to all those heavenly petitions.

He could still hear the chaplain mouthing platitudes to him until the medics arrived to put his writhing, agonized body on a stretcher. Could still remember the torture of the bumping, jostling military ambulance ride, endless miles while his leg blazed with a fire no one could put out. . .except the surgeons at the field hospital.

Those docs put the fire out, all right.

Permanently.

And from there he got a free ride home to America. To get *rehabilitated.* Man, how he hated that word.

❧

" 'If I then, your Lord and Master, have washed your feet,' " Mr. Thomas read, " 'ye also ought to wash one another's feet. For I have given you an example, that ye should do as I have done to you.' "

The passage relating to the humility of Jesus had perplexed Mary since her days in the concentration camp. It seemed an incredible concept then, and still did, to think that the very Son of God had not considered Himself above such a menial task but performed it with the deepest love. The Prince of heaven, with a servant's heart, as the Dutch woman would have said. Even as the priceless picture warmed Mary's insides, her glance drifted idly across the table to Nelson.

Apparently lost in a world of his own, an expression of intense bitterness had turned the young man's features as hard as granite. The sight stunned her. Before supper, he had seemed at ease and quite witty, and during the meal he injected the conversation with a steady stream of humor. He'd been fine until the ensuing

Scripture reading. What could possibly have caused such a change?

Just then his gaze connected with hers, and the severity in his facial planes vanished almost instantly.

Which baffled her even more.

"Well, Son," Mr. Thomas began, "we might find the Dodgers or Yankees playing somewhere on the radio if we turn the dial a bit. What say we get out of here and let the ladies do what ladies do best?" He eased his chair back and got up, pausing momentarily as if giving Nelson a chance to speak if he needed help. Then the two took their leave.

Mrs. Thomas immediately began clearing the table.

"Mom, you've worked enough today," Estelle reminded her. "Mare and I are more than capable of cleaning up. Sit down and relax for a change."

"Well. . ." After a slight hesitation she gave in. "Maybe I'll see if your father would like to go sit outside for awhile. There might not be a game on, after all."

Mary greatly appreciated yet another opportunity to visit with Estelle during the cleanup. Then, once the kitchen had been restored to order, they sought the comfort of the parlor, where they found Nelson at the card table working on a picture puzzle.

He motioned with his dark head toward the front steps without even looking up. "Mom and Dad are outside."

"We know," Estelle commented. "Want to join them, Mary?"

A knock rattled the screen door even as Estelle spoke, and she went to answer it. "Jon! Finished your shift, huh?"

"Sure did, Doll," came a low male voice. "Thought I'd drag that brother of yours out for a soda."

"Good luck!"

They both laughed.

"Well, come in," Estelle went on. "There's someone I'd like you to meet, even if you aren't able to pry Nelse out of here."

Mary's nerves started up immediately at the thought of being in the presence of yet another stranger as the tall, loose-jointed young man with sandy hair accompanied Estelle into the parlor's warm lamplight. He lifted an arm in greeting to Nelson before his attention turned in her direction.

"Jon," Estelle gestured, "this is Mary Malinowski, a friend of mine from Olympic. Mary, Jonathan Gray, Nelson's best buddy. He lives down the street a couple of houses."

"How do you do, Mary?" he said, an appraising smile on his long face. The blue checks in the cotton shirt he wore mirrored the hue of his eyes. Eyes that seemed keenly observant in their perusal.

Automatically, she inched back a fraction for more space. "Pleased to meet you," she whispered, wishing he would at least look away.

He kept up the assessment. "So you work with Stella, eh?"

Mary nodded.

"Good, good. She needs somebody to keep her in line."

Not completely sure what that meant, Mary manufactured as much of a smile as she could, then checked her watch.

"Oh!" Estelle gasped. "I almost forgot. It's time for me to walk you to the trolley stop."

"Need company?" Jon winked at Estelle.

She tilted her head a little, as if trying to decide. "Seeing as how you're a policeman, we probably should accept—but no. I've never heard of a problem on our street. We'll be safe enough."

An alarm shot through Mary at the thought of police escorting her anywhere. She reminded herself that this was America, and law enforcement officers were not to be feared. But not until she'd bid Mr. and Mrs. Thomas good-bye and she and Estelle had walked to the end of her block did she truly feel at ease.

"Jon's a really great guy," her friend gushed while they walked toward the nearest trolley stop.

"And interested in you," Mary pointed out. "I see him watching."

She brushed off the suggestion. "Nah, not really. He knows no one will ever measure up to—" Moistening her lips, Estelle swallowed without finishing the remark.

"About boyfriends we never talk," Mary said, her voice gentle. "A person so nice, like you, must have many."

Estelle craned her neck to peer down the cross street they had reached, but no streetcar was in sight. She turned and met Mary's eyes. "I was engaged, once. My high school sweetheart. The two of us thought we had our whole future planned. But with the war on, he entered the navy, not wanting to 'tie me down,' as he put it, until after the conflict was over. Only. . .his ship was torpedoed and sunk. No one made it off alive."

"I am sorry," Mary whispered. "I should not pry."

"So," Estelle continued, the forced cheerfulness in her voice a little obvious, "that's why Jon doesn't pester me. He knew my fiancé. . .most everybody in our neighborhood knows everybody else. I'm kind of glad he treats me like a sister, actually. It's all I need. Maybe someday I'll change my mind, but for now it's just fine." She drew a long, slow breath, then exhaled. "Best of all, Jon keeps after Nelse as much as he can, trying to get him to get out of the house, but my stubborn brother's being a real stick-in-the-mud."

"Great pain, Nelson has," Mary said quietly. "Inside."

Estelle studied her in the glow of the street lamps. "Well, I sure wish he'd get over it. Very few families in this country came through the war without some personal loss along the way, including me. And we've all tried everything we know to help him. The worst thing is, he won't even come to church—and he used to be there whenever the doors opened, taking part. Now, though, the least little thing, and he's morbid as a graveyard."

Unsure of how to respond, Mary held her silence.

"Funny," Estelle said with a little frown, "he seemed in pretty good spirits earlier, when the two of you talked, while Mom was marking the hem of my new dress."

Mary shrugged, not knowing what to say.

"Well, maybe Jon can knock some sense into him for real. Sometimes I think that's what it's gonna take."

Giving the dark-haired girl's arm an empathetic squeeze, Mary wished she could think of something terribly wise to impart. But all she could hear was Corrie ten Boom encouraging the women prisoners to support each other and help anyone else who bore scars from war, whether inside or out.

She just had serious doubts about being the one to help Estelle's brother.

"Well," Mary ventured, "if not keeping company with boyfriend, maybe some weekend you have free time."

Estelle's piquant face came alive with pleasure. "I have free time every weekend!"

"Then, some shopping we do?" Mary tried not to seem too hopeful. "My apartment. It is—American word—boring. Some pictures I want. Plants. Things to make pretty."

"Oh, that would be fun! I would love to!" Estelle nibbled her lip in thought. "Would you mind if I come over sometime this week to get an idea about what kinds of things you might be able to use?"

"Sure. I make chicken noodle soup for us."

"Super. Well, let's see. I have church and choir tomorrow night, but Thursday's free. Would that be okay with you?"

"Fine. Thursday." The very thought cheered Mary no end. Company at her place, two nights from now. And two more after that, a whole day at the stores with Estelle. What could be better?

The wheeze and rumble of an approaching streetcar drew her out of her imaginings. Meeting her friend's smile, she leaned to give her a hug. "Such fun I have, knowing you. Thank you for supper."

"You're quite welcome. I'll see you tomorrow," Estelle responded.

"Bright and early," they both said in unison, and giggled.

Thoughts of the enjoyable evening with Estelle's family kept Mary from feeling her usual loneliness on the homeward ride. She mulled over the events again and again, remembering the delicious meal, the comforting Scripture, the wonderful oneness of the home.

But the conversation with Nelson she tucked into a different place in her heart, one she wasn't entirely sure she should visit. She'd be better off not encouraging him to talk at all. At least, not to her. She had enough pain of her own to deal with.

# Chapter 7

Wow! What a dish," Jonathan exclaimed after Stella and Mary took their leave. "Gotta get me a job at a sewing factory." He moved closer to the window, hands in his pockets, gawking up the street at the girls.

Nelson cast an unbelieving gaze toward the ceiling.

Jon caught the snide look as he swung around and crossed the room. "Come on, Man. Any guy can see she's a looker—silky blond hair, incredible eyes. . ."

"Yeah, unless he happened to be blind. But Mary Theresa's got a lot more going for her than just that gorgeous face. She happens to be a very sensitive person."

"Ah, now." Jonathan bent to Nelson's level, a knowing grin spreading from ear to ear. "Do I detect a slight note of interest here?"

*A slight note of interest?* It seemed the more Nelson tried to keep his thoughts from wandering to Mary, the less successful he was at it. But even he knew the pointlessness of entertaining any grand daydreams. He branded his friend with a scowl. "No. You're way off base, Pal. Anyway, I thought you were carrying the torch for Stella."

"Let's say I'm biding my time." Straightening, Jon slid his hands back into his trouser pockets and rocked back on his heels. "And no fair changing the subject. We were talking about Mary. How long have you known her?"

Expelling a weary breath, Nelson rattled off the details, his tone flat as a phonograph record. "She's a friend of Stella's who comes for supper now and then. But I'm not interested—in her or anyone else." A corner of his lip curled in disdain. "As if any dame would be desperate enough to want to be seen with a gimp."

Jon plopped his tall frame down to lounge on the couch, his long legs stretched out in front of him. "That's the sappiest thing that's ever come out of your mouth."

"You don't say. Well, it didn't take Nancy long to dump me when she got wind of my little mishap, did it? And she was supposed to love me forevermore, wasn't she?" Feigning indifference, Nelson returned his attention to the half-finished jigsaw puzzle, making an elaborate pretense of finding a particularly elusive piece.

Several uncomfortable minutes ticked by before Jon emitted a disgusted whoosh of air and stood. "Well, it doesn't appear you're in the mood for company tonight. I only came over here in the first place to see if you wanted to go for a ride in my new jitney."

Nelson perked up. "You got yourself a car?"

"Yeah. Well, okay, so it's not much to brag about—yet. Only set me back a hundred and fifty clams. But I figure I can knock out the dents in my spare time. Then, a coat of paint, and she'll be almost good as new."

Forgetting his aversion to leaving the house, Nelson lumbered to a standing position, unmindful of a few puzzle pieces that fell to the floor in the process. "This I gotta see."

"Well, well," Jon mused. "If I'd have known a bucket of bolts would be all it took to get you out of here, I'd have sprung for one months ago."

Nelson grabbed his crutches. "Just shut up and lead the way."

Outside, he gave his friend's '34 Ford Roadster the once-over, from the greyhound hood ornament to the whitewalled spare tire mounted above the back bumper. Though the flashy little vehicle showed its age, he could see obvious possibilities. The interior looked more than reasonable. He blew out a silent whistle. "Rumble seat and all, eh?"

"Yep." The word barely concealed the pride in Jon's voice. "And peppy. She's got a Flathead V-8. Belonged to one of the guys at the precinct, but his wife just had twins a couple months ago, so they needed something bigger. 'Course, it took me awhile to convince him of that," he said with a wink.

"Well, let's see what she can do." Nelson opened the door and eased himself inside, one hand still on his crutches as he inhaled the enticing smells particular to cars. Leather and grease and. . .adventure.

"Here, let me run those sticks up to the house," Jon offered. "I can grab 'em again when we get back."

On his return, he wasted no time in folding down the convertible top. "Might as well get the full effect," he said, his grin just shy of gloating. Taking the driver's seat, he started the engine and maneuvered the knob-handled gearshift into low, tooting a jaunty *aooogah* to Nelson's parents. When he pulled out onto the street, he headed westward.

*This is the life,* Nelson thought, reveling in the engine's purr, the feel of the wind tossing his hair in wild abandon as miles sped by, apartment buildings and shops on one side and the dark waters of the Hudson River on the other. *Too bad my little black coupe has been sitting and gathering rust since I went away. I should sell the thing and give Dad the money, since I'm never gonna use it.*

"How 'bout a soda?" Jon asked, turning to him. "I need some gas." Without waiting for a response, he pulled into a Texaco station just ahead on the right and nodded to the skinny, pimply attendant. "Fill 'er up, Kid."

While the boy pumped the fuel and washed the windshield, Jonathan strode inside the station and emerged with two nickel bottles of carbonated soda pop. He handed one to Nelson before starting off again.

Neither spoke for a short span until Jon braked for a traffic light. "Did you mean what you said back home, Nelse?" he asked. "About being a gimp?" He gulped several swallows of his drink.

"Well, what would *you* call a one-legged cripple?" Nelson groused.

"You don't have to be a cripple unless you wanna be," his friend chided. "So what if you have part of a leg missing? They did fit you with an artificial limb at rehab, didn't they?"

"Yeah. Right. Super deluxe model, flexible ankle joint, the whole bit. Smooth and shiny as a brand-new penny. Even wears one of my shoes."

"So, where is it?"

Nelson glowered at him. "In the closet. The stupid thing hurts my stump."

"It wouldn't once you got used to it. I know other guys who—"

"Look. Lay off, will you?" he railed. "I don't wanna talk about it. I'm tired, anyway. Let's head back."

"Okay, okay." Jonathan raised a hand in defense, a muscle working in his jaw as he clamped his mouth shut. But he didn't remain quiet for long. "But I might as well tell you this, as a friend, before you hear it from somebody else. I'm glad you didn't end up with Nancy Belvedere. She was messing around with Ray Baxter, down at the precinct, while you were off earning Bronze Stars and Purple Hearts. You deserve a whole lot better gal than her, anyway."

That piece of news floored Nelson. Could his fiancée really have been making a patsy out of him behind his back? He'd never once doubted her love. On the other hand, he'd never known Jonathan to lie either. The two of them went back a lifetime. But forcing his thoughts in a different direction during the oppressive silence as they motored homeward, the nagging truth of his friend's admonition regarding the replacement limb wouldn't let Nelson alone. It was his own fault he'd never become accomplished at walking with the thing. He hadn't been one to spend a lot of time practicing. Before, everything physical had always come easily. A little too easily. Maybe he should dig out that ugly contraption, give it another shot.

❧

"Let's run to Woolworth's for some lunch," Estelle suggested. "All this shopping has me starved."

Enjoying the beautiful Saturday, Mary Theresa nodded in agreement. The endless variety of merchandise available in American department stores never ceased to amaze and delight her. Having checked the newest designs in home fashion at Macy's and Gimbel's, she'd chosen only a few small items she could not resist, knowing the less expensive wares of the five-and-ten would be more within her means.

Their purchases firmly in hand, the two of them exited the main entrance to the bustling thoroughfare, then headed straight to the popular dime store, where they took stools at the lunch counter, paying no mind to shoppers browsing only a few feet away.

While her friend perused a menu from the chrome holder in front of them, Mary Theresa scanned the daily specials displayed on a small chalkboard. "Good. Today is hot roast beef sandwich. That I get," she told the slim, redheaded waitress. "And please, a glass of water."

"I think I'll have the grilled cheese," Estelle decided, "with potato chips and a lemonade."

With a crack of her chewing gum, the freckled girl gave a nod and went to fill their orders.

Mary feasted on her meal when it arrived, especially the mound of mashed potatoes with brown gravy. It tasted like a little bit of home. The Old Country.

"I think we've done pretty well so far, don't you?" Estelle commented before biting into the second half of her sandwich. "Those utensils in the rotating stand will look cute on your counter. And the matching towels and hot pads from Gimbel's will brighten that little kitchenette."

"Yes. Very pretty they are. But still I must find pictures to hang. Such plain walls." With a rueful shake of her head, Mary polished off the rest of her roast beef, increasingly eager to survey every remaining inch of Woolworth's store.

A few hours and a fair amount of money later, the two of them emptied their purchases in a heap on Mary Theresa's couch, draped their sweaters across its arm, and kicked off their shoes.

"The pictures I want to hang first," Mary declared, sorting through the stack for the framed pastels she'd chosen. Then her shoulders sagged. "Oh, no! A hammer we forget."

"Not necessarily," Estelle said with a smile. "I knew you wanted to spruce up your walls, so I tucked Mom's steak pounder and some tacks into my purse, just in case."

Mary seized the girl's slender frame in a hug. "Too much, you are. Thank you. Now we must get busy. This picture of wishing well and butterflies I think for over there, don't you?"

Long after they finished, had supper, and Estelle had gone home, Mary Theresa couldn't bring herself to turn off the light. Midnight was fast approaching, and she felt bone weary after the busy day, but she couldn't stop admiring their handiwork. What a difference homey touches like colorful throw pillows, inexpensive figurines, philodendron plants, and sheer curtain panels made in her little place. It looked almost. . .reborn.

With her heart filled to bursting, Mary Theresa slipped to her knees. She could think of no prayer from her years of catechism which could begin to express her deep gratitude, yet she sensed that the good things which had happened to her came from God. But how could she dare to approach Him in the familiar style some people had adopted?

*People like Corrie ten Boom and the Thomases were naturally good,* Mary reasoned. Like saints. They hadn't participated in the abominable acts she'd been subjected to at Ravensbruck. How could she expect a holy God to hear the innermost prayers of someone like her, someone so unworthy?

A fruitless wish rose to taunt her. If only she were pure, like Estelle and the Chudzik daughters. But the vile past could never be undone, and its black shroud bowed her shoulders with an oppressive weight of guilt and shame she could never forget.

*God loves us all,* she could hear Corrie admonish. *No matter how unworthy you may feel, He knows your heart. Each of you is precious in His sight. He wants you to come to Him. He is watching for you and waiting for you to come.*

Hoping that were true, longing for it to be true, Mary clasped her hands before her and swallowed the lump of apprehension clogging her throat. "Thank You, dear God," she whispered. "Thank You." Her prayer couldn't begin to express what she felt, but with her whole being she harbored the hope that it would somehow please Him.

# Chapter 8

"Whatever possessed me to wear my new shoes to work?" Estelle wailed after the trolley's doors whooshed shut and the conveyance pulled away. "I should have saved them for church. I just know I have a huge blister."

Accompanying her limping coworker home for what had evolved into a weekly get-together with Estelle's family, Mary slipped an arm around her. "Slow we walk. Not so much hurt."

Estelle gave a pained smile when they turned down her street. "They looked so stylish in the store window on Saturday. That's what I get for buying in haste." Suddenly she stopped. "Wait, this should help more than anything." Placing a hand on Mary's shoulder for balance, she slipped both shoes and anklets off entirely, revealing an angry, nickel-sized abrasion on one foot. "Mmm, much better." But tiny lines of distress fanned out from her eyes as she gingerly walked the rest of the way barefooted.

Even Mary was glad when they finally reached the portion of the tenement row house belonging to the Thomases. They mounted the steps and went inside.

"Well, well," Nelson remarked in the entry, grinning like the Cheshire cat in Christine Chudzik's favorite story. "Olympic's star seamstresses return home after a hard day at the factory."

Estelle just groaned and headed for the couch, where she collapsed with a sigh onto the slipcovered cushions.

But Mary had detected a decidedly cheerier tone than usual in Nelson's voice and glanced up at him. Then she realized something else. He seemed taller than she remembered. Why, he was standing! Without crutches! An unbidden smile of astonishment teased her lips.

"Thought it was high time I mastered the old peg leg," he quipped with a self-conscious shrug. "They say all it takes is practice, practice, and more practice. Either of you gals up to a little stroll around the block?" He looked from one to the other in speculation.

"Count me out," Estelle moaned. "It was all I could do to stroll home with this swell blister I acquired, compliments of my new shoes."

"Mary Theresa?" he asked tentatively, dark, even brows climbing to his mahogany hair in question. "I gotta warn you, though. I'm not very good at this yet, so I could very likely trip over one or both of my feet. . .in case you'd rather not risk the embarrassment of being seen with a clumsy oaf."

His poignant smile tore at her heart. In truth, Mary would have preferred to remain behind with Estelle. . .but not for the reason he suggested. Her aversion related to being alone with men—period. Still, the fact that Nelson was more concerned with her possible discomfort than his own struck a tender note in her spirit. He'd never given her cause not to trust him. And he looked so vulnerable, wobbling ever so slightly while he waited for her response. How could she refuse?

"Sure thing. I go. There is time?" she asked as he reached around to push the screen door open for her.

"Oh, you mean before supper. Yeah, Dad hasn't come in yet. Besides, I probably can't walk very far." Following her outside, Nelson stopped and turned, poking his head back inside. "Sis? Tell Mom we won't be too long, okay?" He let the door close with a bang.

Mary went down the steps first, then stood aside, trying not to show her alarm as he tackled the same feat, his movements haltingly slow and ungainly, his face scrunched up in concentration.

When he made it to the sidewalk, he flashed a toothy grin. "See? Easy as pie."

She couldn't suppress a smile. "This I see."

Letting him set the pace, Mary did her best to stay out of the way, yet remained close enough to offer assistance, just in case. The coming evening was sure to be a lovely one, with the mild ocean breeze gently stirring the treetops, occasionally tugging stray hairs loose from their pins. She let her gaze drift to the assortment of row homes on either side of the street, noticing the lamplight beginning to glow here and there behind the curtained windows. A sprinkle of children's laughter added a charm of its own.

"It's been pretty nice having you come to supper with Stella," Nelson said between grunts as he hobbled along. "She's been needing a friend. Most of her schoolmates are married now and busy with their own lives."

"Good for me too, she is. Only my host family I know—and yours—in America."

"Did you come from a large family back in Poland?"

A twinge of alarm skittered up Mary's spine, but at the sincerity in his voice, she willed her wariness aside. "Two brothers, one sister, our parents." Speaking of her departed loved ones didn't sting as much as she'd expected, though she knew the sadness would never completely go away.

"I'd like to hear about them someday," Nelson said, "when you feel like talking."

Mary slanted him a glance, noticing how the brown plaid shirt deepened his

174

eyes to a rich chocolate shade. "Perhaps. Someday."

He smiled then, a smile slow and gentle and filled with understanding.

She stifled a gasp as the world came to a sudden standstill.

Turning the next corner, Nelson stumbled. His hands flailed madly about, finally latching onto Mary in a desperate move to keep from falling.

She tamped down a rush of unwelcome memories and held her ground until he'd regained his balance.

"Sorry," he murmured, abashed as he released his grip. "Please forgive me. I was stupid to attempt this without a cane."

Still fighting for her own composure, Mary tried to ignore the lingering traces of his touch. Amazingly, she felt strangely bereft as they faded away —despite her loathsome experiences at the concentration camp. "Home you have the cane?" she blurted out. "I could get it."

Guilt colored Nelson's strong features as he shook his head. "I broke the fool thing, over my good knee. Pretty dumb, now that I think about it."

He had the most disarming way of making her smile, Mary realized. And she shouldn't be smiling. "Are you hurt?" she finally managed, subduing the uncustomary giddiness she so often felt in his presence. . .even as her practical side reminded her there could never be anything more than friendship between them.

"Naw. Except for my pride." Nelson started forward again, and she fell into step beside him. "At one time I was quite the athlete," he went on candidly. "Played football in high school; ran track for the sheer fun of it." He paused. "I thought my life was over when I found out I was a cr—I mean, lost my leg. For several months in the hospital, I was furious at the doctors for pulling me through."

"Some people were not so fortunate," Mary whispered, her eyes fixed on the sidewalk.

♦

The quiet reminder sliced through Nelson's conscience. Here he was, strong and healthy and walking around—however clumsily—in two shoes. While beside him was an angel-spirited beauty who'd had her whole family senselessly ripped away, yet she gave no murmur or complaint. What right did he have to gripe? Or more important, to blame God? Estelle had been right. So was Jon, and so was Mary. It was time he smartened up.

"Thanks." He looked at her with a half-smile. "For the reminder, I mean."

She lowered her lashes and kept the slow, laborious pace.

By the time they turned the final corner and were nearing home, Nelson's stump ached. He should have been content just to go to the corner and back on his first try, instead of overdoing things.

But he wouldn't have missed this walk for anything.

Enticing supper smells met them as he and Mary climbed the steps and went inside.

"Oh, good," his mom said. "Everything's ready. Soon as you two come to the table, we can eat."

&

"How is blister?" Mary Theresa asked as she took her place next to Estelle.

She gave her an agonized look. "The same. Sure hope I can find some comfortable shoes to wear to work tomorrow."

"I hope too."

Mr. Thomas waited until he had everyone's attention, then folded his hands and bowed his head. "We thank You, dear Lord, for Your wondrous provisions. Thank You for bringing our Mary back to us for another evening. Please continue to keep Your hand of blessing upon her day by day. And please touch Stella's foot and ease the discomfort she's feeling. Help us to be faithful to You always. Now bless this food so lovingly prepared for us all, in the name of Your precious Son. Amen."

Once again, Mary was touched by the prayer—and by the amazing concept that Almighty God would concern Himself with such trivial matters as blisters! Such a spirit of love pervaded this home, this family, she found herself counting the days until she could be here again. *Our Mary*, Estelle's father had called her. And heaven help her, she truly wished she were a part of them.

But she knew that could never be. Christians or not, some things simply could not be shared with these dear people. She couldn't bear the look she knew would be in their eyes. To be precious in God's eyes, that would have to be enough for her.

"Help yourself, Dear," Mrs. Thomas said, passing the stuffed cabbage. "I hope it's the way you like it."

Shaking off the cruel reality which had dampened her pleasant reverie, Mary smiled and took the bowl. "Delicious, it looks. Like back in Poland."

"Mom even made bread today," Estelle commented. "Since it goes so well with the dish."

"Enough chatter," Nelson teased. "There's a couple of hungry men waiting for the food to come our way."

Estelle tossed her thick hair and gave a mock salute. "Yes, Sir! Right away, Sir!" After placing two cabbage rolls on her plate, she passed the bowl to her father.

"How was the walk, Son?" the older man asked, his expression colored by a mixture of surprise and satisfaction. He nudged his bifocals a bit higher.

"Not too bad. Mary Theresa only had to carry me the last stretch." Filling his own plate, Nelson winked at her.

Mary decided she'd better give her whole concentration to the task of buttering the fresh, cloudlike bread.

After the meal ended, she helped her hostess clear the table while Estelle elevated her sore foot.

"I'm so happy to have you to supper with us," Mrs. Thomas said, putting on her apron and removing a second from the drawer for Mary.

"This I not need," she tried to protest.

But the older woman wouldn't be dissuaded. "No sense spoiling that pretty dress," she insisted, tying the strings snugly around Mary's waist, mothering her. "You have such lovely clothes."

Mary swallowed down a rush of emotion. "Thank you. Host family, the Chudziks, help me dress American."

"Well, they taught you well. Still, it can get quite warm here in the city in the summertime. You might consider some dresses with short sleeves. It's much cooler that way."

"Maybe new dresses I buy next summer," she placated, knowing the day would never come when she would expose those disgusting concentration camp identification numbers to the world.

"How long have you been in New York now?" Mrs. Thomas asked while the dishpan filled with water.

Mary fought to regain her serenity. "I think seven, maybe eight months."

"I do hope you like it here. There are lots of things to do in the city, places to go." She added dinner plates and glasses to the sudsy water.

"Yes. To museums the Chudziks are taking me sometimes. And parks."

"I'm glad. We really love having you here with us and would like to think you're happy in America."

Nodding, Mary reached for the first item set on the drain board. "Peace there is here. Not like back home. This I like. And your family."

With a teary smile and soapy hands, the little woman hugged her.

Not until the time came for Mary to leave did she remember that Estelle wouldn't be able to walk her to the trolley. Mary wasn't exactly fearful of navigating the streets at night, and it was only two blocks to the stop. Surely she could manage that short distance.

But Nelson lumbered to his feet as she headed for the door. "Thought I'd keep you company."

"Safe I am. Truly. No need to come."

He raised a hand to quiet her protests. "I need all the practice I can get, remember?"

"Are you sure, Son?" Mr. Thomas asked from his customary parlor chair. "I could drive her home in my car."

"Yeah, Dad. I intend to walk as much as I possibly can."

Alarm jolted her heart, but what could she say? A quick good-bye to Estelle and her parents, and Mary again started up the street with the one young man in the world she knew she'd be wiser to avoid.

Nelson's gait was still quite awkward, and Mary sensed this walk caused him even more discomfort, but they had plenty of time before the next streetcar arrived.

When they finally gained the stop, Nelson reached inside the sweater he'd put on and drew out a book. "I have something for you. Sort of a thank-you for putting up with a clumsy oaf. It's not much."

Mary took the volume he held out, its leather cover soft and flexible beneath her fingertips. "Oh!" she gasped. "A Bible it is! I cannot—"

"Yes, you can. It's not that great, Mary. Just my old one. It's pretty marked up and all, so I hope you don't mind. Mom and Dad bought me a new Bible not long ago. It's silly letting this collect dust on my bookshelf. And the way you seemed to admire Mom's. . .I'd like you to have it."

Fighting against a stinging behind her eyelids, Mary Theresa could barely utter a word. "Thank you," she somehow said around her tight throat.

When the night breeze tossed a stray lock of hair into her eyes, Nelson reached to brush it away, the touch of his fingertips warming her to her toes. The subdued light revealed a longing in his eyes that she'd never glimpsed before, and it changed the rhythm of her pulse.

The approaching trolley rumbled to a stop just then, and Nelson handed her up. "Good night, Mary Theresa."

She smiled past the mistiness in her eyes and stumbled blindly to a seat, silently voicing her thankfulness to God that the streetcar had come along when it had. . . because otherwise she might have kissed Nelson Thomas.

# Chapter 9

Aware that she was beginning to nod off, Mary Theresa blinked and peered through heavy eyelids at the alarm clock beside her bed. Two A.M. already? But it was worth the loss of sleep. She closed the Bible Estelle's brother had given her and hugged it to her heart. *Thank You for granting my dearest wish.* Like a soul coming out of a famine, she'd already struggled through a portion of the New Testament, flipping through in search of familiar passages, laboring over the outdated English words, yet determined to conquer them.

She noticed that Nelson had underlined verses here and there, often with an addition of a written note or related reference along the margin in a neat, strong hand. Even though some of the comments were beyond her understanding, she still stopped to peruse them whenever she came to one, pondering new meanings and concepts.

So far, she admitted with a yawn, all seemed to coincide with the wonderful things Corrie ten Boom passed along to her and the other women at the death camp. And that only increased her hunger to know more.

"A new day is tomorrow." Then with supreme reluctance, she laid the treasured Book on her night table. A Bible all her own. No reason to hurry. She would read slowly, as her limited command of the language necessitated, starting with the Gospel of John, where she'd discovered the sewn-in ribbon marker had been placed. And she would savor every word.

Turning to her side, Mary snuggled into her pillow, her thoughts a delicious blend of Scripture verses and the evening stroll with Estelle's very charming brother. His voice still rang in her mind, and her heart skipped at the memory of the longing she'd seen in his eyes in that unguarded moment. Even yet, it reawakened yearnings she had buried long ago and never planned to resurrect.

Inside, she knew she should not dwell on even the smallest of such forbidden pleasures. But still. . .what could it hurt just to think about him for a little while, to imagine she was just like other young women, just for tonight. . . ?

❧

Nelson rose from the upholstered chair when his parents came downstairs dressed for prayer meeting. "Thought I'd tag along this time—if you don't mind a slowpoke, that is." He'd practiced walking throughout the day and already could detect marginal improvement since those first two attempts last night with Mary Theresa. She'd been very enjoyable company, and he'd appreciated the opportunity of getting to know her a little. He'd never met anyone so shy. Something about her plucked an unplayed chord inside his spirit, though he still doubted that any woman could find him appealing, least of all someone as perfect as she. No, better to think of her as a friend and be grateful for that much.

Aside from that, he rather hoped for a chance to talk to the pastor after church.

A look of elation passed between the older couple before his dad grabbed him in a bone-crushing hug, wrinkling Nelson's best suit. "Remind me to thank Jon and Mary for whatever they did to get you to return to the land of the living," the older man teased.

"Hey, did I miss something?" Stella asked, straightening the waistband of her pleated charcoal skirt as she traipsed down from her room, a false pout on her lips. "I thought I heard someone mention Mary."

Mom just smiled. "Your father just commented on how indebted we are to that dear girl. Leave the parlor light on, Nelson. I don't like coming home to a dark house."

Stella shot a glance to Nelson and placed a hand over her heart in pretend shock. "Don't tell me you have deigned to honor us with your presence at the Wednesday night service."

"Shut up, Squirt," he countered, purposely flicking a lock of her curly hair into her face.

Hardly offended by the brotherly prank, she wrinkled her nose at him and followed their parents out to their old four-door sedan, with Nelson lagging behind.

A reasonably short drive took them to the stately brick church a stone's throw from Central Park, where the older couple had met, married, and remained members in the ensuing years. Nelson couldn't have imagined his family going elsewhere.

"As I live and breathe," Pastor Herman said, striding to meet their little group when they entered the sanctuary a scant few minutes before the service. Of medium height with a wiry build, the man ran his long fingers through his thatch of white hair and headed straight to Nelson, a warm smile revealing perfect dentures. "Welcome back, young man. It's good to see you again. This is an answer to prayer."

"Yours and everybody else's," Nelson supplied with a droll grin while they shook hands. "Sorry it took so long."

"The Lord has all the time in the world, Son," he returned kindly, then greeted the rest of the family before turning his attention to Nelson once more. "You're with the rest of your 'family' now, my boy. A few of our brave servicemen didn't make it back from the war, I'm sad to say, but I'm sure you'll see some familiar faces. It's time to get started, so have yourself a seat, and I'll steer a couple folks your way after the service."

Only too happy to oblige, Nelson followed Stella, taking the spot between her and his mom, with his father occupying the aisle seat. After nodding and waving to a half-dozen individuals whose attention their arrival had roused, he let his gaze drink in the familiar painted and paneled surroundings, walnut pews and altar, high ceiling, and burgundy-carpeted aisles. A sight he'd sorely missed during the European conflict.

Before he'd chosen to study engineering, he had often pictured himself occupying a similar pulpit, commanding the attention of a large congregation who hung on his every word. But those youthful dreams no longer held appeal. Now he was content just to listen to a man of God passing on the rich nuggets of truth gleaned from hours of study and prayer.

From the opening of the service, when the organist played "Shall We Gather at the River?" to the end of this installment in the minister's sermon series on the cross of Jesus as foretold throughout the Bible, Nelson sensed his spirit absorbing the presence of the Lord as a dry sponge soaked up water.

"So you see," the preacher said in conclusion, holding his open Bible aloft, "we have in Isaiah fifty-three yet another vivid word picture of our suffering Savior, one written hundreds of years before His birth in Bethlehem. From Genesis to Revelation, God has provided unmistakable portraits of His Son, the 'Lamb slain from the foundation of the world.' His wondrous plan for reconciling fallen man unto Himself is revealed from cover to cover throughout His holy Word. Let us bow in prayer."

Afterward, the congregation broke up into small groups to pray for the individual needs of the members and others. Nelson, however, caught the pastor's eye, and the white head tipped in the direction of his study, an invitation Nelson promptly accepted. He made his way there as quickly as his uneven gait would allow.

"What can I do for you, Son?" Pastor Herman closed the door behind them, gesturing toward an armchair facing his massive desk before taking the worn leather one behind it for himself.

The man's appearance, Nelson noted, was as neat and orderly as the room had always been as far back as he could remember. Small things, yet they instilled trust and confidence. And those sharp blue eyes, though discerning, always put a person at ease. "I'm not sure. I just need to talk to somebody who doesn't live with me. Confess, maybe. That's supposed to be good for the soul."

"Quite. It's another example of obedience. The New Testament encourages us to confess our faults to one another."

"I understand." He paused. "I guess what I have to say is, it's finally gotten through my thick skull that I've been blaming God for letting me lose a leg, when I should have been thanking Him for saving my life. All these months I've been wallowing in self-pity. What a waste. I really need to make things right and start living for God again. Just wanted you to know."

A gentle smile appeared on the pastor's mouth. "It's very gratifying to hear that, Nelson. The folks here at church have been praying for you for a long time. I'd suggest you consider making your rededication public some Sunday, letting them know their prayers have been answered."

"Thank you, Sir. You're right. I probably should do that." Limping down that long carpeted aisle while everyone watched would take some courage—and that he was starting to regain, thanks to Mary Theresa's willingness to help him practice. Had she opened and read the Bible he'd passed along to her? Would she search the pages until she found the peace she so needed?

The minister's smile widened into the grin Nelson remembered. "I'm real glad to have you back, Son." Rising, he came around the desk and clamped an encouraging hand on Nelson's shoulder.

ra

Mary Theresa gave her finished work a final count the following Tuesday, before returning it to the basket to be turned in.

"Another long, long day," Estelle commented, covering her own machine. She placed a hand on her spine and arched her back a little. "Time for us to go home for supper."

"Getting tired of me your family must be," Mary said, expressing one of her fears.

"Not a chance. They look forward to having you eat with us every week. In fact, Mom and Dad have really taken to you. They talk about you as if you're their long-lost daughter—which is fine with me. I always wished I had a sister." Picking up her production quota, Estelle headed for the clerk's counter, the skirt of her floral print dress swaying.

*And Nelson,* Mary wanted to ask. *What about him? Does he speak of me too?* She was eager to know how the walking was coming along, among other things. Spending much of her free time in his old Bible gave her a clearer picture of the man inside, and the deeply spiritual person he'd been before the war awed her. A large part of her envied that intimate relationship he'd had with God before he'd been severely wounded. Would he ever recover it? Would she ever find her way to her own peace? Expelling a breath, Mary leaned down for her basket, then followed her friend.

"Is everything okay with you, Mare?" Estelle asked over the rumble of the trolley on their way home. "You've been quiet for days."

Mary patted her friend's hand, noticing that she and Estelle both sported on their fingers the ever-present traces of pinpricks so common among sewing factory employees. "On my mind there is much. Every night, staying up late, reading, reading."

"Must be a swell book!"

"Yes. The Bible."

"Oh." Estelle seemed a bit taken aback for a second. "Well, if you come across anything puzzling, Nelson's a good one to ask. He usually knows the answer. At least, he always did before he left for the war. In our church's youth group, he was the captain of the quiz team, forever drilling everybody else in memory verses and Bible facts."

*Interesting*, Mary thought. But she really couldn't bother him with her trivial questions. She needed to put distance between them again, concentrate on her friendship with Estelle, as she had in the beginning.

"Thank goodness he finally started coming to church again," her friend continued. "He went with us last Wednesday night and twice last Sunday. I've even been seeing him studying his Scofield the way he used to."

That last bit of news filled Mary with unexpected joy. Up and around on his artificial leg, and back at church? Perhaps he truly had made his peace with God. "And you?" she probed. "In your room a Bible I see. Do you read every day?"

Estelle shifted in her seat, her cheeks taking on a pinkish hue. "I, um, don't always give it the time I should, I'm afraid."

"In Poland, no Bible I have," Mary said quietly. "The priests only have them. But I think, in country with so many Bibles, everybody read."

"Not as many as one might expect." Turning to her, Estelle spoke with candor. "I used to read through the Scripture from cover to cover every year. But when Ken, my fiancé, was killed, I hit a pretty low spot. After that, I didn't pick it up for ages."

"Yes," Mary agreed. "To part with loved one is not easy."

"I might have known you'd understand." She lowered her gaze to the worn floorboards. "I must admit, I questioned the purpose to life—all the while seriously doubting there was one. Of course, I still went to church during those dark days. Heaven forbid my parents should see how weak their darling girl's faith was."

Mary nodded but didn't respond.

"Now," her friend babbled on, "I've gone back to reading through my Bible again. As far as delving into the heavy stuff, though, I kind of leave that to guys who want to be preachers." She flashed an embarrassed grin. "I know, I shouldn't feel that way. And my conscience has been niggling me about it. The Lord expects His followers to be able to provide answers regarding their faith."

Mary really wanted more than that. She wished Estelle would also provide more answers about her brother. But plying her with endless questions would hardly be wise. The man was already on Mary's mind a little too much. When she studied his Bible, it seemed she could hear his voice doing the reading. Somehow, that had to stop.

Arriving at the Thomases', she found Nelson looking comfortable and way too appealing in the easy chair by the radio, his legs propped on the matching hassock. His new black Bible lay open in his lap.

He glanced up with a smile as they disposed of their purses. "Hi, Sis. Hi, Mary. What's new?"

"New? At the salt mines?" His sister snickered. "You've got to be kidding."

Obviously unaffected, he switched his attention from her and zeroed in on Mary, a twinkle in his wide-set eyes. "How about you? Read any good books lately?"

"One only," Mary answered evenly, knowing he understood.

But Estelle filled in the blanks. "She's been reading the Bible. And I volunteered you, O knowledgeable one, to help her with all her questions."

Mary didn't know whether to blush or blanch, she had such a rush of anticipation, mixed with fear and embarrassment.

Nelson, however, displayed a mouthful of healthy teeth with his easy grin. "I was just about to go out for another daily constitutional—which, thanks to Dad, shouldn't be such a chore this time." Producing a cane from beside the chair, he waved it with a flourish. "Want to keep me company, Mary Theresa? Any questions you might have, just ask away."

Mary figured she'd probably come to regret spending more time with the object of so many of her wayward thoughts. But surely she had things in their proper perspective now. If she kept her focus on biblical questions only, maybe it would be all right. Or so she told herself. "Sure. I go."

# Chapter 10

That's quite the cloud bank rolling in off the ocean," Nelson commented upon reaching the sidewalk outside. "We've been needing a good rain."

Mary checked the sky, then matched his pace as they set out on their trip around the block. She immediately noticed a new smoothness in his steps now that he had the aid of a cane. Obviously, he had been practicing, and the extra effort showed. And she didn't mind admitting he looked wonderful, despite his limp. So manly and appealing as the slanted rays of the sun gilded the planes of his face.

With an inward sigh, she diverted her gaze to the row houses lining the road. A variety of delectable suppers emitted their mouth-watering smells into the early evening air, to be blended together occasionally by the breeze from a passing car. Any minute and her stomach was sure to growl and embarrass her.

"So, you've been reading the Bible, eh?" Nelson asked casually.

Mary had wondered how and when he'd bring up the subject. "Yes."

"So have I, thanks to you."

The unexpected statement caught her by surprise. She swung a glance his way and saw a warm grin reflecting its glow in his light brown eyes. And for a precious few seconds, she imagined they were like any other couple out for a pleasant stroll.

His voice brought her back to earth. "Before you started coming home with Stella," he began, "I'd resigned myself to spending the rest of my days in that easy chair in our front room, feeling sorry for myself. I'd shut the Lord out of my life, feeling it was all His fault I'd lost a leg. He was supposed to take care of me, you see. Or so I believed. It took you to make me realize He really had looked out for me, after all."

A little unsure of his meaning, Mary gave him a questioning look.

"The shell that wounded me took my army buddy's life. It could have just as easily taken mine too."

"Oh." Thinking of the raft of relatives and friends who had been wrenched out of her world, Mary Theresa had no trouble at all relating to his loss. "You lose the friend. That pain I know." She averted her gaze to a noisy group of children in the street who'd ceased their game of kick-the-can until she and Nelson passed.

"Somehow I doubt my losing one pal measures up to what you've gone through," he added, once they were beyond the range of activity.

Not about to illuminate him on that understatement, Mary stared straight ahead, content to let him do the talking. As long as he was the topic instead of her, she had no fears.

They turned the next corner, and Nelson resumed where he'd left off.

"Just knowing that you understand has helped me. Got me moving again, at long last."

"I am glad."

He stopped abruptly and turned to her. "By the way, Mary Theresa, I hope you don't mind me butting in between you and Stella. I know she's the reason you come over. I'll try not to monopolize you from now on. But I just wanted you to know I appreciate your letting me ramble on. It's like having another sister." He started forward again.

Rambling was the last thing Mary would have called the moving account he had just shared. . .but the "sister" part burst the tiny bubble she'd allowed to start growing in her dreams. She let out a stoical breath and caught up to Nelson. After all, she knew better than to dream in the first place.

As if sensing the change in atmosphere, Nelson reverted to the original subject. "Stella says you have some questions pertaining to the Bible?"

Mary relaxed and shrugged a shoulder. "Not a big question. Just a little one."

"And it's about. . . ," he said, coaxing her on.

"The notes you are writing on the sides of the pages. Such as at the supper, when Jesus is washing the disciples' feet."

"Oh, yeah," he said with a wry grimace. "Sorry about all my scribbling. I should have gotten you a new Bible."

"No. The writing, this is fine," she quickly assured him. "Sometimes a big help, especially with English words I not understand."

He appeared to contemplate her statement for a moment. "Then what's the problem?"

She cocked her head back and forth, wondering how to put her thoughts into English. "About Judas you write. Jesus knows he is enemy, but still He washes the feet."

"Oh, that," Nelson said, his expression one of relief. "That thought was from one of our pastor's sermons at church. He was preaching on forgiveness, on how the Lord ministered even to His worst enemies. How He knew the heart of man, yet loved mankind in spite of it. He was always ready to forgive."

Mary slowly shook her head. "I do not know about this forgiving of the enemies. Sometimes that is a very hard thing."

While the setting sun turned Mary's hair to spun gold around her lovely face, Nelson watched an array of emotions play over her exquisite features. His heart went out to her. He could not imagine someone so fragile in appearance having to deal with enemies as vile as the Nazis. If anyone had deserved to be spared from the horrible things that had befallen her country, Mary had. There was something incredibly special about her. And whatever it was, it convinced him that if he had known her before the war, he would have gladly protected her— even single-handedly—from the entire German army.

Of course, before those events occurred, he had been able-bodied. Strong. Whole.

And it wasn't true that he thought of her like a sister. Quite the opposite. But he couldn't allow himself to entertain foolish notions of a more personal nature. One rejection was more than enough to get past. He swallowed a lump in his throat. *Dear Lord, help me to find the right words. Speak through me to help this searching soul.*

"You're right, my friend," he told her. "It is hard to forgive people who've wronged us or caused us harm. It goes against our nature. I felt exactly that same way when I fell on the battlefield. In fact, until the last week or so, I doubted I would ever find a shred of forgiveness inside for anyone I felt was responsible for maiming me."

"But now?" she asked. "You can forgive?"

The depth of pain in her blue green eyes was almost more than Nelson could bear. Her entire family, dead. Such awful suffering had been forced upon this angel-woman. "Yes," he said gently. "But only because the Lord gave me the strength I needed. I couldn't have done it otherwise."

A sad smile softened her lips, and her eyes took on a faraway look. "Those words someone else said. We forgive because God forgives." A ragged breath came from deep inside. "Still, is a hard thing."

Without even thinking about it, Nelson reached over with his free arm and hugged her. "I know, Mary Theresa. I know."

❧

In reflex, Mary almost stiffened and shrugged out of Nelson's embrace, even though she knew it was only a gesture of comfort. But then, she remembered. He considered her just another *sister*. He had no designs on her. She had nothing to fear from him.

As quickly as it occurred, the hug ended.

She tried not to assign to his action any more importance than it deserved. Drawing on one of the most valuable talents she'd acquired at Ravensbruck, she kept her expression passive and did not display any emotion whatsoever.

"Was there anything else you were wondering about?" he asked, as though nothing had happened.

"Small things."

"Well, if you'd like to spell them out, I'll do my best to explain them."

Noticing they were approaching the house, Mary just smiled. "Next time, maybe."

"You got it." His expression took on a sudden brightness. "Say, if you're free on Sunday, you might consider coming to church with us. Our pastor is wonderful in explaining spiritual matters, and he lays things out so simply, even a blockhead like me can understand them."

She met his gaze. "Maybe. Some Sunday."

"Great. Hey, we made it back already." Nelson turned onto the walk leading to the front steps.

Mary put on her best smile and followed, preceding him inside when he paused to open the screen door for her.

"Oh, you're back, you two," Estelle remarked from the dining room. She came toward them, several pieces of silverware still in her hands as she peered outside. "Are we in for a storm? I've been watching the sky."

Mary had completely forgotten the clouds they'd mentioned earlier.

"Wouldn't be surprised," Nelson said. "The radio announcer said a squall might be headed this way."

Wondering if it could possibly compare to the one raging inside her, Mary effected her original cheerfulness and turned to Estelle. "Needing help?"

"Sure. Extra hands are always welcome here."

❧

The ticking of the bedside clock was barely audible against the pounding rain. Feeling utterly worn out, Mary Theresa made no attempt to read her Bible into the late hours. She lay curled up beneath all the blankets she possessed, summer or not, trying to dispel the chill inside her as she mulled over her visit to the Thomases, the more-than-pleasant walk with Nelson.

*You have no right to feel slighted,* she lectured herself. *You forget you must not think about Estelle's brother.*

"But he is so nice to think about," came her reply in the stillness.

*He is a good man. Not like the others. A man of pure thoughts. Too pure for you.*

There was no argument against the truth. Clenching her teeth, Mary turned over, covers and all, and expelled a weary sigh.

The aggravating jangle of the alarm clock jolted her awake. Astonished that she'd dozed at all, Mary wondered how in the world she would get through this day. She got up and washed with cold water to help revive herself, then grabbed the first dress she touched and put it on.

Shortly thereafter, when she arrived at the factory, she took comfort from knowing Estelle would be there. She headed straight for the machine.

Mary's spirit took a nosedive. Mrs. Hardwick stood waiting for her. What on earth could she want? "Good morning," she ventured, wishing Estelle had come early. But her friend's machine still wore its muslin cover.

"Malinowski." No actual smile ever made an appearance on the supervisor's mouth. In fact, Mary decided, the only variance in the woman's demeanor occurred when it revealed anger rather than irritation. "You'll be moving to an electric machine today. One of the girls quit yesterday."

"I will? I–I mean. . .yes, Madam." A better machine. Faster work. That meant more pay.

It also meant a different location.

Any elation she might have felt vanished like hoarfrost in the hot sun.

"Come along. We'll get you set up."

Clutching her purse to her chest, Mary trudged behind the surly matron, counting machines as they went. One, two, three. . . How far from Estelle was she going to end up? Fifteen, sixteen. . .

Eventually Mary quit counting.

When Mrs. Hardwick finally halted their march, Mary looked back across the cavernous room. The new—or rather, better—machine couldn't have been farther from her old location unless it had been in an entirely different building.

"Those are your supplies," the woman announced, gesturing toward a metal rack lining the end wall. "You'll find your new quota posted on the machine." With something akin to a smirk, she turned on her heel and strode away.

Mary hugged herself as she took a deep breath and slowly let it out. Olympic Sewing Factory suddenly reminded her a whole lot of a forced labor camp.

# *Chapter 11*

Just finishing up another shirt collar when the noon bell rang, Mary added the article to the others in her basket, then turned off her machine. She snatched her lunch bag and thermos from the bottom drawer and made a beeline for Estelle, approaching her friend from behind. Mischievously, Mary leaned over to peek into the brunette's face.

"There you are!" A look of profound relief subtracted frown lines from Estelle's perpetually cheerful expression. "I've been getting a stiff neck all morning trying to find you."

Smiling, Mary cast a wistful look at her old machine, still bearing stacks of unfinished sleeve parts, as if waiting for her to sit down and get to work. Perhaps it was being serviced and oiled for its next attendant. "A nice day, it is. Outside we eat?"

"Sure. Just let me grab my stuff."

Not wanting to waste any of the limited time available, they hurriedly exited the factory. Along the exterior of the drab, tan building, other Olympic workers stretched their legs and chatted. A few smoked cigarettes. Mary and Estelle filled their lungs with the fresh ocean breeze, appreciating even a short respite from the stuffy confines of the workplace as they made their way toward a shaded bench half a block's distance away.

"Where on earth did you end up?" Estelle asked on their walk. "When I arrived at my machine and saw a stranger occupying yours, I felt like I'd lost my only friend."

"My machine? A new girl there is?" After all the effort Mary had put forth to meet her quota on the old relic, she'd nevertheless harbored a slim hope that her move would prove temporary. And the fact that no one had been occupying it when she reached Estelle gave the impression that it was vacant. Now she knew she must accept the grim reality of permanence.

"Yes," Estelle moaned as they took seats. "Gertrude something or other. She's nice enough and all, but the girl is all thumbs, and that's no exaggeration. Maybe it's from trying too hard or something, but so far, she's managed to break two needles, chip a tip off her scissors, and she has yet to do a single sleeve properly."

Remembering how awkward she'd felt on her own first day, Mary couldn't help chuckling.

Estelle rolled her eyes. "Old Lady Hardwick's been breathing down our necks all morning, barking orders. Needless to say, I didn't want to risk drawing even more attention by asking after your whereabouts." She reached into her lunch sack and took out an apple.

"Poor you." Mary Theresa sympathized as she unwrapped a ham and cheese sandwich and began eating.

As always, Estelle bowed her head for a brief prayer before biting into the crisp fruit. "Poor me!" she exclaimed afterward. "What about you? Where'd she stick you?"

"Other end of world," Mary quipped wryly. "Against back wall. Too much we were liking work together, I think."

"No doubt." Estelle's light laugh somehow lacked mirth. "Well, at least on sunny days we can come here and have a short visit. Have you made a friend at your new station?" She crunched into her apple, a teasing gleam in her eye. "It probably won't take much to replace me, sad to say."

A sheepish grin broke across Mary's lips. "English I pretend not understanding. What good is to make friend, if just to split up?"

At that, Estelle smiled and shook her head. "You're right." Then she sighed. "Lunch is the only time we'll have now. And I'd really started enjoying our snatches of conversation each new day. It made coming to work much more pleasurable."

"For me too." The hot tea which usually perked Mary up during the break now only made her sleepy. Considering her restlessness throughout the previous night, she knew it would be a struggle to stay awake until quitting time. She poured out the contents of the thermos cup and recapped the bottle, then brushed the crumbs from her lap onto the sidewalk for the pigeons cooing about them. So much leisure time the birds had, strutting about in the mild, clean air.

"Well, you'll still be coming to supper on Tuesday nights. Okay?" Estelle asked a little too brightly. "At least we'll have something to look forward to in this new, otherwise colorless existence."

Mary feigned a smile, her best attempt to match her friend's levity. "Maybe. Sure."

Mutually disappointed at this new turn of events, they lapsed into a short span of silence, watching the passing traffic as they ate.

Suddenly Estelle stopped chewing. "Hey! I have an idea!"

"What is it?"

"On the other hand," she said tentatively, "I guess it depends on whether you already go to church somewhere on Sundays. Does your host family come to get you every week?"

"No. Other direction is Saint Hedwig's. Not to bother, I tell them. Other churches near me." Mary shrugged. "But go, I do not. To walk in alone, sit alone. . ."

Estelle's chocolate eyes focused on her. "Then it's settled. You're coming with me and my family to church on Sundays. We'll come by and pick you up. Afterward, you can have dinner with us. It'll help make up for being separated at work. What do you think?"

Mary hesitated. "More bother I would be."

"Are you kidding?" With a look of disbelief, Estelle leaned closer and hugged her. "You couldn't be a bother if you tried. But—" She sobered. "If you think you'd feel uncomfortable attending worship with us, don't think you have to come just to please me. I'll understand."

"New to me is this Protestant church," Mary admitted. "How to know if I like or not like?"

"You mean, you'll actually give it a try?"

At the hope in her friend's dark eyes, Mary didn't have the heart to refuse. *Besides,* she told herself, *perhaps it won't be so very different from what I am used to.* After all, they did worship the same God. And what could it hurt, to spend an extra day with these dear people who made her feel so at home? Or to be around Nelson. . .

❧

"This must be it," Nelson heard his father say as he steered into an empty space along the right curb. He applied the hand brake, then turned off the engine.

"Right, Daddy. I'll go get Mary." Seated behind their father, Estelle opened her door and jumped out. In a matter of seconds, she disappeared into the broad foyer of a squat two-story building whose ground floor housed a watch repair shop on one side and a millinery on the other. Above were a number of apartments.

Since his door was on the passenger side, Nelson also got out to wait by the car. No sense making Mary Theresa walk around the entire vehicle to get in. He slid one hand into the pocket of his dress slacks and idly assessed the neighborhood, noting other neatly kept establishments interspersed by occasional large dwellings. Fair-sized maples and box elder trees provided mottled shade to the sidewalks lining the street.

Detecting the approaching chatter and giggles that invariably preceded his bubbly sister, he turned to see her emerge and start down the steps. The squirt looked particularly appealing with her dark waves gleaming against the vibrant cranberry red dress Mom had finished a few days before. Her white hat and high heels accented the tiny polka dots and white trim, enhancing her shapely legs. *Not bad,* Nelson decided, *even for a sister.*

But when Mary Theresa stepped into view, a ray of sunshine lit upon the fairest rose in all the kingdom. In a filmy long-sleeved dress of delicate pink, she needed no adornment but the strand of pearls gracing her neck. Beneath a small, straw-colored hat, and freed from the normal confinement of rolls and pins, her side-parted hair fell to her shoulders in a soft honey-gold pageboy. A pearl barrette rested behind one ear.

Nelson had to remind himself to close his mouth.

Maybe this wasn't such a great idea, taking her to church. . .where any guy with eyes in his head was certain to snap her up.

The loveliest of smiles parted her lips as she and Stella approached. "Good morning, everybody," she said, oblivious to the glorious vision she made.

"Morning," they all chorused.

Nelson gave himself a mental shake, then cleared his throat. "Hope you don't mind the middle." He moved aside to allow Mary enough room to climb in while Stella went around to her seat.

"Is fine," she said softly, lifting her lashes to meet his gaze. Pausing, she handed him her Bible to hold, then turned and lowered herself to the seat. "Oh!" she gasped, as the narrow ruffle at her wrist snagged on his watch.

"No problem." Nelson freed the errant thread almost as quickly as it had caught.

But not quickly enough to prevent that glimpse of her delicate forearm.

Or the numbers tattooed in black.

Feeling as if he'd just taken a punch to the stomach, Nelson climbed in beside Mary. A barrage of questions, like the rat-tat-tat of an enemy machine gun, shot through his mind. What untold horrors had those remarkable eyes witnessed? Had her own family been slaughtered in front of her? And what about her? What kinds of tortures had those inhuman Nazi animals inflicted on this fragile creature, with no one to protect her from harm?

Why hadn't bigmouth Stella made some mention of her friend's background. . . unless Mary had kept the fact that she'd been imprisoned in a concentration camp a secret even from her.

And if so, why?

In any event, a lot of things suddenly made a whole lot of sense.

&

"Oh, isn't this just the grandest of days?" Estelle gushed, straightening her skirt as the car pulled out into the light Sunday traffic. Retrieving her slim shoulder bag and Bible from the window ledge behind the seat, she placed them on her lap.

"Yes, simply delightful," her mother replied. She turned to Mary, a gracious smile plumping her cheeks. "We're so happy you could come with us this morning, Dear."

Returning the older woman's smile, Mary Theresa nodded. Her insides quavered as she tried to ignore being crammed a touch too closely to Nelson in the backseat of the family car. She could feel the warmth emanating from him. Or was it her? Had he seen the loathsome brand she'd been so careful to hide from the world? Did he know her shame?

She doubted she could bear knowing if he'd discovered her dreaded secret, yet the possibility of not knowing seemed somehow even less bearable. Hesitantly, she raised a timid gaze in his direction.

Nelson seemed absorbed in the passing scenery. But as if sensing her attention, he turned to her, the typically friendly smile on his lips and in his eyes.

His face revealed nothing!

Mary dared to relax. Somewhat.

"Oh, look, Mom," Estelle said. "They've painted that charming little shop we like so much. And added shutters. Doesn't it look absolutely divine?"

Mary tuned out the exchange between mother and daughter and concentrated instead on how incredibly dashing her friend's brother looked in the navy serge suit he wore. The tie knotted at his throat had flecks of the same light brown as his eyes, and his shiny mahogany hair had been neatly slicked back. All that walking in the sunshine had added an appealing light bronze cast to his clear complexion, only increasing his appeal.

Mary barely suppressed an unbidden sigh.

If circumstances had only been different, had she been born in America instead of Poland, perhaps she could have been Nelson's girl.

*What are you thinking?* she berated herself. *You are here to attend church with this family. For you, that is more than you should have expected.*

"Well," Mr. Thomas announced in his usual pleasant way, "we're here." He turned the car onto a street running alongside the church and parked in the first available spot.

The men got out first. Nelson gave no indication it had been a struggle. He'd certainly made remarkable progress since the last time Mary had seen him. He opened his mother's door, offered a hand to her, and then to Mary.

Placing her cool fingers into his much warmer ones, Mary again chanced a look at him. Surely he must have caught a glimpse of the wretched tattoo. How could he not? It practically shouted out her shame. He had to know.

But if he did, he gave no sign of it.

# Chapter 12

This small, but tidy, place of worship seemed nowhere near the size of the churches which Mary Theresa had visited during her lifetime. But she found the pristine white steeple crowning the red brick structure quite charming, with its plain metal cross gilded by sunlight against the cloudless sky. She sensed a cordial welcome among the other arrivals greeting one another with smiles and handclasps. Nevertheless, a tiny niggle of unfamiliarity fluttered inside her like a flock of butterflies, and she wondered what to expect.

The bell in the tower pealed as the family headed for the steps leading to the main entrance. "Late again," moaned Estelle as she picked up the pace.

Once inside, Mary caught only the briefest glimpse of the sanctuary upon entering the foyer. Estelle grabbed a hand and drew her to a downward staircase, with Nelson following cautiously behind. Mr. and Mrs. Thomas headed in an entirely different direction. "We have Sunday school before the main service," Estelle explained, "with other people in our age group."

Somewhat winded after mounting the outside staircase and then descending this one, it took Mary a moment to catch her breath as they paused outside a closed door, waiting for Nelson.

With a scarcely noticeable limp, he caught up and opened it for them, and the threesome stepped inside a carpeted room whose plain walls held only a blackboard, a calendar with a painting of Christ, and a few colored pictures of Bible scenes in matching wood frames. A bulletin board near the door sported a mishmash of notices and pictures of missionaries thumbtacked to its cork surface.

Two dozen strange faces peered up from the circle of folding chairs ringing the room.

Unpleasant experiences from the death camp, of times when too much attention was centered on her and a few fellow prisoners, assaulted Mary's mind. She felt vulnerable and exposed, and unconsciously she shrank backward. Into Nelson.

"They don't bite," he whispered, giving her shoulder a reassuring squeeze.

Drawing on that encouragement, Mary followed Estelle to three empty chairs. With her friend seated on one side and Nelson on the other, she felt a little of the tension inside her abate. Now if only everyone would stop staring. . .

A young man with freckles and a crew cut, obviously the leader, spoke first. "Hi, Stell, Nelson, and. . .?"

"My friend, Mary Theresa Malinowski," Estelle supplied.

"Glad to have you with us, Mary," he grinned, initiating smiles and interest from the others. "I'm Lennie Richards. I'll let the rest of this mob introduce themselves at the close. To catch you late-birds up, our study of the Gospel of John brings us to the account of the condemned woman, in chapter eight, if you'd like to turn there."

Estelle and Nelson found the passage quickly, but Mary had to resort to checking her Bible's table of contents first, all the while detecting more than a little scrutiny from some of the young men in the group. Finally reaching the specified chapter, she swallowed and tucked her pinpricked fingers beneath her Bible, wishing she'd at least remembered her lace gloves.

Lennie leaned forward, an open Bible in one hand as he took up where he'd apparently left off before their arrival. "Remember, there was no question about guilt here. None whatsoever. The case was cut-and-dried. The gal had been caught in the act of adultery and brought before Jesus. There she stood, in the middle of the crowd He'd been teaching, all eyes upon her. Now the question was, what punishment should she receive?"

Completely relating to the victim in the story, Mary wanted to crawl into a hole and die.

"Wait, wait, wait," Estelle cut in, raising her arm to halt the proceedings. She wagged her head. "And where was the man, I ask you? Honestly. Since way back in the Garden of Eden, we women have had to take the blame for everything. Did Eve hear God state the rules of the place? No. She got it all secondhand, from old Adam. It was all hearsay."

The other young ladies present stifled giggles behind their hands as they exchanged surreptitious glances between themselves. They seemed more than willing to allow her to be their voice.

"Yeah," a gap-toothed fellow with prominent ears piped up. "But even so, she embellished it, didn't she? Women always have to tack something on to a story, make it a little juicier, and it started at the beginning of time. Things haven't changed much either."

A collective snicker of agreement came from the male segment.

"Humph." Estelle crossed her arms. "Well, I have to admit, something has always bothered me about certain passages. How do you justify that all through the Old Testament, kings and patriarchs thought nothing at all of wedding a few dozen wives and taking a multitude of concubines on the side?" Her voice raised momentarily. "What's fair about that? It's the old double standard, plain and simple."

"I agree," a fair-faced redhead with blond eyebrows said, a rosy glow advertising her reticence to speak out, especially on such a sensitive subject. "Why must women always take the blame, and never the men?"

" 'Cause that's the way it's supposed to be," said one of the guys who'd been less than discreet in his bold appraisal of Mary.

Quite aware of that fresh perusal as she listened to a few more arguments along that line being bandied about, Mary felt a warm flush of her own, as if she were the woman standing before that judgmental mob. What if Nelson truly had seen her tattoo, guessed what she had done? She clasped her hands in her lap, wishing she could get up and walk out, find someplace to hide.

As if picking up on her discomfiture, Nelson finally stepped into the fray, his voice firm, yet gentle. "I think we're all getting offtrack here, people. The whole point of the passage is not guilt or punishment, per se. The Pharisees were attempting to trip Jesus up in the matter of Jewish law. The fact is, in God's perfect plan, He advocated one man and one woman, in marriage for life. And in Israel's covenant, the law dictated death to both parties in almost all cases of adultery. But Rome had taken away the right of the Jews to inflict the death penalty, which in this case happened to be by stoning. They were hoping to trap Jesus between His allegiance to the law—which ran counter to Rome's decrees—and His mercy and love toward even those who violated it—which would lower the moral standard. Either way He decided, they figured they had Him."

"Amen," Lennie breathed, relief written all over his freckles. "Say on, Nelse."

"But, as always, Jesus knew the hearts of those dignitaries," Nelson continued. "And He knew the one thing that would trip *them* up. Which is why He suggested that whichever one of them who was without sin should cast the first stone. Can't you picture all those proud teachers of men, their faces turning red, slinking quietly away?"

Heads nodded in agreement around the circle.

"Even today, we must consider our own faults and failures before we jump onto someone else's. All of us have something in our lives to be ashamed of. Let's not be so quick to condemn others."

Just then the bell in the tower signaled the call to worship.

"Well said, Nelson," Lennie declared with an emphatic nod and clapped his Bible shut. "We're sure glad to have you back. Now let's close in prayer."

Mary Theresa let out a slow breath. The class had finally ended. Her heart swelled with gratitude over the way Nelson had come to her rescue like an undeclared champion.

Then the other shoe fell. For him to have defended her, he must have seen the tattoo.

After the morning worship service, as their little group headed homeward, Nelson let the other members of his family compare their impressions of the finer points of the pastor's sermon without any input from him. He had other things on his mind. Conscious of Mary Theresa's presence beside him, his ears perked up a little whenever she spoke, but the rest of the time he tuned everything out.

He felt rather pleased with his performance in Sunday school. He hadn't intended to take over the discussion and, in fact, had planned to sit back as he had done last week and listen to those younger guys talk. But when it became apparent that the class had gotten out of hand and that Mary Theresa was in distress, a need to protect her rose to the fore.

And she'd had every reason to be uncomfortable, Nelson concluded bitterly, the way Barry Sanders had stared at her. And Rob Denton hadn't been very subtle in the way he'd ogled her either, considering the young man was supposedly going steady with Pastor Herman's granddaughter, Melody.

Of course, Nelson reminded himself, both those guys had excellent jobs. Promising futures. When it came right down to it, they had a whole lot more to offer someone like Mary than he did.

Whoa! What was he thinking? His own former true love had dumped him the instant she learned about the loss of his lower leg. What made him think someone perfect—much less rare and exquisite, like Mary—would give serious consideration to a guy who'd been maimed, and who spent most of his time sitting on his backside, letting the savings from his allotment checks rot in the bank?

Fact was, he felt a whole lot better about himself now that he'd tossed the crutches and started using his artificial leg. It seemed incredible how much more relaxed people were around him, how they treated him the same way they had before the war. Maybe it was time to consider going to work again. At least do that much.

"What did you think about that, Nelson?" Dad was saying.

"Hmm? Oh. Sorry, I wasn't listening. My mind was elsewhere."

"Asleep, more than likely," Estelle chided. "After using up a year's supply of brainpower in Sunday school."

"How's that?" his mother asked.

"Just the usual male versus female thing," she answered. "No sooner do I get to put in my two cents than Nelson charges forward like a knight ready to do battle. Nobody got a word in edgewise after that."

"Probably scared little Mary to death, with such goings-on," Mom said.

"Oh, I don't know," Estelle returned. "She was really quite a hit. The guys were all admiring her. A couple of them in particular."

"Do not say such things," Mary said quietly, her head lowering.

Picturing that bunch of young guys leering at Mary Theresa, like wolves circling helpless prey, Nelson ground his teeth. He looked up at his father. "Say, Dad, I've been wondering. Suppose Mr. Gavin's still holding my old job open, the way he promised? Think I might try going back to work."

"Well, that is good news," his father said, meeting his gaze in the rearview mirror.

"An answer to prayer," Mom added. "A real answer to prayer. We'll have to celebrate." She turned around to Mary. "I do hope you still have an appetite, Dear. You will be coming to dinner, of course, won't you?"

"A. . .headache I have," Mary said, with that trapped look about her. "I should go home."

Nelson's spirit flagged. She had to know he'd monopolized Sunday school for her benefit and hers alone. Or was it just him she wanted to avoid? Thank heaven he hadn't humiliated himself by asking her out. One small blessing he could be grateful for.

"Oh, nonsense," Mom countered. "That's nothing a little bit of aspirin won't cure. We have plenty of that at home. We'll get you fixed up right and proper. See if we don't."

≈

Mary knew exactly how a mouse felt when the trap snapped on its tail. She hadn't exactly disliked her foray into the different style of worship. Granted, that plain sanctuary with its simple wooden cross backlit behind the pulpit could have used some sprucing up. A few statues, some embroidered cloths on the altar, a bank of flickering candles. . . But all in all, she'd liked the hymns with their lovely music and words, and the soloist had performed flawlessly as well. And the pastor's sermon, in English rather than Latin, had stirred her heart, taking her back to those Bible readings she'd found so comforting in the barracks.

And even that class—what did they call it?—Sunday school. Especially Nelson's standing up for her. Even now she felt his very real presence next to her on the seat. She tried to shift a little closer to Estelle.

*Except for the topic which had hit a bit close to home,* her thoughts rambled on, *it was quite an experience to hear young people discussing religion and its practical application to one's life.* She'd never had much interest in such things in her younger years. Her parents and siblings attended Mass only sporadically, and none of them seemed to feel a lack.

Not until Ravensbruck did Mary begin to grasp how very deeply Almighty God loved mankind, how precious and real His presence seemed to those who trusted Him with their very lives. Even in that hellish place, amid the indescribable suffering, His peace was available to anyone who reached out for it. Where one worshiped God wasn't the most important thing. It was a matter of the heart that counted.

But still, all of that happened in the past. What about the present problem? Now that she'd gone to church with her friend's family, even enjoyed some portions of it, she wanted to go home. Be by herself. Ponder everything she'd heard.

And that was the one thing she couldn't do. In misery, she looked out the corner of her eye at Nelson. . .who strangely didn't appear any more thrilled about her coming than she was.

Of course, he'd had more time to think about that hateful brand. He'd surely guessed her shame. Perhaps he knew. . .everything.

# Chapter 13

Nelson brought up the rear of the oddly quiet group as his family and Mary Theresa trailed into the house after church.

"I'll change and get dinner going," his mom announced, heading for the stairs. Already tugging his tie loose, Dad clomped after her.

"Come on, Mare," Estelle said. "Soon as I put on a more comfortable dress, I'll go find you some aspirin for your headache."

Nelson slipped off his suit jacket and watched in sullen silence as the two girls started up the steps. When he heard his sister's bedroom door close, he ascended to his own room at a slower pace.

No wonder Mary Theresa had a headache, he told himself, after so much attention was drawn to her at Sunday school, then sitting through a long worship service that probably seemed strange and foreign to her. And of course, Stella invariably talked the girl's ears off all the time. But then, why should he complain about that? It kept him from having to make so much conversation himself.

Changing into casual slacks and a short-sleeved cotton shirt, he continued mulling over the day's happenings.

By the time he came back downstairs, he discovered that the others had already beaten him. He crossed to his chair, bent to pick up the Sunday paper on the floor beside it, then took a seat.

Stella's impatient voice drifted from the kitchen. "That's what I've been trying to tell you. It's all gone. Really. The bottle's in the medicine cabinet, but it's empty. I looked for another one, but there wasn't any."

"How odd. I know we just bought that a few weeks ago," Mom replied, her voice somewhat muffled by the door she closed whenever she had the oven going. "Maybe Nelson's been taking it to ease the pain of walking with that wooden leg. I know it bothered him quite a lot at first. You'll just have to run to Murphy's and get more. I believe this is his Sunday to be open for emergencies."

"Oh, Mom. . . ," Stella groused. "It's hot out. Are you sure there's no other aspirin in the house? Maybe in your purse?"

"No, Dear, that was all we had."

"Is no problem," Mary Theresa said. "Only small headache I have. Fine I am."

But Nelson doubted his mom would allow anything to dissuade her from that inborn compulsion to mother their guest. She reveled in it. He almost smiled when he heard her reply.

"Small headache or not, I'm sure you're very uncomfortable. The drugstore is just down at the corner. It'll only take Stella a few minutes. She'll be back in no time."

"Then I too go," Mary Theresa offered. "I'll keep her company."

"In that bright sun? I won't hear of it." The kitchen faucet ran momentarily, then ceased. "Now, I've wrung out a nice cool cloth for your head. You just come sit down in the parlor and close your eyes. Put your feet up. We'll have you better in no time." The kitchen door opened, and three sets of footsteps came down the hallway.

While Stella took her leave, Nelson watched a white-faced Mary being guided into the front room, right past him, to his father's favorite overstuffed chair near the fireplace. "Here," Mom insisted, gently pushing her down onto the seat cushion. "Lay your head back. Yes, like that. And put this washcloth on your forehead. Here's the hassock to rest your feet. And you won't need these high heels on either." One by one, she slipped Mary's shoes off, then placed them together on the floor, within easy reach.

The whole scene would have been comical, Nelson supposed, if he hadn't been in such a mood. Stella pouting her way out the door, Mary Theresa approaching the parlor as if to face a firing squad, Mom so absorbed in the chance to fuss over somebody, she was completely oblivious to all else. That left only Dad out of things. Where was he, anyway?

Just then, the older man's heavy footfalls echoed along the upstairs hall and down the risers. Nelson's eyes widened. Instead of the typical Sunday afternoon attire his father wore in case relatives dropped by unexpectedly, he had on his grubby chore clothes. "Thought I'd change the oil in the car," he said, meeting Nelson's gaze. "It seemed to idle a little rough this morning; did you notice?"

"Who, me? No."

"Well, no sense waiting till old Jenny gives out on us altogether, when there's plenty of time today to set her to perking again." With a conspiratorial wink at Mom, he sauntered toward the rear of the house.

"Guess I'll see about dinner," she said with a little shrug and traipsed up the hall again.

The back door closed with a click. The kitchen door whooshed shut.

And the loudest silence Nelson had ever experienced settled over the front room.

Across from him, with her forehead and eyes shrouded beneath a worn, pink washcloth, Mary Theresa sat so still she scarcely appeared to be breathing.

The mantel clock ticked, ticked, ticked.

Nelson gave a silent huff. "Nice day today, wasn't it? Always did like midsummer in New York."

Mary Theresa moistened her lips.

A few more minutes passed.

*So that's how it's gonna be, is it?* Well, he wasn't about to take on sole responsibility of entertaining the troops. That was the USO's job. Picking up another section of the Sunday paper, he snapped it open.

"You saw, didn't you?" she finally asked.

"Excuse me?" Having a fairly clear idea what Mary meant, Nelson didn't have the heart to come clean, not after all the trouble she'd gone through to keep that tattoo hidden from the world. Always wearing long sleeves, no matter how hot the weather. Protecting her from the truth would be easy enough. After all, it was the gallant thing to do and all.

Then again, perhaps he'd misread her. Maybe she meant something else entirely. That was marginally possible, wasn't it?

She raised a corner of the cloth, peeking at him through one eye.

"Oh. You mean the way all the guys at class were gawking at you?" he hedged. "They weren't exactly subtle about it, you know."

Mary hesitated for an instant, then lifted her head, and the washcloth dropped to her lap. She toyed with it as she focused on Nelson. "Uncomfortable it makes me, to have people looking at me. I do not like."

"Well, you might as well face it, Mary Theresa," he said with a half-smile, "the Lord didn't exactly cut corners when He made you. I don't know when I've ever come across a more beautiful woman in my life."

Expecting her to warm to the compliment and perhaps even blush a little, Nelson watched her expression deflate instead. Incredibly, the edges of her lips wilted sadly.

"A curse it is," she disclosed. "Too much it draws attention."

How was a guy supposed to respond to that? All the women he knew seemed to want a man to notice them, to appreciate the effort they'd put into looking attractive and appealing. Otherwise, there'd be a lot less in the way of coy looks and short skirts around, wouldn't there?

Mary Theresa expelled a tired breath. Tipping her head back once more, she closed her eyes and replaced the pink blindfold.

Watching her withdraw into that private shell, Nelson allowed himself a leisurely evaluation of her glistening hair, slim curves, tiny feet. . .and for the life of him, could see nothing remotely resembling a curse. Yet she wore shyness like a feather quilt about herself. What could possibly have happened during the war to make her feel she had to keep hiding?

He'd seen newsreels of the pathetic souls who'd been confined behind all that barbed wire, their emaciated forms, hollow eyes, hopeless faces, shaved heads. He glanced at Mary's crowning glory, wondering if she'd been made to suffer that humiliation. But in any event, at least she came out of the camp alive. *That must count for something,* he reasoned.

But then his more sympathetic side took over. From the few things Mary had told him and the family, Nelson knew she had no living relatives. That had to hurt more than anything else. And, judging from her age and the years Poland was involved in its struggle to survive, she'd likely missed out on a goodly chunk of her education, which could account for her lack of confidence in herself. And as far as resources, he had no clue about how she'd managed immigrating to America or what her financial situation might be now. He did know that job at the sewing factory didn't pay much—he'd seen Stella's paychecks. Maybe all those things, plus her limited proficiency in English, made her feel inadequate.

But why would she feel that way here, of all places, among people who truly. . . cared? Because, he might as well accept it, he already cared about Mary Theresa more than he'd ever intended. And that was the problem.

By the time the screen door squeaked open and his frazzled sister came in, the distinctive aroma of fried chicken floated deliciously through the house. She held a paper sack high in triumph. "Success at last!"

Mary Theresa sat up.

"Sure took you long enough," Nelson mused.

Brushing a sheen of perspiration from her forehead with her fingertips, Stella arched her eyebrows. "Well, I ended up having to go all the way to Jenkins's Drugstore. Murphy's wasn't open today after all."

"Oh. So sorry I am for the trouble," Mary crooned.

"It wasn't any bother, really. Only another couple blocks. The breeze kept me cool, and part of the walk was shady. The important thing is we can now take care of that headache. Come on. Time's a wasting. Mmm. Dinner smells good. I'm starving."

Nelson couldn't help noting how quickly Mary Theresa made her escape.

Nor did he miss the wary glance she flicked in his direction as she went by.

*Oh, well,* he decided. A lot of serious stuff was going on in that pretty head of hers. Some other time maybe he'd probe a little more, next time he had her alone. Find out what all she was hiding.

☙

Later that evening, soaking in a hot bath, Mary relived that unbelievably long day. She'd rather enjoyed the church service, if not the Sunday school class—and she might have liked even that, had the topic been something a little less personal. It seemed no matter where she turned, her past was thrown in her face. Was there no escape from it, ever?

Yet, as her thoughts drifted back to the Reverend Herman's message, she found herself drawing on its comfort. She'd never thought about Jesus' crucifixion as being God's plan from before the dawning of time. But, the pastor explained, only a perfect, innocent sacrifice would satisfy a holy God and cover the sin of mankind. For that purpose, He gave up His own Son to come to earth as a babe and to die that awful death on the cross. Mary's heart swelled at the thought of such immeasurable love.

*But then again,* her conscience taunted, *there were sins, and then there were sins.* Maybe some offenses were too vile to be forgiven. And she suspected hers might be among those.

On that bleak thought, Mary stepped out of the tub to towel off. Then in her blue flannel robe, she padded out to her sofa and sat hugging her knees to her breast.

Today had been a close call. Too close. She didn't relish putting herself in that kind of situation ever again. Maybe Nelson knew about her identification number, and maybe he didn't. If he did, Mary could only hope he'd keep her secret from his family. After all, what purpose would it serve for the horrible truth to become common knowledge?

But even if he didn't know about it, there was every possibility that somehow, someday he'd discover it anyway. . .unless she stopped going to the Thomas home entirely.

That wrenching thought filled her with a loneliness as deep as the one she'd felt when she and Rahel had kissed one another's cheeks and embraced in final farewell in Switzerland. Neither of them could bring themselves to speak aloud, but to her dying day she would hear her Jewish friend's whisper. *Kocham Ciebie. Do widzenia. . .I love you. Good-bye.*

Could she bear to give up these special times with this precious new American friend who'd become as close as a sister? Be satisfied only to chat with Estelle at lunchtime and let it go at that? Never to see the parents who had made her feel as special as a daughter? Or the brother, Nelson. . .whose own wounded soul had somehow reached out to hers from the moment they met?

With a shuddering sigh, Mary Theresa knew it was time to give that unthinkable resolution some serious consideration.

A heavy weight descended upon her spirit. Hoping to find strength and solace, she picked up the Bible that Nelson had given her and opened it at random. But her blood turned cold. Instead of the peace she so sorely wanted, her eyes focused on the admonition from the fifth chapter of James: *Confess your faults one to another. . . .*

# Chapter 14

Bright and early the next morning, Nelson followed the tantalizing smell of bacon down to its source.

" 'Morning," Stella said, passing him on her way to the door.

"Squirt," he returned good-naturedly. "Work up a storm."

She wrinkled her nose at him. "I liked going to work a whole lot better when we were making army uniforms. It seemed so much more important, back then." Snagging her purse and lunch bag from the hall tree, she left.

Nelson watched after his sister for several seconds, appreciating the way she looked in her violet jumper and print blouse. She had tamed her curls a bit with the addition of a twisted scarf, tied ribbon style, with the ends dangling behind one ear. *Jonathan could do a lot worse,* he decided. Stella had taken her fiancé's death at sea pretty hard, but maybe she was finally getting beyond it. Nelson thought he'd detected a few lingering glances in Jon's direction the last time his friend was here. And it was about time. She needed to get on with her life.

And Sis wasn't the only one. He'd be hiking to the trolley himself, shortly, then catching the subway across town to talk to his former boss and see about getting his old job back. If that worked out, perhaps in time he could start giving some thought to getting married and settling down. Other guys like him had found girls willing to look beyond their handicaps.

And children. He'd like that. Thoughts of Mary Theresa flew into his mind and so did the admiration she'd gotten from the other guys at church. When a woman was as perfect as she and could have her pick of men, why would she consider him? Filling his lungs and exhaling slowly, Nelson continued on to the kitchen, where he could hear his parents' voices as he approached and entered.

"Hi, Mom. Hi, Dad."

" 'Morning, Son. You're looking chipper today."

"Yes, isn't he?" At the stove, his mother smiled. "Good morning, Dear." She broke two more eggs into the frying pan to sizzle, then put bread into the toaster. "Breakfast will be right on."

Nelson caught a mysterious glance pass between his parents as he took his usual spot at the kitchen table but didn't think much about it until his dad tacked on a sly wink. That added to the definite undercurrent Nelson sensed in the room. He cleared his throat. "I decided today was as good a day as any to go see Mr. Gavin about my old job. In a little while, I'll go hop on the trolley."

The older pair just grinned.

Tucking his chin in puzzlement, Nelson threw his hands up. "Okay, I give. What's going on?" He looked from one of them to the other.

"What do you mean?" his father asked in all innocence.

Mom brought over the plate of food and set it before Nelson, her smile looking ready to explode from ear to ear any second.

"I know something's up with you two, or you wouldn't look like cats who'd just swallowed canaries. Come on, come clean."

His dad nodded in acquiescence. "Well, no sense letting your breakfast get cold. Eat up. When you're done, your mother and I have a surprise for you."

After bowing his head for a brief prayer of thanks, Nelson dug into his meal. But it was hard to enjoy it with those two waiting with bated breath for him to finish. He finally wolfed it down without tasting any of it, then scorched his throat on two gulps of hot coffee. He wiped his mouth on the napkin.

"Guess it's time," Dad said, getting up and crossing to the back door, Mom only a step behind. "Come with us, Son. We have something to show you."

His parents led him out the kitchen door and down the steps to the alley, where they turned in the direction of MacDougal's Garage on the corner.

Nelson had known barrel-chested Sean MacDougal practically all his life. A redheaded giant with a heart as big as the world, the Scotsman loved to tinker around with cars. He kept almost all the cars in the neighborhood running their best and never seemed too busy to instruct any lad interested in taking up the trade. When Nelson joined up with the army, Mac generously offered to keep Nelson's car at the garage for him until his return.

The little black coupe had been Nelson's pride and joy. During his time in Europe, he'd often pictured it sitting idle behind MacDougal's, collecting rust and spiderwebs. Not wanting to learn the extent of its deterioration, he'd purposely avoided going to see the man since he'd come home. He had no use for the car, anyway. And now Dad wanted to rub it in?

Nelson held back a little, trying to prepare himself for the moment he would see this sad reminder of his former life. But his parents walked right toward the antiquated garage with its peeling exterior and opened the wide, wooden door to the shop.

Daylight fell across the interior of the grimy work area cluttered with tires, car parts, and smelling of metal and grease. Everywhere there was an available spot, things were either piled on it, stacked under it, or suspended above on wall hooks.

The Scotsman looked up with a grin, still holding a polishing rag as he finished shining the hood of Nelson's all-too-familiar Chevy. "Nelse, me lad. 'Tis grand to be seein' ye." Wiping his smudged fingers on the rag, he extended an arm.

"Mac." Nelson grabbed the beefy hand and shook it, still not entirely sure what was happening, why his folks had brought him here.

His father patted a fender as he strode around to the driver's side, a smug expression on his face. "Looks pretty good, huh?" He opened the door.

"Sure does," Nelson had to admit. But that only made him feel worse. Surely they realized it was completely useless to him now.

"We rigged her up with a hand clutch, Mac and me," Dad went on. "Thought if you were going back to work, you'd be needing a car."

"A hand clutch?" Had he heard right? Nelson moved around to peer inside, where the sight of the new addition rendered him nearly speechless.

"Your father worked all yesterday afternoon on this," his mother supplied. "He wanted to surprise you."

"I. . .don't know what to say." He should have thought to do that himself. . . and would have, if he hadn't been wallowing in self-pity. Some aspiring engineer he turned out to be.

"We love you," she replied, as if that explained everything.

Blinking away the stinging behind his eyes, he grabbed them both in a big hug, while Mac beamed on from the side, nodding his head. "Well, I love you too. You guys are the best," Nelson declared, his voice hoarse. "All of you."

"What say we go try her out?" his father suggested.

Nelson itched to do just that. "I'm game. Might take me awhile to get the hang of it, though."

"Take all the time you need, Son. I'm in no hurry. Bill's covering for me at the shop this morning. I called him last night and told him I'd probably be in late."

While his dad went around to the passenger side, Nelson leaned over to give his mom one more hug, then eased himself into the coupe, finding the key already in the ignition. The engine caught on the first try. He cut a glance to his father.

"Mac and I started her up every so often while you were away. We knew you'd need her sooner or later."

Nelson could only shake his head, wondering if he'd ever stop grinning like a sap. They rolled down the windows, his father resting an elbow on the ledge of his. Then with a jaunty wave to Mom and Sean MacDougal, Nelson eased the coupe cautiously out of the shop and into the street, past rows of houses he'd about memorized over the years, past shops he'd frequented since his boyhood, heading for parts unknown.

So quickly it came back, this feeling of normalcy. He grinned at his dad, whose grin mirrored his own. Just wait till Jonathan saw this. And Mary Theresa. . .

Somehow it mattered for her to approve. After all, she was largely responsible for his being up and around again. Dare he imagine her occupying the passenger seat, golden hair blowing in the wind, enjoying a drive in the country? He emitted a silent sigh.

Nelson adapted amazingly quickly to the process of applying the clutch by hand to change gears, a feat he could only attribute to his experience of riding friends' motorcycles occasionally during his able-bodied days.

Had it been only a short while ago he'd lain in a hospital bed, certain this part of his life had ended for good, that he'd never experience the freedoms he'd always taken for granted? Now it seemed the Lord planned to give it all back to him, perhaps might have done so before this if Nelson had trusted Him a little sooner. This unexpected and undeserved blessing humbled him greatly.

"Well, what do you think?" his father asked after they'd driven half the length of Manhattan.

"That God gave me the best parents in the world, and I have a lot to be thankful for. I'm gonna make you and Mom proud of me, I promise."

Dad reached over and gave his good knee a squeeze. "We've always been proud of you, Nelse. We just want you to be happy."

❧

Another cloud drifted across the sky, masking the face of the sun, momentarily shading the bench Mary Theresa and Estelle had come to think of as their own. Mary wondered if it was her imagination that every time she looked up into the blue, she counted more clouds, perhaps indicating another storm.

"You seem quiet today," Estelle commented before biting into her egg salad sandwich.

Mary shrugged a shoulder. "A little tired I am." She broke a few chunks of bread crust and tossed it to the growing number of pigeons who'd discovered they could get handouts if they ventured close enough.

"I don't doubt it. For what's supposed to be a day of rest, yesterday turned out to be quite busy for all of us."

Not particularly wanting to rehash all of that, Mary decided to change the subject. "How is new girl? Gertrude."

Estelle arched her eyebrows, an incredulous expression coming forth. "You won't believe the latest. This morning she managed to sew right through the tip of her finger and fingernail."

"Ouch."

"Yes. Which, of course, sent her traipsing off to the company nurse. And set her quota back another considerable degree. Of course, to make matters worse, Old Personality-Plus Hardwick is forever breathing down the poor girl's neck, making her even more nervous and frazzled. She can't do anything right."

"How sad," Mary commiserated. "Not for faint of heart is sewing factory."

"You said it." Estelle chewed thoughtfully for a few seconds. "I really can't fault Gertie for a lack of effort, though. I think she just tries too hard. It wouldn't surprise me if she ends up going somewhere else, soon, to find a job."

Mary wagged her head, remembering her own difficulties in making the quota. Already it seemed a long time ago.

"Oh!" Estelle brightened. "Speaking of jobs, my big brother was up first thing this morning. Remember he mentioned something about going to talk to his old boss and see if he could get his position back?"

Even as she nodded, Mary wanted to ask more details but couldn't bring herself to pry. She had no idea what kind of work Nelson had done before the war.

"He worked at Lawson Engineering," Estelle went on in her chatty way. "Nelse always dreamed of designing wonderful bridges and great buildings. From the time he was a kid, he filled sketchbooks and drafting tablets with the most incredible drawings. To say nothing of notebooks crammed with all these complicated mathematical equations. He's really quite the brain, you know. Not like his mere mortal sister, who had to study and cram and sweat over every test at school."

Mary smiled to herself at her friend's lowly opinion of herself. But it was not hard at all to envision a youthful Nelson absorbed in his drawings. She only prayed today went well for him, and that he could, in fact, get his position back again. Then his life could start returning to normal. He deserved that much, if not more. A man needed to settle down, get married. . . . Any woman would be proud to have such a fine, smart husband. Her chest rose and fell on a silent sigh.

Just then the factory bell trilled the back-to-work signal. Wadding up their lunch sacks, the girls rose and hurried back to take their places.

"Well, back to the old grind," Estelle quipped. "This little break seems shorter every day. I'm sure glad tomorrow's Tuesday, and we have supper at our house to look forward to."

"Yes," Mary agreed. But inside she'd already decided not to go home with Estelle anymore. She just didn't know how to break the news.

## Chapter 15

How could it be Tuesday morning already? Mary Theresa peered at her alarm clock to determine if it had gone off at the set time. She had no idea when she'd dozed off, having watched hours pass by one after another. Kneading her temples, she padded to the bathroom to wash her face and freshen up. It took a light touch of makeup to cover the grayish circles below her eyes, but Mary hoped the evidence of yet another sleepless night would be less noticeable.

She should have simply told Estelle she wouldn't be coming anymore. But now her mother would be expecting her, have extra food planned and in the making. It vexed Mary to remember that on previous occasions with Estelle's family she'd taken extra care to choose just the right dress, hoping to look especially nice for them. Or to be more truthful, for Nelson. But even as she acknowledged the fact, she could see the utter futility of such nonsense. What could she have been thinking?

"The problem is, when it comes to Nelson, you forget to think," she lectured herself around her toothbrush. "You forget he deserves much better. Useless daydreams; they must stop."

Yesterday's clouds had been the prelude to another summer storm, and the steady rain which had battered the windows throughout the night would likely continue all day. Intending to choose an outfit that wouldn't spot easily, Mary went to her closet and picked through the lot, finally selecting a charcoal gabardine skirt with a matching cardigan and a plain blouse. Dull enough to match the day and her mood, she mused. After throwing a small lunch together, she bagged it, picked up her purse and umbrella, and left for the trolley.

Amazingly, Estelle's bright face and grin met her from the middle of the streetcar as Mary entered and paid the fare. Returning her friend's smile, she went to join her. "Early today you are."

"I got ready a little quicker than usual, I guess." She grinned. "What a morning, huh? Looks like there'll be no shady bench for lunchtime today."

Mary opened her mouth to respond, but Estelle continued with scarcely a breath. "Hey, wait'll you hear. Dad and a mechanic from our neighborhood rigged

Nelse's old car up with a hand clutch, so he can drive now. Isn't that great?"

"Yes. Great." Though she hadn't started out the day with enthusiasm, somehow the good news about Nelson did raise Mary's spirits a little.

"It would appear his old boss will take him back too. So starting next week, big brother will be a working man again."

"Happy for him I am." But the words were barely out of her mouth before Estelle cut in once more.

"Yeah, he and Dad went out for some practice drives that day and the next. I think they were both amazed at how quickly Nelse picked up applying the clutch with his hand instead of his left foot."

Having no idea what that even meant, Mary only smiled and diverted her attention to the rain-slick world outside the windows. Much as she yearned to know anything and everything about Nelson, she couldn't afford to spend much time thinking about him. . .not when she planned to wangle her way out of having to see him again. The only thing she hadn't figured out was how to tell Estelle. Mary didn't dwell on the anguish she'd incur by letting their beautiful friendship cool. . .but far better to do it that way than to have the truth of her past deal the mortal wound to their relationship. And it would, eventually.

Soon enough, the girls arrived at the factory, took their stations, and threw themselves into their work. With the doors closed against the dampness, the cavernous interior of the place quickly grew sticky and amplified the cacophony of noise from all the machines as well. Mary did her best to ignore the discomfort and concentrate on making the quota back in her own corner.

Something about the stiffness of the new fabric and the way the shirt collars turned out reminded her of her late father, dressed ever so fastidiously, as befitted his position at the university. Mama had taken pride in starching and ironing Papa's white dress shirts just so. And he'd had such plans for his offspring. Mary couldn't help wondering what he would think of his daughter now, so far away from home, slaving away in such a wretched place. The thought brought a sad smile. But at least she was alive. Perhaps it would be enough for him to know she had escaped the horrors that had claimed the rest of their beloved family.

The lunch bell shattered Mary's pensive thoughts. Clipping the threads on the piece she'd just finished, she turned off her machine and plucked her lunch and thermos from the bottom drawer. Instead of losing herself in remembrances of the past, she wished she'd have spent the time rehearsing what to say to Estelle. But it was too late now. She drew a fortifying breath and made the long walk to her friend's station.

"Oh, Mare. Hi," the bubbly brunette sang out as Mary approached. She tapped the machine beside her. "Gertie's out with an infected finger, so you can sit here in your old spot while we eat. It'll be like old times, almost." She unwrapped the food she'd brought and laid it out.

With a nod, Mary tugged out the vacant chair and sank onto it, then reached into her own lunch sack.

"How're those collars coming along?" Estelle teased. "Knowing you, every one that goes through your machine comes out perfect."

"Not always," Mary confessed. "One I hide sometimes."

"I know just what you mean. I've had my bad moments too. And by the end of the day I'm just anxious to get out of this place and forget about it for awhile." She nibbled a celery stick. "If it weren't for Tuesdays and knowing you'll be coming home with me after work, I'd dread the entire week."

Mary swallowed a chunk of her sandwich without chewing it and regretted it immediately. She grabbed for her tea to help wash it down.

"Is something wrong?" Estelle asked.

It seemed the ideal chance to start manufacturing the excuses she might need to build on later. "I. . .I. . .not very good I am feeling." It wasn't exactly a lie, Mary reasoned. Doing this to her best friend inflicted more than a little guilt, and she felt positively awful about it.

Especially when she saw Estelle's cheery demeanor collapse before her eyes.

"You're sick? Oh, no. I kind of thought you looked a little tired on the trolley this morning."

Nodding with just a touch more misery than she needed to, Mary wrapped the remainder of her uneaten lunch and tucked it into the bag.

"Well, Mom is really good at fixing what ails people. Maybe when we get home—"

"Please," Mary fudged, "maybe tonight my home is better for me to go."

Her friend's lips sagged at the corners. "Oh, and I so count on your visits." Then her lips softened and lifted with a forced smile. "Oh, well. If I must live without you one week when you're not yourself, I guess I'll get over it. After all, there's always Sunday, right?"

"Yes," Mary agreed, feeling like a skunk. "There is Sunday."

Which gave her a couple days to come up with an excuse to bow out of that too.

❧

Nelson steered onto a dead-end street to demonstrate how smoothly he could use the hand clutch during a perfect turnaround, then pulled back out onto the busy avenue, merging with the other Wednesday night traffic. The coupe purred like a kitten, and the breeze pouring in through the open windows felt balmy and wonderful. He grinned at Jonathan.

With a futile attempt to smooth his windblown sandy hair, Jon nodded. "Not bad, Buddy. Not bad at all. It's great to see you tooling around again. I was about to give up trying to light a fire under you anymore."

"Yeah, don't remind me what a sap I've been. I'm trying to make up for it."

"So what did it?" Jon probed. "Or maybe I should make that *who*. That pretty little Polish chick? Is she the reason for this new resolve?"

Nelson's irritated glance caught his pal's suggestive wink. "Why is it, whenever you come around, it's Mary Theresa this, Mary Theresa that? I do have my own life, you know, and did even before she got here."

"Well, pardon me," Jon snapped back. "I used to be able to kid around with you in the old days." His tone gentled. "It's just that you've started coming back to life lately, and as far as I know, she does happen to be the only new factor in the equation."

Nelson shook his head in chagrin. "You're right. I didn't mean to fly off the handle. I'm being a jerk. And right after prayer meeting too. Guess I should've paid more attention to that sermon."

"So," Jon began a little more cautiously, "are you saying she is or isn't a factor in all this? She does have supper at your house every week, doesn't she? And Stella says Mary's started tagging along on Sunday morning with you guys too. Are you telling me you're not interested?"

Passing a slower vehicle which pulled out into the road, Nelson shrugged. "I don't know. And that's the truth."

"What do you mean? We used to talk, Nelse. Open up."

Conceding that his friend was right, Nelson tried to imagine putting his feelings into words when he still had to figure things out for himself. He inhaled a troubled breath and released it. But he really did need to talk to somebody, and who better than his best friend? He finally took the plunge. "I thought at first there might be some kind of. . .attraction there—"

"On your part, or hers?"

"Both," Nelson admitted. "The first time Mary Theresa came home with Stella she seemed like a scared rabbit. But then she started warming up. She's the one who came walking with me when I needed to get used to my peg and all. And we'd talk a little. She's. . .got a lot of problems, you know?"

Jonathan gave a thoughtful nod. "She came from overseas after the war, right? She must've seen a lot."

"I'm sure she did. Mary doesn't talk much about it, but I thought she was starting to open up with me."

"Starting?"

"Yeah. Told me a couple little things I don't think she's even told Stella, or I'd have heard them already." He smirked.

A chuckle burst from the passenger side, and Jon's grin took awhile to disappear. "So what happened? Why'd you say you 'thought' she was opening up?"

Nelson grimaced. "Because all of a sudden she made a U-turn. Last time she came over, on Sunday, she gets this sudden headache. Then last night, when we all expected her to come for supper, she begged off, saying she was sick. Well, it'll be Sunday again in a couple more days. If she gives Stella another convenient little excuse, it won't take a genius to figure. It's me she's avoiding."

Jon tipped his head, doubt written all over his face. "Not necessarily."

"On the other hand," Nelson continued, "it's just as well. I'm heading back to Lawson's come Monday morning. To my old job."

"So I hear. That's terrific."

He nodded. "Figure I'll have enough on my hands with getting back into that routine, keeping my car running, going to church. Guess I don't need another complication right now. Later there'll be plenty of time to find some gal willing to put up with me and—" He tapped his artificial leg and shrugged. "So for now. . ."

"Whatever you say, Buddy." Jonathan clammed up and looked out his side window.

The sudden silence didn't sit well with Nelson. He took a different tack. "So what's with you and Sis? Gonna give her another shot?"

Jonathan winced. "Who knows? Think she's ready?"

"Only one way to find out."

"I suppose."

Funny how much easier it seemed to give advice than to take it, Nelson mused. But something had definitely changed with Mary Theresa. Ever since they'd gone to church. Since he caught a glimpse of her tattoo. The way she kept it hidden, a person would think being thrown into a concentration camp was something to be ashamed of. Something that was her fault.

Or was it him. . .him and his leg? Maybe she thought it too painful a reminder of a time she'd prefer to forget.

Whichever it happened to be, Sunday would either be the beginning. . .or the end.

First, however, there was something he needed to do.

# Chapter 16

C urled up on her couch with her fingers wrapped around a cup of hot tea, Mary lost herself in the quiet music playing on the radio. In a little while she'd run a bubble bath and soak away the weariness of the day, but for now it was enough to relax and clear her mind of all troubling thoughts regarding letting go of Estelle. . .and even sadder, Nelson. She'd grown so easily fond of his rich voice, of kindnesses so like his sister's. Their sweet friendship was among her greatest treasures, and her visits to that loving home, the brightest spots in her world.

A few light taps sounded on the front door.

Startled, Mary almost spilled her tea as she jumped to her feet. She hadn't heard anyone come up the steps. She set the half-empty cup on the lamp table and padded to answer the summons. "Who is outside?"

A pause. "It's me. Nelson."

*Nelson!* Mary swallowed her surprise, then unlocked and opened the door.

A sheepish grin met her in the dim lamplight spilling out the opening. "I hope it's not too late. I happened to be passing your street and thought I'd drop by. I have something to give you."

Words failed her. Should she invite him in? Was that proper? Or wise?

"May I come in? I promise I won't stay long."

"O–of course," she stammered. Hoping she'd made the right choice, she stepped aside.

"Nice little place," he said with a disarming smile as he glanced around the small living room with an expression of approval.

"Thank you. With decorating Estelle helped me."

"Ah, yes, the famous shopping trip. She talked of nothing else for days."

"I too had fun."

He nodded.

"Some tea you would like? I am having." Gesturing toward the couch and her own cup, she gave a questioning shrug.

"Sure. Thanks." With that, he settled into the adjacent slipcovered chair.

Mary hastened to the kitchenette and took a second cup and saucer from her drainer. Once she'd poured the tea and added a few cookies to a plate, she brought them to her guest. "Are you taking sugar or cream?"

"Black is fine, thank you."

Reclaiming her seat, Mary did her best to relax, despite the fact that her pulse insisted on doing silly things.

Nothing seemed to fluster Estelle's brother. He raised the cup to his lips, his gaze riveted to her as an instrumental rendition of "Something to Remember You By" filled the silence.

She wished she'd turned the music down or even off. It lent a kind of intimacy to the moment she didn't feel she had a right to.

"We've been missing you lately."

"Yes, I–I'm sorry." She fluttered a hand, a hapless substitute for an explanation.

"Anyway," he went on, "I saw something in a bookstore near where I work and thought you might find it useful." Reaching into an inner pocket of his jacket, he withdrew a gilt-edged book and leaned forward to hand it to her.

"Always gifts you are bringing," Mary said softly, then gazed down at it. She gasped. "A Bible! In Polish!" Her mouth parted in shock as she looked up at him again, her heart swelling in response to yet another display of his thoughtfulness.

"I know it can't be easy for you to muddle through King James's English," he said, his tone gentle. "Even we have problems understanding some of those old words. But I thought maybe if you could read in your own language, it might help you find clearer meaning to the verses."

"Oh, Nelson," she breathed. "Too kind, too generous you are. I will love this. How much you cannot know."

With a gratified grin, he drained the remainder of the tea in his cup, then stood. "Well, that's all I hoped. Maybe sometime we can talk over a few passages again. I enjoyed the questions you came up with. They made me think."

Mary felt her cheeks warming under his scrutiny. "Maybe the day comes when I not bother you with questions," she murmured, grateful beyond words as she rose to her feet to walk him to the door.

Reaching the tiny entry, Nelson hesitated, his hand closing around the knob without turning it as his eyes made a leisurely perusal of her flushed face. "I hope we never reach that point, Mary Theresa. I really do." Then with a last heart-stopping grin, he left.

Mary sagged against the closed door, fighting tears as she turned the lock after him. Such a loss he would be.

≈

If Mary Theresa imagined that disappointing Estelle had been tough to do on Tuesday, her dread of going to work on Friday about doubled that discomfort. She knew that with its arrival would come lunch with Estelle, as would the inevitable discussion leading to the Sunday service. Mary wracked her brain trying to fabricate a plausible way to evade spending time with the Thomases—after she'd practically promised to start going to church regularly with them. She hadn't mentioned Nelson's visit a few nights ago, and since Estelle hadn't either, Mary could only assume he hadn't said anything himself. Which was fortunate.

Facing herself in the mirror, she practiced maintaining an even expression while mouthing a few pretexts. "Cramping I have. My cycle. . ." No, not that. "A big tooth in back is. . ." Mary shook her head in disgust. "How about the truth? I cannot come because your brother I lo—"

Even without finishing the word, the certitude of what she'd almost said shook her down to her toes. . .it wasn't a fabrication. Despite all the noble plans she'd made to remain aloof from Nelson Thomas, to save him and his family from her wretched past, the unthinkable had happened. Mary had grown to love her best friend's brother.

Now more than ever, she knew she could never return to Estelle's home. What if her feelings somehow emblazoned themselves across her face or radiated from her eyes. . .or worse yet, came tripping out of her mouth? How humiliating it would be to reveal her whole heart, only to have it and her impossible dreams crushed forever. To see the affection that precious family had shown her turn to horror and loathing would be much more shattering than all the agonies she had endured at Ravensbruck.

Straightening her shoulders, Mary Theresa reaffirmed her decision to withdraw from Estelle and her family. . .or at least the family and Nelson. Working with Estelle, she would still have some measure of friendship with her. Or so Mary hoped. She could not bear to hurt the girl any more than necessary.

To avoid running into her before working hours, Mary dressed quickly and caught an earlier trolley, then loitered out of sight in the solitary confines of the lavatory until the start bell.

If ever there had been a shorter morning at Olympic Sewing Factory, Mary Theresa didn't know when it could have occurred. When the lunch signal pierced the air, only the stack of completed collars in her basket belied the notion that she'd barely sat down to work.

She drew a cleansing breath and effected her most casual expression. Then, gathering her lunch, she went to meet her friend, and the two of them exited the factory.

"Gertrude's back at work," Estelle commented as they sat eating on their bench a few moments later. "Her finger's still bandaged, but she's determined to stick this out and prove to Hardwick that she can do her job."

"Good. Glad for her I am."

"Me too. It seems a new employee needs that kind of gumption to make a quota. You had it, and look at you. You've been promoted already." Smiling, Estelle finished the last of her hard-boiled egg.

Mary shook her head. Right from the first, it had felt more like a demotion than an advancement, being moved so far away from Estelle, electric machine or no. After all, it only happened because some other girl had quit. Noticing a gray pigeon inching tentatively closer to her shoe, she carefully broke some crumbs from the cookie she'd been nibbling and let them fall from her fingers.

"I've been asked to sing a solo this Sunday," Estelle said, her eyes soft as she watched the birds coming to Mary's feast. "Well, actually, the choir will back me up with some *ooohs* and *aaaahs* in several measures of the song. But it's one of my very favorites: 'The Old Rugged Cross.' Do you know it?"

"I do not think so."

"Well, then, you're in for a treat. Pardon my modesty," she giggled.

Mary drew a deep breath. "I. . .on Sunday I cannot come."

"You can't?" One of the few actual frowns she'd ever seen on Estelle's face creased her smooth forehead. "Really? I thought you enjoyed coming with us last week."

"I did."

"Is it because we're Protestants? And you were uncomfortable in our style of worship?"

*That would make it easier,* Mary reasoned. Only it wasn't true. "Not that. The Chudziks I want to visit," she blurted. And once it popped out, the idea sounded quite good, so she added to it. "Veronica and Christine I am missing."

Estelle's delicate features smoothed out again, like waves at sea after a storm had passed. "Oh, of course you would, after living with them all those months. I should have anticipated that."

Breathing an inward sigh of relief, Mary didn't feel quite as bad now herself. She tossed a few more crumbs to the birds.

"Well, we'll expect you as usual then, on Tuesday. Okay?"

Mary knew she just had to tell Estelle she would no longer come home with her at all. Ever. There was no getting around it. She opened her mouth and drew a breath to get the words out.

"You can't say no this time," Estelle cut in, her dark eyes sparkling with mischief. "It's my birthday."

Mary's spirits plummeted to the sidewalk. Once again she could not refuse.

❧

"This is just the loveliest surprise," Mrs. Chudzik gushed when Mary Theresa showed up on their doorstep. "If you had a telephone, we could have called and taken you to Mass with us."

"Next time, maybe," Mary hedged, easing out of the woman's embrace. No sense alluding to having missed church altogether.

As she followed her inside, two sets of footsteps skittered toward them, and Veronica and Christine let out a squeal. "Mary! Mary's here!" And they surrounded her with loving arms.

"We were just about to sit down to dinner," their mother announced. "There's plenty. Are you hungry?"

"A little," Mary confessed. "May I help?"

"No, everything's on the table. All we need is you. We want to hear all about how you're doing out on your own, how your job is going, what friends you've been making."

With an appreciative glance around the familiar surroundings of her first home in America, Mary followed her two "little sisters" to dinner, trying very hard to appear happy.

"Sissy and I have started taking dance classes," Christine said during dinner.

"How nice," Mary said. "Fun it must be."

"I used to take ballet when I was little," Veronica explained. "But I've always wanted to learn tap. We're giving a recital soon, and you can come see us dance."

Mary nodded, enjoying hearing the girls' experiences again.

"And how is your job going?" their mother asked.

"Good. Everything I like but supervisor. This woman I must show." Mary got up and offered an imitation of a perpetually scowling Mrs. Hardwick skulking through the rows of sewing machines, an imaginary magnifying glass poised to search out flaws in people's work.

The family roared with laughter, and Mary couldn't help but get caught up in it herself. For a few moments, it almost felt as though she'd never left them to go off on her own.

"Child," stout little Mr. Chudzik said from the head of the table, "it does our hearts good to see how well you've adjusted to life in this country. If I'm not mistaken, even your English seems to be getting clearer." He rested his elbows on the armrests of his chair and nodded approvingly.

"Thank you. Hard I try, to sound like others. I do not think always in Polish now."

"Oh! Speaking of Polish," his wife gasped, placing a pudgy hand to her heart, "a letter came for you the other day. I almost forgot."

"I know where you put it, Mother," Veronica said, and jumping up from the table, she bolted to retrieve the envelope from the parlor.

Mary Theresa held her breath, wondering who could have written to her.

The postmark revealed the missive had come from Florida, which added even more to the mystery. But then the return address caught her eye. "Rahel! From my friend Rahel!" she exclaimed, delighted beyond words. She smiled and tucked the mail into her skirt pocket. "For later I must save."

It seemed to take forever until the meal ended and the dishes had been washed and put away. And all the while, Mary could feel Rahel's letter in her pocket. From time to time she touched it with her fingers just to be sure it didn't disappear. But Florida! Why Florida?

Finally, the Chudziks drove her home and waved good-bye. Mary slipped inside and ran up the stairs to her apartment. Then she tore into the message from her Jewish friend:

*Dearest Marie Therese,*

*I hope this letter finds you. I have been trying for a long time to learn where you are. I wrote to Josep and Ania for help, and they told me they believe you went to live with one of their American contacts named Chudzik. I am trying them first. If I do not hear from you, I will write to Josep for other names.*

Still overwhelmed at having received this unexpected word from her dear friend, Mary smiled to herself. Rahel had not changed. The determination which had enabled her to survive the death camp would likely see her through the rest of her life as well. She returned her attention to the pages in her hand, realizing how strange it seemed to be reading Polish again after having been so thoroughly immersed in the English language since her arrival in New York.

*There is so much to tell you, I do not know where to begin. The ship I took to Palestine was not permitted to dock. Too many refugees already, they told us, so my grand plan of settling there and making jewelry did not come to be. Many places I went after that. Too many to write. But at last I came to Miami.*

*I work now for a family named Goldberg, in their store. The owner, Mr. Goldberg, likes the pieces I make, so he lets me design others. But most amazing is that even with a Jewish name and heritage, he and his wife have become Christians. They believe Jesus to be the Messiah promised centuries before His birth in Bethlehem. It reminds me of hearing the Bible at the camp. I am starting to believe it was true, all those things we heard.*

Mary's eyes widened as she reread that paragraph. Rahel, becoming a Christian believer! An added sense of joy filled her. She had begun to accept those teachings herself but had never brought herself to share that with anyone. She read on:

*It seems strange to live in a place where there is peace. Peace all around, and now peace growing inside my heart. But I am very lonely here. How I wish my family were alive to enjoy this with me. That is why I am writing. I feel as if you are my family now. My sister. And I think how wonderful it would be if we could live in the same place, be happy together.*

*If you get my letter, please write to me. I know you might like being in New York and not want to leave there. That is fine. But think about how much fun we could have together. It is always warm in Florida. We could learn to swim in the ocean. Even if you cannot come to live here, you could still visit me. I long to learn about you and your life in America. I will wait to hear from you.*

*Your friend always,*
*Rahel*

Hugging the letter to her breast, Mary Theresa laid her head against the back of the couch. How very precious to know that Rahel was safe and doing well and in the trade she loved. So many prayers had been answered. And Rahel wanted Mary to join her. That would take some consideration. Florida was a long way from New York.

It would also be a long way from Nelson. That would be hard.

But to stay in Manhattan and face the possibility of running into him, knowing all the while that nothing could ever come of it. . .that would be much harder still.

Perhaps, she mused, this might be the solution for her dilemma.

# Chapter 17

A late summer breeze ruffled the hem of Estelle's green-and-white-striped cotton dress and toyed with a wisp of shiny sable hair. Mary Theresa watched her brush it away from her face to munch the ham and cheese sandwich she'd brought for lunch. "I thought today would never get here," Estelle remarked.

Beside her on their bench, Mary only wished she shared that sentiment. For her, the days leading up to this one seemed to have wings. There'd been nothing she could do to slow its coming. *And after those well-laid plans to stay away from the Thomases too,* she thought scornfully. All for naught. Somehow she would have to weather one more long evening at Estelle's.

Thankfully, her friend didn't pick up on her angst. "This is the first birthday in ages that my whole family will be together. Nelson missed the last couple, being off at war, you know."

Mary just nodded. *Nelson.* How would she survive the upcoming hours in his presence, knowing how she felt about him?

"Do people celebrate birthdays in Poland?" Estelle asked casually.

Sloughing off her troubled thoughts, Mary tried for an outward show of enthusiasm. "Yes. This custom we have. But now, most have no means to a celebration of the day."

"Oh, I'm sorry. Well, Mom always bakes a special cake when it's somebody's birthday and usually makes some really thoughtful gift we had no inkling she had in the works. Once in awhile it'll be something store-bought." She stopped suddenly and glanced at Mary. "When is your birthday, Mare? I've never asked you that."

"Sixteen of April."

"Oh, rats. We'll have to wait over half a year for it to get here. I just know my mom will want to make you a birthday cake too. You're like part of the family."

Even as Mary tried to ignore the pang of guilt that followed her friend's last comment, part of her still sought an escape. Something to prevent her from having to go through with this. But the friendship she and Estelle shared meant far too much to her, and Mary just didn't have the heart to disappoint her. Not on the day of her birth. She would get through this somehow. . .this one last time before she left here forever. Could she muster enough courage to move to Florida?

Mary's thoughts naturally drifted to Rahel. She'd read and reread the treasured letter so many times over the last two nights, she nearly had it memorized. She'd even started on a reply, wanting it to be as informative as possible without actually making a commitment. But now, anticipating the swift arrival of yet another family get-together at Estelle's, the notion of going somewhere far away grew in appeal.

A pair of pigeons cooed in the background while a particularly venturesome one pecked its way through bread crumbs at Mary's feet.

"I know you had a swell time with your host family on Sunday," Estelle said, gazing at the birds, "but will they be expecting you every week now? Maybe to go to church with them again?"

"That we did not discuss," Mary answered truthfully, then brightened. "Guess what? A letter they had for me. From Polish friend, Rahel Dubinsky." An easier smile came to her lips.

"Really? How interesting. Had she written you before?"

Mary shook her head. "Contact we lost when to Holy Land she sailed and to America I come."

"Well, how splendid that you've found each other again." Estelle grew pensive. "It must be lovely to be in that part of the world. Imagine walking on the very roads and paths the Lord walked along. Or climbing hills where He must have preached to the crowds, seeing the Sea of Galilee. What a feeling that would be."

"Palestine is not taking her. In Florida is Rahel now. To live there."

"Oh." Estelle tilted her head with a puzzled frown. "I'm sure it must be nice there too."

Mary nodded. "She. . .wants for me to visit." *Maybe stay forever,* she added silently.

"Too bad you have a job here," Estelle crooned. "Old Hardwick has a conniption when any of her workers dare to take time off—except in cases of death, of course." She snickered. "And even then, it had better be their own. She'd have to allow at least a half-day in that case."

Mary smiled but did not answer.

With the lunch bell ending their noon break, the girls rose and brushed off their skirts, then returned to their workplaces.

Hoping to keep her mind off how swiftly the afternoon would end, Mary threw herself into her work. She'd found the making of collars incredibly simple, and the process had so quickly become automatic, she imagined she could do them with her eyes closed. While adding steadily to her stacks of finished pieces, she mulled over her answer to Rahel. Anything to keep her mind off how much she longed to see Nelson and be with him.

Mary knew the supervisor would never permit an extended absence to a relatively new employee, and she had not earned any vacation time. In order to go to Florida to visit Rahel, she would have to quit her job. And if she quit her job, she might as well make the move permanent. Could she bear that?

But. . .could she bear not to?

All too soon, the quitting bell startled her from her dilemma. Gathering the completed articles together, she turned them in, then went to meet Estelle.

And face the dreaded gathering which lay ahead.

"At last!" her friend exclaimed, bubbly as ever. "What a long day, huh? Well, it's finally over. Now we can go home."

As the girls disembarked the trolley at Estelle's stop, the setting sun cast a soft peach blush over the rows of tenement houses lining the street, blending variegated textures and colors into a softer palette. Mary's gaze wandered along the tiny yards that had become so familiar in the short time she had been coming to dinner with her friend. She'd chosen a few favorites among them, knew which ones had the loveliest rosebushes, the prettiest curtains, the sweetest children. Knowing she wouldn't pass this way again after today, she found herself committing the familiar sights to memory. She'd call them to mind often when she went to live with Rahel.

But one, tucked between a unit with asbestos siding and another trimmed with brick face, would forever stand out above the rest. As Mary approached the Thomas home, she drank in the neat pale yellow exterior and tidy window boxes overflowing with brilliant geraniums. She imagined she would hear the slap of that screen door in her sleep, recall the good-natured banter that filled the rooms, smell the delicious meals Estelle's mother inevitably prepared.

"Mmm," Estelle murmured as they went inside. "Chocolate. I knew she'd bake my favorite cake." She looped her purse strap over a hook on the hall tree, and Mary followed suit.

"Well, well," Nelson grinned, coming to his feet from the easy chair. "If it isn't the birthday gal. Hi, Squirt. Mary."

Estelle sent him a sisterly grin.

"Hello." Unable to sustain his warm gaze, Mary lowered her lashes and smiled. It wouldn't do for him to read her feelings. She schooled her features into what she hoped was polite reserve.

"Dad home yet?" Estelle asked.

"Nope, but he called a few seconds ago to say he's on his way."

Just then Mrs. Thomas breezed in, her cheeks rosy as the pink print housedress she wore. "Oh, hello, girls. We're so glad you could join us, Mary. And don't you look pretty. We missed having you around here lately."

"Hello, and thank you." Smiling, Mary did her best to stifle a flush. She hadn't especially planned to dress for the occasion and had donned a dark floral print skirt and complementing blouse. Obviously, even the simplest outfits in her wardrobe reflected Mrs. Chudzik's good taste and Veronica's eye for fashion. Mary had never taken off the fine chain Rahel gave her, except to add a crucifix to the Star of David. Though most days it remained out of sight, today it did not. "Delicious, something smells," she said, hoping to divert everyone's attention away from her.

"That would be the chicken and dumplings Stella requested," Mrs. Thomas supplied. "Birthday people choose the menu on their special day. It's kind of a tradition we adopted over the years." She glanced to Estelle. "Your father should be home any moment, Dear, so we'll be eating shortly."

"Great, Mom. And it does smell good—as usual."

She stepped nearer and gave her daughter a hug. Then with a light laugh, she embraced Mary as well, patting her back. "My two girls."

Mary had to swallow a huge lump in her throat but did manage a smile.

"Think I hear Dad," Nelson said, moving to the window. "Yeah, that's him." Turning back, he rubbed his palms together and grinned. "Finally. I've had to sit here smelling all this stuff ever since I got home from work. A man can take only so much, you know."

The usual clomping up the outside steps brought Mr. Thomas through the door, which clapped shut behind him. "Hi, all," he said with a glance that encompassed everyone. "Happy birthday, Snooks. Nice to see you here, Mary. Smells like supper's waiting."

"It is," his wife announced. "Go wash up, and we can start right in."

Not needing instruction as they all filed into the dining room, Mary Theresa claimed the spot which had been hers from the first. She chanced a quick look across at Nelson while he sat down, and he grinned, sending the butterflies inside her into chaotic flight. Did he have to be wearing the brown-checked shirt she liked so much?

"Well," his father said, his bifocaled glance making a circuit and settling on Mary, "the whole family is together again." Immediately he bowed his head. "Dear Lord, we are so blessed. Thank You for Your boundless love and provision for our needs. Thank You for Stella and the bright spot she is in all our lives. Grant a special blessing at this special time set aside to commemorate the day You gave her to us. And bless our Mary as well. Thank You for bringing her back to us. We give You our praise. In Your Son's name, we pray. Amen."

Too caught up in the touching grace to echo his amen, Mary crossed herself and opened her eyes, more than aware of Nelson's focus on her.

"This does look luscious, my dear," Mr. Thomas said, gazing down at the china tureen all but overflowing with its bounty. "If everyone will pass plates, I'll see that you get served."

Welcoming even that small diversion, Mary gave hers to Estelle to pass on. Within moments, a generous portion of the chicken mixture and a fluffy dumpling came back. She couldn't believe the cloudlike softness as she cut into the moist, steamed dough. . .and the taste of it and the accompanying stew seemed like a dream. "Very good this is," she told Mrs. Thomas in all sincerity.

"Why, thank you, Dear. I'm glad you like it."

"How was work today, Nelse?" his father asked. "Starting to fit in yet?"

He chuckled. "I kind of feel like the new kid on the block, actually. But things are coming back. I can connect the names to the right faces pretty well already. Mr. Gavin's letting me go slow. Yesterday and today, he had me refining some blueprints for a project he has in the works. Shouldn't be long before I'll be going out to job sites with the rest of the guys."

Stella shook her head. "I never could figure out what all those lines and diagrams mean." She turned to Mary. "Engineers and architects can look at that stuff and somehow envision an entire building, basement to roof."

"We are geniuses. Just plain geniuses," he quipped, forking a carrot chunk to his mouth.

"And how about you girls?" Mr. Thomas went on. "Quotas coming along at the factory?"

Estelle nodded, then shot a glare to her brother. "Of course, we do more than merely scribble stuff on paper, like some geniuses I know. But our favorite time is lunch hour." She returned her attention to her father. "That's when we get to put aside our grand endeavors and go sit in the fresh air with the pigeons. They like Mary."

"My food they like," she corrected. "Watching them is. . .nice."

"I'd imagine the feeling is mutual," Nelson teased.

Meeting those merry light brown eyes, Mary almost couldn't swallow.

"Anyone care for more?" Mr. Thomas offered, the ladle ready in his hand.

"No thanks, Daddy," Estelle said. "I need to save room for cake."

Nelson, however, didn't hesitate in the least and handed over his plate, his eyebrows waggling in a comical fashion. "Some of us are just getting started."

At the close of the meal, Mary and Mrs. Thomas cleared away the main course while Estelle reveled in her lofty position as the birthday girl. Then Mary returned with a stack of cake plates, and the lady of the house brought in a triple-layer cake, iced in white frosting and decorated with colored sprinkles and lighted birthday candles.

"Good grief! A regular inferno," Nelson teased. "You're gettin' old, Sis."

She gave a playful kick under the table.

But when the others broke into "Happy Birthday," Mary could only mouth the unfamiliar words. She had to smile when Estelle made an elaborate display of blowing out those twenty-two rapidly melting candles.

Mary couldn't remember enjoying a moister chocolate cake in her life and felt so full she had to force down the mound of chocolate ice cream on the side. From the sparkle in Estelle's eyes, she sensed her friend had chosen the flavor in her honor.

Finally, dessert dishes were whisked away, and a small pile of presents replaced them at the center of the table. Mary got caught up in Estelle's delight over the bounty of thoughtful gifts. . .a hand-embroidered blouse her mom had made, a new alarm clock from both parents. She held her breath when her friend opened the present she'd brought, hoping it too would please her.

"Oh, Mare. Thank you. I've been needing a new silk scarf. It's just beautiful and my favorite shade of green." Estelle reached over and hugged her.

"You have one more thing, Squirt," Nelson reminded her, nudging a small gift her way.

Mary watched Estelle's eyes grow misty as she gazed inside the narrow jeweler's box and drew from the cotton lining a tiny gold cross suspended on a delicate Figaro chain. "Oh, Nelse." She sprang up and ran to hug his neck from behind. "You remembered I broke my other one. Thank you."

"Anytime, Sis," he grinned, patting the arm nearly choking him.

Estelle straightened. "And thank you, everybody. This has been my best birthday ever. I love you all."

Against poignant memories of her own childhood birthdays, Mary's heart ached at the atmosphere of love in this home. . .and the priceless joys that had been ripped away from her so long ago. She could hardly get beyond the clog of emotion in her throat.

"Well, Mary, dear," Mrs. Thomas said, providing a most welcome distraction, "it looks as if you and I will be dealing with the aftermath."

She took a deep breath and plastered on a smile. "Fine. To help I like." Detaching herself from old griefs she could not afford to dwell on, Mary stood and began gathering the discarded wrapping paper and ribbons, wondering if her relief was obvious to anyone else.

She braved a shy glance at Nelson and felt somehow encouraged to see a gentle smile on his lips. And Mary knew she would miss that sight most of all. . . .

# Chapter 18

Nelson began taking stock of Mary Theresa from the moment she and Stella arrived, weighing her expressions, tone of voice, her manner, the way she responded to questions and comments. He'd been convinced she'd quit coming around because of him, but he had to find out for sure. He figured if he waited long enough, watched closely enough, she'd trip up somehow, and the truth he sought would be evident. Perhaps painfully so.

But, man, the girl was good. Whenever she knew she was the center of attention, she appeared completely composed, ever so polite, and typically pleasant. Her smile seemed genuine. Obviously she felt real affection for Estelle and their parents, and even offered Nelson a few smiles that looked sincere. But those other times. . .when she didn't know the microscope was focused on her, that's when Nelson caught brief flashes of sadness in her eyes. A sadness so profound it seemed almost tangible. And it did unspeakable things to his insides.

Seated in the parlor after supper, with his father reading the evening paper in his overstuffed chair, Nelson could hear the good-natured banter drifting from the kitchen. He pictured Estelle perched on the step stool while Mary Theresa and Mom did the dishes. Sure sounded like a happy enough group. Maybe his instincts were wrong. But if they were, it would be the first time.

Still mulling over the events of the evening, he turned the radio on and searched the dial for music, then adjusted the volume down.

Francis Langford's "Harbor Lights" flowed smoothly and low in the background as the ladies finally left the drudgery and came to join the menfolk. Mom picked up her knitting and took her usual spot in the cushioned rocking chair by the fireplace, while his sister and Mary chose opposite ends of the couch. Stella immediately leaned forward to the birthday gifts she'd left on the coffee table and began examining them, this time more closely.

"This scarf will look so pretty with my winter coat," she said breathlessly, running the emerald silk through her fingers. "I can hardly wait for the cooler weather to come."

"In New York are the winters cold, like in Poland?" Mary asked.

"Oh, we may get a few blizzards that are real doozies," she replied. "But, fortunately, here in Manhattan the weather can be pretty mild, a good part of the time. At least now that big brother's around, I won't get stuck shoveling all the snow this year." She crimped her nose at him.

"Hmm," he returned in stride. "I was thinking of digging out my crutches, come winter. . . ."

"Ha. That's what you think. I turned them into firewood just the other day."

"If you did, you'll regret it."

Looking from one to the other, Mary laughed softly.

Dad peered over the top of his newspaper and nodded to Mom. "I think we just relinquished our peace and quiet to the younger generation. How about we seek solitude in the kitchen? Sure could go for a cup of coffee, maybe another slice of that cake?"

"I think I can accommodate you, Love." Putting aside her project, Mom rose with him, and they traipsed down the hall. The door swished shut behind them.

"Well, apparently we've perfected the art of clearing a room," Nelson said with a wry grin.

"Time for me to go home, I think," Mary said tentatively.

"Just let me make a quick trip upstairs," Stella said. "I'll only be a moment."

Nelson saw Mary's blue-green eyes widen as she watched after his sister. Then she settled back against the couch.

A few measures of an introduction, and Jo Stafford's rich voice issued from the speaker. "I'll be seeing you in all the old familiar places. . . ."

Mary's lips curved into a bittersweet smile. She reached to the jeweler's box on the coffee table and took out Stella's necklace, fingering the delicate cross. "Very pretty," she said, her words barely audible.

"I kinda thought she'd like it."

Mary moistened her lips, then hesitated, drew a breath, and spoke. "Why do Protestants wear plain the cross? The death of Jesus they do not like remembering?"

Turning the song down another notch, Nelson met her gaze. "Oh, we remember it, all right. It's a precious thought to know the Lord of creation became a man and died for our sins. But you see, the story didn't stop there. The fact that He rose again three days later is what's amazing. It's the basis for all our hope. The empty cross is a reminder that all who come to Him will live again one day with Him in heaven."

She appeared to consider his words, then replaced the jewelry in its box. "For good people that is," she said softly. "People who do not sin."

"We all sin, Mary Theresa. Ever since the Garden of Eden. No one is good. The only way any of us can be sure where we'll spend eternity is to ask for God to forgive us and to accept the free gift of salvation He provided through His

Son's death on the cross."

"But. . .my past you do not know," she whispered. "Things I have done. No one could forgive such things."

Astounded that she could be so hard on herself, Nelson prayed for wisdom before he answered. "God can, Mary. He promises that though our sins be as scarlet, He will make them white as snow. Here, I'll show you." Plucking his Bible from the lamp table beside his chair, Nelson got up and crossed to the couch. Sitting a respectful distance from her, he showed her the passage in Isaiah and waited for her to read it. "He also promises that no one who comes to Him will be turned away."

"*Too* bad are some things."

"Nothing, little one, is too bad."

"You are sure of this?"

"Sure enough to bet the ranch on it. God cannot lie." Taking a tract from inside the cover, he gave it to her. "Here, Mary. Keep this and read it at your leisure. If you'd like to know for certain that you have peace with God, there's a sample prayer on back. But you can make up your own prayer instead, if you prefer. It's not the words that count; it's the heart behind them."

Those troubled eyes raised to his, and they brimmed with trust. "Much Bible I have read already, now that I am reading in Polish. I. . .this peace I would like now," she whispered.

With the greatest joy he had ever experienced, Nelson took the hand of the woman he loved and knelt beside her while she prayed.

❧

There were no words to describe the lightness of her spirit when Mary Theresa allowed Nelson to assist her to her feet after her prayer. She felt as if a great weight had been removed from her being.

He looped an arm around her shoulder and hugged her. "Welcome to God's family."

She could have hugged him back. Almost. But one conviction still remained. God had forgiven and accepted her. . .but she was still the same person, with the same past. People would not be so forgiving. She braved a smile through moist eyes and eased out of his chaste embrace.

Estelle came tripping downstairs just then, humming to herself.

"I'll let you tell people your good news whenever you're ready," Nelson whispered, moving away.

"Okay," Estelle sang out, entering the room. "We can drive Mary home now."

"Drive?" Mary echoed. "Trolley is fine."

Nelson grinned. "No sense hoofing up the street anymore when I've got a perfectly good car sitting right outside. You'll be safe. . .I've been practicing. And Stella will come too."

Unsure, Mary looked to her friend and watched her nod. "Well, okay," she said in her best American. "But thank you and good-bye I must first say to your parents." She couldn't possibly leave here without doing that. Not with her future plans to consider. Those had not changed.

Moments later, the threesome headed out front to Nelson's coupe. The girls got into the backseat, while Nelson took his place and started the motor. "Hang on to your hats, ladies," he teased over his shoulder.

Mary darted an alarmed glance to Estelle but received only a reassuring pat on the arm. "Don't mind him. He's just feeling his oats now that he can tool around town at a whim."

As he pulled away from the house, Mary settled back and relaxed, watching the passing scenes in the fading twilight.

"Nelse?" Estelle asked before they'd gone half a mile.

"Yeah?"

"Could we stop at Mickey's for a root beer float?"

"What? After all that cake and ice cream at the house? You gotta be kidding."

"No, I'm not," she insisted. "Please? Can we? I'm dying for a root beer float. It is my birthday, remember."

He let out an exasperated huff. "Sisters."

"Is that a yes?" she asked hopefully.

"Yeah." But his wagging head showed his disdain.

Mary too thought it incredible that slender Estelle, who rarely consumed her whole bag lunch at work, could possibly yearn for something else after the huge cooked meal and birthday desserts. But it didn't matter all that much. Surely he'd drop her off before they went to Mickey's, wherever that was.

But her street whizzed by without Nelson even slowing down, let alone turning into it. Captive that she was, she held her peace. What other choice did she have?

Mickey's Soda Shoppe, she discovered, turned out to be a charming ice cream parlor not far from Woolworth's, right around the corner from a movie theater. No doubt most of its clientele consisted of young people who frequented the theater and came after the shows.

Nelson parked in front of the establishment, and they exited the car for the restaurant.

Mary couldn't help but gawk at the red-and-white-striped cushions on white wrought-iron chairs surrounding a smattering of tables. . .all the more striking on the black-and-white linoleum floor. A jukebox in one corner blared a lively new song she'd never heard before as they strode to a table in the far corner.

A petite blond waitress in a ruffled white apron and black dress brought menus, then left.

They barely had a chance to open and study them before a familiar voice interrupted. "Well, well. Fancy meeting you guys here."

"Jon!" Nelson exclaimed. "What brings you to Mickey's?"

His mischievous grin split his long face. "Oh, just had a hankering for some ice cream. Hi, Mary. Hi, Birthday Doll." His blue eyes locked on Estelle's.

Mary slanted a glance at her friend and caught an uncharacteristic blush. And a smile the girl couldn't seem to contain.

Nelson, obviously on to something, tucked his chin at his tall, sandy-haired friend, then at his sister. "Okay, what's up?"

Estelle, all innocence by now, only shrugged.

But Jon pulled up a chair. "So, what is it? Hot fudge sundaes all around? Chocolate milk shakes? Or do we go whole hog on the banana splits?" He winked at Estelle.

"We were about to have root beer floats," she supplied.

"Great. Then let's get ours to go. Game?" he offered her his hand.

Hesitating the briefest of seconds, Estelle smiled. "Game." She placed her fingers in his. "See you two," she said gaily, and hand in hand they went to the order counter.

"Methinks we've been had, Mary Theresa," Nelson said evenly when the pair left without a backward glance, carrying their treats out to Jonathan's car.

She had the same impression herself but couldn't express it as eloquently.

"Hungry?" he asked.

Mary shook her head.

"Me neither. I could go for a soda, though. How about you?"

"Sure. Soda I like too." But she couldn't help wishing she had her hands around her friend's slender little neck. That girl had to be the rudest, most brazen, downright— She couldn't even think of an English word to fit.

Flagging down the young waitress, Nelson placed their order, and she brought the drinks over almost immediately.

"Well," he said after taking a long draught through his straw, "my sister appears to have finally decided to give my good buddy Jon a tumble. It's about time, really. She's been mooning over her dead fiancé long enough." A slow grin widened his mouth, and he raked fingers through his reddish-brown hair, leaving paths among the shiny strands. "Poor old Jon's been carrying a torch for her since high school."

"Good together they look," Mary had to admit, smiling. Then she sensed Nelson's gaze searching her face. There seemed to be some quality in his eyes she'd never noticed before. . .and she couldn't afford to find out what it was.

Neither could she afford to reveal her own feelings. That was the absolute last thing she needed right now. She lowered her eyelids and gave her full concentration to her soda. The time had come to make arrangements to move to Florida. She'd do it as soon as possible. Sooner.

But first things first. Tomorrow, when she saw Estelle at work, she would throttle her.

Nelson leaned closer. "How's your drink?"

# Chapter 19

Aware that Nelson had finished his soda, Mary Theresa quickly gulped hers down, then blotted her lips on the paper napkin.

"Ready to go?"

She nodded. "Thank you for buying me drink."

"Anytime." They rose, and he allowed her to precede him. Reaching around to push open the door, he then walked her to the car.

So wonderfully attentive. Too much so. She would remember this always.

Still, Mary couldn't help her relief that the evening would soon end. She did appreciate its beauty, with the first stars appearing in the darkening sky, the mild summer breeze. It would provide precious memories to look back on someday, when she could bear to. For now, she would just pretend tonight was like any other, with her heading home from supper at Estelle's. Yet how could she completely ignore the fact she was with Nelson, or the incredible peace which filled her heart? The peace, at least, was hers to keep. God loved and accepted her, exactly as she was, and He'd gifted her with an extra few sweet moments alone with Nelson. . .entirely unplanned and more than she'd dared to dream.

Neither spoke as they reached the car. Nelson handed her inside, closed the door, and went around to his side. He started the motor and pulled away from the curb. But he didn't turn in the direction of her apartment.

Mary felt a twinge of panic and sent him a questioning look.

"Thought we might take a little drive," he said. "Seems a shame to waste such a pretty night."

*Well, okay, I can do this,* she assured herself. *He is the one who gave me the Bible, knelt with me in prayer. I can trust him. And I will have another memory to cherish. A few moments more.* The city did look lovely, with subdued lights here and there inside the tall buildings, a sprinkling of colored neon signs at gas stations and diners. She tried to concentrate on those things.

"Feel like walking a bit?" Nelson asked casually as they neared Central Park. "Just because I can drive now doesn't mean I want to revert to sitting around all the time."

"Maybe a short walk," she replied. "Work is tomorrow."

"Sure, I understand. I'm a working man myself now." He pulled into one of the main drives, found a spot to park, then got out and came around to assist her.

*He couldn't have chosen a more perfect night,* Mary decided, inhaling the fragrant perfumes of the late summer plants as they strolled along one of the walkways. Black-purple fruit of the elderberry glistened from nearby lights, and she could easily imagine the glory of all the chrysanthemums in the sunshine. The whole world seemed brand-new somehow, and she appreciated God's handiwork in an entirely different way.

Just beyond a wooden footbridge, they came to an open pavilion, dim but illuminated by standing lights positioned around the grounds. They mounted the steps to the circular stage. Hands in his pockets, Nelson gazed over the well-kept greenery and shrubs surrounding them. "I used to come here pretty often. That is, my family did. For the outdoor concerts. People would bring chairs or blankets, and we'd sit and bask in the music of the big bands. It was great. Maybe they still give concerts, who knows?"

Mary leaned back against the railing, admiring the twinkling stars against a blue velvet sky as he talked. She loved the way Nelson's voice sang across her heartstrings, and if he wanted to stand there forever and talk, she'd be content to listen that long.

A few moments of silence passed before he emitted a silent chuckle and turned to her. "You know, lately I was starting to think you were avoiding us. Or to be more precise, avoiding me."

The fine hairs on her arms prickled, and the breeze suddenly felt chilly.

"Was I wrong?"

Mary could find no reason to hide the truth. He'd find out soon enough, anyway. She lowered her gaze and shook her head.

"So, which was it then? The family or me?"

"Both."

He released a sudden rush of breath, and his shoulders flattened.

"But not for reason you think," she elaborated.

"You mean, we didn't do anything to offend you then."

"No. Never. Very. . .loving is your family." *Too loving. I love all of you too much.*

"That doesn't make a whole lot of sense, Mary," he said, a frown creasing his forehead. "If you're happy around us, why would you feel you needed to avoid us?"

"Be—because too close I am getting." She paused. "Away. I must go away. To Florida."

"To visit someone?"

She shook her head. "To live. Soon. Before too hard it is."

"Well, that's a relief," he blurted sarcastically, raising a hand and letting it fall to his side. His droll tone indicated an attempt to lighten the moment. "I thought maybe you were uncomfortable being around my. . .injury. Women generally don't flock around a guy like me, you might say."

"The injury? No. To me this is not important," she answered in all honesty. "A man like you many girls would want."

"Would you?" He locked his gaze on hers.

Mary's heart thudded to a stop. She had to look away.

He stepped closer, placing his hands on her shoulders. "Because I might as well level with you, Mary Theresa. I lov—"

"No!" Mary gasped, pressing her fingertips to his lips. An inexpressible ache crushed her spirit, and her broken heart throbbed so, she wondered if he felt the pulse in her touch. Tears welled up inside, but she suppressed them by sheer force of will. She had to hold herself together a little while longer. She would have the rest of her life to cry. "You must not say that," she whispered. "Not to me. Never to me." She tried to ease out of his grip.

But Nelson only held tighter, confusion etching his finely honed features. "Don't be ridiculous. Why shouldn't I say that to the woman I want to marry?"

*To marry.* Mary had relinquished that dream long ago. It was far too late to consider something so utterly hopeless. Her head drooped in defeat. "Reasons are. . .too many."

A ragged breath issued from him. "Name one."

She searched his face in the subdued light, hating the pain she saw there, hating that she was the cause. . .and most of all, hating that if she did tell him her reasons, she would inflict even more hurt. The crushing weight of the words she knew she would have to say to him almost suffocated her.

But it was the only sure way to make him understand.

*Father, please give me the strength I need to do this.* Mustering every ounce of fortitude she possessed, she steeled herself against the love for Nelson which had been growing inside her from the moment they'd met. She tugged herself forcefully from his grasp and turned away a little, to avoid having to witness the brutal blow she had no other choice but to administer. She would never be able to live with herself if she watched the effects of her confession. *Just take me home,* her heart begged. *Let us leave now. Please. I cannot do this. I cannot.*

But he stood there, feet planted, not moving. Waiting.

The rate of Mary's heart intensified until it throbbed in her ears, each beat a death knoll to her relationship with Nelson Thomas. She could feel the pounding in her neck, could feel the heat rising to her face. It seemed a struggle even to breathe, to swallow. "Like others I am not," she finally choked out. "Not like Estelle, not like woman you should marry."

"What are you saying?" he probed.

A dark pain clutched her heart, filling her throat. How could she speak the words? How could she dredge up the horrific memories which could take years to banish completely from her thoughts and nightmares? Even as the battle raged within her, Mary chanced a tiny look—a last look—at the only man she had ever loved. The man who had led her to the Lord and helped her to trust again. This man of whom she was not worthy, could never be worthy.

*How can I not tell him?*

She drew a shuddering breath and plunged ahead, before her love for him could make her change her mind. "In Ravensbruck, in death camp," she heard herself whisper, "I was. . .*comfort girl,* for German officers. M—many officers. They—"

"Stop! Stop!" Nelson shrank back several inches, his head shaking in refusal, his jawline hardening. Mary sensed his eyes piercing her very soul.

Renewed loathing for herself and those faceless beasts in uniform flowed through Mary like vomit, withering her heart. It hadn't been worth it, to survive. She should have refused. Fought. Let them gas her. Death would have been better than having to endure this.

A sound issued from the depths of Nelson's being that was not human. A sound Mary Theresa had heard often during her confinement, from prisoners whose loved ones were tortured and murdered before their eyes. It would haunt her as long as she lived. On the edge of her vision, she saw his head sag into his hands, and his broad shoulders began to shake.

This time, *he* turned from *her.*

Her heart dropped within her with a sickening thud. Only the things she had survived before enabled her to live through his shuddering sobs. She blinked back the tears trembling on her eyelashes.

She'd known from the beginning that the two of them could never become involved. That when he went, so would his family. . .including Estelle. She should not have cultivated those friendships, yet she could not help herself. They had shown her the love she'd been so hungry for. And she'd needed it so.

"To tell you I did not want. You make me tell," she lamented, knowing it didn't matter. Nothing mattered now. "I knew you would hate me. I. . .I am going now."

He swung back, his face ravaged with tears. "Hate you?" he asked incredulously. *"Hate you?"*

Mary swallowed, trying to think of what could be worse, what degree of contempt lay beyond even hatred.

Nelson swiped the wetness from his face. And with the tenderest smile she had ever seen, he reached for her and drew her close, crushing her to his chest, rocking her in his strong arms. "I could never hate you, Mary Theresa," he murmured huskily against her hair. "Never. I love you more than life itself. Those months at the death camp, those. . .terrible things you endured. . .none of that was your fault, your doing. It was all done *to* you. You had no choice. You were the victim. If I abhor anybody," he grated, "it's those animals that could do such deplorable, inexcusable, inhumane things to an angel like you. But I can only leave their ultimate judgment to God."

Closing her eyes against an exquisite pain cinching itself around her heart, Mary still doubted the words she'd never dreamed she'd hear in her lifetime.

"Both of us were victims of war, my love," he went on. "Things were done to us that we had no control over. But it's time to let go of the past and forgive those who caused our suffering. Only then will our healing be complete."

Mary had not prepared herself for this. She'd braced herself for his utter disgust, for his ultimate rejection. She'd expected Nelson to turn his back and walk out of her life forever. But, this! This was the unconditional kind of love Corrie ten Boom had spoken of. The kind of love God had for the people who repented of their sins and accepted His Son. "Y–you still love me? Even now?"

The realization completely shattered the floodgates behind her eyes.

With a strangled sob, Mary sought Nelson's comfort, losing herself in those strong arms. Burying her face in his solid chest, she wept for the first time since she'd been taken into captivity. Great, huge sobs for herself, for her relatives, for the torment and shame of her past, for losses which could never be recovered.

On the fringes of her consciousness, she felt him scoop her up into his arms and cradle her there like a child. He eased down to the banister and sat stroking her back, her hair, making no move to stem the cleansing tide, as if he sensed her need to relinquish those hurtful memories once and for all.

Mary relaxed a little in his embrace, then a little more, drawing comfort and sustenance from that stalwart heart beating against her own. Slowly, gradually, the chains that had bound her for so long melted away. Her slowing tears took a new turn, becoming a wellspring of joy over the new life she had found in the Lord, with the Thomases, and best of all, with Nelson. No matter what the future held for them, it would never seem as hopeless as before. Because of him. Because of God.

At last, she fell silent.

Nelson continued to hold her closely, rocking her tenderly, his wordless solace infusing her with even more peace and hope. Then he gently set her to her feet and stood facing her. With the edge of his index finger, he raised her chin and looked deep into her soul. "My dearest Mary, don't ever hang that lovely head again. You became a new creation earlier this evening. Old things are passed away, and all things are become new. God has erased your past and made you pure in His Son.

He's given you an inner beauty that radiates from your eyes and shines out at me whenever I look at you, a beauty even beyond your outward appearance." His thumbs brushed away the last traces of tears from her face, and he smiled into her soul. "And I'm asking you to stay. Please. Don't go away. Because if you'd deign to consider a guy with a bit of a limp, I'd be honored to have you for my wife."

He still wanted her! Despite everything! Her lips curved into a tremulous smile. She tested her voice, surprised to hear it when it came out. "For a long time, I am loving you, Nelson. The honor is mine. I will stay."

"I'm glad you said that," he breathed, the circle of his arms tightening around her. "Oh, Mary, nothing in this world will ever hurt you again. This I promise with all my heart." Lowering his head, he covered her lips with his, in a kiss that said far more than mere words ever could.

Mary snuggled closer as he deepened the kiss. *Thank You, dear God,* her heart sang, *for teaching me forgiveness, for giving me love.* Despite those old feelings of unworthiness, her past no longer mattered. The Lord had graciously given her far more than the desires of her heart, and she didn't know how to begin expressing her praises.

"Come on, my angel," Nelson crooned, hugging her to his side. "I know a few people who're gonna want to hear about this. And on the way, we can start making some plans."

And the two of them stepped out into the beautiful night.

# Epilogue

A few late-falling snowflakes danced on the wind beneath a sky of clearest blue, adding even more frosty glory to a city blanketed in white. Peering out at the beauty from the lace curtains on Estelle's bedroom windows, Mary could hardly speak. Everything looked so pure, so pristine. . .just the way she felt.

"Stand straight," her friend coaxed, "or I'll never get these pearl buttons fastened."

Doing her bidding, Mary gazed down at the lovely bridal gown Mrs. Thomas had poured all her love into making. Of purest white satin, with long lacy sleeves and a bodice trimmed with seed pearls and sparkles, she felt like a princess.

Stunning in her own radiance, Rahel stepped close enough to give her a mute but fiercely emotional hug. "*Kocham Ciebie,* I love you," she whispered, her deep brown eyes shining with moisture. Her long, dark hair and olive complexion glowed against a rich emerald gown with a complementing headpiece of satin and tulle. "Fortunate you are. Be happy." Having come expressly to stand up for Mary, she was quickly forming an attachment to the rest of the family and would find it hard to return to her solitary life in Florida. . .if she could bring herself to leave at all.

"Now for your veil," Estelle said, misty-eyed as she stood by in a gown identical to Rahel's, her shining curls even more glorious next to the fabric's deep color. Picking up the beaded Juliet cap and veil her mom had fashioned, she set it in place and pinned it to Mary's hair, unfolding the blusher veil over her face.

Mom Thomas rapped on the door, then opened it to peek around, her cheeks pink against a deep wine-colored suit. "Oh, my pretty girls," she murmured, all teary and flustered. "I couldn't be more proud of you." Crossing to them, she gave all three a hug, unconcerned about crushing the satin and taffeta creations she'd labored over. "Everything's ready downstairs for our Christmas wedding. Let's get your flowers." She bustled to the florist's box on Estelle's bed to pass out bouquets of red carnations and white roses whose fragrance filled the room.

Estelle stood back to admire Mary, then gave her a hug also. "Now you'll be my real sister, you know. I've never been so happy."

"I too," she whispered, unable to trust her voice.

241

Piano music drifted from downstairs in prelude to "The Wedding March," and her soon-to-be father-in-law appeared and offered his elbow. "You look lovely," he assured her. "Let's not keep poor Nelson waiting any longer."

The scent of pine drifted upstairs from the long-needled evergreen the family had decorated last night. Large poinsettia plants lifted brilliant faces from several spots throughout the downstairs, lending an even more festive air, as did the tall red candles burning so brightly on the mantel. One by one, the women started their measured descent down the stairs whose railings sported red velvet bows and holly.

Mary, trailing a few steps behind, reached the landing, her hand on Dad Thomas's black-suited arm.

Her gaze immediately sought Nelson's and almost melted from the depth of love and admiration she saw in his light brown eyes. In his new charcoal pin-stripe, he looked tall and resplendent, standing beside the lovely Christmas tree hung with tinsel and shining ornaments. She couldn't help believing she was getting the better end of things. . .not only in her betrothed's masculine appearance but in his spiritual maturity.

## SALLY LAITY

Having successfully written several novels, including a coauthored series for Tyndale, several Barbour novellas, and numerous **Heartsong Presents**, this author's favorite thing these days is counseling new authors via the Internet. Sally always loved to write, and after her four children were grown, she took college writing courses and attended Christian writing conferences. She has written both historical and contemporary romances and considers it a joy to know that the Lord can touch other hearts through her stories. She makes her home in Bakersfield, California, with her husband and enjoys being a grandma.

# Remnant
## of
# Grace

Susan Downs

*To my beautiful Korean-born daughters,*
*Kimberly (Moon-Young) and Courtney (Jeong-Ok).*
*I thank God for intertwining your lives with mine and thereby*
*expanding our family's cultural heritage to include*
*Korea—Land of the Morning Calm.*

# Chapter 1

Friday, June 23, 1950

Eun-Me scrubbed a year's worth of accumulated dust off the cabin's yellowed linoleum. Her strokes kept cadence with the gentle waves as their natural rhythm lapped a tireless, steady beat against the stretch of Korean shoreline known as Taechon Foreigner's Beach.

While she worked, a constant tide of memories, emotions, and questions flooded her thoughts. Eight years had passed since she stood on the Inchon pier and waved good-bye to Philip as a prisoner of war exchange ship carried him away from Eun-Me's homeland and out to sea.

In those torturous, sweet days before the Japanese expelled all remaining Americans from Korea during World War II, she, her brother, and the missionary's son had been an inseparable trio of best buddies. But, when Philip Woods returned today, would he greet her like a long-lost friend? Or like his parents' household servant—the *ajumoni*—she had since become?

She scolded herself for fretting over such senseless musings. She was foolish to give Dr. Philip a second thought. Yesterday Clarence and Ruth Woods had gone to the Inchon shipyards, not only to meet Philip but to also meet their future daughter-in-law, Philip's future bride. Today, after a night's rest at their Seoul home, the Woods family planned to drive down to their cabin at the Foreigner's Beach along the coast of the South China Sea for a few days of vacation together. For this purpose, Eun-Me had been sent ahead on the train with instructions to air out the cabin and prepare a homecoming celebration feast fit for a king—or a recent medical school graduate who was soon to start his residency.

Eun-Me couldn't imagine a more pleasant assignment. The term "cabin" painted a more rustic word picture than the reality of this beautiful place. She trusted Philip would return with fond memories of the native stone, two-story structure, which included a fully-equipped kitchen with American appliances and more modern conveniences than any Korean home.

The clutch of towering firs surrounding the house obscured the waterfront from her view. However, the moment she had removed the winter shutters from the screened porch that ran along the back of the house, fresh ocean breezes lifted the curtains like sails and sent fresh sea air throughout the downstairs rooms. She knew from her previous visits here that the sandy trail leading from the back porch would take her to an isolated swimming beach reserved for missionaries and other expatriates.

Sitting back on her haunches, Eun-Me tossed her scrub brush into the bucket of blackened wash water and looked up to check the time. Two o'clock. The Woods family could arrive from Seoul any minute now, and she had not yet started supper.

She put away her cleaning supplies and scurried about the kitchen, gathering ingredients for the bean paste soup and setting a cast-iron pot full of water on the stove to boil. The spicy meal had been Philip's favorite Korean dish when Eun-Me's mother served as the Woods family's *ajumoni*, and she had helped her mother prepare the aromatic broth for them countless times.

After her mother died of a stroke, Eun-Me had stepped into her position as the Woods family's *ajumoni*. So, now, Eun-Me was the one preparing Philip's favorite dish. And now, instead of being on equal social footing with the missionary's son, she was nothing more than a servant. Or worse, a charity case. An orphan.

Yet, harbored within her deepest desires, Eun-Me dreamed of someday cooking all of Philip Woods's favorite foods, not as an *ajumoni*, but as his wife. In her secret fantasies, she saw herself standing close behind *Moksanim* and *Sahmonim* Woods as they greeted the homecoming Philip. Allowing her imagination free rein, she closed her eyes to picture the young doctor running down the gangplank, scooping her into his arms, begging her to be his bride.

However, Eun-Me knew she would never see her yearnings come true. More than years and miles accounted for the wide gulf that separated them. She couldn't marry anyone—much less Philip Woods. With no relatives left to arrange a marriage and no dowry to offer a husband's family, her prospects for a marital union appeared nil. As an orphan, she would never climb any further than the bottom rung on the ladder of Korean society. She was destined to spend a future of lonely days as an *ajumoni*. And Philip was destined to marry another. An American.

Eun-Me stood and swiped at the front of her baggy *mom-pei* trousers. She both looked and felt like she fit the part of a lowly *ajumoni*. If Philip saw her in these ragged work clothes, he'd most definitely feel sorry for her. She couldn't bear his pity. She decided to change.

Before tending to her personal needs, she surveyed the cabin's interior and smiled. She'd done an admirable job of preparing the place, despite the fact that she'd arrived on the train only the day before.

Eun-Me changed into the only dress she owned besides her traditional Korean *hanbok*—a stylish gold shirtwaist dress that Mrs. Woods had ordered for her last year from a Stateside catalog. Although she probably should have chosen something more conservative, Eun-Me liked the dress's rich color and the stares it solicited when she walked through the South Gate Market on her weekly shopping trips.

She hurriedly tucked and pinned her wayward strands of hair back into place. Then, swiping at the smudges on her face with a palmful of cold water, she shot a cursory glance toward the mirror before heading back to the kitchen to resume her duties at the stove.

The pungent broth of garlic, hot peppers, and bean paste had just come to a rolling boil when the crunch of automobile tires on the gravel road jarred Eun-Me into a kinetic frenzy. Philip had arrived. And he was calling for her.

≈

Philip struggled through the cabin's screen door with Jennifer's oversized suitcase. "*Yoboseyo?* Hello? Grace? You here?"

Without waiting for a response, he dropped his burden in the entryway, shucked off his loafers, stepped over the neat row of house slippers, and padded quietly down the hallway in his stocking feet toward the kitchen. The sinus-clearing smells of long-forgotten Oriental delicacies greeted him, and in that mouthwatering moment, he knew he had come home to Korea.

He recognized her soft voice before she appeared in the kitchen doorway, and he couldn't help but smile at her unique blending of Korean and English—"Konglish," they had called it as kids.

"*Anyong haseyo, Paksanim* Philip! Welcome home." She shuffled toward him, her form already bent in a deep bow.

"Hey, Grace. Don't waste those honorific titles on me." He engulfed her dainty shoulder in his palm, hoping to still her incessant dipping and nodding. "I'm not 'Doctor' to you. It's just me, your ol' buddy Phil. Now, stop your kowtowing and come give me a good American-style hello hug."

Philip bit back a smile as he stooped over to gather her into his arms. He almost told her that she was just as short as he remembered her but decided this was not the time. He pulled her close and buried his face in her hair. Her sweet essence stirred within him pleasant remembrances of his dear childhood friend, and he drew a deep breath, savoring the memories. Yet, even in the midst of the nostalgic pleasure he found in Grace's embrace, guilt stabbed at his conscience to find such joy in the arms of any woman other than his fiancée.

He could feel tension emanating from Grace, making him wonder if she felt his sudden attack of conviction, or if her stiff reaction was simply a result of his breach of Korean etiquette. He hoped their reunion held the same significance for her as it did for him. The last thing he wanted was for Grace to feel that their friendship must end since he would soon be a married man.

He released her, and she immediately backed away two short steps. He heard Jennifer and his parents clamoring through the front door, and he knew he should hurry to help them with the luggage, but he lingered to study Grace's face.

Over the course of his lengthy absence, she had passed from adolescence to adulthood. Her unblemished complexion and rosebud lips still needed no assistance from cosmetic jars or lipstick tubes to enhance her beauty. Yet, her almond eyes, which once sparked with mischievous fire, now radiated a silent sorrow.

Philip couldn't help but question why God had permitted wave after wave of tragedy and suffering to sweep over one as gentle and meek as Grace. At the age of ten, she'd been forced to witness her pastor-father's execution by the Japanese occupying forces when he refused to bow to the Shinto shrine. Surely that was enough trauma to last a lifetime, yet there was more.

Shortly after his parents reentered Korea following Japan's surrender to the Allied forces, they wrote Philip with news about Grace's brother, Eun-Soo. Evidently, about the same time the Woods family was forced to leave Korea during World War II, the Japanese had conscripted Eun-Soo to work in a Manchurian coal mine. Soon after, Grace and her mother received a one-line telegram announcing that Eun-Soo had died in a mining accident. No further explanation ever came concerning his mysterious demise.

The impact of his good friend's death had not fully hit him until this moment. Never again would he laugh at Eun-Soo's antics. Their "Trio of Trouble" was no more.

Now, Grace had been forced to bear the grief of her mother's death as well. Even though he had sent her letters expressing his sympathies, he wanted to further convey his continued sorrow.

"About Eun-Soo—and your *omma*—" Philip's throat clogged with emotion, and his words tapered off to a whisper.

"No, no, *Paksanim* Phil." Grace shook her head back and forth and raised her palms toward him. "Don't say anymore. Save your sadness for another time. This is a happy day, and you mustn't spoil it by dwelling on things we can't change." She then hid her brilliant smile behind her hand, in typical Korean fashion, yet she seemed to deliberately avoid eye contact with him.

"I'll unpack your things, and you can rest." Her words came at a fast clip. "I have your old room all ready for you." She moved to slip by him, but he stopped her before she could escape his reach.

"Wait. I can unpack my own things. Besides, there is someone I really want you to meet." His fingers softly encircled her forearm, and he led her down the hall to the entryway.

Eun-Me forced a smile. She wasn't sure she was ready to be introduced to the woman he had pledged to marry.

She nodded and bowed in greeting to *Moksanim* and *Sahmonim* Woods, who stood in the stairwell leading off the entryway. They sloughed effortlessly out of their street shoes and clambered up the stairs, each lugging a suitcase behind them.

A slender figure sat in the middle of the shoe-cluttered entryway, struggling to untie the laces of her shoes. Hoping to catch a quick glimpse of the woman, Eun-Me craned her neck from side to side, then up and down. The stranger's chin-length, curly blond hair fell into her face, preventing Eun-Me from getting a clear view, yet that which she could see looked stunning.

From beneath the hair, Eun-Me heard a shaky voice. "I don't know how my shoelaces got so tangled. And I don't think I should have to trade my own sneakers for some used straw slippers, anyway. Who knows who wore them before me? Just think of the germs! As I recall, you said this place would be just like an American home. I never have to take off my shoes at home in San Francisco."

The woman abandoned her attempts to untie her shoes and yanked them off, tossing them toward the door. She donned a pair of woven bamboo slippers, then stared at her feet in a lengthy silence.

Abruptly, the American lady tipped her head back and sniffed at the air with a crinkled nose. "Has there been a skunk nearby?"

Eun-Me leaned to whisper to Philip. "I don't know. What is a skunk?"

At her words, Philip's lips tightened, and his cheeks darkened.

Eun-Me squirmed, hoping against her common sense that the question bore no correlation to the smell of the bean paste soup simmering on the stove. In her eagerness to provide a warm welcome for Philip, she hadn't stopped to consider how someone unaccustomed to Korean food might react to this particularly puissant odor while it cooked.

She longed to slink off and hide. If she made a hasty retreat, she could postpone these introductions until Philip's pretty fiancée had recovered from her exhausting journey and was in a better mood.

Eun-Me frantically glanced around the room, planning her getaway. However, before she could slip out of the room, Philip cleared his throat in readiness to speak. Eun-Me waved her hands in a frantic attempt to stop him, but he replied despite her protests.

"The skunk is a unique animal that is native to North America. I'll explain later." He turned to Jennifer and gave her a smile that Eun-Me knew was forced. "Hey, Jennifer. Forget about the shoes and the smells for now. There's someone here I'd like you to meet."

The woman rose from the floor to tower over Eun-Me. With one hand, she flipped her blond hair out of her face, then raked her fingers through her curls to smooth them into place.

Eun-Me waited for Philip to begin the honors of a formal introduction, but before he could speak, his fiancée stepped forward. In response, Eun-Me automatically dipped in a low honorific bow, but as she straightened, Jennifer's descending hand smacked her in the nose, bringing stars to her eyes.

She stood quickly, blinking away the sting and forcing herself to keep her hands at her side instead of checking for blood, which would further bring attention to the woman's awkwardness.

Jennifer rubbed her own hand as she spoke. "Oops. Sorry. I'm a bit off-kilter and not used to all this bowing," she said, her voice increasing in volume and slowing in tempo with each word.

"Can you speak English?" Jennifer shouted. Jennifer pressed her index finger into the center of her chest. "Jennifer." She pointed to Eun-Me. "What's your name?" Her voice slowed even more, but the volume of her voice leveled. "Do. You. Understand. Me?"

Eun-Me stretched to her full height, but she was still much shorter than the tall, slender Jennifer. Before she could speak, Philip rested his hand on Jennifer's shoulder.

"Jennifer, you don't need to shout," he said in a flat, even tone that Eun-Me had only heard him use when he was very, very angry. "I'm the only one in the room with a hearing loss, and I can hear you loud and clear." While he spoke, he fingered the thin scar that split his cheek in front of his ear, and his subtle motion served as a forceful reminder to Eun-Me of his old prisoner-of-war injury.

"Grace isn't deaf, and she speaks English better than many of the kids in our own schools in the States. Jennifer Anderson, this is Cho, Eun-Me."

Eun-Me forced herself not to bow again and at the same time did her best to control her voice so that it held no hint of an Asian accent, especially after Philip's high praise of her language skills. "I am very pleased to make your acquaintance, Miss Anderson."

Jennifer stiffened, her mouth tightened, and her eyebrows rose. First she glanced at Philip, then back to Eun-Me. "I'm pleased to meet you, Miss Me. You are the first real Korean I've met, except for the crew on the freighter coming over. You don't mind if I call you Cho Eun, do you?"

Not sure how to respond, Eun-Me stared at the floor until Philip broke the silence.

"Her name isn't Miss Me. If you want to use her Korean name, you should address her either as 'Miss Cho' or 'Eun-Me.' Koreans place the family name first and the given name last, and each given name has a special meaning. Eun-Me's name means grace and beauty. So, when she asked my dad to give her an English biblical name, as many Korean Christians do, 'Grace' seemed to be the perfect fit for Eun-Me.

"Rather than using her Korean name, you might find it easier to call her Grace. And, in return, she should call you Jennifer. You wouldn't mind that, would you, Grace?"

Grace raised her attention from the floor, back to Jennifer. "No. Not at all. Philip has always called me 'Grace,' and I'd be honored if you'd do the same." Eun-Me tried to smile in encouragement toward Jennifer. However, the gesture of friendship was not reciprocated. Instead, Jennifer turned to glare at Philip, and as she spoke, tears slid down her cheeks.

"How could you embarrass me like that, Philip?" She shook visibly as she spoke. "I thought the servants weren't to call us by our first names. And now, this last-name-first thing! I can't be expected to know all these funny little rules."

At the word "servant," Philip immediately stiffened from head to toe. Before he could speak, Eun-Me stepped forward and laid her hand lightly on Jennifer's arm. Jennifer flinched at her touch, so Eun-Me backed up a step, completing the break in contact. "There is no need to feel embarrassed. The Korean culture and language are very different from yours, and you are in a strange land. No one expects you to know these things immediately. I've been studying English since I was ten, but I still make many humiliating blunders."

"Your English is impeccable, Grace," Philip interrupted. "And I'm not ashamed to take a good part of the credit for teaching you." He turned to face his fiancée, his posture remaining rigid as he spoke. "You've heard my stories about Grace and her family since the day we met. She's not just a housekeeper or *servant*," he said, enunciating the word very clearly. "She's an old family friend."

Distress clouded Jennifer's eyes. Eun-Me wished there was something she could do to set the pretty lady at ease but couldn't think of anything other than to show the honored guest to her room.

"You must be exhausted after such a long boat trip from America. I can turn down your bed so you can rest."

Philip suddenly relaxed his posture and stepped up to Jennifer, laying an arm around her shoulders.

"I'm sorry. I didn't mean to embarrass you. I suppose it's my fault for not explaining some of these cultural differences better. I keep forgetting how new all this is for you. And you may not have realized that Grace was the childhood friend I'm often talking about. Come on. Give me a little hug and show me that you accept my apology."

When Jennifer turned in to Philip to receive his hug, it was Eun-Me's turn to feel embarrassed.

She looked away and squirmed uncomfortably as she witnessed Philip's tenderness toward Jennifer. Their embrace reminded Eun-Me of the welcome hug that Philip had given her just moments earlier. His touch had ricocheted through her like a jolt of electricity that left her trembling from head to toe.

She couldn't remember the last time she'd been held by another human being. Certainly not since her *omma* had died. . .

*Oh, how wonderful it would be to rest in the arms of another. In Philip's arms.*

She had loved him since they were children and had suffered an obsessive teenage crush over him even after he left the country when she was fifteen. Since then, no man had ever shown her the respect and admiration that Philip had.

No man paid her any attention at all. In his absence, she had allowed her love for him to grow untethered in the secret places of her heart. She craved his touch, any show of affection, no matter how small.

But, he belonged to another now. She could never enjoy his caress. Besides, only in fairy tales could a housemaid win the heart of a doctor.

Eun-Me shook her head to clear away the nonsensical thought. She didn't have time for such absurd daydreams. She had work to do. Easing away from the private exchange between Philip and Miss Anderson, Eun-Me excused herself with a muttered explanation that she never expected them to hear.

"If you'll pardon me, I'll just run along and turn back that bed for Miss Jennifer now."

❧

From over the top of Jennifer's shoulder, Philip watched Grace disappear down the hallway.

The sound of his father's deep baritone voice above him made him jump.

"Hey, you two, knock it off. You aren't alone, you know."

Philip released Jennifer and looked up to see his parents descending the stairs. "Sorry, Dad. But I had some apologizing to do. I seem to recall you having to beg forgiveness from Mom a time or two."

"No comment." Philip's dad ducked his head to avoid a playful slap from his mother as she came up behind him.

"Watch it, Mr. Missionary, or I'll go sunbathing without you. I saw our bachelor missionary, Richard Spencer, lying on the beach when we pulled into the compound. I bet he knows how to treat a missionary mama right."

"I'm not about to let a gorgeous dame like you out of my sight."

Philip watched as his dad flicked a beach towel at his mom. Two years had passed since his parents returned to Korea, leaving him in San Francisco to finish medical school. His heart warmed to watch them banter playfully with one another again. He breathed a silent prayer that his marriage would be as strong as his parents' union after thirty years together.

He turned to Jennifer, a wide grin spreading over his face. "Looks like the old folks are heading for a swim. You feel up to a dip in the drink?"

"Sure," she responded. But the smile she returned seemed to tax her energies to their limits.

"Hey, if you're too tired, I understand. If you want, I'll set up the beach umbrella, and you can take a nap in the fresh ocean air. I could lie beside you and work on my tan awhile. With the hours I've been keeping at the hospital lately, I've not seen the sun for months."

"Truth is, Philip, after two weeks on an ocean liner, I've breathed about all the sea air I can stand, and my stomach is doing flip-flops. Why don't you go to the beach with your parents? I'll catch up with you after I've had a chance to rest a bit."

Philip's mother wagged a finger in his face. "Son, you may have all the fancy letters after your name and an expensive doctor education, but you need to listen to a little advice from ol' Mom and let this girl sleep as long as she wants in a real, on-solid-ground bed. She was too keyed up to get a good rest last night in Seoul, and she looks plumb worn out."

She stroked Jennifer's hair with a mother's tender touch as she continued her lecture, and although she'd not been back to her native Texas for more than thirty years, a strong south-Texan twang still peppered her speech. "We've got all summer to visit, and you can stand to be away from her for an hour or so. Why don't you carry her suitcase into her bedroom and help her get settled, then join us at the shore by the boat launch in just a bit? Eun-Me will take good care of Jennifer while we're gone. Goodness gracious, we won't be far."

He was about to ask Jennifer if that was what she would prefer, but when he looked at her, the dark circles under her eyes and her drooping shoulders told him all he needed to know.

"All right, Jennifer. As your personal physician, and after consultation with my esteemed colleague, I am ordering complete bed rest for you." Her suitcase stood just inside the entryway where he'd abandoned it earlier, and he moved to pick it up. His words trailed after him while he dragged the weighty luggage down the hallway. "I'll have to answer to your dad when we return Stateside, so I've got to take good care of you. When we get back to San Francisco in August, it wouldn't do to present a sickly daughter to the doctor in charge of my residency."

Jennifer shuffled her feet as she walked behind him but paused at the bathroom door halfway down the hall. "Don't be ridiculous, Philip. You can do no wrong in Daddy's eyes. Now, if you'll excuse me for just a moment—"

She closed the bathroom door behind her while Philip craned his good ear toward the other room to catch his mother's words. "We'll run along and see you in a few minutes, Son." The screen door screeched closed behind them, and he could hear their flip-flops slapping against the sandy path as they headed down to the shore.

When he entered the guest bedroom, he found Grace in front of an open window, waving a towel. "What on earth are you doing, Grace?"

"I fear that these cooking odors have made your fiancée sick, so I'm trying to shake out some of the smell. I should have stayed with my plan to serve the *bulgogi*. But I remembered how you liked the bean paste soup—I didn't even stop to think how your fiancée might react to our more potent Korean foods."

"Grace, the sooner Jennifer acclimates herself to Korea, the better. And the soup smells wonderful to me. I can't wait till supper. I've not had a decent Korean meal since I left Seoul eight years ago. And Dad says your *kimchee* is even better than your *omma*'s." Philip watched as the secondhand compliment sent a shy smile tugging at the corners of Grace's lips.

"In fact," he continued, "I wish you'd teach Jennifer your secret to making good *kimchee*. That's one of the reasons I brought her to Korea—so she'd learn how to cook Korean food. A basic prerequisite for any woman who hopes to marry me is the ability to produce a tasty pot of *kimchee* now and then."

An undercurrent of a chuckle tinted her reply. "I am happy to help you in any way that I can. You know that. But we'd better postpone the cooking lessons awhile. Miss Jennifer doesn't look like she could stomach much more of our culture today."

At that moment, Jennifer walked into the room and sat on the corner of the bed, her shoulders sagging. "You've got that right, Honey. My tummy's upset. And my head is killing me. If you'd fetch me a glass of water and a spoon, I could stir up a bicarbonate of soda. Then, I really need to sleep."

Philip tightened his lips, not liking the way Jennifer again summarily dismissed his old friend. As he watched Grace obediently bow out of the room to retrieve the requested items, he determined to discuss the matter with Jennifer after her nap.

"Rest well, Jennifer." He paused at the doorway as he spoke. "Since things seem to be under control here, I'm going to change into my swim trunks and spend a bit of time with my folks on the beach."

In less than three minutes, he had rifled through his luggage for his swimsuit, changed, and grabbed a clean beach towel from the bathroom on his way out the door. As he rounded the corner of the cabin and stepped onto the sandy trail leading to the beach, a volley of rifle fire rang through the air. And a woman's scream sliced through the cabin walls.

# Chapter 2

Jennifer's shrieks brought Eun-Me racing back to the bedroom from the kitchen.

"Oh, God, have mercy on me! We're under attack! I don't want to die! Where's Philip? Why did he insist on bringing me here?"

Eun-Me rounded the corner to see the distraught American on her knees in the middle of the bed, clutching the bodice of her housecoat. Eun-Me froze in her tracks as she tried to decide how to handle the situation.

Philip couldn't have gotten far down the trail to the beach. However, if she ran to catch him, she'd have to leave Jennifer alone. That didn't seem like a wise idea in light of Jennifer's distraught condition.

Eun-Me hesitantly approached the bed, one arm outstretched. "Everything is all right, Miss Jennifer."

As Eun-Me continued to approach her, Jennifer recoiled. Not knowing what else to do until Philip arrived, Eun-Me decided to speak from across the room. She lowered her voice in an attempt to calm Miss Jennifer without touching her. "We're not under attack. Listen to me. No one is shooting at us."

"What was that then?" Jennifer narrowed her eyes to a harsh squint, making Eun-Me feel that Jennifer somehow held her personally responsible for the commotion.

"The gunfire comes from the military outpost on the back side of the beach. The troops practice maneuvers there every afternoon. You'll get used to the ruckus soon enough. Please. Trust me. We're all right. Everything is all right."

Jennifer's chin quivered when she spoke. "I want Philip. Find him for me. And hurry."

As though cued, Philip burst into the room. Jennifer's tears erupted again when he gathered her in his arms.

Eun-Me offered a hurried repeat explanation of the explosion to Philip, but before she could go into more detail about the military exercises, Jennifer interrupted her as she pushed away from Philip. "I can't take this. Why did I ever let you convince me to come? I'm already a nervous wreck. I'll never survive a whole summer."

"Listen, Jennifer. This is the first I've heard of any military exercises, but rather than fussing about the noise, let's thank God for the protection and safety these troops give us."

Eun-Me watched Jennifer send Philip an incredulous glare, then sputter, "But. . .but. . ."

He held up a hand to silence her. "You've gotten yourself all worked up. Let me get my bag and dig out a mild sedative to help you sleep." Philip darted out of the room, leaving Eun-Me to watch over Jennifer. He returned within seconds, however, clutching two white capsules in the palm of his hand.

A staccato *rat-a-tat* of rifle fire sounded in the distance as he persuaded Jennifer to lie back down. Minutes after downing the pills, her breathing became rhythmic and steady as she dozed off.

Philip waited a few more minutes to make certain Jennifer was sleeping soundly before he excused himself to join his parents at the beach.

"I don't expect Jennifer to wake up for hours," he said to Eun-Me as she walked with him to the back door. "But if she does, just ring the dinner bell, and I'll come running."

❧

Long after Eun-Me had cleared the table and put away the leftovers, Philip and his parents remained in their seats. Eun-Me snatched glimpses of the laughing, reminiscing family as she washed the dishes and tidied the kitchen. There could be no denying that Philip was his parents' son. He had inherited his mother's sandy blond hair and pewter gray eyes, his father's imposing six-foot, three-inch height and dimpled chin.

When a loud belch escaped from *Moksanim* Woods, Philip tipped back his head and roared with laughter. "You sure know how to compliment the cook, Dad. And you have proven once again that you are more Korean than American."

*Moksanim*'s chair screeched against the linoleum floor as he pushed back and rose to loom over Eun-Me. "I can't find words to say it any more eloquently, Grace. You really outdid yourself on that fantastic dinner." Philip stood and sandwiched Eun-Me between the two of them.

"Add my amen to that, Grace. I wish I could have polished off the last of that *kimchee,* but I'm too stuffed. Don't be surprised if you hear me raiding the refrigerator in the middle of the night, though." He picked up his coffee cup and motioned to his folks with a jerk of his head. "What do you say we take our coffee to the davenport and relax awhile? I'd like to see if I can pick up any stations on my transistor radio. I need to brush up a little on my Korean listening skills."

As Eun-Me poured fresh coffee into their cups, her muscles ached with such fatigue that she had to steady the pot with both hands. After fighting back several yawns, she finally found the courage to ask *Sahmonim* Woods if she could retire early for the evening.

"Should Miss Jennifer wake up, I've left a light supper for her in the icebox."

"You run along to bed, Dear," *Sahmonim* urged. "We can take care of Jennifer."

Philip stood in polite deference to Eun-Me as she bowed and backed out of the living room. "Judging from the looks of Jennifer when I checked earlier, she may sleep the rest of the night, but thank you for all you've done to make her feel comfortable. And, Grace—it's wonderful to see you again."

A shiver of excitement raced through her as she looked into his eyes. She swallowed hard, licked her lips, and whispered a breathy, "You too."

Dropping her gaze, she fled to her makeshift sleeping quarters in the storage room off the kitchen. She latched the door behind her and buried her head in her hands. If her *omma* were here, she would have undoubtedly launched into Eun-Me with a rapid-fire Korean tongue-lashing by now.

"Remember your station, Daughter," she would have said. "Master the art of self-control. Never allow your emotions free rein." And *Omma* would have been right on all counts.

Yet her heart refused to listen to logic and reason in matters concerning Philip Woods.

She unrolled her pallet and smoothed the bedding before climbing under the covers of the thick *yoh*. The stiff, rice-hull pillow rustled noisily when Eun-Me burrowed her head into a comfortable position. Filtering under the door, a static-laced broadcast of a traditional folk song crackled from Philip's radio. Eun-Me pictured him on the sofa, his feet propped up on the low coffee table. The image sent another warm shiver through her. He was here. In the next room. She couldn't take her mind off the delightful fact.

For the longest time, she had convinced herself that her remembrance of Philip was much more idyllic than the real man. She felt certain that, once she saw him face-to-face, the reality of him would shatter the sainted status he held in her mind. In fact, the flesh-and-blood Philip sitting on the sofa far exceeded her revered memory of him.

Yet, even as she contemplated all of Philip's wonderful attributes and relived her joy at seeing him again, a pang of guilt seized her. He belonged to Jennifer.

She needed help in sorting out her feelings, and there was only one place she knew to turn for wisdom and guidance. Eun-Me reached into the kerchief-bound bundle of her belongings, which sat on the floor by her mat, and withdrew her Korean/English Bible. The pages fell open to the bookmarked place in the Book of James.

Breathing a prayer for inspiration, she picked up her reading where she'd left off yesterday. As she'd gotten into the habit of doing, she focused first on the English version of the passage and tried to see if she could catch the meaning of the verse without reading the Korean translation. Despite her weariness, the wealth of insight contained in the few phrases she read grabbed her attention, and she tried hard to concentrate, but she read no further than the first chapter, when her eyelids drooped shut. She weakly tried to open them again, but the effort proved too great.

❧

Eun-Me blinked back to wakefulness and stared wide-eyed into the blackness for several long seconds as she struggled to place her whereabouts. Not until she heard whispered English coming through the wide crack beneath the storage room door did she remember that she was at the beach cabin. She recognized the voices of Philip and Miss Jennifer and the light, which jabbed at the darkness from under the door, seemed to carry their speech. For, despite their lowered pitch, she understood their every word.

"What are you doing up in the middle of the night, Philip? I'm too keyed up to sleep, and my growling stomach doesn't help either. I'm starving." With a vacuum-sealed thump, the refrigerator slammed shut. "Isn't there anything in this kitchen that I can eat besides that skunk-smelly soup, fermented cabbage, or globby, sticky rice? Where's the peanut butter?"

Eun-Me bit her lip to stifle a rising bubble of indignation. Despite her professed hunger, Miss Jennifer couldn't even bring herself to taste a single bite of the Korean food, yet she was quick to criticize. Either Miss Jennifer fancied herself an extremely finicky eater or she was rather stubborn and set in her ways. Regardless, pleasing her presented Eun-Me with a formidable and unwelcome challenge.

The repeated creak and slam of cabinet doors told Eun-Me that Miss Jennifer's search for food had not yet proven successful.

"Knock it off, Jennifer."

Philip's clipped command caught Eun-Me off guard.

"What?" Jennifer stretched the word into a whine. "What'd I do?"

"You've expressed loud and clear your unhappiness about coming here. That's what."

She pictured Philip in her mind's eye as he drew a long, deep breath, hesitant and uneasy in the task of admonishing his fiancée.

"Jennifer, what's gotten into you? I've never known you to behave like this. Where is that perky, sweet girl who stole my heart? Can't you make the slightest effort?" The intensity of his obvious vexation rose with each question until all indications of his awkwardness were quickly smothered by blatant ire.

"I don't know what you were expecting, but I tried to prepare you. You just didn't want to bother to listen. Don't you realize how condescending you seem? I've held my tongue until now, because I know how stressful this trip has been on you. But you have to realize that when you belittle the food and customs of Korea, you insult me. And another thing—"

Evidently, Philip had realized his growing pitch, for his words suddenly dropped back to a hoarse whisper, and Eun-Me had to strain to catch the next sentence.

"Whether you meant to or not, you've degraded an old family friend by putting on pompous airs. I highly doubt that in the entire course of your lifetime you will ever have to experience the hardships that Grace has already endured."

Once again, Philip abandoned his efforts to keep his voice down as his volume rose with his emotions. "I owe a lot to Grace, and I won't have you demeaning her. She's one of the most selfless people you'll ever meet. In fact, she's even sleeping on the storage room floor right now so that you could have some privacy."

When she heard him say her name, Grace's ears heated with embarrassment. His words weren't meant for her to hear, and she felt like a spy, eavesdropping like this. Still, she couldn't very well interrupt their discussion now. She rolled to her side and covered her head with one arm in an unsuccessful attempt to block out Philip's diatribe. No one had asked her to sleep in the storage room. She had made the choice in order to afford Miss Jennifer some comfort and privacy as she adjusted to her new surroundings. And she did not regret her decision, nor did she expect Miss Jennifer's gratitude. Yet, she knew that if she had done the same for Philip, he would have gone out of his way to express his thanks.

"Let me remind you that, up until the prisoner-of-war exchange, Grace was the one who brought us word from home along with our meals every day during the six months that Dad and I were imprisoned. She nursed my wounds and bandaged my ear after each interrogation and beating. During that time, she and her mother stayed, at the risk of great peril, to look after my mom while she was under house arrest. And, long before her mother came to work for us, her father was my dad's best friend."

At the mention of her father, tears stung Eun-Me's eyes, and she whisked them away with a quick swipe of her elbow while Philip's voice took on a tender tone.

"When Pastor Cho and his wife became Christians, their parents disowned them for refusing to worship Buddha or practice Shamanism and ancestor worship. So, our family took the place of the Chos' own flesh and blood. After Pastor Cho died a martyr's death, we brought Grace, Eun-Soo, and their *omma* into our home, since their kin had rejected them. Grace is no servant to us. She's family. Do you understand?"

Gooseflesh erupted on Eun-Me's arms when she heard Philip refer to her as "family." Perhaps she wasn't as alone as she had assumed herself to be after *Omma's* death. She heard a distinct tinge of brotherly affection in Philip's words as he continued.

"So, if you can't find it within your self to befriend her, at least grant her the respect she deserves. Neither she nor her mother have ever been treated like servants, and I won't stand for your condescending airs now. I love you, Jennifer. But I have to tell you, I felt pretty disappointed in you today."

In the long silence that followed, Eun-Me tried to picture Jennifer's reaction to Philip's scolding. She rose up onto one elbow and listened for sniffles that would indicate an encore of this afternoon's tears. Was she crying? Pouting? Or cowering? Expecting to hear a soft, apologetic response, Eun-Me winced at Miss Jennifer's sharp rebuttal.

"Look. I'm sorry. Okay? I know I've been cranky and critical. But you have to remember, I've never been outside of California. Give me some time to get used to all this. Nothing makes sense to me. On one hand, I'm scared to death, and on the other—well, frankly, I find it all so pathetic. Oxen and field workers in funny hats and thatched roofed huts and primitive conditions, just like a page out of a *National Geographic*, but with machine-gun-toting military guys thrown in. You grew up around here. You're used to all this noise and smell and war-game business."

"You're wrong there, Miss Jennifer," Eun-Me muttered to herself, for she knew from a lifetime of personal experience that no one ever gets used to war. She had spent her whole life under the heavy-handed rule of the Japanese, and she felt certain that, until her dying day, she would cringe at the sight of a pea green uniform. Surely, Philip must feel even more fearful than she for, following Japan's bombing of Pearl Harbor and their official declaration of war against America, Philip had been arrested and interned on trumped-up spy charges. He had suffered through six months of physical beatings and emotional tortures before his repatriation back to the States.

"We probably ought to postpone this discussion until tomorrow." Philip's voice held a note of weary resignation. "I'm afraid that we've already disturbed Grace's sleep, and you need to eat something before you make yourself sick. Although you aren't likely to find anything to your liking in the cupboards. They don't sell peanut butter anywhere around here. However, you should be happy to know that I had the foresight to pack a couple of jars of peanut butter. I'll run upstairs and grab a jar from my suitcase so you can make us both a sandwich."

As his footsteps carried him away from the kitchen, the volume of his words dropped. "While I'm gone, why don't you go and rest on the davenport? Flip on my radio if you want. That's what I do when I'm keyed up and having trouble sleeping. But, Jennifer, please. . .try to learn why it is that I love this land and these people so."

"Okay, Philip. I'll try harder. But I'm still so nervous and shaky. Could I get you to give me another dose of that mild sedative you gave me this afternoon? Maybe everything will look better after a few more hours of sleep."

❧

*Saturday, June 24, 1950*

The clapper on Eun-Me's windup alarm clock jangled obnoxiously to signal her 4:45 wake-up time. Despite the short night, she wanted to slip over to the open-air tabernacle for her daily dawn prayer time before she began her workday.

She changed from her nightgown into her *mom-pei* trousers and a shapeless work shirt, then crept softly through the house with her shoes in hand so as not to disturb the others. The skies, although dry at the moment, couldn't be trusted to stay that way in the middle of rainy season, and the trees still dripped with the vestiges of a midnight shower. She sprouted her umbrella, then tucked her Bible into the crook of her free arm and set out down the sandy path.

Eun-Me veered to the left when she came to a fork in the trail, and her steps fell silent as she traveled over a blanket of pine needles, picking her way through the underbrush that had yet to be cleared for the summer. The chapel, situated on a bluff, overlooked a rocky portion of shoreline and afforded a breathtaking view of the sea as slender shards of predawn light splintered the dark waves.

Entering the back of the simple sanctuary, Eun-Me discovered that, unfortunately, she was not alone. As her eyes adjusted to the dark room, she recognized the unmistakable silhouette of Philip kneeling at the mourner's bench in front of the pulpit. From what she could see of him, he didn't look like he had slept at all during the night.

Hoping not to disturb Philip's time of prayer, she quietly slid into a seat on the wooden bench nearest the rear door. She debated whether or not she should leave the building altogether and grant Philip total privacy, but before she could decide what to do, the door spring squeaked softly, and *Moksanim* Woods stepped inside. She nodded in greeting as he passed her on his way down the aisle. Then, folding her hands in her lap, she bowed her head and hunched her shoulders, assuming her customary praying posture.

Try as she might, however, she could not channel her thoughts heavenward, for Philip's supplications filled the morning air, and all of Eun-Me's attentions focused on him.

"Dear God, please show me what to do." His rich voice echoed across the chapel. "Oh, Father, I've made such a mess of things. None of this has turned out like I'd hoped. How can I possibly tell her now?"

She jerked forward in an effort to rise. Concern for her troubled friend compelled her to stay. Yet, she didn't want to embarrass him, and Eun-Me felt certain Philip was unaware that others were privy to his prayers. She looked up in time to see Philip's father move in beside him and slip an arm around his shoulder.

"*Hahnahnim, kamsahaomnieda*—Oh, Lord, thank You." She breathed a prayer of gratitude that *Moksanim* had the sensitivity to make his presence known. No doubt he would counsel Philip concerning whatever mess he felt he had created. She couldn't fathom what it could be. Nor did she feel comfortable knowing unless he shared the matter directly with her. As the two men huddled in holy conversation, Eun-Me noiselessly tiptoed outside.

Not yet ready to return to the cabin, she stood overlooking the steep staircase that led from the chapel to the beach.

Philip's prayer played repeatedly in her mind. Who was this "her" he had mentioned? What information did he feel hopelessly unable to disclose?

Breathing deeply, she captured a gust of salty wind in her lungs. This guessing game was a waste of her time. If the matter concerned her at all, she'd learn the answers in due time. Until then, she'd redouble her prayers for Philip.

For the moment, she needed to concern herself with the more pressing urgency of breakfast preparations. Fish head soup with steaming sticky rice comprised a typical morning's menu. Usually a guest would be granted the honor of receiving the fish's eyes in their bowl. However, Eun-Me didn't think that Miss Jennifer would appreciate the time-honored tradition. For today, she decided that she would serve a breakfast of biscuits and gravy and scrambled eggs as something that would better suit Miss Jennifer's taste.

Eun-Me traipsed down the steep stairs and onto the beach, headed toward the row of market stalls on the distant horizon. Despite the early hour, she hoped that the egg lady might be open for business.

❧

Throughout breakfast, Philip listened to Jennifer as she gushed on and on with effusive praise of Grace's cooking. He doubted that he was the only one to question the sincerity of her feast-or-famine kindness. Still, he realized she was making a concerted effort to rectify her behavior of yesterday, and for that he was thankful.

His overly animated fiancée had sashayed out of her bedroom and plopped a hefty stack of ladies' magazines and bridal catalogues on the kitchen table. With one look at the pile, he knew why he'd been forced to drag her suitcase all the way down the gangplank.

When Jennifer asked his mother her opinion of pink organza for the bridesmaids' gowns, Philip took her question as his cue to leave. His dad was tinkering with the temperamental hot-water heater in the bathroom and couldn't break away. Grace had left the cabin on an undisclosed errand minutes before. So, collecting his beach towel, folding chair, a half-finished paperback book, and a jug of iced tea, he headed for the shore alone.

He looked forward to burrowing into the warm sand for a snooze under the midmorning sun. The Lord knew he had not gotten much rest of late, but he couldn't blame his sleeplessness on the grueling schedule he'd kept as an emergency room intern. The root of his insomnia stemmed from a growing and dreadful fear that he may have made a horrific misjudgment in his choice of a life mate.

Within the safe haven of her hometown, the daughter of a prestigious San Francisco doctor had seemed like the ideal match for him. He'd found so many reasons to fall in love with Jennifer. Witty and pretty and at ease among the city's most elite social circles, she drew admiring glances wherever they went, and Philip was always proud to be seen with her. Of even more importance to him, she professed a relationship with Jesus Christ and claimed Him as her Savior.

Since that evening last September, when Dr. Anderson had introduced them to one another at a hospital fund-raiser, Jennifer had always acted enthralled when Philip related one of his childhood adventures as a missionary kid. He thought she found his Korean heritage fascinating and unique. But they had no sooner pulled away from San Francisco Harbor than she set about subtly belittling and berating his adopted motherland. When he described a centuries-old custom, her blank stare plainly conveyed her disinterest. If he tried to teach her a Korean greeting, she floundered like a fish on dry land.

He attributed her anomalous responses to an attempt to mask her ignorance concerning this culture so foreign to her own. Or perhaps she felt a genuine fear of the unknown. Regardless of the cause for her insensitivity, over the course of the two-week voyage, his patience had been stretched tissue-paper thin. And after coming ashore yesterday, their relationship appeared to be deteriorating at an alarming speed. Jennifer's calloused treatment of Grace had dealt a crushing blow. Yet, he couldn't fully explain to her why.

Long before he had invited her to Korea to meet his parents, he had wanted to share with her the other reason he wanted to make this trip. The most important reason. Yet, the right moment for such a disclosure just never seemed to come.

Philip laid his armload of beach paraphernalia on the sun-warmed sand and spread out his towel. Then, stretching his arms toward the sky, he dipped left and right, backward and forward, popping the kinks out of his neck and back. Yesterday when he'd come here, he had been so involved in visiting with his parents that he hadn't paid much attention to the view. Now, as he paused to study his surroundings, a flood of childhood memories washed over him.

Not much had changed since the last time he'd vacationed here, although he didn't recognize any of his fellow sunbathers. Several other "big noses," as the Koreans so affectionately called Americans, lay scattered about the beach. Compared to the handful of small-framed, darker-skinned natives who were busy digging clams from the freshly exposed shore at low tide, the pasty-white, flabby foreigners looked uncomfortably akin to beached whales.

His gaze rested on the form of a lone clam-digger skirting the foamy edge of rolling surf, and he laughed aloud when he recognized that the distant figure was Grace. With her pant legs rolled up around her knees and a pail dangling from her arm, she appeared childlike, unscathed by the eight-year passage of time since he'd been gone.

He left his gear and jogged toward her. As he drew closer, he cupped his hands around his mouth to form a makeshift megaphone before calling out her name.

"Grace!"

She turned to look in his direction, responding instantly by waving her free hand in a sweeping arc. He increased his speed from a jog to a run, and Grace waited for him to catch up to her. His quick sprint left him breathless, and he grabbed his knees, gulping air before he attempted to speak.

"Need. . .some. . .help?" He tipped his head up to look at her, then he straightened to his full height as he took one final lung-filling swallow followed by a quick exhale. "I bet I can remember the best clam-digging spot on the beach. Follow me."

"The only help I need from you is your help in eating them. You must be exhausted. I don't think you've gotten any sleep since you arrived at Taechon." Grace's brows knotted as she straightened and turned her head to gaze upward at him.

Without asking, he took the pail from her arm and motioned for her to follow him. "Well, the more we gather, the more I can help you eat. Come on. Let me show you where the clams hang out in this neighborhood. That little run invigorated me, and I couldn't sleep now if I tried. You know, don't you, that they don't allow anyone to graduate from medical school until they've mastered the ability to function on little or no sleep?"

Grace, in typical Oriental fashion, fell into step two paces behind him. "Then that's just one more reason I could never be a doctor," she answered with a chuckle. "But, if you insist on helping me, then lead the way." They walked in comfortable silence past the bank of stairs going up to the chapel and on until the sand turned into a rocky stretch of shoreline, accessible only at low tide. A shallow, surf-carved cavern jutted into the overhanging cliff, and Philip briefly crouched in the shadows of the opening. When he straightened again, the sound of shellfish clanking against the sides of the metal pail echoed through the cave. Grace joined him in the harvest, and within minutes the bucket brimmed to overflowing.

"You can't carry this." Philip refused to allow Grace to take the pail from him. "Let me deliver this back to the cabin for you." He retraced their shoe-print trail but stopped at the cement stairs and plopped himself down on the bottom step, sinking the clam bucket into the soft sand between his feet.

"Dad told me you were in the chapel this morning." As Grace approached, he patted the place next to him. "I hope my ranting prayers didn't drive you off. You didn't have to leave. Actually, I am grateful for the chance to tell you about a couple of things that are really eating at me. I could use some advice, and you always had a level head about you. I'd appreciate your prayers too. I couldn't bring myself to talk to Dad. For one thing, I don't want him to be disappointed if things don't work out like I'm thinking they will."

Instead of sitting beside him, Grace sank to her knees in the sand next to him.

"I don't know about the levelheaded part, but I'm honored that you would confide in me, and I certainly will pray."

His eyes met hers for a fleeting second before she dropped her gaze and intently studied her folded hands. Her humble posture and sweet spirit filled him with a warm pleasure and sent a small smile pulling at the corners of his lips.

"Thanks, Grace. I knew I could count on you. Here's the deal. . ."

Philip raised one hand to rest it on the back of his neck, then straightened and drew a deep breath before he began to speak. "Jennifer's father is the chief of staff at a private hospital in San Francisco, and he's in charge of my residency. Dr. Anderson has really bent over backward to help me. He had to do some creative scheduling so that I could take enough time off to make this trip. Plus, he's already hinted strongly that he's put in a good word for me with a doctor friend of his, and apparently, I have an 'in' to become a junior partner as a general practitioner with him. Of course, the idea of settling down close to her folks thrills Jennifer to no end."

"Oh, that's wonderful—" Grace pressed her fingers to her lips.

"Well, yes and no. There's just one little glitch in this seemingly perfect plan. One big glitch, actually. . ."

He gulped another big breath before continuing.

"You see, for the past couple of months, I've been sensing that God is calling me to be a missionary doctor back here in Asia—either Korea or Japan. I already know the languages, and the need for doctors is so much greater here than back in the States. So, this trip to Korea involves more than introducing Jennifer to my folks. For weeks I've been praying that God will use this trip to confirm or deny my missionary call, and the minute I set foot back in Korea, I felt an undeniable assurance that this is where God wants to use me."

A rush of excitement swept over him as he voiced, for the first time, his surety of God's call on his life to mission service. Yet, the dawning of a sadder revelation tempered the thrill of this one.

"I'm still waiting for the right moment to share all this with Jennifer. She's reacted so negatively to everything about Korea since we arrived. She seems downright miserable. I couldn't possibly spring on her now the idea of moving here permanently. Grace, you don't think God would call me to be a missionary without calling Jennifer too, do you? The way I see it, a missionary's life is so tough, both the husband and wife need to know without a doubt that God is calling them to serve."

Grace's eyes widened more than he'd ever seen, and she gasped.

"*Paksanim,* do you mean to tell me that you haven't discussed all this with Miss Jennifer? She needs to know immediately."

Before he could defend his position, Jennifer's voice cracked through his thoughts.

"Philip, what are you two talking about down there? What is it I need to know?"

He twisted around to see his mother, with Jennifer beside her, overshadowing them at the top of the stairs.

Jennifer perched her hands on her hips, and her eyes narrowed to a tight glare. "Are you keeping secrets from me?"

# Chapter 3

Eun-Me had already jumped to her feet and was brushing the sand from her britches when *Sahmonim* Woods called down to her, "Grace, why don't we leave these two alone? Sounds like they might need to chat awhile."

She responded with a quick nod.

"I'm praying for you, Philip," she murmured into his good ear as she retrieved the pail from between his feet and inched past him on her way up the stairs.

At the halfway point of her descent, Miss Jennifer breezed past Eun-Me without acknowledging her proffered "Excuse me" or extending the courtesy of the same.

"That poor dear," *Sahmonim* rasped in a loud whisper when Eun-Me fell into step behind her. "She's a beauty. That's for sure. But she's more skittery than a Mexican jumping bean."

"Yes, Ma'am," she replied, certain that she'd never seen a jumping bean of any nationality, but just as certain that the graphic description must fit Miss Jennifer perfectly.

The full pail swung awkwardly back and forth, forcing Eun-Me to clutch the metal handle with both hands in order to steady the load.

*Sahmonim* glanced at Eun-Me over her shoulder and slowed her pace. "Well, I can recall feeling mighty scared my first few days in Korea. We just need to give her some time to adjust. Don't you suppose?"

"Yes, Ma'am," Eun-Me parroted her previous response, but she wasn't at all confident that time would improve Miss Jennifer's caustic disposition.

"You don't think this little tiff they seem to be having will amount to anything serious, do you, Dear?"

"No, Ma'am. I hope not, Ma'am," she replied stoically, refusing to respond in any more detail to *Sahmonim*'s not-so-subtle dig for information.

Fortunately, the genteel missionary respected Eun-Me's unspoken plea not to pry any further, and the two women fell silent for the remainder of their walk back to the cabin. Eun-Me seized the opportunity to pray in earnest for Philip, asking God to grant him the wisdom that she'd read about last night in the Book of James.

She shivered as a ripple of excitement swept over her at the thought that Philip might move back to Korea as a missionary. Even if she had to work hard not to expose her true feelings for him, she relished the idea of being near him frequently. Seeing his bright smile. Enjoying the pleasure of his company. But her tingles subsided as she considered the fact that Miss Jennifer would be ever present as well.

"Oh, *Hahnahnim*, give me a double portion of Your patience and understanding as far as Miss Jennifer is concerned," she breathed in concluding prayer when she and *Sahmonim* approached the cabin.

Philip's parents sequestered behind closed doors, and Eun-Me surmised that *Sahmonim* was explaining to her husband about this most recent and uncomfortable turn of events between their son and his future wife. Knowing her employers as well as she did, she knew that they would also spend time in concerted prayer.

When they reappeared in the living room an hour or so later, Eun-Me had busied herself with dusting and sweeping and tidying, chores that allowed her to watch and listen for the return of Philip and Miss Jennifer as well. Both *Sahmonim* and *Moksanim* thinly veiled their own nervous anxieties by dumping a new two-thousand-piece jigsaw puzzle onto the folding table they had set up in the far corner of the living room. Then they lackadaisically sifted through the mountain of puzzle pieces in search of the straight-edged border ones.

Eun-Me dropped all pretenses of busyness when a duet of footsteps sounded on the back porch. Jennifer burst through the door first. With her head down and her hands hiding her face, she streaked across the living room, down the hallway, and into her bedroom, slamming the door behind her without bothering to remove her shoes.

Seconds later, Philip struggled through the back door. The assortment of beach gear he carried under one arm clattered to the floor when he stepped out of his beach flippers and kicked the door shut with the heel of his foot.

He clutched something in the balled fist of his right hand.

Walking over to his mother, he reached down and took hold of her wrist. Turning her palm up, he released that which he held in his grasp.

Eun-Me stared in disbelief at the sparkling object, which lay in *Sahmonim's* outstretched hand. Just this morning at breakfast, she had admired the distinctive pearl-and-diamond engagement ring that graced Miss Jennifer's left hand. *Had he demanded its return? Or had she been the one to break their engagement?*

Her stomach sank at the guilt-pricking realization that her failure to keep her opinionated advice to herself was to blame for this row between Philip and Miss Jennifer. If she hadn't blurted her question at the beach loud enough for anyone to hear, all of this trouble could have been avoided. Philip knew his fiancée much better than she did, and he was surely sensitive enough to know the appropriate time to share with her the news of his missionary call.

When she caught sight of Philip's doleful frown, a fresh stab of remorse assaulted her thoughts. She swallowed hard to stifle her desire to comfort him.

Just because Philip had always confided in her when they were kids did not mean that she should offer her comments now. She told herself to forget the way things used to be. The years had changed their relationship, and it was now too presumptuous of her, an *ajumoni* with only an eighth-grade education, to tell a grown man with a doctor's degree what to do. Regardless of their past friendship, she no longer had the right to counsel, console, or admonish him—particularly concerning matters of romance.

As he addressed his mother, Eun-Me could no longer bear to look at Philip's face. She cared for him too much to see him in such pain. She fixed her gaze on the ring again.

"Please, Mom. Don't say anything. I'm not in the mood to discuss this now. I'll explain to both you and Dad as soon as I'm able." Philip's voice cracked with emotion when he folded his mother's fingers over the tiny golden band. "I need you to hold onto Grandma Carson's ring for safekeeping."

*Moksanim* rose from his seat, knocking several puzzle pieces to the floor with his shirtsleeve. "Don't you worry, Son," he said as he moved to Philip's side and offered him a paternal pat on the back. "The two of you will work through this, whatever the problem may be."

Philip shook his head slowly from side to side. "I wish I could be certain of that. We'll see. But, if you'll excuse me, I think I need to be alone for awhile." Eun-Me watched Philip, his shoulders drooping, as he walked to the staircase. Grabbing the handrail, he looked as though he had to pull himself up the stairs.

When Philip had left the room, *Sahmonim* pinched the ring between her finger and thumb and held it up to the light. "You have no idea how hard it is for me not to order you to tell me what this is all about." Her smile held no joy as she lowered the ring and looked Eun-Me in the eye, but the weight of her statement came through, despite her pleasantness.

"Now, Mama. Stop your meddling." *Moksanim* sidled up to his wife and prodded her arm gently with his elbow. "Exercise the Lord's gift of patience in your life. You don't want Grace to break a confidence. I imagine that her ability to keep quiet is one of the reasons Philip shared his troubles with her. Our son will tell us the whole story in due time. What do you say we get out of this stifling cabin and go for a long walk? The mood is much too heavy in here. Grace, do you think you could rustle up a picnic lunch for Mama and me?"

Eun-Me did his bidding while they went in search of the wicker picnic basket in the storage area under the stairs. She had their lunch ready to pack when the elusive container finally appeared.

"I just peeked into Philip's room on my way downstairs," *Sahmonim* said when she came into the kitchen to retrieve the basket. "He's fallen asleep on top of his bed with his old scrapbook in his hands. I think we should let him sleep as long as he can. I'm awfully worried about him." She plopped a straw sun hat onto the unruly shock of her permed, sandy blond curls.

"Yes, Ma'am. I won't disturb him." Eun-Me laid two ripe persimmons on top of the *kimbap* lunch she had prepared and snapped the lid closed on the full picnic basket before handing it over to *Moksanim*. "I suspect that Miss Jennifer is sleeping also. I've not heard a sound come from her room in quite some time."

"Those poor dears. They'd both be more agreeable and their problems might be solved if the two of them could just get a good night's rest."

"That's your cure-all for everything that ails our world," *Moksanim* interjected. "Now, come along, my missionary mama. I'm sure Grace will appreciate a bit of peace and quiet so she can get her chores done."

≈

Grace stood at the sink washing dishes when Philip walked into the kitchen to get a drink. He paused, not wanting to interrupt her soft singing of his favorite Korean folk song, *"Ariyang."* When she finished the tune, he stepped up behind her and tapped her lightly on the shoulder.

*"Eye-go!"* she squeaked, making him regret sneaking up on her. She grabbed a cup towel from its hook and turned to face him as she dried her hands. Then, leaning back against the sink, she grasped the towel to her chest. "You scared me. I thought you were sleeping."

"Naw. I can't sleep in all this heat and sticky humidity. And when I did manage to drift off, I had the most awful dream. Siberian tigers were chasing me all over the Korean countryside while I searched for Grandma Carson's lost ring. I woke up more exhausted than when I fell asleep." He pulled his hand from behind his back and offered her the paper bag he held.

"Sorry I scared you, but I wanted to give you these. I meant to give them to you yesterday when I arrived, but I forgot in all the hubbub."

She peered into the bag, then reached in and pulled out several packages of chocolate chips. "I remembered how much you loved chocolate chunk cookies as a kid, and I thought my mom could teach you how to make them using these chips, if you haven't already learned."

Philip jumped to sit on the countertop, leaving his feet to dangle several inches from the floor. "Speaking of Mom. . .are she and Dad around? I figured I might as well sit down and spell out this sticky situation to them."

He listened as Grace explained that his parents were out on a picnic but that they should be back soon. He dipped his head toward Jennifer's bedroom door and asked, "Have you seen or heard anything from her?"

"No. Miss Jennifer locked herself in her room, and other than a brief visit to the bathroom, she has not come out. She even refused to open the door to receive the lunch tray I prepared for her."

"That doesn't surprise me," he said with a sigh. "Well, go ahead and say, 'I told you so.' I never should have let things go this far without telling Jennifer about my calling to missionary service. She really lashed into me this morning and said some pretty ugly things." Philip paused the nervous swaying of his feet and sighed, looking away from Grace to stare absently out the window to the dark trees.

"She said I tricked her. Even deliberately misled her about the possibility of going into private practice with her daddy's friend. She accused me of planning to marry her first, so that I could gain her father's financial backing, then she'd have no choice but to let me drag her to the other side of the world to live in what she called 'a grass hut.' I tried to tell her that we could have a regular house just like Mom and Dad, but she refused to listen. She said she's not about to tag along in my shadow while I act like some kind of savior to the heathen. Then, she practically threw my engagement ring at me."

He heard Grace gasp, so he turned back to look at her. Her black eyes brimmed with tears of sympathy, and he struggled to maintain his own composure when he saw the compassion she felt for him. Jennifer might have rejected him, but he knew that he could always count on Grace to be a supportive and faithful friend.

She nodded. "So what are you going to do?"

"I've got no choice. I hate to spoil my folks' summer vacation by cutting it short, but Jennifer hates it here and can't seem to stand the thought of spending any more time with me. I guess I'm going to have to ask Dad if we can head back to Seoul tomorrow and see when the next freighter is scheduled to leave Inchon for San Francisco."

Rifle fire whistled through the air to signal the start of the daily military exercises. Just then, Jennifer stepped into the kitchen. Philip chuckled to consider the irony as he braced for some caustic remark from her. He imagined the crack of firearms outside served to warn him that mounting hostilities inside would soon explode again.

"Uh. . .Philip. I'd like to have a word with you." She tipped her head and looked down her nose at Grace as a not-so-subtle cue to her that her presence was not wanted. Grace muttered something about a matter that needed her attentions outside and left the kitchen before Philip could tell her that she didn't have to leave. He jumped down from his perch on the kitchen counter and waved his hand, indicating for Jennifer to take a seat on the davenport in the living room.

He sat facing her on the edge of the easy chair's cushion, and when he finally collected enough courage to look her in the eyes, she offered him a weak smile.

"I may have been too hasty when I gave you back the ring." As she spoke, she rubbed her tanned finger where the sun had tattooed a pale imprint of the missing engagement ring.

"My emotions got the best of me. Now that I've had a chance to cool down a bit, I've reconsidered things." She drew a deep breath and dropped her hands to her lap, then began to nervously smooth the wrinkles from her sundress.

"I know. . . .I've done this a lot lately. . . ." She stumbled on the words when she raised her eyes to look at him and began again. "I've done this a lot lately. B–b–but, I want to apologize." Her eyelids narrowed and made direct, unwavering eye contact.

When he didn't respond, she continued, her apology taking on a defensive tone.

"For starters, I admit, I overreacted a bit. Although you do realize, don't you, that you sprang some pretty big news on me? Everything here is so different, and I've not had a chance to get used to things, then I hear you saying you want to bring me here to live. I'm willing to pray about this missionary thing if you'll give me more time. After all, you have your residency to complete yet. A lot can happen between now and then. And I still think that maybe what you're sensing is really just happiness at being home and not a voice from God at all."

A tinge of enthusiasm lifted her voice as she continued speaking. "You know, if you really wanted to help the Korean people, you could be more effective by providing the funds to build a hospital or clinic, then financially supporting the staff. Think of the admiration you'd get from the medical community. And, with the help Daddy is promising, in no time at all you'll be generating an income that could easily handle that without putting the slightest crimp in our lifestyle."

Philip cleared his throat before he spoke. "First of all, Jennifer, if you're expecting me to return the ring to you right now, I'm afraid I can't do that. I gave the ring back to my mother for safekeeping since, originally, the ring belonged to her and to her mother before her. I figured I had no further use for the heirloom. Mom and Dad have gone for a picnic, so I couldn't give it back to you at the moment, even if I wanted to."

Jennifer's lips pursed into a thin, straight line of mounting animosity, and Philip measured his next words carefully.

"Frankly, I'm not sure I'm ready for you to wear the ring again." Jennifer's emerald eyes flashed at his words.

"I've had time to do a little thinking myself, and I'm not ready to just kiss and make up. You said some pretty nasty things earlier. Obviously, you don't have much faith in my ability to make it on my own, without your daddy's help. And you've second-guessed my spiritual discernment as well." She shook her head back and forth, and he rushed to finish his speech before she could interrupt.

"If your apology still stands, then I accept it, and you are forgiven. In hindsight, I realize I should have shared with you as soon as I began to sense a mission call. So, for that, I apologize to you as well. But, in light of your response today, I was right to worry about your reaction. I think we really need to give this time and talk things through before we rush back into making wedding plans."

Jennifer rose to her feet to loom over him, and the icy glare she gave him erased all hints of her earlier penitence. "So, tell me, Philip, what am I supposed to do in the meantime? Sit around in this miserable place and wait for you to think about it some more?" She tapped her foot and crossed her arms. "Just how long do you plan to punish me and make me wait?"

White-hot anger pounded at his temples at her unpremeditated description of his homeland. He clinched his jaw in a futile attempt to choke back his indignation.

"If you find Korea to be such a miserable place, then it's because you have made it so. The only thing miserable around here that I can see is the misery you've brought." Philip pushed off the arms of the easy chair and stood to look down on Jennifer. "If, in all honesty, you think I could slough off God's call on my life simply by throwing money at a worthy cause, then you don't have a clue about the true meaning of Christian service. I would be happier living here in abject poverty and all alone, even in that grass hut which you speak of with such disdain, than living a life of luxury with some spoiled and selfish socialite." His voice escalated with each incensed word. "I won't be bullied into a hurried decision that I'll regret the rest of my life. Do you understand?"

Yet, even in his anger, Philip sensed that he had settled the issue about his call once and for all. Nothing else—no one else—would stop him from following the Lord's leading in his life. If that meant serving alone, then so be it. Whatever the cost, he would follow God's leading in his life and serve Him.

A sudden peace washed over him, supplanting his exasperation with Jennifer. He exhaled his tension in a puff of breath, and his shoulders relaxed. However, Jennifer's face appeared almost purple in rage at his blunt scorn, and she lashed back at him with fury.

"A spoiled and selfish socialite, huh? Well, you sure didn't seem to feel that way just a few days ago. I didn't know I'd promised to marry such a pompous, pious saint. You can keep your cheap old engagement ring. I wouldn't marry you if you were the last man on earth."

Her lack of originality struck a strange chord of humor in Philip as she continued her diatribe.

"Remember, when you get back to San Francisco you still have a three-year residency program to complete under Daddy's supervision. I'm certain you'll come to regret all this sooner or later. But when that day comes, don't come crawling back to me begging for forgiveness."

She tilted her chin into the air and stomped her foot to punctuate her final demand. "How soon can I get out of here? I want to go home."

A gloomy darkness overshadowed the room, and Philip glanced out the open window to see a bank of murky clouds moving across the late afternoon sun. "First, let me say that I already regret getting so mad at you."

She replied with a low "Hurmph," but he continued on.

"I shouldn't have let my emotions take over like that. You and I both know that I'm not given to such outbursts, but I still need to offer you an apology. It's not my place to judge you, and I wish I could take back that 'spoiled and selfish' remark." He stared at Jennifer until she returned his gaze.

"But the more we talk, the more I realize you and I aren't meant for one another. I don't think you could ever be happy living so far away from your folks, and I am more convinced than ever that God is calling me here."

The racket of war games had stopped, replaced by an eerie, death-quiet serenity. Philip's words sliced through the stillness.

"I'm sorry we had to come all this way to make such an unpleasant discovery, but I promise to do whatever I can to get you back home to San Francisco immediately. As soon as Dad comes in, I'll speak to him about our returning to Seoul tomorrow." He could see tears threatening to spill down her cheeks and a welling pity overtook him.

"Jennifer—" He wavered, then decided to add one last thought. "Let's try to make this unpleasant situation as easy on one another as possible. What do you say we part company on friendly terms rather than as enemies?"

Jennifer stared at him for several long seconds, and when she finally did respond, she ignored his proposal altogether.

"This is awkward, I know. However, I need to ask you for another dose of that sedative. I thought I'd brought plenty of my own when we left San Francisco, but I've run out."

Droplets of perspiration beaded across her upper lip, and she swiped a hand brusquely over her mouth before she continued.

"My mother knew how nervous I was about making this trip and she had shared a few of her pills with me to help calm my nerves. However, I've had such trouble sleeping and my nerves have given me such a terrible time these past couple of months, especially these last two weeks, that I've used up my supply. Would you kindly share just a couple more?"

The impact of her confession caused his jaw to drop in disbelief. "Do you realize what you've done, Jennifer? You've developed a dependency on those sedatives. No wonder your moods have seesawed so. I'm sorry, but I can't let you have any more. You'll have a rough few days until the medicine is out of your system, but I'll try to help you all I can." He reached out to lay a hand on her shoulder, but she yanked away and glowered at him through slitted eyes.

"How ridiculous. I'm not addicted to any drugs. They were only mild sedatives. My dad's a doctor, for goodness' sake. He would never have given my mother anything harmful. And another thing: Whether or not I've had my nerve pills won't change my decision not to marry you."

She signaled her retreat by tossing her hair out of her face in a quick jerk and spinning away from him. "I'll be in my room if you find a shred of decency within you and decide to give me those pills." She tromped down the hall on bare feet as she called out over her shoulder, "Just stay as far away from me as possible until I can get out of here."

*

*Sunday, June 25, 1950*

Eun-Me lay on her *yoh* listening to the early morning cricket songs long before the alarm clock rang. Philip and the events of yesterday so filled her thoughts that her mind refused to rest. She made a mental list in preparation for their hasty departure, for they would all be returning to Seoul after the worship service today. Miss Jennifer was going back to America where she belonged.

After dinner, Philip had insisted on Eun-Me's presence when he explained to his parents about his call to be a missionary, then he filled in the blanks concerning his resulting quarrel and breakup with Miss Jennifer. For Philip's sake, Eun-Me was sorry that things weren't working out between the two of them. Moreover, she pitied Miss Jennifer's nervous condition. But she had to squelch a flash of pleasure at the thought that the American would soon be gone.

Philip did seem to be handling the situation well, however. Much better than Miss Jennifer, who had locked herself in her room throughout the remainder of the evening. Even *Sahmonim* couldn't coax her out.

Throwing back the heavy quilt, Eun-Me slid her feet onto the hard linoleum and stood. To remain in bed and fret about all that needed to be done was simply a waste of time, regardless of the hour. Since they would all worship together later this morning, she wouldn't be going out for dawn prayers, but if she worked quietly, she could use this time to get a good start on packing things away in the cabin.

She felt her way through the dark room until she found the light switch and flipped it on. She stood still and blinked away the ensuing temporary blindness until her eyes adjusted to the stark, bright light, then she slipped into her shirt-waist dress. Before beginning the work she knew must be done in preparation for them to leave, she quickly rolled up her *yoh* and tucked it neatly under a shelf of canned goods that she and *Sahmonim* had put up last year. With all around her silent, she chuckled quietly to herself with the knowledge that she wouldn't have to wait in line for the bathroom at this time of day.

Toothbrush in hand, she began her journey to the bathroom, but her feet skidded to a halt in the open doorway. Philip, already dressed in khaki slacks and a white oxford shirt, sat crouched on the davenport with his transistor radio held close to his good ear. Her heart went out to him. He must still be having a hard time sleeping because of the time differences between America and Korea, or perhaps because of worry over Miss Jennifer.

She tried to smile, knowing she'd surprised him, but a second glance showed more than mere surprise in his eyes. Eun-Me laid her toothbrush on the kitchen counter and moved toward Philip as he rose, still clutching his radio, to meet her halfway across the room.

His brow knotted, and his face was strangely pale, even for an anemic-looking American. His voice came out as barely a whisper. "From what I can make out between my rusty Korean and all this static, Communist forces from the North invaded Seoul less than an hour or so ago. The city is under attack."

# Chapter 4

Eun-Me's knees buckled, and she grabbed hold of the dining table to steady herself. "How could this be? All the reports lately seemed to be saying that the threat of invasion appeared minimal."

Philip pulled a chair out from the table and motioned for her to sit. Accepting the offered seat, she rested her elbows on the table and briefly buried her face in her hands. When she dropped her hands into a fist on her lap and looked up at Philip again, he had pulled a chair away from the table and sat facing her, backward in his seat and straddling the ladder-back.

"Apparently, the Communists took advantage of that element of surprise. Let's hope and pray that our forces repel them quickly and send them packing back up North." He set the transistor radio between them on the table, and Eun-Me's gaze traveled back and forth between Philip and the squawking, barking black box. The frantic voice crackling over the airwaves reported tanks and artillery plowing at an alarming and steady rate into the city north of the Han River.

"Oh, Philip, we live north of the Han." She fired a rapid volley of questions at him without giving him an opportunity to respond. "Do you suppose they've reached our *dong?* What are we going to do? Should we waken the others and prepare to evacuate?"

Philip raised his palms to her and shook his head. "We shouldn't overreact just yet, Grace. You know how news reports tend to exaggerate these rumors of war. This may turn out to be nothing more than another skirmish along the 38th parallel."

Eun-Me tried to relax at his calming tone.

"I'll go and roust my folks here in a minute to get their advice. Dad's usually awake by now, anyway. However, I do *not* think we should disturb her." He jerked his head in the direction of Jennifer's bedroom. "There's no telling how she's going to react to this news. This certainly puts a kink in her plans to leave. The chances aren't looking too good that we'll be going back to Seoul today."

Philip gently encased her hand in his grasp. "Whatever happens, Grace, I'm confident that the Lord is going to watch over us. And I promise to do my best to take care of you."

Eun-Me couldn't speak through her emotion-clogged throat, so she only nodded. Philip's touch as he held her hand enabled her to push aside the fearful threat of impending war for a few seconds.

He gave her hand a final, gentle squeeze before releasing his grip and rising from his seat. As he passed behind her, he rested his hand on her shoulder. "Now, I'd better go see about waking Mom and Dad. If you don't mind, I think we'd better turn off the radio to preserve the batteries. I've just got a couple of extras, and who knows when or if we'll be able to buy more. I don't imagine they'll be able to confirm or deny these invasion reports until daylight anyway."

Eun-Me also stood and reclaimed her toothbrush from the kitchen counter, her hand still warm from Philip's touch. "Go ahead and switch it off. I need to finish getting ready. Then I'll start cooking breakfast right away."

When Philip headed for the stairs, Eun-Me hurried to the bathroom and, within minutes, had returned to the kitchen to start breakfast. Once the rice came to a boil on the stove, she turned the fire down to maintain a slow simmer and began to rummage through the top drawer for a pencil and small notepad.

She jotted down a list of things to do in the event that they were forced to flee. Most of her list dealt with the preparation of food that they could carry and eat easily in the car. Eun-Me chewed on the end of her pencil and looked out the kitchen window while she thought. A light drizzle dripped from the early morning sky, filtering the first light of day.

At the sound of footsteps descending the stairs, Eun-Me left her list-making and set out a traditional Korean breakfast for the Woods family. She would wait until Miss Jennifer emerged from her room before preparing a plate of fried eggs and ham for the sullen guest.

As Philip and his parents took their seats at the dining table, their demeanor mirrored the gravity of the early morning news. They ate in silence while Eun-Me tended to their needs.

After breakfast, *Sahmonim* volunteered to help Eun-Me tackle the items on her "to do" list. They started by baking a batch of cookies using the chocolate chips that Philip had brought from America. They worked for an hour or so, while Philip and his father moved to the living room to huddle over the radio.

"Mama, Grace," *Moksanim* called to them from the living room, "the news from Seoul sounds grave. I think we should all gather around and kneel for a season of prayer. I doubt if we'll be having church services in the chapel in light of these developments, but I need to spend some time talking to the Lord."

Eun-Me and *Sahmonim* left the kitchen and joined Philip and his father in the living room. They all dropped to their knees on the floor around the coffee table. *Moksanim* led, then each one took a turn praying aloud.

While Philip prayed, Eun-Me took comfort from the familiar manner in which he spoke to the Lord. Obviously, prayer was not just a ritual for him but communication with a close Friend. Her admiration for him grew as he concluded his prayer with a plea that Jennifer would find happiness.

When he asked for divine help in getting Jennifer safely and quickly back to San Francisco, Eun-Me grimaced with guilt. Philip expressed compassion for the woman who had hurt and rejected him. Her own thoughts and concerns had centered on how today's events might affect her life alone.

She'd given little or no consideration to how an enemy invasion might terrify Miss Jennifer. Instead, she viewed her as a bother. A burden. A hindrance should they need to flee to safety. If Philip could demonstrate such a Christlike attitude, despite a broken heart, surely she could find it within herself to do likewise. In quiet petition, she vowed to be more loving and kind.

Eun-Me waited to pray aloud until each of the others had taken a turn. She couldn't hold back her tears as she abandoned her use of English and poured out her heart to the Lord in her native Korean. She echoed the Woodses' previous prayers, expressing her fear at the thought of war. She cried out, questioning how it could be that their own countrymen were waging battle against them. She pleaded for peace and the Lord's protection over them, as well as safety for their friends and church family back home in Seoul. She begged for a quick end to the fighting.

Despite the harsh realities of war that now stared them in the face, her panic dissipated and a calmness overtook her while she prayed. She sensed God's undeniable presence and His peace in their midst.

As *Moksanim* pronounced the final "amen" and they stood to their feet, the wild clanging of a bell pierced the early morning air. "Someone's sounding the alarm, calling us all to gather for an emergency meeting," he said, pushing back from the table and rising to his feet. "We need to go to the chapel right away. Mama, you'd better get Jennifer up. She needs to be in on all this."

But before *Sahmonim* could move, Miss Jennifer opened the door to her bedroom and stepped into the hall. She wore the same powder blue shift she'd been wearing yesterday, but deep wrinkles now creased the dress.

"Is this Sunday morning bell ringing another Korean custom that Dr. Woods forgot to tell me about, or is something going on?" She looked from *Moksanim* to *Sahmonim*, then to Eun-Me, with deliberate care not to look in the direction of Philip. *Sahmonim* rushed over and gave the willowy blond a quick hug.

"Dear, the bell is used to summon everyone on the compound. We're to gather at the chapel as soon as possible. We didn't want to alarm you until we'd learned more of the details, but by all indications, Communist forces from the North invaded Seoul around four o'clock this morning."

Jennifer raked her hair from her face with a trembling hand, and Eun-Me watched as her fair skin paled to an ashen gray.

"But I've got to get home. Philip, what have you gotten me into? My nerves can't handle this." Her words hissed with venom as she glared at him through narrowed eyes. "Daddy will hold you personally responsible if anything happens to—"

"My son can't be held responsible for acts of war, Miss Anderson." *Moksanim* interrupted her before she could finish her threat. He walked across the room and put his arm around his wife's shoulder as she stood next to Jennifer. His size alone gave him an air of authority, but never in all the years that Eun-Me had known *Moksanim* Woods had she heard him speak in such a stern manner. His words were almost harsh.

"Situations like this require full cooperation from all of us, not criticism. Please bear this in mind. I promise you that we'll do our very best to see that you are safely delivered home. Right now, all of us—including you—need to get over to the chapel and discuss this crisis with the others. I hope I've made myself clear. Come along, Mama. Let's go."

Jennifer cowered as though she'd been slapped and lagged behind the others as they put on their shoes and headed down the path to the chapel.

ﾀ

Philip led their little entourage into the chapel, where a tense hush settled over the group of foreigners already assembled. As his parents, Grace, and Jennifer passed by him to take their seats, a solemn-faced, rigid figure in a U.S. military uniform approached him with his hand outstretched.

"Woods, Russell Barnard here. It's unfortunate that we meet again under such tenuous circumstances, but I'm pleased to see you after so many years. Have you gotten word of the Communist invasion?"

He pumped the soldier's hand up and down. "Rusty, glad you introduced yourself. I would have never recognized you in that uniform. I remember you as that scruffy, redheaded shortstop on our mission school baseball team. Guess we've both changed a bit since then." Philip noticed the GI's parents sitting on the front row, and he nodded to them in greeting when they looked his way. "I didn't realize you and your folks were here."

Turning back to the lieutenant, he lowered his voice to a near whisper. "But, to answer your question, yes. I've had my radio on most of the morning, trying to catch the reports. As a member of the armed forces, do you have any inside information that the radio announcers aren't telling us?" He fell into step beside the lanky soldier, and together they made their way to the front.

"I'll be sharing with the rest of the group here in a minute, but I fear the worst.

I am currently assigned to the Korean Liaison Office, Far East Command, in Japan, and I just happened to be taking a two-week leave to vacation here in Taechon with my folks. I'm going to evacuate the three of us back to Japan on the first military transport we can catch. Until this crisis blows over, I'd advise you to do the same. We're leaving for Kimpo right away in hopes that we can beat the Communists there." The soldier's advice sounded more like a command than a suggestion.

"Unfortunately, we don't have the connections or access to military transportation that you do, and I'd be a little nervous about heading toward the action, even if I did. But I need to find some way to get my friend here back to America." He made a cursory nod toward Jennifer, who sat scowling, with her arms folded, in the pew behind his parents. His heart warmed to see that Grace had moved to sit beside his poor, pathetic ex-fiancée.

"Maybe someone among the group will have a suggestion," he added, shrugging his shoulders.

"I wish I could help you out, but my hands are tied. However, if you can find your way to the US-KMAG compound at the Daejon Air Field, they should help you to safety, if need be."

Philip scrunched his forehead in bewilderment. "That's quite an acronym. What does it mean?"

"We've taken to calling it 'K-mag' for short. Stands for our American Army's Korean Military Assistance and Advisory Group," Lieutenant Barnard said as he stepped up onto the platform. "They are designated as a gathering point and would be responsible for the task of evacuating our American refugees, should the situation warrant that. I'll be happy to give you directions after the meeting." Philip took the cue to excuse himself and took a seat next to his father as Rusty addressed the group.

"Well, I believe everyone's assembled. Let's get this meeting under way. Since I rang the bell, I'll assume the responsibility of serving as the unofficial chair—unless someone objects."

Philip's childhood schoolmate briefed the group on the latest accounts of the invasion. In conclusion, he reiterated his earlier statement he'd made privately to Philip—that everyone should consider leaving Taechon as soon as possible and head south, away from the advancing troops. He pointed out that enemy forces could traverse the distance from the capital city to Taechon in a matter of hours.

As the gravity of the situation unfolded, a woman seated on the front row with her family raised her hand for attention, then stood. "My name is Helen Carroll, and my husband, Tim, and I and our two boys, Michael and Caleb—" She nodded in their direction while she spoke. "We arrived in Korea six months ago to serve as independent missionaries. We are living in Seoul until we finish language school and brought our sons down here on the train for a long weekend. . . ."

Her voice cracked with emotion, and she covered her mouth with her hand to stifle a sob. She regained her composure after a couple of deep breaths and continued. "We're out here in the middle of the boondocks. Literally." She dabbed at her cheeks with a handkerchief and patted the back of her young son, who had come to her side and wrapped his arms around her legs. The older of the two boys, whom Philip guessed to be about six years old, sat at stoic attention on the other side of his father, but he brusquely swiped away his own tears with the back of his hand at the sight of his mother weeping.

"The trains run sporadically, and the schedules are chaotic at the best of times. How do you propose that we get to this evacuation place you suggested? We don't have a satchel full of money to bribe our way to safety." She lowered herself back into her seat and pulled her child onto her lap. Her husband pulled her close, and she buried her head into his shoulder.

Philip's dad stood and moved toward the front. "First of all, let me say thank you to Lieutenant Barnard for his report."

The GI left the podium and sat on the front row, yielding the floor to the veteran missionary.

"And, Ma'am—" He addressed Mrs. Carroll directly, but his words were meant for the entire assembly. "I'm committed to seeing that everyone here reaches a safe haven. I have a car, and if we have to, we'll cram into it like sardines." He looked back and forth over the audience. "How many here would want to go with us in our Studebaker to Daejon?"

A show of hands indicated seven people, not counting the Woods family group. Included in that number were Richard Spencer, the unmarried missionary professor from their own mission, and Frank and Gloria Taylor, career missionaries with the OMA mission board, as well as the four members of the Carroll family.

Philip's dad drew a deep breath, then released a low whistle through his clenched teeth. "That'd make twelve of us in a two-door sedan. A tight squeeze, even for sardines. Perhaps we men should go into town and at least check on the train schedules. We won't know unless we try. Doesn't Jesus teach us that we have not because we ask not?"

While his dad arranged a meeting time and place with the other men for their trip to town, Philip felt a tap on his shoulder. He twisted around in his seat to see Jennifer, her face shrouded in seriousness. "I need to speak to you and your father," she rasped into his right ear. "Right away. Before you go to town."

He studied her green eyes, searching for clues to explain her request, praying that she didn't have any other bombshell surprises to drop on them.

"All right," he whispered back at her, "I'll meet you at the cabin before we head into town, but we'll have to make it quick. I have to get directions to the Daejon evacuation center from Rusty before we go, and Dad wants to leave for the station in ten minutes or so."

"A minute is all I need."

As Jennifer slid back into her seat, Philip stole a quick glance at Grace sitting next to her. The two women provided a startling study in contrast. One short, the other tall. One blond and fair, the other black-haired and olive-skinned. One calm, the other a nervous wreck. Yet, while the physical differences were stark, he marveled at the spirit and attitude differences even more. When surrounded by the affluence and high society of San Francisco, he'd been blind to Jennifer's self-consuming and superficial ways. But now, compared to Grace, those negative traits glared apparent.

The cadence of his heartbeat quickened to see Grace, with her head bowed, hands folded in her lap, and her lips moving in silent prayer. He admired her quiet strength and tender spirit. She owned nothing. She had no one with whom she could share life. She'd lost everyone near and dear to her. By all rights, she could be bitter and disillusioned. Yet, she was an example of trust. Sweetness. Kindness. Love.

Philip jolted out of his reverie when his mother tapped him on the knee. "If you will let me by, I will escort the girls back to the cabin so we can get right to the work of packing."

"Oh, sure. I'll be coming right behind you. I just need to get those directions from Rusty." He followed his mother into the aisle, where they headed in opposite directions. While the women left the chapel, he joined his dad at the front and waited for the cluster of people around Rusty to leave. When they were finally able to approach the GI, he sketched a simple map for them on the back of a piece of scrap paper, and they wished each other well as they parted company.

On the way back to the cabin, Philip told his father about Jennifer's request to speak with them, but he didn't expect to find her waiting on the back steps when they approached. Clutching something in her hand, she ran toward them while they were still several yards away.

The firs dripped with the residue of the morning's light rain, and the rising summer heat left the air heavy and uncomfortable to breathe. "Reverend Woods. I had hoped for just the right moment to make a special presentation of this gift to you, but this crisis supersedes such ceremony. My daddy wanted you to have this for your mission work." She handed him a black velvet pouch, and Philip looked over his dad's shoulder as he unsnapped the fastener to reveal a one-inch stack of crisp and new U.S. currency.

"That Mrs. Carroll said something about not having a satchel full of money, and, well, I figured you might be short on cash too. If you need to use this three thousand dollars to get us out of here, I'm sure Daddy will reimburse you for any expenses you incur in getting me home."

Never had Philip seen so much cash all together in one place. He felt rather certain that his dad hadn't either, for his voice cracked when he spoke. "I hardly know what to say. A mere 'thank you' isn't nearly sufficient. Your father is more than generous, Miss Anderson. We will certainly take great care to use this gift wisely."

"Daddy considers himself quite the philanthropist. He does this kind of thing all the time. I only hope there's enough to get me home."

Grace could live for more than several years on the tithe of this amount. How sheltered Jennifer's life must have been if she didn't realize just how far these funds would go or comprehend the risk of carrying so much money, even without the threat of war. She could practically charter her own freighter to carry her to San Francisco with the money in that pouch. Then again, cash might prove worthless in protecting them from the adversaries and adversities they might face in the days ahead.

Despite the fact that Jennifer had offered the gift, in part, to save her own skin, Philip knew that her father was a truly kind and generous man. A twinge of regret passed through his thoughts when he considered the financial support he could provide to the mission effort if he followed Jennifer's advice and stayed in the States to practice medicine. If he patched things up with her and married into the Anderson family, he had no doubt that this cash gift would be just the tip of the iceberg when it came to her father's generosity. With the doctor's influential backing, he could be generating a hefty income of his own within no time.

Yet, he sensed a growing assurance that God had called him to be a missionary. He couldn't turn his back on his call now, no matter how much the decision cost him. And since their "discussions" and subsequent breakup yesterday, he realized he would forever regret marrying Jennifer.

He only prayed that there would still be a place for him to serve in Korea at the end of his residency program. For, although he had announced to Grace his willingness to live and work in either Korea or Japan, he struggled with lingering bitterness toward the Japanese. He had wrestled against the temptation to be glad that the Korean aggressors, and his personal tormentors, had been humbled and defeated in the recent world war. While the people of Japan desperately needed the gospel message, he wasn't sure he was up to such a task. God still needed to do a mighty work in his life concerning his animosity toward the Japanese. The most he could muster was a willingness to be willing for a change in his prejudiced heart.

He felt a nudge and looked to see his dad holding out the velvet pouch for him to take. "Son, I'd feel better if you were to take half of this. The thought of carrying so much cash scares me, but I don't think we have a choice. I think I'll ask Eun-Me to sew a secret pocket into my pant leg. You might want to consider doing the same."

He could picture Grace, sitting cross-legged on the floor of the living room, meticulously stitching money into his slacks. With the thought, he couldn't help but compare the two women once more. He swallowed against the welling emotion the comparison brought. While he was grateful for the funds, he realized that Jennifer's idea of being of service to others was to throw her money around. Her talent in sewing was limited to what she could do with a safety pin. But Grace. Grace lived to serve the needs of others. She found joy in being useful. Such assets could prove to be more valuable than cash in the end.

"The hidden compartments will have to wait until this evening." Philip rushed to divvy up his portion of the funds into three bundles and crammed them into the pockets of his roomy trousers. "Here come the other men. We need to head into town. If you'll toss me the keys to the Studebaker, I'll start the engine. Oh, and Jennifer, thanks again."

She shrugged off his gratitude and began to walk back to the cabin. "No need to thank me. I had nothing to do with it other than to make the delivery, and I promised Daddy that I would."

❧

When the screen door slammed, Eun-Me looked up from her job of packing away the beach and picnic gear in the storage closet under the stairs to see Jennifer crossing from the living room to the kitchen. She grimaced at the sight of the American wearing shoes on the spotless linoleum floor that she had worked so hard to clean. Yet, she gave Jennifer the benefit of the doubt by assuming that she simply wasn't accustomed to removing her shoes at the door and hadn't stopped to think. Jennifer came up alongside *Sahmonim* as she stood at the counter, wrapping in waxed paper the cookies they had made.

"Mrs. Woods, if you're finished looking through my bridal catalogues and magazines, I ought to pack them away. Even though it appears that I won't be needing them anytime soon, several of my sorority sisters are getting married within the year, so I might as well take them back home and give them away. Hopefully, someone else can make good use of them." The inference to the recent breakup charged the air with uneasiness.

"Certainly, Dear. Go ahead and take them. But if we're forced to cram twelve people into our car, I doubt that we'll have room for suitcases and the like. You might need to pack a separate, smaller bag with just a change or two of clothes and the bare necessities. I'll loan you my canvas shopping bag to use if you'd like."

The idea seemed to shock Jennifer even more than the announcement of the Communist invasion. "I can't leave my suitcase behind. I bought a whole new summer wardrobe for this trip. Who knows if or when my things would ever make it back to San Francisco should I be forced to abandon my luggage here? I'll get Philip to strap it to the top of the car with rope. Grace, while you're digging around under the stairs, find a length of rope for us to use."

"We'll leave that to the men to decide." A hint of irritation laced *Sahmonim's* voice. "Why don't you run along and get your things together? We may have to leave at a moment's notice, so we need to be prepared."

Eun-Me latched the hook on the storage cabinet and rose to her feet. Every encounter she had with Miss Jennifer left her in need of fresh air. She moved over to the entryway and gathered up the rug in order to carry it outside and shake out the sand. Pushing the front screen door open with her hip, she stepped onto the cement step. Then, closing her eyes and turning her head to one side, she released the dust from the rug with a flick of her wrists.

The blare of a horn made her jump, and she opened her eyes to see a battered, open-bed military truck pulling into the compound ahead of the Woodses' car. Philip waved to her from behind the steering wheel. Despite the seriousness of their circumstance, she couldn't stop the ripples of joy that made her smile at the sight of him, and a silly grin split his face in return.

She dropped the rug by the door and ran to the passenger side of the truck. When it screeched to a halt, she laid her hands across the open window frame and stood on her tiptoes to peer across the truck's cab at Philip. *Moksanim* Woods brought his sedan to a stop behind the truck. He and his companions piled out of the car, but they continued in deep discussion, paying no attention to Philip or Eun-Me.

"Here is your knight in shining armor, come to rescue the damsel in distress astride his trusty steed."

She didn't really understand what he was saying, but she laughed anyway. "Where did you get this?"

"As we feared, the train schedules have been thrown into total chaos. So, Dad coerced the local police chief into selling us this pile of junk. He vowed that it'd make the trip to Daejon without a breakdown or he'd give us our money back. Of course, we'll have to find him first. But the tires are good as new, and we didn't see any other options, so we thought we'd take the chance."

Eun-Me shot a glance behind the cab to the flatbed. "Miss Jennifer will be happy to hear that she can carry her suitcase along."

"Miss Jennifer better think again if she thinks I'm going to lug that trunk of hers all over the Korean countryside. I think we need to establish some ground rules before we set out on this journey. And rule number one is, each one must carry their own gear."

"Then I suppose I should be thankful that all I own fits nicely in a knapsack." The prospect of their imminent departure sobered her, and she looked at the men standing next to the car behind them.

"Are we leaving right away?"

"No. We plan to set out at first light tomorrow morning. We don't want to be caught out in the middle of nowhere after dark. We men will each take a turn as a lookout through the night, and if anything suspicious occurs, we'll ring the chapel bell. In the meantime, though, Dad and I have a little sewing project that requires your experienced hand. Can you scrounge up a needle and thread?"

## Chapter 5

When he had finished changing his clothes, Philip stepped out of the bathroom and looked down at the hem of his trousers. "You did a great job, Grace. Even I wouldn't know there were secret pockets along the cuff if I hadn't watched you sew them in."

She sat on the floor beside the living room coffee table with her legs crossed, already stitching a similar pocket into the lining of his dad's pant leg. He found himself alone in the room with her. Jennifer, pleading a headache, had asked for a dinner tray in her room, and his parents had excused themselves right after the meal so that they could finish packing and rest up in preparation for the coming journey.

"There's nothing to this kind of handwork. I started mending our family's clothes when I was seven years old." She lowered her sewing to her lap, and her face lit up with a wide smile as she looked up at him.

When they were kids, he had always teased her about her eyes disappearing when she smiled, and now her almond-shaped eyes reduced to mere slits as she grinned. The vision and associated memory filled him with warm pleasure. It was good to see his old friend again.

He sat facing her in the easy chair and pulled his leg up by the ankle onto his other knee. "Knowing that rough-house brother of yours, I imagine Eun-Soo did his part in making you an expert seamstress." He picked a stray thread from his pants and balled it between his fingers, then flicked it into the air.

"I never minded." Eun-Me's smile faded to a pensive pout, and she shook her head slowly from side to side. "He always treated me better than any little sister deserved. Unlike most *oh-pah*, my brother always showed me respect—something most Korean men won't do for any woman, let alone a younger sister. I've got you to thank for that."

He raised a hand in protest and leaned toward her to emphasize his words. "His kindness to you isn't something I can take the credit for. He really loved you, you know. And he felt such a responsibility to look after you and your *omma* when *Moksanim* Cho was killed. He had a kind heart. This world needs more men like him. I really miss the guy."

"Me too. But I never had a doubt about his faith or his salvation, and I'm sure he and my parents are enjoying the rewards of heaven right now."

Her features softened. Her eyes took on a pensive, unfocused glaze. And, although she looked straight at him, he felt that her spirit was far away.

"I often cry to think that I'm all that's left of our family." She spoke so softly that he had to tilt toward her with his good ear to catch her words. "I feel like just a piece of scrap. The salvage. A remnant of the rich heritage my family left to me. I'll never be able to pass that heritage on to another generation. I'm uneducated and unmarriageable. What good am I?"

The question stunned him. Sweet-spirited Grace personified beauty and ability and goodness. He didn't understand how she could possibly feel so insecure. Women would always be a mystery to him. He'd never once known Jennifer to question her self-worth, yet Grace had so many more gifts and talents to offer than Jennifer.

He planted both feet on the floor in front of him and leaned forward until his eyes were mere inches from hers. "You can't let yourself think like that. I can't honestly say that I understand why God would allow you to endure the suffering you have had to face in your lifetime. I can't fathom why He would take your family from you and leave you orphaned. However, I do know that you remain here on earth for a reason. You are a constant blessing to my family—for what that's worth. But beyond that, God has a special plan for you. When you start to feel overwhelmed and insignificant, remember the potential of a tiny mustard seed."

She nodded, yet he had the strong impression that he hadn't gotten through to her. He had to find some way to convince her that he wasn't just offering platitudes. He pushed himself off at his knees and stood to loom over her.

"Hey, I drew the first shift of the night watch duty. Why don't you come along with me and catch the sunset on the ocean one last time before we leave? If the war situation continues to escalate, we may not have another opportunity like this for a good long time."

And he may not have the chance to speak with her alone for a good long time either, but he kept this thought to himself.

❧

Eun-Me fumbled with her sewing as she picked it up and returned her full attention to her work. Again, she had let herself get carried away with her loose tongue and had said more than she should have. She could feel the burn of her cheeks, and she kept her head down as she replied. "I'd like to, but I have to finish this, and I still have several other jobs to do." She knew Philip was watching her, but she refused to look his way.

"I don't want to keep you from your work, but I wish you'd reconsider. My guard shift doesn't start for awhile, so if you change your mind, come get me. I'll be outside checking the oil in the truck."

She jabbed her needle into the stiff fabric of the pant leg, pricking her finger and drawing a bead of blood. As she sucked on the puncture wound, she chided herself for not refusing outright Philip's offer for a sunset walk on the beach. At the risk of further vulnerability, she dared not trust herself to be alone with him.

With just a raised eyebrow or a show of concern, he had the power to draw the most intimate of disclosures from her. She couldn't allow herself to invest any more emotionally. She had already said far too much. Revealed too many of her private thoughts. Exposed feelings too tender. She possessed enough good sense to know that nothing could ever develop between the two of them. They were worlds apart in every way. If she allowed their relationship to progress any further, she merely raised her risk of heartbreak.

At all costs, she had to guard her heart.

When she had finished her sewing, she locked herself in the bathroom and hand-washed her work clothes, hanging them to dry over the tub so that she could wear them tomorrow. Before exiting, she cracked the door open a sliver and made certain that she was not going to face Philip when she stepped into the open area of the kitchen and living room.

&

*Monday, June 26, 1950*

Eun-Me set her kerchief-tied bundle on top of her rolled *yoh* in the corner of the entryway as the first weak rays of light broke through the black, predawn sky. Then she walked into the kitchen to retrieve the wicker basket she had filled with foods they could eat on the road. In order to avoid the need to wash breakfast dishes, she had fixed a light meal of hard-boiled eggs and apple slices, and she added these items to the foodstuffs that she and *Sahmonim* had prepared the day before.

After she deposited the basket next to her mounting pile of travel necessities, she moved from window to window throughout the living room and kitchen, first lowering, then latching the shutters in preparation to leave.

She had yet to see anyone stirring about the cabin, but the upstairs floorboards creaked under heavy footsteps, and earlier, the shower had been running for a good long while, so she surmised that Jennifer was also awake and getting ready.

Eun-Me wondered if everyone else had slept as fitfully as she had during the night. She had tossed and turned, with her ears tuned to listen for a warning clang of the chapel bell. Yet, when her alarm clock sounded to signal a new day, she had breathed a prayer of thanksgiving that the night hours had been calm.

A knock sounded at the cabin's front door at the same moment that the three members of the Woods family came down the stairs toting their suitcases behind them. "I'll get that," Eun-Me said, skirting around them to answer the door as they fumbled to don their shoes.

*Moksanim* and *Sahmonim* Carroll stood in the shadows of the porch stoop. They each held a lethargic boy. A tall duffel bag drooped between them. Eun-Me flung the door open wide and invited them inside.

"We won't bother coming in," *Moksanim* Carroll said, patting his son's back. "The Taylors and Professor Spencer are coming right behind us. But if we could get the keys to the car, we could lay our boys in the backseat while we load the vehicles."

Philip jangled a key ring above his head. "Follow me. I'm ready now." He scooped up Eun-Me's *yoh* and tucked it under his arm as he headed out the door.

"I'll be back for the rest of this stuff in just a minute. Mom, can you rouse Jennifer and tell her to get her suitcase out here? I'm sure hers is the biggest piece of luggage we'll have to deal with, and we need to pack it first."

"Here I come. Just hold your horses." Jennifer skulked out of her bedroom, pushing her suitcase ahead of her in swift shoves. "Actually, I could use your help." She straightened and arched her shoulders back.

*Moksanim* Woods left his own baggage by the stairs in order to assist her, and she followed him outside. Eun-Me hoisted her pack across her back and held the door open for *Sahmonim*. Together, they joined the others by the vehicles. The Carrolls were situating their boys in the back of the car, while everyone else watched Philip and his father wrestle to lift Jennifer's suitcase into the trunk of the car.

"I don't know what kind of seating arrangements you had in mind, but I'd be grateful if our family could stay together," *Sahmonim* Carroll said as she approached the group. "I'm so frantic with worry that I can't bear the thought of being separated from my husband right now. Besides, I need his help with the boys."

Philip wiped the dust from his hands as he straightened. "We haven't really considered who will sit where, other than the drivers' seats. I'll be driving the truck, and Dad will be behind the wheel of the car."

"I call dibs on the car too," Jennifer interjected. Eun-Me caught Philip rolling his eyes at this latest demand.

Eun-Me kept silent in the ensuing shuffle for seats, while *Moksanim* and *Sahmonim* Carroll each scooped a child in their lap, then eased into the backseat of the car. After the stout, gray-haired *Sahmonim* Taylor wedged in beside the young mother, Philip's father returned his seat back to its upright position and took his place behind the wheel. *Sahmonim* Woods straddled the gearshift next to her husband, and Jennifer hopped in beside her to occupy the seat next to the window. The car door slammed shut with a thud, leaving Eun-Me standing in the drive.

She didn't feel as though she had any right to demand a certain place or position. However, she squirmed uncomfortably when she found herself seated between Philip and the tall and lanky Professor Spencer, with *Moksanim* Taylor sitting next to the passenger door. She would have offered to ride in the open back rather than the close confines of the cab, but the men had loaded the truck bed with gas cans and hurriedly gathered tarps and camping supplies.

"I hope you won't be too miserable riding with us guys, but we're running short on open seats." Philip reached around the wheel to the steering column and turned the key in the ignition. He looked at Eun-Me with a sympathetic smile while the engine chortled into action. "Besides, I need to be able to reach the gearshift, and you're by far the most petite one among us, so you're elected to sit by me."

His hand brushed her knee as he took hold of the stick shift and ground the gears from neutral into first, then eased his foot off the clutch, lunging the vehicle forward. The casual sweep of his hand across her leg sent an electrifying shiver through her.

Philip extended his arm to adjust the rearview mirror, and Eun-Me lifted her gaze to catch him looking at her. She could see only the reflection of his eyes, but she knew from his crinkled squint that he was smiling at her. The brief magnetic interchange that ensued brought an instant heat to her cheeks, and she had to willfully avert her eyes.

Acting rather discombobulated at the tender moment, Philip cleared his throat and twisted his head to look out the back window. "Looks like Dad's right behind us. I guess we're off."

Eun-Me scoffed at herself for reading more into Philip's actions than he meant to convey. She hastened to convince herself that he was trying to put her at ease. Nothing more. She would never be, *must* never be, anything other than an old family friend turned *ajumoni*. For that privilege alone, she felt unending gratitude. Yet she would harbor this fresh memory of Philip's comfort and concern long after he was gone.

He steered the truck through the compound gate, leading their small procession due east down the rutted road of soggy earth. The route that Philip and his father had mapped out the day before avoided the main roads in hopes of dodging any troop movements. As the crow flies, *Moksanim* Woods had said, the distance between Taechon Beach and the city of Daejon spanned roughly sixty miles. But he anticipated that the journey would take them eight or nine hours, or more, as they traversed the back roads around and through the mountainous countryside.

Eun-Me stared at her folded hands in silence while the three men carried the conversation. When they switched topics from the encroaching enemy armies and the prospects of war to Korean and American politics, she didn't even try to follow their discussion, for they used too many English vocabulary words that were unfamiliar to her. But *Moksanim* Taylor's words jarred her from her daydreams when he leaned around the professor to address Philip.

"So, tell me, Son. What is the story behind the pretty young blond riding back there with your folks?" The elder missionary ran a hand over his bald head. "She blew my theory that she was your future missus when she chose to ride with your parents rather than next to you. Is she a new missionary recruit?" He elbowed the bachelor professor in the arm and chuckled. "There may be hope for you after all, Spencer."

Without turning her head, Eun-Me cast a sideways glance at Philip, and her stomach knotted to see the bloodless pallor that had settled over his face.

A quick snort preceded Philip's response.

"I think I can predict with certainty that Miss Anderson is not the answer to our good professor's prayers for a wife. Let it suffice to say that she is my boss's daughter, and she came to Korea on a fact-finding mission. Thanks to this Communist invasion, I'm now faced with the unpleasant responsibility of seeing her transported safely back to San Francisco."

A sudden and sad realization gripped Eun-Me as she considered for the first time that Philip might accompany Miss Jennifer back to the States. For some reason, she had assumed that he would find her an escort or send her on alone while he stayed the remainder of the summer with his parents, as planned. She wasn't ready to say good-bye to Philip yet. He'd arrived only days before. They had so much catching up to do, and she had waited so long.

Up until his arrival last Friday, she had almost convinced herself that what she felt for Philip was nothing more than the remnants of a teenager's affection. She'd heard the Americans describe these feelings as a "crush" or "puppy love."

After all, she'd been brought up to believe that romantic love was just another cockamamie American idea. In Korea, love came long after the wedding day—if it ever came—after years of growing comfortable with the mate chosen by one's parents.

Eun-Me stole a flickering glimpse at Philip. The jumble of emotions she felt for him caused her to question everything she had been taught about love. Despite their lengthy separation, her affections for Philip had blossomed rather than withered from the neglect of years and miles. She could neither explain nor understand this connection between them. Often, through a simple exchanged glance, they read the other's thoughts. Without saying a word, they were able to acknowledge that the other knew.

The longer he stayed, the deeper the connection grew. Just being with him made her happy. He filled the empty spaces of her soul.

She allowed a secret smile to play on her lips at the thought of how special he made her feel. He never treated her as a lowly servant or acted condescending toward her. He treated her like she was special. Like a lady. A queen.

What she felt for him went far beyond comfort and sometimes felt far from comfortable. Sometimes the sight of him set her heart racing in a way she'd never experienced before, and she knew she'd never experience this with another. This had to be love. However, such feelings held no future promise of fulfillment. He could never know the extent of her affections. Philip would go back to America and find a new bride or patch things up with Jennifer. And when he went, he would take a piece of her heart with him.

She consoled herself with the thought that, perhaps, God in His mercy knew her heart couldn't withstand the humiliation she would encounter if Philip were to learn of her true feelings for him. Her affections were getting harder and harder to hide. His speedy departure might be a blessing in disguise.

Eun-Me jumped when the deep bellow of a car horn sliced the air, and in syncopation with her fellow travelers, she turned her head to look back at the Studebaker. The car slowed to a crawl and pulled to the side of the road but had not yet come to a complete stop when the passenger door flew open and Miss Jennifer jumped out.

&

Philip pumped the brakes and brought the lumbering truck to a halt. Then, shifting into reverse, he twisted around and slid his right arm across the seat back behind Eun-Me so that he could see out the back window. Within seconds, he closed the distance between the two vehicles and parked the truck in the middle of the road.

He jumped from the cab and ran back to the car. His mother had already climbed out, waving for Philip to catch up to her as she made her way toward Jennifer.

"She's been really quiet since we left the cabin. Then, all of a sudden, she said to stop the car. That she was going to be sick."

Philip and his mother came up behind Jennifer, who had fallen to her knees on the edge of a barley field and was heaving up her stomach's contents.

"Mom, she's going to need a drink of water and a wet cloth when she's done. Would you mind asking Grace to dig those things up while I stay here and watch over Jennifer?"

His mother nodded her assent and began to walk back toward the road.

Philip knelt on one knee at Jennifer's side and pulled her hair away from her face.

When her retching stopped, she leaned back and hugged her knees to her chest.

"I feel like I'm coming right out of my skin," she said, resting her head on her knees.

"I worried that something like this might happen. You're going through the worst of the withdrawal symptoms as you flush those sedatives out of your system." He started to pat her on the back, but she shrugged his hand away. "I'm really sorry for you, Jennifer. I wish there was something I could do to help, but you should start feeling better soon."

"You could help me if you really wanted to." She lifted her face to reveal tears spilling down both cheeks. They dripped from her chin, leaving dark wet splotches on her red pedal pushers.

"I'll fetch the milk of magnesia from my bag to help settle your stomach, but if you're asking me to give you another sedative—I just can't do that." He shook his head emphatically.

"Please, Philip. Won't you take into consideration these extenuating circumstances? I'll never survive this grueling car trip. We're bouncing all over the road." Suddenly, her head dropped down, and she covered her face with her hand. "Oh, I feel faint," she mumbled.

As Philip took her in his arms to keep her from lying in the soft, black dirt, he felt an overwhelming sympathy for her. Real compassion. Pity for the poor little rich girl. But nothing more. The feelings of love he had held for her until very recently had been replaced with a cumbersome sense of duty to deliver Jennifer, safe and sound, back to her daddy. A silent prayer of gratitude flowed through his thoughts when he considered that this discovery came before he had married her.

He looked up to see Grace and his mother approaching, and his heart pounded in his chest at the sight of his dear old friend.

Philip shook his head, wondering if he was going crazy. He'd known Grace practically his whole life. He'd never viewed her as anything other than a real buddy and pal. He struggled to think of a reasonable explanation for his emotional reaction to watching her approach. He certainly could not begin to entertain any romantic notions. Especially now. Probably never.

There were far too many reasons why a relationship with Grace would never work. For one thing, he still had a residency program to complete in the States. And if he'd learned anything from his breakup with Jennifer, he learned that he shouldn't expect any woman to pick up roots and follow him halfway around the world.

Grace would be as miserable in America as Jennifer was in Korea.

He rose and hovered over the women as they assumed their nursing duties. With the utmost care, Grace tended to Jennifer's needs. She eased her head forward and offered a sip of water, then mopped her forehead with a damp hand towel. She was born to be a mother. She needed a husband and children to pamper and coddle. How unfair that this culture's traditions would deprive her of the privilege because she had no family to strike a marriage deal and pay a dowry.

Maybe, just maybe, he could pursue these romantic feelings when he returned as a missionary doctor after his residency. However, until then, he could not allow himself to even dwell on such things. In the meantime, the Lord might mercifully and miraculously bring some Korean man into her life who would accept Grace for his wife despite her orphan status.

For now, he needed to purge himself of any thoughts about women and romance and concentrate on the problems at hand. He had to get Jennifer back in the car and all of them back on the road. They hadn't received any updated reports on the invasion since yesterday. Neither his transistor nor the car radio could pick up anything but static. And he had no idea whether or not their forces were successful in pushing the Communist troops out of Seoul. Everyone in their little convoy would be on edge until they were able to get to Daejon and hear the latest news.

He crouched next to Grace and studied Jennifer's face. "How's the ailing passenger?"

Ignoring his question, Jennifer waved off Grace. "I just shouldn't have tried to eat anything in the car." She pointed her comments to his mother as she accepted her assistance to stand, then looped an arm through her crooked elbow.

Either she had decided the effort to push him for another sedative was useless, or she didn't want his mother and Grace to know the true reason behind her sudden illness. Whatever her rationale for dropping her appeal, he was grateful for the unspoken truce.

"Well, I'll race to the truck and dig out that milk of magnesia. You just take your time and let Mom and Grace help you." When he came over the rise at the roadside, he found all the other passengers milling about and stretching their legs. His dad and Professor Spencer had spread a road map across the hood of the car and were deep in discussion about possible detour routes should the need arise.

Philip pulled back the tarp on the truck bed and was opening his bag on the tailgate to retrieve the medicine for Jennifer when he felt someone tugging on his pant leg.

"Hey, Mr. Doctor," Caleb, the younger Carroll boy, called out, "why'd that pretty lady urp over there?" Instantly, his mother clapped a hand over his mouth.

"Don't mind him. He's not yet mastered the art of tact." Mrs. Carroll allowed her hand to drop to her son's collar as she spoke, but she still maintained firm control over him. "I explained that some people get a little queasy when riding in a car, but I guess he wants a second opinion."

The youngster looked up with brown eyes as round as silver dollars, and Philip stooped to ruffle the boy's auburn hair. "Your momma is right, Caleb. Miss Anderson's tummy is just a little upset from the bouncing and jostling is all. She'll be fine. But you could help her feel better if you'd sit still and quiet in the car. Do you think you could do that for me?"

His little head wobbled up and down in exaggerated assent. "Know what? I got to water the trees. And my dad's takin' Michael—"

*"Caleb!"* Mrs. Carroll's hand smothered her son's mouth once more in an effort to silence him, but he still managed to mumble the remainder of his announcement.

"—to water a tree too."

Philip tipped back his head and laughed. "Actually, Mrs. Carroll, I was just about to suggest that we all ought to do the same before we get back on the road."

The women had not yet come into view, so he deduced that they must have stopped at a discreet clump of bushes at the edge of the barley field for just such a purpose. Across the road and a short distance away, he saw Michael and his father stepping from behind a piney knoll.

Once everyone's needs were tended to and Philip had administered a dose of the chalk-white medicine to Jennifer, they resumed their earlier positions, and the caravan started off again.

At every chuck hole they confronted for the next several miles, Philip would snatch a quick glance in the rearview mirror to check on Jennifer's reaction and make certain that the Studebaker hadn't pulled over again. But she maintained a granite expression and a statuesque pose. No one in the truck seemed to want to bother with conversation, each one withdrawing into their own private thoughts as the truck creaked and groaned over the bumpy road.

They stopped on the outskirts of a rural village for lunch, refueling, and a "tree-watering" break, but the skies were heavy with rain and not even the little boys dawdled over their meal.

The further inland they drove, the more dramatically the scenery changed. The flat fields of barley gave way to terraced rice paddies, ripened to a verdant green, cut into rolling hills. Philip had expected to encounter scores of fleeing refugees. Instead, they saw only farmers standing behind an oxen-driven plow, goading their beasts forward through the mud. The only uniforms they sighted were those of the occasional stooped-shouldered *haraboji* as they strolled alongside the road. Each old gentleman wore an identical long white robe, with the outline of a top-knot visible through his opaque horsehair hat. They all shuffled as though their feet were heavy, their eyes scanning the distant hills.

With even less frequency, they would drive past a *halmoni*, dressed in traditional ballooning skirts of bleached muslin, a baby tied up in a blanket on her back.

"These folks seem oblivious to the events going on in Seoul," Philip said to no one in particular. Inwardly, he cringed to think that they might go barreling into Daejon like a bunch of wild-eyed refugees only to discover that the crisis had been squelched no sooner than it had begun. Even so, he concluded that he would rather be a safe dolt than a dead hero.

"News travels slow out here, so they may very well not know," Grace whispered. "But more likely, even if they have heard, people out in the countryside would refuse to leave their land unless the enemy is in sight."

"Let's pray that none of us faces such a time," Professor Spencer interjected as a final amen, and they fell silent again.

When the terrain shifted from rolling hills to steep mountains, driving required all of Philip's attentions, and he was thankful for the lull in conversation. He squinted in such intense concentration whenever they crept around the precipitous hairpin curves that his temples throbbed. The dirt road frequently dwindled to nothing more than an ox path, and the clutches of both vehicles began to emit an acrid smell from the constant downshifting.

The repeated blare of the Studebaker's horn broke Philip's concentration as they chugged up the side of a mountain. He looked into the rearview mirror in time to see the car disappear around a curve, rolling backward down the dirt lane they had just traveled.

# Chapter 6

What's the matter? Are they okay?" Grace shifted in the seat next to him and craned her neck to see out the rear window.

"My guess is he's burned out his clutch," Reverend Taylor answered for Philip while he maneuvered the truck to a stop. "Pray his brakes hold."

Philip cut the engine and his door squeaked open while he scrambled out of the cab. "I don't like the idea of driving this monster in reverse. Everybody stay here while I run and find out what the problem is. Hopefully, Dad was able to stop just around the bend." He left the door ajar and followed the fresh tire tracks down the hill in the direction the car had just gone.

Gravel skittered down the hill ahead of him, forcing him to shuffle to keep from losing his footing. His dad had managed to pull the car into a scenic turnout and was lifting the hood when he approached. Even though Philip had asked everyone to wait in the truck, the other men caught up to him, and they all gathered around to gape at the steaming engine, while Grace joined the women and children clustered behind them.

"This buggy won't be going on to Daejon today." Philip's dad whacked the fender with his fist. "And who knows where or when we'll ever find a replacement clutch in these parts. God bless the women of the Texas Diocese Missionary Society, but when they gifted us with this automobile, I don't think they considered the difficulty of finding parts for a Studebaker on a mission field."

"Whatever will we do, Clarence?" asked Philip's mother as she squeezed in beside his dad and circled his forearm between her hands.

"We've only got one option that I can see." Scratching his head, he turned away from the car and looked up the road. "Somehow, we'll all have to pile into the back of the truck."

"You can't be serious!" Jennifer growled, crossing her arms. "I'm barely able to manage the car ride. You might as well shoot me here and now rather than force me to endure even an hour in the back of that junk heap."

Tempted to take her up on her offer, Philip let loose with a snide retort. "You're free to walk the rest of the way if you'd rather—"

"Don't you think she could ride up front?" Grace's voice drifted out from behind the others and interrupted him, deflating his escalating anger.

"I'll be glad to give her my seat. She is sick, after all."

Sweet, gracious Grace displayed more Christian charity than he could ever possess. He didn't want her to give up her place next to him. His right side still radiated from the closeness of Grace after riding side by side for the past several hours. He treasured the memory of her nearness.

Even if he hadn't stated his feelings for her in words, he knew she understood how he felt. For, despite his resolve not to become any more emotionally involved with Grace than he already was, they had traded countless quick glances and silent exchanges in the rearview mirror throughout the course of the day.

He felt certain Grace shared his growing affection. She conveyed as much each time she caught him looking at her. He cringed to think that Jennifer might be riding beside him for the duration of their trip to Daejon. After their breakup, the thought of sitting next to her for even a minute or two sent ice water through his veins.

Philip looked from Grace to Jennifer and back again as he tried to think of some way to accommodate Jennifer without making himself miserable.

"Son, you look like you could use a break." While he spoke, his dad wiped the grease off his hands with a faded red rag he had pulled from under the driver's seat. "If you don't mind riding in the back, I'll drive the truck."

Philip made a mental note to thank him for his merciful intervention at the first chance he got.

Mrs. Taylor waved her hand to summon his dad's attention. "What do you propose we do with all our baggage? We couldn't possibly squeeze into that truck with all our suitcases too."

"I think we should take our example from Grace and gather a small bundle of one change of clothes and basic toiletries." While he spoke, Philip's dad twisted his rag in his hands and kicked at the dirt, sending a small stone tumbling over the side of the precipice. "We'll pack as much as we can in the car with the hope that we will be able to return within the next twenty-four hours to repair the clutch and retrieve our—"

The other missionaries nodded their assent, but Jennifer launched a vehement protest before he could finish his proposal. "That's fine for all you folks who live around here, but I'm on my way back to the States. Couldn't we enlist one of these little guys to sit on top of my luggage?" She ticked her head toward the Carroll boys, who each clutched the legs of a parent. "That wouldn't take up too much space. Or couldn't you tie my suitcase onto the roof? I asked earlier for someone to bring a rope for me. Did anyone do that?"

Philip grimaced at the thought of having to lift Jennifer's suitcase onto the top of the truck. Even if they were able to get the thing up there, the weight might cave in the roof. With a lot less effort, she could take her daddy's money and replace her fancy clothes. Besides, those now-useless bridal catalogues accounted for most of the bag's weight. When her time came to marry someone more in keeping with the lifestyle she sought, she could and would buy a brand-new set of catalogues and magazines.

He kneaded the inside of his bottom lip between his teeth in an attempt to bite back a bitter retort, but his dad interceded for him once again when he turned toward Jennifer, his expression shifting to a frown. "I understand your predicament, but we're in a crisis situation here, Miss Anderson, and any extra space we can eke out around the passengers must be filled with essentials, not your wardrobe. We'll be straining the truck's transmission enough trying to carry twelve passengers up and down these mountain roads, and we'd have a mighty long walk to Daejon if that vehicle breaks down too. You'll need to follow the same restrictions that we're imposing on everyone else."

"Fine, then." She glared at Philip through slitted eyes. "Can I trouble you to unload my bag so I can pull out my necessities?"

As he spun away from her and walked toward the trunk of the car, she muttered loud enough for all to hear, "I might as well kiss the rest of my belongings good-bye."

❧

Eun-Me gave her head a quick jerk to dispel the mental picture sparked by Miss Jennifer's remark. She believed that the act of kissing ought to be reserved for someone much more precious than possessions.

Even though she had never kissed nor been kissed by any man, she often fantasized about the prospect of her first kiss. Philip's kiss. The mere words made her mouth tingle with the sweet, tangible illusion of his lips pressing tenderly against hers.

She forced herself to tuck away her intimate reveries and return to the real world. Such daydreams could never be fulfilled. With Philip or any man. She reached out from her position behind the others and tapped Miss Jennifer on the elbow. "I could help you, if you'd like. I don't have any repacking to do."

"I believe I'll take you up on your offer." Miss Jennifer pressed her fingertips into her temple and closed her eyes. "I have such a pounding headache. I don't think I could bend over right now." She dropped her hand to her side and turned to follow after Philip, while Eun-Me fell into step behind her.

As Eun-Me culled through the stacks of carefully folded clothes in search of something practical, Miss Jennifer towered over her, tapping at her mouth with a red-polished fingernail. "Uh-uh," she grunted each time that Eun-Me's hand lingered on an article of clothing she thought might be appropriate.

The only undergarments she found were lighter-than-air scraps of lace-trimmed silk. By comparison, her own cotton pantaloons seemed so. . .well, *utilitarian*. No wonder the American seemed to glide when she walked, while Eun-Me crinkled and plodded along. She'd never seen such delicate apparel among Mrs. Woods's laundry. She decided that only the richest of "big noses" could afford these flimsy, fancy fineries. A small sigh escaped her lips when she patted three pairs of the panties into the bottom of the straw beach bag Miss Jennifer had given her to pack.

By the time Eun-Me had gleaned two complete outfits and essential toiletries from Miss Jennifer's suitcase, the others had finished shuttling all but the most crucial supplies from the back of the truck and into the car. Philip stood at the truck's open tailgate and motioned for her to hand him the overstuffed beach bag.

"Here, Dad." He tossed the parcel up to his father, who was rimming the truck bed with everyone's knapsacks. "This should be the last."

Turning back to Eun-Me, Philip's eyebrows raised in question as he spoke. "I hope you don't mind. We took the liberty of spreading your *yoh* out flat to give our backsides a little extra padding."

"No, of course not. Whatever I can do to help." She noted that they had lined the rusty sheet metal floor with a canvas tarp before laying down her bedroll. "Is there anything else I can carry back to the car?"

"Naw. You've done more than your share just by assisting Jennifer." He sent a quick wink her way, and the innocent gesture made Eun-Me's pulse race. "Dad estimates that we're no more than an hour and a half away from Daejon. We should pull into the city about dusk—if we don't run into any more trouble, that is. I think we're all ready for a rest stop and a hot meal."

Only an hour and a half away. And then what? Eun-Me wrestled with the possibilities. If the invading Communists continued to push south across the peninsula, not only would Philip flee Korea with Jennifer, but his parents might accompany them as well.

Then she'd be left utterly, totally alone.

Yet, even as the thought slashed into her mind, her father's favorite and oft-repeated scriptural promise brought comfort to her soul. *"Be strong and of good courage, fear not, nor be afraid of them: for the LORD thy God, he it is that doth go with thee; he will not fail thee, nor forsake thee."* She closed her eyes and inhaled deeply, drawing strength from the knowledge that her Lord would not forsake her, no matter what the future held.

❧

When *Moksanim* Woods bellowed, "All aboard," everyone but Eun-Me and Philip began jockeying for position. *Sahmonim* Woods sat beside her husband in the truck cab, and *Sahmonim* Taylor squeezed in next to her. Miss Jennifer, whining that she might need to make another emergency exit, occupied the seat by the door.

Philip stayed back to offer a steadying hand while the remaining passengers climbed into the truck bed, and Eun-Me hoped that she appeared humble and deferring as she waited off to one side. She would have let the others go first anyway, but this time she had an ulterior motive for lagging behind. If she managed things just right, she would be sitting next to Philip for the remainder of the ride.

She watched *Moksanim* Taylor crawl into the center of the truck and lean his head back against the rear window of the cab. Next, the Carroll family spread out across the left side of the flatbed so that Michael and Caleb would have room enough to wiggle away their nervous energy. Finally, Professor Spencer hoisted himself into the truck bed and nestled among the knapsacks in the corner directly behind Miss Jennifer.

"Madam. Your carriage awaits." Philip held one arm across his waist and bowed low while cutting a wide swath through the air with his outstretched hand. She accepted his assistance but knew if she looked in his eyes, she wouldn't be able to maintain an appropriate expression of solemnity, so she glanced forward instead, just in time to catch a look of disgust from Miss Jennifer.

The split-second interchange left Eun-Me feeling like a fool. She scrambled to make room for Philip, and while he yanked the tailgate shut behind him, she drew her knees up under her chin.

Sometime during their repacking efforts, the sun had evaporated the rain clouds. Oppressive midday heat soaked the moisture from the steaming earth like a poultice, and a fog of exhaust billowed around the truck when the engine rumbled to a start. Once they were under way, a dust cloud enveloped them, forcing Eun-Me to bury her face in her hands.

At first, she was grateful for the opportunity to recover from her embarrassment without the risk of Philip wondering why she had withdrawn so suddenly. But the more she thought about Miss Jennifer, the more she resolved to hold her head up high. She wasn't about to let that sophisticated crank rob her of these snatches of joy she found in Philip's company.

Every few minutes, she tried to lift her head and take in her surroundings. She wanted another opportunity to look Miss Jennifer straight in the eye and smile ever so sweetly. But each time the irritating haze clogged her throat and made her eyes fill with cleansing tears.

Catching quick glimpses at her traveling companions, she saw that they had all chosen to sleep rather than fight to see through the gritty haze. She refused to succumb to the tug of drowsiness. She wanted to cherish each moment she had left with Philip until he departed for America. The memories she gathered now might have to last her another several years. Or forever.

Eun-Me marveled at Philip's ability to sleep, for he looked terribly uncomfortable. He had tucked his knees up under his chin and laced his fingers together across the back of his head. But his relaxed body bobbed and swayed with the rocking motion of the truck. Each time a tire bounced into a pothole or over a rock, his form leaned into her leg, sending goose bumps prickling up her left side. The farther down the road they traveled, it seemed to Eun-Me that the jostling encounters with Philip occurred with greater frequency. She pondered the possibility that Philip was intentionally knocking into her. However, she decided that, with her eyes closed, her senses were merely heightened and her imagination had gone wild.

The next time his weight pressed into her knee, she noted with surprise that they hadn't hit any bumps in the road. She spread her fingers apart from her covered eyes and stole a peek at him. Poking his head out from under his arm, his eyes sparkled with mischief as the distinguished doctor twisted his features into a funny face and stuck out his tongue at her.

Eun-Me quickly closed the gap between her fingers, and her palms felt the heat rising in her cheeks. When they were kids, Philip had always played such childish pranks on her when attempting to take her mind off a tense situation. Yet, even though she knew all this, she couldn't control the flush of pleasure flooding over her—until the unwelcome memory of Miss Jennifer's earlier sneer attacked her thoughts.

Despite her resolve to do otherwise, Eun-Me berated her giddy reaction to Philip's teasing and forced herself to regain a modicum of dignity.

With a final bone-jarring jolt, the truck bounced off of the dirt path and up onto a stretch of paved road. Philip jabbed Eun-Me lightly with his elbow and leaned toward her to whisper in her ear. "You are probably safe to put your hands down. Looks like we won't have to eat any more dust for awhile. We should be pulling into town soon."

Lifting her face out of her hands, Eun-Me could see Philip stretching his arms above her head and working the stiffness out of his limbs. Rather than the occasional thatch-roofed farmhouse rising up from the rice paddy landscape, now black-tiled rooftops surrounded by whitewashed courtyards sprouted like mushrooms along the pedestrian-clogged street.

"This paved road adds a whole new meaning to the saying, 'A sight for sore eyes.' I don't think I could have endured another pothole."

*A sight for sore eyes.* Eun-Me committed the new English phrase to memory as Philip reached for his back pocket and pulled out a clean, folded hanky, then handed it discreetly to her. "You look like you've had about all the traveling adventures you could stand for one day too."

She grimaced to think what she must look like and accepted the handkerchief with a silently mouthed "thank you." She'd heard some of the other *ajumonis* say that the Americans they worked for used a handkerchief to blow their nose, then would actually return the soiled article to their pockets. Eun-Me knew Philip would never do anything so uncouth. After a couple of swipes over her face, she tucked the dust-coated cloth up into her sleeve. Provided they stopped in Daejon long enough for things to dry, she intended to rinse it out once they reached the military compound. She ached in places she'd never even noticed before and wondered if she would be wrong to pray for a good hot bath.

A child's shrill wail drew her focus back to the truck. "Momma, Michael's lookin' at me." Caleb Carroll poked at his mother with a pudgy finger to punctuate his whine. "Make him stop."

The weariness expressed in his mother's response reflected Eun-Me's own utter exhaustion.

≈

When his father pulled to the side of the road a second time to study Lieutenant Barnard's hand-scribbled directions to the KMAG compound, Philip wondered if they had made a wrong turn. He worried even more when, instead of taking the highway toward downtown Daejon, they headed northwest onto a hard-packed gravel road leading into a small village. He was ready to crawl up to the window behind the driver's seat and ask if he could help when they fell into line behind a camouflaged U.S. military jeep. Both vehicles ground to a stop in front of a barricade at the end of the isolated road.

The few remaining splinters of daylight illuminated an American MP as he stepped from a small guardhouse. He raised the barricade and waved the jeep through but blocked their path by standing directly in front of their vehicle with his rifle gripped in both hands and ready to use.

"Halt. Who goes there?"

Philip leapfrogged over the truck's tailgate and joined his dad beside the truck, while the MP approached. The closer he got, the less intimidating the soldier became. Philip thought the young buck private looked more like a kid dressed up to play army in his father's old fatigues than a modern-day warrior trained to kill the enemy.

In the fading light, Philip could make out several wooden structures and a number of Quonset huts situated on the compound in neat rows. Gusting winds unfurled the Stars and Stripes atop a flagpole that towered just beyond the guardhouse, and the flag's hooks and grommets clanked loudly against the metal mast.

"We are a group of American missionaries and our dependents." Philip's father looked the soldier in the eye without flinching. "We were sent here by an officer with the Far East Command's Korean Liaison Office. He said you'd be able to advise us as to the current military crisis and provide us with food, shelter, and an escort to safe haven, if necessary."

"I'll need to see passports and proper identification before I can admit you onto the compound. We're under tight security." The GI tilted his head to look past Philip and survey the truck's passengers. Philip could tell when his gaze reached Jennifer, for his eyebrows raised and a fleeting smirk of lecherous admiration crossed his face.

Philip developed an instant dislike for the private, and his blood boiled to see pond scum like this kid looking at Jennifer—or any woman—with such blatant lust. The fact that the guy was serving his country far away from home still didn't give him license to be disrespectful. Regardless of Philip's personal feelings about Jennifer, he wouldn't hesitate to defend her honor.

The soldier made brief eye contact with him and grinned, confirming Philip's interpretation of the man's expression, then he continued to scan the rest of the truck's passengers. Philip knew the moment the GI noticed Grace, huddled by the rear wheel well.

The soldier's smirk dropped into a frown. His entire face hardened. He cleared his throat. "I can't let the civilian *gook* pass. We have no way of telling which ones are the enemy and which aren't. Like I told you, we're under tight security, and I'm only supposed to let verifiable Americans in until Major Denton tells me otherwise."

Seething even more at the private's use of the racial slur aimed at Grace, Philip couldn't keep the sarcasm from his response. "I'm sure you meant no discourtesy to our Miss Cho, but the proper term for a Korean in their language is *Hangook saram*, and to my knowledge, there is no abbreviation. How would you like it if I were to call you a—"

"Son, this isn't the time or place for a language lesson." His father laid a hand on Philip's shoulder. "Why don't you collect everyone's passports and Grace's registration card while I arrange to discuss this matter with the private's commanding officer?"

He started to walk away to gather the documents, but his step faltered when he heard his dad address the young MP. "Before I joined the Lord's Army, I served as a master sergeant in the U.S. Army myself, so I understand the chain of command and your need to follow orders. . . ."

Philip looked back in time to see the private stiffen at his dad's subtle rank-pulling pronouncement. He continued on his way, grimacing to think of the trouble that he'd be in about now if not for his father's levelheaded intervention. He had allowed his quick temper to get the best of him again—even though he knew full well that a gentle reply like his dad's, which related to the annoying soldier's predicament, might have garnered a more accommodating response.

As Philip returned from assembling the requested bundle of documents, he rubbed his thumb over the black-and-white, solemn-faced photo of Grace attached to her registration card.

"Oh, Lord," he prayed with his eyes open while he walked, "protect Your precious Grace from further tragedy."

He deposited the official papers into the MP's outstretched hand and watched while the soldier turned on his heels and reentered his guardhouse. After thumbing through their credentials, he began to mumble something into a walkie-talkie. But, no matter how hard Philip strained to hear the GI's monologue, his words were still unintelligible.

His dad tugged on his sleeve to draw him toward the front of the truck and out of the MP's line of vision. "When I go to meet with the major and discuss our situation, why don't you pull the truck over and encourage everyone to get out and stretch their legs? The troops are getting rather restless, and Michael and Caleb appear to have declared war on one another."

High-pitched squeals split the early evening air.

"At times like this, I'm reminded why we only wanted one child. Whenever you fought with Eun-Soo or Grace, we could just shoo them off to their *omma*." His father shot a quick glance over his shoulder toward Grace. "I hope Grace didn't catch wind that she's the reason for our delay. She'd feel terrible if she knew."

"And I hope I didn't compound our problem by spouting off to the MP." Philip snatched a sideways glimpse at the guardhouse, and when he did, his father whispered into his good ear.

"If God and your mother hadn't been watching, I might have decked the bum. Might still if he doesn't wipe that seedy grin off his face whenever he looks at Jennifer. Don't worry, though. He's low man on the totem pole at this dinky outpost. Let's just pray that his commanding officer is a man of reason and integrity."

"Excuse me, Sir." The MP slung his rifle over his shoulder as he approached. "Don't mean to interrupt, but Major Denton has agreed to speak with you immediately. He's ordering the mess sergeant to rustle up some grub for your group, and they can go on to the mess hall while you meet with the major." Philip hiked his eyebrows in suspicion at the soldier's about-face in attitude.

"I'm not allowed to leave my post, and we're shorthanded, since most of our men have already been called out, so you'll have to go unescorted, but both buildings are easy enough to find. The large Quonset hut in the center over there is the mess hall." He held their documents in his hand, so he pointed with a nod of his head toward the half-moon-shaped corrugated metal building as he spoke. "Located just north of that you'll find the major. There. Where the jeep is parked. If you have any trouble, just look at the signs." The soldier handed the thick pile of passports back to Philip's father, then snapped his right hand away from his forehead in salute. "You're all free to pass."

"Including Miss Cho?" Philip hesitated to ask, but they had to know.

"Yes. Including Miss Cho."

⁊⦁

Eun-Me eased down from the tailgate with Philip's aid, then she leaned against the spindly trunk of a gingko tree while he helped the others disembark. She knew she ought to follow custom and rush ahead to hold the door for her superiors, but the unfamiliar surroundings left her frozen in fear and nervousness.

She felt more and more out of place among all these foreigners. She had caught the angry expression on the guard's face when he first noticed her among the missionaries. And, although she couldn't hear his words, his eyes had shouted that she wasn't welcome here.

"Are you feeling a bit uncertain about eating dinner in a place called a 'mess hall'?" *Sahmonim* Woods came alongside her and patted her lightly on the forearm. "You'll see. It's not as bad as it sounds. Come on. Walk with me."

She must have noticed Eun-Me's searching gaze for Philip, because *Sahmonim* answered her question before she could ask. "Clarence had asked to speak with the man in charge, and Philip went along. I'm sure they'll bring us an update concerning the invasion, but there's no sense in us waiting for them. I'm so hungry I could eat a team of oxen about now." She had to raise her voice to be heard over the ruckus the Carroll brothers were creating as they ran past them toward the entrance, arguing over which one should get to enter first. Their father settled the squabble by serving as the doorkeeper himself, and he made both boys wait next to him.

"Excuse me. You'll have to excuse me." Miss Jennifer shuffled and danced her way to the front of the group and through the open door. "I've got to find the little girl's room. Quick!" The others ignored her dramatics and filed in behind her.

A blast of bright light and loud music engulfed them when Eun-Me and *Sahmonim* stepped across the threshold and into the wide hall filled with tables and chairs.

"Welcome to our little piece of America right here in *kimchee* land." A short and round man dressed all in white stepped from behind a work area surrounded by a serving counter in the back of the room. As he approached, he wiped his hands on his apron, which left an oily brown smear across the hem. "My orders are to make you feel right at home, and I've already thrown a couple dozen hamburger patties on my grill. I'll keep 'em comin' until you've had your fill. You folks go ahead and make yourselves comfortable." He headed back behind the counter and picked up a greasy spatula. "Burgers 'n' fries will be comin' right up. If you need anything in the meantime, just holler, 'Sarge.'"

He began to flip the sizzling meat, and while he worked, he sang a slightly off-key version of the record that had been playing on the jukebox when they entered the hall. *"Some enchanted evening, you will meet a stranger. You will meet a stranger, across a crowded room. . . ."*

In all her days, Eun-Me had never once seen anyone so strange as this man wearing an apron who could cook. She still had a lot to learn about Americans, even after living and working with them for many years. The thought of how her dinner might taste made her lips curl and her nose crinkle in disdain. She was anxious to see the look on Miss Jennifer's face when she discovered her dinner had been cooked by a man.

While she waited for her meal to be served, Eun-Me positioned herself beside *Sahmonim* at the end of a long table, in a spot where she could watch the door.

"Yum. Those fries smell wonderful." Miss Jennifer set her purse onto the table and plopped herself into a chair on the other side of *Sahmonim* Woods. "From the looks of our chef, he knows how to cook, and am I ever ready to eat some real food."

"I'm glad to see you're feeling better," *Sahmonim* replied. "Just be careful not to overdo too soon." She leaned toward Eun-Me and gave her a cheery smile. "Personally, I'd rather have a bowl of your bean paste soup."

Eun-Me decided then and there that she would never understand Miss Jennifer.

When "Sarge" set in front of her a paper-lined plastic basket brimming with the American-style fried potatoes and hamburger sandwich, Eun-Me bowed her head and thanked the Lord for the food, but she still hadn't mustered much of an appetite. Instead, her attentions were focused on the door, knowing she wouldn't be able to relax until Philip returned.

She pushed her picked-over supper away and sat up straight in her chair when the door finally opened. Although her heart sank briefly to see a uniformed American army officer standing in the doorway, she perked up again when Philip and *Moksanim* followed him into the room. With one look at their solemn expressions, Eun-Me knew the news wasn't good.

"Ladies. Gentlemen. If I might have a word with you?" The military man stood directly over Eun-Me, while Philip and his father took the seats *Sahmonim* had reserved for them across from her. Above her head, Eun-Me heard the officer clear his throat, but he waited for everyone to quiet down before he began to speak. The Carroll boys, who sat with their parents at the other end of the long table, had been practicing their fencing skills with French fries, but they dropped their "swords" immediately when their father snapped his fingers.

"I'm Major Randolph Denton, and this small compound is under my command. I won't bother with pleasantries because I know you're all anxious to hear the latest news from Seoul. Let me get right to the point."

Eun-Me longed to turn and watch the major while he spoke. She didn't want to miss the meaning of any of this crucial announcement, but she didn't want to interrupt, so she focused her full attention on listening to his words instead.

"The South Korean troops have not succeeded in repelling the Communist forces as we'd hoped. In fact, the enemy is sweeping across the 38th parallel, pushing south at a rather alarming speed."

The clipped manner of his speech heightened Eun-Me's nervousness, and she could feel the muscles in her shoulders tense.

"Today I received word that U.S. Ambassador Muccio has ordered the evacuation of all American civilians. The train station here in Daejon is already in a state of mass confusion, but we were able to send the local missionaries out on a Pusan-bound train. And more than five hundred of our fellow countrymen who reside in Seoul left this afternoon on a Norwegian fertilizer ship headed for Japan."

At any other time, she knew Philip would have made some joke about the vessel's cargo, but he still wore the same solemn expression she'd seen when he walked in the door.

"Before you begin to worry unduly, let me hasten to say that I believe we are far enough south of the fighting that we are in no immediate danger now, but we are prepared to transport all Americans to safety as soon as possible."

*All Americans to safety.* That part of the message rang in her ears, leaving her to wonder what would become of a Korean girl like her.

# Chapter 7

Eun-Me strained to concentrate on the rest of the major's speech, but worries over her own dilemma kept distracting her. She knew the Woods family would do everything in their power to protect her and keep her close to them, but from the way the major talked, the decision to stay in Korea or evacuate might no longer be up to them. She wasn't naïve enough to think that the U.S. military would show any consideration or concern for her. She'd be just one more homeless Korean refugee among the masses trying to flee the horrors of war.

From behind her, she heard the major say something about putting everyone up for the night and sending them out with a convoy headed for Taegu at 0600 hours tomorrow and onto Pusan by train from there. Did this mean that within hours—or minutes—she'd be put out on the streets, abandoned in a strange city? Eun-Me's heart pounded in her chest at the very real possibility. Even though she was an orphan, at least back in Seoul she had a home and a livelihood. Here she knew no one, and worst of all, she had no place to go amid the outbreak of war.

The sound of chairs scraping across the floor jarred her from her fretful reverie. The major was backing toward the door and motioning for them to come.

"If you'll follow me, I'll show you to a barracks so you can catch a few hours' sleep. I wish we had better accommodations to offer you, but as tired as you all must be from your travels today, an army cot is likely to feel as good as any feather bed."

She slumped in her seat as the others moved to obey Major Denton's command. Philip came around from the other side of the table and tugged on the back of her chair. "Come on, Grace. I know you're exhausted, but you can't sleep here. Why don't you walk with me?"

"B–b–but, I'm not an American. The U.S. military won't take care of me." Hard as she tried to hold back her welling tears, they began to stream down each cheek and drip onto her lap. She buried her face in her hands, and her chest rose and fell with quick, quiet sobs.

"Please. Don't cry. I watched you while Major Denton spoke, and I knew you were upset." Philip dropped to one knee next to her and drew his face so close that she could feel his breath on the back of her hand. "I'm not at liberty to divulge the reason right now, but I have it on full authority that you will be allowed to go with us when the convoy sets out for Taegu tomorrow at dawn. Trust me on this. I promise I'll explain everything once Dad has had a chance to talk with Mom."

She lowered her hands from her face just far enough to look at him, but he looked so blurry through her tears that she had to swipe at her eyes with her fingers before she could get a clear view of him. His eyes confirmed his sincerity.

She couldn't begin to guess what secret plan he and his father had plotted to grant her the privileges afforded the Americans, but her gratitude knew no bounds. She wouldn't pry for any information until he was ready to share.

"Here. Let me loan you my hanky so you can dry your tears. You know I never could bear to see you cry." He stood and patted at all his pockets in search of his missing handkerchief. He had obviously forgotten that he'd loaned it to her in the truck earlier that afternoon. She withdrew the soiled linen from up her sleeve.

"Is this the one you're searching for?" She smiled through her sniffles as she dabbed at her remaining tears with the one corner of the handkerchief that was still fairly clean. Despite her added grime and tears, it still held the essence of Philip. Eun-Me inhaled a deep whiff and held her breath. She wanted to keep the cloth forever, dirt and all, as a memento of today. She may have a precious few such days left to spend together with him.

A light rain had begun to fall when they caught up with the others. They tagged onto the tail end of their processional and filed past Major Denton into the barracks that he had assigned to them for the night. Not a single one of the Americans bothered to leave their shoes at the door, so Eun-Me reluctantly followed suit and kept her street shoes on as she walked across the concrete floor.

The Quonset hut's one large room, devoid of any decoration, caught Eun-Me off guard. She hadn't expected to share sleeping quarters with the men, but the major made no mention of a separate facility for the women.

Other than the canvas army cots that lined both the walls, no other furniture occupied the room. At the end of each cot, a stripe-ticked pillow sat atop a neatly folded blanket. The blanket's olive green wool looked scratchy and uncomfortable, and Eun-Me didn't share Michael's and Caleb's enthusiasm for the idea of sleeping like real-live army men. She longed for the thick softness of her *yoh*.

Miss Jennifer had already shaken out a blanket and collapsed onto one of the beds. By all appearances, she had fallen asleep fully clothed, right down to her shoes.

"You'll find the showers and latrine out back. Like I said, I wish I could offer you something a bit more comfortable, but at least you'll be out of the elements for the night." Major Denton peered out the doorway and into the night sky. "More rain's moving in. These monsoons may be great for the rice crops, but they wreak havoc on the roads. You may be in for a rough go tomorrow, and reveille will sound before dawn, so I'd advise lights-out right away."

"You've been most accommodating, Major." Professor Spencer thrust out his hand as he stepped forward from the ring of missionaries that had formed around the officer. "Thank you for all your help."

The others added a hearty "amen."

Eun-Me ached from head to toe, so while all the men left to bring in the knapsacks, she decided to lie down on the cot next to Miss Jennifer and wait for them to return. She told herself that she would only rest her eyes for a minute or two, then she'd shower and shake out her dusty clothes before putting them back on again.

ॐ

"Philip. Son. I hate to do this to you, but you've got to get up."

"What? What is it? Did you find Grace?" Philip bolted upright on his cot when his father's voice and gentle shaking broke into his nightmare. The dream was a repeat of one he'd had a few days earlier—running from a tiger in the woods. But this time, he'd lost Grace and not his grandmother's ring.

"You must have been dreaming." His father gave him a comforting pat on the back as if he were still a little boy. "Grace is still sleeping soundly on her cot right next to Jennifer." For a quick second, he cast the beam of the flashlight he carried to illuminate their sleeping forms. "I don't believe either of them has budged one iota since they fell asleep three hours ago. However, thanks to Kim Il Sung's army, they won't get to sleep much longer. We've had a change of plans. Major Denton wants us all to assemble at the mess hall immediately, and you're to be ready to evacuate."

"What time is it? Did I sleep through reveille?" Philip looked for signs of daybreak coming through one of the narrow windows, but blackness was all he could see. He thought that perhaps the heavy rain, which pounded on the sheet metal roof with a deafening clamor, prevented any sunlight from shining into the room.

"No. According to my watch, the time is just a few minutes after midnight. However, a reconnaissance team pulled in a few minutes ago, and they've heard reports that the invading troops from the north may reach Daejon as early as morning's light. To make matters worse, all this rain caused a rockslide near Okchon, rendering the highway to Taegu impassable from here. If y'all expect to get south before the back roads are cut off, you're going to have to leave as soon as we can get you out of here. I'll waken the others in a minute, but I wanted a chance to speak with you first." The soft glow from the flashlight cast long shadows against his father's face and made him appear very old.

"Guess this means there'll be no turning back in my decision to stay on as an interpreter until they can get their own men in here. I'd make Dick Spencer stay with me if he hadn't limited his Korean vocabulary to theology. If I get my hands on one Lieutenant Rusty Barnard, I just might strangle him for sending word to the major about my so-called 'excellent language skills.' With friends like him, who needs. . .oh, never mind." Philip knew that his father took the recommendation as a high compliment, despite the empty threat and mock stern tone of his words.

"Your mother agrees with me, though. I owe our beloved Korea my best efforts to bring peace back to our land. And if by staying to help with negotiations I can play a part in ensuring Grace's safety. . ." His dad had to clear his throat before he could finish his thought. "Well, you know I'd lay down my life for that dear girl."

He shuffled a large manila envelope from under one arm to the next. The beam of his flashlight danced across the floor as he reached for his back pocket and withdrew his billfold. "I've carried this business card around in my wallet for a couple months. Kept meaning to take it out but always forgot. I guess the Lord knew we'd need it today." Philip accepted the card from his dad, who pointed his flashlight to illuminate the words.

"This has the address and phone number of an old friend by the name of Tanaka. Tanaka *Sen-sei* in Japanese, but he prefers that you use the Korean title, *Hwangjangnim,* instead. I want you to contact him as soon as you get to Japan. He'll take good care of you. I don't know if you remember him, but he and his wife came from Japan some fifty years ago to open an orphanage in Seoul. He had to return to his homeland during the war, but by then they were both more Korean at heart than Japanese. I saw him just a couple of months ago. He was back in Seoul for a few days in order to bury his beloved mate. As her last request, she asked to be buried in the foreigners' cemetery. That's a story for another day, but after the memorial service, he said if I or my family ever had occasion to pass through Beppu, the coastal town where he lives, we'd have a place to stay. Beppu is the closest Japanese port from Pusan. You'll probably drop anchor there. After you leave for San Francisco with Jennifer, I am confident he'll watch after your mother and Grace until I can travel over to bring them home."

Philip watched his dad pull the manila envelope from under his arm and offer it to him.

"The major kept his end of the bargain we struck when we met with him. Here are the U.S. military pass and identification documents he had promised to prepare for Grace. But I'd still feel better about her safety if you were to stick close beside her until you arrive in Japan. Folks are liable to get desperate if this war continues to escalate. Grace may be in danger if the knowledge of these special papers and permits were to fall into the wrong hands."

His father leaned in close and whispered into Philip's good ear. "I've been watching you the last few days. I don't think you'll find the task of sticking close to Grace too difficult a chore. I'm glad to see the two of you have picked up your close friendship where you left off back in '42. She's needed a confidante, and since we're the 'big bosses' now, she's too tied to convention to confide much in your mother or me. Grace has done your heart some good too, I do believe."

Philip felt ill at ease to learn that he and Grace had been under his parent's scrutiny. Or maybe his discomfort came from knowing his dad had hit the nail on the head. The very mention of her name sent a warm happiness flooding over him. He swung his feet over the side of his cot and donned his shoes, then stood.

"You can count on me to take good care of all the womenfolk, Dad. I just wish I didn't have to say good-bye to you so soon."

"I understand the necessity of getting Jennifer back to San Francisco. And who knows how long I'll be deterred here. I'm certain we'll see the Lord's hand in all of this someday. But, Son, if I don't get another opportunity to say so, I want you to know I'm proud of you. I'm praying that God will protect us all until the day that you're back in Korea and we're working together for Him on the same team."

Philip's father threw his arms around him, and they pounded each other on the back in a bear hug. "Well, we'd better shake the others out of bed. I want you to put as many miles as possible between you and the Communists." With a final slap on the back, his dad stepped back and handed him the flashlight. "I hereby bestow on you the honor of waking Cinderella and Sleeping Beauty over there."

Guided by the flickering luminescence of the dying flashlight, Philip crossed the room and paused between the two cots where Grace and Jennifer slept. His head volleyed back and forth as he contemplated which of the women he should waken first.

Jennifer slept with her mouth open. All traces of lipstick had long ago been wiped clean. A trickle of drool trailed down her pale, gaunt cheek and into her blond hair.

Pity welled within him, and Philip wondered what had ever attracted him to her. Any beauty she possessed seemed so superficial compared to Grace. And he didn't mean just the effects of cosmetics on her outward appearance.

As he thought about his relationship with Jennifer, he realized the stormy end to their engagement had been brewing for many months. He'd simply chosen to be blind rather than read the warning signs.

Even though she'd been faithful in attending church with him, whenever he had tried to draw her into a time of prayer or Bible study, she had always had something "important" to do. She seemed more concerned about planning a fancy church wedding featuring the beautiful bride than in building the foundations of a Christ-centered marriage. Life revolved around *her*—not *them*.

Yet, he had to accept a good portion of the blame and not be so quick to judge Jennifer. He'd been wrong to try to force his call to ministry on her or assume that if he could just get her over here, she'd have a change of heart. Jennifer couldn't help her self-serving attitudes and self-centered disposition. An indulgent heritage and egocentric environment were hard to overcome. The undertow of materialism had nearly sucked him in as well.

Grace, on the other hand. . . Her face radiated an inner peace even while she slept. She had chosen to allow God to strengthen her character through the tragedies of life rather than become embittered and sad.

Wisps of raven hair had come loose from her braid and blown across her face. Philip bent to lightly brush the wayward strands back into place. At the feather-soft sensation of her skin against his fingertips, he felt compelled to caress her forehead again. Her eyes flew open, and she gave him the most enchanting smile he'd ever seen. He felt certain his heart stopped beating for a brief moment or two. The look they shared implied more than a trade of neighborly affection between two old friends.

*Oh, dear Lord,* Philip prayed in silent desperation, *don't let me break this wonderful woman's heart. No good can possibly come by encouraging these romantic feelings I have for her. We are worlds apart in every way.*

Jennifer's sniveling effectively broke the sweet tension he and Grace had just exchanged. "Dr. Woods. Whatever has possessed you to go stomping around in the middle of the night and scaring me half to death? I don't know about *her,* but I, for one, need my beauty sleep."

Philip gritted his teeth. Not so long ago, he had considered marrying this woman. Now he had to force himself to even be civil to her. "Put a sock in it, Jennifer," he grumbled. "I'm not doing this for my health."

❧

Eun-Me clutched the packet that bore her name and the official seal of the U.S. Army tightly to her chest as she prepared to go out into the midnight rain. She had argued that she couldn't possibly accept these documents, knowing what *Moksanim* Woods had promised in exchange. Yet *Moksanim* refused to listen to her and had insisted that he would stay no matter what. He assured her that the Lord had chosen this way to work all things together for her good.

*Sahmonim* stayed behind in the mess hall with *Moksanim* for a time of private good-byes while the others proceeded to their assigned vehicles. As if providing Eun-Me with travel passes weren't enough, Major Denton had arranged for his personal driver to transport Eun-Me in his jeep, along with *Sahmonim* Woods, Philip, and Miss Jennifer. All the others had to climb into the back of a troop transport truck for the trip to Taegu.

However, they hadn't traveled very far until a fresh wave of overwhelming weariness transplanted any feelings Eun-Me had of preferential treatment. They took so many twists and turns around the dark, mountainous countryside that their arduous journey from Taechon Beach the day before seemed like a Sunday afternoon joyride now. And this time, she didn't have her previous pleasure of sitting next to Philip and exchanging clandestine smiles. Instead, she had wedged herself in between *Sahmonim* and Miss Jennifer. The soldier who was driving offered only his name and rank when Philip tried to speak to him. Corporal David Frye made it clear that his job involved transporting them to Taegu. Any conversation was optional. His silence set the precedent for the duration of their nighttime ride. Occasionally, Eun-Me heard *Sahmonim's* soft humming of a favorite hymn, but only slow and steady breathing came from Miss Jennifer.

Torrential monsoon rains followed them from the time they left the compound, and the open sides and convertible top covering the jeep provided them with little protection from the elements. Eun-Me felt wet all the way down to her bones.

The darkness of night merely served to amplify her fears. She held her breath at every bend in the road, watching nervously behind them to make certain that the other vehicles in the convoy stayed in her view, terrified to watch the road ahead for fear that the Communists would pop out from behind some rock and ambush them. Such a choke hold of terror gripped her at times, she thought she might scream if they didn't arrive at their destination soon.

She kept herself from breaking down by focusing her gaze on the silhouette of Philip's face outlined by the dashboard lights. As long as he sat in front of her, she knew she could survive.

Then, as if Someone shut the spigot off, the rain stopped. Morning's first light split the black horizon with glorious brilliance. And Eun-Me offered spontaneous praise to the Lord for seeing them safely through the night.

Beside her, Miss Jennifer squirmed in her seat and twisted her head to look out the window. "That has to go on record as the longest night in history. Are we getting close yet? I've got the most awful crick in my neck."

She hadn't asked the question of anyone in particular, and Philip showed no signs of answering her, so for the first time since they'd left the Daejon KMAG compound, Corporal Frye spoke.

"By my estimation, we should be pulling into Taegu in another hour or so." He shot a quick glance in his rearview mirror at Miss Jennifer, and his voice brightened considerably, as though he'd just noticed his pretty passenger for the very first time. "But if you need me to, we can pull over and let you stretch your legs by the side of the road. Even better, I know of a roadside *shik-tang* up ahead where we can grab a bite of breakfast if you don't mind Korean food."

"I could really go for a bowl of that yummy sticky rice. Dr. Woods, you don't mind if we stop, do you?"

Philip swiveled in his seat. His mouth dropped open, and he stared wide-eyed at Miss Jennifer. "N–no. I don't mind. I'm always ready to eat, but we ought to ask the others. They may be anxious to get right to the train station. We can pick up something to eat there. Mom. Grace. What do you gals prefer?"

Eun-Me absentmindedly nodded her head in support of *Sahmonim*'s "Sure, let's stop." Her mind was busy trying to figure out what had brought about the change in Miss Jennifer's opinion toward Korean food. She didn't want to be judgmental, but she suspected that the remark wasn't purely innocent. Had she intended to poke fun at her? Or was she trying to stir up jealousy in Philip by acting flirtatious with another man? In either case, Eun-Me didn't think Miss Jennifer had achieved the desired effect. She no longer cared one whit about what Philip's old girlfriend thought of her, and Philip didn't seem to show any signs of jealousy. Instead, he turned his attentions to her, not Jennifer.

"I'm going to order you a cup of ginseng tea and make sure you eat a big breakfast. I know you hardly touched your dinner last night, and there's no telling how many days we'll have to travel before we make it to Japan." Eun-Me felt her cheeks warm under his close examination.

꽃

"That tea looks and smells just like dirt. How can you drink that stuff?" Rather than taking offense at Miss Jennifer's remark, this time Eun-Me covered her mouth with her hand and chuckled aloud. Then she put the cup to her lips and finished the last earthy dregs of her ginseng tea.

"I personally don't like the taste, but ginseng's good for your health. Are you certain you won't try just a spot?" Eun-Me pretended to tip the pot toward Miss Jennifer's cup.

"No, no. That's quite all right, but thank you. I'm feeling just fine this morning. There's not a thing wrong with my health."

Another round of laughter rippled across the foreigners. From the moment they had entered the roadside *shik-tang* to eat breakfast, Miss Jennifer had entertained everyone, beginning by making fun of herself as she attempted to sit on the floor Korean-style. This was a side of Miss Jennifer's personality that Eun-Me had not seen until now. Eun-Me could understand how Philip might have fallen in love with *this* Miss Jennifer—delightful and witty and at ease in a crowd. Could the bitter remarks and crotchety disposition displayed by Miss Jennifer all week simply be due to her not feeling well? If so, and the true Miss Jennifer had shown herself again, then Philip would soon be racing to make up with her.

The thought occurred to Eun-Me that her tender exchanges with Philip may have come to an end. Suddenly, she no longer felt enthralled by this new Miss Jennifer. She cast an inquiring glance across the table toward Philip. Like the others, he was watching Miss Jennifer, yet he did not appear to be wooed by her charm. Instead, he eyed her suspiciously.

Even so, Eun-Me felt certain that their inevitable reunion was just a matter of time.

From the far end of the table, where the three military drivers had been entertaining the Carroll boys, Corporal Frye cleared his throat and tapped lightly on his teacup with a metal chopstick. At the signal, everyone looked his way. "I think we'd better load up again and hit the road. We've been stopped way too long." He stole a quick peek at his watch. "Major's orders were to deliver you all directly to the Taegu train depot."

The long-legged Americans untwisted themselves from their awkward positions on the floor, settled up their bill with the proprietor, and headed out the door. The breakfast and the morning's frivolity had invigorated the group at a critical time, and as they climbed back in the jeep and trucks, most of them seemed in good spirits and ready to endure the remainder of their trip to Taegu.

Miss Jennifer hooked her arm through *Sahmonim* Woods's, and they walked together toward the jeep. Walking alone, Eun-Me started to follow them across the dirt-packed yard of the *shik-tang*, but she paused when Philip called, "Grace. Wait up."

As he fell into step beside her, Eun-Me crooked her neck to look at Philip and caught him staring after Miss Jennifer. Her heart sank.

"She's the life of the party when she wants to be."

Eun-Me managed to squeak an "Um-hum" through her emotion-clogged throat, but even if she could have thought of a more detailed response, she would have choked on her words.

"I hope and pray this is the Jennifer who shows up on the boat when we leave Japan headed for San Francisco. My trip might be bearable, if so."

This time, Eun-Me couldn't even choke out a monosyllable reply, and Philip stopped in his tracks the second he looked at her.

"Grace, are you all right? Did I put my foot in my mouth again?"

His foot was nowhere near his mouth, so Eun-Me assumed the comment to be another unfamiliar American idiom. The time that she spent pondering the phrase took her mind off her faltering emotions just long enough for her to regain sufficient composure to speak. "I'm fine. Really. Don't pay any attention to me. I was just thinking about how 'topsy-turvy' everything has turned, as *Sahmonim* would say. Once again, life proves to be totally unpredictable."

"Yes. Life and Jennifer Anderson."

Eun-Me could feel Philip looking at her as though he wanted to say something more, but she avoided his gaze and quickened her pace. "I'd better hurry. *Sahmonim* has already climbed into the jeep, and Miss Jennifer is waiting for me to sit in the middle so she can take her seat."

The corporal kept the jeep's speed at a crawl until the other two vehicles clattered up onto the paved road behind them. Even then, his feet kept tapping the brakes and working the clutch in an attempt to dodge the people walking alongside and down the middle of the street.

As Eun-Me expected on any given morning at this hour, some of the pedestrians appeared to be typical provincial citizens going about their daily routines. Yet, unlike most mornings, refugees comprised most of this throng. The women carried all of their worldly possessions tied in big bundles and perched on top of their heads. The children, clutching a sibling's hand, raced their feet in double-time to keep stride with their parents. Rice-filled gunnysacks were slung over the shoulders of many of the men.

Since Philip's transistor radio first crackled with the initial invasion reports, this surreal scene of commonplace mixed with chaos personified for Eun-Me the terrifying reality of an approaching war.

When their convoy reached the outskirts of Taegu, Eun-Me thought she heard music. She looked through the front windshield to see uniformed schoolchildren lining both sides of the road. They waved Korean flags high above their heads. Their young soprano voices surrounded them, and the strains of Korea's national anthem filled the air.

Tears fell unimpeded down Eun-Me's face as she joined in singing the melody. When she reached the chorus, she could no longer find voice to repeat the words, so she hummed along. And sobbed.

*Sahmonim* leaned across Eun-Me's back and began to whisper a translation of the lyrics for Jennifer:

*Until the East Sea's waves are dry and Paektu Mountain worn away,*
*God watch o'er our land forever! Our Korea we stand and cheer!*

*Rose of Sharon, thousand miles and range and river land!*
*Guarded by her people, ever may Korea stand!*

However, at the last verse, *Sahmonim*, too, had to pause and swallow her tears before she could continue.

*With such a will; such a spirit, loyalty, heart and hand,*
*Let us love, come grief, come gladness,*
*This our beloved land!*

# Chapter 8

Philip raked his fingers through the front of his hair in an attempt to mask his own moist eyes. Even while he watched the scene unfold, he knew that he would look back on this moment as a pivotal point in his life. His soul welled with pride at the thought that these people were his people. This land was his land.

Only one overriding motivation kept him pressing toward America instead of staying here with his father to work for peace. He knew he had to complete his residency so that when he returned, he'd be fully qualified to serve the Korean people and fulfill God's call. No matter what the future held in store for Korea, he vowed that he'd be back to his adopted motherland someday.

Grace's cries filtered up from the rear seat. He longed to hold her in his arms and comfort her. She had looked so distressed back at the *shik-tang*.

He worried that he had upset her by bringing up the fact that he would soon be going on to San Francisco with Jennifer and leaving Grace and his mother alone. After all, the realization must be sinking in that within a matter of hours, she would be leaving Korea and going to Japan.

He shook his head, disgusted with himself for his insensitivity. His petty problems with Jennifer paled when compared to the ordeals facing Grace.

Given how she struggled with feelings of bitterness toward the Japanese, the prospect of finding herself surrounded by the lifelong enemies who had killed her father and brother, with no way home, might be almost as terrifying as the invasion of the Korean Communists from the north.

He buried his head in his hands. This time, not to hide a few tears but to bring to the Lord his mental list of prayer requests: Grace, his father, his mother, traveling mercies to Japan, Jennifer's safe transport home. Then, his prayers went back to Grace again.

"Sir, we're nearing the Taegu train depot, but I'm worried about dropping you off in the middle of this mob." The corporal's tight grip on the steering wheel made his knuckles deathly white, and Philip realized they hadn't moved in traffic for quite some time. "I don't see how a group of your size could possibly all stay together. Any suggestions as to what I should do?"

Philip scanned the sea of black, bobbing heads that moved with tsunami force toward the station's row of ticket windows. "We don't appear to be going anywhere fast. Let me jog back to the transport truck and poll the other men. Wait right here." He meant the remark as a wisecrack, knowing they weren't likely to budge, but the pinch-lipped Corporal Frye gave a quick nod and kept his eyes peeled on the road.

Philip eased himself out of the jeep and began to wedge and push his way upstream against the shoving crowd toward the truck.

❧

"Isn't there a special station for Americans?" Eun-Me jumped at the touch of Miss Jennifer's hand on her arm when she leaned forward to address their driver. Her emerald eyes sparkled and grew rounder with fear, darting in every direction as she scanned the pressing crowd. "I've never seen so many people in one place in my life. We'll be crushed to death for sure."

"You'll be fine, Dear." *Sahmonim* reached across Eun-Me to offer a calming pat to Miss Jennifer's knee. "Such crowds aren't all that unusual in Seoul, and I've always survived. You've got one big advantage over these folks. With your height, you'll stand head and shoulders above the rest. Thank goodness the rain has stopped, or we'd have to fight to keep the umbrella spokes from poking out our eyes. Let me offer one suggestion, though." *Sahmonim* shot a quick glance at the corporal, then leaned in farther and lowered her voice to a raspy whisper. "Tuck your passport and any cash you might be carrying down in your underwear. Pickpockets thrive on situations like this."

Eun-Me recalled the skimpy underthings she'd packed for Miss Jennifer, and she didn't think that her foundation garments could provide sufficient support for such a task, but she kept her opinion to herself.

"Thanks for the advice, but I'm wearing a money belt. I should be fine on that front."

While Eun-Me still wore the same clothes as the day before, Miss Jennifer had postponed their departure from the compound an extra fifteen minutes so that she could change. The black flared skirt of her two-piece traveling suit could very easily hide such a bulge. Perhaps Miss Jennifer's decision to wear a skirt on their evacuation journey, rather than her form-fitting dungarees, was not as illogical as Eun-Me had originally thought. Of course, she would have no trouble hiding her packet of documents down a wide leg of her *mom-pei* pants, and she had no money to worry about.

In a flurry of movement, Philip shoved their knapsacks and Miss Jennifer's beach bag into the jeep's floorboard ahead of him, then jumped back into his seat. A spike of sandy blond hair stood straight out from the crown of his head, and the collar of his shirt had flipped up on one side. His disheveled appearance seemed to bother no one else but her, so Eun-Me fought the urge to set him right again.

"Looks like this is where we'll say good-bye, Corporal Frye," Philip said as they exchanged a handshake. "The consensus reached after my quick powwow with the other men is that we'll stand a better chance of getting tickets on the train if we split up and queue in different lines. We've decided to all go our separate ways from here."

Eun-Me caught sight of the pale-skinned and light-haired Carroll family before they were swallowed up in the jostling swarm. Each parent clutched a boy in one arm and yanked their duffel bag between them with their free hands.

"The Carrolls said to tell you folks that they hope to see you on the train." Professor Spencer stuck his head in the jeep's open doorway on the passenger side. "Reverend and Mrs. Taylor have already taken off too. But, just in case we don't connect again, I wanted to wish you all Godspeed. Mrs. Woods, Grace, I'll see you back in Seoul as soon as this nasty mess is settled, if not before. Philip, don't let this experience keep you from visiting your folks again soon, you hear? Glad to have met you, Jennifer." He waved in salutation, then was gone, his balding head floating on top of the wave of humanity.

"Okay, ladies. No sense postponing this any longer. Have you secured all your valuables?" Philip waited until he heard a distinct yes from each one before handing them their respective bags.

"Pay attention, Jennifer. The minute you set foot out of the jeep, I want you to get between Grace and my mom and lock your arms in theirs to form a human chain. Don't let go for anything. No arguments."

If Miss Jennifer had been inclined to protest, she wouldn't have dared after the steely glare Philip shot at her. Eun-Me squirmed in her seat when his focus shifted toward her, but his scowl lifted into the slightest of smiles when their eyes met.

"Grace, since you're the only Korean among us, you'd be the most likely one to get lost in this crowd, so I'm going to hold your hand and keep you close to me while I lead the way. We aren't going to worry about what people think." Her face warmed to know he had read her mind yet another time, and she dropped her gaze away from his clairvoyant stare.

"Are we ready?" He didn't wait for a response but jumped out and offered his hand while first Miss Jennifer, then Eun-Me climbed from the back of the jeep, followed by *Sahmonim*.

Before Eun-Me could plant both her feet on the ground, Miss Jennifer had looped her straw bag onto the crook of her elbow and locked arms with her. Philip, upon seeing Eun-Me struggle with one free arm to adjust her own pack, bent down and murmured in her ear, "I'd say she's taken my instruction a bit too seriously. Let me help you with that." He slipped her arm through the cloth ties of her knapsack and pushed the bundle up onto her shoulder, then he offered his open hand.

He engulfed her tiny palm in his and intertwined their fingers, finalizing the act with a soft squeeze. Eun-Me allowed herself to be pulled into the current of refugees with Miss Jennifer and *Sahmonim* in tow. She paid no attention to the strangers pressing in on her. She felt only the tingling touch of her hand wrapped securely in his. She would gladly follow Philip to the ends of the earth if he did this the entire way.

"Thief! Stop! I've been robbed!" Eun-Me's ears rang from Miss Jennifer's piercing screams. Philip immediately stopped their processional and spun around. She still clutched Eun-Me in a viselike grip, but from the crook of Miss Jennifer's arm, where her straw beach bag had hung moments before, now only the strap dangled in the breeze.

In vain, Eun-Me surveyed the crowd around them in search of the thief. Any purse-snatcher or pickpocket with the skill to go unnoticed while cutting a swaying bag from someone's arm stood a good chance of making a clean getaway.

Philip pulled the strap away and examined Miss Jennifer's arm for any signs of injury. "You don't appear hurt, so we need to keep moving."

He tugged Eun-Me's hand and took a step, but Miss Jennifer refused to budge. Eun-Me, caught in the middle, stretched in both directions.

"You've got to call the police so they can catch the dirty pilferer." Miss Jennifer no longer displayed any signs of her early morning good humor.

"Just forget it, Jennifer. We have to hurry."

"I need my stuff." She growled at Philip with an angry snarl. "It's bad enough that I had to leave most of it behind in the broken car, but now all I've got is what I'm wearing!"

"Jennifer, we're in the middle of a war. The police aren't about to drop what they're doing because some rich American lost her pajamas. If there's time, we'll try to buy you a new toothbrush when we get to Pusan. We'll figure out the rest later. But, please. Let's go."

Eun-Me ran through a mental inventory of the things in her knapsack. She didn't think she possessed a single item that would interest Miss Jennifer. Not here or at home in Seoul.

People shoved and prodded their way toward the ticket windows. No one bothered to stand in a line. The only rule that applied in this cacophony seemed to be "He who shoves hardest wins." Philip gave up on being polite after a dozen or more stooped *halmonims* cut in front of him. "If that's the way they want to play, watch this," he mumbled at Eun-Me. And he wormed them through to the ticket clerk.

*"Pusan gachee sae-jang chusaeyo."* As Philip stated his request for the tickets, Eun-Me noted with pride that his accent remained perfect after all these years.

The man behind the counter didn't even look up when he replied, *"Opsumnida."*

"What did he say?" Miss Jennifer shouted to Eun-Me over the din.

"He said the tickets to Pusan are sold out."

Without saying a word, Philip pulled back the *won* he'd shoved into the slot beneath the window bars and added a crisp American ten-dollar bill on top of the Korean currency. The clerk finally raised his head. A second later, Philip stepped back from the window with four tickets squeezed in his left hand.

They snaked their way from the plaza area and through the turnstiles onto the platform to wait for the next southbound train. Philip led their cadre to a remote corner of the depot and away from prying onlookers. He dropped Eun-Me's hand and motioned them into a huddle.

"In case we get separated, I want us each to carry our own ticket." Philip handed one to each of the women and slipped his inside his shirt pocket. "Mom, you're in charge of making sure Jennifer never leaves your side. You, Grace, and I can get to Pusan by ourselves if we have to, but she's totally dependent on us."

Even now, away from the teeming masses, Miss Jennifer held tight to the sleeves of Eun-Me and *Sahmonim.* Philip's words made her pinch a bit harder.

"If one of us misses this train, I think the others should go on to Pusan and wait. We'll rendezvous at the taxi stand in front of the train station. If two trains come in and the missing party still hasn't arrived, then go to our nearest church and ask the pastor to put you up for the night. We'll catch up with one another there."

In the distance, a breathy train whistle started low and rose to a shrill crescendo. The piercing blast sent all the waiting passengers scurrying for a post near the edge of the platform as a cloud of soot darkened the morning sky.

"Okay. Here she comes." Philip, clutching Eun-Me's hand, waded into the throng once more. "The ten o'clock southbound is only forty-five minutes late. Mom, you and Jennifer go ahead of us so we're certain you get on board."

Miss Jennifer released her grip on Eun-Me to cling onto *Sahmonim* with both hands, while the drab green train bellowed into the station and chugged to a stop. From what Eun-Me could count where she stood, she estimated the rail engine pulled eight cars—each filled to capacity.

Everyone converged at the landings in front of each car door to wait for the porters to open the floodgates and admit new passengers. Philip stood at Eun-Me's side, clasping her hand painfully tight. The prodding and jostling intensified, propelling Eun-Me into *Sahmonim's* back with such force that she thought she might suffocate if she couldn't catch a breath soon.

No one in front of them seemed willing to allow this car's lone departing passenger off the train, lest they lose their hard-earned position. The porter resorted to kicking into the barricade of bodies to punch out an opening large enough for passage of the young *omma* with a baby tied to her back.

Once his charge had left the train, the porter stepped back and permitted the melee to resume in the push to board. Eun-Me felt her feet leave the floor, and sheer momentum carried her toward the small opening.

Ahead of her, she watched *Sahmonim* and Miss Jennifer step, as one body, over the threshold onto the train. Eun-Me released her hold on Philip and reached out to grab the railing on either side of the door to pull herself on board. Before she could snatch a firm hold, two middle-aged men pushed their way in front of her. Eun-Me fished for the railing again but felt only air.

The train pitched forward to signal its imminent departure, and the press of the crowd eased. Suddenly left without support, Eun-Me began to flail her arms in every direction, searching for something—anything—to hold onto that might steady her teetering balance. The train began to roll.

A rising sense of panic sent a squeak of fright from her lips as her leg slipped into the crevice between the platform and the locomotive. From the corner of her eye, she saw Philip reaching out for her, but he couldn't catch her in time.

She fell forward, hitting the platform with her open palms. Her knapsack slipped off her shoulder and lay by her hands on the floor. Her right leg still dangled dangerously close to the lurching train. At the screeching blast of the train's whistle, Eun-Me froze.

Before she could think what to do, Philip reached under her arms and yanked her to her feet. He tugged a bit too hard, and they both stumbled this time. But he quickly regained his balance, retrieved her knapsack, then steadied Eun-Me by wrapping her in his arms. Philip stepped backward, drawing her away from the platform, as the train increased its speed.

"Dr. Woods, Grace!" Caleb Carroll waved to them from the departing caboose. "We're goin' to Pusan!"

Eun-Me leaned into Philip's embrace, and together they watched the train shrink on the horizon, then disappear around a curve.

❧

"You're bleeding, Grace. Let me see your hands." Ignoring the quizzical stares of the Koreans who waited for the next train, Philip set their bags at his feet and wove one leg through the straps. He turned Grace to face him and pulled her forward until she was between his knees. Then, he lifted her palms to examine them.

"Are you hurt anywhere else? How about your leg? Is it painful to put weight on it? Do I need to examine you for a break or a sprain?" She responded to each question with a quick shake of her head.

He stopped talking long enough to blow the loose dirt away from her open wounds.

As a doctor, he knew he shouldn't feel this way, but his hands were trembling. He decided he still hadn't recovered from the scare Grace had given him.

"Someone borrowed my handkerchief, and I never got it back, or I'd already have you fixed up as good as new." Philip gave her a quick wink and grinned, then he began to blow again, this time caressing her delicate fingers with his thumbs. He hated to think of the hard labor that such dainty hands had been forced to do.

Without thinking, he raised her hands and gently kissed each tiny fingertip. Her hands started trembling, like his own had been doing since he first reached for her. "What are you doing. . . ?" Her voice trailed. But she didn't pull away.

A cold shiver raced through him at the thought of the tragedy that had nearly occurred. He'd come so close to losing his beautiful Grace, not briefly in the crowd, but to death beneath the iron wheels of the train. He circled her dainty wrists in his hands and guided her arms around his waist to wrap himself in her embrace. Releasing her hands, he reached his arms around her and pulled her close to him. Philip longed to keep her there forever, safe from harm.

He bent down and began to search her onyx eyes, unsure if they glistened with the vestiges of fear or the seeds of the same overpowering force that now drew him to her. Philip lifted his hand to stroke the outline of her cheek. Then, tipping her chin, he gently raised her face toward his.

There in the middle of the Taegu train station, jostled by the never-ending stream of travelers, he lowered his mouth to hers. Drawn to the softness of her quivering lips, he kissed her with all the love in his heart.

A whistle's sharp blast severed the fragile moment and brought Philip back to the reality of where they were. He could feel the renewed press of the crowd as they rushed to catch the approaching train. Grace dropped her arms, and he loosened his hold on her, effectively completing the break.

He cleared his throat, trying to ignore the awkward silence that hung between them. His mind raced to find the appropriate words to explain or defend what had just occurred.

Philip desperately wanted to tell her that he loved her. Her response confirmed in his heart the fact that he had suspected for a long time. Yet, he couldn't bring himself to admit his love out loud. He would be gone from Korea for at least another three years. She deserved more than a long-distance love. Regardless, he didn't have time to make sense of it now. Another southbound train was pulling into the station, and he had to get them on board.

He looked down at the petite form of Grace. The top of her head came only as high as his chest. Philip took one more glance toward the slowing train and the sea of black heads pushing past them.

"Let's go," he said, and without waiting for her to approve of what he was about to do, he slung their bags over his shoulder and scooped her into his arms.

"Quick. Wrap your legs around me. I won't let you fall." He had shamed her sufficiently by kissing her in public. If it meant seeing Grace safely onto that train, he would gladly breach this bit of decorum as well.

In a flash, Philip boosted her up and held her like a large child. Clutching her tightly with his right arm, he used his left as a battering ram to push his way forward to the open doorway of the railcar.

≈

Eun-Me hardly noticed her skinned hands and bruised knee, for her lips still burned with the tender pressure of Philip's kiss. That much-dreamed-of experience was all she'd imagined—and more. She would savor the sweet memory for all eternity.

Despite her desire to remain in his arms, now that he had carried her safely aboard the train, she knew the inevitable moment had come when she must release her hold on him.

"We've created enough of a stir. You'd better put me down now." She loosened her grasp and eased her feet to the ground.

In the short span of time Philip had taken to push their way on board, the train had filled to standing-room-only capacity. They jockeyed for a place to stand where they wouldn't get trampled by the rushing current of oncoming passengers. With her face still buried in his chest, they shuffled together, wedging themselves into a small space between the last seat and the back wall of the car.

Eun-Me had been surprised to see another locomotive arrive so soon after the other had departed, until she overheard the porter who stood guard at the door behind her explain the reason to another puzzled traveler. From what she could gather as the onslaught of riders pushed their way past, the railroad authorities had pressed into service every available locomotive to try to accommodate, while they could, the urgent demands of the evacuees flooding south.

After a couple of jerking false starts that bounced Eun-Me's head into Philip's chest, the train started to move. The porter used his shoulder to force the door closed against the tide of people still trying to board. Eun-Me looked out the window to see a handful of men so desperate to flee that they were climbing onto the roof of the train to ride. She breathed a prayer of thankfulness that Philip had gotten them inside.

Eun-Me lifted her head up toward him, and he offered a thin smile in return. This wasn't the time or place to discuss what had happened just moments before.

She wasn't sure she could have found the words to express her feelings for him, even if they had been all alone. Nor was she sure if she could bear to hear Philip's explanation for what had occurred. She wanted to believe that he'd kissed her as an expression of his true love, but she feared the real reason stemmed from his being overcome with emotion after the heroic rescue he'd performed.

She was almost glad the circumstances wouldn't allow the truth to come out right now. She wanted to hold onto her fantasy as long as she could and believe that he loved her as much as she loved him.

Eun-Me relaxed as the clacking of the iron wheels played their unique lullaby. Her knees suddenly felt so weak that she might have collapsed to the floor if there'd been room to move. She could have easily dozed as she stood, for the catastrophic events of the past few days and minutes were beginning to take their toll on her. But she refused to succumb to sleep.

By this most recent twist to the week's cataclysmic turn of events, for the next several hours she'd been thrust into Philip's arms. She planned to savor each second; preserve each moment in her memory. She knew that each mile they traveled brought her another mile closer to the place and time that she would have to tell Philip good-bye.

When the train pulled into the station at Pusan, Philip slipped his arm about her waist and guided her down the steps from the train. He kept his hold on her while they made their way through the terminal and across the open plaza toward the taxi stand.

"Oh, wait just a minute. I can't let *Sahmonim* and Miss Jennifer see me looking like such a mess." She paused and brushed at her trousers, dismayed to find a rip at the knee, which must have happened when she fell. "I'm beginning to look more and more like a refugee."

"You look beautiful to me. Why do you care what they think, anyway? We're all pretty scruffy by now." Philip waved his free hand high in the air, keeping a firm grasp around Eun-Me's waist with his other. "There's Mom and Jennifer. Mom seems to want us to hurry. I wonder what's going on."

*Sahmonim* was waving frantically in the air, so they began to jog toward her. "We've got to rush to get to the pier. I'll explain on the way. We don't have time to wait for a taxi. We'll have to take a tram."

With Miss Jennifer in tow, *Sahmonim* led the way to the corner stop to wait for the next streetcar headed for the pier. Judging from the heavy smell of fish that filled the air, Eun-Me didn't think they would have too far to ride. While they waited, *Sahmonim* began to explain the reason for the rush.

"We got off the train here in Pusan and were milling around the taxi stand with all the other missionaries, trying to decide what to do, when a young American soldier with the local KMAG approached us. He said that arrangements had been made for two boats to evacuate American citizens this afternoon and this evening. The others ran to catch the first one. If they left on time, they should already be at sea. But if we hurry, we can probably still make it aboard the boat that's scheduled to leave at six."

"That's not all the soldier had to say." Miss Jennifer interrupted *Sahmonim* as the trolley car approached their stop. "When he heard that I was going on to San Francisco rather than staying in Japan, he advised us to check the schedules as soon as we landed in Beppu."

She paused long enough to follow *Sahmonim* aboard the tram and grab hold of one of the safety straps that hung from overhead. "He said we ought to leave for America immediately if that was our final destination. They expect General MacArthur's army to be called in to settle this skirmish, and the seas will be teeming with troop carriers. According to him, any commercial ships that can, will want to leave the area as soon as possible. We may be on a freighter headed home as early as tomorrow. Wouldn't that be good?"

Even though Philip had guided Eun-Me safely aboard the tram, Philip's hand still rested on her waist, and she caught Miss Jennifer staring at his arm. The hint of a snarl curled her lips, and the flash of anger in the American's green eyes made Eun-Me squirm and want to pull away, but Philip gave her a gentle squeeze and drew her closer to his side.

"I'm not looking forward to leaving Mom and Grace so soon. And I'm not in any hurry to make that long voyage. I'm beginning to think that this journey will never end. However, the sooner you are safely home, the better. That's for sure."

*Sahmonim's* voice took on the tone she used when speaking to a child. "Now, Son, watch your tongue. We're all tired, but that's no excuse to be rude." Eun-Me couldn't keep the hint of a smile from playing on her lips.

The last trolley stop deposited them within several hundred yards of the pier. Several dozen Americans, both civilian and military, milled about the dock, making it easy for Eun-Me to immediately locate their outgoing vessel.

Along the gangplank leading onto the military transport that would ferry them across the East China Sea to Japan, a line had formed, and a stern-faced Korean port authority official checked passports and documents before permitting the passengers to board.

Everyone passed unceremoniously until Eun-Me stood before the clerk. He took one look at her and snarled in brusque Korean something to the effect that only Americans were allowed on board. A U.S. military policeman stepped forward from his guard post with his rifle poised. "Step aside." He barked the order into her face.

# Chapter 9

Philip's hand on her back prevented her from instinctively following the command. "She's with me, and she carries the proper documents to allow her entrance into Japan. Show them your papers, Grace."

She turned her back on the men and fished the envelope from its secure hiding place. The official snatched the credentials from her hand and held them close to his eyes, then up toward the sun.

The clerk didn't bother to speak. He shoved the papers at her and jerked his head toward the boat. The American soldier stepped back and allowed her to join *Sahmonim* and Miss Jennifer, who were waiting for her at the top of the gangplank. Philip followed close behind.

"That's one fortunate little lady you've got traveling with you." A heavyset man in a business suit nudged Philip and jerked his head at Eun-Me while they stood at the railing with *Sahmonim* and Miss Jennifer. "We'll probably pass hundreds of Koreans at sea trying to sneak into Japan illegally. Those that make it that far will be caught and sent back." The stranger shoved his right hand toward Philip.

"Name's Conway. Joseph Conway. Own an import/export business back in the States. Was standing behind you folks in line back there. You're the only American I know who brought their *ajumoni* along for the ride to Japan. You must have some pretty good connections to pull the strings necessary for such a thing. You aren't with the embassy, are you? No offense, but you don't look like a diplomat."

Eun-Me watched Philip as he tried to answer, but the man never paused long enough for Philip to respond with more than a shake of his head. An ivory toothpick bobbed from the corner of the man's mouth while he spoke, and he paused between sentences to suck air through his teeth.

"I hope you don't fancy taking her back to America with you. The permits she's got won't work. I'm always haggling with immigration officials, trying to get permits for my Korean business associates to enter Japan and the States. Entrance into Japan is difficult, but nigh on impossible back home." He pinched the toothpick between the fingers of his left hand and slid it from his mouth.

"We are aware of the immigration restrictions. She'll be staying in Japan." Philip offered no further explanation, but that seemed to be enough to satisfy Mr.

Conway. He bit on his toothpick again while he backed away. "Listen, nice talkin' to you folks. I'm gonna see what they've got cookin' in the galley on this tub. Good luck to you all."

"A pleasure doing business with you, Sir," Philip muttered under his breath.

"Oh, children, that reminds me." *Sahmonim* pulled a package wrapped in newsprint from the top of her knapsack. "I forgot in all our rush to get to the boat. I knew you two wouldn't have had time to eat, so I bought some *kimbap* and dried squid as well as a few apples from the street vendor outside the train station while we were waiting for you. We can have our own little dinner cruise right here on the deck. Let's stake out that cozy spot over there." She pointed to an out-of-the-way corner that was protected by the overhang of the engine room.

"Count me out." Eun-Me watched Miss Jennifer crinkle her nose in a now-familiar way. "I think I'll follow that Mr. Conway to the galley. Maybe they have American food on their menu."

An earsplitting blast from the ship's horn echoed across the harbor and signaled their departure. From what Eun-Me could tell, she was the lone Korean passenger on a boat that didn't appear to be even half full. After the press of the crowds they'd endured all day, the relative solitude brought a welcome reprieve.

Against the backdrop of an evening sun melting into the sea's horizon, Eun-Me spread the simple meal out before the three of them, then Philip offered to pray. While he thanked God for the food and His watch, care, and protection throughout this long and difficult day, Eun-Me felt the ship pull away from Pusan's shore, and the burn of tears stung her eyes.

Only God knew what the future held for her homeland and when, or if, she'd be able to return. She swallowed hard against the rising knot of emotion that clogged her throat, as she echoed Philip's "amen." Lifting her head, she watched her beloved Korea slip from view.

After dinner, Philip rounded up some blankets from a deckhand, and they made pallets under the stars. They'd no sooner gotten settled than *Sahmonim* announced she was going in search of Jennifer. She disappeared around the corner before either of them could volunteer to go for her.

"Grace, come with me." Philip stood and extended a hand to help her to her feet. Her body ached all over from her day's travails, and her spirit ached from emotional exhaustion too. Yet, she didn't even consider refusing Philip's request. They had such precious little time left.

Together they walked to the railing, and Philip moved in close to her as they both looked into the ocean waves. "This may be my only chance to be alone with you before I leave. I suspect Mom was thinking the same thing when she hurried off. She wanted to give me a chance to tell you good-bye." Eun-Me's heart pounded wildly, and she had to breathe deeply to fight off the dizziness that the silhouette of his solemn smile produced.

"By most standards, this past week has been pretty awful. I certainly wouldn't have guessed when I left San Francisco just under three weeks ago that I'd be headed back to the States within a matter of days, racing to get my former fiancée out of Korea before the Communists cut us off." Philip gripped the railing tightly in both hands.

"I have to say, though, as strange as this sounds, that the lessons I've learned through this whole gruesome ordeal have made the trauma worthwhile for me. For one thing, I've gotten my priorities straight again. I'm committed to keeping my promise to return after my residency and serve as a missionary doctor, wherever and however God sees fit. I won't let anyone or anything deter me from my commitment to fulfill His call to follow Him."

He dropped his hands from the railing and turned to face Eun-Me, taking her hands in his. "Grace, there's another important lesson I've learned in the short time I've been here. . . ." He paused and drew a deep breath as though the weight of his words clogged his throat. A shiver of anticipation ran through her as she waited for him to continue.

"I've been reminded of how valuable you are to me. I wouldn't trade this time I've spent with you for anything in the world."

He drew his face closer to hers, and she stared into his gray eyes. "I wish more than anything I could take you with us, but you and I both know that's not possible right now. I do vow to keep in close contact and will pray for you night and day. I promise. I'll be back as soon as I can." In a tender act reminiscent of his gesture earlier that day, he lowered his head and tipped her chin toward him. She closed her eyes, and her lips prickled in anticipation of the kiss she was about to receive.

He gently kissed her, not once, but three times, each one lasting longer than the one before. When he pulled back from her, she longed to reach up and pull him toward her again, but she somehow found the discipline to refrain.

He watched her with such intensity, she knew he was waiting for her to respond. Yet, she groped for the right words to say. She had anticipated Philip's arrival for so long, but never in her wildest dreams or worst nightmares could she have possibly imagined that things would turn out like this.

She wanted to admit her love for him and confess that she had loved him for years. She longed to pledge to wait until he came back for her. She knew she couldn't or wouldn't marry another, even if Philip never returned. She would wait a lifetime for him.

Still, he hadn't come right out and said the words "I love you." And, even if he did love her now, at least three years would pass until he would return. A lot could change before then. She had already exposed too much of her soul to him.

The time had come for her to pull back and shelter her heart.

She averted her gaze and stared into the sea. "I think you know I share the same feelings that you've expressed. I wish we didn't have to say good-bye so soon, but knowing that you'll return gives me something to look forward to." She fell quiet, her thoughts, hopes, and wishes such a tangled mess that she couldn't sort through them.

They stood for a long time, feeling the brush of the salt-air breezes and listening to the ocean waves' rhythmic hammering against the boat's hull. The tempo reminded Eun-Me of an old folk song her mother used to sing to her, and she began to sing. Philip accompanied her by humming along, and his low tones combined with the sounds of the sea to soothe Eun-Me's frantic thoughts and frazzled nerves. Their voices tapered to silence when they reached the end of the tune.

ॐ

*Wednesday, June 28, 1950*

The boat's air horn jolted Eun-Me from her sleep as the first pink slivers of morning light danced on the ocean swells. She stood and looked across the water to see dozens of fishing boats heading out to sea. Tracing the wake of their boats, she saw the coastline of Beppu, Japan.

Japan. To Eun-Me, the very name represented bitterness. Resentment. Suffering. Fear. While the boat docked and they prepared to disembark, she prayed, begging God to bring a swift end to the conflict with the Communists so that she could hurry home.

The pier teemed with activity, despite the early hour. The sound of fishmongers screaming in Japanese as they hawked their catch made Eun-Me cringe. She hadn't stopped to consider that she'd have to revert to the use of Japanese. She'd tried to purge her vocabulary of the despised language after Korea was liberated from Japan's rule. Even though they had all been forced to speak Japanese in public and had been required to take Japanese names, she remembered with pride how her parents stubbornly continued to speak Korean in the privacy of their home. Eun-Me considered resorting to one of Philip's old childhood ploys to speak very fast in English when anyone addressed her in Japanese, pretending like she didn't understand one word of what they were trying to say.

Philip settled the women in an oceanside cafe and left them to eat breakfast, while he went to check on the schedules of freighters heading for San Francisco. Eun-Me had no appetite. The realization of what this day might bring had just begun to sink in. Philip might be leaving her today. Leaving her alone with. . . alone with *Sahmonim* amidst a people she despised.

Philip returned and tossed an envelope onto the table in front of Miss Jennifer.

"Just as you ordered. Two tickets for the *Maiden Voyage*, headed for San Fran." He pointed toward a rusty freighter anchored offshore. "You'll have to suffer with my company for just two weeks more—starting today. We're to be here at four this afternoon to board."

Eun-Me had to bite her bottom lip to hold back an escaping gasp. She could feel her life spinning quickly out of control. In less than a day, just hours away, Philip would be gone.

Philip gulped down a quick, now-cold bowl of fish soup and rice and pushed back from the table. "Mom, let's hope we can find this friend of Dad's and get you two settled at his place before we take off. If not, we'll bring you back here to the evacuation center that our military has set up for all the Americans. They should be able to get word to Dad of your whereabouts right away, and I imagine we'd find the other missionaries there, unless they've decided to go on to Tokyo to wait."

"We'd better get going if we hope to be ready to leave by four o'clock." Miss Jennifer dropped her spoon in her empty rice bowl and stood. "Don't forget you promised to take me shopping before we left for America. I can't abide this dress another day!"

They walked out of the café and waited on the curb, while Philip hailed two pedicabs. While he showed the first driver Tanaka *Hwangjangnim*'s business card to make certain that he could find the address, Miss Jennifer rushed to climb into the second cab beside *Sahmonim*, leaving Philip to share the cab with Eun-Me.

After a wild ride through a maze of pedestrian-clogged streets in the city's business district, their pedicabs turned down a narrow lane, lined on either side with walled courtyards, which surrounded traditional Japanese homes. They came to an abrupt stop in front of an unadorned iron gate, and *Sahmonim* caught up to Philip before he could set both legs out of their cab.

"Son, let me ring the bell and announce ourselves." She motioned him to sit back in his seat. "If he is home, Tanaka *Hwangjangnim* will recognize me."

From the open-air carriage, Eun-Me could hear the gate's chime echo through the small courtyard. Within moments, the sound of shuffling feet preceded the click of a latch. The gate opened just enough for the person on the other side to identify the caller, then it flew wide open.

"*Sahmonim! Ohsoh-oseyo!* Come in! Come in! What brings you to Beppu?"

Eun-Me's mouth fell open in surprise to hear the words of this white-haired, grandfatherly Japanese man, dressed in an American-style business suit, white dress shirt, and tie. He spoke in Korean and English, and not a word in Japanese.

"*Moksanim?* Is he not with you?" While *Sahmonim* explained that her husband remained in Korea but had sent his greetings, Tanaka *Hwangjangnim* craned his neck past the gate to peer into the two rickshaws.

"Please. Everyone, come in." He motioned to them, and Philip helped Eun-Me down.

"You must be *Moksanim*'s son. Philip, is it not? Your father spoke to me of you so often, I feel as though I know you well." Their host offered his hand in greeting to Philip and turned to give a traditional bow to Eun-Me and Jennifer. His English showed the stilted speech patterns and heavy accent of one who had learned the language later in life. "We must get you out of the street. Follow me."

He led them through the garden and slid open the latticework door, then waited for them to leave their shoes on the high step before ushering them into an austere room. Scattered cushions and a low table of black lacquer with an intricate floral design made of inlaid mother-of-pearl were the room's only furnishings.

"You must excuse," he said, gathering up an open Bible, notebook, and pen from the table. "My housekeeper does not work Wednesdays, so my home is a mess, and I have little to offer in way of refreshment." He pointed to the wall. "My dear wife, God rest her soul—you see her in the photographs there—she would have been embarrassed for visitors to find her house so."

Framed, grainy prints of a *hanbok*-clad, sweet-faced *halmoni* adorned the walls. In each picture, the woman's arms either held two babies or they were wrapped around a huddle of children. Eun-Me was beginning to feel as though she'd never left home.

Instead of taking a seat on the floor as Tanaka *Hwangjangnim* pushed them all to do, she bowed deeply and said, "Sir, I am the Woods family's *ajumoni*, and I feel more comfortable working in the kitchen than having someone wait on me. If you would allow me the honor, I'd be happy to prepare some tea."

His nervous chatter ceased, and relief showed in his smile. "You shouldn't have any trouble finding whatever you need. Everything is in full view," he said as he directed her to the tiny alcove kitchen off of the front room. She lit a burner on the two-burner butane stove and set a kettle of water to boil. Then, making as little noise as possible, she gathered teacups from the open cabinet. On the countertop, a small ripe melon rested on top of a package of *dok,* and she took the liberty of arranging the rice cakes and fruit on a plate.

While she worked, she listened to *Sahmonim* explain to the gentleman the reason that her husband did not accompany them. Immediately upon hearing about their predicament, he insisted on their staying with him as long as they had need. He said that the guest quarters out back sat unused, and he would be grateful for the company.

"The place is far too quiet since my wife died." He looked longingly toward the photographs on the wall as he spoke.

He had read a day-old local newspaper report of the invasion yesterday, but the account didn't indicate any crisis of this size, and he had assumed that the fighting was just another border skirmish along the DMZ. Throughout *Sahmonim's* account of the invasion and their hurried evacuation, Eun-Me heard him interject time and again, with an emotion-cracked voice, "My orphans. Oh, *Hahnahnim*, have mercy on them."

Guilt stabbed at Eun-Me's conscience as this elderly Japanese man expressed his love and concern for the Korean children he had devoted his life to serve. She had been so quick to judge and hate all the citizens of Japan for the actions of a few. She'd never stopped to consider that God can change the heart of anyone who comes to Him—even if he or she is Japanese—while evil wasn't limited to one race but is found in every unrepentant heart.

Whenever *Moksanim* faced an obstacle in his ministry, Eun-Me always heard him quote the Scripture, *"All things work together for good to them that love God."* Could it be that God wanted to miraculously use this most horrid circumstance of war and her exile to Japan to perform a healing work in her soul? She sensed that, for her own spiritual good, He wanted and needed to purge her of the prejudice and hatred she felt toward the Japanese. And she feared she wouldn't have listened to His tug on her heart to repent had she not been forced into just such a circumstance as this.

Before she left the kitchen with the tea tray in her arms, she breathed a prayer of willingness, asking God to do His work of love in her heart and make her more like Him.

æ

Miss Jennifer showed no interest in refreshments, and her frequent sighs betrayed her boredom at the never-ending talk of war. She threw repeated glances at her watch. When *Sahmonim* stood and asked the way to the facilities, Miss Jennifer seized her opportunity.

"Dr. Woods, we really should be going soon if I'm to have any hope of finding what I need before we disembark. As it stands now, I think we'll need to plan on going directly to the pier. I don't think we'll have time to come all the way back here."

Eun-Me threw a furtive glance at Philip, and her heart pounded in her chest to think that his departure was at hand. His mouth curved downward in a frown. "You won't give up, will you, Jennifer?" Although he addressed the American, he was watching Eun-Me.

"Son, her request is logical." *Sahmonim* laid a hand on Philip's shoulder as she spoke. "She does need at least a few basic necessities. And you did promise."

Philip shrugged his resignation. "Tanaka *Hwangjangnim*, perhaps you could direct us to a market where we can buy Miss Anderson some clothes. Her bag was stolen at the train depot yesterday, and she isn't prepared for an ocean voyage."

"If you don't mind, I'd be happy to go along and help you barter for the best price. If you go alone, they'll think you are tourists and raise the price considerably. Being Japanese, I am more likely to get a better bargain. Also, I'll be along to escort the women safely back here after they see you off."

"It's settled then." *Sahmonim* patted Philip's shoulder and moved toward the door. "We'll all go. Just let me freshen up a bit. I won't be more than a minute or two."

The teacups rattled in Eun-Me's hands as she cleared the refreshments away. "Here, let me carry that for you, Grace," Philip said as he lifted the tray and followed her toward the kitchen. They excused themselves from their captive host, while Miss Jennifer regaled him with the tales of her agonizing journey.

"Perhaps you and I can sit in a café and talk while Mom and Tanaka help Jennifer shop." He set the dirty dishes in the sink, and Eun-Me began to pour the remaining hot water from the teakettle over them.

"I've been thinking, Philip. Maybe I should say my good-byes here instead of going shopping and to the pier. I don't imagine Tanaka *Hwangjangnim* would mind my staying behind in his home."

Eun-Me swished her hands through the sink water to avoid looking at him. She had made up her mind to try to handle things this way when he first handed the boat tickets to Miss Jennifer. Up until then, she had wanted to relish every last second she could have with him, but now she questioned the wisdom of abandoning all her customary reserve and allowing her emotions free rein. Each rich moment she had shared with him only served to increase her present pain. She knew she'd have to speak fast before she broke down.

"I can't bear the thought of making a public spectacle of myself like I'm afraid I would."

Already she could feel a huge knot forming in her throat, and he had to lean his good ear toward her to catch her whispered words. "A—a—and your leaving won't seem so final if I don't have to actually see you board the ship."

"Okay, Grace. I think I understand."

When she trusted her emotions enough to turn and look at him, she found her own pain reflected in his eyes.

*Sahmonim's* voice filtered from the other room. "Philip. Grace. Come on. We're all waiting."

"I'll be along in just a minute," Philip called out. "Why don't you three go on down to the corner to hail a pedicab?"

"Don't dawdle, Son. We really haven't much time." The sound of the others donning their shoes filtered through the open window.

"Oh, shouldn't I tell Miss Jennifer good-bye?" Eun-Me hurriedly dried her hands on a dish towel and started toward the door.

"I'll give your regards to her later, Grace. Let them go." He stayed her with his hand and lifted his head to listen for the house to grow quiet. Their voices trailed into the garden, followed by the clank of the gate latch. Philip bent to face Eun-Me and took her hands in his.

"I know you want to avoid a long, drawn-out good-bye, and I won't prolong the agony." Eun-Me watched the knot in his throat move up and down while he spoke. She could not look in his eyes. "I'll let what I said last night serve as my farewell."

When he leaned down so close to her that she was forced to meet his gaze, she was startled to see tears shining in his eyes. She squeezed her own eyes shut tight and pursed her lips to try and stifle a threatening sob.

"Good-bye, Grace. God watch over you 'til we meet again."

His lips brushed against both her cheeks in gentle kisses, and when she opened her eyes again, he had gone.

❧

Eun-Me covered her face with her hands and tried to cry quietly at first, but she couldn't contain her pain. Rolling waves of grief swept from her in loud wails, and she dropped to her knees on the floor. Three years would pass at a slow, excruciating pace. And anything might happen in the meantime. Just this week she'd seen her life turned upside down in a few seconds' time.

The many crises of the past few days had not seemed overwhelming, as long as Philip had been there to share them with her. But now. Without him. She didn't know if she could bear her burdens another minute—much less three years.

At last, she reached the point of such exhaustion that she had no strength left to cry. Her weeping had weakened to hiccups when she rose from the floor.

Eun-Me reminded herself of one of the most important lessons her *omma* had taught her. She could hear her voice saying the words, "When life's troubles are too hard to handle, one should keep thoughts and hands busy with work." So, she washed her face and tried to complete a few simple housekeeping chores. Yet, no matter how hard she tried to think of other things, her mind kept returning to Philip and the void he had left in her heart.

In anticipation of the Tanaka *Hwangjangnim*'s and *Sahmonim*'s return, she was in the middle of meal preparations when she heard the gate latch click. She quickly patted her eyes in a futile attempt to wipe away the traces of her crying spell and went to greet the visitor at the door.

Before her hand reached the handle, the door slid aside. There, alone on the stoop, stood Philip, a handful of brilliant pink *mugunghwa* in his hand. The sight of Korea's national flower surprised her almost as much as the sight of the bearer of the bouquet. She couldn't imagine where he might have gotten them, nor could she fathom what mission brought him back within two hours of saying good-bye.

Shucking his shoes at the door, Philip stepped inside and handed her the flowers. Eun-Me was speechless as he swept her into his arms. Her feet left the floor as he pulled her into a tight hug. Just then, she didn't care what brought him back, only that she was with him again. He loosened his hold so that her feet could once again touch the floor and backed away just far enough to look at her while he spoke.

"Grace, there's been a change of plans. I've been discussing them with my mom and Tanaka *Hwangjangnim*, but they all depend on you and we haven't much time, so I need you to hear me out before you respond."

Eun-Me couldn't have said anything at that moment anyway. She still hadn't recovered from the shock of seeing Philip at the door. She nodded her assent.

"I love you, Grace. And I believe you love me too—beyond just being best of friends."

Silent tears forced their way from her eyes, and she swallowed hard, confirming his supposition with another nod. He paused just long enough to smile, then took her bouquet of *mugunghwa*, set them on the floor, and took her hands in his.

"I can't bear the thought of being separated from you for a single minute. We've been through too much together to face the uncertainty of these coming days apart." He lifted a hand to her face and began to gently stroke her cheek.

"I've made some of the toughest decisions of my life this week, and I have you to thank for giving me the courage to see them through. You encouraged me to be honest with myself and examine my hopes and dreams and visions for the future. Because of that, I found the strength to sever a relationship that I now know would have only led to catastrophe for me. I'd lost track of what really matters and had allowed the lure of this world to blind me temporarily, but coming home and spending time with you reminded me of the important things in life—things money and status can't buy. I think God knew I needed you to keep me pointed in the right direction."

Eun-Me didn't feel worthy to take any of the credit he tried to give to her. She felt certain he would have reached the same conclusions eventually, as he allowed the Lord to speak to him and work in his heart. She started to shake her head and protest, but he laid a finger on her lips and silenced her before she could speak.

"I know you well enough to know that you feel self-conscious and insecure about your position as an *ajumoni* and lack of schooling and all. But, Grace, the spiritual wisdom you possess is far more priceless than a formal education, and your insight far surpasses mine. We complement and complete one another, you and me. I need you and I love you with all my heart. That's why I've come to ask you if you would be my wife." Philip fumbled in his shirt pocket for a moment but never took his eyes off her. When he withdrew his hand from his pocket, he held his grandmother Carson's pearl-and-diamond ring.

"Grace, will you marry me?"

Eun-Me stared first at Philip, then at the ring, then back to him. As much as her heart rejoiced to hear him proclaim his love for her, she feared that fatigue had made him lose all common sense. Finally, she found her voice.

"I love you, Philip. And I'd be so honored to be your wife. . .but I don't have anything to offer you. I'm orphaned and poor with no dowry to bring to a marriage, unlike Miss Jennifer. Besides, even if I said yes, I can't go to America, and you must leave right away."

She dropped her head to hide the fresh sorrows that threatened to overtake her. She knew when he had time to think all this through, he would come to his senses and see the impracticality of his proposal. And when he did, Eun-Me would force herself to be content with the cherished knowledge that he loved her just as she loved him.

Philip tipped her chin up and gave her no choice but to look at him. "I won't take no for an answer that easily, Grace. Finish hearing me out. I haven't yet told you about my plan. While immigration laws won't permit a single, young Korean woman like you entrance into the States, they will admit you as my wife. And, even if we need a few weeks to get your visa approved, I've still got until September before I have to return." His words came faster and faster, and Eun-Me began to catch a glimmer of his hope as her own.

"Mom and I had a little discussion while Jennifer did her shopping. She offered to escort Jennifer to the States in my place if you agreed to marry me. And Tanaka *Hwangjangnim* offered to let us stay in his guest quarters as long as necessary. He'll take us to the provincial office to register our marriage right away so we can start your visa processing."

His eyes pleaded for understanding as he studied her face. "I don't want you worrying that you don't have a dowry and that your parents aren't living to arrange a marriage for you. When I told Mom I wanted to marry you, she said that she and Dad had often talked about who they would have selected for my wife had our family followed the Korean custom of matchmaking. And, Grace, they would have chosen you. Your name was divinely inspired, for grace is with you, and you leave a remnant of that grace wherever you go. We all can see that the dowry you bring to our marriage is much larger than superficial, material things. Your inner beauty, spiritual strength, and giving, helpful spirit are worth far more than gold."

He dropped to one knee and took her left hand in his. "I'll ask you one more time before I say good-bye again and race to the pier. *Cho, Eun-Me, saranghaeyo.* Will you marry me?"

Eun-Me leaned to whisper in his good ear, "*Nye,* Philip. If you'll have me, I will marry you. Together, we'll pray that God brings us home to Korea soon, where we'll work side by side."

He slipped the ring on her finger and stood to pull her to him. She rose onto her tiptoes, circled his neck with her arms, and they sealed their covenant with a kiss.

# Glossary of Korean Words

| | |
|---|---|
| *Ajumoni* | (literally means "aunt") housekeeper |
| *Anyong haseyo* | (literally translated, "Are you living in peace?") Welcome! Greetings! |
| *Ariyang* | title of a traditional Korean folk song |
| *Bulgogi* | seasoned, grilled beef (a favorite Korean dish of many foreigners) |
| *Dok* | a sweet rice cake |
| *Dong* | neighborhood |
| *Eye–go!* | exclamation, e.g., "Oh, my!" |
| *Hahnahnim* | Almighty God |
| *Hanbok* | traditional Korean dress |
| *Hangook saram* | a Korean person |
| *Halmoni* | (honorific form: *Halmonim*) Grandmother |
| *Haraboji* | (honorific form: *Harabohnim*) Grandfather |
| *Hwangjangnim* | honorific title for orphanage director |
| *Kamsahaomnieda* | Thank you |
| *Kebun* | mood, state of mind |
| *Kimbap* | (sushi) seafood or meat rolled in rice and held together by a sheet of seaweed |
| *Moksanim* | honorific title for Pastor/Reverend |
| *Mom–pei* | everyday work pants |
| *Mugunghwa* | also known as Rose of Sharon; Korea's national flower |
| *Nye* | yes |
| *Oh–pah* | older brother |
| *Ohsoh–oseyo!* | Come in! |
| *Omma* | Mother |
| *Opsumnida* | "I have none," or "All gone." |
| *Paksanim* | honorific title for Physician |
| *Pusan gachee sae-jang chusaeyo.* | Four tickets to Pusan, please. |
| *Sahmonim* | honorific title for minister's wife |
| *Saranghaeyo* | I love you. |
| *Sen–sei* | Japanese title for Teacher |
| *Shik–tang* | restaurant |
| *Yoboseyo?* | Hello, is anyone there? |
| *Yoh* | sleeping mat |
| *Won* | money |

346

## SUSAN DOWNS

Susan and her pastor-husband can often be heard speaking Korean in their home. For, although they now reside in Canton, Ohio, the Downs' spent five of their twenty-five years in the ministry as missionaries to Korea, and they adopted two of their five children from Korea. Susan's former career as an international adoption program coordinator expanded her vocabulary to include a few words of Chinese, Vietnamese, and Russian, as well. These days, however, Susan sticks primarily to the use of English for her many fiction and non-fiction writing projects and in her work as a freelance copyeditor.

# Remnant
## of
# Victory

Jeri Odell

*With deep gratitude to my friend and editor, Debra White Smith,*
*and with deeper gratitude to my Lord and Savior, Jesus Christ.*

# Prologue

## Vietnam, 1974

"Mama, Thai and I are going out to play," Loi said to their tiny, almond-eyed mother.

Bending down, Mama hugged Thai. Her long black hair fell forward and tickled his cheek. He loved the way she smelled like fresh flowers. Then lifting Loi's chin, she said, "You behave and avoid trouble. Watch out for Thai."

Loi nodded. "Of course, Mama." He wrapped his skinny arms around their mother's tiny waist for a quick hug before he ran out the door.

Four-year-old Thai followed his older brother into the sunshine of a brand-new day. In his haste to keep up, he slammed the door of the small room they rented. He chased after Loi, who, at six, was Thai's hero. Thai considered him to be a man of courage, curiosity, and imagination. Cautious, Thai dreamed of being more like Loi.

The scent of the wet grass beneath his sandals filled the air, and Thai sucked in a deep breath. With Loi as his leader, life resembled one big adventure, unless Mama found out. Trailing behind Loi toward the Saigon River, they probably faced another day of mischief. Then the adventures would end because they'd be forced to stay indoors for their disobedience.

They scurried through the crowded streets. Thai and Loi counted the soldiers they passed on their journey to the river. Thai couldn't count past ten, so he started over several times. The military was as much a part of their lives as the sun rising and lighting up the deep blue sky each morning. In Saigon, uniformed men walking around town was normal. Thai knew no other way of life.

When they arrived at the river, the boys found a spot to sit on a sandy bank and watch the boats come and go. The sand stuck to the back of Thai's bare legs, making them itch. "I don't like the war," Thai said as he brushed sand off the back of his knobby knee. "The killing makes me afraid."

"You're a baby. Nothing but a baby. I'm not afraid of a thing," Loi said, puffing out his chest.

"I am not a baby! Mama says I'll grow big someday, and she says being afraid is okay. She's scared too, sometimes." After all, they'd lost most of the people they loved because of this war, including Daddy.

"Mama said the war and its dangers are a long way off from Saigon," Loi reminded him.

His statement seemed true enough. Constant gunshots no longer echoed around them.

"She says most of these city dwellers have never seen or heard the war. That's why she moved us here, remember?" Loi spoke with absolute certainty.

Thai nodded. He missed the small fishing village they'd once called home; he longed for the family they'd once lived with. Now there were only the three of them. Everyone else had died: their grandmother, grandfather, two uncles, and their families. Just like Daddy, they were all gone because of the stupid old war.

A few of the American solders—the ones with the tan uniforms—came over and asked the boys to play kick the can. Thai kicked off his sandals, and the warm sand squeezed between his toes. He played hard, trying to keep up with Loi. When the soldiers returned to work, Loi and Thai walked along the riverbank. The water surged by in a noisy and powerful display. Thai stayed several feet away from the edge, while Loi tempted fate and walked mere inches from the precipice.

Loi's eyes sparkled. "I like the soldiers. I'm going to be a soldier too when I'm old enough. I'll march and carry a gun just like Daddy used to."

Thai hoped he was never old enough. He didn't voice the thought because Loi would again call him a baby.

On the walk to their mother's flower cart to get their lunch, Loi ducked through a rough district. Goosebumps trickled along the back of Thai's neck. He disliked going this way, so he ran to catch up with Loi's longer, faster stride. But Thai wasn't fast enough. Someone grabbed him from behind and pulled him into a back alley. A large hand covered his mouth, and he gagged against the smell of sweat mingled with dirt. Loi kept going, never realizing that Thai no longer followed.

"I have a present for you, little boy," the uniformed Vietnamese soldier whispered. Though Thai could understand the man's Vietnamese, he talked slightly different than the people Thai knew. "Was your daddy a soldier?"

Thai nodded. His heart thumped in his chest. He struggled to breathe with the large palm covering most of his face.

"I won't hurt you," the man assured him. "If you promise not to scream, I'll remove my hand. I have a present from your daddy."

Thai nodded his agreement, and the large hand dropped from his face to a viselike grip on his arm.

"He asked me to give you this." The man pulled out a small red item from his pocket. Thai had never seen anything like it before. When the man pushed a button, fire shot out. He patiently showed Thai how to operate the lighter, as he dubbed the red object. Thai relaxed, realizing this man offered friendship.

"The red one is mine," the man said. "This blue one is for you. Don't use the lighter until you have many people around to see the present. The fire might only work once." Thai nodded his understanding. "Go." Then he waved his hand toward the street, "And remember, save the lighter until you can share the fire with lots of people."

Thai ran from the alley gently cradling the present in his hands. *A gift from Daddy! A gift from Daddy!* As he rushed toward his mama's cart, the chant bubbled within him. Desperately, Thai hoped to catch up with Loi before he arrived alone. They'd both be in trouble if Loi got back without him. He spotted his brother sitting on the curb about a block from the cart.

Excited, Thai showed Loi his surprise. He demonstrated how to press the button without actually pushing down. Thai explained about the soldier who knew their daddy. Clutching his hand tightly around the treasure, he said, "I'm saving the present to surprise Mama someday when she's sad."

Just as he began slipping the lighter into his pocket, Loi grabbed the prize. He raced off, leaving a sobbing Thai in his wake. When Thai rounded the corner, he caught a glimpse of Loi standing near Mama on the sidewalk, next to her flower cart. Then several pedestrians blocked them from his view.

Thai ran around them and spotted Loi as he held up the lighter. "No! It's mine. It's mine," he screamed. "That's not fair! I'm supposed to show her!"

Loi glanced his direction.

Thai yelled again. "Mama, don't let him push the button. That's my surprise—"

A flash of light preceded the explosion. The flower cart splintered into fiery pieces of debris. Thai fell to the ground. The unyielding sidewalk tore into his knees and palms. The screams of pedestrians crashed against his ears. Fire and smoke blocked all sight of Mama or Loi.

"No!" Thai screamed as sobs racked his body, and a cloak of desolation covered his soul.

# Chapter 1

Thai parked his white Mazda Miata curbside in front of a sprawling brick home in an older Pasadena neighborhood. He double-checked the address and hopped out. A manicured lawn caught his attention. Only in California. Back home, in Illinois, nothing green grew in January.

A basketball hoop hanging above the garage and a wide sidewalk winding through the neighborhood suggested that this house was the perfect place for a kid to grow up. Pastor McCoy's raising seven children here underscored the truth. He'd told Thai that afternoon during the job interview that all seven were girls. He'd also offered Thai the position of college minister at Christ Community Church.

Thai rang the doorbell and watched two neighbor girls bicycle by. Their giggles and chatter drew a smile. He glanced at the cloudless sky. In his hometown, warm days like this didn't happen until late spring. Life in California looked promising.

"Hello, you must be Thai," a lilting voice greeted him.

He turned back to the doorway. A pair of chestnut brown, almond eyes welcomed him. His breath caught in his throat. His heart pounded. His nightmare from last night returned. Four-year-old Thai stood in Saigon, looking at his mother for the last time. Visions of the explosion filled his mind.

"Are you all right?" Her brows drew together.

He swallowed hard, forcing himself back to the present. "I'm fine. Is this the McCoy residence?"

"Yes." She smiled, extending her hand in a friendly gesture. He forced himself to offer the same courtesy, taking her small, soft hand in his. "I'm Kinsy, Karl's second daughter. Come in. The family is expecting you." He followed her petite frame—clad in jeans and a sweatshirt—through a tiled entry hall and into a large family room where Karl watched a UCLA basketball game on a big-screen TV.

Karl rose and shook his hand. His gray, thinning hair added to his distinguished appearance. "Thai, welcome. Did you meet Kinsy?" Karl smiled proudly at his petite Asian daughter, and Thai nodded. "You'll meet the rest of the crew at dinner. Do you like basketball?"

"Very much, Sir."

"Then join me for the end of the game. Only five minutes left, and don't be so formal. Call me Karl. The rest of the staff does." His warm blue eyes offered friendship.

Thai joined Karl on the large taupe sectional, made to accommodate a dozen or so people. Kinsy took the cushion next to his, and he caught a whiff of apple blossoms. He tried to focus on the game but ended up wondering about Kinsy instead. *Was Karl's wife Asian? Maybe he'd served in the war and married a Vietnamese woman. God, what are you doing to me?* The farther Thai tried to run from his Vietnamese roots, God seemed to keep bringing him full circle. Would he ever succeed in his goal to bury the past and forever forget?

During a commercial, Karl informed him, "Kinsy is on staff at Christ Community too. You'll work together a lot, I'm sure. She's the missions director and worked closely with our last college minister." Thai's heart plummeted farther. She'd be a constant part of his ministry here, making her hard to avoid.

"College kids are the most eager and available for short-term missions work." Kinsy grinned, and her amiable overtures both repelled and attracted him. "Of course you know the facts."

"Mission trips are a large part of my ministry philosophy," Thai said. "I like to see the kids involved and growing in service. I find that, while serving, many of them realize their gifts and God-given potential." Thai wasn't going to let one little woman with a gumdrop nose steal this chance at his dream job. Known as a cutting-edge church, he'd desired to serve on staff at Christ Community since his seminary days in Dallas. Somehow, he'd avoid Kinsy and tolerate her—and the memories she resurrected—only when he had to.

"I agree." Her hundred-watt smile shined upon him. "On a mission trip in eighth grade to Sells, Arizona, I led several of the Indian children to the Lord. The experience changed my life. I knew I didn't want a day to go by that I didn't share Christ's love with someone." Her eyes danced with a passion for God.

"That's my girl," Karl declared. "Her heart's desire is for all to know Him."

"Someday I hope to return to Vietnam, find my birth mother's people, and tell them about Jesus." Her words resonated with a longing ache.

The statement also answered his question about her parentage. She must be adopted.

"Have you ever been back?" she asked.

"No." He paused, wondering how much he should reveal. "I have no plans to return, ever."

Her eyes rounded, but she didn't miss a beat. "I do. I long to see my mother's homeland, learn of their customs, embrace my heritage." Yet her steady gaze asked, *How can you not long for the same?* "I don't remember Vietnam," she continued. "I was adopted as a baby. Do you—"

"Too well, Kinsy. I remember too well."

"Dinner's ready," Mrs. McCoy called from the hallway as the tantalizing smells encouraged ready response. Relieved by her impeccable timing, Thai rose.

Karl flicked off the TV and led the way to the dining room where a long cherry-wood table dominated the room. "Thai, this is my wife, Kettie, and our two youngest daughters, Kamie and Kelsy."

"Good to meet you ladies." Kettie looked remarkably young for having daughters as old as she did. The only signs of age were telltale crow's feet fanning out from her brown eyes as she smiled. Kelsy had her father's blue eyes and looked just like him. Kamie, also Asian, wore her hair long and straight, and Thai recalled that last morning when his mother's long hair tickled his face.

"Smells delicious." He tried to sound normal, but the memory unsettled him. His hand automatically went to his cheek. "I haven't had a home-cooked meal in awhile."

"Excuse the huge table," Kettie said. "We just gather at one end rather than removing the leaf. I never know when all the girls will be home, or when we'll have company." Thai noted at least a dozen chairs flanking the table. Then the plump roast caught his eye, sitting on a platter like a king surrounded by the rest of the feast. His stomach growled, and he hoped no one noticed.

Karl took the seat at the end, and Kettie claimed the chair to his right. He motioned Thai to the place on his left. Kinsy sat next to Thai, and the other two girls seized the chairs beside their mom. When Kinsy reached for his hand, he jumped. *What is she doing?* Then Karl clasped his other hand and started praying. Thai expelled a long, slow breath.

For a second, he wondered if the pastor's daughter was making a play for him. She was pretty, intelligent, but Asian. If she weren't Asian, he wouldn't have minded holding her hand. She possessed what he most admired in a woman: a fervor for evangelism. But she also represented what he most wanted to avoid: Vietnamese roots. As her fingers moved in his, Thai determined all the more to forget Vietnam or die trying.

❧

Kinsy passed Thai the mashed potatoes and wondered about the horror on his face when he met her. Maybe she'd caught him off guard. After all, he'd faced the street when she'd opened the door. And who, after meeting her blue-eyed, fair-skinned dad, would expect an Amerasian daughter?

But somehow she knew that her nationality didn't just surprise him. Kinsy spooned gravy onto her potatoes and continued unraveling the mystery. Again, Thai had looked uncomfortable when he met Kamie. The two of them seemed to trigger unpleasant memories from his distant past. And she'd never forget the pain in his voice when he vowed never to return to their shared birthplace. His reasons for not wanting to go back plagued Kinsy.

"Thai, tell us about your American family," her mom encouraged in a warm, interested tone. She sipped her iced tea and waited expectantly.

A tender smile touched his lips as his brown eyes softened. Kinsy admired his high cheekbones and thick midnight black hair. "My dad was a lifer in the Air Force. He served in Vietnam, and God gave him a compassion for the people and their plight. When he returned after the war, he and his wife adopted Tong and me."

Thai paused and cut off a bite of his roast. "This is delicious—tender and juicy."

"Mom's a great cook," Kelsy bragged.

"How old is Tong?" Kettie continued in the tone her daughter deemed interrogation, but Thai seemed comfortable with the questions.

"He's twenty-eight. Two years younger than me." He buttered his roll.

"Same age as Kinsy," her mother observed. "Is he a blood relative?"

"No."

Kinsy hoped Thai might share more, but he didn't.

"Where are you from?" Kinsy asked.

"Chicago area."

"My sister Kally went to school at Trinity. She's a teacher."

Thai nodded. "I went to Wheaton."

"Kylie, another sister, almost went there," Kelsy informed him. "Then she decided to buck tradition and go to a state school."

"How in the world do you keep track of all these Ks?" Thai asked with a chuckle. "Do all seven of you have names beginning with K?"

"Karly, Kinsy, Kally, Korby, Kylie, Kamie, Kelsy," all three sisters recited at once.

"Don't worry, you're certainly not the first to be confused," Karl assured him. "Seemed the thing to do at the time, since Kettie and I are also Ks, but I think we've regretted the decision more than once." He paused and lifted a forkful of mashed potatoes to his mouth. "Did your parents have any biological children?"

"Three, but they are much older than Tong and me. My parents were around forty-five when they adopted us, so they are well into their seventies now."

"Healthy, I hope," Karl said while slicing off another piece of roast. He offered Thai a slice, which he gladly accepted.

"Yes, thank the Lord. Dad retired from the military about fifteen years ago, and once Tong and I finished college, they started traveling in an RV. They have a ministry of sorts, holding Bible studies in each campground they visit. They've led countless elderly people to the Lord." He looked at Kinsy. "They share your passion for the lost."

Since first meeting at the front door, he'd avoided direct eye contact with her—until now. Her heart did this crazy little flip-flop, sending electricity clear to her toes. His ebony eyes reminded her of chips of coal, and in their depths, deep wounds smoldered.

"Anyway, they're happy." He turned back toward her parents. "I'm sure they'll pop up here one day soon. They have to make sure I'm fine and check out the new church where I'm serving. You know how that is."

Both Karl and Kettie nodded. "You bet we do," they said in unison.

Dinner conversation continued to flow comfortably until the meal's end. As everyone stood, Thai expressed his thanks. "The meal was beyond wonderful, Kettie. Let me help clean up."

"Traditionally, we play a game of basketball to decide who gets the honor," Karl informed him.

"But first we put the food away," Kettie reminded. "So if everyone will grab a dish. . ."

Thai carried the mashed potato and gravy bowls into a large country kitchen decorated in blue checks. In no time, the perishables were covered and stored in the refrigerator, and everyone headed out front for the game.

They played several games of Rock, Paper, and Scissors to choose the team captains. Kinsy and Kettie won the honors.

"Karl," Kettie said without hesitation.

"Thai," Kinsy called. Then Kettie took Kelsy, and Kamie joined their team.

Asian versus non-Asian, Thai thought. Of course, he found himself stuck with the two he least desired to team up with.

Since Kettie picked the first player, Kinsy's team started with the ball. Kamie threw it in, and Kinsy gracefully headed for the basket. Karl blocked her shot, spun around, and shot for two.

Kamie tossed the ball to him this time, and he dribbled to the basket. Karl planted himself in Thai's path, so he passed the ball to Kinsy. Open, she took the shot. "Two-two." She grinned and gave him a high five.

Thai really got into the game. Both he and Kinsy were competitive, so they made great partners. In a short amount of time, they left the other team behind. Thai admired her courage on the court—a little hundred-pound dynamo, energetic and fearless.

"Looks like Kettie, Kelsy, and I have dish duty," Karl announced through puffs of breath. "You two won't be on the same team again." He grinned at Thai and Kinsy.

*I hope you're right.*

Kinsy gave Thai one last high five.

"Dad, don't forget I need a ride home," Kinsy said.

Two little frown lines marred the space between Kettie's two perfectly arched eyebrows. "Where's your car?"

"In the shop. Dad brought me home from work with him."

"Thai, would you mind dropping Kinsy off? Her apartment is near where you're staying."

His fists clenched. *I'd rather not.* "Sure, but my offer for cleanup still stands."

"Absolutely not," Karl declared. "You won—fair and square. No dish duty tonight."

"Okay. Thanks for everything—the job, the dinner, and the fun." Thai shook Karl's, then Kettie's hand.

"Our pleasure," Karl assured him. "I always like to have new staff over to get acquainted with my family and vice versa."

"Well, thank you. I had a good time." He turned to Kinsy. "You ready?"

"I'll grab my things and be right out." She hugged her dad, mom, and sisters, dashed into the house, and returned a minute later with her purse and briefcase.

Once they were inside the car, Thai asked, "Where to?" He started the engine, turned on the lights, and pulled away from the curb.

"Hop on the 210 and head east. Do you know how to get to 210?"

He nodded. Somewhere deep inside, he acknowledged she was the cutest, perkiest, most fascinating woman he'd met in ages. She loved God, played basketball like a guy, and her eyes—warm pools of melted chocolate—invited him to wade on in. After a few minutes of quiet, Thai searched for something to say. "I liked your family."

"Aren't they wonderful?" Her tone reflected a smile of approval and pride. "I was so blessed. My growing up years were great. Not perfect—but filled with love."

"I feel the same way about my American parents." His home had been filled with love too, but the pain of his early years always overshadowed the present. He didn't want to remember his mom and Loi, yet their memories wove themselves around him like a second skin. "Did you like growing up in a large family?" he asked, ready to voyage into any realm of small talk to avoid his past.

"I did. We had fun, crazy, frustrating, and maddening times. I will tell you this, I plan to have at least four kids, maybe as many as eight. Some will be adopted, of course."

"Of course. I have the same goal to adopt, but eight kids? I hope your future fellow's desires match yours." He wondered if she had a special guy in her life. *Why do I care? She's Asian!*

"He will, or he won't be my future fellow. Kids are very important to me. Some things in life are nonnegotiable. Take the next exit and go left."

"What else is nonnegotiable?" He glanced at her pretty profile, barely visible through evening's shadows.

"I only have three—Christ, kids, and cherished."

"Only three? Makes you pretty low maintenance," he teased. Her light tone put him at ease, and Thai enjoyed their easy banter. "Christ and kids are pretty self-explanatory, but cherished?"

"Right at the light. My dad," her voice took on a dream-like quality, "says God created all women to be cherished, adored, and loved beyond belief. I won't settle for less. Neither will my sisters."

In the dark, with no reminder of her Asian heritage, he longed to be the man who'd cherish her. Different from most girls he'd met—she seemed open and real. She stirred something within him—his own yearning to be loved and cherished.

"Pull over by the curb. This is my complex. Thanks for the ride, Thai. See you at work tomorrow."

Wishing the evening didn't have to end, he considered walking her to the door, but the dome light illuminated the car. He looked into her almond eyes. *Oh, those eyes. . .just like Mother's. . . .* Her cropped hair gleamed in the limited light, indicating that it was as silky as his mom's. Thai touched his cheek. Instead of offering to escort her, he bid her an abrupt good night and drove off into the darkness.

# Chapter 2

Kinsy watched Thai pull away from the curb and drive from her peaceful, tree-lined neighborhood. Heading upstairs to her apartment, she unlocked the front door. Kally, her next-youngest sister, sat cross-legged on the couch, grading papers. "Hey, Kal." Kinsy hung her purse and briefcase on the hall tree. "How come you didn't come for dinner tonight? Did you get my message?" She plopped down in a matching blue-plaid armchair.

"Yeah, I did, but Danielle made pasta, so I stuck around here. I needed to do laundry and get these reports graded."

"I figured she did. The garlic and onion met me about halfway up the steps." Should she say anything about Thai? Dying to talk the situation through with somebody, she plunged in. "I met a guy. . . ."

She now had Kally's full attention. "The new college minister?"

Kinsy nodded. "Something about him really intrigues me. Problem is something about me apparently repulses him."

"Oh, come on."

"No, I'm serious. I saw the dislike in his eyes. He's also Vietnamese. I wonder if he's prejudiced against his own people. He reacted oddly to both Kamie and me."

"Why are you intrigued then?"

"I'm not sure. He's very good looking for one thing," she joked.

"Kinsy, you've never been swayed by looks."

"No, but they don't hurt." She grinned. "I'd like to know what makes him tick. Sounds rather corny, but he seems like this great guy with some big, hidden secret. I'd like to solve the puzzle."

"Always love a challenge, don't you?" Kally's dark eyebrow shot up, daring her to deny the truth.

She didn't bother. "I don't understand. How can he not yearn to know about his homeland? Why isn't he at least curious about his Asian heritage?"

Kally watched with those intense brown eyes of hers. Her hair and eyes were the darkest of all the McCoy's natural children.

Kinsy paced between the living room and dining room. "Kamie and I ache to know more about Vietnam. Why wouldn't he?"

"At what age was he adopted?" Kally set her students' reports aside and stretched.

"Six, I think Dad said."

"Maybe he remembers things he'd just as soon forget. Those six years must have been right smack in the middle of the Vietnam War. He would have been affected just like all the American soldiers who fought there."

Kinsy spun around to face her sister. "I bet you're right! You just solved the mystery of Thai Leopold. Maybe that's why he gets a haunted look on his face whenever he sees Kamie or me. Tonight in the car—surrounded by darkness—he acted more relaxed. When I opened the door and the light came on, he turned cold as ice." She returned to her favorite spot in the house, the old, worn armchair. Plopping down, she dangled her feet and legs over one arm.

"He probably lived through some horrible atrocities of war," Kally said. "No wonder he has no desire to return. You don't remember Vietnam. He probably can't forget."

"You know, he said something about remembering too well. I wonder how can I help him?"

"Pray for God to bring healing. And maybe the kindest thing you can do is stay away from him."

"Yeah, like that's an option. We're going to be working side by side." Besides, Kinsy didn't want to stay away, but deep inside she knew her sister had a point. If she caused him pain, what kind of friend would she be to keep hanging around? "I will pray for him." She raised her chin with determination. "A lot."

Kinsy wandered into the kitchen and poured herself some water. "I know!" Taking a sip of the cold liquid, she continued, "The Bible smuggling trip I'm working on for the college kids may be to 'Nam. He probably just needs to face his skeletons."

Kally came around the corner. "You'd better pray about this first. If looking at you and Kamie is difficult, I don't think forcing the poor guy on a trip is the answer."

"Don't you think God brought him here for a reason?"

"Absolutely," her sister assured her. "But you just met the guy, for Pete's sake, and God may not have brought him here for your reason. Only God can change him, Kinsy. You can't."

"I know, but God can use me in the process."

"Slow down. That's all I'm asking. You know how you tend to plow ahead under your own steam."

Kinsy nodded. Kally was right. Sometimes she struggled to discern whether God led her or if she'd run a mile ahead of Him. Her tendency to jump in and get things done often got her into trouble.

"I'll be careful and prayerful, I promise." She hugged her sister. "I think I'll turn in."

" 'Night, Kins. I'll pray too."

After she readied for bed, Kinsy read a Psalm and a chapter of Proverbs, part of her nightly routine. Then she prayed for Thai. "I don't know what Thai needs, but You do. Touch him, Father, please." She lay awake for a long time, thinking about a man she barely knew. A man she hoped to help.

෧

Thai tossed his keys on the hotel dresser. Hating the stuffy smell of hotel rooms, he opened the window. The church had rented him the moderate room while he visited L.A. for his interviews. Now the job officially belonged to him, so he'd have to find a place to live. As he moved toward the bed, Thai noticed the message light blinking on his phone, and the red flash blurred into images of a grenade's blowing up his grandparents' home. He balled his fists and shoved the images to the back of his mind.

Hand shaking, Thai hit the message light. After listening to his brother's voice, he punched in the frequently-dialed number.

"Hey, Tong," Thai said, reclining against the headboard of the queen-sized bed.

"I called to congratulate you, but you don't sound like a man who just landed his dream job. What gives? Your voice is dragging the ground like a worm's belly."

"I don't know. Maybe I made a mistake. Maybe this isn't God's plan for me."

"What are you talking about?" Tong exclaimed. "This position has been your prayer for six years."

"I don't know. I'm just having some doubts, I guess."

"Isn't that normal? I felt the same when I got on the force. Don't you remember? And you told me that when I had prayed about something that long that the open door just had to be God."

Thai sighed and ran his hand through his hair and grimaced at his brother's use of his own words against him. "Yeah, I remember."

"What gives? Don't you like Pastor McCoy?"

"Very much. He's as warm and gracious in person as he is in his books. He took me home for dinner to meet the fam."

"So, why the doubts? Didn't like his wife, family, other staff members, what?" Tong released his battery of questions with his usual determination to get to the bottom of every case.

"Kinsy and Kamie—his daughters. They're Vietnamese."

"Oh." Tong's quiet response echoed with understanding. They'd shared a lifetime of confidences, friendship, and respect.

"Every time I looked at Kinsy, all I could see was my mother dying in the explosion. She's just another reminder that I'm to blame."

"Thai, that explosion—it. . .it wasn't your fault."

"I just need to forget. How can I do that here? Kinsy is on the church staff. The missions director! We'll end up working together on a couple of projects a year. There's no possible way to avoid her."

"God knew all this before He led you there," Tong assured.

A twist of irritation slithered through Thai's midsection. He didn't want answers, just someone to listen. "How are Lola and the kids?"

"Fine. We're planning a trip this summer to visit you and Mickey Mouse."

*If I'm still here.* "Ah, I get the picture. Living near Disneyland is an asset to draw visitors. I figure Mom and Dad will be here in the next few months."

"You figure right. They're headed west, and I'm sure you're a bigger draw than even old Mickey. I don't blame them for not hanging around here in the winter, but we sure miss them. Hang on a second. . . . 'Night, Hon. I'll be there in a minute. Okay. . .Lola sends her love."

"And I send mine. You're sure a lucky man." A touch of envy crept into Thai's heart. "You have a nice life and a great wife. I wouldn't mind meeting a little blond dream like Lola."

"Why does she have to be blond, Thai? Maybe God has a brunette for you. Maybe God has an Asian wife for you." The hint of impatience rising in Tong's voice reflected their previous discussions on this very topic. In a heated conversation, Tong even accused his older brother of putting limits on God.

"You don't remember Vietnam, but I do, and I want to forget," Thai snapped. "Part of my plan to leave the past behind is to marry American. If she's blond, all the better.

"Remember when I was in junior high and the kids called me names?" Thai continued. "I promised myself right then that no kid of mine would live through any of those experiences. When I met Tyler Evans, I knew I'd found my answer. Even though he was half Asian, no one teased him because he looked like a blond California kid with a great tan."

"You know, God has used Lola's nightmare for His glory," Tong said, as if Thai's argument meant nothing. "Maybe He can do the same for you."

"I don't know. . ."

"Neither did she, but look how God has used her rape to help others find healing. It's really weird, but I met her because she was raped. Don't you see how different her life would be if she hid from her past?"

"But—"

"She often says, 'Only God can take our tragedies and make them triumphs.' I'm not denying that you haven't had your share of tragedy, but. . ."

Thai let out a long, slow breath and ran his hand through his hair. "I can't make any promises right now. Just pray for me—tons."

Tong chuckled. "I will, big brother. Uh. . .so, care to tell me about Kinsy McCoy?"

"Not really."

"Don't sound so threatened."

Thai sat up on the edge of the bed and untied his shoes. "I never said I was threatened. I've only met her once and just spent this evening with her."

"And?"

"She seems terrific. Okay, maybe more terrific than anyone I've met in a long time, but—"

"But?"

"She's Vietnamese, Man, I already told you."

"And her nationality supersedes everything?"

"For me, yes."

"Is she beautiful?"

"Umm."

"Love the Lord?"

"Passionately."

"So God has brought you to a new church where there is a beautiful, terrific, in-love-with-God woman, and you're complaining?"

"Things aren't so simple."

"I know, Thai." Tong sighed. "Lola went through a lot after her experience. I just wish you could—"

"You don't wish half as much as I do." Thai rubbed the base of his neck.

"Do you mind if I share this with Lola? I think it's time the two of us change our praying for you."

He gripped the receiver. Was Tong right? He'd spent the last twenty-six years running from memories. *I think I need help, Lord. Enable me to look at Kinsy without the painful flashbacks. I'm so weary.*

"Thai?"

"Yes. That's fine. Go ahead and share with Lola."

"Thanks, and hey, enjoy your first day of work tomorrow."

"I'll try. . .I'll try."

"I love ya, Bro."

"Me too."

❧

Later in the night, Thai awoke, yelling, "No!" He sat up, drenched in sweat. His heart pounded. He gulped in air as if he'd jogged several miles. The explosion mixed with terrified screaming reverberated through his mind.

Thai turned on the hotel lamp and grabbed his Bible. He'd read a few Psalms to temporarily erase the memory. He'd killed his mother and brother, and the guilt weighed heavier in the night than at any other time.

The words blurred. Thai closed his eyes, seeing fire and smoke. The scent of burning flesh smelled as real as it had twenty-six years ago. The shrieks of horror rang in his ears. Visions of people running in every direction, yet going nowhere.

Thai lay in a crumpled mass of misery on an unyielding sidewalk. "Mama, Mama," he screamed over and over, but she didn't answer or come to him. People yelling, children crying, women screaming, and sirens rang out around him, but he dared not open his eyes, afraid of what he might see.

He lay with his knees curled under him, his face buried in his forearms, his side pressed tightly against a building. Continual sobs racked his thin body. Smelling the smoke, he wondered if the fire would get him. Taking a deep breath, he forced himself to raise his head just a little. He peered through one squinted eye toward Mama's flower cart. Gone, and in its place laid pieces of charred debris.

"Mama," he screamed again. Then he caught a glimpse of her, recognizing a torn piece of her bright pink dress. Two men loaded her tiny frame onto a stretcher. He ran to her. "Mama, Mama." His little hand reached for her, but she didn't reach back. He touched her stiff, still hand, and he knew Mama was dead, gone just like Daddy.

A piercing scream wrenched itself from the center of Thai's being. He held tight to Mama's hand.

"Somebody get this kid out of the way!" a soldier yelled, trying to maneuver the stretcher into an ambulance.

Another soldier lifted Thai by his upper arm, carrying him several feet away, and unceremoniously plunking him down. "Get lost, Kid."

Frantically, he searched for Loi, spotting his brother's unmoving body against the curb. A melted piece of the blue lighter lay mere inches from his arm. One of the soldiers picked it up. He smelled it. "The kid blew the place up with a V.C. lighter."

"They trick kids with these all the time," the man who'd moved Thai said, shaking his head.

More screams tore from Thai. His surprise killed Mama and Loi. His entire body shook from the force of his pain.

Finally, a man standing nearby yelled at him. "Shut up, boy! Just shut up!"

But Thai couldn't stop. His agony, too deep, too real, poured out in louder wails.

The man walked over to him, grabbed him, and shook him until Thai thought his teeth would fall out. "I'm sick of your noise. I said stop!"

Thai bit his lip. His loud weeping turned to silent sobs.

"Leave him alone!" someone warned in broken Vietnamese. Thai recognized Sarge, one of the American soldiers who played with him and Loi down near the river. He lifted Thai into his arms. "Tell old Sarge what's the matter with his little buddy."

Thai pointed to Loi's lifeless body and the weeping broke out again. Sarge hugged Thai close and let him cry. He patted his back and whispered soft words near Thai's ear. Though Thai didn't understand the meaning of the English words, he understood the comfort Sarge offered.

When Thai's screams quieted to hiccuping sobs, Sarge asked about his family. Thai told him they were all dead. Sarge's eyes teared up, and he hugged Thai tighter. "I'll take you to the American orphanage. They'll care for you well," Sarge promised.

# Chapter 3

Two-and-a-half months had passed since Thai joined the staff at Christ Community, and Kinsy evaded him day after day. After more of Tong's coercing, Thai promised his brother and himself that he wouldn't avoid her. Therefore, her avoiding him proved bewildering, with a twist of ironic humor.

She came to meetings late and left early. No matter where he sat, she chose the opposite side of the room. Whenever he almost passed her in a hall, she ducked into someone's office or into a restroom. CC—a church with a staff of over fifty—had his and Kinsy's offices in separate corridors, making eluding him easy for her. But why did she, and why did he care?

In truth, something about the greatly respected woman fascinated him. Her avoiding him only heightened the fascination. The staff sang her praises. She did her job well. Kinsy was almost perfect. Her only visible flaw, her nationality, even seemed less important.

Thai had been praying a lot, spending extra time in the Word. Now stronger, and ready to test his strength, he wondered how he could with Kinsy avoiding him. He'd been learning to take captive his thoughts and tell himself the truth. Kinsy looked nothing like his mother, except her eyes. Looking at her didn't have to trigger a reaction.

Today, during their regular Wednesday chapel service and staff meeting, he planned to corner her about the Bible smuggling trip she planned for the college group. April lingered only a week away; time to get moving on details. She'd sent out promo material, but the destination remained unknown.

Thai waited at the chapel entrance, next to the double wooden doors with the stained glass crosses embedded in them. Chapel service had started about five minutes before, and the staff's voices rang out in a chorus of "I Love You, Lord." Kinsy rounded the corner, stopping abruptly. She wore a navy blue suit, and the tailored lines showed off her tiny waist.

"Thai." She recovered quickly. "How are you? I haven't seen you in ages."

*Of course you haven't, because you're avoiding me like a bad disease.* "I'm well. How about yourself?" He leaned on the chapel door, crossing his arms. Inwardly, he dared her to ditch him this time. She stopped in front of him. They stared at one another for a second. His mother's face flashed before him. The explosion came next. Thai stopped the resulting flinch. *I can do this, in Your strength.* He blinked and focused on Kinsy.

"I'm fine too," she said. "We'd better go in. We're already late."

He straightened. "Mind if I sit with you?"

Her mouth fell open. "Not at all."

≈

Thai held the door open for Kinsy and followed her to a row near the back. She tried to focus on the praise and worship but struggled to forget the man standing next to her. She closed her eyes, enjoying his rich tenor voice, wrapping around her like a warm blanket.

Kinsy attempted to listen to her father's teaching as he continued leading them through a study on the book of Isaiah. Her confused mind kept thinking about Thai. She'd taken Kally's advice and, for his sake, avoided him. And Kinsy had prayed faithfully and daily for him. Now, he sought her out.

The college kids were already his fans, including her two youngest sisters. Most of the girls considered him cute, and the guys labeled him cool. Her dad referred to Thai as a gifted Bible teacher. Nobody had to convince her. Somehow her heart knew that wonderful described him adequately, but he still had problems that Kinsy seemed to increase. She tried not to take offense, although she couldn't deny the pain in his eyes just moments ago.

He passed her a note. *Can we have lunch?*

She smiled. A bubble of hope rose within her. God must be answering her prayers. *When?* she scribbled back. *And why?* she wondered.

"As soon as we're through here," he whispered, looking right at her.

Today he wore his wire-rimmed glasses, and he looked as good in them as he did in contacts. His striped dress shirt and blue tie looked casual with the sleeves rolled up a couple of folds. Something about the way he gazed at her made her heart almost forget to beat. "Sure." But she wondered if going was the smart thing to do since she already liked him too much for her own good.

As soon as the meeting ended, Thai swept her away to Baja Fresh, a little Mexican restaurant that smelled like fajita heaven. "Hope you like this place," he said, as they stepped toward the line.

"One of my favorites."

"Mine too. I discovered this one on my second day of work. I come here like three times a week. We never had Mexican food like this in Chicago."

"Exactly what Kally said."

After they ordered, he led her to a corner table. "What other culinary treasures have you discovered?" she asked.

He still avoided eye contact with her most of the time, fixing his gaze on his drink. "In and Out Burger and California Pizza Kitchen. My other two hangouts."

"To cover the other four days of the week?" she teased.

"Just about. I don't cook much, but I sure appreciate your mom's occasional invitations. Hers are the only three home-cooked meals I've had since I got here."

"How pathetic." She wondered if he was hinting for an invitation from her.

He cleared his throat. "Have I offended you?" Now he looked directly at her with an intensity that bore into her soul.

Kinsy choked on her soda. "What?"

"You've avoided me since the night we met. I wondered why."

"Number seventy-four," the counter help called out.

"Excuse me." Thai went to claim their order.

*Oh, great. Thanks, Kally! Now what do I say?* she stormed. *The truth. The truth is always good.* Kally's voice echoed in her head.

Thai returned, placing Kinsy's burrito in front of her. She fingered the paper wrapper, hoping Thai had forgotten his question.

"So, what gives?" he asked. "Am I imagining things or have you spent the last two months running from me?"

Kinsy tore the burrito's wrapper. Taking a deep breath, she blurted out, "Yes, but my sister told me to."

"Your sister told you to avoid me?" He cocked one eyebrow, challenging her to convince him. "Which sister?"

"Kally."

He wrinkled his forehead. "Kally? Kally doesn't even know me. We've never even met." He flung up his hand.

"I told her about meeting you and how uncomfortable you seemed around Kamie and me. She figured your reaction has something to do with your past in Vietnam." The smell of grilled onions and peppers wafted around her.

"I didn't realize I was so obvious." He sipped his soda as if he were trying to swallow a lump in his throat.

"Seemed to hurt you to look at either of us, so Kally said the kindest thing I could do was stay out of your way. And I've really tried."

"I'm sorry, Kinsy. Don't take my problem personally. It's just that. . .when I look at you, I remember things I've tried a lifetime to forget." His face tightened into a mask of anguish.

She nodded her understanding, and her throat constricted. "Don't worry, Thai. I've gotten good at staying out of your way." She made a weak attempt at a joke. "We don't have to spend time together."

The slight smile suggested that he appreciated her sensitivity. "The problem is my brother says we do."

"Your brother?"

"He thinks the time has come for me to quit running from the past."

"Sounds like we have a face-off between my sister and your brother."

Thai chuckled and unwrapped his burrito. "He thinks practice makes perfect and the more time I spend with you, the easier being around you will get."

"So you expect me to ignore Kally?" Kinsy chided. "She'll not appreciate your brother taking precedence over her." Not sure she liked Tong's prescription, Kinsy excused herself and went to the salsa bar.

The problem was that spending time with him put her heart in danger, more than ignoring him did. During the past two months, the more she avoided him, the more she yearned to stop avoiding him. Everything about him—even his painful past—appealed to her. Developing a friendship, opening her heart to him, placed Kinsy in risky waters.

His cautious eyes suggested that Thai only needed her help to get over his past. No promise of a relationship or hope of commitment lingered in their inky depths. Was she willing to play the guinea pig in his experiment?

Kinsy settled at the table with several types of salsa she didn't even remember dishing up.

"Let's pray," Thai said.

Without thinking, Kinsy reached for his hand. A spark ignited at their touch. His startled gaze preceded a stiff prayer. By the time he tacked on the amen, her hand felt singed.

She busied herself with her lunch, hoping Thai didn't recognize the attraction she knew must be pathetically displayed all over her face. She noticed his questioning gaze in her peripheral vision but didn't look up.

❧

Thai returned to their previous conversation. Anything to take his mind off the 110 volts that had just passed between them. "So what do you say to Tong's plan?"

She hesitated. Probably thinking the whole idea was insane—just as he did. But he'd promised Tong he'd at least try.

"I'm not asking you to be my best friend, Kinsy," Thai assured.

"Well, what a relief," she said flippantly, "since I already have one. I don't think Danielle would appreciate your usurping her spot."

"I promise, I'm no threat to Danielle. Will you just quit avoiding me? Maybe we can share an occasional lunch."

She hesitated again. "Sure—I guess."

He didn't understand the tinge of distrust in her voice, and they finished their lunch in silence.

"March in L.A. is great," he commented on their way back to the car, hoping to regain the easy camaraderie they had shared briefly in the restaurant. "No snow to shovel, no coats, no boots."

"Just a warm breeze," Kinsy said. He opened her door, and she slipped into his leather seat.

On the drive back to the church, Thai concentrated on the passing hotels, restaurants, and various businesses. What could he say now since he'd accomplished his mission? Finally, he grasped at a new topic. "So tell me about this big staff retreat coming up in a couple of weeks. The one everybody's talking about."

"Once a year in April, the whole staff goes to Yosemite for five days. We stay at Emerald Cove near Bass Lake. The whole point of the trip is to build unity and refresh us spiritually. Each year, we take a new trail. This year the plan is conquering Half Dome. Have you ever been to Yosemite?"

"No."

"I don't think there's a prettier place this side of heaven. Do you like to hike?"

"I'm not an avid hiker, but I enjoy hitting the trail occasionally."

"Me too," she admitted.

"I do enjoy the outdoors and nature. Your dad said this year's theme is team building."

"Yeah. His goal is for those of us who work together on a regular basis to strengthen our bonds, thereby strengthening our ministries. My guess is you'll be teamed up with the youth ministry leaders."

"How about you?"

"I'm not sure where he'll put me. Maybe with you guys. I work with the college, high school, and junior high ministries a lot."

He hoped not. An occasional lunch was one thing, spending a week together seemed a little more than he desired to tackle. At once, his friendly overtures mocked him. He planned to call the shots—spend time with her on his terms, when he so desired. Now, he wondered if Tong was right. Maybe God had other plans. Thai again fought an urge to run from Kinsy—far and fast.

"I think they are posting the list today. Shall we check?" she asked when they pulled into the church parking lot. "The trip is only a couple of weeks away."

Thai and Kinsy made their way to the office bulletin board behind the receptionist's desk. "Hello, Sally," they both chimed in unison. She nodded, busy answering a call.

Kinsy spotted their team first. "Looks like Tong's getting his wish. We are on the same team."

Thai nodded but didn't say anything. He and Kinsy were paired with Chris and Rob, the high school and junior high ministers. Four people made up each team.

Talk about intimacy. Dread rose like bile in his throat. His newfound strength vanished like a sand castle whisked away by the tide. Had anything really changed inside of him?

"Thanks for lunch," Kinsy said, glancing at her watch. "I've got to run. I'll see you around." She started to walk away but stopped. "And no ducking," she whispered and winked. Then she was gone.

Trouble, no doubt. She sent his heart reeling in two directions. Half of him really liked her and liked the idea of spending time together. The other half hated looking into those eyes. . . . He glanced back at the team list and sighed. Tong had been praying again.

&

"I remind him of something or someone he's been trying for years to forget," Kinsy informed Kally and Danielle at dinner. Aimlessly, she pushed the peas around her plate. "The problem is he reminds me of someone I hope never to forget."

"You've got it bad, Girl." Danielle grinned and took a sip of milk.

"I do." Kinsy groaned, taking a bite of rice. "I've got a major crush on a guy who can barely stand to look at me. Now I have to spend a week with him. The teams will do everything together, from the time they get up until lights out."

"Gives you about seventy-five hours to win his heart," Kally informed her in her no-nonsense schoolteacher voice.

"No hope there. His goal is to tolerate being around me, not fall for me." Kinsy pushed her half-eaten dinner away, no longer hungry. The smell of the grilled chicken didn't even tempt her. "To make matters worse, the Bible smuggling trip this summer looks more and more like we'll head to Vietnam. He'll hate me if that happens."

"Kinsy!" Kally's exasperation rang through loud and clear. "I told you not to manipulate the situation."

"I didn't. Honest. At least not completely. There were four places open last fall when we applied, and I told Steve to pray about where to send us. I said our team would go anywhere but picked Vietnam as our first choice. I never retracted the request, even after learning of Thai's aversion. As Steve and I both prayed, the Lord is closing doors elsewhere and flinging them open for 'Nam."

"Who's Steve?" Danielle asked.

"He organizes the trips."

"I sure hope you're hearing God and not your own will," Kally said. Sometimes her to-the-point personality irked Kinsy.

"You apparently have your doubts." Kinsy's annoyance laced the clipped accusation.

"Well, you have been known to jump the gun."

"Kally, I really care about Thai. I don't want to hurt him. Believe me, at this point I'm begging God to send us anywhere but Vietnam. I'm sure—just like you—Thai will assume I manipulated the whole thing." *Then I'd never stand a chance with him—never. Not that I really do now!*

"So when will you know?" Kally's tone now held a trace of sympathy.

"Not until May. I'm sure Steve will know before then, but they don't like the teams to have too much advance notice. Security and all."

❧

Thai hadn't spent time with Kinsy since their lunch two weeks before. He'd passed her in the hall twice, and she didn't run the other direction. She actually smiled and said hello. They'd exchanged E-mails about the upcoming Bible smuggling trip, but no personal contact.

Monday morning—retreat day—showed up right on schedule and proved to be another warm L.A. day. Thai donned a pair of khakis and his favorite Chicago Bears T-shirt. He sighed on his way out of his apartment. From now until late Friday evening, he and Kinsy were expected to be connected at the elbow. If he could erase her disturbing presence from the equation, a great trip awaited him.

As he pulled into the church parking lot, he spotted Kinsy unloading a sleeping bag from the trunk of her frog-green Del Sol. She bounced over and deposited her bag in the pile with about twenty others. Perky. The word described her from the tip of her short molasses-colored hair to the toes of her white Nikes. Petite. Perky. Asian.

Thai parked his car and unloaded his own things. About half the staff had already arrived. With a grumbling engine protesting all the way, a rented bus pulled into the parking lot. The hissing brakes brought the beast to a halt. Diesel fumes filled the air, and Thai wrinkled his nose.

He and a few others helped the driver load everything in the storage area under the bus. Then Karl called the staff together for prayer. After praying, he said, "Let's load up. Pretend you're Siamese quadruplets for the next five days."

Chris and Rob were the first two on the bus, so they claimed the back seat. Thai settled next to them. Kinsy boarded almost last. Thai watched her come down the aisle all smiles and sunshine. She wore a pair of jean shorts and a pink T-shirt. Emotions warred within. He was simultaneously torn between his attraction to her and a need to run from her.

Their gazes met when she was halfway to the back of the bus. She paused for a microsecond, as if to tenderly say, *I know this is hard for you.* Like one of those slow-motion commercials, he sat mesmerized as a beautiful girl moved toward him. Their gaze lengthened, and he didn't have the will-power to look away.

Kinsy smiled—just for him. Thai discovered a growing fondness for her smile, and he grinned back at her. She stopped in front of Thai, Chris, and Rob and peered at the three of them. "Don't the bad boys ride in the back of the bus?" she asked with a lifted brow.

"You got it, Babe." Rob grabbed her wrist and pulled her down on the seat between him and Thai. "And you're our bad girl for the week," he teased.

A twinge of jealousy shot through Thai.

Kinsy stood up and faced Rob with hands on hips. "I'm nobody's babe, bad or otherwise. Understood, Buster?" she joked, poking him in the chest with her index finger.

"I like a woman with spirit," Rob countered, grabbing the offending finger.

"Too bad, she said she'd be my woman this week," Chris informed them, winking at Kinsy.

"Fellows, fellows. You'll have to share. Now who will let me have a window seat?" She batted her eyelashes.

Thai rose, and she slid in next to him. Both Chris and Rob complained.

"I know a gentleman when I see one," Kinsy informed them. "Now, you two need to practice losing gracefully and quit your bellyaching." She faced the window, ending the conversation.

After the bus started rolling, Kinsy leaned toward Thai and quietly said, "I wasn't sure you'd want me this close."

*Part of me does—more than you could ever know.* "I figured I'd better protect you from the sharks," Thai quipped.

"Well, thank you, gallant knight."

"My pleasure, damsel in distress."

Thai wondered if Kinsy had ever dated either one of those two; both were flirty and familiar. *But I shouldn't care.* Nonetheless, Thai did care.

"I'm not getting in the middle of something, am I?" Thai asked a few minutes later.

"What do you mean?"

"Rob seems interested."

Kinsy laughed. "Rob flirts with anything female. He's definitely not my type."

"So what *is* your type, Miss McCoy?"

"Tender, sensitive. You know."

"Why are all women looking for a sensitive man?"

She giggled, reminding him of tinkling bells.

"I don't know," she said. "But I guess most of us are."

"Do you have a boyfriend?"

"No. Haven't for years."

Why did those words please him? She was not at all what he was looking for.

At least not the outer package. "Your mom said you're twenty-eight. How many years could it have been?"

"I'm embarrassed to tell you. Way too long. How about you? Anyone waiting in the wings?"

"You're not fooling me with the old bait and switch tactic. You tell me how long, then we'll talk about my pathetic love life."

"Sounds promising. Here's the deal. I fell in love briefly my freshman year of college. For about ten minutes, I thought he might be the one. For right now, God's plan seems to be singleness."

"Are you fine with that?"

"Most of the time, at least until my younger sister—four years younger, mind you—got married last year. Suddenly, I felt like an old spinster."

"Which sister?"

"Korby."

"Is she the only one who's married?"

"Yes."

"Where does she fall in the lineup?"

"Fourth. Just after Kally. Now, your turn to spill the beans."

"I've never been in love. Dated lots of women, but can't ever seem to get past the third date."

"Three strikes and they're out?"

"Yeah, I guess. By then I always know they aren't the one woman I'm looking for."

"And what will she be like—that one woman?"

"She'll love God, me, and life." He realized he'd just described Kinsy, except the "love him" part. "And she'll be blond."

"Blond?" Kinsy frowned. "Oh—as far from Asian as possible?"

He nodded. "Yep."

Kinsy squinted, then turned to gaze at the passing Calfornia countryside. Although the sun brushed the plowed fields around Fresno with sparkling diamonds of light, the brightness faded from his day. Why did he make the blond comment just when they were enjoying each other? Was it a reminder to him or to her?

Neither spoke the rest of the trip. Thai recognized the resemblance between the barren plowed earth lying just past the freeway and his own life. Both appeared bleak, empty, and filled with deep ruts. A little boy with a life just as bleak, just as empty, surfaced.

The American orphanage loomed at the end of the driveway like an imposing gray monster. The old three-story building appeared cold and uninviting. Thai wrapped his arms tighter around Sarge's neck where he sat on his lap in the passenger seat of the camouflage-colored jeep.

They bounced along the rutted drive, dust billowing behind them. The jeep rolled to a stop near the front door. Sarge carried Thai into the front office where a stern, red-headed woman with a tight bun typed on an old machine.

Sarge spoke to her in English. Thai knew by Sarge's compassionate tone and his frequent glances toward Thai that he told her about Mama. The woman's face remained professional, unmoved. Fear gripped Thai. This didn't seem like a nice place. No one would love him here.

Sarge picked up Thai. "This is good-bye, little buddy. You be a good boy for old Sarge."

Tears pricked Thai's eyes. He held tight to Sarge. The strong man buried his head against Thai's bony shoulder. His body shook, and Thai pleaded, "Can't you keep me?"

Sarge raised his head, his red, tear-filled eyes begging for Thai's understanding. "I wish I could, little buddy, but the army won't let me. I'll try and come back for a visit, though. I've got to go now."

He tried to place Thai on the floor, but Thai held tight to his neck. Sarge pried Thai's little hands loose, but he only grabbed hold again. Finally, the woman held on to Thai while Sarge left. Sarge turned and waved, tears running down the big man's face. He said something, but Thai couldn't hear the words because of his own wails.

When the woman finally let him go, Thai ran out the door to where the jeep had been. It was gone. Only the dust of departure remained. Thai ran up the long driveway until his legs would go no farther. At last, he collapsed on the dirt drive, a rock digging into his knee. He lay in the dirt and sobbed until someone carried him back to the orphanage.

# Chapter 4

Kinsy didn't turn toward Thai or invite conversation again. His blond comment hurt. Just another reminder she'd never be anything more than someone he was learning to tolerate as a means of overcoming his past. She refused to let his subtle rejection ruin this trip. *I'll show you, Thai Leopold! You'll never meet a blond like me, and it'll be your loss.*

As the bus groaned up the last steep hill, camp waited right around the bend. Kinsy said a quick prayer, sucked in a deep breath, and decided to forget Thai's mindset toward her. She'd be charming, friendly, and as normal as she could manage. He'd not put a damper on her mood or her hopes.

The bus squealed to a halt. The staff, chatting and laughing, crowded into the aisles. Since they were in the back, Kinsy and Thai were the last two off the bus. She stopped just before exiting and turned to him. "The first thing you should do is take a huge sniff of this mountain air. Nothing like the stuff we breathe in L.A."

"Yes, Ma'am." He gave her the thumbs-up sign.

They both stopped and inhaled a hearty dose of diesel exhaust. Choking, sputtering, and laughing, Thai said, "This, Miss McCoy, is the last time I take your advice about anything."

"Sorry, I forgot about the bus. Wait until you get a whiff of the pine scent, guaranteed exhaust-free. You'll think you've died and gone to heaven. But look around. Have you ever seen such a great place?" This was her third staff trip up here, and her love for the camp and the mountains grew each time.

"I've got to admit, you're right. Lots of trees, lots of mountains in the backdrop, and lots of sunshine. I'd forgotten how blue the sky really is. After three months in L.A., I thought it had permanently turned gray."

Kinsy chuckled. "Some places in the world, blue is still the color." She looked up to prove her point and shivered against the slight breeze.

"Over here for cabin assignments," James, the administration minister, called out. "Lunch is ready now in the dining hall. Then you'll have an hour to get your things, unpack, and settle in. We'll meet back here at three. Come in grubby clothes, preferably long pants and long sleeves."

"I'll meet you for lunch in a few minutes. See the large wood-sided building?"

Kinsy pointed off to her left. "That's the place."

"Meet you there," Thai agreed.

Kinsy searched for her bags. After digging through a pile, she unearthed her things. Then she got her room assignment. Since there were fewer women on staff than men, the men got the larger dorms up the hill and to the right.

Kinsy and the other seven women were assigned the house and a trailer off to the left, just beyond the dining hall, hidden in a clump of trees. She headed for the trailer and plopped her stuff on a top bunk in the back bedroom. After a quick lunch with her team, she unpacked.

Then she found a quiet spot on a log to sit and contemplate life. Well, at least to contemplate Thai. His eyes verified that he was aware of the undercurrents between them. With each minute she spent in his company, she liked him more. *Wonder how I'd look as a bleached blond?* She'd experienced prejudice many times but never expected bias from another Vietnamese person. If only he'd let God heal his past, maybe—just maybe—they'd have a future.

At three, she found the guys from her team. Her dad passed out colored scarves; theirs were red. "Tie those around your necks," he instructed. James started passing out paintball guns, goggles with nose- and mouth-guards attached, and paintballs. Each team got little marble-sized paintballs to match their scarves. About half of them fit in Kinsy's gun canister, the rest she shoved into the various pockets of her overalls.

He explained the rules of the game and the boundaries. The object was to splatter as many people as possible with red paint while not taking a hit. Points were given for the number of hits, and bonus points went to the team with the least paint splatters on them.

Kinsy and her team huddled together, discussing strategy.

"Let's stay close together, watch each other's backs," Rob whispered. He grabbed her hand. "Kinsy and I will partner. You guys keep us in sight." He led her off through the tall pines toward the playing field.

Kinsy glanced back at Thai, who scowled at Rob. A warm glow spread through Kinsy. She hoped he was jealous.

"Are you dating Thai?" Rob asked when Chris and Thai were out of sight.

"No. What prompted you to ask?"

"The vibes. The way you two gaze at each other. The way he looked just now when I took your hand."

"You're imagining things. We barely know each other." Yet it seemed like she knew him better than others, like Rob, whom she'd known much longer.

"But you'd like to," Rob suggested. His hazel eyes dared her to deny his claim.

"I never said that."

"You didn't have to. Hey, how come we've never gone out?"

"Oh, Rob, you know you're like a brother to me."

"No, I can't take it!" He covered his ears with his hands. "Not the dreaded B-word, every guy's worst nightmare."

He pulled her behind a tree, giving her the quiet sign. They got their guns in position and fired on the enemy. *Splat, splat, splat, splat.* The orange team now had a few red blotches. Kinsy and Rob ran through the forest, dodging low tree limbs, before the orange team retaliated.

Thai and Chris caught up with them. They'd gotten the same three guys from the other side. They were whispering and laughing. *Splat, splat, splat.* Blue paint splotched their legs. Chris shot a couple of them in the rear as they retreated.

"Follow us," Thai said. He and Chris led out this time. A twig snapped behind her. She spun around and raised her gun. She got a green ball in the belly and hit a tree with her return shot.

"Ouch, these things sting, Rob," she whispered.

He motioned her to follow. They came up on Chris and Thai being bombarded from several directions with several colors. They ducked and ran since they were out-numbered about two to ten.

Kinsy and Rob took cover and opened fire on the other teams. They both got several good shots. She'd completely lost track of Chris and Thai. There was no way to find them without trekking through heavily dominated enemy territory, so they went back the way they came.

"Do you get the feeling they're ganging up on us?" Kinsy whispered. "They didn't shoot at each other, but they all shot at us."

"You noticed too?" Thai asked from behind them. "Am I being dragged into some vendetta from a previous year?"

"I'll bet the staff is getting you two goons back for all the practical jokes and Super Soaker episodes." Kinsy pointed to Rob and Chris.

"I think Kinsy and I will follow you two for awhile," Thai informed them. "I'm not interested in paying your debts, Rob. Lead on."

Rob looked at Kinsy. "Sorry, but Thai's right," she said. "This war has nothing to do with us. We'll be a few paces behind, help when we can, but we're not taking the brunt of this. You're on your own."

Chris and Rob started out. Kinsy looked at Thai and laughed out loud. "You look like a Christmas tree with a variety of different colored bulbs hanging all over you."

He yanked her downward, and she fell in a heap beside him. The ground's dampness seeped through her overalls, while the smell of wet grass filled each breath. Several paintballs whizzed over them, hitting a tree. "Those were meant for us," he whispered.

His gaze fixed on hers and neither moved. Whether a second or several minutes passed, she had no idea. His smoldering eyes sent her heart pounding, and her mouth went dry. He hesitantly touched her face, running the tips of his fingers over her high cheekbone. His tenderness sent an ache through her, an ache for him to care about her the same way she'd begun caring for him.

He plucked a twig from her hair and tossed it aside. Entwining his fingers in her hair, he began closing the inches separating them. With every fiber of her being, she longed for his kiss, but at what cost? So she could cry herself to sleep every night when he replaced her with his American dream?

Kinsy forced herself to break the spell he'd unknowingly cast over them. She rose up on an elbow and aimed for a lightness she was miles from capturing. "The gallant knight routine again, huh?"

"Yes." He brushed the dirt off her cheek. "My poor, distressed damsel."

She replayed his words. *My poor distressed damsel.* He'd said *my*, not *the* or *a*, but he called her his. *I'm overreacting and having a bout of wishful dreaming.*

❧

Rising slowly and searching the horizon for other teams, Thai spotted no one. He reached down, took Kinsy's hand, and helped her up. Her hand rested snug and safe in his, and he realized he liked touching her. He'd almost kissed her! Where did his brain go when she was around? He released her hand and immediately missed the warmth. They quietly made their way down the hill, in the direction Rob and Chris had headed.

Thai grabbed Kinsy and pulled her behind a tree. He raised his gun. *Splat*, he got an orange guy's arm. Another *splat*. Kinsy got him too, in the leg. They crept on through the dense forest. "Watch your footing," he whispered when he slid a couple of feet down the hill, causing a few rocks to roll down ahead of them.

Suddenly, they were being hit from all sides. He tried to shield and protect her. They ran as fast as they could, but hit after hit slammed against their backs with a rhythm that mimicked a machine gun's staccato release.

❧

Mama took the boys for a morning walk down river. They laughed, skipped, and sang songs. But unexpected explosions dashed aside their revelry and riveted their attention on the village. Smoke billowed across the sun-filled sky. Grabbing their hands, Mama ran fast—faster than Thai's legs would go—away from their little fishing village.

Thai fell, hitting the unyielding earth with a thud. He screamed out in pain. Mama yelled at him to hush, and her horror-filled eyes scared him into silence. She swept him up into her arms, grabbed Loi's hand, and kept running. He looked back over her shoulder as the remains of their village collapsed wall by wall, while fire destroyed building after building.

Mama fell to her knees, too tired to run any farther. Lying in the tall grass, they remained hidden until sunset. Mama's quiet weeping wounded Thai more than seeing the burning village. The rest of their family was most likely dead. Thai cried until he fell asleep. When he awoke, near-darkness surrounded them, and his stomach gnawed with hunger. An eerie silence penetrated his spirit, leaving him empty and cold.

&

The whistle blew, signifying the end of the war. Relief flooded Thai as he stopped running. An exhausted Kinsy, her breathing heavy, leaned against him. She stumbled to the nearest log, where she plopped down. "Now I understand being saved by the bell!" Scrutinizing him, she asked, "You okay?"

"Fine," he barked. The memory that shook him to the core made his words more brusque than he intended. Kinsy's imploring gaze made him force a smile he was far from feeling. "Let's find Chris and Rob," he said more gently. When they did, all four of them resembled clowns in polka-dotted attire. Laughing, they all shared their tales of war. Thai joined them, but his laughter rang hollow.

"They hurt worse when they bounce off and don't break open. Look at this welt," Kinsy said, rolling up the right sleeve of her navy blue turtleneck.

"Oh, poor baby," Rob said with no sympathy.

When the scores were tallied, the red team came in dead last. They all protested they'd been ganged up on. No one had much sympathy because at one time or another, they'd all been the butt of a Rob-and-Chris-style joke.

"I'm hitting the shower, fellows. I'll see you at dinner," Kinsy informed her team. "Hopefully without green hair."

"I'll walk you back," Rob offered.

Thai watched Kinsy walk away with Rob. An uneasiness settled in his gut. He tried not to notice them as they laughed and joked together, but his attention kept wandering in their direction. At her door, Kinsy rose up on tiptoe and kissed Rob's cheek. Envy—an emotion he was unaccustomed to before meeting Kinsy—shot through his veins. *Why should I waste time on jealousy? She's a long way from the blue-eyed blond you're waiting for, Pal.*

After a long, hot shower, Thai met his team for dinner. Kinsy, her usual eager, energetic self, didn't give Rob any more attention than she gave him or Chris. Thai almost asked her about her relationship with Rob but figured the same question twice in one day was too much. Being male, he sensed Rob's interest, and the kiss on Rob's cheek made him wonder about Kinsy.

After dinner, they met up at Star Rock for a praise service. For the next hour, they did nothing but sing praise songs to the Lord. Then each team went off to pray for their ministries. By the time they'd finished, Thai decided he was crazy to care what happened between Kinsy and Rob. Thai certainly wasn't interested in her. Not in the least.

*Then why did I almost kiss her?* The moment just caught him off guard. Nothing more than being close to a beautiful woman whose lips begged him to taste their sweetness, touch their softness. *Yeah, and pigs fly.* His attraction for Kinsy went way beyond her lips. The woman exemplified everything he'd dreamed of. *Except the added bonus of her Asian heritage,* he thought bitterly.

They spent the next morning playing wild and crazy team games. The red team fared much better, though they still didn't win. In the dining hall after lunch, Karl announced each team had free time until chapel at seven. He gave them a list of some ways to spend the afternoon and several options for dinner.

"Golf!" Chris said with excitement.

"Definitely," Rob agreed.

"No question. Who would fish when they could golf?" Thai asked.

"Me," Kinsy threw out weakly.

"You? What are you thinking, Woman?" Rob asked.

"I don't know how to golf." Kinsy looked at each of them suspiciously. Eyes squinted, she asked, "Did you guys bring your clubs?"

All three nodded.

"You conspired behind my back?" She stood, placing hands on her hips.

"No," Thai assured her. "Rob sent Chris and me an E-mail suggesting we drag our clubs along, you know—just in case."

"How come Rob didn't include me in the E-mail since I'm part of this team?" She raised her eyebrows.

Rob had the decency to blush. "I knew you weren't a golfer."

"And yet you expect me to spend my afternoon with you on a golf course?" she challenged.

Thai knew Kinsy was only giving Rob a hard time, but Rob chewed his lip in uncertainty. "She's got you there, Pal," Thai said.

Rob held up his hands. "Now wait a minute, three of us voted for golf and majority rules. We've already made a deal, whoever wins the first hole will be your personal tutor."

"Fine. I'll be a good sport, even though this whole thing seems underhanded to me. But if there are any more choices, I'd better be included from the onset." She emphasized her point by waving her index finger under Rob's nose.

"Yes, Ma'am." Rob saluted.

Thai loved golf. Him, God, and a ball out in the wide-open spaces—not much in life better than that. Especially on a beautiful course with the backdrop of the Sierra Nevadas surrounding him.

He pulled his club from his bag, lined up his first shot, and swung. The ball soared toward the hole, landing neatly on the green, just feet from the desired destination. With a mixture of dread and anticipation, he was certain Kinsy was his for the afternoon. He exchanged his nine iron for his putter and sank the birdie.

Chris managed to par, and Rob bogied. "You can have the girl." Rob did a gangster impression. "She's yours, Pal. You teach her to play—if you can. Meanwhile, Chris and I will see you two later." They hopped in their golf cart and headed over the hill.

"What are par, bogie, and birdie?" A light breeze played with her hair, and Thai remembered its silky softness from yesterday.

He pulled out a wood for Kinsy to try. "Par is when you break even. This hole, a par three, meaning a golfer should get the ball into the hole in three shots. Chris managed that, so he got par. A bogie is one shot over par, and a birdie is one shot under par."

"Seems to me the worst guy should have gotten stuck with me."

Thai tensed at her statement. "Would you rather golf with Rob? I could finagle a trade." He hoped his disappointment didn't seep out with his words.

"Not necessarily. I just thought you might enjoy the game more if you weren't saddled with me."

Thai decided now looked like a good time to test the water. He casually leaned on his club. "You know, I think Rob might like to meet a damsel in distress, especially if she were you."

"Oh, and what makes you think so?" She cocked her head to the right, raising her eyebrows.

"Guys know these things."

"Oh, they do, huh? Well, then you also know I'm not interested in Rob, and he's not interested in me either. He's just lonely and between dates. He's another guy who goes for blonds." Her pointed look chided him for his narrow thinking. "I may have to become acquainted with Preference. I'm sure I'm worth it. Now teach me to hit this silly ball."

"Blonds, huh?" he asked, handing her his wood.

She took the club, and he placed a ball on the tee for her. "Those are the kinds of girls he dates. Blonds. Air-headed, breathy types." She lined up her shot and actually looked like she knew what she was doing until she swung. She clipped the top of the ball, and the thing barely moved. However, her club flew several yards into the air and landed with a thud against the emerald-colored grass.

"The goal is for the ball to fly out there and the club to stay in your hand." He grinned at her and realized he no longer thought of his mother and the explosion every single time he glanced at Kinsy. As a matter of fact, on this trip the memories had only plagued him during that paintball game. The rest of the time, his mind had been preoccupied with a sassy gal who claimed she might try Preference. But Thai didn't think blond suited her—not in the least.

She rolled her eyes and retrieved her club. "I thought you were my teacher." She handed him the club. "So teach me."

Another group of golfers drove up. "We'll let them go first." He and Kinsy moved out of the way. "Do you know any nice girls for Rob? Non-bimbo types?"

Kinsy thought a minute. "My roommate, Danielle, would be perfect. Unfortunately, she also has the wrong hair color."

He ignored her jab. "Maybe we can do something as a foursome sometime. See if your prediction proves correct." He wondered if he were using Rob as an excuse to spend more time with Kinsy.

"Maybe," she said, distracted as she studied each golfer teeing off. When they finished and drove their cart on, Kinsy moved back to the tee. She stretched her neck muscles by tilting her head from side to side. "I'm ready. What are the basics?"

Thai stepped up next to her. "Eye on the ball."

"Check."

"Feet shoulder-width apart."

She adjusted her stance. "Check."

"Knees bent."

First-time golfers usually looked corny, so Thai tried not to laugh.

"What now?"

"Swing easy. Don't try to kill the ball."

She swung, made contact, the ball sliced to the right and only rolled about twenty-five yards.

"Much better!" Thai hoped to encourage her.

"Don't lie to me!" Her face set, she marched out to reclaim her ball. "I'd say that was a pathetic improvement at best."

She set the ball on the tee and tried again. The results were much the same. After three more tries, Thai offered to help at a closer range. He'd hoped to avoid this scenario, but Kinsy's mounting frustration made eluding physical contact impossible.

Thai stood behind her and wrapped his arms around hers, gripping the club with her. Her hair smelled like apple blossoms, and a silky strand of her short locks blew against his cheek. A flash of his mother's hair tickling his cheek was blotted out by the memory of yesterday's near-kiss. As Thai had imagined, Kinsy fit perfectly in his arms, and concentrating on his swing challenged him to the max.

"Eye on the ball, feet apart, knees slightly bent, now we'll swing easy. Relax, let me lead." He led her through the swing. They connected with the ball and followed the shot through. Neither of them moved. The ball went much farther and higher than Kinsy's previous shots and almost hit the green.

"Did you feel the poetry in motion as you followed through on your swing?"

Kinsy nodded. Thai slowly loosened his hold and moved away from her. His true desire was to turn her in his arms, look into those almond eyes, and see if he affected her the way she did him. Did she experience all the crazy things he did? Did her heart beat like a tom-tom when he held her? Did she almost forget to breathe?

"Now what?" Kinsy asked softly, seeming a bit unnerved.

"Now you take your second shot." He threw his golf bag over his right shoulder.

"I think I'll try this one by myself." She began walking the distance toward her ball.

*Good idea.* Thai glanced toward the golf cart but decided to follow Kinsy on foot. The walk would help him work off some of the tension from that close encounter.

When they arrived at the ball, he handed her the correct club. She lined herself up with the hole. "Eye on the ball, feet apart, knees bent, swing easy," she reminded herself. After four more tries, her ball rolled into the hole. Thai admired her tenacity.

"Double bogie. Not bad for your first-ever hole of golf."

She smiled up and him. "Shall we move on?"

"We shall."

They walked backed to the golf cart. Thai had some thinking to do. Kinsy wasn't anywhere close to the woman of his dreams, or at least the one he thought he dreamed of. Yet he could no longer deny his growing emotions. Everything about her captivated him. Everything except her Vietnamese heritage. *But is that even important anymore?* Memories of that exploding village rushed upon him. His mother's gentle weeping swept over his mind as if she were with him. Thai cringed and forced himself not to bolt from all that Kinsy represented.

⁂

Kinsy lined up her next shot. *Did you feel the poetry in motion?* Thai's question echoed through her mind. Yeah, but the poetry she encountered when he wrapped his arms around her had nothing to do with her swing. The question was, did she affect him at all?

Other than occasional small talk, they finished their next few holes in quiet contemplation. They hadn't even started the fifth hole when Rob and Chris showed up. They'd already finished their entire game on the nine-hole course.

Thai and Kinsy decided to quit. Rob told Kinsy she could pick their dinner spot since she'd been a good sport about golf. She chose Ducey's. They drove to The Pines Resort where the restaurant sat overlooking Bass Lake. Requesting an outdoor table, they admired the evening sun, ducking behind the mountains and tall pines. The serenity calmed Kinsy's jumbled emotions.

After they'd ordered, they sat quietly while the waves lapped upon the shore. Taking a deep breath of the crisp mountain air, Kinsy admired God's handprint on the sky; He'd brushed hues of orange, pink, and lavender across the western expanse.

Soon the waitress returned with their iced teas, and Chris ended their contemplative moment. "I hate to break the silence, but Karl asked us to share with each other the best part of our jobs on staff at CC," he said, stirring a packet of sugar into his tea.

"For me," Kinsy said, her gaze never leaving the sunset, "getting to travel to places I've never been and tell people who've never heard the good news about Christ." She smiled. "God gave me the perfect job because traveling and evangelism are my passions." She squeezed her lemon into her tea glass.

"College kids are at the brink of many major decisions," Thai said. "If I can encourage one of them to make a better choice about dating, friendships, or their futures, it makes my week. Every choice we make either moves us toward God or away from Him. My goals are to help them understand that concept and to equip them through the study of God's Word to make decisions and strengthen their tie to Christ."

Kinsy and Thai exchanged a glance of mutual respect. He no longer shied away from looking at her, and the pain crossed his face less frequently. Her chest tightened. She refocused her gaze on the lake. Kinsy yearned for him to fall for her as she was falling for him. Yet maybe for Thai this was all part of his brother's experiment. Her stomach clenched.

"Rob, what's your favorite part of working at CC?" Chris asked.

"Eating peanut butter from my armpit."

"Gross!" Kinsy scrunched up her nose.

"The junior highers love gross. Seriously, watching God change the heart of a rebellious middle-schooler tops anything. Many of them come into my department with an adolescent attitude, and they leave two years later desiring to live their lives for God."

They all looked at Chris. "Baptizing a new believer. I can't ever immerse someone without getting teary. Here is a high schooler willing to publicly proclaim to the world he's chosen to follow Christ and now is moving forward into a new life. Chokes me up every time."

While the waitress passed out the plates, Kinsy thought about how extraordinary each of these men was. They'd committed their lives to shepherding God's flock, and they loved what they did. Their faces reflected their joy. Even though each of them was special to her, only Thai pulled her heartstrings.

She took a bite of her salad. "Chris, how are Miranda and the baby?"

"They are great. My favorite thing in life is spending time with my wife and baby daughter."

"You're married?" Thai asked. "I had no idea."

"Five years next month. I highly recommend tying the knot." He grinned at Thai and winked.

Kinsy cleared her throat. So both Chris and Rob had noticed the sparks between her and Thai.

"So how'd your golf game end up today?" Thai asked.

The three of them spent the rest of dinner talking golf. Relieved that she didn't have to carry on witty conversation, Kinsy ate in silence, watching the sun sink out of sight. Her emotions were on overload, and she relished the time to think things through. Did Thai even have a clue about the way he affected her? Probably not. Kinsy's heart sank right along with the sun.

When they got back to camp, they headed up the trail toward Star Rock. Tonight her dad taught on the ministry gifts and how God used them all in His body, the Church. Kinsy thought about the three guys on her team, how different they each were, yet how perfectly suited they were for their ministries.

Tired, Kinsy bid her teammates good night as soon as chapel ended. Thai offered to walk her up the trail, but she declined. Her ravaged emotions couldn't take being around him for another minute.

*Oh, God, what am I going to do? I like him way too much, but I'm the wrong nationality and have the wrong hair color.*

Deep within her heart, Kinsy was reminded that God knew the plans He had for her. She'd hang on to Him.

# Chapter 5

Thai rose before dawn the next morning, needing some solid God-time before he faced Kinsy and Half Dome. He slipped out of the cabin, leaving behind a symphony of seven snoring men. He spent the next hour sitting on a tree stump, praying and studying the Word. He told God all about his confusion regarding Kinsy. No answers came, but the time with his Father refreshed him.

At five-thirty, they all boarded the bus and headed toward the drop-off point that would begin the hike of a lifetime. During this journey, his team sat in the very front and were the first to enjoy the breathtaking view. Kinsy took the seat next to Chris, so Thai claimed the window seat across the aisle. He enjoyed the ride, drinking in all the sights along the way.

They passed through Wawona Tunnel and into Yosemite Valley. On the left was El Capitan, then Yosemite falls. Walls of sculpted granite intensified the majesty of God's creation. Off to the right, Thai spotted Sentinel Dome. Kinsy's describing Yosemite as awesome seemed almost inadequate.

The bus stopped near Curry Village. Thai grabbed his backpack. Chris and Kinsy waited for him and Rob, and they exited together.

"What do you think?" she asked.

He shook his head. "I can't find the words."

She nodded her agreement.

"Shall we start our ascent?" Chris asked. "Sad thing is we start by going down, then we have a longer uphill trek." He led out with Rob on his heels.

"After you, Kinsy." He planned to watch out for her, in case she got into trouble.

"I'm not fond of heights. I may slow you down."

"I don't mind." Even more reason for him to keep an eye on her. Thai followed her down the narrow dirt trail, eyeing Half Dome in the distance. "Hard to believe we'll be on top of that rock in a few hours."

"My mind is saying, 'yeah, right, seems impossible.' It looks so high and so far away."

"Hey, where's the Kinsy I know? The one who rises to every challenge?"

"I think I left her back at camp," she joked. "What if I can't, Thai? What if I'm too out of shape? I'm so inadequate. Look at that mountain of granite. Who am I to think I can conquer the magnificent Half Dome?"

"You can, Kinsy. You're in great shape." He believed every word he said. He'd never met a more capable person. "Don't you accomplish everything you set out to do?"

"Usually."

"Remember you and the golf ball yesterday? This is just another challenge set before you. Think of the excitement cresting the last ridge. We'll be on top of the world."

"You're right. I know you are." The words belied her lack of conviction.

Thai almost chuckled at the irony of his words. Kinsy struggled with the physical aspects of the climb, but he struggled spiritually with his ascent toward Christlikeness. Inadequacy seeped from his pores. In all honesty, he didn't trust God with his past, or his future. That's why he'd figured everything out for himself, down to the type of person he'd even consider dating. Kinsy didn't fit his ideal, but did she fit God's?

"I'm anxious to have this climb behind me." She grinned back at him. "I won't think about the distance. I can do everything through Him who gives me strength, even this."

"That's my girl."

Kinsy glanced back again, a question on her face, and he realized his faux pas. A part of him yearned for nothing more than for Kinsy McCoy to be his girl. An energetic little dynamo, she'd blown into his life like a fresh breeze and turned his world topsy-turvy. All the things he was sure of now seemed questionable.

Thai had decided years ago he'd date only the all-American girl—blond and blue-eyed, so he'd have a chance at American normalcy. A chance to forget his painful past, maybe even forget he came from Vietnam.

A great plan he'd stuck to since age twelve. He'd never even dated a brunette. Then this little fresh-faced Vietnamese beauty with a heart bigger than she was caused him to doubt his decisions. Thai prided himself in being a striver. He fixed his eye on the goal and never veered. How did one tiny woman manage to push him so far off course?

Kinsy stopped and leaned against a boulder. Rob and Chris had disappeared, hidden from their view by the surrounding forest. A bunny hopped across the path, and chirping birds serenaded them with their song of spring. Kinsy took a few sips of water, rubbed her right calf, and they continued.

By the time they reached Heartbreak Hill, the trees had become sparse and rocks lay everywhere. She smiled weakly and looked at the trail ahead. He followed close behind as she began the extreme uphill trek. About halfway up, Thai realized this hill was appropriately named. His heart broke watching Kinsy fight her way to the top. They climbed for what seemed like forever, dirt crunching under their feet with each step. This was definitely the most intense part of the journey so far.

Thai wasn't sure exactly how long this portion took, but he was certain they'd climbed at least two hours, going straight up toward the sun. His legs wobbled, and he wondered if they'd carry him the rest of the way. Kinsy must wonder too. Her steps had slowed to a snail's pace.

When they crested Heartbreak Hill, Thai said, "We're almost there."

Kinsy stopped. He put an arm around her, and she leaned against him. She laid her head against his chest and closed her eyes.

"You're doing great," he crooned.

"My legs feel like rubber."

"Mine too."

She took a deep breath. "Let's go."

He gave her a squeeze and released his hold. They went down for a short way—a welcome change to his aching calves. Then the trail headed up again. Finally, they reached The One Thousand Steps. Rocks in the mountain created steps leading to the base of Half Dome.

"Do you really think there are actually one thousand of them?"

Thai shrugged. "I have no idea."

Kinsy led out again. When they reached the base, she said, "There were at least a thousand, if not two."

Thai chuckled in appreciation of her attempt at humor.

ଈ

Kinsy studied the two thick wire cables, running from the base to the top of Half Dome. Fear knotted her stomach. Terrified of heights, how could she do this?

Thai wrapped her in another hug. He must have read the terror she knew was written across her face. "I'll be right behind you," he promised.

She nodded. Inside she longed to head down the mountain as fast as she could run. Instead, she grabbed a pair of gardening gloves from the huge pile on the ground near the cables and slipped them on.

"Pull yourself up the face of the rock using your arms and the cables," Thai stated the obvious.

Kinsy bit her lip and grasped the cables. She tugged herself slowly higher, placing her feet wherever they'd plant. *God, please don't let me lose my grip. And don't let me think about falling.*

Two climbers were coming down using the same two cables.

"Thai?" Her raspy voice echoed her fear.

"Don't worry. Just move to the right, and let them pass."

She nodded and followed his instructions, heaving a big sigh once the other hikers passed her.

"I'm right behind you. You're doing great. Not too much farther. Keep moving up."

She nodded, searching for another solid place to stick her foot. A loose pebble caused her foot to slip slightly, and she nearly screamed.

"Good job, Kins. Keep going, Baby. Keep going."

His endearment touched her heart. She had to make it to the top, just so she could fall into his arms.

"The view is beautiful from up here. Can you believe how far we can see?"

"I'm not looking. I'm only staring at my shoes."

"Just keep looking at those shoes. You're doing great. I'm so proud of you."

Finally, the top. Every muscle in Kinsy's entire body ached, and her arms throbbed. "Thank You, Lord. Thank You," she wept softly.

Thai held her. "Now you can look. Breathtaking is the only word for this." He waved his arm as if he owned the grand expanse before them.

Breathtaking was right. An eagle soared overhead. The air seemed lighter and thinner, the clouds much closer. Looking over the vista, toward the peaks and valleys, Kinsy recognized God's signature in every direction. The Creator of the universe must have smiled when He carved out Yosemite.

"Thank you, Thai," she whispered. "I couldn't have made it without you. I'd have missed all this." As she glanced at him, she saw the tenderness radiating from his eyes. "Once again, you're my gallant knight."

He brushed away her tears with his thumb. "And once again you're my beautiful distressed damsel. Rescuing you is becoming a habit." His gaze intensified. "A habit I'm not sure I plan to break."

Kinsy thought he might kiss her, but Rob cleared his throat, reminding them they had an audience. Thai kept his arm around her, and together they admired the view.

"It's incredible," Kinsy whispered. Then her gusto returned. "We're on top of Half Dome! What a sense of accomplishment!"

Thai beamed at her.

"I can see forever! Is the view amazing or what?" She held tightly to him and turned carefully, looking out in all directions. The loose gravel under her feet made her think slipping off the edge wouldn't be too difficult, so she used Thai as her anchor.

"You're what's amazing," he whispered near her ear. Goosebumps covered her arms.

"I'm Amerasian," she solemnly reminded him.

"I know, but that doesn't seem to matter. . .much."

"But it still matters?"

"I don't know. All I know is you're terrific."

She smiled. "So are you, Thai."

"I want to kiss you right now," he said, caressing her face. "But I won't. Our first kiss should be a sacred moment—just between us."

His words touched her heart. His eyes promised that, in not too much longer, she'd know the tenderness of his lips against hers.

"Over here for a team shot," Rob motioned.

Kinsy clung to Thai. They inched their way toward Chris and Rob. "Go slowly," she whispered. "I feel like we're going to slip off the edge."

"What would you do if you didn't have him to hold on to?" Rob asked.

"I'd crawl." And she had no doubt she would. They all laughed at her honesty.

Other teams were arriving now. Some of them had a member or two quit and turn back. Kinsy had no doubt she would have been one of them if it had not been for Thai.

She looked up at him and knew the possibility existed to love this man. *God, please don't let him break my heart. Somehow, let him love me too.*

After half an hour and many pictures, the time to leave arrived. Kinsy couldn't wait to have her feet on flat ground. Though the scenery was beautiful, she was ready to head back down. Thai stayed by her side, keeping her safe. Her dad gave her a knowing wink, and Kinsy smiled at him.

Both she and Thai put their gloves back on for the climb down the cables. "Going down won't be as bad," he assured her. "I'll go first."

He started down the rock the most common way—face forward. A couple of guys just ahead of them even ran down the cables. Kinsy's head spun just watching them. She opted to back down, facing the rock. Going forward and seeing everything, including the heights to which they'd climbed, was just too much. Again, she kept her eyes fixed on her feet. Thai coached her down, telling her where to place each step.

*He said going down would be easier. Boy, was he wrong!* Even after she finished with the cables, the trek remained difficult. Bone tired, she didn't voice her discouragement. At least going up, there was a goal, the prize of accomplishment waiting to greet her at the top of Half Dome. Her knees ached from the constant downward motion. Weary, she longed to see the end of the trail. When they finally arrived at the bus several hours later, Thai hugged her and kissed her temple.

"I'm so proud of you! Look at all the men from CC who quit, but you didn't give in to your fears."

She smiled. "Definitely a hard day, but a great one." *Mostly great because of you.* "I'm glad we're back on semi-flat ground. Thank you for not letting me quit."

Thai pulled her behind a massive oak. He touched her hair and her face, gently tracing her jaw line. She couldn't believe this was happening. "You are my inspiration."

"For what?" Her voice quivered.

"Kinsy, I've spent my life running from my past, and I'm getting tired of running. I don't want to give in to my fears anymore. I'm beginning to think I'm ready to take a chance on you—on us. I'm not going to say I'm free of everything that happened to me, but I do think I'm starting to grow. . .at least, some. Is there any way you would be interested in—"

"I am. I have been since our game of basketball."

He lowered his head. Their lips met. For Kinsy, Thai's kiss was the fourth of July and Christmas rolled into one. When the kiss ended, his expression matched the emotions dancing in her heart.

He drew her to him and held her close. Neither spoke. Words proved unnecessary. None were capable of describing all the sensations manifesting themselves within her. But thanks to God poured from her heart. He'd heard and answered her prayers: Thai saw past her Asian features to the woman inside.

# Chapter 6

Thai whistled on the drive to work the following Monday morning. Spring was here. Flowers bloomed, birds sang, and he just might be in "serious like." The silly ear-to-ear grin plastered across his face witnessed his delightful dilemma. Since last Wednesday afternoon when he'd kissed Kinsy, the grin had become an almost permanent part of him. If not for the occasional nightmares that were a regular part of his sleep pattern, Thai wondered if the smile would have remained intact even when he slept.

With his usual precision, Thai buried the pain and chose to focus on Kinsy. *Ah, Kinsy.* Man, was she terrific. They hadn't kissed again—yet. He planned to be careful, go slow, set good boundaries. They also avoided public displays of affection; PDA, as the college kids called it. But just the secret looks and her just-for-him smile curled his toes.

Last night after church, they strolled along Kinsy's favorite stretch of beach. Hand in hand, they walked for a couple of hours. Neither said much. They didn't have to. Being together was enough.

Thai parked next to her car. Even seeing the Del Sol brought him pleasure. He decided to drop by her office before heading to his. He'd start his day with a ray of her smile to carry him through.

"Good morning, Miss McCoy," he said as he rounded the corner into her office.

She looked up from the papers on her desk. No smile greeted him from her pale face. He knew immediately something was wrong—very wrong.

"Kinsy?"

"Thai, I'm glad you're here." She rose from her desk. "We need to talk. Please, have a seat." She motioned to the padded chairs facing her desk, her words stiff and formal. Walking around him, she shut her office door. Her blue plaid jumper swished around her ankles with an ominous finality.

Kinsy's face was drawn and tight. Even her movements seemed wooden and unnatural. She returned to the chair behind her desk, keeping distance between them.

"What's going on?" He tugged at the collar of his denim shirt, suddenly choking him, even though the first button was open.

"I talked to Steve this morning." She took a deep breath. "Our Bible smuggling trip is set. We're going to Vietnam."

He felt like she'd stabbed him in the back. The explosion flashed in his mind. He pictured Loi's and his mother's bloodied, stiff bodies in a heap of smoke and ash. Thai's heart pounded, and every breath hurt.

The present swam before his eyes, and anger flooded him. He rose, leaning over Kinsy's desk, hitting it with a clenched fist. "You did this on purpose!"

"N–no, Thai, not on purpose. Steve was ultimately responsible for our destination. I just—"

"You just cooperated!"

Kinsy reached for him, but he instinctively jerked back before she made contact. She looked down. The pain on her face in no way compared to the hurt and betrayal slicing his heart to shreds.

"I told you the day we met I would never return—not ever!" He leaned farther across her desk and got in her face. "Just because you have some fantasy about returning to your homeland, don't drag me into your plans. Vietnam was a nightmare I don't plan to relive."

"Thai, I'm sorry." A tear crept down her cheek. Her eyes begged for understanding, but Thai was incapable of anything but personal agony. Her shoulders sagged with the weight of a bad decision.

"Why?" he asked in a pain-filled voice. "Why did you do this to me?"

"I told you I wasn't responsible for the final decision, except prayer. You'll have to take this up with God." A defensive edge hardened her words.

He ran a hand through his hair and paced her small office like a caged animal. Finally, he returned to the chair.

Looking her square in the eye, he said, "I can't—I won't go back. Even if it costs me my job. If need be, I'll turn in my resignation today."

"No, Thai. Please don't. We'll try to work around this somehow."

"Kinsy, you don't seem to understand. There is no working around it. I will not—I repeat—will not ever set foot on Vietnamese soil as long as I live!" With his vehement declaration, Thai left Kinsy's office, closing the door more forcefully than he'd intended.

He headed down the hall to his office corridor. His conscience pricked. *What if God asked me to go? Would I tell Him no? Surely, He wouldn't ask that from me.*

Thai spent the morning arguing with himself and struggling with guilt over his reaction. Why did he assume the worst? Maybe she really had nothing to do with it all. He'd never known her to lie. He picked up the phone and dialed her extension.

Kinsy's voice greeted him. "I'll be out of the office Monday afternoon. You may either leave a message or press 135 to speak to my secretary."

He pressed 135. "Judy, where's Kinsy?"

"She decided to take a personal day about ten this morning. Did you keep her out too late last night? She didn't look well."

"How did you know I was with Kinsy last night?"

"You two are the talk of the office. Did you think you could date the pastor's daughter and no one would notice?"

"I suppose not." He sighed and hung up his phone.

*Great.* The entire office probably also knew they'd had a fight. Their first. He decided to go buy an I'm-sorry-I-was-a-jerk card and leave it on her desk. Nothing had changed. He wouldn't be a party to the trip, but he shouldn't have blamed Kinsy. He'd practically called her a liar. After purchasing the perfect card with a pathetic looking dog on the front, he returned to the office, sat at her desk, and scrawled a short note.

*Kinsy, I'm sorry. I overreacted. I know this isn't your fault. Forgive me for insinuating it was. Though I won't go on the trip, I hope we can still be us. Fondly, Thai.*

Some of the heaviness lifted. He sealed the envelope and leaned it against Kinsy's phone. Picking up a framed picture of her and her six sisters caused his heart to warm. He replaced the frame and rose to leave. A letter on the corner of her desk caught his eye. The letterhead indicated it was about the Bible smuggling trip.

Thai hesitated. Since he was supposed to be a co-leader on the trip, reading the contents probably wouldn't hurt. He picked up the letter, his hand shaking slightly. Guilt pricked his conscience, but he read on. The last paragraph caused him to sit back down. He read it again.

*I so appreciate your openness and even your suggestion that the CC team take the humanitarian aid trip to Vietnam. Your excitement about the possibility of visiting Vietnam when we spoke on the phone two weeks ago confirmed what I already suspected. I am confident this is where the Lord is sending your team, so congratulations, Miss McCoy, your dreams and prayers are coming to fruition.*

He stared at the letter, disappointment and hurt battling within. She'd known all along—not only known but requested the destination. He scanned to the top of the page and read the date. April 1. Within the past couple of weeks she'd asked for Vietnam as the team's destination, knowing full well Thai's repulsion about returning. Obviously, she didn't care.

Steve may have ultimately chosen the destination, but she suggested it and even encouraged the decision. Thai swallowed hard. Kinsy McCoy wasn't at all the woman he assumed. He shut his eyes, hoping to close out the pain as well. She was a liar and a manipulator. All his hopes for overcoming his past now mocked him. Even more important than Kinsy's participation in this farce, she was also Vietnamese. *I should have never veered from my decision to marry an all-American blond.* He tossed the card in the trash. *I have been a fool. An utter fool. Kinsy McCoy won't dupe me again. Not ever.*

❧

Kinsy jogged along the beach. Boy, her life had gone from perfect to disaster in four point seven seconds. She hoped the run would clear her head, rid her of a nasty headache, and let off some steam. Just last night she and Thai had strode this same beach, and today he marched out on her in a huff.

She really wasn't surprised at how the scene played out. Even though he'd learned to accept her, he withdrew whenever Vietnam was mentioned, and his eyes were by no means void of the glimmer of pain. His words before that kiss near Half Dome now plagued her. He had said he couldn't make any promises. Perhaps today ended any hopes of even the beginning of promise. She'd give him a couple of days to think, cool off, then they'd talk. Her stomach knotted. What if he refused to talk? *Don't borrow trouble, Kinsy.*

When the possibility of this trip presented itself almost a year ago—long before she met Thai—she sensed God answering her long-prayed prayer to find her birth mother's people. Disguised as a humanitarian aid trip, its true purpose lay in smuggling Bibles to the underground church. They'd stay at an orphanage run by a Christian couple and bike Bibles to nearby villages.

Kinsy hoped to trace her family history since the orphanage was the one where the McCoys had adopted her. She already knew her mother came from a small fishing village; her father was an American G.I. The entire village had rejected both mother and baby.

Somewhere in the back of her mind, she believed this trip would free Thai from his past so he could embrace the plans God had for his future. From her perspective, this looked like the perfect opportunity to make her dreams come true and help Thai at the same time. The only problem: He didn't want her help.

She probably needed to warn her dad about this. He would know what to do, and he'd pray. She jogged back to her car for the forty-minute drive home. Because of the distance, she indulged herself in a beach jog only once a week. Her dream was to someday live on the beach; she loved the ocean and its powerful reminder of her Creator. He was still in control, even though her life had hit a bump in the road.

Kinsy dropped into the car seat and punched in her dad's extension on her cell phone. "Hi, Dad." She filled him in on the earlier disagreement. "What should I do?"

"Why don't you see if you can get the trip changed and keep me posted? I don't want to lose Thai over this. Maybe God still has work to do before he can face the past. He's come a long way in a little over three months. Be patient, Pumpkin."

Kinsy smiled. Her dad had been saying those three words to her since before she could remember. Patience—the elusive ability to wait. "I'll try. I love you, Dad."

"Goes double for me."

Snapping her cell phone shut, she decided to head back to the office, pick up Steve's home number, and try reaching him tonight. The sooner the better. Kinsy pulled into the parking lot. No sign of Thai's Miata. He must have left for the day.

She unlocked a back door, hoping to bypass as many eyes as possible. She still wore her jogging attire—tank top and shorts—not very appropriate for the church office. Slipping into her office, unseen, she closed the door behind her. She flipped on the light. Her chair was pushed away from her desk and turned sideways. Someone had been in there. Prickles danced up her spine and the back of her neck.

Moving slowly, cautiously toward her desk, Kinsy wished she could control her heart's increased pace. She peeked around the corner, making certain no one was hiding there. With relief, she sat down, glanced around the room, and rolled forward toward her desk. The message light flashed on her phone. She decided to ignore the voice mail until tomorrow.

Steve's letter with his home and office number lay in the middle of her desk—one corner crumpled as if someone had held on too tightly. She smoothed out the crinkles, knowing she'd left the letter on the corner of her desk, unwrinkled. Some sixth sense suggested that Thai had been snooping.

Kinsy reread the incriminating evidence in her hand. If Thai read this letter, he'd never believe she hadn't finagled the destination of this trip. Her suggesting Vietnam had taken place last summer, but from the sound of the letter, it might have happened just a couple of weeks ago. However, her encouraging Steve to continue pursuit of Vietnam had occurred after she met Thai and after she knew how painful the trip would be. She had known—almost for certain—this was their destination when she was with Thai last week in Yosemite. Yet Kinsy, fearful of his disapproval, had chosen not to mention even the possibility to him. Perhaps she had been naïve. Kinsy had far more to fear than merely his disapproval. Would one dream cost her another?

She stuck the letter in a file folder to take home and decided to call Steve later tonight. Maybe Thai could forgive her if she got the trip changed to somewhere else, anywhere else. Rising to leave, something purple protruding from her trash can caught her eye. Bending down, she pulled out an envelope with her name scrawled across the front in Thai's bold script. So, he had been in there.

Tearing open the flap, she removed a greeting card. The saddest looking basset hound she'd ever seen looked back at her. Inside the card simply said 'Sorry.' Sitting back down, she read Thai's note to her. She rested her head against the back of her chair, closing her eyes and imagining the scenario unfolding.

Thai must have regretted their tiff as much as she had, even going out of his way to buy a card and write a note. He must have come in here to leave it on her desk, the letter caught his eye, and the desire for them to still be an "us" went straight into the garbage.

❧

Thai's sparsely furnished living room seemed as empty as his heart. The lone recliner that usually brought comfort now ridiculed his single existence. Thai muted his big screen TV. Even basketball, his favorite sport, couldn't capture his attention. He grabbed his cordless, punched in his most frequently-dialed number, and paced restlessly.

"Hello."

"Tong, it's me."

"Thai! How was the trip to Yosemite? I've always hoped to go myself someday."

"The trip was great. Beautiful, incredible, amazing."

"And?" Tong asked, reading the unsaid, as always.

"Kinsy and I hit it off—too good, as a matter of fact."

"What do you mean?"

"She reeled me in." He plopped into his brand-new hunter green recliner.

"Reeled you in? So, you're a fish now?"

"No, a fool." He moved the handle on his chair, and the footrest rose. "I should have never veered from my determination to stick with blonds. Kinsy and I can never have a relationship. There's too much in the past—and maybe even in the present."

"You and Kinsy have a relationship now?"

"We had the beginnings of one until today, but not anymore."

"So, what happened?"

"I ended the thing. She's a smooth operator, fooled me completely, but the truth shined bright and clear this morning. For one week this woman had me right where she wanted me, but never again." He picked up the remote and surfed the muted channels.

"What in the world did she do?"

"Our Bible smuggling trip is to Vietnam! Vietnam! The very place I don't want to go, and she knew it!"

Tong's silence spoke of Thai's own shock.

"But topping that, she wasn't completely honest about the whole thing. I found a letter proving her deception."

"No kidding? From what you said, she didn't impress me as the type."

"She wanted her own way—despite how I felt. She manipulated things." Thai let the footrest down and rose from his chair. "Now she expects me to go!" He started his pacing again, all the while wondering if his reaction was really an easy escape. After all, the nightmares hadn't gone away, just because he had declared himself in "serious like" with Kinsy. Despite his silly smile when he remembered that kiss, their relationship still stirred the old fear that tainted his past.

"Wow. I don't know what to say."

"Well, I know what to say! She's not forcing me to go! Period!"

"Will you be able to get out of the trip and keep your job? I mean, isn't going your responsibility since the trip is for the college kids?"

"Yeah, as the college pastor, I'm expected to participate. But I am not going. If I have to resign, I will."

"Thai, this is your dream job. Think things through."

"I have, and I'm furious with her for putting me in this spot by using blatant female manipulation. She knows how I feel about Vietnam. Look how hard I struggled letting her into my life, and quite frankly, there are times it's still a struggle. Now, she thinks I should embrace the whole country."

"Maybe going back will set you free to move forward."

Thai sat in one of his two kitchen chairs. He rested his head in his hands. "I can't," he said in a quiet, pain-filled voice. "I just can't."

"I know going would be hard. . . ."

He swallowed. "It would be more than hard."

"At least pray. What if this is more a God thing than a Kinsy thing? What if He's orchestrating these circumstances?"

"I have my doubts." Thai opened his sliding glass door and stepped out on his balcony. Crisp, cool April air blew lightly against his heated cheeks. The sun lingered low in the western sky; in Vietnam, the sun would be rising soon. But Thai's heart was filled with inky darkness.

"So you really liked her, huh?" Thai didn't miss Tong's tactful change of subject. Tong always hit Thai between the eyes with something difficult and just left the seed to germinate. He never nagged or harped, only subtly sowed a kernel of an idea and left Thai alone to grapple over the issue.

Thai looked at the smoggy sky. "I liked her—a lot. And her betrayal hurts, Man."

"Are you sure this isn't a resolvable misunderstanding?"

Thai told him about his intent to reconcile and about the contents of the letter.

"Sometimes things aren't as they seem. Don't you remember with Lola and me, we had a few miscommunications? I thought one thing, and she thought another."

"Very different. This stared me in the face in black and white. I read the letter. No misunderstanding; believe me, the thing would stand up in a court of law. Besides all that—it's like this whole episode has reminded me of just how opposite Kinsy and I are. She wants to embrace Vietnam, and when all the dust settles, I still want to run from it."

"So, what now?"

"I'm going to go talk to her dad—explain why I can't go. If he asks for my resignation, I'll type it for him. Can I crash on your couch for awhile if I become unemployed and homeless?" He hoped to lighten Tong's concern.

"You know you can. I'll be praying, and, Thai, you do the same."

He sighed. "I will." The niggling doubt resurfaced. Would God require him to return to Vietnam? The whole notion made him want to shut Kinsy out all the more.

"You can't leave California yet. Samantha is set on visiting Uncle Thai and Mickey come June. You wouldn't break the heart of a three year old, would you?"

"Never! Give her a hug from her favorite uncle."

"I will. Love you, Bro."

"Back at you." Thai hit the end button on his cordless. Returning inside, he replaced the phone in its cradle and picked up his mail from his tiny table for two. Settling into his recliner, he unmuted the TV, flipped through his mail, and yelled at the Bulls for allowing another turnover.

This place definitely had the look of a bachelor pad. His living room had a recliner, a nice stereo system, and of course, a TV. The stark white walls cried for a decorator's touch, but no decorators lurked on his horizon.

He tried to ignore what Tong had said, but as usual, he couldn't forget. He just hated Tong's ability to calmly place a thorn of doubt in the midst of all his notions. If only Tong would nag, shutting him out would prove an easy task. Instead, he made these profound statements and prayed they'd take root. The words swarmed around and around in Thai's head. *What if this is more a God thing than a Kinsy thing? What if He's orchestrating these circumstances?* And on the heels of these questions, the old memories flooded Thai anew—recollections of a tormented four year old who might never find peace.

# Chapter 7

Kinsy stomped up the steps to her apartment, undecided as to who'd made her the maddest, Thai, herself, or the driver who just cut her off. The aroma of something Italian and wonderful hit her the minute she unlocked the front door.

"You look like you had a day. Good thing I fixed Chicken Parmesan," Danielle said.

"I did have a day. If my favorite meal can't make me feel better, nothing can." Kinsy glanced at the table. "Candles, linen napkins, fresh flowers, and six places set. . ." *Please, God, tell me we're not having a dinner party.* A knock at the door confirmed her suspicions. Kinsy glanced down at her jogging attire and sent Danielle a the-least-you-could-have-done-is-told-me look.

"Would you get it?" Danielle smiled sweetly. "I'm busy with the salad."

Kinsy mentally added Danielle to the list of people who'd annoyed her today. She swung open the front door, and her jaw dropped. "Thai, Rob, Chuck!" Danielle's name just moved to the very top of the list of today's annoyances.

"Aren't you going to invite us in?" Rob asked.

She opened the door wider, and Rob led the three of them into the apartment. He carried a bouquet of mixed flowers. Thai's tortured expression left her in no doubt he'd rather be in the hospital with gangrene than here. Somehow he'd been tricked into this little adventure, of that she had no doubt.

"Aren't you going to introduce us?" Rob asked, looking pointedly at Danielle working in the kitchen.

*Idiot,* she chided herself. She'd stood in the doorway, gaping, as if she didn't have a manner in the world. "Rob, this is my roommate, Danielle. Danielle, Rob."

Danielle gave him a bashful grin. "Nice to meet you."

"You too." Was Rob blushing? "I brought these for you." He held out the flowers.

Certain she'd missed some major clue as to the unfolding of these events, Kinsy shot Danielle a questioning look. Chuck stepped forward. "Danielle, I'm Chuck, and this is Thai. I speak for the three of us when I tell you how much we appreciate you inviting us for a home-cooked meal." He glanced at Thai. "Well, at least

I speak for two of us."

*Danielle invited them? Why?*

Kally walked through the front door, carrying an armload of books and a filled-to-capacity book bag slung over her shoulder. Her eyes widened upon spotting their dinner guests. "Hello," she said, looking at Kinsy with raised eyebrows as if to say, *What's going on?* Then Kally looked at her attire, and Kinsy noticed her lips quiver. She almost laughed!

"Kally," Kinsy said in an artificially sweet voice, "I'd like you to meet Thai. You already know Chuck and Rob. Thai, this is Kally, sister number three."

"Nice to meet you, Thai." Kally smiled, then nodded at the other two.

"Danielle, Dear," Kinsy continued in her carefully modulated tone, "how long before dinner? Since I've been caught by surprise, I'm hoping I'll have time to shower."

Danielle had the decency to look guilty. "Go ahead."

"Kally, may I help you carry those into your room?" Kinsy asked, taking the stack of books from her. Kally followed her down the hall. The minute they were in Kally's room, Kinsy shut the door. "I have no idea what's going on here, but the timing stinks."

Kally started laughing. "Glad to see you dressed for the occasion."

"This is not funny." Tears came from nowhere. "Our trip is to Vietnam, and Thai hates me." She sat on the edge of Kally's bed, wiping her eyes. The emotions she'd held tight all day threatened to burst forth. "We're through."

Kally sat next to her, putting a comforting arm around her shoulders. She hugged her and never said 'I told you so,' making Kinsy grateful. Finally, Kally said, "Run and shower. You'll feel better. I'll entertain the troops."

"Would you bring me my briefcase? I need to make a phone call."

Kinsy slipped into her room and took a fast shower. Then after she threw on jeans and a sweatshirt, she called Steve.

"Hi, Steve, this is Kinsy McCoy."

"Hello, Kinsy. I assume you got my voice mail. You must be thrilled with the news. Vietnam, here she comes! Your dream come true."

Kinsy sighed. Under any other circumstances, she would be thrilled, but her dream wasn't worth Thai. She'd thought about the whole ordeal all day. She wished for a chance at forever with him. This trip would ruin any possibility, if it hadn't already.

"Kinsy, are you there?" Steve's voice brought her out of her reverie.

"Yeah, I'm sorry. I need you to reassign our team. We can't go to 'Nam." She lay on her back across her bed, staring at the ceiling.

"Too late. We've already purchased the plane tickets in each team member's name.

We bought them today, as soon as your secretary e-mailed the list of participants."

"There's no way?" Her words rang with desperation. She laid her hand across her forehead.

"I'm sorry, Kinsy, there's not. I thought you'd be thrilled. You said there was nothing more important than finding your mother's people."

That was then. Now Thai seemed more important. "True, but I ran into a problem on this end. Don't worry. It'll work itself out," she said in a hollow voice.

"Well, have a good evening then."

Saying good-bye, Kinsy didn't know whether to laugh or cry. She had an evening ahead of her all right, but the good part seemed doubtful.

∞

Thai sat stiffly on Kinsy's sofa, staring at the TV but not really watching the game. Seeing her, being here, brought extreme discomfort. Rob and Chuck had shown up at his doorstep, uninvited and unannounced. He knew better than to leave with them, but he had no idea they'd bring him here. Having heard about the quarrel, they said they came to take him out for a bite, get his mind off his misery. When they pulled up here, he'd almost stayed in the car. However, sitting alone with his memories appealed less than facing Kinsy.

Kally and Chuck both watched the game with him. Rob stayed in the dining area, keeping Danielle company. From the smell of things, he'd at least get a decent meal out of this miserable evening. He wondered where Kinsy was. Maybe she was dolling herself up to make the grand, breathtaking entrance. No matter how good she might look, his decision wouldn't be swayed one iota.

When Kinsy came back in, he didn't even look up. His nose, however, verified her presence by the apple blossom scent of her shampoo. He had no choice but to notice her when she padded barefoot across the blue living room carpet between him and his game. She sat cross-legged in the armchair.

"Dinner's ready," Danielle announced.

Kally flicked off the TV.

Chuck protested.

"Dad says TV has no place at the dinner table. It stifles conversation," Kally informed him.

Thai ended up seated across from Kinsy. He'd been wrong about her dressing to kill. She did just the opposite. She wore a gray sweatshirt, no makeup, and damp hair. She'd been crying. *Probably for my benefit*, he reminded himself after a pang of regret hit his heart. He'd have to stay on his toes.

In all honesty, she left him vulnerable, with an aching need to fill the lonely life he'd carved out for himself. And that vulnerability had made him pretend that his past might not affect them. But Thai had been wrong. Dead wrong. Their first fight had involved the past. Those moments on Half Dome had been nothing more than a surreal removal from reality. Regardless of how he had grown to care for Kinsy, or even his attempts at spiritual growth, she was still Vietnamese. She wanted to embrace her heritage—something Thai could never do. Today's argument had been nothing more than a foretaste of what the future would hold for their relationship.

After Rob said grace, everyone dug in. At least the food was good, even if the atmosphere was strained.

"Danielle, this is delicious," Rob complimented. "Can your roommates cook like this?"

"No," Kinsy and Kally answered in unison.

"We work out the details, though," Kally said. "We buy the groceries, and Danielle figures out what to do with them."

Rob chuckled. "I'd be willing to buy, if you'd cook for me."

Danielle smiled and blushed. Kinsy had been right. Danielle did seem perfect for Rob, and the chemistry between them nearly sizzled, just like it had between him and Kinsy.

Dinner passed in small talk. Neither he nor Kinsy said much. Apparently, Kally and Chuck were old friends, and they carried the conversation with tales from high school.

After everyone devoured their homemade cheesecake, they played Rock, Paper, Scissors for cleanup. Thai and Kinsy lost. They cleared the table in silence, avoiding accidentally bumping each other in the small kitchen. When he'd loaded the last plate in the dishwasher, Kinsy had just finished wiping off the table. She stood between him and the kitchen exit.

She swallowed hard. "Can we talk?"

They faced each other, and tension clenched his fists. "There's not much to say."

Her lip quivered. "Please." She barely whispered the word.

"All right," he agreed. Part of him longed to hold her and promise things would be okay, but could they ever be?

"Do you want to walk, so we have some privacy?"

"Lead on."

Thai followed her out the door. She led him to a grassy area under a big oak tree. She sat down, pulling her knees up near her chin. He settled next to her, keeping some distance.

"I'm sorry. I know how this looks to you, but I didn't set out to hurt you." Sad brown eyes pleaded for his understanding. "I know you read the letter on my desk, and the way it's worded sounds incriminating, but that's not exactly what happened."

He didn't say anything. He just stared at her, wondering how he could voice his own jumbled thoughts.

"Thai, please believe me. Yes, when I first talked to Steve—almost a year ago— I shared with him my desire to return to Vietnam one day. When he mentioned 'Nam as one of the Bible smuggling destinations, I said our team would be more than willing to participate."

She paused, apparently waiting for a reaction. With his jaw clenched tight, he had none.

She continued. "That was last fall, before you ever came into the picture. He and I both committed to pray about where God would have this team to go. I should have called him immediately last January when you told me how you felt about Vietnam, but I didn't. I just figured since everyone was praying, God would take care of the details, and I thought if we ended up there maybe you could find freedom and healing from your past."

He resented her pat answers to his childhood pain. The only thing Thai needed freedom and healing from was her. He disliked Christians who blamed God rather than taking responsibility for their own actions. He maintained the cool stare. "You knew about this at Yosemite, didn't you?"

She squirmed under his unyielding scrutiny. "Maybe in my fervor, I forgot to let God be God. I'm sorry. I never meant to hurt you. I should have been more up front with both you and Steve. As Kally frequently reminds me, I have a habit of running about a mile ahead of God and His will for my life." Her eyes glistened with the tears brimming in them.

"I tried not to worry about what would happen between us if Vietnam ended up being our assignment. Anyway, when I learned our destination, I knew you'd be unhappy, but I didn't know you'd end up hating me." She looked away, taking a deep breath.

"Kinsy, I don't hate you. I—I guess I'm just disappointed that you weren't completely honest."

The threatening tears now rolled freely down her cheeks. "I said I was sorry." Her pain-filled eyes made him wonder for a brief moment if he were off base.

"But you never answered my question. You knew at Yosemite, didn't you?"

She nodded and bit her trembling lip.

"Yet you let me kiss you anyway." He shook his head.

"I—I was afraid you'd be angry."

"Angry? If that's all you were afraid of, then—"

"I didn't—didn't realize this would completely jeopardize our relationship. I guess I was naïve." She rested her forehead against her knees. "I found your card in my garbage." Her gaze returned to him. "I guess you decided our relationship was over when you learned the complete truth?" Bitterness dripped from each word.

Thai rubbed the base of his neck. "I think it's all bigger than just this deal with the trip," he muttered, realizing he hadn't been exactly honest with Tong either. Thai had placed more of the blame on Kinsy for their breakup than where blame should squarely rest—with his continual struggles with the past.

"It's still all about my being Vietnamese, isn't it?" she rasped.

"Yeah. Afraid so."

"You said at Yosemite you couldn't make me any promises. . . ."

"Yes. And I'm beginning to see that, no matter how attracted I am to you that there's just too much to overcome. You want to embrace Vietnam—"

"And you don't, and you don't want to be close to anyone who does."

Thai examined the grass between them.

Amidst new sniffles, she rose and walked back to her apartment.

He waited a full fifteen minutes before following and was relieved to find Rob and Chuck in the doorway, saying their good-byes. Thai decided to wait at the bottom of the stairs. He should go up and thank Danielle for dinner, but he didn't relish facing Kinsy again tonight.

Rob bounded down the stairs two at a time, his face covered with a mile-wide grin. Thai recognized the symptoms. The falling was great, but the thud when a guy hit bottom left too many bruises.

"Wow, can she cook! A man could get used to her real quick." Rob patted his stomach, stopping on the bottom step.

"But she's not a blond bimbo, Rob. Kinsy says those are more your type." Thai let the sarcasm fly, wondering if Rob's disappointment would hit as quickly as his had.

"Speaking of Kinsy," Rob studied Thai, "what did you do to her? She came back from your walk sobbing. Went straight to her room. A little early in the relationship for those kind of tears, wouldn't you say? You two should still be in the honeymoon period." Rob headed toward the car.

"We're finished." Thai didn't intend on discussing Kinsy with these guys.

"You broke up with her?" Rob persisted.

Thai nodded, planning to skip any explanation, but Rob's questioning glance prodded him on. "We aren't right for each other."

"Seemed pretty right to me," Rob stated.

"Sometimes reality is different than it seems."

❧

Thai's stony expression had crushed Kinsy. Now, sitting in the middle of her bed, she blotted away the final tears and wondered if she knew him at all. The closing of the front door brought Kinsy out of her room, and she glared at Danielle. "What was that I just sat through?" she demanded, her voice grumpier than intended.

"A dinner party." Danielle guiltily shifted in Kinsy's favorite chair.

Hands on her hips, Kinsy challenged, "You just decided out of the blue to invite three guys you've never met over for dinner—one of them being my ex-boyfriend."

Danielle sighed. "Yes, for your own good. Rob called and said you planned on getting the two of us together—"

"I mentioned that to Thai, but I never said a thing to Rob." Kinsy paced to the other side of the room.

"Well, apparently Thai did. Anyway, he suggested tonight might be a good night because you and Thai had a spat. He hoped to give you two a chance to make up. Since I'm off on Mondays, the plans worked out fine."

"They did?" A bitter chuckle escaped her lips. Kinsy let out a sigh and dropped onto the sofa. "I'm sorry. You're not the enemy, and I know you tried to help."

"I'm sorry too. I shouldn't have meddled," Danielle said, flicking off the TV with the remote.

"Your heart was right. It's just been a lousy day." Beyond weary, Kinsy buried her face in her hands.

"Thai seems nice enough. What happened?"

"I told him this morning our summer trip is to Vietnam. He thinks I arranged the destination—which I guess I did, at least in part. Then, he found out I didn't tell him at Yosemite. It all looks really bad." She sighed. "But the bottom line is that he can't get past his past, and he sees me as a representative of the whole thing."

"I thought he was moving away from all that."

"Yeah, me too." Kinsy didn't want to discuss Thai anymore. Just thinking about him depressed her. "What's your opinion of Rob?"

Danielle's face lit up. "I liked him."

"It appeared the feeling was mutual. Where's Kally?"

"In her room grading her stack of papers."

"I need to call my dad. I'll see you in the morning. Thanks for trying, but next time will you clue me in?"

Danielle nodded, and the two friends exchanged an all-is-well-between-us smile.

Back in her room, Kinsy hit number one on her speed dial. "Hi, Daddy, it's me. I need to let you know things have worsened with Thai. Can I ask Rob to replace him on the trip?"

"Do what you think best."

"Okay." She appreciated his confidence in her. "Thai's not ready to face Vietnam. I see that now. I talked to Steve, and it's too late to change our itinerary. Maybe Rob can clear his schedule and come."

"Fine. Let Thai know he's off the hook, with my blessing. I don't want him to worry about any fallout from this."

"Thanks, Daddy."

"You sound low. Has this affected your relationship with Thai?"

Kinsy tried to swallow the lump in her throat. She answered with a strained "Yes."

"I'm sorry, Pumpkin. I wish I could make everything work out, but Thai's a smart man. He'll figure things out in time, but I'm sure he's struggling right now. Give him a little space."

"I will. Thanks."

"Sleep well."

"You too."

Certain all was lost between her and Thai, Kinsy began to accept that he had indeed used her as a guinea pig and that the experiment had failed. No matter what the future held, Thai wouldn't be a part of her life. Acknowledging the truth didn't make the bearing any easier. She'd lost her heart to a man who viewed her as everything he needed to avoid.

# Chapter 8

Thai hadn't slept well. He'd almost taken a day off, but what for? To sit around brooding about yesterday? Not too appealing. He thought maybe work would take his mind off the rest of his life, but here he sat, and yesterday hung around him like a dark cloak.

He walked to the window. The sunshine didn't dispel his gloom. He returned to his desk just as Kinsy stuck her head into his office.

"Do you have a minute?" she asked.

At his nod, she came in and pushed the door closed. Telltale circles peeked from under her eyes. Even though he didn't plan to, he reacted at the sight of her—first with a pleasurable rush, then with a disappointed pang.

She sat in one of the two burgundy padded chairs across from his desk.

"What do you need, Kinsy?" he asked, more abruptly than he'd intended.

She looked down at her hands, folded in her lap. She drew her lips together in a tight line. For a moment, he thought she might cry.

Then she looked him straight in the eye. "You're off the hook. I found someone else to accompany us on the trip. My dad said to tell you you're appreciated and respected. This will in no way affect your position here at CC or reflect on your record."

He nodded his acknowledgment. Guilt stabbed him in the midsection. He'd wrestled with God all night about this decision. Now free to back out, he wasn't sure what to do.

Kinsy rose to leave. She stopped halfway between the door and the chair she'd just vacated, and turning back to face him, she said, "I'm sorry, Thai. For everything. Please believe me." She didn't even try to hide the anguish in her voice. Her eyes shined with unshed tears.

He looked away, hands gripping the edge of his desk, fighting the urge to go to her. "Kinsy. . ." He glanced up, but she was gone. The rest of his sentence died on his tongue.

In the aftermath of that encounter, Thai decided to talk to Karl; after all, he was not only his boss but also his spiritual shepherd. Of course, he was also Kinsy's father. Thai entered the small alcove where Karl's secretary sat behind her desk. She buzzed Karl and sent Thai right in.

Karl rose from behind his desk, came around it, and shook Thai's hand. Then he and Thai each sat in the two straight-backed chairs.

"Kinsy gave me your message. Thank you," Thai said. He appreciated the compassion on Karl's face.

"I'm sorry this happened. My Kinsy-girl is a selfless person who really does love God with her whole heart. In her fervor, she sometimes plows ahead and runs over a few toes."

Thai's toes were more intact than his crushed heart. "I know she longs to go back so much, she can't understand my hesitancy to face my worst nightmare again. I thought I was clear with her about my never returning. I don't understand why she did this to me." He shook his head.

"She means well, Thai. She really does. She gets an idea and runs straight ahead. Convinced facing your demons would free you, she hoped you'd go for your own sake."

"I know, but that's my decision to make. I may never feel the way she does about my Asian heritage."

Karl nodded. "You're right, and she was wrong. She admits it. Her tendency is to embrace everything about life and expect others to do the same. She hasn't walked in your shoes, so she can't know your pain. Kinsy's had an easy life. Adopted as a baby, no memories of the war, she grew up with love and acceptance." Deep wisdom shone from Karl's eyes.

"I appreciate your understanding." Thai already held the graying minister in high esteem, and he just moved up a notch.

"From the discussions I've had with Kinsy, I know she now realizes the error of her ways," Karl said. "In her excitement to finally fulfill her long-held dream, she figured God provided a great opportunity for you as well, so she didn't mention any of this to Steve, thinking she left the whole situation in God's hands. I don't believe she intended to deceive you, but I know she pushed you between a rock and a cliff."

Thai sighed. "She sure did. I just don't want this to affect my relationship with you, the rest of the staff, or my job in any way."

"I assure you, it won't. I've spent almost three decades reminding Kinsy to slow down and practice patience. She's learning but, like all of us, has room to grow. I do think you should know she tried to give up her dream for your sake."

"What do you mean?" Thai asked.

"When Steve announced the destination, she immediately called him to get the itinerary changed. By then, she realized she'd rather lay down her dream than put you in a spot you weren't ready to be in."

Surprised, Thai asked, "She did?"

Karl nodded. "Unfortunately, too much time had lapsed. The airline tickets were purchased."

"So there's an airline ticket in my name?" Thai had been asking God to confirm His will about this trip, leaning toward being obedient instead of obstinate, if this were indeed more of a God thing than a Kinsy thing. Karl's words brought a stab of confirmation to Thai's heart.

"Don't worry about it, though. Kinsy offered to pay for Rob's ticket since she's responsible for the problem. She wouldn't allow the church to bear the financial burden of her mistake."

*Great!* Thai momentarily wondered if he should call her Saint Kinsy. Yes, she had her flaws, but through Karl's eyes, she seemed pretty special, a selfless woman of integrity. "So Rob's going in my place?"

"He'll know for sure in a couple of days. He's trying to clear his calendar and get everything covered."

"Well, hopefully everything will work out." Thai rose to leave. "Thanks for understanding."

"You're welcome, Thai. Any time." They shook hands.

Thai headed straight for Rob's office, more confident with each step.

"Hey, my man," Thai greeted Rob.

"Thai, so you're still talking to me. After last night I wondered if you'd forgive me for butting into your and Kinsy's relationship."

"Forgiven and forgotten. I know you were only trying to help. Now I need a favor."

"Name it. I guess I owe you big time," Rob replied.

"Will you wait a day before clearing your calendar?"

"Are you thinking about going?"

"I'm experiencing pangs of conviction. I'm spending the rest of the day in prayer and fasting. I don't plan to say anything to anyone else until I'm sure. Especially not Kinsy."

"Does this mean you're going to give her another chance?"

"No, it just means I intend to be certain I'm obeying God. I think Kinsy and I both realize it would never work between us. We're just too different." *And she's still too Asian.* Even if God gave Thai the strength to return to Vietnam, he doubted that he could ever be completely free of his past.

❧

Kinsy drove back to the church after a quick dinner with her roommates. Wednesday evening had arrived and so had their first training for the Vietnam trip. She hadn't seen Thai since yesterday morning, but she had done a lot of soul searching since then.

Thai was right to be disappointed in her. She should have never hidden the truth from him at Yosemite. Finally, Kinsy had admitted that to herself and God. Deep inside, she'd hoped Vietnam would be their ultimate destination. Both of her reasons were purely selfish. The first—she wanted to go, plain and simple. The second—she knew in order for her and Thai to have a future, he needed to face his past. How could he ever love her when he had so many hang-ups about the Vietnamese people?

She'd let go of any hope for a future with Thai. Her heart ached, and her only hope was that he would someday forgive her. Even friendship appeared impossible, and maybe too painful.

Kinsy parked her car close to the youth building where the college, high school, and junior high classrooms were located. Tonight, she and Rob were meeting with the team of ten to start their training. She grabbed her briefcase and walked to the correct room. No one had arrived yet. Placing twelve chairs in a circle, she then laid a handout on each one. The team trickled in one or two at a time. At seven o'clock, Kinsy decided to go ahead and start. Since Rob was only a stand-in, she'd not given him much responsibility.

Taking one of the two empty chairs within the circle, she introduced herself, then each of the students introduced themselves. All the faces were familiar except one. Everyone briefly shared what had drawn them to this trip.

Kinsy glanced at her watch. 7:15. *Where's Rob?* She decided she might as well break the news: Thai wouldn't be part of the team. "Thai—"

"Is running late and apologizes," he blurted, rushing through the door and taking the last chair in the circle. "Tonight I thought I'd share an overview about Vietnam, after Kinsy explains what she needs to about the packets."

Kinsy's mouth fell open. Shock, surprise, amazement, and disbelief all shot through her. Where was the angry, hurt guy she'd left yesterday morning? This fellow looked like a man without a care in the world. He wore his favorite Bears T-shirt and a Bulls cap, and her heart reacted with a painful longing.

"Kinsy? Are you with us?" he asked, lifting his eyebrows.

"Sorry. I guess my mind wandered." She had lost her focus and forgotten her entire mental agenda for this meeting. "Tell you what, why don't you take the floor? I can cover the packets next week. Everyone take them home and study the information. We'll discuss any questions at our next meeting."

They all nodded their agreement.

Thai took over. "Most of the Vietnamese are Buddhists who desperately need Jesus. An underground church meets in homes. Hungry for God's Word, they tear a Bible into many sections, so each person can have a few chapters to read. Then they trade them back and forth, reading them so often they wear out in no time. The point of our trip is to supply the church with more Bibles.

"We'll leave LAX, change planes at Tokyo's Narita International Airport, and end up at the Tan Son Nhut airport in Ho Chi Minh City, better known as Saigon. Pack light because of the Bibles. We're allowed three large suitcases apiece. Two-and-a-half of them will be filled with Bibles, leaving half of a suitcase for all your personal effects."

Kinsy watched Thai, amazed at his metamorphosis. *What was he doing here, and what in the world changed his mind?* He'd apparently studied all the information thoroughly and paid attention to what she'd previously shared.

"We'll actually only leave the airport with the one suitcase—the one filled with half Bibles and half clothes. The other two will be whisked away to places unknown. We're traveling under the guise of a humanitarian aid trip, and our home base will be an orphanage, run by a Christian couple, and situated about ten miles outside of Saigon.

"They'll provide us with cyclos, better known as bikes. Those will be our transportation to visit small villages in the vicinity, under the guise of sightseeing. While in those villages, we'll connect with the contact person for the underground church and bless them with the Bibles."

Kamie's best friend, Lindsay, raised her hand. Her pale blond hair would definitely earmark her as a foreigner. "What would happen if we got caught delivering the Bibles?"

"We are in little danger," Thai assured them. "But the Vietnamese receiving the Bibles could be in grave danger, even face a prison sentence. So we need to present ourselves as model tourists and be wise and careful, for their sakes."

Everyone nodded their understanding.

"My dad said it's really hot there."

"He's right, Justin. The humidity and temperature run neck and neck, so a ninety-degree day with ninety percent humidity isn't uncommon. The summers are hot and wet—wet with rain and soggy with humidity."

"Are you from Vietnam, Thai?" asked Kristen.

"Originally." He glanced at Kinsy and she knew the horrors still plagued him. "As are Kinsy and Kamie."

"Do any of you remember the country at all?" Melissa asked, her almost black hair pulled back into a ponytail.

"I have some memories." Thai paused, pain flashed in his eyes. "I don't think Kamie or Kinsy remember anything. Right, ladies?"

Both nodded.

"Tell us about it and your life there. Maybe share a favorite memory," Kristen requested.

Thai glanced at Kinsy. He'd gone slightly ashen, but he recovered quickly. She wondered if he had any favorite memories.

He cleared his throat and began. "I was almost four. My family lived in the coastal fishing town of Phan Thiet. My father, uncles, grandfather, and many generations before them were fishermen. Year 'round the smell of fish hung in the air. When my mother, brother, Loi, and I moved to Saigon, I missed the aroma of fish almost as much as I missed our family. For me it had been the smell of home. Fourteen of us lived in Grandma's house, a warm place filled with laughter and love.

"Anyway, this memory sticks in my head. Loi, our five cousins, and I walked down the shady avenue from Grandma's toward a kiosk resting under an old tamarind tree. Our sandals crunched on the sand as we went. We all held hands and sang." A faraway look stole over Thai's face. "I was the baby of the group. I remember thinking life just didn't get any better than that. I felt safe, loved, and protected. We each bought a breadfruit milkshake."

He paused, and Kinsy thought she caught sight of the glimmer of tears in his eyes. "A week later, all of them but me, Mama, and Loi were dead." The wooden words held no expression or tone, and the muscle in Thai's jaw tightened.

Everyone in the room gasped and a silence fell over them. Kinsy longed to comfort him in some way but knew only God could really heal and comfort Thai.

"I'm sorry. I didn't mean to shock you. I guess part of our going is facing the pain and destruction this country faced. Some of the people will hate you because you're American. Many believe America deserted them before the war was finished. Most have lived through loss, pain, and devastation. The more you know about their past, the more compassion and care you can show the people."

Amidst respectful silence, Kinsy distributed some Vietnamese language tapes for the team and encouraged them to begin learning the language. After a few more questions, the first training session ended.

Everyone left, and Kinsy gathered her belongings. Thai filed the paperwork in his briefcase. Words of comfort filled her mind, but she had no idea what to say or not to say. She longed to take his hand in hers, squeeze it with compassion, and offer tender expressions of sympathy, but remembering his rejection the last time she reached for him stopped her.

Even "I'm glad you changed your mind" might lead him to believe she gloated, though gloating was the last thing on her mind. There was nothing she regretted more than the pain she'd caused Thai because of this trip. So in silence, they worked side by side returning the chairs to their original places.

❧

Although Kinsy toiled near Thai, hundreds of miles emotionally separated them. When the room was neat and tidy, they shut out the lights and walked outside.

Overwrought, Thai didn't have the strength to explain how he ended up here at the meeting or why he was suddenly back on the team. Instead, he simply said, "I guess I'll see you next Wednesday."

"Guess so," she agreed. Her lip quivered, but she kept her chin high, not giving in to the tears shimmering in her eyes.

The night ended. Kinsy turned right and walked down the sidewalk toward the north parking lot without looking back. She'd not said a thing, though he'd seen a million questions in her eyes. She was hurting. He was hurting, and it didn't appear either would get better. He headed toward his car in the south lot.

During his prayer and fasting yesterday, he had finally accepted facts. God desired for him to face his past, and He wasn't going to let Thai rest easy until he did. Both Kinsy and Tong were right. Sometimes you have to look back before you're free to move into the future. Ready for God to heal him, he knew healing included pain.

He also realized the next couple of months would be the hardest of his life, but once he'd decided to go on this trip, peace flooded his soul. Choosing God's will instead of his own way empowered him. He would get through this, but he needed all his focus and energy on God. He refused to be diverted by Kinsy and his conflicting emotions in regard to her.

# Chapter 9

Throngs of passengers crowded the terminals at LAX the morning of their departure for Vietnam. Thai arrived early, finding the designated meeting place by the ticket counter where they could all check in together. Tong, Lola, and their two children had been visiting for a week and insisted on accompanying him. They wouldn't be flying out for a couple more days and planned to take the kids down to Sea World today after Thai left.

Fascinated by the large, rolling suitcases, one-year-old Thomas held on to them and used them to navigate. He wasn't quite ready to trek off on his own yet. Uncertain whether or not she wanted to be awake this early, three-year-old Sammy sat quietly on Lola's lap.

Thai didn't know for certain if he wanted to be awake this early either. The closer the trip grew, the more nightmares had disrupted his sleep, and last night he'd barely dozed. He spent much of the night in prayer, trying to take captive his thoughts. He reminded himself over and over that God did not give him a spirit of fear.

He spotted Kinsy coming. Both Kally and Danielle were with her. He rose to help them with the suitcases and recalled the final understanding in her eyes when she met Lola and saw how her blond features produced children who weren't strongly Asian. At last she seemed to understand Thai's cry for a blond wife, and the emotional wall between them had grown all the thicker. Except for the training sessions, Thai had avoided her. Yet all night thoughts of Kinsy had mingled with his Vietnam past. . .holding Kinsy, kissing Kinsy, everything about Kinsy.

As he approached them, he noticed her tired eyes. She must not be sleeping well either. They didn't see him because they were laughing and struggling with the big, heavy suitcases.

"Let me help you with those, ladies," Thai offered. Tong was right behind him to carry another one. Kinsy's smile vanished the moment she saw Thai. All emotion left her eyes, as if she'd closed the door of her soul against him.

Thai and Tong each carried one of the large cases back to their destination. The three women managed to tug and slide the last suitcase to the growing pile before Thai could get back to help them.

Thai introduced Kinsy's roommates to his family. The team began drifting in, and Thai and Tong helped with the heavy suitcases. Just as Thai and Tong had rounded up all thirty-six suitcases, Karl and Kettie arrived. Thai checked the suitcases with the porter and gathered everyone. Family and friends accompanied each of the team members, and they created a large huddle.

"Karl plans to share a few parting words with us," Thai announced.

"We're here to dedicate each member of this team to the Lord. May each fulfill the special work He's planned for him. Just like the believers in Acts, I'd like us to lay hands on them, pray for them, and send them on their way."

The team formed a tight circle, with intertwined arms. Everyone moved closer around them, placing their hands on the travelers' backs and shoulders. Peace washed over Thai's weary soul.

After prayer time, everyone said their good-byes to friends and family members. Thai, overwhelmed with uncertainties, hugged his brother tightly. "I love you, Tong."

"I know."

"I still miss Loi, but I'm so grateful God gave me you for a little brother."

Tong hugged him back. "And I love you, Thai. I'll be praying. I sense God's going to do a great work in you while you're there."

"I sense that too, and it terrifies me." Thai chuckled. "I'm not sure why I always dread God's scalpel. After the pain of His surgery, the blessings flow. I just hate the pain."

"Don't we all," Tong said.

Thai bid farewell to his sister-in-law, niece, and nephew, then Karl was his last good-bye.

"I'll be praying for each of you by name," Karl promised, first shaking Thai's hand, then hugging him. "Especially you."

"Thanks, Karl." Thai appreciated his sensitivity.

Thai took an index card from his pocket and called out each name. "Kamie, Lindsay, Melissa, Kim, Kristen, Daniel, Eddie, Justin, Nick, Nate, and Kinsy, it's time." His gaze drifted over each face; the excitement and anticipation he saw warmed his heart. He sensed the Lord's presence with them, and God's peace filled Thai's soul.

"Time to get our boarding passes." They all turned for one last wave to their loved ones standing nearby. Thai smiled at Tong. With his arm around Lola, he held her close to his side. Thai looked forward to the day he had a Lola in his life. Kinsy caught his eye as she ran back to give Kally a last hug. He almost wished she'd been the one.

"Kally is moving to Phoenix to take care of an elderly lady who is like a second mother to her." As they walked toward the security booth, Thai strained to catch Kamie's every word. "Kally lived with her while she was in college. The lady has cancer now and doesn't have a soul to help her. Kally will be gone before we get back. She and Kinsy are very close since they've lived together the past three years. On top of that, Danielle—their other roommate—is getting married."

"Poor Kinsy," Lindsay said with sympathy.

After they passed through security and obtained their boarding passes, they claimed the vacant chairs in the waiting area. Kinsy stood on the other side of the room, and Thai gazed toward the planes on the runway, trying to convince himself that he was better off with Kinsy out of sight. But Thai soon found himself rising and approaching her against the demands of his common sense.

❧

The airport waiting area was crowded. Kinsy made certain all the participants were seated with at least one other member of the team. Then she found an empty chair herself. She closed her eyes. Kally's moving to Phoenix troubled her. Telling her sister good-bye proved difficult. She didn't want to think about her future or Kally's. Both probably faced a tough year.

"Mind if I sit here?" Thai's voice broke into Kinsy's thoughts.

She opened her eyes, and there he stood, looking uncertain as to what her reaction might be. She shrugged. "Suit yourself." She slid as far to the other edge of her chair as she could.

"I heard Kamie say Danielle is engaged."

Kinsy nodded, not even looking in Thai's direction, hoping he'd get the hint. She wasn't interested in idle chatter. The farther away from her he stayed, the happier she'd be.

"Rob?"

Again, she only nodded.

"Wow! He didn't even tell me! They moved quick, didn't they?"

"I guess when you meet the right person, it doesn't take long to figure it out." Thoughts of her and Thai's rocky relationship twisted her words with bitterness.

"And Kally's moving to Phoenix to take care of a friend?"

"For awhile."

A man's voice came over the speaker announcing the boarding of their flight. Thai stood, and their ten charges gathered round.

"Let's move over to a corner for some last-minute reminders," Thai said.

He looked like a mama hen with all her chicks trailing behind. Kinsy brought up the rear.

Thai spoke quietly, so they all surrounded him in a tight circle. "Remember, when we land in Vietnam, Kinsy will lead us through customs. We don't want to give the appearance we're traveling as a group, so mingle with the other passengers. Spread out going through immigration. Don't talk to or look at each other. That's why all our suitcases look very different, so if they catch one, they hopefully won't catch us all."

"What would happen if we got caught going through customs?" Concern laced Kamie's question. Her face paled a shade or two.

"Don't worry. Like I already told you, they'll just confiscate your luggage. Remember, we are more of a threat to the people we meet than to ourselves. We'll just pray our way through. Determine to look and act natural and pray all the way."

As their rows were called for boarding, they all made their way to the gate. After storing her backpack in the overhead bin, Kinsy sat with Kamie and Lindsay. Thai took the seat directly behind her, next to Eddie and Daniel.

"Thai, what happened to your mom and brother?" Eddie asked.

"They were killed in an explosion."

"Where were you?"

He sighed. "Down the block, watching it happen." Pain filled his words, and Kinsy cringed. At last, she had gotten what she wanted. Thai was facing his past. Now, Kinsy wasn't sure if she'd be strong enough to go back to the scene of such devastation.

"How horrible. Sorry, Man."

"Me too," the other participant said.

"Hey, let's find another subject," Thai injected with false cheerfulness. "Did you guys see the game last night?"

The conversation took off on sports. Kinsy quit listening. The engines revved up, and the plane started rolling away from the terminal. They taxied to the runway and waited in line for takeoff.

Her mind returned to Thai. Everything she learned about him only made her love him more. He'd been through so much. *God, please give him a happy life filled with Your blessings. . .and a wife, Lord, a good wife as well. He deserves someone who will understand him far better than I have.*

The plane sped down the runway. Its nose lifted, and Kinsy asked God to hold them in His righteous right hand. Her heart beat a little faster. She was going home!

ঝ

The sports conversation died, and Thai closed his eyes in an attempt to catch up on his sleep. Yet the memories began to play out in slow motion. *Take captive my thoughts,* he reminded himself, only to have his thoughts roam toward Kinsy. Something deep within him yearned for them to find a peace with each other. Her eyes assured him that she was hurting as much as he was. Thai sighed, punched the little pillow he'd received from the stewardess, and tried to find a comfortable position. He prayed about Kinsy and promised God he'd at least offer a token of friendship. Kinsy was special and deserved someone better than a man whose past marred his present.

Thai somehow managed to get a few hours of exhausted, dreamless sleep before changing flights in Tokyo. By the time Vietnam Airlines Flight 742 touched down in Saigon, his adrenaline pumped, and his exhaustion fled. He was back in Vietnam, whether he wanted to be or not. His stomach knotted, yet he was also excited about delivering the Bibles.

When the fasten seatbelt sign shut off, Kinsy rose and grabbed her backpack and headed into the aisle. She glanced in his direction, and her eyes reflected the same fear and exhilaration he was experiencing. He winked at her, and her eyes widened. As she glanced away, Thai didn't take the time to question his spontaneous gesture. Instead, he hoped and prayed she'd get through customs without a hitch.

A few passengers followed Kinsy down the aisle, then Kamie moved into the crowd waiting to disembark. They continued the process until only Thai remained seated. He stood. It seemed like forever since Kinsy disappeared toward the front of the plane.

Thai continued to pray for each of them as they moved ahead to board the shuttle bus. Thai kept his eye on Eddie, Daniel, and Kristen. They were the only team members in his line of vision. He longed to catch a glimpse of Kinsy and know she was safe.

He nodded and smiled to the stewardesses. Both were Vietnamese but not nearly as pretty as Kinsy. For the first time, Thai realized, he had looked at Asian women without the stabbing pain searing his heart. He moved quickly toward the shuttle bus that would carry them to the airport. The team members sat exclusively to themselves, never acknowledging that they knew each other. They unloaded, and Thai again lost sight of his companions. His heart pounded in anticipation of the unknown lying ahead. He continued to pray, and Kinsy weighed the heaviest on his heart.

The man who cleared his papers was curt. Thai moved on to the baggage claim area. He spotted about half of his team, also awaiting luggage, and caught a glimpse of a few others heading toward the baggage X-ray. Finally, Thai's first bag came by; he grabbed it and loaded it on a cart. After snaring the rest of his luggage, he moved toward the baggage X-ray and prayed all the more fervently as he witnessed each member's bags being cleared. At last he followed the team members to the exit.

When Thai left the airport through the glass doors, humid air, hot and thick, closed in around him. His lungs worked harder, and sweat beaded on his forehead. Traffic noises and voices rang loud as he passed through the wall of waiting people.

Off to the left, he spotted the white van which would carry the Bibles to their planned destination.

"You last one? Number twelve?" the driver asked in broken English as Thai approached with his luggage.

"Yes," he replied, and the driver heaved the luggage into the van.

Thai smiled. Gratefulness welled up in his chest. The whole dozen of them had safely arrived! *Thanks, Lord, and please enable the rest of the smuggling to go this smoothly.* The driver slammed the van door and crawled behind the steering wheel. Thai watched as the van pulled away from the curb and into traffic. He prayed for each of the almost one thousand Bibles they'd smuggled in. *May each one fall into the hands of a hungry Christian and not into the wrong hands.*

Thai looked around, taking in the sights and sounds of his homeland. A lump rose in his throat. Emotions he'd buried twenty-six years ago bubbled just below the surface. *God, we need You so much. Protect our team. Carry me through the days ahead. Heal my heart. And somehow help me sort through all this confusion over Kinsy.*

He walked across the parking lot, following the directions to where the orphanage van waited to whisk them away. When he spotted the team standing beside the light blue van, he jogged the rest of the way, anxious to hug each one of them.

"We made it!" he stated the obvious. He pulled Nate and Nick into a hug. "We made it!" Relief washed over him, and the apprehension over customs faded into the past.

"Thai," Kinsy said from behind him. He turned and fought the urge to hug her as well. "This is Cadeo and Lan. They run the orphanage." He shook Cadeo's hand, then remembered to bow low. *It's paramount that in your ignorance you don't give offense* is what the literature Steve had sent to the team said. He also bowed low to greet Lan. They both looked close to his age.

"Welcome, *ban*, or friend," Cadeo said in English. "You are most honored guest, and you are also Vietnamese?"

Thai's defenses rose. He almost shouted, *I'm an American!* Instead he nodded his agreement. He hated that question but hid his distaste. He'd spent his life correcting people. Now was not the time to continue in that vein.

Cadeo invited Thai to sit in the front of the van with him. "Lan and Kinsy will enjoy visit."

Everyone climbed in, finding a spot. As they pulled out of the airport, Thai's stomach knotted tighter. Things looked familiar, yet unfamiliar. He'd forgotten how green the countryside was. Stray vendors here and there sold food from baskets. Billboards dotted the skyline advertising familiar products like Honda, IBM, and Coca-Cola.

The streets were crazy, people honking, yelling, and making obscene gestures. Most intersections bore no traffic signs or signals, so the right of way went to the most daring and persistent. Thai gripped the handle above his door, praying all the way. "This is nuts," he commented. At each intersection, people, bikes, scooters, jeeps, ox carts, trucks, and animals jockeyed for position.

"We barrel through," Cadeo said confidently, barely missing a woman on a bike.

"Why isn't she wearing a helmet?" Thai asked.

Cadeo chuckled. "People here can't even afford eyeglasses, and you wonder about helmets? They cost sixty American dollars—twice what a teacher earns in a month. It's too hot anyway. No one would wear them, even if they could afford them. It's not surprising that head injury is the number-one cause of death here in the city."

A man on a scooter glared at Cadeo as he fought him for the right of way. Neither backed down, and Thai wondered if the man had a brain since their van would mash his scooter into the ground. That made no difference. He insisted on going first, and Cadeo swerved at the last second to avoid flattening him.

The victor moved ahead, already engaged in another battle of the wheels with a taxi. "Driving in Saigon is a contest of the will," Cadeo stated. "It's part of the Vietnamese way of life."

Thai remembered in amazement how he and Loi ran through the crowded streets, only now they seemed more crowded and louder. With painful clarity, he saw two little boys, traipsing through the town like they owned the place. Pain shot through him. *Loi, I miss you so much!* His eyes burned, and swallowing proved impossible.

## Chapter 10

The van crunched over the gravel drive leading to the old two-story building housing the orphanage. Kinsy's heart pounded. This worn building, or Lan's parents, might hold the key to her past. Anticipation fought with fear. On shaky legs, Kinsy rose from her seat.

Thai offered his hand to help her down. She accepted. His touch sent even more emotions reeling within her. "You okay?" he spoke softly near her ear. His warm breath against her neck caused goose bumps to shoot up her spine.

She disliked needing him, but a part of her longed to collapse against him and let his strength be her own. He tightened his hold on her hand as if he'd read her mind. Kinsy smiled up at him. He blurred slightly, and she swallowed hard.

The slamming of a door brought her attention back to the orphanage. About ten smiling, shouting children bounded toward them. A small girl got knocked down in the process. No one stopped to help her; they just skirted her and kept going until they reached Cadeo.

Thai ran and picked up the crying girl. He held her close and kissed her cheek. His tenderness touched Kinsy. He said something, and the little girl laughed; her braids bobbed up and down. He carried her toward the van, and she rubbed her eyes with her fists.

"Kinsy, will you hold her while I help Cadeo and the boys with the luggage?" He tried to pass the child to Kinsy, but the little girl wrapped her arms tightly around Thai's neck, refusing to let go.

"Cai, are you okay?" Lan asked.

The little girl nodded.

"Cai, this is Mr. Thai and Miss Kinsy. They've come to help us for a little while."

"Do the children speak English?" Kinsy asked, surprised.

"Since many of them are adopted by families from the U.S., we only speak English here at the orphanage. They learn Vietnamese as a second language when they start school," Lan said.

"Cai, I love your braids," Kinsy told her. The little girl smiled and touched her hair. She was an adorable child—sincere brown eyes, a pug nose, and a rosebud outh. "Would you like to come show me your house while Mr. Thai carries in y suitcase?"

Cai looked at Thai, then back at Kinsy. Kinsy held out her arms. Cai hesitated, oking at Thai again.

"I'll come get you as soon as I'm done," he promised. "Miss Kinsy's a very nice dy." He looked at her with warm eyes.

Kinsy swam in a pool of confusion as his recent wink plagued her memory. *hy are you doing this to me?* she wanted to blurt out. *I thought any chances between were over.*

Cai finally said, "You can put me down now."

Both Thai and Kinsy laughed. He put her down and squatted at her level. You're not such a little girl after all. How old are you?" Thai asked.

Cai held up four fingers. "And a half," she added proudly.

"How about a tour while the guys unload?" Lan asked Kinsy.

"Sounds great."

"I'll lead," Cai announced.

"Come on, girls, and I'll show you around," Lan called. She followed Cai, with insy and the five girls on her heels.

The orphanage, shabby on the outside, was in better shape on the inside than insy expected. They housed about fifty children in two large dorm-type rooms. he children decorated their own spaces. Cai proudly led them to her purple rea. She'd painted the wall purple, her quilt was purple with white daisies, and he had a purple dresser.

"I bet I know your favorite color," Kinsy said.

"I like pink too," Cai informed her. "What color do you like, Miss Kinsy?"

"Pink—definitely pink." She winked at Cai.

"I love the way you've managed to let each child capture his own individuality a dorm-like setting," Kinsy commented, running her hand over Cai's silky hair.

"I'm just following my mom's lead," Lan said. "She wanted each child to know e was unique and special to God. She helped them find and develop their gifts. try to do the same."

"Sounds like your mom's a wise lady."

"She is."

"How did you meet Cadeo?" Kinsy asked as they toured the boys' dorm. She ved a good love story.

"He grew up here in the orphanage. I fell in love with him when I was about ight. My mom insisted he must feel the same way, but you couldn't prove it by ne. He teased me unmercifully, pulled my pigtails, and hit me every chance he ot. Mom said that's how ten-year-old boys show affection.

"He was almost adopted at twelve, by a Canadian couple. I cried myself
sleep every night, begging God not to let him go. A couple of years later I f
horrible and selfish for cheating him out of a family, so I confessed to him wh
I'd done." Lan's eyes misted over.

"He told me he'd prayed the same prayer. He reached out and gently ran h
fingers over my cheek. 'I would have come back for you,' he'd said, and from th
day on, I knew he was my soul mate. He never hit me or pulled my hair agai
Instead, he started being gentle and thoughtful." Lan grinned. "How about yo
and Thai? How did your love story begin?"

Kinsy looked at her dirt-smudged Keds. "Thai and I aren't. . ."

"I'm sorry. I just assumed," Lan stammered. "I mean the way you two look
each other. Anyway, what do you think of the old place?" Lan asked as they con
pleted the tour.

"It's wonderful," Kinsy said, trying to stifle a yawn.

"You must be exhausted after such a long flight and many time changes."

"I am. It's about three in the morning back home."

"And here it is almost dinner time. Are you hungry?"

Kinsy nodded. Their last plane meal was hours behind her.

Lan stepped outside and rang a large dinner bell. Children came from eve
direction. Lan led her to a huge room filled with tables and chairs. Along o
wall, a counter laden with huge urns of soup, bowls, and spoons beckoned ther

Cadeo and Thai entered with the five boys. Thai's gaze caught hers. He smile
and her heart responded with gladness. She smiled back, wishing he loved he
As much as she planned to treat him with cool disdain, she couldn't pull it off f
more than a few minutes. He walked toward her, Cai's hand in his.

"How's everything?" he asked.

"Fine. How about you?"

"Grab a hand for prayer," Cadeo said loudly over the dull roar of conversatio
Thai took Kinsy's, and Kinsy reached for the hand of a little boy about ten. H
glared at her, said something hateful in Vietnamese, and moved away. Stunne
Kinsy didn't understand. Then all the children moved away from her, and sl
recalled the training material mentioning Vietnamese prejudice against Amerasian

Lan stepped up and took Kinsy's hand, and Cadeo blessed the food. Kinsy did
hear his words, though, because she was so hurt by the children's rejection.

"I'm sorry, Kinsy," Lan whispered after Cadeo said amen. "Some of the childre
have learned prejudices at school. I will have Cadeo speak to them later tonight

"But I'm half Vietnamese," Kinsy said, as if that would somehow end genera
tions of ingrained attitudes.

Thai still held her hand, gently massaging it with his thumb. Through blurre vision, she watched Cai run off and join the other children in line to get her soup. Two young girls spooned the soup into the bowls for the children.

"The problem is you are also part American. Many Vietnamese hate the Americans for leaving us and blame them because we lost the war and our freedom. The children pick up these attitudes from peers and teachers."

"Yes, I know," Kinsy whispered. Somehow she had naïvely assumed that because she was coming to help, the children would accept her.

❧

Anger sparked in Thai. No one should be so rude to Kinsy. He thought about grabbing the kid by the scruff of his neck and setting him straight. The hurt clouding her eyes only intensified his protective instincts. Thai wrapped his arm around her shoulders. "Cadeo will take care of it." He led her toward the chow line. "Let's eat. I'm starved."

"Hope you like rice and catfish soup," Lan said from right behind them.

"I think I do," Thai said, as they took their place in line. The smell of the soup caused a memory to surface. He could see his grandmother in her kitchen, cooking for the family. A longing flooded him for those carefree days of childhood.

Kinsy got her bowl and spoon, taking a chair as far away from anyone else as possible. Thai knew she made a choice to avoid another scene. He took his food and joined her. Cai got up from her seat across the room and sat on Kinsy's other side. Grateful, he didn't know if Cai calculated the move or not, but Kinsy needed a little love and acceptance about now.

After dinner, Cadeo said, "We'll show you to your rooms."

"What about cleanup?" Kinsy asked.

"Tonight you are our guests—our very tired guests. Tomorrow will be soon enough to work."

Cai kissed both Thai and Kinsy good night. He found himself longing for the freedom to also kiss Kinsy and wish her sweet dreams. Not only had she been rejected by the children, she had also been rejected by him.

Lan led the ladies to their room, and watching Kinsy walk away pulled at Thai's heart. All those feelings from Yosemite resurfaced. Thai and the boys followed Cadeo to their room. Cadeo passed out oscillating fans to all six of them. "These not only help with the heat, but they also help keep the mosquitoes away."

Each boy claimed one of the six cots, setting their fans on the small tables beside where they'd sleep. Thai grabbed the last one and placed his things on the empty cot near the window.

"Sleep well," Cadeo said on his way out the door. "Tomorrow we'll tour Saigon."

Thai's heart felt as if it dropped all the way to his feet. Perhaps they would tread upon the last place he'd ever seen his mother. A lump rose in his throat.

"Then we'll get busy distributing those Bibles and doing some repair work around here. I'm so glad you came. You have no idea what a blessing you are to Lan and me."

"Good night," they all clamored at once as Cadeo shut the door.

Though he was exhausted, sleep evaded Thai. After a fitful night, the breakfast bell woke him with a start. Thinking about touring Saigon today caused his heart to lodge in his throat. Was he ready to walk her streets again? Truth be known, he didn't think he'd ever be ready. Nonetheless, the heavenly insistence suggested that God was ready. *I can do everything through Him who gives me strength.* The verse that Kinsy quoted at Half Dome echoed through his mind. *If she could face her fear of that mountain, I can face Saigon*, he thought with new resolve.

"First, we'll take Ly Thai To Boulevard," Cadeo said as they all loaded into the van. "It's now one of Saigon's major thoroughfares. Then we'll walk in order to get a feel for the life here."

The humidity hung around Thai like a heavy cloak. His damp clothes clung to his wet skin. On their drive, they passed tons of minuscule eateries. The streets were sometimes cluttered with discarded trash, crowded with people everywhere, and loud with the noises of cars and the drone of voices. He spotted a group of children playing soccer with a tennis ball. They seemed oblivious to the danger of the nearby traffic, just as he and Loi had been.

Once Cadeo parked the van, they strolled by numerous dark, thin women lining the streets, selling various sundries from kiosks and baskets. Every sight, every sound resurrected surreal memories that hurled themselves through Thai like rain pelting a huge jungle leaf during a Vietnamese summer. He seemed suspended between the past and present, not able to fully experience either. An old woman who reminded him of his grandmother peddled sweet rice and proved the catalyst that fully hurled him into the past. Suddenly, he was four again, and his grandmother had just nabbed him by the collar for running through the house. But Thai had only been following Loi.

Finally, his grandmother released him, and Thai joined his brother on the street. In an alley, they stopped to watch a mother and daughter fry dough cakes, wrapping them in dirty newspaper to sell. The past merged with the present, and Thai's stomach rolled at the thought of eating something prepared in such filth. But he pictured himself and Loi doing exactly that, spending the money Mama gave them on street food like banana rice cakes, fried bread, or rice porridge.

The past faded into a distant blur as the poverty overwhelmed Thai. Beggars spotted the street, and one undernourished boy stood out in the crowd. Time no longer existed, and Thai's steps faltered. Familiar-looking eyes stared back at him. *Loi,* his heart screamed, but his mind reasoned away the possibility. Tears welled up, rolling freely down his cheeks.

"Thai?" Kinsy spoke from right next to him. She laid her hand on his arm. He grabbed it like a lifeline, squeezing tight.

The little boy moved on through the crowd, and Thai decided he must chase him down. He needed to help him! "Wait," Thai called, knowing the child most likely couldn't understand. "I have to find him, Kinsy," he said before sprinting off.

"Thai, wait!" He dismissed her cry. He had to find the boy, and waiting would lessen his chances. Kinsy shouted something else, but her words dropped from his mind in the face of his heart's insistent demands. The boy turned down a dingy alley, and Thai hesitated before following. This alley might very well be the one where the soldier gave him the lighter. His stomach clenched, and his determination to find the boy overruled his aversion. Finally, he noticed the child at the alley's opening, begging food from a cart in the next street. The woman turned him away, shaking her head.

Breathless, Thai slowed his pace and neared. The boy looked skeptical, wary. Calling to mind the words from the language tapes, Thai struggle to phrase his sentence in the Vietnamese language. "I want to help you." He reached in his pocket and pulled out all the *dong* he'd brought with him for the day. He wished for the rest of his money hidden in his suitcase at the orphanage.

"For you and your family." He held out the notes.

The young boy looked from the *dong*, to Thai, and back to the money again. Shock registered on his face, then gratitude. He slowly took the notes, then bowed. His voice trembled with his thanks as he stuffed the bills in his pocket.

"Take this too," Thai said, offering him a Vietnamese New Testament.

The boy accepted Thai's gift, turned, and ran. He stopped once, waving a last good-bye before rounding a corner, and he was gone.

Thai pivoted to return to where he'd left the team and bumped into Kinsy. Instinctively, he pulled her into his arms, and they clung to one another, both crying, for the country of their births and its people.

❧

With Thai's arms around her, Kinsy knew they both experienced many of the same emotions. Returning was nothing like she'd expected, much more painful and less joyous than she had anticipated. Thai loosened his hold on her. She looked into his watery, red eyes and despised herself for the part she had played in causing him to even be on this trip. No wonder he erupted when he learned that she had hidden their trip's destination. Kinsy marveled that he would even speak to her.

"He looked like Loi," Thai explained. He took a deep breath as if hoping to exhale the memory. "He could be me, Kinsy. . .or you. How were we the ones lucky enough to leave, yet unlucky enough to lose everything before we did?"

She only shrugged and shook her head. She had no answers for him, just her own questions.

"This is my country. These are my people. I wanted to forget, but how can I?" He glanced upward, toward the alley walls. "This might even be the very alley where that soldier gave me the lighter that blew up my mother and brother." The tears trickled onto his cheeks, and Kinsy reeled with the force of his words. For once in her life, she didn't push ahead of God or pry for more information.

"How can I help my people? What can I do to make their lives better?"

Her own feelings mirrored Thai's. Her tears flowed again. She cried for the people who shared her ancestry, she cried for this man she'd grown to love more deeply each day, and she cried for herself.

Thai tenderly draped his arm around her and led her back toward the main street. Her vision still hazy from the tears, she leaned against him, letting him guide her. Thai stopped at the place where he'd last seen their team. "I wonder how we'll ever find them?"

"Cadeo said we'd meet at the van at three. He took the kids to eat at one of the approved places on our list, then to do some shopping. I think he sensed we both needed some time to assimilate being back here. I tried to tell you just before you ran, and that's why I came after you. The team had already departed, and I didn't want to be completely alone in this city all afternoon."

He squeezed her shoulders in brief hug. "I'm sorry. Seeing that little boy made me forget everything else. I would have never consciously left you alone here."

"I know," she assured him.

"Suddenly, I'm famished. How about you?"

"Famished and emotionally spent. Sitting down for awhile would be nice."

"There's a café." Thai pointed across the street. "What do you think?"

"It looks safer than most of these street vendors. Let's check our list." Kinsy shuffled through her backpack. "Yeah, the place is Steve-approved."

Thai took her hand and led her through traffic and into the small, dark building. He held out her chair at a table for two in the corner and took the seat across from her. A young boy came over to take their order. Staring at her, he muttered something in Vietnamese, and quickly left.

Thai's jaw clenched. Kinsy instinctively knew that, considering the boy's glare and derogatory tone, he had said something about her.

"I'm not very hungry after all. Can we leave?" Kinsy stood and hoped to avoid any sort of scene.

An older man approached them. Kinsy bowed. He said something to Thai in Vietnamese while staring at her. Thai's eyes reflected his intent to defend her. She laid a restraining hand on his arm.

"We're leaving." She forced a smile, but more tears burned the back of her eyes. *Thai must think all I do is cry.*

The war Thai fought within battled across his face, but he finally nodded his acceptance of her decision. His pulsating jaw revealed his anger, but he remained outwardly calm, bowing to the man before they left.

Not a word crossed his lips as they strode down the street. He led her to a rusty table, near an alley, and they silently nibbled on a bag of trail mix from Thai's backpack.

"This stuff is a far cry from what we would have eaten. Are you disappointed that I wanted to leave the café?"

He reached across the table and laid his hand on hers. "No, I'm just angry at them for being so rude."

"It doesn't matter, Thai."

"It does to me." He paused as if weighing an important decision. "When I was in junior high, kids who'd been my friends suddenly turned on me because I was different. They called me Yellow-skinned Asian and sometimes even Slant-eyes."

"But Vietnamese eyes aren't really slanted."

"I know. But that didn't matter. They chanted, 'Go home where you belong.' When the kid back there called you half-breed, I wanted to deck him, for your sake, for mine, and for every other kid who's ever been picked on."

Touched by his protective attitude, she also experienced a dawning of fresh understanding about his past. Part of his desire for a blond wife had more to do with protection than prejudice. He intended to shelter his future offspring from what he'd been through. A new spark of respect flared within Kinsy.

A stray dog rooting under their table caught her attention. "He's hoping we dropped a scrap of food. Poor, hungry fellow." Thai dropped a handful of the trail mix near his nose.

"Can I bum some *dong* until later? I gave all mine to Loi's look-alike."

Kinsy granted his request.

"I'll be right back," Thai said. He returned with a fairly long bone. "Ox tail for this old bag of bones." Thai gave it to the dog and patted him on the head. "Cadeo said people don't eat dog much anymore."

"Good to hear." She smiled, loving him for spending money on the poor old thing. "I couldn't bring myself to ever even taste dog."

"My grandmother said the same thing. No matter how hungry she was, she'd never cook or eat dog meat." He smiled tenderly. "You would have liked my grandmother. She was a spunky little thing, devoted to the care and feeding of her clan."

"I'm sure I would have. Lan said many women still dedicate their lives to cooking, cleaning, and meeting the needs of their children, grandchildren, and extended family, especially in the smaller villages."

He nodded. "Have you ever thought about adoption?" Thai's question came out of nowhere.

"Of course I have, since I'm adopted."

"No, I mean about adopting children yourself someday?"

She nodded. "Especially after meeting Cai. I wish I could offer her a family now."

He shot her his heart-melting smile, full of incredulity. "I had the same thought."

# Chapter 11

The next day, fear and anticipation rose within Kinsy. The village they pedaled toward, Cau Hai, was the village her mother hailed from. Today her lifelong dream would become reality. On this very day, she would meet some of her extended family. Anh's daughter was coming home.

Between a letter left for her at the orphanage, some facts the McCoys gathered, and an old file Lan possessed, Kinsy knew a few things about her past. Her grandfather, Bay Le, was a chief and respected elder in the remote village. Her father, an American soldier, died protecting the village. Her mother died birthing her. Now Kinsy was pedaling through a foreign land, going home.

The roads were rough and bouncy, but the beautiful terrain made up for the bumpy ride. The foliage was as green as emeralds, and jungle-type plants grew in abundance. Kinsy's heart soared. She prayed her grandfather would be one of the Christians in the village expecting the Bibles. Since none of the team were avid bikers, they rode awhile and walked awhile. Everyone pedaled in silence, a bit nervous since each carried a pack full of smuggled Bibles and some Bible tracts with them.

Kinsy knew this moment was orchestrated by God, an answer to her lifetime prayers. As they biked off the beaten path, every fiber of her being balked against the strain. When they stopped for lunch, she'd never experienced such relief at getting off a bike; the seat and her bottom lacked compatibility.

"Only a couple more miles," Thai said, looking at the map Cadeo drew. After lunch they rested for about half an hour, then started on their way. Kinsy barely got a bite of food down. Excitement tied her stomach in knots, making eating next to impossible.

When they arrived at the small village, Thai asked for Nghia Hoa. He followed the directions to a shack with walls made from palm branches and a straw roof. An older Vietnamese gentleman, with thinning white hair, greeted Thai and invited the dozen team members into his home. Weeping when they began unpacking the Bibles, Nghia held each one like a fragile crystal vase. Then Thai helped him carry them to a secret hiding place somewhere out back.

Nghia invited them to sit on straw mats, where he served them sweet smelling banana rice cakes and Coca-Cola to drink. Smiling proudly, he told Thai he'd saved his Coke for special American guests. Thai roughly interpreted what Nghia said, understanding some, but not all.

"Most in this village very poor. American churches send shortwave radios, but most stolen before hear God's word. You work hard to get God's Word into hands and ears of people."

Again Nghia got teary, sorrow etching itself across his lined face. "Bless your faithfulness." He prayed for their group. "Now go. I sell refreshment to travelers as a cover, but none stay long, so neither can you."

Kinsy had Thai ask about her grandfather, Bay Le. Nghia looked concerned but gave them directions to the Le home. "He's not a friend of God's people," Thai translated the pastor's warning. "Be careful not to expose the underground church or my work to him."

Deeply disappointed by the news, Kinsy desperately desired her grandfather to be a part of the Christian movement here in this village. Kinsy touched the New Testament in her pocket, hoping to present it to the old man as a gift. Now maybe she shouldn't since they'd been seen with Nghia. The team promised him they'd be careful not to put him at risk.

As they walked their bikes towards her grandfather's, Thai asked the team to wait out front. He would accompany Kinsy to the door. He gave her hand a quick squeeze, and she whispered, "Pray for me."

"I have been all day," he assured her.

Thai knocked, and a young male servant opened the door. Her grandfather lived in a much nicer and larger place than the pastor did.

They bowed low. "May we speak to Bay Le?" Thai asked in his rough Vietnamese. The servant said, "Mr. Le does not accept visitors."

When Thai translated, Kinsy said, "Tell him I'm his granddaughter, Anh's child." The servant nodded and closed the door.

"Is he coming back?" Kinsy asked.

"I think so."

Her heart pounded. Meeting her family would not be easy, if even possible. *God, please make a way.* She rubbed her palms against her pant legs.

❧

An uneasiness crept up Thai's spine even before the door opened. A stooped, white haired man glared at Kinsy. His cold eyes sat deep in a wrinkled face. "You liar and fraud," the old man shouted. "I have no daughter, only sons. Do not ever insult my family name again." The old man spit on Kinsy, called her a half-breed, then slammed his door.

Stunned, Thai removed his outer denim shirt to wipe the spit and tears off her face. He drew her away from the house. "Let's get out of here."

Kinsy stopped halfway to the bikes. An ashen pallor covered her face, blighting her cheerful demeanor. "Tell me what he said," she whispered.

Thai didn't want to repeat the words, knowing she'd only feel worse, but he knew he must. He repeated the truth as gently as possible.

"Why would he lie?"

"I don't know." Thai knotted his shirt around his waist and led her toward the bikes. "Let's go home."

Kamie hugged Kinsy when they got back to the group. "Are you okay?"

"Not yet," Kinsy said in a raspy whisper, "but I will be."

They climbed on their bikes; nobody said much. *Why, God? Why did you let that happen to her?* Thai asked as they pedaled back toward the orphanage. Immediately, he thought of 2 Corinthians 4:10, "Through suffering, these bodies of ours constantly share in the death of Jesus so that the life of Jesus may also be seen in our bodies" (NLT).

How many times had Thai taught on those verses? As we suffer, we identify more with Christ and become more like him. Even though he desired Kinsy to grow in Christlikeness, he hated for her to hurt. But as humans, hurt was inevitable. Then the truth struck Thai. God allowed his suffering for the exact same reason. Already, Thai was experiencing a certain release from his past. But could he relinquish all his sorrow and let God make him whole?

୬

Heartbroken, Kinsy pedaled on, aching to the very marrow of her bones. A scooter roared past them and stopped. Thai rode up beside the petite woman wearing the pointed hat many of the Vietnamese women wore. He dismounted, and the rest of the team stopped a few feet back. Kinsy heard the woman say, "I am Chi, Anh's cousin." Chi's English was coarse but understandable.

Kinsy got off her bike and went to the woman, taking her hands. After being spit on, she wasn't sure she should be so trusting, but this woman appeared to be an ally. "I am Kinsy McCoy. Anh was my mother. She died giving me life."

Chi's eyes shifted. "Anh not dead. Lives in Vung Tau."

Stunned by the woman's fear-filled words, Kinsy said, "No. My mother Anh Le is dead. The note left with me at the orphanage said so."

"Excuse me, Kinsy," Thai interrupted, "we'll be over there under those palms." He pointed toward his destination. "Holler if you need me."

"Will you stay?" She already needed him.

Thai nodded and sent the participants off, but he stayed next to Kinsy.

"I wrote the note. I know what it said." Shame wove itself through Chi's words and across her face.

Kinsy's knees felt like wet noodles. She reached for Thai to steady herself. "What are you saying? I don't understand."

Chi sighed. "My Uncle Bay convinced me it would be best. He is an important chief in our village. His daughter having child by American soldier embarrassed the family. He disowned her. He did not lie today when he say he have no daughter. As far as he's concerned, he does not."

"How do you know what he said to me?"

"My pastor, Nghia, sent for me and told me your story. Then I went to my uncle's, and his servant disclosed what I had already guessed. Your grandfather— my uncle—rejected you. I am sorry."

Kinsy nodded. "You are a Christian?" She was almost afraid to ask. What if this were some sort of trap?

"Yes, I follow Christ. Only the past few years, though, as you must already presume."

"Does my mother follow Christ?" Her biological mother lived somewhere in this country! She was alive!

Pools of sorrow swam in her ebony eyes. "No, she does not."

"My grandfather?" she asked, fairly certain of the answer.

Chi shook her head.

"Did my mother not want me?" Kinsy asked, trying to piece it all together.

"Very much. She love your father. When he was killed, she wanted his child very much. Then your grandfather learned the truth and sent her away. He is powerful man, and he made certain Anh believed you died at birth. He arranged with the doctor for me to take you to the orphanage. I lied and told them your mother died."

Kinsy leaned against Thai, no longer having the strength to stand. "Why?"

"Your grandfather believed she deserved to lose the child because of the shame and disgrace she caused him."

"Does my mother still think I am dead?"

"I told her the truth after I become a follower of Christ. She wept and threw me out. I have not seen her since. But she is only about 120 kilometers from Saigon. Perhaps you can visit. Perhaps you can beg her for my forgiveness."

Kinsy hugged Chi. "I will. I promise. Thank you, Chi. Thank you."

With a furrowed brow, Chi asked, "For what do you thank me?"

"For coming after me today and telling me the truth." Kinsy hesitated. "Will my mother want to see me?"

"Very much. She long to see you very much." Chi smiled. "Even though she hates me for what I did, she's happy you live in beautiful, free America."

Chi and Kinsy hugged and cried. Kinsy promised to write her new grandcousin, as they are called here in Vietnam. She took the paper with Chi's address, tucked it in her front pocket, and bid her good-bye. Kinsy watched Chi ride away on her scooter, bouncing along the washboard road.

"I have a mother!" She turned to Thai, knowing there was no one she'd rather share this moment with than him. She loved him with all her heart. She loved him enough to let him go. She loved him enough to wish for all his hopes and dreams to come true, even the ones excluding her from his life forever.

He smiled. "You're amazing." Hugging her close for a brief moment, he then whistled for the kids, motioning for them to join him and Kinsy. Soon they all pedaled toward the orphanage. Kinsy nearly floated, no longer dwelling on her sore leg muscles. "My birth mother is alive!" she repeated on the ride home.

In the evening after dinner and cleanup, Kinsy joined Thai out on the porch. Just seeing her, having her near brought him pleasure. The rest of the team read stories to the kids and helped tuck them into bed, while he and Kinsy gazed at the star-filled, inky sky.

"Feels good to get our first set of Bibles delivered," Thai commented.

"Sure does," she agreed.

A breeze played with her hair, and he wished for the freedom to do the same. During their trip, the chains of Thai's past seemed to be dropping away from his soul, link by link. Yet, a haunted little boy was still locked away in the recesses of his heart.

"And I have hope for my grandfather to someday find Christ, since there is an active, growing church right within his village."

"And both you and Chi will be praying," Thai said. "I'll pray too." He paused before adding, "I spoke to Cadeo and requested the next two days off and the use of the van. He gave his blessing for me to drive you to Vung Tau. He'll keep the rest of the team busy with chores around here. I even called your dad and made sure we got his blessing. I hope you don't mind."

Grateful, almond-shaped eyes gazed into his. She smiled slightly. "I don't mind at all."

# Chapter 12

Midmorning rain pelted the van. Drops beat on the green leaves of the surrounding jungle plants. Water gushed from a gray sky and reduced the road to a series of endless brown puddles.

Kinsy remained silent as Thai concentrated on the slick, wet road. On Highway 1, a concrete divider kept the chaos going in the same direction. Thai turned onto a smaller road heading out toward the coast. Shanties lined the road. The terrain was flat. Rice paddies, swampy and green, and fruit groves filled the land on either side of them. The mountains stood regally, far off on the horizon behind them.

Kinsy wondered how different her life might have been had her Vietnamese grandfather not interfered. She wouldn't be a McCoy or have ever met Thai. She might not have even ever met Christ. Kinsy clung to God's sovereignty, knowing He knew from the beginning of time how her life would turn out.

They passed a strip of settlements. "Fisherfolks' homes," Thai said. The huts built with grass roofs sat on stilts raising them high off the water below. Driving by a tiny, grandmotherly woman with wrinkled hands and face, Kinsy wondered what her own grandmother Le might look like. She thought back to the grandfather she met just yesterday and prayed for him again.

They rolled past some ancient buildings with paint peeling off in large chunks. Windows were thrown open wide, probably in hopes of catching a cool breeze off the sea. Children. Everywhere children ran and played.

"That was my life," Thai said, nostalgia filling his voice. "Loi and I ran freely through the village streets with our cousins." The ache in the words pierced her heart.

Thai followed Chi's directions to the home of Anh Le—the home of Kinsy's mother. The small beach cottage sat apart from the large front house. After parking the van, they walked side by side to door. He touched her arm briefly as if to say, *I'm here if you need me*, and she squeezed his hand in appreciation. Her stomach knotted, her hands trembled, and her pulse accelerated. A film of sweat dampened her palms.

Thai knocked on the door. Sucking in a deep breath, Kinsy held it. A woman with dyed red hair and excessive makeup answered their knock. Kinsy's heart dropped in disappointment. This wasn't the motherly image she expected.

"We're looking for Anh Le," Thai said in English.

"Who wants her?" the woman asked in near flawless English.

"I do. I have come from America to visit her," Kinsy answered.

The woman's face softened, but she didn't let her guard down completely. "Why would you come so far to visit Anh Le?"

Kinsy knew this was her mother. She'd seen the hope flash in her eyes when she'd mentioned America. She bit her bottom lip, afraid to say the words. She took a deep breath. "I am her daughter, Kinsy McCoy."

The woman's eyes filled with tears, and she leaned against the door jam. She tenderly looked at Kinsy, and tears ran freely down both of their faces. Kinsy reached to the woman, and she clung to her.

"I am Anh—your mother," she whispered in a broken voice.

Kinsy moved toward her, pulling her tiny mother into her arms. She had no idea how long they stood there, hugging, crying, and laughing. Her mother pulled back, taking her hand. "Please come in."

Kinsy looked back at Thai. His eyes glistened with tears as well, and she knew he must be longing for his own mother. "This is my *ban*, Thai. This is my mother," Kinsy said with pride, "Anh Le."

"Welcome, Kinsy's friend. It is my pleasure to have you both in my home."

The cottage perched on the edge of a cliff over the beach. Her mother led them out onto the balcony jutting out over the water. Waves lapped against the rock embankment a few feet below. Two coconut palms shaded the side of the house.

"It's beautiful here," Kinsy whispered.

"It's my sanctuary." Her mother turned away from the sea and faced her visitors. "I have soda. May I offer you one?"

Kinsy and Thai answered simultaneously, "Yes, please," and followed Anh back into her home.

Her mother's house was decorated tastefully, much more American than the others she'd seen. When her mother returned with the sodas, she and Kinsy sat together on the sofa. Thai took a nearby chair.

"I used to own the whole estate, but the Communists seized everything. I was only able to buy back this little studio, a fraction of what I once had." Kinsy wondered what her mother did to obtain such wealth. "How did you find me?" Anh asked.

Kinsy told her about coming to this country on a humanitarian aid trip and meeting Chi. She chose not to mention her grandfather, the way he treated her, or his denying having a daughter. If her mother asked about him, Kinsy would be honest, but why cause more hard feelings between them if she didn't have to?

"Chi sends her love and continues to beg for your forgiveness," Kinsy said.

"Let's not talk about our unhappy pasts, or our wretched, deceitful relations. Tell me all about you, your life from as far back as you can remember. Come talk to me while I prepare lunch for us."

Kinsy followed her mother into the corner kitchen area. Thai excused himself and went out on the balcony. Kinsy leaned against the counter dividing the tiny cooking area from the main room.

"Thoughtful, considerate, and handsome young man," her mother said when Thai left. Kinsy decided not to answer. Instead, she gave her mother a brief, thirty-minute overview of her adoptive family and her life in the States. Anh got teary a few times.

"I'm so glad you live in beautiful, free America with a good family and a happy life." She hugged Kinsy. "Lunch is ready. Go fetch your young man."

As Kinsy stepped toward the balcony, the words *your young man* clenched her heart. She thought back to their kiss at Yosemite and wondered if she would ever feel his lips against hers again. Thai napped in the sun on a lounge chair. His tranquil expression tugged at her heart. She sat on the edge of the chaise and longed to trace the outline of his cheek.

Thai's eyes opened; their tenderness stole her breath. Smiling, he asked, "So what do you think of your mom?"

"She seems wonderful." *Just like you.* "Lunch is ready."

When they were all seated at the table, Anh served them steamed rice cakes filled with pepper pork and sweet beans. Kinsy liked the spicy food very much. Anh asked Thai about his background and how he ended up in the U.S. Giving a brief overview, he didn't expound on anything Kinsy didn't already know. She wondered about what happened between the time the soldier gave him the lighter and his mother and brother were killed. But once more, Kinsy covered her curiosity.

❧

Anh Le reminded Thai of his mother and his responsibility for her death. She didn't look or act like her, yet they were both petite Vietnamese women who loved their children. Bile rose up Thai's throat, and he thought he would choke. If only he had hidden the lighter from Loi, perhaps his mother and Loi wouldn't have been killed. Thai might himself have died, but anything would be better than knowing he was in any way connected to his mother's and Loi's death.

"Tell me about you now," Kinsy pleaded. "Tell me about my father."

Anh's eyes misted over. "Your father. . ." Affection radiated on her face and her voice. She dreamily stared past Kinsy as if she were ensnared by another realm, a time she could never relive and only visit in her memories. "Your father was Sergeant Major William Harlow, United States Marines. His dark hair and sparkling green eyes made him the most handsome man I'd ever met."

Anh rose and went to a small chest sitting on a dresser. Removing several pictures, she handed them to Kinsy. Kinsy studied each picture, running her fingers over the faces as if touching them made them more real. She bit her lips in an attempt to stop the threatening tears.

"He was handsome, and you were very beautiful. Is the baby in this picture me?"

Anh nodded. "Chi gave me the picture when she confessed her wrongdoing."

After several more minutes of staring at the pictures, Kinsy passed all but one of them to Thai. She continued to stare at it.

He looked at the beautiful Asian baby—Kinsy—and imagined what her children would look like. An unexpected longing for children of his own with dark hair and eyes filled Thai. He would give to them something Thai never knew: the security of his approval.

Thai had been loved but not secure. His adopted dad was a military man and didn't have much tolerance for teary-eyed boys. "Take it like a man" was his motto. Thai's cautious and sensitive nature got on his nerves. Instead of grieving for his mother and Loi, he tried to bury all the pain and fear because he didn't intend to upset his new dad.

All the grief from all those years suddenly bubbled up, and he could no longer contain his emotions. Abruptly, he rose from the table. "I think I'll take a walk."

❧

Kinsy knew Thai wrestled with his own demons from the past. She ached for him. At least part of her past could be resolved. His never could because everyone had died. She said a quick prayer for him.

"Let me help you clear these while you tell me about your life." Kinsy rose and started carrying dishes to the sink.

Anh started farther back than Kinsy had expected. "My parents married without the blessing of either family. I hoped because they did, they'd understand my love for Bill was as intense and real as theirs had been. However, they neither understood it or accept our relationship." She paused and swallowed hard.

Kinsy filled the sink with soapy water and started to wash. Her mother, while rinsing and drying, continued her story.

"My father told us they lived on rice and love under a leaky roof in a one-room shack. Moving to a little village to escape the hostility of their families, my father was eventually elected a chieftain and became an important man. I think somewhere along the way he forget his humble roots and their passionate beginning. Anyway, I was born first, followed by seven brothers."

"Eight children. Quite a clan." And Kinsy was a part of the clan, tied by blood. She handed her mother another plate.

443

"It's not unusual for Vietnamese families to have lots of children, especially in those days. My parents, they worked hard, scraped by, and saved, proving to their families they'd made something of themselves."

"Did they ever make peace with either set of your grandparents?" Kinsy washed the last pan.

"Sadly, no. In Vietnam one must always respect and honor one's parents. Even at forty or fifty years of age, a person must never disagree with their elders. It is expected of us to bow, nod, and obey. A marriage without blessing is the same as a death. My parents died to their families when they chose to wed."

"How tragic," Kinsy said, saddened by all the division in her newfound family. She wiped down the counters and stove with her wet dishrag.

"I did meet my grandparents. By my own father disowning me, they accepted me. Funny how that works. They are all dead now, though, but I got to know them a little." Anh stood on tiptoe to slide the plates into their rightful place.

"Did you ever fall in love again or marry?" Kinsy asked when they settled back on the sofa.

Anh shook her head. "I am a prostitute, Kinsy." She held her head high, raising her chin as if to say, *I am not ashamed of it either.*

Kinsy's heart dropped, as did her mouth. Her weak, quiet "Oh" said more than a thousand words might have.

Her mother rose and walked to the balcony door. She faced Kinsy. "When I lost Bill, my family, then you, nothing mattered. All love and happiness had been stripped from me. I didn't desire to love again because I didn't want to feel that much pain again—not ever. Rather than risking heartache again, I chose a life of distance and wealth. And I'm sure somewhere inside me I intended to hurt my father as much as he'd hurt me. Having a prostitute for a daughter brings much shame upon the family. Now, it's nothing more than a way of life—and my livelihood."

She paused, looking out to sea. Kinsy noticed Thai leaning against the front door. His face reflected the same surprise and sorrow she wrestled with.

Anh continued her story without turning around. "Men don't fall in love with prostitutes. They only use them for their pleasure and pay them well. In no time, I'd amassed a small fortune and bought this lovely estate. After the American soldiers left, I rebuilt my clientele with wealthy businessmen. I lost it all in 1975 to the Communist regime. As I told you before, I'd saved enough cash to buy this little beach house back."

She turned back to Kinsy. "Now will you disown me too?"

Kinsy went to her, taking her hands. "You are my birth mother. We share a tie stronger than your career choice." Her vision blurred. "I feel sad you've spent such a long time without knowing or being loved. Money may buy you beautiful things, but it doesn't buy happiness. And things don't fill a lonely heart."

Anh stroked Kinsy's hair. "You are much too wise for your young age, my beautiful daughter." She returned to the sofa. "You are right. I'm a lonely middle-aged woman with no love in my heart or life, at least not until today." Her words and smile warmed Kinsy.

❧

"Thai, welcome back," Anh said. "Why don't we stroll down the beach, so you two can see more of my little tourist town? Designed with the foreign oil workers and executives in mind, it beckons all to relax and enjoy life," she said in a singsong voice as if she were reading a brochure.

*Her clientele,* Thai thought. "I'd love a walk, and the beach just happens to be your daughter's favorite place in the world."

Anh sent Kinsy a warm look. "Mine too." She reached for Kinsy's hand. "I'd like to hear more about both of you. I've talked much too much already," Anh said, leading them out the door.

"And I still want to hear more about you and my father," Kinsy added.

The three of them strolled down the beach toward the tourist area. Kinsy carried her sandals, and Thai remembered her doing the same thing in L.A. Then she waded through the lapping waves. Since arriving in Vietnam, everything she did intrigued and impressed him, and Thai wondered if he was truly falling in love for the first time in his life.

They walked in silence, enjoying the afternoon, the beauty surrounding them, and digesting all that had transpired today. When they hit the tourist beach, a mob of vendors descended on them, pulling at their sleeves and pushing bowls of clams and snails into their hands. Teenage girls shoved warm cans of soda, baskets of fruit, and bottles of water at them. Sellers outnumbered prospective buyers about five to one.

All three shook their heads vigorously. Finally, the vendors left and found new prey. "Most of the tourists are Russian businessmen. Many are part of the Russian oil interest headquartered in our little resort town," Anh said.

Thai noticed that several men recognized Kinsy's mother. The way they looked at her made him sick. They didn't see Anh as a human with feelings, only entertainment for themselves. One younger man eyed Kinsy. Thai grabbed her hand, letting the fellow know she wasn't on the market.

Kinsy smiled up at him. Her hand rested in his, her skin velvet soft. Anh rented sun chaises, and they settled on them.

"Here in Vietnam, most take an afternoon nap." Anh yawned and closed her eyes. "Americans don't have time for such frivolity, do they?"

"Not often," Thai said. "We're much too busy to enjoy life."

"How is that saying? Something about Rome?"

Thai and Kinsy laughed. "When in Vietnam," they both said, "do as the Vietnamese."

"That is the one." Anh smiled. "Join me in a nap, then I'll tell you about your father and me."

"You've got yourself a deal," Kinsy agreed, closing her eyes.

# *Chapter 13*

K insy woke up first. Her mother and Thai both still slept. She padded along the water's edge. So much had occurred in the last few days she was on emotional overload. She'd need months to process it all.

Noticing Thai and her mother awake and talking, she returned to her chaise.

"Tell me about your orphanage experience, Thai," Anh requested.

"After my mother's death, everything is a blur." Thai looked away from Kinsy and Anh, staring out across the water. "After I lost my family, an American soldier took me to an American-run orphanage that was overcrowded. I slept on the floor with one blanket."

"Kinsy, do you remember anything about your orphanage experience?" her mother asked.

"No. I was adopted before I turned a year old." Kinsy gazed at Thai, thirsting for every detail he provided. However, she knew from the few bits of past he had already shared that he was glossing over many gut-wrenching details.

"My adoptive family said, as near as they could tell, I was there about six months. Shortly before Saigon fell, they herded us like little animals onto a cargo plane and flew us to the U.S. It was another nine months or so before my adoption."

"Was Tong there too?" Kinsy muttered.

"He slept next to me on the cold, hard floor, and we ended up on the same plane. When he cried at night, I tried to comfort him the way I remembered my Mama did for me. We almost got separated and sent to different orphanages, but someone recognized the bond we shared and kept us together. At that point, I think we became a package deal."

"So the Leopolds adopted you together," Anh asked.

Thai nodded. "Tong adjusted better to life with our new family than I did. I closed myself off from them, not wanting to take a chance on loving more people who might die. For some reason, in my little boy mind, it was only safe to love Tong."

Thai sighed and looked back at Anh. "Anyway, about all I remember about the orphanage is Tong, a cold, hard floor, then the plane ride. Not much else."

Kinsy longed to comfort him, but what could she possibly say or do to help?

Instead she stared out over the water, her heart aching for the little boy who had lost too much.

"Say, it's almost time for dinner." Anh switched the subject. "Shall we walk to a little café I know?"

Kinsy and Thai stood up, and both stretched. "Now it's your turn, Anh. Tell us how you met Kinsy's father."

The three walked side by side with Anh in the middle. "The village of Cau Hai, where I grew up, had a dozen American marines assigned to protect it. Your father was one of the dirty dozen, as they liked to call themselves. Their mission, Bill told me, was the protection of village elders and chiefs and politicians favorable to the democratic regime in the South."

She turned down another street. "This way. Anyhow, Bill was stationed in our village for almost three years. The first year, my seventeenth, he stayed to himself and just befriended other soldiers. We had no contact, except I and about every other girl in the village thought he had the dreamiest eyes we'd ever seen. We'd watch him from our windows. He was by far the best looking Marine to come our way."

She stopped in front of a small café. "Here we are."

Thai held the door. Smells from America, steak and hamburger, increased Kinsy's hunger. Both Kinsy and Anh stepped inside. Once they were seated, Anh requested English menus.

"I've decided on a good old juicy T-bone. No rice, vegetables, or soup for this boy." Thai closed his menu.

"I think I'll follow Thai's lead," Anh said.

"Might as well." Kinsy laid her menu on the pile.

After their orders were taken, Kinsy asked, "What happened the next year?"

"Because the Viet Cong raided our village at night taking our young males as *volunteers* and stole our food and other supplies, the marines started night missions to ambush the V.C. It helped for awhile until they figured out the game plan. During one week near the end of Bill's first year, ten out of the twelve marines were killed. Bill said over those next couple of years the squad never reached full strength again, and over the next six months, thirty-six Americans died defending our village."

A tear slid down her cheek, followed by another, then another. Kinsy thought of each life represented by those tears, men protecting her grandfather and the other important men from this small village. Anh blotted the glistening moisture from her cheeks with her napkin. "Most of the villagers appreciated the Americans, but a few had the nerve to complain. How can you complain about someone giving their life for you?"

Thai's eyes met Kinsy's. She saw the same spark in them she experienced. A window of opportunity presented itself for them to share Christ. "Have you ever heard of Jesus?" Thai asked.

Anh looked suspicious. "Chi mentioned Him. I am not interested."

"But He gave His life for you," Kinsy interjected. "What you said about the American soldiers made me think of Jesus. He did the same thing. He died in our place." Kinsy pulled a thin Bible from her pocket and held it out to her. "Will you at least read the book of John?"

She shook her head. "I cannot read English."

"This Bible is written in Vietnamese," Kinsy said.

Her mother tentatively reached for the book Kinsy offered. "I will think about it. No promises, though."

"Agreed." Kinsy nodded her head. *Father, please open her eyes to the truth. May she see her need for a Savior. Open her heart to You, Lord.* "So when did you and my father become friends?" Kinsy changed the subject, careful not to push her mother away.

"Just after those ten men died. I was angry with my own father because he didn't like the boy I was seeing and forbade me to see him again. I'd taken a walk to cool off. Near the edge of the village in a thick grove of trees, I heard wailing. Thinking someone was hurt, I ran and found your father sitting on a fallen log, head in his hands, crying like a baby.

"I approached him slowly, fearing he'd been shot. Kneeling before him, I gently touched his arm and asked if he was hurt. He shook his head. Uncertain what to do, I rose to leave. In a broken voice and hard to understand Vietnamese, he said, 'Don't go.' He patted the log next to him, so I sat beside him while he wept. Soon I was weeping too.

"At that moment, our hearts and lives bonded irrevocably, though nothing happened between us for many months. We met each afternoon on our log. I helped him improve his Vietnamese, and he taught me English. Ah, our dinner is here." She seemed relieved to get a break from the painful story.

They all *ooed* and *ahhed* over the steak. "Good choice, Thai," Anh said. "Now tell me how you two met."

Thai and Kinsy took turns sharing their story, both making certain to leave out the romantic parts, just as Thai had left out so much about his past. After dinner they walked back to the beach house. While Thai unloaded their things from the van, she and Anh stepped out onto the balcony. The water reflected the moonbeams as they danced along the rippling waves like fairies sprinkled in gold dust.

"I'm so glad you're spending the night. Two days isn't long to catch up on a lifetime, is it?" Anh asked. The breeze lifted tuffs of her red hair and feathered it around her cheeks.

Kinsy reached for her hand. "No, but we can write and call each other."

Her mother kissed her cheek. "I'm glad you came."

Kinsy smiled. "Me too." She yearned to hear the rest of the story about her father but stopped herself from pushing too much. For the first time, Kinsy was finding herself content to wait for God to naturally unfold the events of her life.

Later, Kinsy found her things in a room, decorated in white eyelet. Feminine and beautiful, the room made her feel like a princess. After a shower, she lay in the middle of the big four-poster bed, swallowed up by a soft feather mattress. She was sure she fell asleep with a smile on her face.

❧

Thai, too tense to sleep, stepped out onto the balcony. The cool night air somewhat refreshed his battered emotions. The ocean beat against the rocks below, reminding him of God's awesome power. His soul was still hollow in the aftermath of the afternoon release of his solitary grief. He stood still, breathing in the salty air. The rhythmical waves felt as if they bathed his soul in a sweet, healing salve. When he rushed out of the house after holding Kinsy's baby picture, Thai had been overcome with a grief more potent than any he had allowed himself to experience. He blindly dashed along the village streets until he once again found himself in an alley. Out of the pedestrians' sight, Thai collapsed against the dingy wall and slid to the ground while sobs erupted from him. For the first time, he opened the door of that dark room in his soul and allowed the four year old within to release all his agony. He no longer lay face-first in the dirt of the orphanage driveway. Instead, he stood up, stepped forward, and began reaching out to embrace the future God had planned for him.

"You love her, don't you?" He hadn't realized Anh was out there with him, until she spoke from the swing.

Thai startled and turned. "I beg your pardon?"

She rose and came to stand next to him at the railing. "Kinsy. You're in love with her."

Thai sighed and gripped the handrail.

"It's written all over your face every time you look at her. I recognize that look," she whispered. "Bill once gazed at me with those same starry eyes."

A kindred spirit, fierce and unrelenting, bound them in new respect. They'd both loved and lost to the Vietnam conflict. Almost three decades later, the pain still lingered for each of them.

"I think I do love her," he said, in awe of his own admission. "I've been really struggling with a lot of stuff." He stared at the full moon. "The last seventeen years—since I was about thirteen—I've been determined to forget my Asian heritage. I promised myself I'd do what my brother has done—marry a blond, have blond children, and live the American dream."

"Then Kinsy came along. . . ."

Thai nodded. "Kinsy and Cai."

"Cai?" she sounded defensive.

Thai chuckled. "Don't worry, she's not another woman. She's a little girl we met at the orphanage. I just keep having this vision of the three of us building a life together, but I've been against the idea of having an Asian wife."

"Are you prejudiced against your own people?" She sounded disappointed.

"No. At least not the way you mean. I'm responsible for my mother's and brother's deaths." He told her the whole ugly story, the one only he and Tong knew. Never taking his eyes off the moon, he avoided the disgust he knew must be present in Anh's eyes.

"It's been hard to look into Kinsy's eyes without seeing my mother and beating myself up all over again for taking that lighter." Tears as hot as his self-incrimination trickled down his cheeks and plopped on the balcony railing like minuscule pools of pain.

Anh wrapped her arm around him with a gentle maternal touch. "You were four years old, Thai. The Viet Cong fooled men much older and wiser than you. Many adults fell for the same trick. You were not responsible. Do you hear what I am saying?"

Thai finally looked at her.

"Maybe this God you believe in spared you for a reason."

Never having considered that, Thai had only believed he should have been the one to die, not his mother, not Loi. After all, he'd been the foolhardy one.

"How old is Cai?"

"Four and a half."

"What if the same scenario happened with her, and an older child took the lighter, blowing up the orphanage? Would you blame Cai or the one who gave her the lighter?"

Worded like that, it sounded ridiculous.

"The one who gave her the lighter would be responsible. Thai, the V.C. killed your mother, not you. You were only a victim of the war. You must forgive yourself and go on."

Her words poured over him like a soothing balm and intensified the healing he knew the Lord had begun to complete that very afternoon. She was right. He was a victim, not a perpetrator. He took her hand, holding it tightly. "Thank you, Anh," he whispered. "I think I was on the verge of realizing all of that, but you just helped me take the final step in dealing with my past."

"You're welcome, and call me Mom. I'm sure one day soon we'll be related." She winked.

Kinsy awoke early to the tapping of a woodpecker. Pale golden light streamed through the eyelet curtains. Rolling over, she buried her head under a pillow. Groggy and annoyed by the intruder, she emerged from her cozy cocoon. Maybe if she threw rocks, the bird would find someone else to aggravate.

She put on her pink terry cloth robe, fumbled for her slippers, and finally arrived at the balcony. "Good morning." Her mother's voice greeted her cheerfully from the porch swing.

"Is it?" Kinsy asked. "I came to kill a woodpecker or two."

"Those aren't woodpeckers. They are women searching for clams."

"What?"

She pointed out over the edge of the balcony. "Go look for yourself."

Kinsy moved to the railing and noticed the beach was much wider this morning than last night. Several women climbed over the newly exposed rocks and chipped clams loose with miniature sickle-like picks. Their wide pointed hats hid their faces in the shadow of the brim.

"Would you like some tea?"

Kinsy nodded and plopped defeated onto the swing next to her mother. "I guess I won't throw rocks at the ladies. They probably wouldn't appreciate that."

Her mother laughed and poured her a cup of tea from the service sitting next to her. "Your father hated being awakened too," she said, a reminiscent twist to her mouth.

"Oh?" Kinsy asked. Reaching for the tea, she held her breath, hoping that her mother would continue the story of her first and only love.

Anh nodded and dreamily gazed past her daughter. "Yes, we became the best of friends. We shared everything. Our first day together on the log, Bill told me he no longer intended to befriend any of the men who were in his unit. A man who had come the day before died within twelve hours, and Bill couldn't stand to lose any more friends. He said he only needed and wanted one friend—me. Instead of learning about the men, he intended to learn about me, embrace our culture, learn our language, and study our history. He asked me to be his teacher and friend. I said yes and cherished the honor."

She smiled as yesteryear's tale continued to unfold. "Those were the most treasured months of my life. We met on our log each day. He absorbed all I taught him like a thirsty sponge. Then he began to teach me about life and love.

"One day during an English lesson, he said the word kiss and pointed to his mouth. I frowned, not understanding what he meant. Asking if he meant lips, he shook his head no. Tongue? I stuck mine out, but again, he shook his head. A devilish grin settled on his handsome face, and he asked if I wished for him to show me a kiss."

Her voice broke, but her face glowed with the happiness of a tender memory. "I nodded, and he taught me to kiss. This was the summer of my eighteenth year, but I'd never been kissed before. Still, I feel like he's the only man I ever kissed. Plenty have kissed me, but I have never really kissed the way I kissed him."

With a pleading look in her eyes, she gazed at Kinsy. "Please do not think your father and I shared a cheap affair. He loved me deeply as I loved him and asked my father for my hand in marriage, but it was denied. My father slapped me around and forbade me to see him again. But it was too late. I loved him too deeply.

"We said our wedding vows to one another. The old log where we met was our witness." Eyes filled with tenderness held Kinsy's rapt attention. "Then I gave myself to him as a wife gives herself to her husband. He only had a year left in the Marines and planned to send for me. Ten months later, just two months before he was to ship home, he was killed in an ambush."

No longer able to hold her tears at bay, Kinsy cried for the father she never knew and for the mother who'd lost so much. She hugged her mom close.

"When you find a man who loves you that much, Kinsy, don't ever let him go. A woman is lucky to be cherished once in a lifetime."

"My other dad says every woman deserves to be cherished. Her value is far above rubies. Is that why you never looked for another love?"

Nodding, she said, "There could be no other love to compare. It would not be fair to expect another man to live up to Bill. He was my once-in-a-lifetime dream come true, and he will live in my heart forever." She walked to the balcony railing. "He believed in your Jesus Christ."

Like rain in a thunderstorm, tears of joy poured forth. Her birth father resided in heaven, and some day they would meet. One day they would worship God together. "Mother—"

She spun toward Kinsy, a smile lighting her teary face. "That is the first time you called me Mother. Thank you. You have no idea what a gift hearing you say the word is."

"You are my mother—my beloved mother." Kinsy rose and went to her, holding her hands. "You can see Bill again. If he believed in Jesus Christ, the Son of God, he is in heaven for eternity. You can join him there someday—if only you will believe."

A tiny flicker of interest danced in her mother's eyes.

"Mother, please read the book of John. You'll get a clear picture of who Jesus is and why He came. John says, 'Yet to all who receive Him—Jesus Christ—to all who believe in His name, He gives them the right to become children of God.'

My father will be in heaven, and so will I. Please be there too." Kinsy stopped herself from begging on her hands and knees.

"I will read John," Anh agreed.

Thai came through the sliding glass door carrying a tray laden with omelets, fruit, and toast. "I thought you ladies might be hungry."

"Starved," they both said at once.

They spent the rest of the morning relaxing and sharing funny childhood memories. After lunch, Thai loaded their things. Kinsy promised to visit her mother twice a week for the next three weeks.

Anh hugged both Kinsy and Thai in a bear hug. She wept as they drove away.

# Chapter 14

Three weeks passed before Thai worked up his nerve and found the right moment to ask Kinsy to marry him. She'd gone to see her mother several times, and yesterday he'd gone along. When they'd found a few moments alone, Thai promised Anh he would propose before they left Vietnam tomorrow morning. He'd put the proposal off in case Kinsy said no. Though her mother assured him Kinsy was his for the asking, his confidence lagged. Sometimes he'd catch glimpses of tenderness in her eyes, but mostly she was guarded in his presence. Thai only knew that he loved her and that his love had been growing since their trek up Half Dome. If she planned to be cherished, he was the man.

Her mother had been reading from John every day. She asked a lot of challenging questions. She had Thai and Kinsy digging to find answers. Kinsy even e-mailed her dad for help. Kinsy and Thai both felt confident Anh would some day give her heart to Christ.

The sun neared the western horizon, stretching golden fingers across the azure sky. Thai and Kinsy meandered along the Saigon River with Cai between them, holding each of their hands. His heart warmed, thinking of the picture-perfect family they resembled.

"Swing me," Cai pleaded.

They each held one of Cai's arms and gently swayed her back and forth.

"Butterfly," Cai squealed. That was their signal that she wanted down to go chase the poor, unsuspecting insect.

Thai whispered a prayer as Cai skipped off after her prey. He took a deep breath. God was handing him the opportunity he'd prayed for. Swallowing hard, Thai hoped to dislodge his stomach, which had somehow crawled up his throat.

He stopped walking and so did Kinsy. They stood together watching their tiny charge running through the tall grass after the elusive creature fluttering over her head.

"I love her." Kinsy's quiet words echoed his thoughts. "Don't you wish we could take her back with us?"

"More than just about anything." Being Cai's daddy ranked second on his list of desires, right under being Kinsy's husband. "And I think you've just come up with the best idea I've ever heard. We could get married and come back to take her home with us."

Her eyes rounded, and her mouth fell open. "I didn't mean that the way you took it, Thai."

"So what." He bowed down on one knee. "Marry me, Kinsy. I—"

"I can't." Pleasure didn't light her face, as he'd hoped. Mortification or maybe even horror more aptly described the emotions flashing from her eyes.

"But. . ." Before he could finish, she bolted toward the orphanage without a backward glance.

Thai rose and brushed the mud off his jeans. His throat burned as he reeled with the confusion over what went wrong. So much for Anh and her certainty about Kinsy returning his love.

Thai held Cai's hand, and they walked back toward the orphanage. Would she be better off here or in a single-parent family with only a dad? If she were a boy, Thai would press forward with confidence, but he knew a little girl needed a mom.

&

Kinsy darted away from Thai, wishing she could run away from her mouth as well. She did it again! Just when she thought she'd learned to let God be God and wait on Him, she'd thrown herself at Thai, forcing a proposal from his lips. *Why? Why, can't I ever learn?* she lambasted herself, not sure she'd ever been so disgusted. *First, I forced him to come to Vietnam, then I used emotional blackmail, implying that if he'd marry me, we could adopt Cai and take her home with us.*

The grass whispered beneath her feet as she rushed ahead. When the orphanage wasn't much farther, Kinsy slowed to a walk, holding her aching side and attempting to slow her breathing. *How foolish to imply Thai had to saddle himself with me to adopt Cai. Single people adopt all the time.* Her face burned with embarrassment. Thai was obviously still dealing with his past, and Kinsy wasn't certain he knew how he felt about himself—much less her. Even for Cai, someday Kinsy would regret forcing Thai's hand in marriage. *Lord, I'm so sorry. Please forgive me for once again running ahead of Your timing, pushing people to get what I want. I thought I was learning. But I still have far to go.* It looked as if Kinsy would be apologizing to poor Thai, again.

&

The next morning, Thai chewed the last bite of his *banh cuon,* a treat that tasted similar to pigs-in-a-blanket. The rice crepes with sausage had been one of his favorite breakfasts as a boy. The team now had two hours to play with the children and say their good-byes. All their belongings were already loaded in the van.

Yesterday, Kinsy avoided Thai until the going-away party. When Thai finally worked up the nerve to approach her at the end of the party, Kinsy muttered a terse apology and confined herself to her room for the rest of the evening. Feeling as if the whole mission team and Cadeo and Lan were watching his and Kinsy's every move, Thai had glanced over his shoulder, only to have his suspicions confirmed. The group at least had the decency to continue in their idle chatter while Thai slipped outside for some time alone.

This morning, Kinsy had risen early to help Lan with breakfast, and Thai had been busy loading their luggage. Regret filled her eyes every time they met his, but with the bustle of their final hours in Nam, they might not get to talk until the plane ride home.

The team passed out the balloons and hard candy they'd purchased for the orphans. Cai asked Thai to read her a book. When they finished, she ran off to see Miss Kinsy. He played soccer with a group of boys in the front of the orphanage.

"There you are, Thai," Cadeo said. "It's time." He tapped his watch with his index finger.

Thai found Kinsy in a rocker with Cai. "We need to round everyone up," he said quietly, hating to disrupt the tender scene.

Kinsy nodded, attempting to ease Cai off her lap, but Cai wrapped her arms around Kinsy's neck. "Please don't leave me here." Cai started crying.

"Honey, we've talked about this." Kinsy lovingly held Cai close.

"We have to go home." Kinsy's eyes filled with tears.

Thai knelt in front of the rocker. Tears filling his eyes as well. "Cai, we'll write to you," he promised.

Her sobs turned to wails, and his heart felt like someone ran it through a meat grinder. Thai helped Kinsy pry her loose, only to have her latch onto him; her death grip around his neck made breathing and speaking difficult. "I'll carry you while I round up the kids, but then you have to be a brave girl and say good-bye." He sent a helpless look Kinsy's direction, but she only shrugged.

Cai nodded her agreement, and her howls quieted to snivels. Thai gathered the team together, they all said their good-byes and gave many hugs on their way to the van.

When everyone was settled in the van, Thai tried to put Cai down, but her arms held his neck for dear life. "Take me with you," she begged. "Be my daddy."

Her words clenched his heart. "I can't. I want to, but I can't."

How do you explain the need for a mother to a four year old? He swallowed hard, hoping to dislodge the lump embedded in his throat.

"Cai, you must let Mr. Thai leave. He has an airplane to catch."

Lan sought to reason with her, but Cai only turned her face away and buried her nose in Thai's shoulder. Lan pried Cai's arms from around his neck. Finally free, he climbed into the passenger seat of the van, unable to tear his gaze from Cai.

She screamed, reaching for him. "Don't leave me! Please, my daddy. Don't leave me." She reminded him of that inconsolable, heartbroken little boy who'd just witnessed the demise of his mother and brother. His heart hurt so much he could scarcely breathe.

Surely, one dad was better than no family at all.

"Wait," Thai said, just as Cadeo shifted into first. He unbuckled his seatbelt. Tears dripped off his chin onto his shirt. He no longer cared who saw him cry. He didn't try to hide the fact that it was killing him to leave Cai behind. He reached for her, and she leapt into his waiting arms. Carrying her to the porch steps, he sat down. "I love you, Cai. I want to be your daddy." The words came out muffled and raspy. "I'll be back for you, I promise. Will you wait for me?"

"You'll be my daddy?" Hope filled her precious face.

"Yes, Honey, I'll be your daddy."

He held her close and wept for the little boy who'd needed a tender daddy instead of the cold floor of an orphanage. And he wept for the little girl who'd now never have to wonder again if someone loved her because she'd have her very own daddy, and he'd love her always.

"Thai, we have to leave." Kinsy's voice was gentle, understanding. When he glanced up at her tear-streaked face, his heart dissolved into a puddle of yearning.

"Run to Aunt Lan. Daddy will be back as soon as he can." He held her tight for a last second, loosened his hold, and she obeyed, running to Lan. *Daddy sure sounded good.*

Thai rose from the step, and Kinsy grabbed his arm. "Stop. This can't wait any longer. I know this is lousy timing, but I've never been good at timing anyway." She glanced at the waiting van. "Thai, I've never apologized—I mean really apologized—for pushing you into this trip." Deep, gut-wrenching humility shown in her eyes, reverberated through her words. "I'm so ashamed." A lone tear slid down her cheek. "And so sorry. I didn't really realize until I heard your story— I don't think I would have had the strength to come back."

Thai wrapped his arm around her shoulders and started walking toward the van. "You remember the promise in Romans 8:28? I needed to be on this trip, so God used your bad choice for my good." He stopped dead in his tracks and faced her. "I forgive you, Kinsy." He gently brushed a strand of hair off her cheek.

"Will you kiss her already?" several boys shouted from the van.

A red flush crept up Kinsy's cheeks.

❧

"Would you mind, 'cause I'd really like to take their advice?" Tenderness radiated from Thai's eyes and melted Kinsy's heart. His hand lingered on her shoulder, near her ear. "I wanted to kiss you yesterday by the river, but—okay, I'll be honest—I've vanted to kiss you every day since we got to Vietnam."

"If you kiss me now, I need to know it's because you want to, not because you eel pressured by anyone—especially not by me." She dreamed of nothing more han Thai's kiss, but not with a high price of remorse attached.

"All regrets are behind me. I settled things with God and buried my past here n Vietnam. I'm moving forward." He traced her lips with his thumb. "Will you :ome with me?"

She barely nodded. Was he saying what she hoped he was? He lowered his head, :overing her lips with his in a long, slow kiss. Wolf whistles erupted from the van.

When the kiss ended, he peered into her eyes. "No regrets," he promised. Grabbing her by the waist, he picked her up and twirled her around. "I love you, Kinsy!" he shouted loud enough for everyone to hear. He stopped twirling and et her down. "I love you!"

The mission team cheered. One of the guys shouted, "You go, Thai!"

"Thai—" She struggled to get the words past the lump in her throat.

"Wait." He gently covered her lips with his fingers. "You need to know, it no onger matters that you're Asian, and I love you more than I ever thought possi- ›le. Cherishing you will be the easiest thing I ever do."

Kinsy looked at her beloved through watery eyes. "And I love you, but. . ."

"No buts. I'm not going to let you get away this time." Thai knelt in the damp grass. Applause broke out in the van.

Kinsy's face grew warm. She laughingly covered it with her hand. "This isn't what I had in mind when I prayed you'd love me with complete abandon."

He only grinned at her. "Kinsy, will you marry me? Not because Cai needs a mother, or for any other reason, but because I can't imagine my life without you. I planned to ask you yesterday down by the river, but things went haywire."

"You planned to ask me yesterday—even after I practically threw myself at your feet and forced you to—"

"You didn't force me into anything. Is that why you ran from me? Because you thought you were pressuring me into—"

"Yes. I just didn't want to make you feel like I was up to my old tricks again. I don't ever again want to push another living soul into anything, especially not you, Thai."

"Well, I had been planning my proposal for weeks. Now will you say yes, so I can get up off this soggy ground?" His eyes danced with pleasure, and her heart sang the same tune.

"Yes!"

Rising, he kissed her deeply, passionately. Everyone clapped and cheered, and Cai ran from the orphanage with Lan close on her heels. "Daddy, Daddy!" Cai squealed.

"Will Kinsy be my mommy?"

"Yes! Yes, she will!" Thai scooped their future daughter into his arms, and th[e] three of them shared a family hug, a precursor of things to come.

After Thai and Kinsy exchanged their final good-byes with Cai, they climbe[d] back into the van. There wasn't a dry eye among the participants. As the van pulle[d] away, Thai and Kinsy leaned out the window, waving to Cai.

She smiled and waved back. "Good-bye, Daddy! Good-bye, Mommy," sh[e] yelled several times.

When they boarded their airplane, Thai and Kinsy finagled a seat trade with [a] couple of the kids so they could sit together on the flight home. "We still have [a] lot to talk about," Thai whispered.

"It's a long plane ride home," she reminded him.

He shared with her about his mother's death and how he'd blamed himself. He told her about his talks with her birth mother and how she helped him see the truth[.]

"I might have never found healing if I hadn't come back here and faced my past. I've been fighting a growing love for you since our basketball game las[t] January, and I think you reeled me in at Yosemite. Denying it had nothing to d[o] with you and everything to do with my skewed perception of my mother's death.["]

"So if a gorgeous blond asked you to marry her—"

"I'd tell her I'm already taken. My heart belongs to a little Vietnamese beauty.["]

Kinsy leaned over and kissed Thai. She didn't think she'd ever grow tired o[f] his lips.

Being cherished was a sweet feeling. Closing her eyes, she thanked God for th[e] work He'd done in her and in Thai on this trip. She loved the Lord and Tha[i] completely. Victory at last belonged to both of them.

## JERI ODEL

Jeri is a native of Tucson, Arizona. She has been married over twenty-five years and has three adult children. Jeri holds family dear to her heart, second only to God. *Remnant of Victory* is Jeri's first full-length novel, and she is thanking God for the privilege of writing for Him. When not writing or reading, she teaches a college girls' Sunday school class and leads a mid-week Bible study for them. Jeri is also attempting to scrapbook twenty years' worth of family photos—a major feat!

# A Letter to Our Readers

Dear Readers:

In order that we might better contribute to your reading enjoyment, we would appreciate you taking a few minutes to respond to the following questions. When completed, please return to the following: Fiction Editor, Barbour Publishing, Inc., P.O. Box 719, Uhrichsville, OH 44683.

1. Did you enjoy reading *Triumphant Hearts?*
   - ❏ Very much—I would like to see more books like this.
   - ❏ Moderately—I would have enjoyed it more if _____
   _____
   _____

2. What influenced your decision to purchase this book?
   (Check those that apply.)
   - ❏ Cover        ❏ Back cover copy        ❏ Title        ❏ Price
   - ❏ Friends      ❏ Publicity              ❏ Other

3. Which story was your favorite?
   - ❏ *Remnant of Light*          ❏ *Remnant of Grace*
   - ❏ *Remnant of Forgiveness*    ❏ *Remnant of Victory*

4. Please check your age range:
   - ❏ Under 18      ❏ 18–24      ❏ 25–34
   - ❏ 35–45         ❏ 46–55      ❏ Over 55

5. How many hours per week do you read? _____

Name _____

Occupation _____

Address _____

City _____ State _____ ZIP _____

# $J$HEARTSONG ♥ PRESENTS

# Love Stories
# Are Rated G!

That's for godly, gratifying, and of course, great! If you love a thrilling love story but don't appreciate the sordidness of some popular paperback romances, **Heartsong Presents** is for you. In fact, **Heartsong Presents** is the only inspirational romance book club featuring love stories where Christian faith is the primary ingredient in a marriage relationship.

Sign up today to receive your first set of four, never-before-published Christian romances. Send no money now; you will receive a bill with the first shipment. You may cancel at any time without obligation, and if you aren't completely satisfied with any selection, you may return the books for an immediate refund!

Imagine. . .four new romances every four weeks—two historical, two contemporary—with men and women like you who long to meet the one God has chosen as the love of their lives. . .all for the low price of $9.97 postpaid.

To join, simply complete the coupon below and mail to the address provided. **Heartsong Presents** romances are rated G for another reason: They'll arrive Godspeed!

## YES!   Sign me up for Hearts♥ng!

**NEW MEMBERSHIPS WILL BE SHIPPED IMMEDIATELY!**
**Send no money now.** We'll bill you only $9.97 postpaid with your first shipment of four books. Or for faster action, call toll free 1-800-847-8270.

NAME _____

ADDRESS _____

CITY _____ STATE _____ ZIP _____

**MAIL TO: HEARTSONG PRESENTS, P.O. Box 719, Uhrichsville, Ohio 44683**